A HAZARD AND SOMERSET MYSTERY

GREGORY ASHE

This book is a work of fiction. Names, characters, places, and incidents either are products of the author's imagination or are used fictitiously. Any resemblance to actual events or locales or persons, living or dead, is entirely coincidental.

Copyright 2018 Gregory Ashe
All Rights Reserved

ISBN #:9781796469554

CHAPTER ONE

JULY 2
MONDAY
11:30 AM

THE DORE COUNTY INDEPENDENCE FAIR was already in full swing. At the perimeter of the fairgrounds, the biggest rides hulked: the Octopods, the Flying Kite, the Free-Swings, and the carousel. Then, moving deeper, the complex machinery gave way to shops, where men and women from four surrounding states sold kettle corn and taffy and carved wooden ducks and the same gag t-shirts you could find at any state fair in three hundred miles. At the center, the games of skill and chance marched along the midway. The air smelled like sawdust and cotton candy, and the summer sun hit like an angry hammer. It wasn't even noon, but Emery Hazard was sweating. And he was, to his own surprise, having a good time.

In his good arm, Hazard carried Evie. The toddler was a blue mess, a controlled experiment of child and spun sugar that had gone terribly wrong, but she was having a grand time licking at the cottony puff and shrieking with excitement. Her blue, sticky hands left a trail up Hazard's shirt, across his collar, and along one side of his face, where he'd fallen into the habit of letting scruff grow. Not a beard; a beard wasn't allowed per department policy. But the scruff came pretty damn close some days.

At Hazard's side walked his boyfriend and fellow detective, Evie's father, John-Henry Somerset. In a linen shirt open at the throat and khaki shorts, Somers looked like a rich boy who might have wandered away from his yacht just long enough to explore the fair. It was a combination of things: golden good looks, mussed hair, and a body like he swam five miles a day. He and Hazard had both grown up in Wahredua, had gone to the same high school, had been in the same classes. But Somers looked comfortable here—out of place, yes, but comfortable. Hazard didn't know if he'd ever been comfortable in the whole county. He'd only come back to save his career, and although some good had come of it—Somers was the best example of that—this part of the world still carried too many unpleasant memories.

"I can carry her for a while."

It was maybe the hundredth time Somers had said that. Hazard ignored him, adjusting Evie's weight, wincing at the sugary glue on her fingers as she clutched at his face to balance herself. He'd have to scrub, really goddamn scrub, when he got home. And pour himself a drink, yes. And check the mail.

He shoved that last thought away. "God, it's hot."

Ahead, at the center of the fair, a children's section was roped off. Although it wasn't yet noon, children swarmed the inflatable jungle gyms, the sandboxes, and the trampolines. Already a line snaked away from an electric train as parents and children waited for their turn. Sweat slicked Hazard's neck, his back, his arm. He shifted Evie again.

Somers frowned, but at least he didn't say anything. This time.

"Here you go," Hazard said, bending over the ropes to set Evie down inside the children's section. "Let me just—yep, I'll take that." He passed the gooey ball, all that remained of the cotton candy, to Somers, and wiped Evie's hands and face with a wipe he produced from his pocket. "All right. Go have fun."

She stared at him with dark, serious eyes for a moment. She had her mother's coloring, but the features were all Somers, and she was a beautiful child. Then, turning slowly, she studied her surroundings: a blow-up castle, a padded plastic see-saw, a fort with a pair of slides. Glancing back at the two men, she took a careful step, and then another. She halted.

"We'll be right here," Somers said.

"Go on," Hazard said.

Her caution broke, and she charged towards the blow-up castle.

"She's going to get trampled," Hazard said.

"Look at you."

"I'm just stating a fact, Somers."

"But you wouldn't have said that two months ago."

"It's a statement. It's obvious."

"You wouldn't have carried wipes in your pocket two months ago."

"It was a practical decision. I was tired of being sticky." He swiped at his own hands, rubbing off the worst of the stick.

Laughing, Somers took the wipe from him, turned Hazard by the chin, and scrubbed at the cotton candy matting Hazard's scruff. Then he kissed him. "There. Better."

A gagging noise from nearby cut through the crowd's hum, and then a long, hocking loogie followed. It hit the grass near Hazard's sneakers.

The picture of an envelope, a simple white envelope, flashed in Hazard's mind. Like the envelopes that had started arriving in the mail a few weeks before. Not today. He wasn't going to think about that today. But it was there anyway, the white rectangle. He blinked, trying to clear the hovering white from his vision.

"Ignore them," Somers said. "It's a beautiful day. It's a holiday. We're spending it together as a family, so just ignore them." And he kissed him again.

There was that word: family. A few months before, that word would have sheared through Hazard. Now, though, it was like pressing on an old wound. It hurt, but there was almost something pleasurable about the hurt, a kind of satisfaction in how the pain had diminished. Family. Always before, family had been a way of trimming Hazard from something larger. Never in his life had he imagined the word might someday include him, that it might mean proximity and intimacy, that it could mean this tangle of emotion in his gut like a ball of twine he was afraid to unravel. He'd never imagined—literally never, not even in the steamiest fantasies he'd

7

conjured as a teenager—that John-Henry Somerset might form such a permanent part of his life.

They stood there, two men taking in the scene before them. Along this portion of the midway, games of skill predominated: shooting galleries with bows and arrows; air pellet rifles and air pellet pistols, modified to be safe—or relatively—for the fair; pitching games; ring-toss; even the crane-operator games that occupied the back corners of family restaurants. The air was full of noises, with the shrieks of delighted girls, the war-whoops of a tribe of boys trying to claim the jungle gym, the calliope music, the groan and grind and rattle of the big rides, and all of it mixed with the late morning heat, the cotton clinging to the small of Hazard's back, the smell of Somers's sweat, the wafting aroma of turkey legs on a spit.

They were, in a way, childhood smells. The Dore County Independence Fair was a tradition, and Hazard had experienced it every year until—well, until the cost of being the town faggot outweighed the pleasure of attending the fair. He hadn't expected to come back here. Maybe he had thought about it, once or twice, when he had been living in Columbia or St. Louis and the Fourth of July rolled around. Maybe he'd thought about it when the fireworks popped, went bright, and the smell of sulfur and black powder and burnt cardboard came in like an invisible tide. But even when he thought about it, he'd never thought he'd be here as part of a couple. He never thought he'd be here as a dad.

And that was stretching things. Hazard knew that. He knew that Somers was being kind and generous, the way Somers was always kind and generous, by including Hazard in Evie's life. He knew that, in the normal course of things, with any other guy it would have gone the other way: Evie might have remained on the other side of an invisible barrier, to be seen but not touched, a way of excluding Hazard while maintaining the fiction of togetherness. Not with Somers though. Somers had let his daughter become part of Hazard's life. And over the last months that fact had gone through Hazard like a world-class thunderstorm: some wonderful, beautiful flashes, while the rest was just about the scariest thing he'd ever faced.

In his head, though, he knew that last part was a lie. He thought about the mailbox, with its little brass door in the mail room. He thought about walking to it today, tonight, his fingers tingling where they gripped the key, breathing the stale cardboard air. He thought about opening the mailbox and seeing another of those envelopes, and he wondered if that was scarier than raising a child. Maybe. Just maybe.

Somers nudged Hazard out of his thoughts. "Look at that."

"You've got to be shitting me," Hazard muttered.

A few yards down the ropes, a woman opened her mouth in shock. "Excuse me. There are children, you know."

Hazard ignored her. His attention fixed on the scene unfolding down the midway. A pack of men was shouting, pressing up against a pair in khaki clothing. The two in khaki were sheriff's deputies, although even from a distance, one of them looked too old to still be pulling fairground duty. The men butting up against them were a type that Hazard had seen all too often: cotton wife beaters, ratty jeans, their wallets clipped to chains that rattled with every step they took. There were four of them, and all four had their hair buzzed short, with the same bad teeth and squashed noses. Brothers. Or cousins. Or both, which was possible the farther out you went in Dore County. Two of them had swastika tattoos low on their necks, which meant they were part of Dore County's own precious little gang of white supremacists: the Ozark Volunteers.

"There are four of them," Somers said.

"I can count."

"It looks like it's getting rough."

"I've got eyes in my damn head, Somers."

The woman at the next fence post, her eyes bulging, said, "Excuse me. Excuse me. Children."

"Don't tell me you're going to get involved in it," Hazard said.

"Nope. You are. I'm going to watch our daughter."

Hazard was suddenly painfully aware of his bad arm. It hung at his side. He could bend it—stiffly and slowly—at the elbow, and he had almost ninety degrees of movement there. He could raise that arm, with a lot of swearing, almost even with his shoulder. But he couldn't throw a punch, couldn't grab a guy, couldn't do anything that took speed and coordination.

For a moment, he was back in the suffocating blackness: the electricity had gone out, and then the door crashed inwards, and the man was there. The man with the knife. And Evie had been there. And there had been nothing Hazard could do. Nothing. And the knife kept coming down, slashing deep across his arm, biting through skin and muscle and nerve. Hazard took a steadying breath. He wasn't going to use the arm as an excuse. Not a goddamn chance.

Down the midway, one of the squash-nosed brothers shouted something and pushed one of the deputies.

"I'll watch Evie," Hazard said.

"No way. I called it."

Another, slower breath. He wasn't going to mention his arm. Not after he'd carried Evie all day, not after ignoring all the times Somers offered to take her, not after the hours and days and weeks of rehab, not after all of that. He wasn't going to do it.

"You called it? This isn't some fucking game, Somers—"

With a loud exhalation, the woman marched towards them. "I can't believe that you would use that kind of language around children. You need to leave, mister. Right now. My brother works for the city, and I'll—"

"For Christ's sake," Hazard growled.

Somers was trying not to laugh, but it was shining in his eyes, and he gave Hazard a little shove. "Better go before she calls her brother."

With a scowl for Somers, and another for the indignant woman, Hazard stalked down the midway. The war-whoops of the boys on the jungle gym had risen in intensity; they were engaged in a full on a battle now, pelting a second group of boys with handfuls of mulch and dirt. One boy, a porker who couldn't have been more than eight and was approximately the size of a beer keg, raised a rock over his head, howling as he rushed at a group of boys. The boys scattered, giggling and screeching in equal parts, and the porker made it about five feet before, red-faced and panting, he stumbled, stopped, and dropped the rock. The boys had never been in any danger from him;

Hazard could have told them that from the beginning. But they hadn't known that. They had —

They had been too shocked and afraid by the boy's sudden, violent rush.

Twenty yards down the stretch of grass, the cousin-brothers were face to face with the two deputies now. From this distance, Hazard could make out their features more closely. He saw that one of the deputies wasn't a man. Neecie Weiss carried her weight with a limp and looked like she could have carried anything else you wanted to put on her ox-like shoulders. The other deputy, though, Hazard hadn't seen before. He was an older man who would probably never see fifty again, beefy, with trim white mustaches and silver hair shining with pomade. Between the two of them, they looked like they should have been able to handle the situation.

Except that those inbred Aryan bastards weren't backing down. In most situations, that was law enforcement's trump card: most people respected cops. Or were afraid of them. If you held your ground, most people would cut the shit. Normally. But the Ozark guys were just getting angrier, and now Hazard could hear them.

"—fat motherfucker—"

"—pig—"

"—stupid piece of shit—"

"—dyke bitch—"

That last one must have cut Deputy Weiss a little too deep because she grabbed at the closest of the men. He got lucky; he managed to twist free of her grip because he was a little faster and because Weiss was pissed, but instead of falling back, he caught a handful of Weiss's short hair and jerked her to the side.

Down the stretch of grass, everything was unfolding quickly. Weiss had gotten in a punch, and blood was running from the squashed nose of the guy who held her hair, and now he was dragging her along the midway. The older deputy had already dropped one of the Ozark boys — Hazard hadn't seen how — but now he was retreating, hands held warily in front of himself as the other two approached with knives.

One thing Emery Hazard had learned growing up in Dore County: bullies never fought fair.

Hazard cut sideways across the midway, moving to the closest tent, a shooting gallery. It had plastic ducks lined up at one end, and the carnie working the tent wore a trucker hat with the words *Crack My Lid* printed on it. He was approaching Hazard, ready to launch into his spiel, but Hazard ignored him. He brought up one of the air rifles, checked it, and set it against his shoulder. His bad arm pinged with the strain, and he ignored that too.

Hazard lined up the rifle and fired. The first shot went too far left; it snapped against a white commercial tent. Hazard had expected the first shot to be crap. That was one of the ways they rigged these games. He calculated the difference, adjusted, and shot again.

Advancing on the older deputy, one of the squash-nosed Ozark boys howled and clapped a hand to his neck. He staggered and spun. Hazard fired again. The man shrieked. It was a high note, and surprisingly feminine, and he flattened a hand over his face.

"My eye, my motherfucking eye."

Hazard fired again. By this point, the second man with a knife had turned too. The pellet got him in the cheek; even from a distance, Hazard could see the impact ripple through the corn-fed flesh. Hazard squeezed off another shot. The man keened, dropped the knife, and wobbled sideways. Blood trickled from his ear, and he wobbled again and fell over. Neecie Weiss took advantage of the distraction to plant her boot in her attacker's crotch, and the last of the Ozark Volunteers hit the ground.

The hub of voices in the midway had evaporated, and the calliope music was gratingly loud in the silence. Neecie Weiss, service weapon in hand, flashed Hazard a look and a grateful nod. The older man, though, simply stared at Hazard without acknowledgment.

But Hazard saw what the big, inbred Ozark boys had hidden before: the brass star shining on the man's chest. So. This was Wahredua's new sheriff. After another heartbeat, the sheriff said something to Weiss, and they began cuffing the fallen Ozark boys.

One of them was still screaming about his eye. The one that had taken a pellet in the ear was vomiting. Hazard settled the rifle back on the counter of the shooting gallery.

"It's five bucks for ten shots—" the man in the trucker hat began, but he wilted under Hazard's stare, and Hazard walked back to the children's area. Voices resumed. Children, for the most part, seemed to realize that the excitement had passed, and their shouts and laughter eased the transition back to normalcy. Then the adults began to murmur in low, excited voices.

"My hero," Somers said, kissing Hazard.

"You're an asshole."

The bug-eyed woman opened her mouth, and Hazard shot her a dark glare. She swallowed whatever she had been about to say, scooped up a bug-eyed daughter, and scurried down the midway.

"Just like Prince Charming," Somers said with a sigh, and then he laughed and kissed Hazard again.

This time, the gagging noise was louder, drawn out and exaggerated until it was almost comical, but Hazard only partially heard it. He was more focused on Somers and on the kiss. It had been one hell of a kiss.

"Faggots," a high-pitched, carnie voice called. "Step right up, ladies and gentlemen. Step right up and see two world-class faggots. We've scoured the globe, searched high and low, and we never found a pair of ass-eating pussies to match the two you see before you. That's right, folks, you're looking at bona fide, genuine, grade A faggots. Two dollars a ticket, no children under the age of ten for propriety's sake."

The words snaked through the crowd like smoke off burning garbage. Men and women turned and then turned again, their faces set with distaste as they hurried their children away. Some of those disgusted looks were for the carnie calling out his hateful spiel. But some were for Hazard and Somers.

Hazard's eyes cut across Somers's shoulder, and his lips pulled back from his teeth. Mikey Grames had changed in the ten months since Hazard had first arrived in Wahredua, and that change hadn't been for the better. For a moment, though, that didn't matter. What

Hazard saw was the past: Mikey Grames, tall and tubby and nasty enough that nobody teased him about the tub. Mikey Grames dragging down Hazard's shorts in P.E. and explaining, in an innocent voice, that he was only checking to see if Hazard really did have a puss or if he just used his ass. Mikey Grames kicking Hazard across the locker room tiles like he was playing air hockey, kicking until Hazard pissed blood for a week. Mikey Grames drawing a knife while Hugo Perry and Somers held Hazard's arms, and Grames slicing through cotton first and then skin, incising three clear lines low on Hazard's waist, the scars still shiny today, where Grames had left a blocky G incomplete.

Hazard dragged himself out of the past. Hugo Perry was dead. Somers was—well, he was Somers. He was different. He was better. He was Hazard's. That only left Mikey Grames, and Grames had grown old. He was the same age as Hazard and Somers, but he looked ten years older. The tub around his middle had melted away, burned off with meth and crack and God only knew what else. Hard living had made a ruin of Grames's face, and the rotten sinkhole of his mouth collapsed inwards. He still had his hair, lank and yellow and brushing his shoulders, and he still looked strong. Even in his carnie get-up, black trousers and a Hawaiian print shirt, he looked like he had the wiry strength that didn't leave most drug addicts until the very end. He was grinning now, the brown stumps of his teeth visible in the morning light.

"Faggots," he hawked again. "Ladies and gentlemen, step right up. Ten dollars a ticket."

"Just ignore him," Somers said. "He's a tweaker; he's not worth your time."

They were too far off for Grames to have heard Somers, but his grin widened, and he stepped to one side and swept out an arm, displaying the tent behind him. At the back, figurines painted like stereotypical Native American warriors rolled along a circulating track, while a row of air rifles sat at the front. It was a shooting game, and Grames was running it.

"You're pretty good with balls, aren't you, Emery? Come on over and handle these." He tugged at his crotch.

"Leave it," Somers said. "I'll get Evie and we'll keep going."

"We're having a nice day," Hazard said, sidestepping Somers.

"Leave it, Ree."

"A really nice day. A family day. Why would I let a piece of shit ruin it now?"

"Ree."

Mikey Grames stayed right where he was, bold as fucking brass, as Hazard advanced on him, but his breathing quickened, and he ran his tongue around and around the decaying rim of teeth.

"You wanted my attention."

"You ain't going to do nothing."

"The last time I saw you, I put you on the ground. Last time I saw you, I could have done a lot worse."

"But I know you now. That's right. I watched you. I know you ain't nothing but a pussy. Got your little boy pussy stretched around Somers's cock, but that's the only thing different about you now. You prance around town. You think you're big shit. But you're still a pussy boy who needs a man to put him in his place."

"What am I going to find if I pat you down? Are you dealing, Mikey? That'd be pretty stupid, dealing at the county fair with all those deputies around. It'd be pretty stupid to carry your own product. But you know what, Mikey? I think you're stupid. I think you've smoked your own shit too long. Should I find out if I'm right?"

Grames's rapid breathing carried the stench of his rotting teeth, but he puffed up like a bantam and took a step. "Why don't you prove it? Prove you're not still a pussy who needs a man's cock up inside him. Prove it. Go on. Prove it. Prove you're not just a cum-rag for every trucker that drives within ten miles of town. Prove it. Hit me. Go on. Prove it." Grames's hand slapped down hard on Hazard's bad arm, and Hazard had to bite back a yell. "Yeah, you little bitch, I know all about you. You can't even jerk your boyfriend off anymore, can you? Can't even wipe your own ass after he drops a load in you. You know what I ought to do? I ought to get your boy and drag him out to the bluffs. I'll take you too. I'll let you watch the whole thing, and when you're done, you'll know what I did to two of your fucktoys: Somers, and that faggot back in high school. What was his name?"

The front of Hazard's mind was wiped clean. White. A perfect, white rectangle of light and heat that took up his whole field of vision. A white envelope. And inside the envelope were pictures that Hazard could never unsee. The pictures of Jeff Langham. Jeff, who had loved Hazard. Jeff, who had been brave. Jeff, who had slid a shotgun into his broken, bloody mouth after Grames finished with him and that had been his way out of Wahredua.

Hazard didn't even realize he'd taken a swing. The punch was clumsy; it was twenty-years of anger breaking through a shitty dam. He knew, even as he followed through, that he'd left himself open, and when Mikey Grames danced to one side and clipped Hazard in the neck, the only surprise was that the little tweaker could move that fast. Hazard stumbled, hand at his throat, choking and trying not to empty his stomach.

"Ree, hey, can you breathe?"

Hazard waved Somers away, forcing himself to straighten, even as he continued to choke for air.

"Well, well, well," Grames said. "You came running right over. Wanted to make sure your prize pussy doesn't get damaged?"

"Long time no see, Mikey," Somers said.

"I should have known you were a faggot."

"I should have let you know. That was my bad. In case you missed the announcement, though, I'll give you the short version: turns out, I'm a big old cocksucker." Somers's voice still had that easy, friendly tone he took with just about everyone. "Mikey, we're going to walk away right now. And if I see you again, even if I see your little cockroach head out of the corner of my eye, I'm going to come down on you so hard there won't be enough left of you to fill a can of cat food. You understand me?"

"He swung first," Grames said, his voice suddenly injured and whining. "You saw him. He swung—"

"Nah. That bullshit's done. This isn't high school anymore, and you can't bitch your way out of trouble. I'm not a dirty cop. I don't like dirty cops. But I'll fucking bury you in pieces if I see you again."

All this, Somers said like he was shooting the breeze, like he could clap Mikey on the shoulder and still buy him a beer. "You understand me?"

Grames curved at the shoulders, his posture twisted and hunched and servile.

"I asked you a question."

"Yes. Yes, I fucking understand you, you fucking cocksucking faggot."

"Good. I just wanted to make sure. Have a good life, Mikey. Glad you grew up so nice."

And without waiting for an answer, Somers spun Hazard around and nudged him away from the shooting game. Hazard coughed again, and the worst of the spasms in his throat eased. Down the stretch of the midway, the sheriff and Weiss were watching them, although neither made a move to help. Hazard stood as straight as he could and cast a backward glance at Grames, who sighted down one of the air rifles at them. He wouldn't do it. He wouldn't, not with two deputies right there, not with so many witnesses, not when the pellet would just leave a welt—not worth the trouble of shooting a cop, Hazard guessed. Mikey was still sighting down the air rifle, though, and his face mottled with red.

"I could have handled that."

"Good Lord," Somers said, leaning over the rope fence to collect Evie, who screamed and kicked. "Say thank you."

"No," Hazard said, "I—"

"No," Evie shouted at the same time, flailing her legs. "I play!"

Hazard froze with his mouth open.

"Yep," Somers said, slinging Evie over his shoulder and bouncing her as he turned back towards the fairground gates. "Sometimes you sound exactly like her."

"I don't sound exactly like her."

Somers rolled his eyes.

"I don't think," Hazard muttered.

"Let's get out of here before you remember how to throw a punch."

They passed Grames from a distance, and he was sighting down the air rifle at them like he might take a shot. But he didn't do anything except at the very end, when Hazard threw a last look back, and then Grames smiled: a brown smile like he'd been chewing shit, and all the tension oozed out of him, and he gave Hazard a cocky wave before he faced the passersby and hawked his game again.

What was that about, Hazard wondered. What was Mikey Grames playing at? His anger and disgust with Hazard had seemed real enough, but at the end, that transformation had been so quick and complete that it made his earlier hatred look like a lie. But why? Why pretend to hate Hazard only to provoke him? And why did he look so damn happy at having succeeded? The envelopes? Were those Mikey?

At the edge of the fairgrounds, Somers's phone rang, and he hooked it from his pocket and spoke quietly into it for a pair of minutes. When he'd finished, he tossed Evie, tickled her, and said, "We've got to get you back to Mom."

"Why?" Hazard asked. "What's happened?"

"Chief Cravens just called. She wants us to stop a murder."

CHAPTER TWO

JULY 2
MONDAY
1:12 PM

DROPPING OFF EVIE wasn't as easy as it sounded. Cora Malsho—who had been Cora Somerset for a long time—had a job as a designer. It was freelance work, mostly for a company in KC, and it left her with relatively little free time. Almost nonexistent free time, in fact. In the end, they had to take Evie to her preschool.

"I don't like leaving her there," Hazard said.

"You threw a punch and ruined our day. You don't get a say."

"Kids need more one on one time. Kids need positive reinforcement from adults in their life. They need—"

"Ree?"

"I was watching this documentary on child development, and they said—"

"Ree, sweetie?"

"I'm trying to tell you something."

"I know, babe. Shut up."

"What?"

"Shut up. Nobody wants Evie to be in preschool all day. Do you have a better idea?"

Hazard decided he should re-watch the documentary before he answered.

They headed back to the Wahredua Police Station. Originally, the building had been a Catholic school, and traces of its youth still survived: although most of the ornamental religious stonework had been removed, rising costs and worker injuries had caused the iconoclastic destruction to stop before it was completely finished. Above the main doors, for example, most of a frieze remained, displaying an angel conquering a devil. Only even that wasn't quite right, because some fool with a chisel had managed to knock off most of the angel's spear, and from the right angle now it looked like the angel was just tickling the devil, and the devil was having one hell of a time.

Inside, the place was as it always was. The smell of coffee stained the building permanently, and over the hum of voices, fax machines screeched and whirred. A few locals sat in the lobby, waiting to speak to an officer, while the oldest police officer in the department presided over the front desk. Jim Murray's nose hairs grew almost to his chin, and he had to be close to eighty, but he didn't miss much. He also didn't like Hazard much, and when he noticed the two detectives, he gave his newspaper a vigorous shake. Beyond Murray, the building opened up, and a bullpen had been erected to corral the desks. Jonny Moraes, a uniformed officer, perched on the edge of one desk, laughing as his partner, the red-headed Patrick Foley, swore at a form he was trying to fill out. Moraes gave Hazard and Somers a thumbs-up and then pointed out another mistake on Foley's form. Foley swore and ripped up the paper.

"Heard you got your ass handed to you," Foley said when he noticed Hazard.

Hazard ignored him.

"Why the fuck didn't you lay out Grames? A piece of shit like that, you outta go after him."

"Word travels fast," Somers muttered.

"Is it true you tried to hit him and he got you in the throat? That's assault on a peace officer. That's what I'd call it."

"Foley, why don't you worry about spelling your name right? We'll worry about Mikey Grames."

Foley's face turned as red as his hair. He looked like he might say more, but Moraes muttered something, and Foley shook his head.

As Hazard rapped on the chief's door, he heard Foley speaking in a low voice.

"Come in," Cravens called.

"—one thing when he was solving cases, but what are we supposed to do with a fucking cripple on the force—" Foley said, his voice rising.

"Let it go," Somers said.

"I'll show him a cripple."

"Let it go." And Somers pushed him into the office.

Cravens was an older woman with long gray hair in a stylish cut. Out of uniform, she might have passed for someone's grandmother, and some of it had to do with her rounded figure. But she'd been Wahredua's first female detective, and after all those years on the force, she had brass balls bigger than most men. Her office was spartan, with only a few photos of her nieces and nephews and an air-freshener odor that probably would have been called fresh linen or something like that.

When they were seated, Somers said, "What's this about? Stop a murder? Is this something domestic? Helping a woman get away from her husband?"

Cravens didn't answer. There were new shadows under her eyes, Hazard noticed, and the nails on her left hand were ragged. In a gesture Hazard had never seen her make before, she pulled the long braid of hair across her shoulder and ran her hand down it.

"Is this about Grames?" Hazard asked. "Are you pissed about that? Because I could have handled him. Whatever those goat-fucking idiots out there are saying, I can take care of myself. You don't—"

Somers bumped his foot, and Hazard stopped when he saw the look on his partner's face.

"This is something bad," the blond man said.

"It's not something good." Cravens cleared her throat, and her jaw creaked and popped, and Hazard wondered how old she was and how many of those years this job had compounded.

"It's not going to get any better waiting," Somers said, but his voice was gentle. "Go on."

"What I'm going to say, you're not going to like."

"We're big boys. We can handle it."

She didn't smile at that, and six months ago, she might have smiled. Instead, she ran her hand down her braid. Hazard's mother wore her hair short. She had worn it that way for most of Hazard's life. And when Hazard's father had come home sloshed, when he had come home after a bad shift, when he had come home and shut himself in their room, in silence, for hours at a time, Hazard remembered his mother running fingers through her short, short hair over and over again. It wasn't the same gesture as Cravens's. If you took video of them and put them side by side, nobody would see the connection. But they were the same thing. The exact same thing.

"When I started on the force," Cravens said, her voice slow, "the chief was Edgcomb. Hal Edgcomb. Before your time, I guess. You two weren't even born. Hal Edgcomb was a lot of things: he was fat and old and a misogynist. He didn't want me on the force, but there was public pressure, and I was too good for him to outright ignore. He gave me the worst assignments every day until he resigned. If I messed up anything—we typed things in triplicate back then, and if the carbon was even the slightest bit smudged—he'd bring me in here and take off my head. The room's changed a little since then. And I'm sitting on this side of the desk. But the truth is that I still think of him every time I walk through that door."

Somers raised an eyebrow at Hazard.

"One day, he sat outside in the heat—it was a day like this—trying to start his car." Cravens laughed. "He had to have been out there hours, just sitting in the car, turning the key, pumping the gas. Honestly, I don't know what kept him out there except that he was as stubborn as a mule. One of the patrol guys found him out there, just about passed out from heat stroke. He never did get the car to start. One of the battery cables had come loose, and he never even thought to pop the hood and check. That happened early on, when I was so green you could have used me for a traffic light, and after that, every time he hauled me in here, I'd think about what a stupid man he was.

"On the desk," she laid her palm down on the wood, "right here he had a plaque. Facing him, but I could read the text at an angle. It's a Thomas Jefferson quote. Do you know what it said? 'Only aim to do your duty, and mankind will give you credit where you fail.' I read that every time he was peeling my hide, and I thought about him passing out from heat stroke, and I would think, 'Who is this stupid old man?' I would think, 'Only Hal Edgcomb would have a quote about failure on his desk to cover his own ass.'" She paused here, lapsing into silence. It was a deep, viscous silence, and Hazard felt it drawing at him. When Cravens spoke again, her voice had an edge Hazard hadn't heard before. "But time makes fools of us all. Maybe I should have that on a plaque."

"All right," Hazard said. "Out with it before I go out of my damn mind."

Somers bumped his foot again, but Cravens only blinked and seemed to come back into the moment. "Yes. All right. A citizen has been receiving death threats for the last few weeks. Nothing written. All of these threats have been verbal and delivered in person. The person who has been doing the threatening is—was—employed by this citizen; he had regular access to the citizen, and in my professional opinion, at least for now, he's a credible threat. I'm assigning you two to a protective detail for the next few days. At least until we can track down this disgruntled ex-employee and figure out what to do with him."

"That's a bullshit job," Hazard said.

This time, Somers kicked his shoe hard enough that the leather squeaked across the vinyl tile. "What my partner is trying to say, Chief, is that this sounds like a job for a couple of uniformed officers. They can rotate more easily, and Detective Hazard and I are busy—"

"You don't have any pressing cases, Detective Somerset. I know what's happening in my own department. And I've chosen you two for a reason. You're the best officers I have, and you're the ones I trust to do this job regardless of your personal prejudices."

Hazard's head came up. *Regardless of your personal prejudices.*

"In any case," Cravens continued, "it's a moot point. You were personally requested for this job, and I intend to assign it to you."

Somers, frowning, said, "We were requested? Who is this citizen? He must have a lot of juice if he can get this kind of treatment."

Regardless of your personal prejudices.

Hazard's mouth dried up. The acrid, burnt-coffee smell that pervaded the station rushed over him. He forced himself through the clues that Cravens had given away, forced himself to reconsider the question. There had to be another answer. Anybody but him.

Cravens was staring at the desktop, her hands flat and spread on the wood.

"The mayor," Hazard said, that burnt-coffee stench flooding his lungs. "You're making us babysit the fucking mayor."

CHAPTER THREE

JULY 2
MONDAY
1:24 PM

MAYOR SHERMAN NEWTON HAD SNOWY HAIR, liver spots, and a suit that probably cost more than Hazard's car. He was old money; the stink of it came off him like mothballs. As he settled into a seat in the chief's office, Hazard had to fight to keep his face impassive. Mayor Newton, through his investment company InnovateMidwest, had been involved in some very shady dealings throughout the area. Hazard was certain that the mayor had been responsible for at least one murder, and he knew that Newton had tried to have him and Somers killed to put an end to their investigation. The bitch about the whole thing was that they didn't have any proof.

The other problem, of course, was that most people saw a delicate, elderly statesman when they looked at Newton. They saw a Harvard man. Or maybe a Yalie. They saw money and class and prestige. They saw a goddamn pillar of the community, never mind that most of the investments Newton made only served to destabilize the surrounding areas, never mind that Newton snapped up properties and let them rot until the value of adjacent lots plummeted, never mind that Newton had been creating his own urban wasteland in Wahredua just to line his pockets. Understanding those effects, understanding the real impact of Newton's actions, required a long-term view, and most people in Wahredua either didn't have or didn't want to have that kind of vision.

"Detectives," Newton said.

"This is bullshit," Hazard said.

"Detective Hazard—" Cravens snapped.

Newton held up a spotted hand, and Cravens sank back behind her desk. The mayor eyed the two detectives. There was nothing venomous or hateful or clever about his gaze. Nothing in his appearance betrayed the monster underneath. His eyes were watery, the irises the color of frozen fish, forgotten and then pulled from the back of the freezer. His head wobbled on his neck slightly, and Hazard was damned if he could tell whether the movement was genuine or fake.

"This is really bullshit," Hazard said.

"Chief Cravens, may I speak to the detectives alone?"

Cravens liked that about as much as she'd like sticking her nose in a paper shredder, but she gathered herself and left. As the door swung shut, the normal noises of the station filtered into the office: the screech of the fax machine, the rumble of the coffee cart as Miranda Carmichael pushed it towards the lobby, the squeak of the broken caster on a desk chair, Mrs. Tuila's braying complaints about the deer eating her blueberry bushes and her demand that they station an officer with a gun to kill the damn things. Then the door clicked shut, and the office was silent.

"I think we can dispense with the niceties," Newton said, and his head was still wobbling on his ancient neck, but his voice had taken on a brusque, business-like tone. "Don't you?"

"You're trying to fuck us over," Hazard said, drilling a finger into the arm of his chair. "Or you're trying to fuck somebody else over. Or both. Probably both."

"And if I tell you I'm not?"

"You're a lying sack of shit. I don't care what you say."

Those watery, fish-stick eyes glided towards Somers.

Shrugging, the blond man said, "Let's hear it."

"You've got to be kidding me. You've got to be fucking kidding me. You really want to sit here and listen to this old bag of shit—"

Somers didn't say anything. He didn't even look away from Newton's watery eyes. He just put a hand on Hazard's arm, and

Hazard choked back the rest of what he'd been saying and dropped into his seat.

"We have a bad history, the three of us," Newton said. "That's my fault. I understand that. Mistakes were made, and some of those mistakes escalated beyond what I wanted."

"You tried to blow up the house we were in." Hazard drilled his finger into the arm of the chair again. "You tried to blackmail us."

"I threatened to blackmail you, Detective Hazard. Not your partner. And I changed my mind about that."

"Or you realized you didn't have shit."

"Trust me, Detective Hazard: when I decide to do something, I do it."

"You changed your mind," Somers said.

Newton inclined his head. "Your father did his best to convince me. And I will admit that as my working relationship with Sheriff Bingham unraveled, I realized that I might be better served by directing my energies elsewhere."

"Somewhere besides trying to kill us," Hazard said.

"I believe that we can help each other, Detectives."

"Help each other? Help each other? I damn near suffocated in that basement. I damn near cut my own hand off. That's the kind of help I need?"

"What do you want?" Somers said

"Somers, you're listening to this old bastard?"

"What do you want?"

"I want exactly what I told the chief: I want you to keep me alive."

"Pass," Hazard said.

"Who's trying to kill you?" Somers asked.

Newton folded his wrinkled, spotted hands, and he shifted in his seat. Hazard noticed a mild scent on the air, and it reminded him of his grandfather. Lectric Shave, that's what it was, and Hazard could see it in his mind, fluorescent green on the Formica countertop in the prefabricated home where his grandparents had lived. And underneath the astringent smell came something else, something fouler, the smell of an unwashed, aging body. And now Hazard noticed the tic in Newton's right eye, and the way his liver-spotted hands trembled, and the way he sat, as though he might slide out of the chair just so he could sleep for a minute.

"Ted Kjar," Newton said.

"Tell us about him," Somers said.

"I've heard that name," Hazard said. "He's the guy with the book."

For the first time since Somers had spoken, Newton's frozen-fish eyes swam towards Hazard.

"What book?" Somers said.

"He's an aspiring author," Newton said. "He was an aspiring author. Before he fell back into bad habits."

"It's a local history book. It's not finished yet, but what he has is good." Hazard frowned, trying to remember. "He gave a presentation on it at the county library in January, I think. He was working on a chapter about—God. World War II, I think. Wahredua's involvement in the war. Wartime life. Give me a minute. I'll think of it."

"This guy doesn't sound like a killer," Somers said.

"The book might kill you," Newton said, "but you'd only die of boredom. Six months ago, I would have agreed with you: there's nothing about Ted Kjar that makes him a killer. He's been a model employee for almost six years. I brought his records with me if you'd like to look." He opened a briefcase on his lap and withdrew a file; as he did, something heavy shifted and clunked inside the case.

"Sounds like you've already taken steps to protect yourself," Hazard said, nodding at the briefcase as he took the file. Clipped to the first page was a four by six photograph, obviously a blown-up copy of a corporate ID, with Theodore Kjar printed along the bottom. The man it showed looked like any other corporate drone Hazard could imagine: thinning, mousey hair; droopy, hangdog eyes; and a paunch developed from long hours of sitting. He had a mole on his chin, but other than that, there wasn't much to make him stand out.

The mayor was still talking, saying, "I have a concealed carry permit, Detective, and I will defend myself if necessary."

"Oh, I'm sure. I'm sure you won't hesitate an instant to pull the trigger. You never have in the past."

The briefcase snapped shut hard.

"Ted Kjar is one of your employees," Somers said, shifting in his seat, his tropical-water eyes fixed on Newton. "And now he wants to kill you."

"Ted is an accountant. Was an accountant. He worked in-house for InnovateMidwest, and as I said, he did an excellent job. You'll see in the file that he had commendable evaluations from his supervisor year after year, and two years ago he received a professional recognition from the local CPA association." Newton sighed; his head was shaking more severely than before, and he rested it now on tented fingers. "He has a wife, Jo. Josephine. And he has a daughter. She's at Drury, in Springfield. Karen, I believe. You can understand how hard this has been for them."

"What?" Hazard asked, glancing up from the file. "What has been hard for them?"

"Ted is an addict. I'm sure there's a more polite way to say it, but that's the truth. You know what they say about addicts: you're always an addict. There's no cure. There's no fix. I suppose I might have told you that he has 'substance abuse problems.'" Newton's prim tone screwed the scare quotes around the word. "But I find that description unhelpful. He's an addict, and he's dangerous. From conversations I've had with a friend who is also a psychiatrist, I believe that Ted may also be self-medicating to treat undiagnosed schizophrenia when he abuses illegal drugs."

"Now you're a shrink as well as a mayor." Hazard turned a page in the file and made a disgusted noise.

Somers shot him a glance.

"Mayor Newton has conveniently provided a history of Ted's mental health." Hazard displayed a clipped bundle of documents. "Ted's been institutionalized twice."

"For addiction recovery," the mayor said. "And depression and anxiety. And yes, Detective Hazard, you're correct: I did pay an investigator to find those documents, and I am providing them to you for the same reason I showed them to Chief Cravens. I believe they are relevant to my situation. They show a history of addiction—"

"What was he addicted to? Coke? Heroin? Marijuana?"

"—a history of addiction, as I was saying, and reason to believe that his mental health is linked to his addictions. You'll notice that Ted's first time in rehab was paid for by his parents when he was in his early twenties. Still in college, I believe." The mayor clucked and shook his head. "It's tragic, but the peak onset for both depression and schizophrenia is the early twenties, and there's a significant link between the two illnesses. College is also a time when many young people experiment with habit-forming substances. We're not doing enough in this country for—"

"Save it for the campaign trail," Hazard said, snapping the folder against his leg. "Smoking some weed in college, that doesn't make him schizophrenic. What do you want?"

"If possible, I'd like to do whatever we can to help Ted, but I'll be blunt: what's most important to me is saving my own life."

"Unsurprising."

"I don't think that's something to be embarrassed about, Detective. I'd like to live a few more years. I'm human just like everyone else."

"That's debatable."

"Detective Hazard—"

Turning to Somers, Hazard spoke over the mayor. "He's got the second hospitalization documented here too. No sign that Kjar was ever diagnosed with schizophrenia, that he ever took medication for schizophrenia, or that anyone ever thought he had schizophrenia. It was another round in rehab. That's all."

"That's exactly my point, Detective. He was untreated, undiagnosed, and an addict. He might have managed to hide the symptoms—"

"Why don't you tell us the rest of it?" Somers said. "Walk me through the events. That's the most helpful thing you can do right now."

Newton watched them each in turn, his posture chilly. The old man smell had grown stronger, and it was cloying now, making

Hazard wish for an open window, an air freshener, even the stink from one of Miranda Carmichael's tomato-cucumber-and-onion sandwiches. From the bullpen outside the office came the low buzz of activity at the edge of hearing, and that noise got under Hazard's skin and itched.

"Very well. In late February, Ted came to my office. It was late."

"The mayor's office?" Hazard asked. "Or your position at InnovateMidwest?"

"InnovateMidwest. I've already explained that he was my employee there; why would he come to the mayor's office?"

"That's convenient. There are security cameras all over City Hall. I don't suppose you have security footage that shows this meeting with Kjar?"

"No. My office is private. I can't prove that this meeting took place. What, exactly, do you suspect me of doing, Detective? What am I supposed to prove?"

"That you're not a lying—"

Somers squeezed his arm again, and to Newton said, "Go on."

"Ted was . . . upset, I suppose I thought. Erratic. He wasn't making sense, but he was talking about people watching him, listening to him, following him. I'd known Ted distantly, professionally, for years, and his behavior was unusual. I listened to him. I didn't really know what to think, but I promised I'd look into the matter, and he seemed satisfied. He left."

"That was it?"

"For the time. A few weeks later, Ted came back. He was angry. Furious. And almost incoherent. Bits and phrases made sense—the watching, the listening, the following—but most of it was rambling accusations. Some of them were directed at me. At first I was worried for Ted, but then he started to throw things, and he grabbed me." Newton gathered a fistful of his suit coat to demonstrate. "He wanted money. I panicked. I dialed security, and they came and removed Ted. I called HR and asked them to terminate Ted's employment." A faint hint of red dusted Newton's sagging cheeks. "I didn't even think that he might be ill. I acted rashly, I know, but I was frightened and angry. I had someone from security remove Ted's belongings and deliver them to his home. I assumed that would be the end of it." Newton paused. The dusting of red thickened, and he said, "Detectives, if I had known he was ill, I wouldn't have done those things. I would have made sure he got help. By the time I realized what was happening, too much had already gone wrong."

"What then?" Somers asked.

"Two weeks ago, I was working late. Ted found me at my car when I left." A smile thinned his lips. "There is footage of this, Detective Hazard. The Kum-n-Go has a camera that caught it on tape. Ted was scratching himself, digging at his skin. He was shouting. He accused me of setting the government on him to spy. He said other things, things I didn't even understand. He hit me." Newton winced, touched his chest, and shifted in his seat. "Nothing serious, thank God. When he was distracted, I managed to get in my car and drive away."

"You didn't tell the police about this?"

"I asked Sheriff Engels to look into it. I asked him to take care of Ted. That's a poor choice of words, I know."

"And how did the sheriff take care of him?" Hazard asked.

"He didn't. Ted had already disappeared. No one knew where he was, not even his wife. Until two days ago."

"Let me guess," Hazard said. "He showed up again at the office."

"No, Detective. He followed me into the bathroom at Riverside Burgers. And before you ask, no, I hadn't seen him. I ordered my burger at the counter and went to the bathroom to wash my hands. He walked right in behind me, and for a moment, I just thought it was my mistake. I didn't lock the door; I was just scrubbing up before I ate. Then I saw that it was Ted. He came at me with a baseball bat. It's a single-user affair, that bathroom, so there wasn't much room to maneuver. Ted shattered the mirror. I went for the door. Ted came at me again, and he slipped on wet toilet paper." Newton smiled, and it flickered like a TV trying to catch a station. "I was going to complain about that wet paper. I was going to go back to the counter and ask for the manager. I mean it's my town, and Riverside Burgers is right on Market. People passing through stop there. People remember things like that."

"This was Saturday?" Somers said.

"That's right."

"What time?"

"Eleven. Eleven ten. Not much past that. I still have the call log on my phone, and you can see I called the chief at eleven-seventeen."

"The chief of police? Not 911?"

"It wasn't an emergency, Detective."

"A man coming at you with a baseball bat isn't an emergency?" Hazard said. "That's an interesting evaluation."

"Chief Cravens and I agreed to meet to discuss the situation. I want what's best for Ted, but I won't lie: I'm worried for myself, too."

"You didn't call the sheriff again?"

"Sheriff Engels believes this is a city matter. He's new to the job, and he doesn't want to step on toes."

Hazard raised his eyebrows at Somers. Dore County's last sheriff had never minded stepping on toes, and, what was worse, had been at the mayor's beck and call. It sounded like Sheriff Engels wasn't dancing to that tune. At least, not yet.

"Saturday at eleven sounds like a busy time for Riverside Burgers," Somers said.

"I suppose. I didn't wait long in line, of course. They're basically fast food, and that's why I decided to stop there. I was on my way to a library event. Storytime for local children. It's a pleasant way to spend some time."

"Good God," Hazard muttered, shaking his head.

"Did anyone else see what happened with Ted Kjar?" Somers asked. "Did you speak to the manager? Did you ask anyone to help?"

"Did you stay long enough to get your burger?" Hazard asked.

"A man had just come at me with a baseball bat. No, Detective Hazard, I didn't stay and eat my burger. I don't appreciate the joke. And no, Detective Somerset, I didn't speak to the manager. I ran to my car and I drove. I called the chief, and she sent Detective Lender over to investigate. He filed a complete report with pictures showing the damage. The broken mirror, I mean. And he has the baseball bat."

Somers hesitated and then leaned forward again. "He does?"

"Yes. I understand they've already taken latent prints from it and compared them to Ted's."

"A perfect match," Hazard said.

"I don't understand your tone, Detective."

"Just so I'm clear," Hazard said, "no one at Riverside Burgers saw Ted Kjar. Nobody heard the glass break. Nobody saw a confrontation between the two of you. You managed to escape—congratulations on that, by the way—thanks to urine on the floor and loose toilet paper."

Newton straightened in his seat. His liver-spotted hands clenched in his lap. "I asked for you two because you're the best. Whatever our issues—"

"You tried to kill us."

"That's enough. That's enough, Detective Hazard. I've told you what happened. You have orders from the chief."

"We haven't actually received those orders yet," Somers said. "Not completely. Just the basics, that we're going to be doing protective duty for you. In rotation, I assume, since we won't be much good if we work round the clock."

"That's correct. The chief has promised a rotation of uniformed officers, but the two of you will be taking control of the operation. I assume that you'll want to work out the specifics of the shifts and the other details." Another of those TV-tuner smiles flickered on his face. "Detective Hazard, you're getting what you've wanted for some time now: my life is in your hands."

"Great," Hazard said. "So if anything happens to you, it comes right back on us."

"I'm sure you don't mean that the way it sounded, but yes, you've got the right idea."

"This is a trap," Hazard said, and Somers began shaking his head. Hazard ignored him. "I know you think I'm stupid. I know you think you're three moves ahead. But I know it's a trap. And I want you to know that I know."

"You sound like you think this is a game, Detective, but I assure you, this is my life. And I don't play games with my life. I hope you won't either."

Hazard met those watery, fish-stick eyes, and then he got to his feet and said, "This is a fucking joke."

"Let's get the first shift scheduled," Somers said. "If you'll give us a few minutes, Mr. Mayor, we'll pair you with the first uniformed officers and let you get about your day."

Newton left them alone in Cravens's office, and when the door had shut behind him, sealing out the smell of old man and Lectric Shave, Hazard jabbed a finger into Somers's chest. "This is a trap. He's giving us the rope, and we're tying it around our own necks."

"For God's sake, Ree."

"Don't tell me you believe that cock-and-bull."

Somers shot him a withering glare.

"Then what are you saying?" Hazard asked. "You're saying we go along with this?"

"I'm saying what choice do we have. If you could keep your mouth shut for five seconds, instead of letting out every damn thought you've ever had, we could have kept an edge."

"I'm not going to kiss his ass—"

"I'm not asking you to kiss his ass. I'm saying if you think it's a trap, dummy, you shouldn't tip your hand. That was about the only goddamn advantage we had."

"I'm not going to let that bastard sit there, smirking at us—"

"Why, Ree? Why does it matter?"

"I—"

"I'll tell you why: you always have to push. You can't stand it, you can't stand feeling like anybody has one over on you, and so you push every goddamn minute." Somers dropped his chin to his chest and took a deep breath. Scarlet highlighted his cheeks, and he looked far more tired than he had an hour before. From the bullpen, the faint shriek of the fax machine penetrated the thick glass of Cravens's office.

"I don't always have to push," Hazard said.

"Lord," Somers said under his breath, "have mercy."

"I don't."

"You're doing it right now."

"I—" Hazard crossed his arms. "All right. I guess I am."

"You're lucky I think you're pretty."

Hazard narrowed his eyes.

With a soft smile, Somers said, "Can we go figure out which lucky bastards get to spend their shifts with the mayor?"

"Simple: we just give Foley twenty-four hours. Every day."

With a laugh, Somers tipped his head at the door, and Hazard preceded his partner out of the office.

But it wasn't as easy as Hazard had hoped, and within twenty minutes, his blood pressure had shot through the roof again. He stood with Cravens, Newton, and Somers in the bullpen. With them now were Jonny Moraes, the dark-skinned beat cop usually partnered with Foley, and Miranda Carmichael. Carmichael's hair, cut short after a nasty encounter with a senior citizen, had grown into a cap of short curls, and her compact, gymnast's body betrayed tension as she waited. Moraes never looked tense; his mother, a Brazilian who had come to Wroxall College and decided to stay when she finished, had passed along some of that infamous Latin tranquility.

"Work it out amongst the three of you," Cravens said, gesturing to Somers, Moraes, and Carmichael. "Three eight-hour shifts."

"What about me?" Hazard said.

"You're with me," Somers said.

"Yeah, but I don't get a say?"

Cravens ignored him. "I want Detectives Hazard and Somerset on the third shift. The rest of it, you can be flexible."

"You said we can work it out," Hazard said.

"She said we could work it," Somers corrected, pointing again to himself, Moraes, and Carmichael. "You don't get a vote."

"What the hell does a vote matter if we get third shift every time?"

"This is why you don't get to help decide," Moraes said with a lazy grin.

"Chief," Hazard said.

"No. I don't want to hear it."

"Every third shift? We're going to work nights until we round up Kjar or until Kjar finally manages to—"

Somers's elbow caught Hazard in the ribs, and he grunted and dropped the rest of it, but Cravens's eyes had gone chilly. "Detective, you may not know this, but most schizophrenics suffer their most severe episodes at night. Mr. Kjar's behavior is in keeping with this; all but one of his confrontations with the mayor happened after dark. Based on that data, I believe that you and Detective Somerset should cover the time when Kjar is most likely to attack."

"If he's going to attack at all," Hazard said. "If he's even drugged up or schizophrenic or whatever story we're supposed to believe, and if—"

"That's enough, Detective. This is an order. If you don't like it, you can sweep Truant Park for six months and I'll see if Officer Moraes wants to try his hand at a detective's job."

"This is—" Hazard began, but Somers elbowed him again.

"Drop it," Somers said. "Or I might see if Moraes wants to take me to dinner, too."

"You're not my type," Moraes put in. "Too skinny."

Miranda Carmichael just shook her head and looked like she wished she'd gone into any other job but this.

"Moraes and Carmichael," Somers said, "why don't you trade off?"

"Fine with me," Moraes said. "You want to finish the first shift today?"

"Yeah, sure. You don't mind catching him at three?"

Moraes shook his head.

"Give me a call a quarter hour out," Carmichael said, "and I'll tell you where to meet us."

Moraes gave a miniature salute, and Carmichael nodded to the mayor. "Whenever you're ready, Mr. Mayor."

"Thank you, Officer. And thank you, too, Chief. And Officer Moraes, you as well. Detectives." Newton nodded, and then he turned towards the front lobby.

Cravens gave the detectives—particularly Hazard—a disgusted look and followed the mayor to the front. Somers slumped against a desk in the bullpen. Moraes, rocking on his feet, gave each of the men a considering look and said, "You'll pick up at eleven, then?"

"Yeah," Somers said. "Same routine. We'll call fifteen minutes before."

Moraes gave Hazard, of all people, another look, and then whistled. "Good luck."

As soon as Moraes had left, Hazard started towards the front lobby.

"What are you doing?" Somers said, tagging after him.

"I want to keep my eye on that son of a bitch."

"That's what we're going to be doing, Ree. Every night. Forever. Or until we catch Ted Kjar."

"No, I mean, I want to keep an eye on him now."

"Jesus Christ. Ree, we should go home. Sleep. We're going to be up all night, and—"

Hazard quickened his pace.

"God damn it," Somers said as he hustled to keep up. "I really might see if Moraes wants to take me to dinner."

"You heard him: you're not his type."

Somers swore under his breath.

At the front lobby, though, Hazard slowed. Newton stood at the front doors and bent to talk to Cravens, while Carmichael stood at a respectful distance. Again Hazard wondered exactly how deep Martha Cravens was in Newton's pocket, and he wondered, too, what Newton was trying to pull. Fake his own death and frame the detectives? Escape with embezzled money, assume a new life, and, just to fuck Emery Hazard over one last time, leave Hazard on the hook for his apparent murder? Hazard didn't know, but he didn't believe any of the bullshit about Ted Kjar, and he wasn't going to let Newton put the noose around his neck that easily.

"Excuse me." The voice came from the front desk, where Jim Murray still sat, peering now over his paper at the mayor and Chief Cravens. "Excuse me, you're blocking the door."

"You've got to wonder what's going on inside his head," Somers said.

"Something devious," Hazard said, his eyes still fixed on the mayor. The old man was focused on his conference with Cravens. "Something that will get someone killed and make him richer, I bet."

"No, I mean Murray."

"Excuse me," Murray said again in that querulous voice. "People have to use that door."

"Do you think he's blind?" Somers said. "Do you think he can't see that it's the mayor and his chief? For what it matters, Murray only has two bosses, and he's yelling at them right now." Somers pulled his lower lip between his teeth. "Do you think he's back in, I don't know, 1958?"

With a nod, the mayor finished his conversation with the chief. He pushed on the station's door, and it swung open. Heat poured in from the outside: muggy, swampy, Missouri heat, pasting the air to Hazard's skin. Through the door, the brick facade of storefronts on the other side of the street watched the station. The afternoon sun blazed where it touched anything reflective: the plate glass, the chrome trim, the antenna above the malingering Family Video.

Newton seemed to remember something. He hesitated, hand propping open the door, and turned back to Cravens.

"Excuse me," Murray said, and now the old man was climbing down from his seat, nose hairs trembling as he shuffled towards the door. "Excuse me, this is a public building, and you can't block the door of a public building. Excuse me. Yes. Yes, I'm talking to you. You can't hold the door open like that, you just can't."

Aside from a quick, irritated glance at Murray, Mayor Newton seemed to disregard him. He bent low, speaking urgently to Cravens again.

"Fuck this," Hazard said. "I want to know what all this cloak-and-dagger bullshit is really about."

Somers caught him by the arm. "This is exactly what we just talked about. Hold on, you big lug. Hold on. If you go rushing in now, you're doing exactly what Newton wants."

"And what's that?"

"I don't know, Ree, but you're dead set on giving it to him."

Murray, with faltering steps, worked his way between Newton and the door. The old cop prized Newton's hand from the door with a bemused smile. Behind Murray, like an angel winking on his shoulder, the antenna across the street caught another blaze of light. Murray hesitated, staring at the mayor as though finally recognizing him, and then let the door swing shut. "Sherman? Oh God, I didn't realize it was you." He patted the mayor on the arm. "But you really can't leave that open. Otherwise this place is hotter than a bitch in rut when the afternoon sun comes in. You just—"

The station's glass door shattered. Murray's whole body jerked, and he took a fumbling step forward. The sound of the second gunshot popped in the distance. Murray jerked again, slumping against Mayor Newton as his legs went out from beneath him. Through the teeth of glass still in the doorframe, something winked across the street atop the Family Video.

Not an antenna, Hazard thought, as he sprang into motion. Glass crunched and slid under his wingtips as he sprinted past the mayor, who was stumbling backward, trying to catch Jim Murray's weight while also trying to scuttle into retreat. Cravens had dropped into a shooting stance, her old revolver pointed at the door as she shouted orders. Somers called after Hazard, swearing.

The thing with a sniper was to keep moving. Erratic. Fast. But always moving.

Hazard leaped through the open maw of glass, and as he did, he caught a glimpse of the mayor's face. Even through the haze of adrenaline, Hazard felt a flicker of shock and then doubt. Because Mayor Sherman Newton looked surprised and terrified just about out of his goddamn mind.

CHAPTER FOUR

JULY 2
MONDAY
1:45 PM

OUTSIDE OF THE STATION, the full heat of summer dropped onto Hazard, and sweat soaked his shirt and jacket immediately. His long legs carried him down the station's front walk and out into the street. A Chevy with a missing side panel screeched to a halt as Hazard raced across the asphalt, stopping inches short of striking the detective, and black wisps of burnt rubber mixed with the exhaust. The driver was shouting something, but the shouting stopped as Hazard drew the Smith & Wesson .38 from its shoulder holster. His left arm bounced painfully at his side, but the pain only filled the margin of his awareness, and the rest of Hazard's mind tried to process possibilities.

The Family Video occupied two units of a five-unit brick stretch that took up the block. The right end unit was a CVS. The left end unit was a coffee shop that had upped stakes before Hazard came back to town. The remaining unit was a FedEx office center. Hazard dismissed the CVS and the FedEx immediately; they would have security protocols, however lax, and the odds were low that the shooter would have used them to access the roof. The Family Video was a higher possibility; it had a back room without a security camera, where Family Video rented out less-than-family-friendly films. They even had three gay pornos, all of them dated 1997 or earlier, all of them consistently checked out, which Hazard found morbidly ironic. But that back room had a utility closet, and it could have provided rooftop access. The most likely way, though, had been the abandoned coffee shop, and Hazard jagged left, his wingtips scraping cement.

"I'm behind you," Somers shouted, and through the adrenaline, Hazard felt a tight knot of satisfaction. He and Somers might not see eye to eye on a lot of things. They had their ups and downs, even as detectives. But when things got serious, everything started to click, and right now, Hazard could feel that click like some enormous switch had been thrown and an electric current ran between the two of them.

With one eye on the coffee shop storefront, Hazard jinked around the corner. Inside, afternoon gloom lay as thick as the dust, and a letter board menu listed the specials for May 18, 2017: tuna fish on rye, a pickle spear, hand-crafted chips. Whatever the hell hand-crafted chips were, Hazard wanted some, but his eye took in the other, more relevant details as well: the locked front door, intact glass, and no sign within that anyone had passed through the store recently. He didn't slow his pace, and another twenty yards brought him to the alley.

The blare of a horn was Hazard's only warning, and he dug in his heels at the last second. A white Dodge Ram shot towards him out of the alley. The leather soles of Hazard's wingtips skidded another six inches, heating the bottom of his feet from the friction, and Hazard steadied himself against the wall. For a moment, it looked like the truck would get away clean.

An instant later, John-Henry Somerset swung the Ford Interceptor across the mouth of the alley in a long, shrieking arc of burnt rubber. The Dodge's tires wailed between the alley walls, the sound of hard braking, and Hazard tore open the SUV's door and climbed up beside his partner.

From his new vantage point, Hazard could see the white Dodge Ram jerking into reverse. The truck shot backward down the alley, and it was obvious that the driver was either inexperienced at maneuvering in reverse, terrified, or both because the Ram caromed off the brick walls of the alley. Metal whined and dinged, grating brick dust from the air and stirring clouds of it down the alley.

Somers didn't wait for Hazard's command; he turned the steering wheel, dropped on the gas, and shot after the truck. The Interceptor was a big vehicle, a variant of the Explorer, but by God's own luck this alley had been designed to accommodate garbage trucks. Or, Hazard realized grimly, not by luck at all. The shooter had chosen this alley on purpose because it was big enough for his truck. As though on cue, the Ram punched out of the far end of the alley, button-hooking left too sharply, and brick and mortar raked the side of the truck.

Punching in a number on the phone, Hazard leaned out the window and fired twice with the .38. One of the shots dinged the Ram's hood, spraying sparks up and across the windshield. He couldn't tell where the other one went.

"Cool it," Somers shouted as he bent over the wheel.

"Last chance before he gets somewhere residential," Hazard said. He pressed the phone to his ear. "Dodge Ram. White. Older model, probably the 90s. No plates. Damage to the sides. Red brick dust. Driver is a black male in his thirties. The truck is headed north on LeClerc." Then he dropped the phone on the seat and took another shot. Glass exploded in the Ram's rear window, and then the truck jerked forward, accelerating down the street.

Somers cleared the alley without any problem, turning hard onto LeClerc and barely missing a VW Bug that was idling on the opposite curb. A blue-haired woman in her sixties—Janey Kappler, Hazard recognized, who had taught him third-grade—stared up at them from the smaller car, clutching a dachshund-embroidered handbag to her chest, and then Somers straightened out the SUV and left the Bug and Miss Kappler and the dachshund handbag in a stream of exhaust.

"No more shooting," Somers yelled over the air rushing through the open window. That air tasted sweet to Hazard: hot, yes, and swampy, but motor-exhaust sweet, asphalt sweet, dandelion-spore sweet.

"Can't you go any faster?" Hazard asked.

Somers didn't bother to reply.

"Where the hell is our backup?"

"It's a small town."

And Somers was right; Hazard knew the facts, but the charge of adrenaline made it difficult to focus on them. Wahredua was a small town, and therefore it had a small police force: with all hands on deck, the city employed twenty-seven peace officers, but two worked exclusively with the city housing department, and another two were resource officers at the local schools. The remaining twenty-three were split across two shifts and spread geographically across town, and with the fair in town, that meant that even with their quickest response time, it would be minutes, maybe longer, before any sort of coordinated response was drawn together, and even longer before they could reach Hazard and Somers's location. If Hazard and Somers hadn't been standing there, and if they hadn't reacted immediately, the shooter might very well have escaped: all he needed to do was drive a few blocks and disappear.

"The bastard planned this."

"Of course he did." Somers frowned. "How'd you know he's in his thirties?"

"He's still young enough to get off that roof pretty damn fast, but not so young he still has good hand and eye coordination. You saw him driving backward; he beat that truck to shit in about fifteen yards."

"I still have good hand-eye—"

"You're a cop. You work at it." Hazard peered at the truck ahead of them. "Damn it, can you go any faster?"

"You already asked that."

Their sirens chirped overhead, and fortunately it was a Monday after the lunch rush, and a city the size of Wahredua rarely had traffic that could truly be described as bad. Still, as they raced through traffic lights and left drivers staring after them, Hazard noticed two accidents already. The shooter didn't have sirens, and it was obvious that when he had blazed through some of the lights, other drivers had swerved to avoid him, causing more problems. In the light of an active shooter who had already shot one cop—shot, not killed, because Hazard wasn't ready to classify Murray as dead, at least, not yet—a few fender-benders seemed like a small deal, but Hazard knew that in political terms, the fallout from today's events would grow exponentially with every injured, or annoyed, citizen.

But at least they were gaining ground. With every quarter mile, the Interceptor crept closer to the Ram. The truck was old, beat to hell, and had never been meant for speed. The shooter had chosen it, Hazard guessed, because it was so unremarkable, especially in a town like Wahredua. The Interceptor, in contrast, specially designed for this kind of work, prowled forward, closing the gap between the two vehicles.

"Shit," Somers swore as the Ram cut left, bouncing over the grassy median and disappearing down a smaller street. The blond man jerked the wheel, launching the Interceptor along the same trajectory. "Smithfield."

Hazard swore too. Now that Somers drew his attention to it, he saw what he had missed with his attention focused on the Ram. Around them, Wahredua had begun to decay. Instead of the well-kept streets and buildings—plenty of brick, plenty of fresh paint—this part of town leaned on sagging wooden supports, with moss growing along huge slabs of asbestos siding. Aluminum carports huddled next to houses on postage-stamp lots, and rust ate its way along acre after acre of chain fencing.

At different times in its history, Wahredua had enjoyed prosperity, peaking with the Missouri Pacific railroad lines and dwindling, more or less, steadily, ever since. But Smithfield had never really been prosperous. Even in its best days, Smithfield had never managed anything more than decent, with a few respectable pockets. And now, with MP lines long since dead and industry all but vanished from the town, Smithfield was a refuge for drug-dealing, sex work, and violence. Its inhabitants mistrusted the police, but Somers, who had cut his teeth here, knew the place better than most cops.

"He's going to try to shake us here," Somers said.

"Obviously."

The hot July sun had baked the streets empty aside from a gaggle of children who lounged in the shade. There were half a dozen of them, two African-American, the other four with skin and hair that suggested a mixture of ethnicities. The oldest wasn't shaving yet, and the youngest was having a hard time staying on her tricycle. They stared as the Interceptor blitzed past them.

Ahead, a massive building rose. It occupied an entire block, and its crumbling brick revealed pale, powdery innards. A stretch of iron fencing ran in front, but where most fences were designed to keep something out, this one looked like it was the only thing keeping the entire structure from falling down. Brown glass flecked the sidewalk in front of the building, and as the Interceptor surged forward, that glass burned with whiskey-colored fire in the sunlight.

"The motherfucking Haverford," Hazard said. "Of course he's going to the Haverford."

The Haverford, the brick structure slumped ahead of them, was an apartment building that should have been condemned. Because of its size and its warren of hallways, the building had become home to a parade of successive drug dealers, as well as anyone else who wanted an easily defensible place to conduct illicit activities. There were, Hazard knew, undoubtedly some decent citizens who lived in the building out of necessity, but they were by far the minority. Hazard had been here only once before, while investigating a murder suspect, but only two fragments of that memory glimmered at the top of Hazard's brain right then. Two facts, one important, and one a tag-along that Hazard associated with this place. First: two cops had been killed inside the Haverford. And second: that Hollace Walker, the closest thing Emery Hazard had to a friend growing up, had come here to buy coke.

Those two thoughts surfaced in Hazard's mind, and he collected them, appraised them, and dismissed them. He wasn't going to die today, inside the Haverford or out.

"He's slowing down," Somers said. "Hold on."

Hazard braced himself against the dash. As the Ram slowed, the Interceptor suddenly seemed to launch itself forward. For a moment, Hazard felt himself floating, as though time and space had suspended him momentarily. Chrome shone in white lines. The Ram's paint glowed incandescent. Hazard's stomach lurched, and the thrum of the Interceptor's tires rattled his jaw, and he tasted the dry, dusty air conditioning inside the SUV. Then the Interceptor connected with the Ram's rear right wheel.

Even steadied against the impact, Hazard slid forward so fast that the seat belt snapped taut and caught him, and his bad arm clipped the dash hard enough to bring tears to his eyes. Metal crumpled and twisted with a long, grating shriek, and there was an odd, hiccupping noise as the Ram hopped the curb. The truck was already spinning, and Somers let the Interceptor's momentum carry the truck forward even as it continued to spin. Then the Ram crashed into the fence. Iron posts clanged as they popped loose of their fittings. The force of the vehicles carried them another yard, and then the Ram settled up against the Haverford's crumbling brick facade and huffed a tiny cloud of steam. The shooter, dazed but managing to keep his feet, stumbled free of the Ram and darted towards the Haverford's door.

"The fucker," Hazard shouted, wrestling free of his seatbelt and dropping out of the SUV. As he circled the Interceptor at a run, he called in their location, and then he and Somers rushed towards the Haverford's door. Intended to be locked, the Haverford's security door had long since been broken, and it opened easily for Somers. The detectives plunged through the lobby and into the hallway beyond.

The corridor split in two directions, following the Haverford's exterior walls and opening onto staircases. There were four directions that the shooter could have gone, but Hazard dismissed the stairs immediately.

"Stay on the ground floor," he shouted, shoving Somers in one direction while he took the other.

It was obvious from Somers's face that he didn't like splitting up, but he loped in the direction Hazard had indicated without another word.

Hazard had the .38 low, and he ran full-out. Part of that was to try to catch up to the shooter. But part of that was the awareness that he was inside the Haverford's maze now, and word would spread quickly that there were police inside the building, and Hazard didn't know what would happen after that. Maybe nothing. But two cops had been killed here.

Ahead of him, the hallway split at regular intervals, crossing the width of the building to maximize the number of apartments. No windows opened onto the July sun; instead, at intersections, electric chandeliers gave miserly pools of light, barely enough to spot the brass paint peeling from the fixtures, and the rest of the hallway was darkness. Not regular darkness, either, but a hot, suffocating darkness, the smell of ancient carpet that has absorbed decades of shit and piss and vomit, the smell of moldering fabric, the smell of a closed-up sickroom.

While Hazard scanned the islands of light ahead of him, he strained to listen. His breathing was quick but steady; injuring his arm had slowed his strength training, but he still ran five miles every day he had a chance. His heart pumped, elevated but sustainable. Those noises made up part of his background, a familiar part. But the rest of the sounds seemed designed to confuse and startle him. TVs blared from within nearby apartments, raucous with canned laughter. A man with a deep voice was yelling about mac 'n cheese. There was a rattling, metallic noise that went on for almost a minute, and Hazard tried to place the sound and could only imagine a wheelchair free-falling down a flight of steps. From ahead, a gunshot clapped down the hallway, and Hazard had already taken cover at the next intersection before his heart slowed and he realized that it had been a door slamming shut.

He kept moving, and his speed was good. The intersecting hallways were dark and empty as he passed them, and although Hazard hoped from time to time that he would catch a glimpse of Somers keeping pace at the other end of the building, the darkness was too thick, and the distance too great, and he had to settle for hoping that his partner was safe.

It was so empty in here. Noises, yes—the long, uneven chiming that Hazard had heard earlier; a TV; the door slamming shut. But the

Haverford had sheltered people for almost a hundred years. It had always been full. Where were they now?

On the next door, Hazard spotted a pre-printed form, white and yellow and red: Building Condemned. And on next stretch of wall, a piece of yellow paper fluttered in his passage, and he glimpsed two words: Unlawful Occupancy. That was an answer to his question, but it only raised another.

Why the Haverford? There were easier ways to lose someone. More public ways, places where police would hesitate to use force for fear of harming a bystander. The Wahredua Shopping Mall. Or Market Street. Or Truant Park. In contrast, Smithfield was a rat's nest of side-streets and alleys, rife with abandoned buildings. In many ways, those were a disadvantage. A fleeing man stood out; aside from those sunbaked children, Smithfield was a ghost town. The only reason to lead them here, to use this as an escape, was if—

Was if he planned on using it for more than an escape.

Hazard stopped running. He dialed Somers on his phone, but he had no service, and the phone stared stupidly and silently back at him. Why bring two cops to the Haverford? Because two cops had died there.

He flattened himself against the wall and took slow, careful steps. Were there three more of those electric chandeliers ahead? Four? Three, he guessed, although the blur and the distance made it difficult to be sure. Only three left. And if the shooter had planned a trap, Hazard hadn't run into it yet.

But Somers—

Hazard quashed the thought before it could get started. He couldn't bear that thought; he couldn't hold it in his head and still do his job.

He forced himself to think: the shooter had drawn them here. He had chosen the Haverford even though better options existed for an escape. And he had done so intentionally. The most plausible reason was because he had set a trap. So. Where was the trap?

If the shooter had planned out as much as Hazard believed, then the trap would have received the same attention to detail. That meant the shooter had a certain amount of logic behind the trap. A wave of panic crested at the thought of Somers walking blindly into a tripwire, a shotgun punching a hole in his chest. Hazard's breathing quickened. His hand was slick along the Smith & Wesson's grips.

That doesn't help him, he told himself. That doesn't help anyone. So stop it. Stop it and think.

Ok. He drew in a breath, tasting the moldering carpet, the heat, the darkness, the flaking brass paint from the chandeliers. Think. What did the shooter know? Well, he knew that Hazard and Somers were cops. No; Hazard forced himself to scratch part of that thought. The shooter might not have known that Hazard and Somers would be the ones to respond. After all, it had been Hazard's own obstinacy that had carried him into the station's front lobby. Somers had wanted to go home and get some sleep.

So, that meant the shooter was most likely expecting other cops. Probably uniformed officers dispatched as soon as the shooting occurred. And that meant the shooter was trusting that these cops would be relatively inexperienced in a situation like this. Wahredua's police received the best training they could, but for the most part, they handled lost cats and public urination and boundary line disputes. A few drunk and disorderly calls. Plenty of domestic abuse. But following a shooter into the Haverford's nightmare warren? That would be new for any of them.

And because it would be a new, unfamiliar situation for those cops, the shooter would expect them to follow standard procedure. Up to a point. Because those patrol cops might have decided to watch the Haverford from the outside and wait for backup. They might not have rushed into the black, stinking darkness, and Hazard felt a dry, brittle grin on his face. They might not be as stupid as Emery Hazard. So maybe the shooter had two traps. Maybe out front—

The explosion was really nothing more than a thud, like one giant fist hammering at the Haverford's front door. This deep in the building, Hazard didn't see any light, but he felt the ripple of force rock the structure, felt it in his own tissue and in the wall and in the ground.

Somers.

He took two steps and then froze.

No. No. Think.

A bomb hidden out front. Or maybe tossed by a friendly neighbor from an upstairs window. Something to take care of cops who might be waiting for backup.

But something else too. Hazard's gut told him that. He loved analysis. He prized himself for his abilities at ratiocination and deduction. But right then, the innermost part of his brain, the part that had evolved over millions of years to keep humans alive, was screaming at him. There was something else. Something inside this building.

But where? He had to narrow the possibilities. Not in these intersections. Not in the cross hallways. There was too much traffic in the Haverford. People lived here, and while the shooter might not care about killing any of them, he also wouldn't be happy if they triggered his trap before the cops. So it had to be somewhere specific, where someone wasn't likely to trip it, somewhere that would funnel the cops so they had to go that way, somewhere the shooter would have access to it, and somewhere the pursuing cops might throw caution to the wind because—

Because they had the shooter back in their sights.

Fuck.

Hazard ran. His left arm flopped painfully at his side, phone in his fingers, and his right hand held the .38. He tried to dial, but those fingers were slow and less responsive, and even when Somers's name came on the screen, the signal was too weak, and the call wouldn't go through. Swearing, Hazard dove into the darkness. That was what it was like: diving. He would reach the edge of the light, granular, sabulous, like land meeting water, and then he was beyond it, in the darkness, his legs churning to carry him towards that next buoy of light.

Where would the cops drop their guard? Where would they feel a renewed spurt of energy and determination? At the end of the building. At the exit. Where the shooter would linger just long enough to be spotted.

Somers.

Oh fuck.

51

Somers was faster than Hazard.

Oh fuck.

At the end of the corridor, Hazard was running too fast. He tried to slide into the turn, taking the corner as fast as he could, but he was moving too damn fast. He didn't fall, and his brain whispered a brief thank you to fate, but he crashed into the far wall, his full weight pinning his bad arm against the drywall. Pain went up like a signal flare. Gasping, Hazard pushed himself off the wall and down the hall.

He could see the exit ahead. The door was propped open, and silver daylight framed the opening. In front of that illuminated backdrop, a silhouette moved, fumbling with the door. That was part of the act; an unspoken justification, in case the cops wondered how they'd been lucky enough to catch up with the shooter. Here was the answer, being pantomimed for them: the idiot got stuck at the door.

Only he wasn't stuck. He was stalling. And as he caught sight of Hazard, he pushed the door open.

Another figure came around the corner at the far end of the hall. He was running. He was moving at full speed. He had the perfect, loping grace that Hazard would recognize anywhere. He had memorized every inch of this man, pieced him together in his mind a thousand times, ten thousand times, over the last twenty years.

"Somers," Hazard screamed, barely recognizing his own voice. "Stop!"

After that, everything happened at once. A muzzle flashed. The light painted Somers in a hundred different shades of red. It picked out every detail, splashing light and shadow, highlighting the perfect lines of his face, the confusion, the surprise, and underneath it all, etching itself into the skin, fear. A boom echoed down the corridor. Somers tumbled over sideways.

Somers.

Then the shooter shoved open the emergency exit door, and summer light flooded into the Haverford's fetid darkness, and Hazard could pick out the gleam of that sunlight on the tension wire running six inches in front of his own shin.

Somers.

Hazard cleared the wire. Ten yards to Somers. Eight.

Somers smiling at him in the park.

Six yards.

Somers swinging Evie and laughing.

Five.

Somers naked on the bed, one hand tracing the dark calligraphy across his chest, and wearing that damn smirk he always wore when he knew he was about to get what he wanted.

Three yards. Three.

And then, to Hazard's surprise, he heard Somers voice. "Go get him. Go get him, Ree. I'm fine. Go after him."

Again, intuition and instinct took over when emotion fried the rational centers of Hazard's brain. He swerved towards the exit door, caught it on his bad shoulder, and howled. He didn't care about the noise at this point. All he cared about was catching this bastard.

The shooter was twenty yards ahead, sprinting full speed down the alley behind the Haverford. In full daylight, seen directly instead of at a distance through a windshield, the man looked different than what Hazard had expected. In spite of the heat, he wore a balaclava, gloves and a long-sleeved shirt. Hazard had already seen in him all that gear, but still, something was different. The difference wasn't anything Hazard could put his finger on, but he was suddenly less certain about his earlier guess. Was the man older? Younger? Was he not even a man at all?

Hazard put on speed. A fresh wave of adrenaline burned through him, incinerating every thought, and the last one, the one that floated up like a cinder caught on a draft of emotion, was simply: Somers is all right. And then Hazard was moving like a truck.

He hit the shooter at full speed. Hazard meant it to be a tackle, but his bad arm refused to respond, and when they hit the ground, the shooter rolled free instead of staying trapped by Hazard's mass. Hazard scrambled after the man. He caught an ankle, dragging the shooter back, and the shooter's other foot shot out and caught Hazard in the chin. Hazard's head snapped back. Black stars spun in his vision.

But he hadn't let go, and he hauled on the ankle again. A second kick connected with his head, but this time, Hazard had been expecting it, and he turned so that the blow glanced along the contour of his skull instead of meeting straight on. With as much strength as he could muster, Hazard hauled, and the shooter skidded three feet back over the gravel. Hazard reared back, trying to get enough weight on the bastard to pin him until Somers got there.

This time, though, the shooter reared back and twisted into a punch. For a minute, Hazard glimpsed the man's eyes: green, glittering. Then the punch connected. Hazard took it as best he could, ducking, but it landed solidly above his ear, and Hazard saw those black stars again. Could feel them, even, prickly against his face. He took another punch, and the third one he managed to knock aside, batting it out of the air like he was Babe fucking Ruth. He just had to hold on. Twenty seconds. Thirty. Somers would be here. Somers was coming.

The next punch was strange; even addled by the blows to the head, Hazard knew something was wrong because the shooter telegraphed the punch loud and clear, and it was obvious that he had changed his target. Instead of throwing another fist or elbow at Hazard's head, the shooter was aiming down.

At his arm, Hazard realized a moment too late. At his bad arm. The punch was clear as newsprint. If he'd been thinking clearly, if he'd had even an extra second, Hazard could have avoided it. But he was rattled from the earlier blows, and waves of adrenaline battered him, and he hated that arm, that was the bottom of it, he hated that fucking arm because it was useless, and so he didn't think about it.

The punch landed perfectly, right where a long, jagged cut was still healing, and Hazard's world went white.

CHAPTER FIVE

JULY 2
MONDAY
2:37 PM

THE AFTERSCHOCKS WERE STILL RUNNING through Somers. Some of it was the shotgun—Jesus Christ, if Hazard hadn't been there. In his mind, Somers saw it again and again: the muzzle flash unfolding in slow motion, a coruscating flower of light and heat. Hazard had forced him to watch a *Nova* episode about stars, and now, in hindsight, Somers could compare it to that, to a beautiful, deadly star being born. He had thrown himself sideways as soon as he heard Hazard's voice, and that was the only reason he had been peppered with three pellets on his side, barely even a flesh wound, instead of being turned into hamburger.

So some of it, yes, some of it was the shotgun, and Somers sat on the back of the ambulance, shirtless because the EMT had cut it away, and he shivered even though the July sun was toasting his back. Some of it was the shotgun. Maybe half. Maybe.

But the other fifty percent, or fifty-one percent, or sixty, or eighty—the number went up, the more Somers thought about it—the rest of it was about Hazard. Emerging from the Haverford, finally free from the smell of cat pee and liniment and rot, Somers had stumbled on the alley's broken asphalt. He hadn't lost his footing. He hadn't slipped. He had stumbled when he saw Emery Hazard sprawled on the ground, unmoving, and a bastard in a balaclava leaning over him.

Somers had been carrying the big .40 caliber Glock that he liked, and he had ignored the fact that the distance was too great and the sun at a shit angle and he had fired. He had emptied all fifteen cartridges from the magazine, which was a stupid move, and as far as he could tell, he hadn't done a damn thing except waste fifteen cartridges. If he were lucky, maybe he'd made that bastard in the balaclava shit himself. If he were really lucky.

Next to him, Emery Hazard winced as the paramedic examined the cuts in his arm. Over two months after Hazard had been attacked in their apartment, the wounds were still red and raw in places, although some of the smaller lacerations had healed and showed shiny new skin. This paramedic, Frannie Langkop, was an older woman, her short gray hair gelled into spikes, and her skin the same color and texture as a good leather coat. She'd patched them up before, and she didn't make much bones about the fact that they were local heroes.

Hazard winced again, and she took his arm more firmly. "Quit being such a bitch about it."

"It stings."

"Of course it stings. About the only damn thing I can do is wipe you down. The damage, if he did any, is going to be deeper. You'll need to see a doctor."

"I'm fine."

She scrubbed with the antiseptic wipe until Hazard growled and yanked his arm away. Then she laughed. "You want me to check your ass for road rash? I could clean you up down there too."

"Fuck you, Frannie."

"I wouldn't mind," she said with a suggestive wiggle of her eyebrows. "You want something? Is it still hurting?"

Hazard shook his head, but pain was still digging a furrow between his eyes.

"He wants something," Somers said. "He's just not going to say it."

"I can give you something local. It'll take the worst of it away for a little bit."

"I'm fine."

"Yeah, give him that."

"I'm fine."

"Then let her give it to you for my sake."

Hazard frowned, but he didn't resist as Frannie injected him near the biggest of the still-healing cuts.

"Thanks," Somers said.

"I only did it because you're giving me a show."

Somers managed to muster a grin, and he even did a little pec show for her, but when Frannie laughed and moved away, he felt the grin slide off.

The ambulance was parked across half of the alley behind the Haverford. Ten of Wahredua's finest had shown up in total, along with the ambulance and a fire truck, although God only knew what the firefighters thought they were going to do. About as much as Somers had, he allowed. Just about as much as that. Now two of the uniformed officers, Norman and Gross, were doing a grid search of the alley, while eight more officers combed the Haverford.

"They're not going to find fuck," Hazard said.

"No. They're not." He reached over and turned Hazard's arm for inspection. "Well?"

He grunted.

"So it feels better?"

He grunted again.

"Because you didn't want her to give you—"

Shifting, Hazard slid his good arm around Somers, and his big catcher's mitt-sized hand slid up Somers's back.

"Jesus, Ree, if you hadn't been there."

He nodded, and his hand flexed against Somers's bare back, and suddenly Somers wanted a fuck. Nothing romantic. Just a wild, hot, still-alive fuck, because he'd just about kissed a shotgun and somehow he was still alive, and Hazard's hand was doing wonderful things to the sun-hot skin of his back.

At the mouth of the alley, Cravens was head to head with Patrick Foley. The chief gestured furiously, and Foley ducked his big red Irish head, and then they separated. The chief's shoes clicked on the asphalt as she came towards the ambulance. When she stood in front of them, her eyes went to Somers's bandaged side. "Are you ok?"

"Hazard's the one who really got hurt."

"Your arm?"

"I'm fine. I keep telling everyone I'm fine."

"This is a cluster," Cravens said. She didn't look like a grandmother anymore. She looked mad enough to chew license plates, but she also looked tired. And old. Older than Somers had ever seen her.

"What about Murray?" Somers said.

She shook her head.

"Christ. I'm sorry."

"Sorry?" Cravens barked a laugh. "You two are the only ones that came close to doing anything. When I saw you jump through the glass—good Lord, Detective, I just about fell out of my shoes. I was still waiting for the shooter to come through the door. I didn't even think that it had been from across the street. I just—I reacted."

"We all did," Hazard said. "I reacted differently because I saw something flashing on top of the Family Video building. The scope, I think."

"And I reacted differently," Somers said dryly, "because I have John McClane for a partner."

The corner of Cravens's mouth twitched, but the rest of her face remained still, as though Frannie had injected her with the local anesthetic instead of Hazard. "You been out front yet?"

Somers shook his head.

"Not much left of the vehicles. Either one of them. He was planning this. He planned this whole thing."

"Not quite," Hazard said. "He didn't plan on us."

"That's a fine sentiment, Detective, but—"

"No. I mean he assumed we would not be the first ones to respond." Hazard laid out the assumptions and deductions he had made, and when he had finished, Cravens was staring at him, her face still droopy and vacant, but her skin gray.

"You thought of that while you were running through the Haverford?"

"Of course not. I stopped to think."

"For a minute," Somers said.

"Two minutes. And a half. Thereabouts."

Cravens shook her head wordlessly.

"John McClane," Somers said, feeling the first real grin since he had emerged into the alley, and he ran one hand through Hazard's long, dark hair, ruining the careful part. "And a little bit of Bobby Fischer."

"I don't play chess."

"I know, Ree. I know."

With what looked like visible effort, Cravens was mustering herself. "Detectives, the events that have happened today mean we're dealing with a very dangerous individual. Or individuals. Ted Kjar—"

"It wasn't Ted Kjar," Hazard said. Somers squeezed his hand, but Hazard kept talking. "This guy was African-American. And don't tell me Kjar might be behind it; just because the mayor says—"

"I know," Cravens said, and her voice wobbled on the edge of shrill. She paused, collected herself, and in a calmer voice said, "I know, Detective. I understand. We're dealing with a dangerous individual at the very least. He was bold enough to attempt to kill the mayor at the police station, and he was clever enough that he almost got away with it. In the process, he killed Officer Murray and might have killed a number of other police. This isn't a protection detail anymore. This is—I don't know. But it's beyond us."

"What does that mean?"

"It means we're going to call in the FBI. This could be terrorism-related. Or drug-related. Or God only knows what else."

"The FBI might not—"

"Or the Highway Patrol. Or the National Guard. God damn it, Hazard, I don't know who we're going to get, but we're going to get someone. What you've done today, it's more than anyone could ask. But I'm going to ask for more."

Hazard had gone still; Somers nodded and met Cravens's tired eyes.

"Whoever's coming, they won't be here for another day. Maybe two. Until then, I need you to keep an eye on the mayor."

"My partner was shot," Hazard said. Bitterness filled his voice. "And I'm useless with my arm like this."

"Ree—"

"I am. If my arm worked, we'd have that bastard in cuffs right now. I'm a liability like this. You need to put Lender and Swinney on it. Somers needs to rest. And I—" He stopped; the expression on his face was so bleak that it shook Somers.

"Detective Hazard," Cravens said, "are you finished?"

He nodded.

"With your arm injured, you still managed to pursue an active shooter faster than any other available officer. You maintained that pursuit, avoided a trap that might have killed you, saved your partner's life, and managed to bring down the shooter."

"And let him get away."

"That wasn't ideal."

"It was a fucking disaster."

"Fine," Cravens said, the word exploding out. "Yes. It was. You fucked up. But you know what, Detective? You're the best I have."

The word was pitched low, but it had a ringing intensity that lingered in the ambulance's cramped space.

Somers smirked, and reached to take Hazard's hand in his own. "And you have me. In case both of you forgot."

Cravens sniffed. Hazard grimaced, but his hand tightened around Somers's.

"Officers Carmichael and Moraes will take their shifts as they've already agreed, but I need the two of you to protect the mayor tonight. Do you understand why?"

Hazard studied her with his scarecrow eyes.

"We understand," Somers said.

"Let me know what you need. Detective Somerset, if those wounds—"

"We'll be in touch."

Cravens nodded and lurched into motion, and something about her seemed stilted and animatronic. Like she'd run to the end of her batteries, Somers thought as he watched her go. Maybe permanently.

"This is a terrible idea," Hazard said.

"Sure. But it's also the only decent option we have."

"My arm—"

"Ree, fuck the arm, if you'll excuse me. Anybody else would have died in there. Christ, I almost died in there."

"I got lucky."

"No, you didn't."

"I'm not always the smartest guy in the room. Today was luck as much as anything."

"I'll remember you said that."

"For fuck's sake, Somers."

"Next time we're having an argument about whether or not federal aid ended the Depression—"

"That wasn't an argument. It was a discussion."

"You ripped two books in half."

"I was making a point."

"Technically, you were making four points."

Hazard growled something, and his arm tightened around Somers. Somers leaned into him, turning his head up, and kissed him.

When they broke, Hazard's scarecrow eyes gleamed. "John, if something happens to you—I couldn't. I can't." His voice shook slightly. "I won't."

"Instead of thinking about that," Somers said, wagging Hazard's chin, "think about the case."

"What?"

"This is a case, Ree. We have a killer on our hands. He wants to kill again, sure, but he's already killed once. And if we can find the bastard, if we can stop him, we can put an end to this before something else bad happens."

"Before we start, I need a few things."

Somers's eyebrows climbed. "Yeah?"

"Food, to start. And time to think. And a men's shirt. Medium."

"You don't wear a medium."

"No, but you do." Those scarecrow eyes were suddenly hotter than the sun. Hot enough to give Somers a sunburn, and the flush that followed ran through his whole body. "And you're making it really hard to think right now."

CHAPTER SIX

JULY 2
MONDAY
2:56 PM

Riverside Burgers was a fixture on Market Street where one of the state highways cut through Wahredua, bringing passersby and even the occasional tourist. The restaurant had started life as a drive-in. Somers remembered, when he had been a boy, coming here in his father's Lincoln Continental and parking under the cement awning next to a menu with a two-way speaker. His father had let Somers press the button on the speaker and then he had ordered two burgers, two onion rings, and two strawberry shakes, and the girl who had brought out their food had long, curly hair and she glided up to the car on roller skates. It was a surprisingly vivid memory, and Somers knew why: it was one of the few happy times he could recall spending with his father.

Today, though, Riverside Burgers had adapted to the twenty-first century. It had knocked down the cement awnings, ripped up the two-way speakers, and replaced the girls on roller skates with a large, air-conditioned dining room. Like just about every fast food place Somers had ever been in, Riverside was decorated with surfaces easy to clean: tile, sealed particle board, and glass. The smell made his stomach rumble, a mixture of frying onions and seared meat.

"You might have been on to something," Somers said, tugging at the collar of the Wahredua Police t-shirt he had taken from Cravens's car.

Cravens herself had driven them here because the Interceptor had been destroyed in the explosion. She had offered to take them through the drive-thru. She had even offered to wait while they went inside. But Hazard had pointed out that they only lived a few blocks up the street, and they would walk home. Cravens hadn't stuck around long enough to argue; she'd had a shit day, and Somers knew it was only going to get worse.

As Somers and Hazard walked towards the counter inside the restaurant, Somers nudged his partner. At the end of a short hall, three doors stood closed: one marked Employees Only, and two gender-neutral restrooms. Police tape crisscrossed one of the doors.

"Like it's a real crime scene," Hazard said, snorting.

"Let's take a look after we eat."

"Good idea. We can watch and see if anyone else is interested in it. Or if we're being followed."

"Right. Plus I'm hungry."

Ignoring Hazard's scowl, Somers ordered, and then Hazard ordered, and they took their food to a table near an arched window that looked over a stretch of ultra-green, well-watered lawn and, beyond the lawn, Market Street. Today's traffic didn't look any different than usual. Word about the shooting and high-speed (well, relatively high-speed, anyway) chase had undoubtedly spread throughout the town. It was difficult to keep any kind of secrets in a place this small. But the city didn't seem any the worse for it.

"Nobody even cares," Hazard said, in that annoying way he had of responding to Somers's thoughts before Somers had even spoken.

"Maybe they just thought it was fireworks."

Raising the burger to his mouth, Hazard said, "Nobody's dumb enough to think those were fireworks." Then, through a huge bite, he said, "Except you, maybe."

Grinning, Somers popped fries in his mouth. "I guess I'm lucky I slowed down. I kept reminding myself how slow you are. Carrying all that extra weight, it can't be easy. Bad for the joints. Your top speed is probably, what, three miles an hour? Two and a half?"

Hazard was downing his chocolate shake—he'd already gone through about half of it—and then he sputtered and frowned and set the paper cup down. "I'm. Not. Carrying. Extra. Weight."

"Of course not."

Face set in suspicion, Hazard toyed with the straw.

"Ree, you look great."

Hazard scooted the cup towards himself.

"All those extra miles you've been running, they're really paying off."

The big, dark-haired man made a satisfied noise and lifted the shake to his mouth again.

"I mean, you'll never get back into those jeans you used to wear, but I'm proud of you for trying."

Slamming the cup down again, Hazard pointed a finger at him. "You're mean."

Somers started to laugh. "Drink your shake."

"No."

"C'mon."

"I don't want it."

"Ree, I was just kidding."

"I know. I just don't want it anymore."

"For heaven's sake, just drink it, all right?"

"I think we have two shooters. No, that's not right. Killers. Assassins. Whatever we're going to call them."

"Do they have anything to do with your shake?"

Hazard shook his head in irritation, and his long, dark hair—too long, really, but just so damn beautiful, especially now that he'd started growing out his scruff—tumbled over his forehead. "What we saw today, what we were dealing with, that wasn't Ted Kjar. At least, not the Ted Kjar the mayor was telling us about."

Somers's face grew serious. "You think the mayor was lying?"

"I thought he was. I thought this whole thing was some bullshit way of making us look bad. Or getting rid of us. But I saw his face when Murray got shot."

"Yeah, so did I. He was terrified. Out of his mind."

"That's what I thought too. And that's a normal reaction to having someone take a shot at you."

"But not if the whole thing is planned. No matter how good of an actor you are, you can't fake that kind of terror."

Hazard nodded, his hand drifting towards the shake without him seeming to realize it. "I agree. So that means we have a few options: a) he was telling the truth about Kjar; b) he was lying about Kjar. Then we subdivide those: a) he was telling the truth about Kjar, and Kjar was the shooter today; b) he was telling the truth about Kjar, but a second person took the shot; c) he was lying about Kjar, but Kjar was still the shooter today; d) he was lying about Kjar, and someone else was the shooter today."

"It's annoying when you do that."

"What?"

"List things."

"The other night, when we were in bed, you didn't seem to mind." Hazard's brows knitted together. "I was telling you all the ways I can make you—"

"Never mind. That's not what I was—never mind. Ok. Four options."

"Right. I don't think option A makes any sense; even if he's telling the truth about Kjar, Kjar couldn't have been our shooter today. If the mayor's telling the truth, if Kjar is a self-medicated, dangerous schizophrenic, then he might have come into the station with a gun, but he wouldn't have had this elaborate plan."

"Drug-addicted schizophrenics can't plan?"

"Of course they can. But they're mentally ill, Somers. Their focus isn't the same, and they'll get caught up in delusions, hallucinations, all of it. What we saw today was someone who is intelligent, ruthless, and deliberate."

Somers nodded, fighting to hide a smile as Hazard took an absent sip of the shake again. "Agreed. All of it, I agree. So B is still an option: Kjar is mentally ill and may have assaulted the mayor, but someone else is also trying to kill him."

"And D remains an option: there's nothing wrong with Kjar, and the mayor is lying for some reason, but there is genuinely someone trying to kill him, and the mayor didn't even realize it."

"What was C again? Why are you leaving it off the list?"

"It's too unlikely: the mayor was lying about Kjar, but Kjar still decides to shoot him. Why? If he's not mentally ill, and if the rest of what the mayor told us is a lie, why would Kjar come after him? The odds would be astronomically against it."

"Does it matter?"

"Statistics are helpful for—"

"No, dummy. Does it matter if he's telling the truth about Kjar?"

"Sure. Either he's planning something, or he's legitimately in danger from someone who is mentally ill."

"Right, right," Somers said, waving this away with one hand. "I mean, does it matter now? In terms of how we go about this investigation?"

For a moment, the only sound was Hazard's slurping on the straw as he tried to get the last of the shake.

"Good?" Somers asked.

Blushing Hazard tossed the empty cup on the table and glared as though it were somehow Somers's fault. "I don't know. And I'm not talking about the shake, so don't say something wiseass about how it's impossible for me not to know how good it is."

"It might be impossible because you drank it so fast."

Hazard threw him the finger. "I'm saying I don't know if we need to decide about Kjar right now. I think we follow the evidence and see where it leads us, and we reserve judgment about Kjar until we know better."

"All right."

"All right?"

Somers jerked a thumb at the taped bathroom door. "Let's start looking at evidence. Unless you want another shake."

"Sometimes you're a real pain in my ass."

"There's a lot of room to be a pain."

After seeing their badges, the manager unlocked the bathroom door, and Somers climbed over the tape. It was exactly as the mayor had described it: a single-user bathroom with a dirty floor. There was even still some old toilet paper on the tile, although it had dried out in the last two days. Over the sink, a broken mirror hung, and the shards of glass still covered the floor.

"Who told you to leave it like this?" Somers said.

"The cop," the manager said. She was probably thirty, bottle-blond, and she had an insulin pump that she checked every few minutes. New, Somers guessed. Or she'd had problems recently. "The one who came and taped it off."

"Do you remember his name?"

"He left a card." She stared at them. Then she blinked. "Do you want me to get it?"

"Now," Hazard growled.

Squeaking, the manager retreated.

"I don't see anything that disproves what the mayor told us," Somers said.

"I don't see anything that proves it either."

"You think he did this himself?"

"I doubt it. He probably had someone else do it and then planted the baseball bat."

"Without anyone noticing?"

"That's the strange part," Hazard said. "It was the beginning of the Saturday lunch rush. Somebody should have seen something."

The manager came back with a card between two fingers, and she displayed it for them without handing it over. Albert Lender, Detective, and then his phone numbers. That was all.

"We already knew that," Somers said to Hazard.

"It doesn't hurt to check."

"Has anyone else been by?" Somers said.

"No. You're the first." Then she blushed, a pretty pink color, and said, "Is it true? About you two?" Somers met her gaze, and then her eyes dropped, and she giggled. "I mean, it's none of my business, but—" She took a deep breath and then said, "It's hot."

Hazard shook his head and brushed past her.

Somers, looking after him, shrugged. "Yep. It is."

"True?" the girl asked. "Or hot?"

With a wink, Somers moved past her, and her giggles followed him down the hall.

They walked three hot, sticky blocks to the Crofter's Mark, a renovated apartment building on Market Street, and they took the mirrored elevator to the fourth floor. The A/C was a relief, and the apartment was dark and quiet. Somers kicked off his shoes and then peeled off the t-shirt, wincing as the pellet-wounds to his side pulled.

Hazard's big mitt caught a handful of his hair from behind, and then another big hand was on his shoulder, spinning him around. Hazard crashed into him, his weight and force carrying Somers into the wall, his mouth hard and needy on Somers's. The kiss seemed to go on forever; there was a violence about it, something primal, that stoked the urge Somers had felt before. A noise was building in Somers's throat, something savage, and he dug his nails into Hazard's back, into his bicep, grinding against the bigger man, desperate for his touch.

"This is just a fuck," Hazard whispered, his voice like river-bottom gravel when he broke for air.

Somers met his eyes. His hand found Hazard's dick still under layers of cotton, and he squeezed. Hazard's yelped, and then he thrust into Somers's hand. "Just a fuck?" Somers asked, forcing his voice to be cool, forcing himself to keep control. One of them damn well had to, at least for a few more minutes.

Panting now, Hazard pressed harder, kissed harder, like he was coming apart. The several days' scruff scraped Somers's chin. As Hazard bent Somers's head to the side, he ran a line of kisses down Somers's neck, and the sandpaper scratch of Hazard's beard was almost enough to make Somers lose it right there.

But Somers dragged himself back from the edge. His voice had a whistling quality when he spoke again. "Just a fuck?"

Groaning, Hazard wheeled the blond man towards their bedroom, marching him backward, shoving down Somers's trousers, his boxer-briefs, until those big, callused hands closed around Somers's dick, and Somers heard himself making a noise he hadn't known he could make. He barely felt it when Hazard shoved him back onto the bed and finished stripping him.

"Just a fuck?" Somers managed to say in a strangled whisper, catching Hazard's jaw, meeting those scarecrow eyes with a challenge. "Tell me. Say it again."

Hazard whined and thrashed.

"Say it."

"Fuck," Hazard panted, knocking aside Somers's arm and kissing him again ferociously. "You're just a fuck. This is just a fuck. Because if I don't have you right now, I'm going to go out of my fucking mind."

After that Somers lost whatever shreds of control he had, and it was just pure, animalistic sex. It didn't last long, but it lasted longer than Somers expected, and when it was over, Hazard slumped over him, his head on Somers's shoulder, and cried. Not sobs, not really. Not even any noise. But the tears were hot on Somers's skin, and the big man's body trembled, the muscles spasming. He jerked upright when Somers touched him.

"Ree."

"For fuck's sake, John, if I lost you, I'd die."

"You didn't lose me. I'm right here."

"But if I did—"

Somers kissed him then, softer now, and he drew Hazard down next to him, and then he dozed. Not long. Fifteen minutes. Maybe twenty. His back and legs ached in a pleasant way, and sleep was inches away, but Somers forced himself back from the precipice and left the bed. He raised the blinds to let in light, and he studied Market Street four stories below. In front of Vicenzi's, the Italian market across from the Crofter's Mark, a rusted-out Scion had nosed up to a red strip of curb, fighting for parking on the busy street. Glass glinted against the sun for a moment and vanished. Then Somers went to the bathroom and cleaned himself up, and when he came back, Hazard lay on the bed, arms and legs akimbo, his scarecrow eyes wide and glittering.

"Come here."

"Good morning to you too."

"It's not morning. It's barely been twenty minutes. Come here; I want you. Right now."

Planting himself in front of the window, Somers turned into the light, letting it fall across him and pick out the taut lines of his body. He ran a hand through his hair and looked out the glass.

"You're a goddamn tease." Growling, Hazard slapped the bed. "Now."

"I thought we were going to get some rest. Maybe do a little background work on Kjar. We can drop by the station, see what Norman and Gross picked up—"

"Fine." Scooting to the edge of the bed, Hazard brought down his big feet with two loud thumps, and he surged off the mattress. Heavy steps carried him towards Somers, a mass of muscle and stiff dark hair and crackling energy. "Fine. But now you made me get out of bed, and I'm going to be—" One hand took Somers by the throat, possessive, almost demanding, and pinned him against the glass. "—grumpy."

"You're—" Hazard kissed Somers's ear, and Somers's next exhalation rattled. "—always grumpy."

"Not like this." The fingers around Somers's throat tightened, rolling his head, flattening his cheek against the glass. Hazard kissed his jaw, his throat. He kissed his neck, the kisses growing rougher, almost bites, and then he did bite, hard, Somers's shoulder.

Somers moaned, his face flattened against the window, his heartbeat so loud it wiped out any thoughts. He opened his eyes, blinked back the sudden brilliance of the sun, and was surprised to find himself aroused by the open window, by the exposure, by the possibility of being caught. No, more than aroused. Hard. Titanium hard.

Below, behind the Scion parked in front of Vicenzi's, something small glinted back at Somers.

Hazard's hand dropped between Somers's legs, and Somers moaned and rocked into him. He whipped his head to the side, cracking against the glass, the dull thrum running through his whole body. He spread his legs for Hazard, letting the bigger man take some of his weight. Sunlight saturated the world outside. It seemed impossible that the world had ever been this bright, and Somers had to squeeze his eyes to slits, his breathing ragged and shallow.

That glint, though. There it was again. Like a needle of light, darting out and then vanishing. Like light catching a small piece of glass at exactly the right angle. And that angle, Somers realized, would have to be very specific. It would have to be glass turned up, directed towards the Crofter's Mark. Like a camera, maybe.

Or a scope.

He shoved Hazard away from the window. The big man swore, stumbled, and fell on his ass, and Somers crashed down on top him. Behind them, the window exploded.

CHAPTER SEVEN

JULY 2
MONDAY
4:39 PM

SHAKING, SOMERS DRAGGED HIMSELF UP and took two limping steps. Behind him, the remaining glass in the frame sagged inwards; a hot summer wind whipped through the broken window, sweeping slivers of glass along the floor.

"Come on."

Without waiting for Hazard, Somers grabbed a pair of shorts and collected his Glock from the holster hanging at the door. He slipped his feet into battered sneakers and ran.

As he ran, he saw that glint of sunlight on glass in his mind. He had thought, at first, a camera lens, maybe. Maybe. But after the day's events, a scope seemed much more likely. Frighteningly likely. And again, Somers felt himself pressed against the glass, naked, exposed. A fraction of a second longer, and—what?

He touched his side where the three pellets had winged him. Being shot through the back with a rifle, even from four stories, would be the end. The absolute end. And it could have happened without Somers knowing. Somehow, that was even worse.

By then Hazard had stumbled after him. "Slow down—"

"He's going to get away," Somers said.

"Somers—"

"I'm not letting him slip."

Somers passed the elevator and sprinted down the stairs. Hazard was still shouting for him, but Somers kept going. The bastard had shot at them. He had shot at them in their home. The one safe place, the one place that was theirs, and he had almost gotten them. Somers wasn't going to let that go. Instead of leaving through the lobby, Somers jetted down a service corridor, past the building manager's office and out into the covered parking. Aside from flies buzzing around the dumpster, the only noise was the muted traffic from the street.

Hazard caught up to him, gulping air, and grabbed Somers's shoulder. "John, he's already gone."

"Maybe not. He was right in front of Vicenzi's. If we—"

"I watched him. He's gone."

"What?"

"From the window, I watched him. Somebody pulled up. A little car, a sedan. Maybe a Ford. He's gone, John. He's already gone."

"Fuck." Somers spun a hard circle on the cement. "That's perfect. Just perfect. Next time maybe he'll walk right up and knock on the door. For the love of God." He kicked at a cement pillar, pulling the blow at the last minute so as not to break his toes. The sweat under his arms was gritty when he shifted, and his heart knocked rapidly against his ribs, and the second surge of adrenaline today, after everything that had already happened, left him dizzy and sick. The sex smell mixed with the stink of the hot, rotting garbage, and he had to fight the urge to squeeze off a few shots at the next thing—just about anything—that moved. Then he scrubbed at his hair. "What do we do now?"

"We get you upstairs."

Somers shook his head. "If we—"

"We get you upstairs. And we get that bandage off because it's soaked through—don't shake your head at me. We get that bandage off, we get you cleaned up—John, I swear by Christ that if you shake your head one more time, I'm going to throw you over my shoulder—we get you cleaned up, and then we get somebody to board up the window until the landlord can replace it."

Somers was holding himself rigid; the urge to shake his head was intense, but he recognized the look on Hazard's face. If Somers shook his head, he was going to find himself being hauled up the stairs ass-first no matter what he said.

"I want to go look around. He might have left something. A casing. I don't know, something."

"We'll find him. I want to get you cleaned up. Right now."

"Ree—"

"We'll find him."

"And how are you so sure? We've got nothing except he's a black male in his thirties. And he likes to shoot people like a goddamn coward. How are we supposed to find him?"

"I told you: I saw him. I watched him from the window."

Something crossed Hazard's face; Emery Hazard was shit at lying, and Somers could see him working up a whopper right then.

"What did you see? Don't lie to me."

Guilt flickered in Hazard's eyes, and he lifted his chin indignantly—too little, too late. "It's our same guy."

"What did you see, Ree?"

"Something I want to run through the computers when we get to the station—"

"Emery Hazard, if you try to weasel out of my question or lie to me or ignore me, you won't be able to carry me because I'm going to put you over my goddamn knee."

Hazard wiped his face, already glistening in the swampy July air. "It was Hollace Walker."

CHAPTER EIGHT

JULY 2
MONDAY
5:03 PM

HAZARD TOOK A BEER and a water from the fridge, opened them, and then stood in the kitchen, listening to splashing in the bathroom. Hollace Walker was here. In Wahredua. With a gun. Hazard stared out the window at the city. The sun sloped west. It lit up everything with opaque light. Flat cement roofs flared white. Dozens of them glowed like lights in a switchboard. Brighter than that. So white that they hurt Hazard's eyes. When he closed his eyes, he saw them against the darkness: white rectangles. Just like envelopes.

The beer was cold in his hands, and he ran his thumbs up and down the neck, and then he put it to his lips and drank. Pounded it, really, the way he hadn't pounded a beer since college. And when it was empty, he rolled it into the sink and got another one from the fridge. And then he stood still again and listened.

Hollace Walker. Hollace fucking Walker.

What Hazard remembered most clearly was the first time he had gone to Smithfield. He had been fourteen. Hollace, a few months older, had already turned fifteen, but he had something about him—bravado, or maybe simply recklessness—that made him older. Dangerous. And alluring. Hollace called this action of diving headfirst into trouble *getting into it*. And there had been plenty of memorable examples of Hollace *getting into it*, evolving in complexity as Hollace's schemes and mechanisms took on larger and larger forms. There had been the cement in the pool. There had been the improvised catapult launching the hornet's nest at the Memorial Day picnic. There had been stolen bicycles, joyriding, and the plate glass window of Morrow's Electronics shattered because Hollace couldn't afford a Walkman. He didn't even steal one; he just broke the glass, and somehow the only one who ended up taking heat for that day had been Rory McEnnis.

But one instance of Hollace *getting into it* had stuck with Hazard. Once, Hazard remembered, Hollace had made it a goal to ride his skateboard down the banisters in the junior high school. All of them. And he had hung confetti poppers along his route and fastened their pull-strings like improvised triplines so that a continuous cascade of colored paper followed him down the stairs. The school, an old brick building with three floors, provided the perfect opportunity. And Hollace had made it halfway down the building before he wobbled, overcompensated, and fell from the second-floor rail. Hazard hadn't been there, but he heard Keith Reher talking about it, with Reher's typical eloquence: "He just fucking fell, man. He just fucking fell." And then, Paul Naranjo's supplementary witness: "He bounced off the railing. It was sick; I swear I heard his ribs crack."

But what Hazard remembered most was what Mary Heintzelman, who was in ninth grade at the time, told everyone in the lunchroom, and she was crying when she told it. She had been at the bottom of the stairs. She had been carrying one of the roboticized infants assigned in the child development class. And she had been feeding it a fake bottle when Hollace ricocheted off the second-floor railings and then fell the remaining twenty feet, his celebratory confetti snowing down around him. A cafeteria table had been smuggled deep in the stairwell by the stoner kids, and it broke his fall. The folding legs snapped inwards, and the relative cushioning probably saved Hollace's life. But Mary Heintzelman didn't talk about the table. She talked about looking straight into Hollace's bloody face and seeing him open his eyes and say, barely loud enough for her to hear, "Did they see?" And then Mary Heintzelman had dropped her test-dummy infant on its head and failed child development.

Hazard's thumb glided over the neck of the Bud Lite, driving beads of condensation towards the neck of the bottle and the molded ridge at the top of the brown glass. The words of a boy with a light-skinned father and a white mother. The words of a boy abandoned by his upper-class, professor father and raised instead by his mother, still a college student when she had him. The words of a boy who lived his whole life in the same town as his father and, as far as Hazard knew, had never so much as crossed the threshold of the man's house.

In the complicated social hierarchy of teenagers, Hollace occupied a slot near the bottom. Part of that was the craziness. It was fun for the other kids, entertaining—"It was sick; I swear I heard his ribs crack"—but it wasn't friend material. More pressing, though, were the two major factors weighing against Hollace in rural Missouri: he was black, and he was poor. Black was black in Wahredua, even in the 1990s. Although Hollace's skin was lighter than a lot of the farm boys after they really got a summer tan going, even though he had those green eyes like spring grass; even though his dark, curly hair came from his mother, he was black as far as Wahredua was concerned. Black simply by virtue of being a black man's bastard. And he was poor. That, at least, was an impartial assessment. Hazard hadn't had much money either, but even in his eyes, Hollace had been poor.

Because of that calculus of social standing, in some way, Hazard's faggotry and Hollace's race and finances marked them as near equals. They were close in age. They were both lonely. And, as Hazard remembered, he had been drawn to Hollace's recklessness. It contrasted with skinny, teenaged Emery Hazard's desire to disappear. The only thing Hazard wanted was to be ignored; the only thing Hollace wanted was attention. And that fascinated Hazard.

At dusk one October, when the air smelled like fallen leaves and last night's rain and the motor oil trickling towards the storm drain, Hollace had suggested going to Smithfield. And Hazard had agreed. It was before he had met Jeff. Or, better said, before he had learned that Jeff was gay and that Jeff had been harboring a crush on Wahredua's only out boy for the past six months. So when Hollace asked if Hazard wanted to *get into it* in Smithfield, Hazard said yes because it was Hollace and because he was alone too often.

Smithfield, in those days, had been dangerous. Maybe even more dangerous than it was today because drug enforcement was still in its infancy and because urban revitalization programs weren't even dreamed of and because Wroxall College was still small and attracting mainly regional matriculation. That left Smithfield as an untended cesspool. They had walked up to Mississippi Street, a boulevard with an overgrown strip of oaks down the middle. They had stopped at the median, where a long branch pointed like a finger: the exact halfway point, as near they could measure it, between civilization and the wilderness known as Smithfield. A few blocks ahead, still visible in the gloom, slumped the Victorian ruin called the Bordello, known to every teenage boy, even the lone faggot, as the site of Wahredua's only operating brothel.

True, it hadn't operated for sixty-odd years, and in the mid-nineties of Hazard's childhood, time and weather and decay had brought the old house almost to the ground. Still, in its sprawl across half a block, in its remaining turret, in its broken gingerbread woodwork, hints of its original beauty remained. And for any boy, but especially for a lonely boy, those hints gave the building a particular gravity, as though it were a dark sun dragging Hazard towards it.

But the two boys had stopped at the median, where the oak branch stabbed towards the ground, marking the point of no return. They had come here once before, and once before Hollace had issued this challenge, and on that time, Hazard had approached the Bordello and an aging woman in nothing but a purple bra and purple tights had offered to blow him for twenty cents. Hazard remembered her balancing pizza boxes in one hand, an old lamp in the other, and he remembered how the tights seemed to magnify obscenely the notch between her legs. And he had run, that time. And now, they were here again, with the same challenge, because Hollace Walker had it fixed in his mind.

Hazard remembered shifting on his feet, leaves crunching under the knock-off sneakers, and waiting for Hollace to take the first step.

"Go on," Hollace said, grinning. "Get into it."

"All right."

"Don't just stand there."

"I said all right." When neither boy moved, Hazard said, "Aren't you going?"

"This is about you. Today, you're getting into it."

"I don't know."

"What do you mean you don't know? I asked you if you wanted to get into it. You said you did. So go get into it."

"I thought—"

"You ever been in there? No. Of course not. Because you're a pussy."

"I'm not a pussy."

"You're a pussy until you're not. That's the thing. You want everybody picking on you? You want everybody pushing your faggot ass around?"

Fourteen-year-old Emery Hazard had clenched his fists and waited. He hadn't come out yet. Not for another year. But somehow Hollace knew. And Hollace knew how to put the screws on.

"Of course not. But you're going to be their little pussy faggot until you get into it and prove you're not. So. How're you going to do that?"

"This is stupid."

"Fine. Pussy."

"Don't call me that."

"Why not? You want me to call you faggot? You want me to talk about that boy pussy you've got?"

"What am I supposed to do?"

"Go in there. Go all the way in. Up to the top. You know what's in there?"

Hazard shook his head.

Laughing wildly, Hollace said, "Shit, nobody does. Grab something. Take something. Bring it back. Prove you're not a pussy."

Even at fourteen, Hazard had wondered at the logic of this. Most of the boys, he suspected, wouldn't be impressed by whatever he took from the Bordello, and even if they were, he knew they still wouldn't be able to overlook the fact that Hazard liked dick. Those were hard, cold truths in his life. They were written in stone. But the temptation was real because Hazard wanted those things. He wanted exactly what Hollace had offered, and he knew that Hollace knew it.

Hazard stepped over that invisible demarcation.

"Go on," Hollace said, poking his back. "Get into it."

And Hazard knew he was going to get into it. Half-remembered fears raced through his mind as he jogged towards the Bordello. Old buildings could collapse, of course. And the floors were often rotted through. And the basements flooded, and suddenly Hazard envisioned crack, split, the ancient wood separating under his weight, and then plunging into the water. And snakes. There would be snakes down there. Water moccasins. And even if the floors held, even if he didn't drop into that snake-filled pit, even if the water moccasins didn't pump him full of poison, there were other things to consider. This was Smithfield. Tramps. Vagrants. Hobos. Winos. Drug-addicts. Prostitutes. Hazard wasn't sure why this last one scared him more than the others, but it did. Anyone could be using the Bordello. Anyone. And if they had a knife or a gun, if they had an old broken bottle or a length of piano wire, if they were just stronger and bigger and could force skinny Emery Hazard to—

—suck cock—

—do something, well, that might be worse than the water moccasins.

But the question that corralled all those thoughts was simple: do you want to be a pussy faggot? And the answer was just as simple: no. So Hazard's thin legs pumped, carrying him towards the Bordello, down the broken asphalt and up the worn, wooden steps, right to the Bordello's door.

It opened, of course. It wasn't locked or boarded shut. It swung wide open, and the hinges didn't even squeak. October dark thickened, but the remaining light showed the uneven floor within. Trash and junk dotted the room: church flyers and a styrofoam Big Gulp with a hole in the bottom and a deflated balloon with a knot tied in it and dead leaves and a long, peacock-colored scarf in a sinuous s that was somehow suggestive to Hazard and made him blush and, in the Bordello's old fireplace, the head of a mannequin with a shaggy brown wig, the plastic melted along one side of the neck. On second glance, Hazard realized the balloon was a condom.

Get into it.

It was either that or go into high school a pussy faggot.

The floor didn't give way under him. He didn't go plunging into a nest of water moccasins. The boards did creak, and there was one ominous pop, although that noise could have been somewhere else in the house, somewhere deeper. Hazard made it to the center of the Bordello's enormous front room and then stopped. Disappointment washed over him. This was it. It was just an empty building with some weird trash. Nothing that would make a good trophy. Nothing to prove what Hazard had done. Get into it, Hollace had said. Get into it to prove you aren't a pussy faggot with a gaping boy pussy waiting to be plugged. Get into it.

But what if there wasn't any it to get into?

Then Hazard saw the stairs. At one point, they must have been enormous, dominating one side of the Bordello's front room. Now, though, only stubs remained. Someone had begun demolishing the house, and the staircase had been torn out almost completely. Almost. Because those stubs were definitely wide enough for someone lightweight, someone scrawny, someone who weighed as much as a length of baling wire. Someone, in other words, like Emery Hazard.

He tested the first five stubs carefully, only trusting them with his full weight when he was certain they would hold, clutching at the Victorian paneling with his hands to keep his balance. Then his confidence grew, and his hands cramped, and he moved faster, giving the remaining steps only a cursory test before climbing. Part of his brain still pictured the potential consequences—snap, crack, water moccasins—but the rest of him was excited. This was stupid. This was dangerous. But it was also fun, and it lit up parts of his brain he rarely used, and adrenaline was pumping and endorphins, and suddenly Hazard did want to get into it. He wanted to get into it bad.

In contrast to the Bordello's main floor, the upper stories were relatively untouched. In one room Hazard found a length of curtain that, although moldy and moth-eaten, he thought might be genuine velvet. In another room, an enormous brooch flashed on the mantle. He assumed the stones were fake, but he pocketed it anyway. And towards the back, in a long room built under the eaves, he found the painting.

It was massive. The oil painting stood on the floor, and it was wedged at an angle under the eaves because it was too tall to stand fully upright. In it, an older, rotund woman with severe hair and a lapdog sat staring out at the viewer. She wore black, and the background was black, and the October darkness was a black gauze that was getting thicker by the minute. But something about the painting entranced Hazard. Part of it was the size. Who wanted a painting that big anyway? And part of it was the fluffy blob of white at the center, the lapdog, and the crooked fingers on the woman's hand where they rested on fur. And part of it was the brooch at her neck, dull and lifeless in oil but looking a lot like the piece Hazard had taken from the mantle. Deeper in the house came another of those pops, and Hazard jumped, and then he heard footsteps.

Hollace came into the room: just a deeper patch of darkness with those eyes like May grass and his familiar wild laugh. "What the fuck are you doing? I thought you got stuck or something."

Hazard nodded at the painting.

Joining him, Hollace knelt in front of the gilt-framed canvas, and in the darkness Hollace bent low, his forehead rasping against the paint as he tried to get close enough to see. Then he laughed again. "This old bitch? You can't carry her out of here."

"What about this?"

Turning the brooch over, Hollace nodded. "It's fake."

"Probably."

"But if it's not, we're splitting it."

Hazard didn't agree with that, but before he could voice his objection, Hollace produced something from his pocket. Metal whirred, and then a tiny flame danced above the lighter he clenched. And, as Hazard watched, he bent and touched the blue crown of the flame to the corner of the canvas.

Hazard nudged his hand away. "What are you doing?"

And then Hollace looked at him and laughed that wild laughter, but none of it came into his eyes. That was the first time Hazard had ever seen that: eyes that looked like they had life but were really dead. Like grass clippings. Still fresh. Still vividly green. But dead, even if they didn't know it yet.

"You either burn," Hollace said, elbowing Hazard clear. "Or you get burned." And then he touched the lighter to the canvas again, and this time Hazard shuffled back a step and watched the oil-thick pigments catch. "They'll be able to see this in St. Elizabeth."

Another pop ran through the room. This time, the sound was close. Immediate. And even through the gathering gloom, Hazard could make out the shadow that filled the doorway.

It was a wino, his brain said, racing to fill in the details. A hobo. A drug addict. He was going to—

—make Hazard suck cock—

—kill them and put them in the flooded basement with the water moccasins.

"Hey. Hey, what are you boys doing in here? Hey!" The man's voice didn't sound drugged or drunk, and he took a heavy step into the room. Then he repeated again, "Hey!" and his tone was one of childish protest, as though his favorite toy had been stripped away. He rushed towards them, and then Hazard saw that in one hand, he held a gun.

Hazard didn't even think about it. He grabbed Hollace by the arm, dragged the older boy to his feet, and launched for the door. The shadow-man was rushing straight at them, his gun a perfect silhouette, and he was still crying out in that tone of childish privation. He didn't even seem to see the boys, but as he passed them, Hazard heard it again, pop, pop, pop. He was shooting at them. He was shooting. Maybe Hazard had been hit and didn't even know it. With his free hand, he pawed at his chest, searching for blood, and then he heard Hollace's wild laughter and, through labored breathing, the word, "Caps."

Pop, pop, pop. The man was behind them now, slapping at the painting, trying to put out the accelerating flames. "Hey!" he whined. "No!"

Pop, pop, pop.

It was a cap gun. Hazard felt dizzy. He'd never had a drink, no more alcohol than children's cough syrup, but he felt drunk. He staggered on the landing, and when he was three stubs down the broken steps, he fell and cracked his elbow hard. But the floor didn't open and spill him into the nest of snakes, and the drunkenness intensified until he could barely stand as Hollace leaped down lightly beside him.

They ran then. The rest of the way out of Smithfield, a few measly blocks, but they ran like the devil was on their tail. At Mississippi Street's overgrown median, they climbed one of the oaks and hooked themselves around the branches and waited.

"Watch that mother burn," Hollace said. "All the way to St. Elizabeth."

But after twenty minutes, the Bordello was still dark, and after another ten, the October night had closed down completely, shutting them into the empty space between the branches.

"Bastard must have put it out," Hollace said when they climbed down. And then they parted ways and went home. And that night, Hazard dreamed about what Hollace had said: *you either burn, or you get burned*. And later that year, when Mary Heintzelman told her story in the lunchroom, a visceral fear had gripped Hazard, and he had dropped the rest of his lunch, uneaten, in the trash can, and then he had met Jeff and it had been easy to avoid Hollace, and they hadn't seen each other much.

It had been easy because Jeff was always so happy, so collected so, so fun. Jeff would take them to the movies, buy the tickets, buy the treats, and find them a spot in back where they could hold hands in the dark. Jeff had money for video games, for dinners out, and once for the bus to St. Elizabeth where they had a picnic. And the money had been nice—and strange, so much money, in hindsight, for a kid without a job—but what Hazard had liked most was that Jeff was confident. It was the confidence, more than anything, that had mystified Hazard. *I've got backup*, Jeff had said. *Big, powerful backup. Just let somebody fuck with me.* And then Jeff would laugh and grab

Hazard's hand and say, *You, you're my backup*. But Hazard hadn't been there the night Jeff really needed backup.

Hazard had wanted some of Jeff's confidence when he had gone to school the next day after the night in Smithfield, when Hazard produced the brooch and Hollace snatched it away and told the story. Only Hollace told it wrong. It had all been about Hollace, with Hazard as a cowardly tag-along and with the shadow-man much larger, much more threatening, and the cap gun was a real gun. By the end of the story, Hazard was forgotten, while a crowd of half-admiring, half-mocking boys ringed Hollace. And Hazard had been right: nothing had changed for him. Nothing. Except having heard those words: *you either burn, or you get burned*. That had stayed with him. It had stayed with him like it had been seared into him, and he knew that was cliché, but it had. Burned right into the flesh. And now in the back of his mind something else was burning: the painting, its frame flashing in the flicker from Hollace's lighter. A rectangular frame. The shape of an envelope. A white envelope bright enough to burn out his eyes.

Hazard's thumb slipped up, bumping the beaded condensation over the rim of brown glass and down into the beer, and all of the sudden Hazard startled, and the bottles clinked together, and he had to take a breath like he hadn't breathed in an hour. The splashing in the bathroom stopped, and a footstep came outside the kitchen, and then Somers's beautiful, perfect face poked around the corner. He'd at least managed to put on a shirt, Hazard saw, and he felt a sudden rush of gratitude. For the shirt. For that perfect face. For everything about Somers right then.

"Are you drinking those yourself?" Then Somers glanced at the sink and raised an eyebrow. "Already got the party started, I see."

"It's one beer."

"What's up with you?"

"Are you done with the bathroom?"

"What's going on? Is there something you want to tell me?"

"We just got shot at."

"You know that's not what I mean."

"He could have killed us. He could have killed you. So I'm upset."

"Ree, what is it? What's going on?"

"We're lucky the glass didn't—"

"You know what? Yeah. I'm done with the bathroom. You go right ahead."

"John."

"I'm going—hell, I don't know. I'll lie down I guess. Or read or something. Go shower so we can head over to the station."

"John."

"No, go right ahead."

The bedroom door slammed shut behind him.

Sighing, Hazard stared at the door. The light reflecting off the rooftops washed into the apartment like flotsam: a detritus of sunspots glowed on the wall, the floor, the door. The white frame of the door. The shape of it. The rectangle. Hazard closed his eyes and saw it there, white and closed, where he could run his thumb along the edge and open it. He knew. He already knew. It wasn't rational or logical, but he knew. So he took his keys and padded down to the lobby, and the little door on their mailbox with the rainbow sticker that Somers had put there and the unicorn sticker that Evie had put there and a grimy patch of dried adhesive where the super had taped a note saying no more stickers, that door squeaked open and rattled when Hazard shook the key loose.

And there it was, lying alone on the stainless steel: a simple white envelope without address, without stamp, without so much as a creased corner. Hazard carried it back to the apartment in both hands, held away from his chest the way someone anciently might have carried an offering to an unknowable, unknowing god. The way a man today might carry a stick of dynamite.

The bedroom door was still closed. Hazard paused as he passed it. He listened. Music played, but it was too quiet for him to make out the melody. Then the bed creaked. And then something hit the door hard, and Hazard jumped.

"I can see your shadow, numskull."

In the bathroom, Hazard forced the door shut; summer humidity made everything swell, even with the air conditioning running full blast, and the bathroom door got a double dose from the shower. Some days, it wouldn't close at all, and that wasn't a problem. Hazard didn't mind catching a glimpse of Somers, naked and dripping when he pulled back the curtain. Somers didn't seem to mind catching a glimpse of him either. In fact, to judge by the number of times Somers opened the door, leaned there, and watched with that cocky smile on his face, he didn't mind it at all.

Hazard slid fingertips behind the mirrored cabinet that hung over the sink. His bad arm throbbed at this angle, and he let out a soft puff of breath as he forced the hanging cabinet up. It slid free from its mounting, and Hazard lowered it to rest at an angle on the counter.

A space had been cut out of the drywall, and normally, the cabinet fit inside this space so that the mirror lay flush against the wall. With the cabinet removed, though, a length of two-by-four was exposed, and on top of the pressure-treated wood Hazard had stacked the other envelopes. Six of them. He slid them into his hands at an angle, and they slanted like a deck of cards ready for him to deal. Six in the wall. And then one today. Six and one made seven.

There was a pattern. There was always a pattern. And if he could figure out the pattern, it would mean something. It would be a step towards the man behind this.

Start at the beginning.

His thumb skipped along the first envelope's flap, and he had to try again before he could open it. The photograph that slid out still made Hazard's heart drop. He had seen it ten times now, maybe twenty times, studying it during stolen moments like this one. He painted it against the backdrop of his mind night after night — each of the photographs, again and again — as he lay in bed and lost sleep. Others were more graphic. Others were more violent. But the first had been the most shocking.

Someone had taken this photograph from a distance, but the quality was good, and whoever had taken it had doubtless used a telephoto lens. The framing and composition weren't anything remarkable, and the shot looked like it had been taken hastily and carelessly. The slight angle might have been due to something else, though—something besides carelessness or haste. It might have been excitement.

In the center of the photograph, a dark-haired boy with the compact body of a wrestler rocked back on his heels. His head was turned to one side, displaying three-quarters of his face. The dark hair, the button nose, the lips. Hazard had gotten his first kiss from those lips. From Jeff Langham. And in this picture, Jeff's lips were split, and gore stained his chin. Two figures stood in profile, most of their features lost in a slash of sunlight, but Hazard recognized them, too. Mikey had been big and ugly and tubby back then, and in the photograph, he looked all of those things. Next to him, like a prototype for the real thing, was the boy who had grown up to be John-Henry Somerset.

Hazard set the photograph on the countertop. His hand was shaking harder now.

The second photograph showed Jeff reeling back, hands in front of his face, as Mikey swung something at his head. The third photograph showed Jeff kneeling on asphalt, his shirt ripped down the front and soaked with blood; in this photograph, Somers was gone, and the boy named Hugo Perry stood behind Jeff, pinioning his arms. The fourth photograph came from a much closer distance. A blow had split the skin low on Jeff's temple, and his eye was gummed shut with blood. His lips were stretched around a penis, his nose was buried in a dense, wiry bush. A hand clutched at his hair. It was obvious that Jeff was crying, but in the photograph, all movement was arrested. In that photograph, for the rest of eternity, Jeff Langham would choke on a son of a bitch's cock, his eye pasted shut with his own blood. Hazard's hand shook so badly when he laid this one on the counter that he knocked the others out of order, and when he tried to straighten them, he only made it worse. The fifth photograph was where things grew strange. The fifth photograph showed Jeff lying on a manicured lawn. The asphalt that Hazard had seen in the earlier pictures, the cinderblock structures in the background, had vanished. Jeff looked asleep. If not for the blood and bruises, he might have even looked peaceful. The sixth photo framed Jeff against the sun. It was obvious from his posture that he was limping, dragging his broken, abused body into the sunset.

And that didn't make any sense. Hazard had wrung the truth about Jeff's death out of Mikey. He had known—everyone had known—that Jeff had killed himself. He had driven out to the bluffs in his father's truck, he had pulled down the shotgun that hung in the rear window, and he had opened an escape hatch in the back of his head. Mikey had confessed to catching Jeff, beating him, raping him. All of that Hazard had known.

A miniature earthquake ran through Hazard's hands now, and he clamped them over the sink, the porcelain cool under his grip. He had known. Yes. He had known. And he had decided that it wasn't worth his career, it wasn't worth his integrity, it wasn't worth killing Mikey and covering it up, even though Hazard thought he might have gotten away with it. But that was before he had seen the photographs. Before they had started arriving in the mail over the last few weeks. Before he had seen Jeff's broken face, before the bloody streaks his lips left on Mikey's dick.

But what did the grass mean? What did it mean that Jeff had walked west after the beatings and rape had ended? What was to the west? His home? The truck? Why send those two pictures?

Another question, Hazard thought, had been answered. He knew now who had taken them. He thought of Hollace Walker setting fire to the Bordello, and he thought of Hollace stealing the brooch and Hazard's story, and he thought of Hollace crashing down two flights of stairs, and he thought of Hollace diving into a sedan after shooting out the bedroom window. He thought of electric green eyes at the Haverford, and he knew too that Hollace had taken the shot at the mayor.

Hollace Walker was here. He was trying to kill Mayor Sherman Newton—and, for all Hazard knew, trying to kill Hazard and Somers too.

All of this, with the envelopes, was no coincidence. He picked up the seventh envelope. His hand trembled so badly that the envelope tutted against the porcelain, tut-tut-tut. He pinned it against the counter to stop the noise.

There was more. Inside this new envelope, there was more, and Hazard wondered how it could be worse. Because it was going to be worse. It was going to be Jeff on the ground, with Hugo's fat foot on the back of his neck, while Mikey shredded his asshole. It was going to be Jeff with his hands tied while Mikey snipped off his balls. It was going to be a wave that would drag Hazard down into darkness, and he didn't know if he could kick hard enough, if he could hold his breath long enough, if he could get himself out of that darkness.

Inside Hazard, deeper than the burn of labored breathing, deeper than the flat-tire whump of his heart, deeper than all of that—in the soul, maybe, or in the subconscious, or between the microfirings of synapses—something stuttered. It was a restrained movement. A frozen, gelid movement. It was a movement of something essential and intangible inside the man; a Hallmark card would have called it a movement of the heart, but that was bullshit. This was deeper than the heart.

Hazard knew what it was, that restricted movement: it was the part of his life that had stalled the day he learned that Jeff had died. It was the part of his life that had never moved forward. Coming back to Wahredua less than a year ago, Hazard had known that his business here wasn't done. He had come back for Jeff. He had come back for the truth. He had thought—a grin tightened his lips until they threatened to split—that he had found the truth in Mikey's confession of abuse and rape and torture and, then, Jeff's suicide.

But these photographs told another story. Jeff had gone somewhere after Mikey had finished with him. And someone had followed him. And someone had been there when Jeff died, and all of the sudden Hazard could visualize it again, the image that had come to him ten months ago when he arrived in Wahredua in an Indian summer, with October as hot as August: a clock with both hands twisted to midnight. A frozen clock. A clock that had stopped. And it had never started ticking again, never, and Hazard had wondered why, and his finger trembled on the back of the seventh envelope, shaking the white rectangle so that it fluttered like a leaf about to fall. That clock. That goddamn frozen clock.

Paper crackled. Glue gave way in stuttering strips. He worked his finger the length of the flap and folded it back with his knuckle.

Three. Three photographs this time. The first showed Jeff Langham in the cab of his dad's truck, his nose flattened against the driver side window, bone and brain and gore peppering the upholstery behind him, and the shotgun sliding down his chest. A hazy reflection in the glass showed a dark-skinned boy with a camera. Hollace, caught in his own photograph. On the reverse, printed on the photograph in blocky letters, he had written, *This little pussy got it.*

The second photograph showed Somers, eyes crinkled, mouth open in laughter, a burger dripping in one hand. Someone had slung an arm around Somers's shoulders, and Hazard recognized the arm: well-muscled, with dark hair, the fingers curled possessively on Somers's arm. It was his own. He had been left out of the picture, though; this was about Somers. Again, Hazard found script on the back: *This little pussy is going to get it.*

The third photograph showed Sherman Newton at a desk, his head down as he bent over paperwork, obviously unaware of the picture being taken. On the left of the image, white stone framed Newton. Limestone. And that bothered Hazard because it meant the photograph had been taken of Newton inside his office at City Hall, and it meant Hollace Walker could have shot him then and there. So why hadn't he? On the back, a final line of blocky letters: *If you don't stay out of my way.*

Fluttering from his hands, the photographs rustled against each other at the bottom of the sink. Hazard stared down at them. He thought about flipping them over, but seeing the words on the back would be worse than seeing the front. He thought about stacking them, all nine of the photographs, and ripping them into pieces. He could flush the shredded paper down the toilet. He could burn it— he could toss the confetti into the stainless-steel sink in the kitchen, dump a bottle of lighter fluid on top, and strike a match. He could—

The door thumped as Somers tried to push it open, but the swollen wood caught on the frame. "What are you doing in there?"

If you don't stay out of my way.

Out of his way? What did that mean? Leave him a clear path to the mayor? Or something else, something—

"You've been in there for twenty minutes, Ree. What's going on?"

"It's a bathroom."

Hazard gripped the edge of the sink again. Porcelain slid under his fingers like ice. *This little pussy—*

"Do you have the shits?"

"For the love of God, can I have five minutes?"

"Yeah. You had five minutes. You had twenty minutes." The door creaked, the warped wood grating against the frame. "Are you looking at porn?"

"Yeah. I'm looking at porn."

"Let me see. Unless it's something—"

The door popped free of the frame; Hazard caught it with his hand, and he grunted as Somers put his weight into it.

"It's not porn. Just let me—"

"What's going on then? It's something weird, isn't it? It's something really weird. It's—is it like a diaper fetish thing? Is that why you're in the bathroom?" The door surged inwards again, and Hazard shouldered it back. "If that's what it is, I won't judge you. I mean, I know I said it was weird, but I really won't judge you. I just want to see." The door wobbled in another inch. Somers's voice took on a note of uncertainty. "Are you wearing a diaper?"

"It's not—I'm not wearing a fucking diaper. It's nothing to do with—fuck, Somers, give me five minutes, all right?"

It might have ended there, except for two things: the mirrored cabinet, leaning precariously against the wall, slid and fell; and, at the same time, Somers gave a final, experimental shove. Hazard turned to catch the cabinet, his attention slid away from the door, and Somers tumbled into the room.

Hazard caught the cabinet before it hit the tile, and then he stood there, clutching the oak and glass to his chest, trying to breathe.

Somers took in the pictures all at once. He paled. Red—ugly, purplish-red—slashed his cheekbones. Then he took in the pictures one by one. With his index finger, he slid the final three—the ones with the writing—towards him, and by some of that same goddamn intuition, he flipped them over. His hands didn't shake. He could have performed surgery, that's how composed he looked, rock-steady except for the violent red vee on his face. And that didn't make any sense because an earthquake was running through Hazard, a 9, a 9.5, and the mirrored glass of the cabinet chittered and rattled against the buttons on his shirt because that goddamn earthquake was knocking everything around.

"How long?"

"John, I was going to tell you."

"How long?"

"Look, my arm was fucked up, I was pissed about rehab, and then this started happening."

Somers closed his eyes. He started to shake his head, but his chin only moved a fraction and then he stopped. "Weeks. This has been going on for weeks, that's what you're saying."

"I just needed to figure it out. It was just somebody fucking with me, trying to mess with me. And when I figured it out, I was going to . . ."

Somers twitched, and the movement silenced Hazard. With one hand—rock-steady, so goddamn steady—Somers reached for the most recent three pictures. *This little pussy is going to get it.* But instead of the picture with his face in it, Somers touched the photograph of Newton. *If you don't stay out of my way.* "This didn't seem important."

"I just got that one. Today. A few minutes ago. I was going to bring this all out to you, tell you about it. Will you—Christ." Hazard juggled the cabinet, trying to find a spot to set it down. "Will you look at me, please? Will you look me in the eyes? I was going to bring it all out, spread it on the coffee table, and talk to you."

Somers nodded. Slow. Really slow. It felt like it took an hour for that nod. And the whole time, Hazard could taste his own lie.

"Which one is it?"

"Hollace—"

Another of those tiny twitches silenced Hazard. "No. You told me you were going to figure this out and then tell me about it. Now you tell me you were going to bring it out right now, lay out all the pieces. Which one?"

"Both."

"It can't be both."

"Hey. Hey. Don't take that fucking tone with me. You know what I meant. You know I meant one and then the other. Why the fuck are you trying to pick a fight about this?"

The sharp red lines in Somers's face vanished. The golden hue of his skin had vanished. He looked sick. In the bathroom light, bruised circles of green and purple swallowed his eyes.

"Fine. I'll be the one who says it."

"Don't fucking talk like that. If you're mad at me, be mad at me. But don't fucking talk to me like I'm—like I'm—"

Like I'm nothing. Like I'm nobody.

"You didn't show these to me for one of two reasons." Somers breathed faster now. "If you open your mouth, if you interrupt me, I'm walking out that door. Two reasons. One: you still think I had something to do with it. With what happened to Jeff. That's one." He was hyperventilating now. The green around his eyes tinged the rest of his face now; his knuckles popped out in white where he clutched the counter, as though to keep himself from falling. "Two: you know I didn't, but it doesn't matter. You can't forgive me. Because I'll always be who I was. For you, I'll always be the kid who pushed you down the stairs, who held your arm—"

"No. No fucking way. I love you." The words were so thick even Hazard barely understood them. "You don't get to make me feel like shit. You know I love you."

"—who held your arm while Mikey cut you. And you can't even keep your mouth shut long enough for me to finish. So I'm walking out right now. I'll—" Somers pried his hand from the counter, tore at his collar, and sucked in air. "I'll be back. For our shift watching Newton, I'll be back. But I need to get out of here for a while."

"Sit your ass down. Sit your ass down, John. Sit your ass down right this fucking minute. John. I'm fucking talking to you. You're acting like a goddamn kid, walking out when we're having a conversation. John, if you fucking walk out that door—"

The front door slammed shut behind Somers.

Hazard took a few tottering steps after him. He made it to the middle of the living room before he realized he was still carrying the mirrored cabinet. He stopped. Then he screamed, and the sound was so raw and so full of rage—at himself, a hundred percent at himself—that it tore his throat. He raised the cabinet and threw.

Oak and glass struck hard enough to cave in the drywall. The cabinet hung there, one corner buried deep enough in the plaster to fix it in place like some bizarre installation of modern art. The glass hadn't even broken, and in the mirror, Hazard saw himself: hair loose and falling into his eyes, chest rising and falling, fingers curling and then spasming into painful stiffness. He saw himself like a dead man, and he walked into his room—their room—and kicked through the closet until he found what he wanted. Then he went back to the living room, raised the baseball bat, and beat that goddamn cabinet into kindling.

CHAPTER NINE

JULY 2
MONDAY
10:47 PM

HAZARD DID HIS BEST to sleep before their night shift watching the mayor. Somers still hadn't come back. Hazard lay in a taut line, and his mind raced, and sleep outraced his mind. Why hadn't he told Somers about the photographs? It had been stupid. It had been needless. It had been irrational. For the life of him, Hazard couldn't put his finger on the reason. And that scared him. It frightened him down to the core because Hazard wanted to believe he was a rational person. But that fear was a tiny flicker next to the bonfire of worry about Somers.

When sleep came, it was gray and restless, tangled with fragments of voices Hazard couldn't understand and shadow-men with cap guns. When he woke, his mouth tasted gray like the sleep, and his eyes had enough sand to fill a playground.

Somers was back when Hazard woke, and Hazard could hear him speaking in the other room. Hazard washed his face and dressed, and when he went into the front room, he found Somers ready to go.

"I talked to Moraes. They're at the mayor's house; he's in for the night. Moraes called a patrol car and had them go around the block a few times."

"John, I want to talk about what happened earlier."

Somers toed the mangled glass and wood that lay strewn across the living room. He rolled the bat with his foot. And he shook his head.

"Moraes told me he had the patrol guys do a complete sweep of the grounds."

"John, please don't do this to me. I'm sorry. I screwed up. I fucked up. I don't even know why I did it, and I'm so sorry."

"I can't do this. Not tonight. We've got a job to do."

"Fuck this job. Fuck Newton. The only thing I care about is you and making this right. Will you tell me that? Will you tell me how to make things right? I'll do it, whatever you want. Just tell me."

"Ree," Somers said, and for a moment, something broke in his perfect façade. Then he shook his head. "This is why partners aren't supposed to be involved with each other. It messes up the job. So let's just do our job."

"You don't want to be my partner?"

"That's not what I said."

But Hazard had heard it. It wasn't what Somers had said, but it had been there anyway, the real message under all the rest of it. And Hazard had heard it. It went through him, sweeping away the detritus from their earlier fight, leaving an Antarctic landscape: pristine, cold, with only the occasional dust-up of snow on the wind. And then not even that. No wind. No gauze of snow. Just ice.

"Patrol cops got out of their car?" Hazard managed to say. That was hard; after that, everything felt easy.

"Yep," Somers said, turning away and rubbing at his face. "It's a miracle."

They drove across town towards Mayor Newton's home. It wasn't far from Market Street. Wahredua had grown inland from the river, and the oldest parts of town—as well, for the most part, as the best parts of town—still formed part of the original settlement. The Newton home stood on a bluff that overlooked the city. They were the same bluffs, Hazard thought as they drove up into the darkness, where his first boyfriend had put a shotgun in his mouth and killed himself. That was the difference that a few odd miles could make. Here, close to town, the bluff was prime real estate: old money, settled nicely with a view of the city it dominated. But go another ten miles, another fifteen, another twenty into the darkness downriver, and it was wilderness. It was the kind of place a boy could be abused and sodomized and raped until he decided he'd rather blast out the back of his head than take another day living.

The Jetta clanked. The temperature gauge was rising steadily, and the poor old car heaved and panted as they continued to climb the hill. Somers was eyeing the dash with what looked like suspicion.

"It's fine. It's just a steep hill."

"This thing sounds like it could barely make it down a hill, Ree, much less up one."

"This is a great car. It's got over two hundred thousand miles on it."

Somers shook his head. "Every time I get in here, I'm pretty sure I'm about to die in a ball of fire."

"I've got a fire extinguisher in the trunk."

"That is absolutely not reassuring."

Just easy, back and forth. Just shitting each other. Like everything was all right.

Then they were rolling up in front of Newton's house, and Hazard forced himself to focus. Like so much of old Wahredua, Newton's home showed the ancestral memory of the mostly-European settlers. Built sometime in the early 20th century, Hazard guessed, the home consisted of a central, pseudo-Victorian structure with two ungainly additions: one on the side, and one on the rear. Although the house proper was dark, electric lights sprang up across the yard like dandelion weeds, and the contrast was unsettling. With so much light outside, especially at night, the void inside the house made it look unreal, almost two-dimensional. It reminded Hazard—not in style or scope but in some other, more essential way—of the Haunted Mansion ride he had gone through on his one trip to Disneyworld's Magic Kingdom at the age of ten. And even at the age of ten he had recognized something important about the Haunted Mansion: it was scary, but it was also meant to be scary.

"Like something out of a Halloween movie," Somers said, opening the Jetta's door and allowing a rush of muggy air into the car. It brought the smell of fertilizer, wet lawn clippings, and the Jetta's hot metal. "You coming?"

"Yeah. Let's check the grounds."

"Moraes said—"

"I know. Let's check them anyway."

So they did a slow circle of the house. Newton's house occupied the prime position on the bluff, looking out with an unobstructed view in three directions. His only neighbor was a similar pseudo-Victorian monstrosity; in a back room on the ground floor, a TV strobed, and as Hazard watched, a woman in curlers and a bathrobe passed the open window. Water beaded brightly on the grass, a stippling of moonlight like someone had gone at the night with a white pen. Footsteps had disturbed some of the water, leaving clear trails where the patrol cops, at Moraes's request, had walked the grounds a few hours earlier.

At the back of the house, the bluff overlooked the Grand Rivere, and the ground dropped to a scrubby slope choked with witch-hazel and sumac and squat little juniper shrubs. The mayor's sprinklers didn't reach this far, and below Hazard, the vegetation was limp and dusty from the long weeks of heat. Then, below that, the river peeled back from its banks, exposing stretches of white, cracked earth that were normally underwater. The river itself, contracted like a span of cold iron, speared along its usual path, and upriver a lone boat moved slowly against the water, its navigation lights betraying it to the darkness.

"Do you see something?"

Hazard shook his head, and they headed back. Tonight, Hazard and Somers both wore jeans and t-shirts, and thanks to the mayor's generous watering of his lawn, Hazard's sneakers were soaked through by the time they had completed their circuit. He went to the door and knocked.

Firm, quiet steps approached the door, and then, after a moment's silence, it swung open. Moraes stood there, still in uniform, and he cracked a grin when he saw them. "Slumber party, huh?"

"You're jealous," Somers said.

"A night with this guy?" He cocked his head towards Hazard. "Definitely."

"All quiet?" Hazard asked, stepping into the house. The foyer was dark, although light gleamed somewhere deeper in the house, and that weak, distant light foamed on the parquet floor. Hazard's next breath brought a chilly, dusty smell that he associated with civic buildings and museums, places that saw a lot of people pass through without ever coming close to being a home. Something else, too, something unpleasant: the smell of old fabric that has been stored too long.

"No problems. He's in his room. I cleared it before he went in there, and I asked him to keep the door open. He didn't like that very much."

"He's probably got a routine," Somers said.

"He's definitely got a routine. The man's practically got a timetable for everything. Tea at this time. Change into robe and slippers at this time. Wash the dishes at this time. Water the grass at this time. That was my job, by the way. I didn't want him going outside, but he insisted, so I did it for him." He must have caught their looks because he shook his head. "It's not like I left him alone. He stayed in the kitchen, right by the door, and I went out the back and turned them on. That's it."

"What if somebody had shot you?" Hazard said.

"That's why I waited until the patrol guys were here." Moraes gave one of those lazy smiles. "I'm not a total idiot."

"But when you turned them off—"

"They were still here. Come on, Detective: cut me a break."

"He's just grumpy," Somers said.

"I'm not grumpy."

"How's the mayor been?"

Moraes shook his head. "His Honor has been fine."

"Between you and me?"

"Scared," Moraes said, and then he held up a hand, as though he needed a moment to think. "But stupid."

"He's always stupid," Hazard said.

"What do you mean?" Somers asked.

"I mean—"

"Not you. Moraes."

"I mean, a lot of little stuff," Moraes said with a shrug. "The sprinkler, for example. Or the tea. He practically ordered me to go buy him licorice root tea. It was six-thirty in Wahredua, Missouri. Where the hell am I going to buy licorice root tea? Never mind the fact that I'm supposed to be keeping him alive."

"He wanted you to leave?" Somers said.

"Not really. He just wanted to pick fights about stuff. He wanted me to do the dishes. Christ, if you tell anybody this, I'll say you're a liar, but I did them. The dishes, I mean. And he wanted to watch TV in his office, but he turned it up so loud I couldn't hear a damn thing, so we had a talk about that."

"He's a bully," Hazard said. "He likes throwing his weight around."

"Maybe."

"You don't think that's it?" Somers said.

"I don't know, man. I know bullies. Hell, Foley can be a bully. I know how to handle a bully. With Foley, I just gave him all his shit right back, with a little bit extra, and after a few weeks we were cool. But this didn't feel like that."

"What did it feel like?"

"It felt like somebody that's used to having control and doesn't have it anymore. Or maybe not even that. Maybe somebody that's never had control and wants it right now. Like a little kid, you know? Like my niece. She's three, and all of the sudden, she's in charge. Of everything. You do something stupid, like you cut up her hot dog, she's going to rip your head off because she's in charge." Moraes shook his head. "After I checked his room, I stayed in the hallway for a while. His bedroom is on the second floor, and I didn't like the idea of being down here. The house is too big. So I dragged a chair into the hallway and sat there. And probably, I don't know, twenty minutes later, I hear his window open. So I walk down there, and he's standing right there, right in front of the window, with the thing wide open. So I shut the window and pulled the curtains and I asked what he was doing. And do you know what he said?"

"I can guess," Hazard muttered.

"He said it was his house. He said he liked the night air. He said he slept better with the sound of the river. And he said the humidity was good for his skin."

"He's either out of his goddamn mind," Hazard said, "or—"

He cut off when Somers elbowed him. "Yeah, that's crazy."

But now Moraes was watching them, and Hazard could see the wheels turning inside the other man's head. "You think, what? He's faking this? You think he's not scared at all? What about Murray? I mean, fuck, Murray got killed today, and if he hadn't been right where he was, the mayor would have bought it. If this is some kind of—"

"I'll tell you what I know," Somers said, "and that's jackshit. Listen, we saw the whole thing with Murray. I saw the mayor's face, I saw him ten seconds after Murray was down, and the mayor was scared out of his mind. You can't fake that kind of fear. Not like that, anyway."

"But tonight," Moraes said slowly, obviously still thinking, and Hazard wanted to kick himself. "I mean, the sprinklers and the window, that's crazy, right? Somebody took a shot at him, and he decides to play human target practice in the window because the night air is good for his skin?"

"You know what I think? I think it's like you said: control. He's the mayor, Moraes. He's been in charge of just about everything for the last, God, how many years? Twenty? Twenty-five? And then today, it's all out of his hands. He's not even allowed to go outside to water his lawn. What do you think that does to a guy?"

"Makes him an even bigger pain in the ass than he already was," Hazard said.

Moraes flashed a smile. "You got that right. You're lucky I didn't leave the dishes for you." Then he rubbed the back of his neck, and it was obvious that he was still thinking about the unspoken suggestion in Hazard's earlier words.

"Moraes," Somers said.

The dark head came up.

"Go home. Get some sleep."

"Yeah. This work, it messes with your head. I couldn't even sit in a damn chair and read. Oh, damn it. I almost forgot." He jerked a thumb toward the back of the house. "Chief brought by some stuff for you. Everything they've got on Murray's shooting so far."

"Thanks."

Moraes didn't linger; he clapped Somers on the shoulder, nodded at Hazard, and let himself out. Hazard locked the door behind him. Now, standing inside, he saw why the house was so dark from the street: either Carmichael or Moraes had drawn the heavy curtains across all of the windows, and where there weren't curtains, they had taped thick layers of newsprint. It was a good idea, especially after the earlier shooting, and Hazard wondered which of them had come up with it. Carmichael was a good cop, efficient, smart, and alert. But right then, his gut told him it had been Moraes.

"He's smart," Hazard said.

Somers gave him a sour look. "You think?"

"I know. I shouldn't have said what I did."

"Ree, you didn't even say it. That's worse, in some ways, because now Moraes is going to fill in a lot of blanks, and he might fill them in wrong."

"I made a mistake."

"You got angry and you started flapping your mouth."

"Moraes won't say anything."

"Maybe. But maybe he will."

"He likes you."

Somers, shaking his head, started deeper into the house, and he spoke over his shoulder. "Ree, he likes everyone. He's that kind of guy. But he's smart, as you said, and he's a good cop, and if he thinks we've got beef with the mayor, he's going to remember that. And if something bad happens to the mayor, he might decide he needs to say something about what he heard."

Hazard followed him into the kitchen, which looked like it hadn't been updated since the 1980s. Propping himself on the yellowing Formica, Hazard said, "I get it. I fucked up. It's not going to happen again."

Somers scooped up a packet of documents and crossed his arms. "It keeps happening. It happened today with Cravens. It happened the first case we worked together. It happened back in high school."

"I don't care what people think of me. I'm going to do what I think is right. I'm going to say what I think is right."

"It's not about caring about what people think. It's about—"

"Manipulating people? Telling them what they want to hear?"

"It's about being politic. Being smart. You don't have to kiss someone's ass, but you also don't have to be an ass, you know? You catch more flies with honey, that kind of stuff."

"All right."

"Can you just try? For me? Just try letting things slide."

"I said all right."

For a moment, they just watched each other. Under the counter, a mustard-colored dishwasher swished and chugged and thumped. There was the slightest smell of vinegar and brine in the air, leftover from whatever Newton had eaten that evening. Somers was the first one to drop his eyes, and he shook his head and started towards the stairs.

Hazard didn't follow, not right away. He checked the first floor, making sure the doors—there were three: one to the garage, one to the deck behind the house, and one at the front—were locked, and then checking the windows one by one. He left off the lights as much as possible, and so his impression of the house was that of a series of dark spaces, and the odor of stale cotton and polyester, and stubbing his toe in the darkness and biting back a swear. When he was sure that the bottom floor was as closed-up as possible, he followed the stairs and found Somers sitting on the floor, documents stacked beside him.

"I checked," Somers said in a low voice. "He's sleeping. Windows are shut, by the way, so I guess Moraes finally got some sense into him."

Hazard tilted his head at the hallway and the remaining rooms.

"I walked through, but feel free to make sure."

Instead, Hazard settled himself cross-legged next to Somers. His arm hurt again; whatever local anesthetic Frannie had applied, it had worn off. Worse, though, was the stiffness of the limb, its slowness to respond. It didn't matter how many hours of physical therapy and rehabilitation Hazard did; the arm remained only partially functional, and as the day had proven, it left Hazard weak. Vulnerable.

Somers slid his fingers into that bad hand, and Hazard tried to squeeze. That's all. He didn't say anything. No apologies, no explanations, nothing. Just his hand. As Somers read, he passed sheets to Hazard, and Hazard began to construct a picture of what had happened that day.

It quickly became obvious that, in spite of all the work that had gone into the day's investigation, no one really knew anything. Or, Hazard reconsidered as he looked at the stack of papers, they knew a lot of smaller things. Based on interviews and a sweep of the shooting area, Cravens was fairly sure that the shooter had accessed Family Video's rooftop by means of the derelict coffee shop. The lock on the service door facing the alley had been broken, and the cops had identified footprints in the dust inside the storeroom. Men's size nine. The shooter had broken a second lock on the trap door leading to the roof, and then he had climbed across the building to reach Family Video.

Accompanying the typed report were photographs of the broken lock on the service door, the storeroom floor, the broken trap, and then shots from multiple angles of the flat, tar-paper roof where the shooter had taken up position and fired. It was easy to read in those photographs the care that the shooter had taken in finding the right spot and, in contrast, the haste with which he had fled when Hazard and Somers had charged out to catch him. The best example of this was the cartridge casing ejected by the rifle, which one of the investigating officers had discovered in the Family Video gutter.

"Careless," Somers said, tapping the photograph of the recovered casing. "What do you think about that?"

"I think it's bullshit."

Somers nodded and, without another word, went back to reading.

And the casing was bullshit; Hazard stood by that opinion. The shooter had been bold enough to try to kill the mayor in the Wahredua Police Station. He had been clever in planning his escape and in executing the traps intended to kill the police pursuing him. The only thing he had not accounted for was Hazard and Somers; it wasn't exactly a modest thought, but Hazard believed that if it had been any other cop, those traps would have been successful.

All of that was exactly why Hazard thought the shell was bullshit. Someone as bold as this shooter wouldn't have panicked when Hazard came charging out of the station. And someone as clever as the shooter wouldn't have overlooked the significance of the ejected casing. So why leave it behind? There had been two shots; why abandon only a single casing?

Those, Hazard found, were yet more questions without answers. The casing belonged to a .270 Winchester cartridge, which matched the Remington 700 recovered from the burned-out truck. It also matched the bullets, according to Murray's autopsy report, that the new, provisional ME had recovered from the body. But neither the Remington nor the casing had any recoverable prints.

The truck, too, seemed to be a dead end. The vehicle had been reported stolen a week before the shooting; it had vanished from a Farm & Home Supply parking lot thirty miles outside Wahredua, and the owner, Carl Trauffer, had immediately called the police. And unless a seventy-six-year-old man was spry enough to jump down from a roof, lead police on a high-speed chase, and then escape into a booby-trapped building, Hazard didn't think Carl Trauffer had anything to do with what had happened.

Even the explosion told them nothing; the explosive device had been stored in the white truck, and it had been homemade. It had also been strong enough to destroy the white truck, cripple the Interceptor, and punch a two-story hole in the front of the Haverford. Only now, studying the pictures of the gaping brick facade, did Hazard realize how extensive the damage was. It was a miracle no one else had died, although the report listed several injuries, some serious, to people living in the Haverford's front apartments. The building had been evacuated of the few citizens defying the unlawful occupancy notices, to the relief of Wahredua's upstanding citizens.

Hazard also noticed that the investigation of the building had been cursory—nothing more than a quick up-and-down. The report listed the findings: doors boarded shut; passages closed off with plywood; windows blacked out. And then the report ended. Painfully, visibly short. Too short. Because manpower was in short supply. Because the fair was in town. Because it was a holiday. Because the building was structurally damaged, and Cravens didn't want to risk her men. Because it was the Haverford, in Smithfield, and they had more important things to do.

What was Hollace playing at? Why the elaborate moves? What did he want, and why was he taking this circuitous route to get there?

"Ow," Somers complained.

Hazard realized he was squeezing the other man's hand and relaxed his grip.

"Looks like some of the strength is coming back in that hand."

Hazard grunted.

"What do you think?"

"We've got nothing."

"We've got a suspect, the weapon, and the escape vehicle."

"We've got Hollace in the wind. We've got a weapon and casing with no prints—none, Somers—and an escape vehicle burned down to the metal. That's all. And it's a stolen truck. And even that damn explosive didn't give us shit."

"What about these?" Somers held out photographs of the booby-trapped shotguns that had waited at the end of the Haverford's maze. "No prints on them either. They're Berettas. A300s. And they're sawed off."

"For maximum damage in a tight space."

"For killing cops stupid enough to run right into them." Somers passed over the photographs, and his hand dipped down to his side, where three pellets had tagged him, and Hazard wasn't sure the blond man even knew what he was doing. "Like me."

"It was almost both of us."

"Almost, Ree. But only almost."

"Nothing." Hazard tossed the photos onto the pile next to him. "The bastard gave us nothing."

"Not quite."

"Somers, look at what we have. Cravens printed off, what, a hundred pages? And what do we have in those hundred pages? Nothing. She could have printed off her shopping list for all it matters."

"I would have liked to see her shopping list. You can learn a lot from a person based on their shopping. If your boyfriend only likes coconut-infused hair products—"

"You promised you weren't going to bring that up. And anyway I don't only use them. I use other stuff."

"Ok."

"I do."

"I believe you."

"I have some pomade that doesn't have any coconut in it."

"Right. I just meant, what you've bought exclusively since we've been together. Since that night I was licking your ear and told you I liked how your hair smelled. Since then. That's all I meant."

"You want me to paddle your ass. That's what this feels like sometimes. Like you want it."

Somers's smirk could have started a fire. "I definitely want you to try." Then the smirk cooled, and he patted Hazard's cheek. "Anyway, you're missing my point."

"What's your point besides getting me riled?"

"My point is that everything is a clue. A shopping list. An entire linen closet of coconut-infused hair gunk."

Hazard could feel the growl building in his chest.

"And," Somers said hastily, "all of this." He tapped the pile of documents.

With a frown, Hazard turned his attention to the papers. "All right. Let's hear it."

"Hollace is smart."

"I already said that."

"Will you just listen?" Somers frowned, drawing his lower lip between his teeth, and his tropical blue eyes went a long way off.

"He's smart about tactical things: stealing the truck, entering through the abandoned coffee shop, the position he took on the Family Video roof, the escape plan, and the booby traps at the Haverford. But he's also . . . I don't know. Arrogant. Maybe even new to this."

"New to assassinating mayors?"

"Don't be an asshole. You're right about the casing. He left it there on purpose; it's a bullshit clue. But it tells us something about him: he knows he's smart, and he thinks he's smarter than us. The photographs prove that. The casing, too. That's to rub our noses in it. Or, if we're really as dumb as he thinks, to tie us up worrying about evidence like that."

"But he's not going to leave evidence like that. That's the whole point."

"Exactly. And the casing isn't the only time his ego slipped through. Think about the whole set-up at the Haverford. He planned for us to follow him there. He wanted to kill some cops. But if he only wanted to kill some cops, he could have stayed on top of the Family Video and plugged you when you came charging through the glass. Don't make that face; I know you calculated the whole thing out, and I know you think you had a good chance of avoiding him as long as you were quick on your feet and kept the element of surprise. But he could have gotten you. Or he could have put a few rounds in Cravens. Or me. Jesus, Ree, he didn't even try. He got those two shots off and ran."

"He might have—"

"Hold on. Even the way he ran tells us something about him. He went to all that work getting an old white Dodge Ram. There're probably fifty trucks exactly like it on the streets of Wahredua every day. He could have disappeared into the city. But he didn't. He took just long enough to get into the truck that we were able to follow him."

Hazard was nodding; he was remembering his own thoughts during the chase, his analysis of the shooter's decision to use a white, older model truck. "I assumed that he had been planning on using the truck as camouflage, but that we were too quick."

"All he had to do was buy himself an extra five minutes—say, planting an explosive near the station's parking lot, then blowing it when he needed to make an escape—and he could have done exactly what you said. But he didn't do that, Ree. He wanted cops to follow him. He wanted the big scene at the Haverford. He wanted everyone to see how smart he was and how stupid the Wahredua PD is."

"Do you think he shot Murray on purpose? Do you think he intended to hit the mayor?"

Between them, then, the only noises were the house settling and a night bird calling in the darkness, and then the bird's song cut off.

"I hadn't thought that far," Somers said. "I think he wanted to get the mayor. I think everything else was going to be icing."

"Assassin kills mayor in police station. That's a big headline."

"And a bigger headline if he lured the cops chasing him into a deadly trap."

"And then he escapes. He leaves a few pieces of evidence—the guns, the casing, the truck—and they lead nowhere, and then time stretches on, and every day the cops look stupider."

"Does Hollace hate cops? Does he hate the mayor? What's this about? Does he hate you; is it all about you?"

"It's not about me."

"Something like this," Somers said, rubbing at his forehead, "it's got a lot of emotion behind it. It might not even be the kind of emotion that usually drives murder. It might be something else, something more cerebral. Arrogance. Pride. Conceit. Ree, those photographs—he sent those for a reason, and that reason wasn't to warn you off, no matter what bullshit writing he put on them."

Nodding, Hazard squeezed Somers's hand once. "So we do what we've always done. We work the case. We'll talk to the mayor and find out why someone might want him dead. And we'll find out the names of anybody who might have hired Hollace to kill the mayor."

"Besides us," Somers added with a lopsided smile.

"Besides us. We'll make a list and start crossing off names. And we'll find him. We'll find Hollace, and we'll stop him."

"Ree, what I said earlier. I was pissed. But I want to know why you didn't show me those pictures—"

And then glass shattered inside Mayor Newton's bedroom.

CHAPTER TEN

JULY 2
MONDAY
11:45 PM

THE SOUND OF SHATTERING GLASS froze Hazard for only an instant. And in that instant, he strained, listening for more noises, as his brain considered possibilities: Newton had bumped a glass of water from the nightstand; Newton had tipped over a standing mirror; Newton had hurled something at a TV. But the analytical part of his mind slashed through the possibilities, and only a single, crystalline thought remained: the window.

In the following moment, glass tinkled, and Hazard envisioned it being knocked from the frame, falling to chime against the larger pieces that had been broken initially. Those were the noises of someone clearing the frame so that he could climb through it without being cut. They were the noises of someone breaking into the mayor's room.

Hazard rolled to his feet, and from inside the mayor's bedroom came a shout. "What are you doing? No. You can't—" And then Mayor Newton's voice cut off.

Somers was still scrambling to his feet, papers flaking off him and spiraling down. Hazard was closest to the door, and he reached it first, his .38 in one hand. When he tried to open the door, it was locked. He took a step back, planted himself, and drove his heel into the wood directly beneath the handle. Wood splintered, staving in under the blow, but it didn't break completely.

A man screamed inside the bedroom. Hazard slammed his heel into the door again. The frame bent, fractures webbing across the wood, but it held. From under the door came a whoosh, and then the smell of kerosene and a ruddy, flickering light.

"Shit," Somers said, and then the blond man turned and ran.

Hazard didn't spare a second thought for his partner; he trusted Somers, and everything else could wait. He kicked at the door again. As he did, he forced his mind to stillness, and then he began to think. The door was locked. From the inside. But Hazard remembered Moraes saying that he had told the mayor to leave it open, just in case. Had Somers shut it? Or the mayor? Hazard thought of Moraes's account of the mayor's behavior, and he thought he had his answer. He kicked again. And who had locked the door? The mayor? Or the killer? He drove his heel into the wood; it was an old house, and the door was old too, and it had been made when solid wood doors were still the norm. Around the lock, distressed wood showed the force of Hazard's blows, but this was taking too long. Much too long.

Inside the room, the screams escalated, taking on a shrieking intensity. The stink of the kerosene grew thicker, wafting under the door in waves, leaving Hazard dizzy and breathless as he worked on the door. The red light brightened.

Then the screams stopped. Hazard kicked once more. Wood shattered, spraying splinters, and the door wobbled and rocked inward, torn free from the frame. Hazard kicked again, and the door flew open and crashed against the wall.

Within the bedroom, a scene that might have merited a place in Dante's *Inferno* played out. Fire burned along the walls, obviously tracing the path of an accelerant and fanned by the swampy air rushing into the room through the broken window. Glass sparkled in that firelight, gathered it, and seemed to regenerate it, so that the fire was everywhere, burning inside every gleaming sliver.

Against the fire's backlight, a dark shape knelt over the mayor's bed. The mayor lay there, motionless. Dead, Hazard thought. Or almost dead. But that didn't matter to the man on top of him. That man brought up the knife. Firelight scrolled along the metal, and then the blade came down and buried itself in Newton's chest. The knife came up.

The knife.

The firelight on the knife.

The way light had ribboned on the knife that night in April when a man had come into Hazard's apartment and tried to murder a little girl. The night Emery Hazard had almost lost an arm.

The knife came up.

The kerosene seared Hazard's airway. It fogged his brain. Hazard knew he needed to say something. He needed to identify himself. He needed to command the attacker to stop. He needed to warn him. But every breath was pure kerosene, and his vision had contracted to the scintillating tip of the knife, sparking like a star. And then that star started to fall.

Pop. Pop. Pop. Over the crackle of the flames, the gunshots were still loud enough to hurt Hazard's ears, and he felt them like concussive taps to his own chest. The .38 kicked in his hand. And the man—

—with the knife—

—on the bed spasmed, one, two, three, a herky-jerky twist with each shot moving him, pulling on him like he was the puppet and Hazard held the strings, like this was some horrible puppet-dance. Then the man slipped off the mayor, sliding onto the bed, and he slid from the bed too and fell to the floor, and he was still.

"Ree!" Somers shouted from the broken window, as though he had flown into the air and decided to stop and take a look. A ladder, part of Hazard's brain realized. Somers was standing on the same ladder that the killer had used to get into the home. The blond man took in the scene, holstered his big Glock, and then reached down. Lifting the large-tank fire extinguisher that he had brought from the Jetta, he directed the nozzle and released the spray. The extinguisher's powder gouted along the walls, smothering the kerosene-fueled flames. Clouds of the powder dispersed outward, filling the air, a heatless smoke and ash that dusted the dresser, the painting of a log cabin that hung on the wall, a framed lace doily, everything. It settled on Hazard's arms like he stood in the cold ashes of a burnt-out building, and when he turned his bad hand up and rubbed the powder between his fingers, he hated how slick it was.

Then the extinguisher emptied itself, and the flames had vanished under the drift of powder. In the distance, sirens blatted, and the night bird called again. Or maybe that was just the ringing in Hazard's ears—the aftershock of the gunfire combined with the rush of his pounding heart.

"Ree, are you all right?" Somers was climbing through the window now, knocking shards of glass from his path with the fire extinguisher, and the glass and metal sang out sweeter than the night bird. When he landed in the room, he gave his partner a questioning look before moving to examine the mayor. Over his shoulder, he said, "Ree?"

Hazard nodded. He was all right. His fingers slicked more of the ash against his palm. He was fine. Hazard picked a path across the room, and his sneakers left dark, wet tracks in the chemical powder.

The sirens were louder now. The bitter, chemical taste of the extinguisher filled Hazard's mouth. It was in his hair. In his eyes. He could feel it powdering his lungs with every shallow breath. He held the .38 at the ready as he bent over the man who had broken into the mayor's home. In Hazard's mind, it was that April night again, and he was helpless, unarmed, and he saw the knife glittering with the light from the sodium lamps, and the knife was coming down, coming down, coming down, and there was nothing he could do to stop it.

Not tonight, though. His sweaty finger, slick with the extinguisher's powder, stuttered along the trigger guard. Tonight he wasn't helpless. Tonight he had the .38. He buried the muzzle in the dead man's shoulder and used it to roll him onto his back.

Hazard recognized the thinning hair, the hound-dog eyes, the mole on his chin, the paunch. He let out a breath, and the chemical agent whirled away and spun back angrily and stung his eyes.

"It's Ted Kjar," he called to Somers.

CHAPTER ELEVEN

JULY 3
TUESDAY
1:51 AM

THEY WAITED A LONG TIME. Separated at first, as Liz Swinney, Wahredua's only female detective, took statements from each of them and began yet another officer-involved shooting investigation. Only when this was complete did the red-haired woman allow them to join each other. Somers, who had spent most of this time sitting in the back of Hoffmeister's patrol car, was ready to kick down the wire partition and climb out the front door. He kept seeing in front of him the look on Hazard's face as he knelt over Ted Kjar. He kept seeing the realization, like a match flame eating up paper by inches, as Hazard knew who he had shot and killed. And he saw, too, what he would never tell anyone else about. Ever. He saw guilt.

So he needed out of this car. He needed out of the back seat of Hoffmeister's black and white, which smelled like Funyuns and greasy farts and Lysol. He needed to be done with Swinney and her shitty questions, even if it wasn't her fault, even if she was only doing her job. And he needed to get to Emery Hazard, the big brute, before Hazard said something stupid.

When Swinney finally squeezed out of the back seat, Somers had to force himself to act cool. He knew how to act cool. He'd acted cool most of his damn life, and most days, it was easy. But tonight, tonight Hazard was a hundred feet away, and he might be saying something stupid, he might be saying something—

—that look on his face, like fire taking black-rimmed bites out of paper—

—that could ruin his life. But instead of running, instead of sprinting to Hazard's side, Somers stretched his legs. He arched his back. He ran fingers through his hair and asked Swinney if she had a bottle of water, which she did, and then he drank it, perched on the hood of Hoffmeister's cruiser until he felt like he could walk like a normal human and not run towards the man he loved.

Hazard stood apart from the rest of the assembled cops, near a clump of dogwood whose leaves were brown and falling. The chemical powder from the extinguisher grayed his hair, and a fine layer of it had settled into the lines around his eyes, on his shoulders, between his fingers. It made him look old. Old and ruined. His scarecrow eyes wouldn't meet Somers's.

"Tell me you didn't say anything."

Hazard's gaze snapped up, but not all the way. "What do you mean?"

"Ree, tell me you didn't."

"I told them the truth."

"For fuck's sake."

Now his eyes did come up, eyes the color of straw at the end of summer. "You didn't?"

"This isn't about me, dummy. You told them you shot him to save the mayor. That's what you told them. Ree, tell me that's what you told them."

He shifted, crossing his arms and staring out at something in the distance. The truth, Somers thought with a sudden wild surge of bitterness. He thinks he's staring out at the motherfucking truth, all noble and martyred.

"Look at me. What did you say to them?"

"It's done, Somers."

"What did you say?"

"I told them the truth. I told them that I broke down the door. I told them that I saw the mayor and I assumed he was dead."

Somers groaned.

Ignoring him, Hazard continued in the same affectless voice, "I told them that I saw the knife, that I lost control, and that I shot Kjar three times."

"You didn't lose control."

Hazard uncrossed and crossed his arms. He was still looking off at the motherfucking truth.

"You didn't. Don't give me that bullshit. You saw a man with a knife. A dangerous man. You saw him attack another man with a knife. You knew that the mayor's life was in danger—"

"He was already dead."

"No. He's alive. He's alive because of us. Barely, but he's alive."

"But I thought he was dead. I told Swinney that because it's important. I thought he was dead, and when I—"

"Shut up, stupid. You knew that his life was in danger, and you knew that your life was in danger—"

"It was that knife, John. It was the fucking knife." The words broke out of Hazard, so soft and low that Somers barely heard them, and they stopped Somers like a brick wall. "I saw that knife and I was there again. I was alone. I was in that room, in the dark, with the knife. And I shot him. I shot him because I was scared."

"Of course you were scared. He had a knife. He could have killed you, Ree. And I'm talking about tonight, too. He killed Newton. He would have killed you if you hadn't stopped him."

Hazard shook his head. Those scarecrow eyes were liquid, now, and their sheen caught the steady blue pulse of the squad car lights.

"Ree—"

"I killed him because I was scared, Somers."

"But, Ree—"

"Please don't do this right now." Hazard swallowed. "Please."

And something about his voice, about the pain in it, about the pleading, made Somers's furious. "This is you all over again. This is you doing the goddamn noble thing because you think you have to. This is you fighting a fight nobody else would even think about. Ree, for Christ's sake, he was a murderer. He would have attacked you."

"Would have. If he'd had a chance."

There it was again: that look. The guilt on his face, a hot, black line where the guilt was already eating away at him.

"You're insane," Somers said. "You're fucking insane, and I can't deal with your bullshit right now."

Hazard's posture changed only slightly, but it was enough to put his back to Somers.

"Fuck you then."

Somers turned and marched towards the knot that surrounded Chief Cravens. The chief looked like she'd gone through the ringer a few dozen times. Her face, waxy now, was set in resolve, but resolve could only carry you so far. Somers was starting to learn that. He was starting to realize that right-fucking-now with Hazard. It was bad enough that Hazard felt this compulsive need to be right, this unrelenting need for everything to be right and true and exact. That was bad enough when you were his partner and you had to watch him turn your canoe up shit creek and willfully—motherfucking intentionally—toss the paddles aside. That was one thing.

Somers could deal with that. He liked his job. He wasn't looking for a promotion. At least, not anytime soon. So he could deal with shit creek. He could deal with the paddles tossed aside. Hell, not just tossed. Goddamn launched into the next county. He could deal with that. He could deal with the angry looks from colleagues. He could deal with walking into the break room, with the awkward silence that told him Hoffmeister and Peterson and Carmichael had been bitching about Hazard. He could deal with the slow erosion of relationships he'd been building over a lifetime in a small town. He could. He honestly could deal with all of that because in exchange, he got Emery Hazard, and there wasn't really anything he wanted besides Hazard.

But what the fuck was he supposed to do when Emery Hazard was doing just about everything in his power to fuck over Emery Hazard? That was a riddle. That was a mind-bender. That was one of those awful lateral thinking problems that Hazard liked to do, the ones in that goddamn book of them that he'd taken when they'd gone to the lake. It was like that. And just like that, Somers wanted to break his head against a wall. Or strangle Hazard just to shut him up. Or maybe both.

Swinney must have seen him coming across Newton's lawn because her crop of coppery hair bobbed towards the chief, and Cravens glanced at Somers and began pushing her way free of the crowd. A few of the patrol cops followed, but Cravens barked something, and they melted away. By the time she reached Somers, they had a good ten yards of privacy in any direction.

"Your partner looks bad," she said.

"We all look bad."

Cravens laughed bitterly and scrubbed at her face. "Is he ok?"

"He's fine."

"You're sure?"

No. No, Somers wanted to say, he wasn't sure at all, but unlike Hazard he had the sense not to say everything that came into his head. "He's fine."

"And you?"

"I don't really feel like tap dancing, but I'll make it."

"This is about as bad as it gets, John-Henry."

That made him pause. He didn't know the last time he'd heard her use his name. John-Henry. Not Detective Somerset. Not even, simply, Detective. John-Henry. And he looked closer at the chief, saw the lackluster eyes and the gray flesh and the tic of her pulse in her throat, and he saw a time bomb. Only this was going to be an implosion, he realized with an intuitive flash. This was going to be a woman who blew apart on the inside without harming anything around her.

"The mayor?"

"Who knows? They life-flighted him to University Hospital. Maybe that'll be enough. God knows he wouldn't have had a chance if you hadn't been here."

"Does his family know?"

"I have no idea. Lender's trying to track someone down. He has cousins, I think. No siblings. No spouse. No children. Parents have been dead for fifty years."

"About Kjar. The shooting. What Hazard said—"

Cravens held up a hand. "I don't care, John-Henry. I never thought I'd say that, but it's true. I just don't care. I don't have the luxury of caring right now. Today. This kind of day. It seems like a joke, do you understand? Murray's shooting. That nightmare at the Haverford. And then, while I've got everybody on the force working doubles to try to lock down those crime scenes and keep the town from falling apart, the sheriff starts calling me about a noise complaint at the Deluxe Drive-in. A noise complaint at a fleabag motel, like he's never worked the job a day in his life. He wants to know how we've handled them in the past. Just when I think I've got that sewn up, kids are shooting each other at the fairgrounds. Shooting each other in broad daylight. So I've got to send Swinney and Lender over there to keep that fuse from reaching the powder keg, and when I think I can take a breath, this happens. So when I say I don't care. I don't care. There will be an investigation; as far as I'm concerned, it'll be open and shut."

"Chief, Hazard might have said something to Swinney. Something that isn't true, but he thinks it is. Or he's afraid it is."

For an instant, Cravens's eyes sharpened, and she looked something like her old self. "Then I trust Detective Swinney will be smart enough to choose only the most relevant pieces of testimony for her report."

"And if she isn't?"

"If she isn't, Detective, then I will be." Somers let out a breath he hadn't been sure he was holding, and Cravens spoke, pretending not to notice his relief. "I need both of you working this case. I need every piece of evidence you can get so we can put Kjar to bed and never look at this again. It's got to be airtight, John-Henry. It's got to be so tight nobody can say we overlooked anything. This is the mayor, for heaven's sake. We're going to have eyes on us, scrutinizing every move, until it's over." That intensity focused her gaze again. Focused it on Somers. "Your partner will have eyes scrutinizing his actions over the last twenty-four hours. Do you understand me?"

"Yes."

"Then do it. Put together the whole story, everything about Kjar, everything about tonight. Go back to the day Ted Kjar was born if you have to. Hell, go back to when the mayor was born if you have to. Airtight, John-Henry. That's what this has to be."

"Yes, Chief."

"Then get the hell out of here."

Somers made his way back to Hazard. The big brute was still staring off into space, arms crossed over his chest, like a statue to the most pig-headed human in existence.

"You ready to work?"

Hazard's jaw flexed. "What about the investigation?"

"Consider yourself provisionally cleared."

"What did you—"

"Nothing. I didn't do anything."

Hazard's amber eyes flicked to Somers's face and then away. "I should be at a desk until we're sure I'm safe to be in the field."

"In the field?"

"You know what I mean."

"Well, you're not going to a desk. Do you understand that?"

Hazard narrowed his eyes.

"Do you?"

His arms dropped to his sides, and his hands closed into fists.

"I'm asking you a simple question, Ree: do you understand me when I say you're not going to a desk? Yes or no. It's a really simple question. I think you can answer it. Yes or no: do you understand that you're not—"

"I fucking understand." Hazard's words exploded in a shout, and he made an obvious effort to control himself before speaking again. "I understand. But I'm telling you that I shouldn't—"

"Stop. Right there. No, just stop and listen to me." Somers softened his voice, and he let his hand trail down Hazard's arm, leaving tracks in the chemical powder of the extinguisher until his fingers hooked Hazard's. "You're smart, Ree. You're so damn smart it scares me sometimes. And you're brave, and you're kind, and you're honest. So be honest with me right now. Use that brain and be honest with me: what do you think would have happened if you had warned Kjar to drop the knife?"

The emotion tripping across Hazard's face was so strong, so raw, that Somers wanted to look away, but he kept his gaze locked with Hazard's.

"I would have shot him," Hazard said, his voice contorted with emotion, his breathing heavy. "He would have come at me and I would have shot him. But, John, that doesn't change the fact that I—"

"It was justified, Ree. You're smarter than I am. You know more than I do. But even I know that it all boils down to one of two things: your life is in danger, or someone else's life is."

"I thought the mayor was dead."

"But you were in danger."

"But that's not why I shot. I shot because of this." And he tried to lift his injured arm.

"You're splitting hairs," Somers said. "I'm not going to argue with you. I'm just going to ask you one more question. Use your brain and be honest. If you put yourself at a desk, what's going to happen?"

"Fuck you."

"What's going to happen?"

"Fuck you, you manipulative fucking prick."

"You want to yell at me? Fine. Yell at me. Call me names. You can even knock me around if it'll make you feel better. But first you tell me what's going to happen if you go sit behind a desk?"

"You'll still investigate. You'll—"

"Don't do that. Don't patronize me."

Hazard's breathing was so loud and labored that it blocked out everything else. Somers stayed where he was, unmoving, eyes locked with Hazard's scarecrow gaze. He caught a whiff of Hazard's sweat, and then, more distantly, the scent of bug repellent. Clouds of midges drifted into floodlights, and then Hazard's breathing eased, and the low buzz of the insects became audible again.

"You would work the case," Hazard said, the words sounding like they'd been dragged out of him. "You might solve it. You're a good detective. One of the best. But you might not. Or the chief might kick it to Lender and Swinney."

"If that happens, the case won't get closed. Or they'll close it with whatever story Lender finds convenient. No matter how much Swinney might wish it otherwise, that's how it would go down. Now tell me: what happens if you don't sit behind a desk?"

"We have a chance at it."

"A good chance."

"We have a chance, John. That's all."

"You know it's more than that. You know we work well together. The things we've done, nobody else here can do those things. So which is it going to be? Are you going to sit behind a desk because you're still dealing with trauma? Or are you going to solve a murder?"

"That's not fair."

"I wish I could make it fair, Ree. You have no idea how much I wish I could. But it's just the two of us, and I can't do this without you."

"You could."

Somers shook his head; he could feel the smile on his face, could feel the sadness behind it. "Whatever comes down the road, you can handle it. Just like you handled tonight. You might think that what you did was because of your past, but it wasn't. You did it because it was the only thing you could do and because it was the right thing to do."

"And how the fuck do you know that?"

"Because I know you, dummy. Now. What's it going to be?"

The clouds of midges darted across the light. Hazard turned his head slightly, and those scarecrow eyes caught crescents of the moon, and his shoulders came down and he nodded. "Let's go solve a murder."

CHAPTER TWELVE

JULY 3
TUESDAY
2:20 AM

HAZARD HAD SHOT A MAN. He had shot plenty of men in his life. Too many men. And while there was truth to the statement that killing changed a man, in his experience, it hadn't changed him too much. He had only killed to protect himself or to protect others. Killing was a hard thing, but it wasn't an impossible thing, and, after all, Emery Hazard had made a habit out of doing hard things.

As he followed Somers towards Newton's house, with a sickle of moon hanging overhead and the humid smell of a Missouri summer, of the river, of trampled witch-hazel everywhere around him, he tried to figure out how to say what was different about this time. Somers, for the most part, was good at saying things. Somers had a way of understanding things, of seeing to the heart of things. The way he had done earlier that evening, looking at the scanty evidence and using it to assemble a profile of the killer. And the way he had spoken to Hazard. There wasn't anybody else in the world Hazard would have allowed to speak to him like that; there wasn't anybody else in the world who could have spoken to Hazard like that. And, yes, Hazard loved Somers, and that was part of it. But it was more than the nature of their relationship; the realizations that cost Hazard so much effort to deduce, the careful working out of logic and sequence, all those things came so easily to Somers, in those intuitive flashes that left Hazard baffled.

And so Hazard was faced with the frustrating knowledge that what was so very difficult for him would have been easy for Somers. He just needed to find a way to say it. A way to explain to Somers why tonight had been different. The first time Hazard had shot a man, he had still been on patrol in St. Louis, and he had been working the overnight shift in north city, one of the most dangerous parts of the city and, for that matter, of the country. Two boys—he had thought, at the time, they were men—had been trying to jack a car. Hazard and his partner had flashed their lights, but the boys had stayed and kept working. Then Hazard and his partner had called in, asked for backup, and stopped the car. Instead of running, at that point the boys had turned and opened fire on the patrol car. The rest had been simple for Emery Hazard. Even as a relatively new cop, it had been simple. Frightening, yes—he wouldn't lie about that; he had been terrified—but also simple. He had followed his training, and when an opportunity presented itself, he took a shot. He hadn't killed the boy—that was a relief, and the intensity of the relief surprised him—but he had been willing to. He had understood his situation, and he had known what to do, and he had done it. More or less for his entire life, that had been how Hazard handled everything. But this, tonight, this had been different.

A radio squawked in a nearby car, and Hazard shot a glance over. Most of Wahredua's police were busy with various tasks: reports, interviews, canvassing the surrounding area for evidence. Some of it, they didn't have to go far to find. Ted Kjar had arrived at Newton's home in a Honda Accord, late model with an expensive trim. Some of the cops were working it now, dusting it for prints, ripping out upholstery, looking for any kind of clue that might make sense of tonight's events. Hazard left them to it, following Somers into the darkness behind Newton's house, thick with the scent of dwarf juniper, where the water beading on the grass balanced tiny points of reflected light.

What made it so difficult to tell, what made it so hard for Hazard to find the words, was that he himself didn't fully know. That, more than anything, was what scared him. And yes, there was some guilt about having shot Kjar, but that guilt was . . . incidental. Hazard didn't know how else to put it. It was secondary. A side-effect of the larger problem. And the larger problem wasn't the shooting. It wasn't the fact that Hazard had ended a man's life. Somers was right about that much; even if Hazard had given the warning, Kjar would doubtless have turned and attacked. No, the problem was larger than that. More systematic than that. And it pointed to something fundamentally flawed in Hazard's process: he didn't know why he had pulled the trigger.

The grass was wet, and as it soaked his sneakers, some of the chemicals from the extinguisher pasted the green blades together. Of course, Hazard told himself, he knew why he had pulled the trigger. He had pulled it to kill Kjar. To stop him. But there was something before that. Something in the moment, maybe the fraction of a moment, before the shot, when Hazard had chosen to act based on emotion instead of decision. He had acted out of fear; and yes, Somers was right, that fear was rooted in a very real trauma that had cost Hazard the use of his arm. But he knew that was an excuse; the reality was that in the final moment, Hazard had refused to decide. He had let himself act based on the past, not on the present. He had let a memory determine his future. It had been so much easier to do that. And he didn't know why he had done it, and that was what terrified him. That was what he couldn't explain to Somers; he could barely explain it to himself.

"And our fourth child will be named Matilda if she's a girl or Matthew if he's a boy."

"What?"

"Oh. So you were listening?"

"What are you—" Hazard swallowed. "Our fourth?"

"Of eight," Somers said. "There's the ladder Kjar used."

"Hold on. Eight?"

Somers just beamed at him and then got down to business. "He came down the hill over there—you can still see the tracks in the wet grass—and walked the ladder right up to the house. He must have been careful because we didn't hear him set the ladder there. Then he climbed up, broke the window, and attacked Newton."

"No."

"What do you mean no?"

Hazard ignored him, studying the scene.

"Ree, what do you mean no? That's exactly what happened."

"How did you come?"

"What?"

"With the fire extinguisher, which way did you come?"

"Over there. You can see where I was running."

"So what's all this?" Hazard indicated crisscrossing paths in the wet grass.

"We were down here earlier."

"I know, but I saw it then too."

"The patrol cops. The ones Moraes sent around the house. Now will you tell me—"

"No, they came before the sprinklers were turned on. Moraes told us that, remember? He said they watched while he turned on the water. So who came down here?"

"Could it have been an animal? Deer?"

Hazard shrugged. "Maybe. It doesn't seem like it. They walked right up to the house—see?"

"So somebody else was here? After Moraes turned on the sprinklers, but before you and I did our walk around the house? That's—Jesus, who?"

"Tell me your version of the events."

"No. You're going to be a dick and tell me how I'm wrong."

"Just tell me again." Crickets chirped, and one of the cops in front of the house must have hit the wrong button because a siren whooped once and then clicked off, the second, interrupted whoop sounding more like a cough. "It helps me think."

"You get off on this."

"On what?"

"Telling me how I'm wrong. Fine. I said he came down the hill, set up the ladder, broke the window, and killed Newton."

"Pick up the ladder."

"Am I your gopher now?"

"Just pick it up."

"I'll mess up the prints."

"Somers, pick up the damn ladder."

With a scowl on his beautiful face, Somers stomped over to the ladder, grabbed it at the height of his shoulders and lifted it. It didn't seem to cost him much effort, but its length made it cumbersome, and the far end of the ladder wobbled.

"All right."

Grunting, Somers set the ladder back in place, and it clunked against the siding.

"Heavy?"

"Not when you've got guns like these." Somers flexed, and his t-shirt tightened around what he was now calling his guns. And they were, in Hazard's opinion, damn fine guns at that. With a grin, Somers dropped out of the pose. "It's aluminum. Strong and light. A guy, even out of shape, could carry it easily."

"But not quietly."

"It's not like it has bells strung up on it."

"I'm talking about setting it against the house. You just did it, and it made a fair amount of noise. Not because it's heavy; because it's awkward."

Somers cocked his head, studying the ladder, and then he walked over to it. He lifted it again. This time, when he set it against the house again, he took care to ease the ladder into place, but it was obvious that this was much more difficult than his first effort. Frowning, he turned back to Hazard. "It's not impossible."

"But think about Ted Kjar, supposedly schizophrenic and drugged-out and frantic to kill Newton. Is he thinking carefully and rationally enough to foresee that kind of problem? Would he even have the patience to settle the ladder in place the way you did?"

"It's not impossible," Somers repeated, but Hazard could see the doubt on his face. "Damn. I didn't hear the ladder hitting the house. I didn't hear anything until the glass broke. You?"

"Same."

"Hollace could have done something like this. He's smart enough and careful enough that he could have gotten the ladder in place without making any noise. And with two people, it would have been a lot easier to do."

Hazard blinked. "You think they were working together?"

"Not necessarily. But it's worth holding on to the possibility. We've got a problem with the tracks back here. Somebody, maybe multiple people, came back here after Moraes ran the sprinklers but before you and I walked around. And we also have a problem with the ladder: either Kjar wasn't schizophrenic, or he had help getting the ladder quietly in place. Then he climbed the ladder, and he broke through the window."

Hazard opened his mouth to say something, but a shape trotted towards them in the darkness, the features resolving into Jonny Moraes's darkly handsome face, now lined with worry and exhaustion. He wore sweatpants and a tank top, with his badge clipped to his waistband, and he looked like shit.

"What are you doing here?" Hazard said.

"I heard. What the fuck happened?"

"We've got some questions for you," Hazard said.

"Yeah," Somers said, cutting off Hazard again before the big man said too much. "Jonny, this has been a shit show tonight."

"He climbed up a ladder? A fucking ladder?"

"We think—" Hazard began again.

"Can you give us that timeline again? Really carefully, though. Like, down to the minute as much as you can."

"Jesus." Moraes blew out a breath. "I got here a few minutes late. Like three-oh-three, maybe three-oh-four. Carmichael had already gotten the windows covered, and I—"

"I don't know if we need that far back. Why don't you start with the lawn? Or the patrol boys you sent around the house. Around there."

Moraes gave them a curious look, and he nodded slowly. "Yeah, all right. George Orear and that girl, the trainee. They're the ones who came. They got here about eight."

"Can you be any more specific about that?"

"What's going on, Somers? What's this about?"

"It matters; that's all I can tell you. Can you be any more specific?"

"Really close to eight. Maybe a few minutes on either side of it. What's going on?"

"So they got here. And?"

"And they cruised the street a few times, checking out parked cars, talking to neighbors, that kind of thing. They came back here just to fill me in. I took advantage and sent them around the outside of the house. That bluff out back is steep, but it's not impossible to climb, and I wanted them to take a look. They did. Orear wasn't happy; he bitched for ten minutes, I'd say, but he did it. Mostly because that trainee, Ehlers, was staring at him like he'd grown a second head. And when they'd finished, I asked them to wait while I turned on the sprinklers. They did. Orear didn't like that either. And then they took off. They swept the grounds about eight-twenty. They didn't spend too long, so I bet I had the sprinklers going by eight-thirty. That's probably around when they left."

Without a word, Hazard pulled his phone from his pocket and walked towards the street.

"What about putting the mayor to bed?" Somers said.

"Not long after that. Nine. No, that's not quite right. I went up there about nine-fifteen. It was a commercial break on whatever TV program he was watching. I checked out the room, made sure the windows were covered and closed, looked in the closets, the bathroom, all of it. By nine-thirty, he was up there."

"And the window?"

"What?"

"You said he opened the window and was standing there for God and country to see him."

"I sure as hell didn't say it like that."

"What time?"

"Jesus. Not very long after he went to bed. Nine-forty. Nine-forty-five?"

"Not later than that?"

"I don't know." Moraes shook his head. "No, it couldn't have been much later than that."

"Why?"

"Because I remember after I got him to close the window, after he threw his hissy-fit, I looked at my watch and I thought I still had more than an hour of dealing with him. So it had to be, I don't know, at least a quarter to ten."

"And that's it? You didn't hear anything else?"

"What the hell is this?" Moraes said.

"Did you?"

"No. Maybe I heard him moving around, but nothing that sounded strange. What is this? What's going on?"

"I told you: a shit show. Look, I'm sorry I can't say more."

"You're boxing me out."

"No."

"You are. You're boxing me out. Why? Because Hazard thinks he's got something figured?"

"No. Jonny, you're taking this the wrong way."

"You're interrogating me like I'm a suspect, Somers. How the hell am I supposed to take it?"

"You're not a suspect. Hazard shot the guy that did this; that part's closed."

"So what? You think I did a bad job? Is that what this is?"

"Nobody is saying that."

"Are you going to haul Carmichael down here? Are you going to grill her too?"

"Grill her? Jesus, Jonny, don't you think you're overreacting?"

"I think this is a fucking joke, that's what I think. And fuck you."

With that, Moraes spun and marched back towards the cluster of police lights. Somers sighed and followed. Hazard, still on his phone, stood right in Moraes's path, and Moraes swerved at the last moment. The smaller, dark-skinned cop made sure that his shoulder caught Hazard, though, and from the flash of pain on Hazard's face, Somers knew that Moraes had caught Hazard's bad arm. And he guessed that it had been on purpose.

"Moraes," Somers called, running after him. "Get back here. Moraes!"

Cradling the phone against his shoulder, Hazard caught Somers with his good hand and shook his head. *Let it go,* he mouthed. And then, into the phone, "All right. All right. Thanks."

"He knew. He knew what he was fucking doing."

"The times check out."

"I don't care if the times check out. I'm going to drag his butt back here so he can apologize."

Wincing, Hazard pressed the edges of the bandage, but he shook his head. "It's fine. He's pissed. I don't blame him. We're just the tip of the iceberg, Somers. When more of this starts getting out, he's going to look like he was part of it. Or, best case, he's going to look incompetent. So are we."

"Jesus fuck," Somers swore, scrubbing both hands through his hair. "What the hell happened tonight?"

"What always happens when we catch a murder like this: everything went sideways."

"Moraes's timeline?"

Hazard nodded. "I just talked to Orear."

"And?"

"Pissed. Pissed that I woke him up, pissed that Moraes bullied him out of his patrol car, pissed that he's got a trainee. But his version matches."

And that gave them nothing, Somers thought. Nothing that helped, anyway. He sighed, and together, the two men started up the hill.

Shaking his head as they walked, Hazard started several times to say something, stopping himself each time.

"What? Just spit it out."

"Why did the mayor open the window and stand there?" Hazard asked. "Did he hear something?"

Somers shook his head, but he couldn't shake the question. That, Somers thought as dew soaked through his sneakers, felt like the key to all of it.

CHAPTER THIRTEEN

JULY 3
TUESDAY
9:48 AM

THEY LEFT NEWTON'S HOUSE for the patrol officers to process, with Norman and Gross taking the lead. Somers had to do some convincing to get Hazard to go with him. Hazard had never trusted Norman and Gross to do a decent job with forensics, but as far as Somers could tell, there was very little reason for his prejudice. And eventually Somers won out, and with Chief Cravens's permission, they went home to catch a few hours' sleep before picking up the investigation again.

But when they got back to their apartment, when they lay in bed, sleep came fitfully, and when it came, it brought horrible dreams. They were dreams that Somers thought he had left behind a long time ago. They were dreams that he thought he had buried—especially since he had found Emery Hazard again, since he had fallen in love with him, since he had tied his life to Hazard's. Somers had convinced himself that the dreams were gone.

But he stood in the bathroom, squeezing toothpaste onto his brush, and his eyes had raccoon rings in the replacement mirror they'd tacked above the sink. His hand shook. Just a little. Just enough that the toothpaste slopped onto the side of the bristles, smeared a blue line along the molded plastic base, and then jagged back up. And his hand shook when he set the brush against his teeth and began to scrub.

In the dream, his hands had been shaking too. In the dream, he had been sixteen again. Sixteen and perfect. At least, that was how everyone had seen him. But he hadn't been perfect. He had been sixteen years old, and the weight of everyone thinking he was perfect had crushed him. It made him think of the pressurized chambers that scientists had used, of how one wrong calculation could shoot the pressure up to the danger zone, and how organs would crumple under that invisible force. That's what it had been like, being sixteen and perfect: feeling like his insides were being squeezed, feeling like his lungs were compressed, feeling like he could never take a full breath, not ever, not when anyone was watching.

In the dream, he had been sixteen and perfect and unable to draw a real breath. And he had stood at the edge of the clay pits. And it had been a hot day. Hot, even though it was May, even though it wasn't even Memorial Day yet and the pools were still closed, and because the pools were closed they had decided to ride their bikes out towards the clay pits past the Tegula factory. It wasn't far, not really. It was only a few blocks off the far end of Market Street. But it felt like the other side of the moon to three boys riding their bikes.

It wasn't summer, but it was hot, and the day had been full of summer smells: the green of new leaves, and the bristle of fresh mulch, and the dusty, hot metal of their bikes, and the clay. God, the smell of the clay was like a wall marking the edge of the pits, and beyond that wall, the summer smells couldn't pass.

They had ridden their bikes out there. They had ridden their bikes for fun. It had been Mikey's idea; that made sense because everything was Mikey's idea. John-Henry Somerset was the golden boy. He was sixteen. And he was perfect. But Mikey Grames was— God, what? A lightning bolt? An earthquake? A hurricane? He was wild. He was angry. He was violent. He frightened Somers, and he frightened Hugo Perry, the third member of their trifecta, but that fear also worked like a magnet, binding the other boys to him. There was something special about being singled out for Mikey's attention. He was unlike every other boy, and so his attention was unique. Valuable. And poisonous.

That part of the dream always received the least development: the bike ride. The bike ride didn't matter. In the dreams, it was of indeterminate length. Sometimes, in the dreams, the bike ride was something that had already happened. A necessary but boring precondition to what the dream was really about. And now, with toothpaste foaming at the corners of his mouth, Somers bit down on the bristles, bit down so hard that the molded plastic dug into the tender flesh of his palate, and tried to remember what the bike ride had really been like. Because if he could focus on that, if he could remember that the bike ride had been on a hot day, with the sun supercharged against his back, with sweat dripping under his arms, with the smell of the fresh mulch bristly in his nose, he could remember that it had all started out with a bike ride. They had been kids. They had just been going for a bike ride.

But Somers had known, hadn't he? He'd known that there'd been more when Mikey suggested the bike ride. He'd known that Mikey thought bike rides were kids' stuff. He'd known that Mikey was a little tubby, that he didn't really get up to much exercise, and that riding bikes on the hottest day of the year didn't fit with what Mikey liked to do. And there had been something in Mikey's face. Something in the way he crunched his ugly, crooked teeth together like a smile. Something in his eyes. One time Mikey had stopped their little band at the edge of a road where a car had struck a German shepherd. The dog's back had been broken, but it was still alive, and Mikey had looked at the dog the same way he looked that day he proposed a bike ride down Market Street to the clay pits. Dead-dog eyes. That's how Somers thought of them as he bit down on the toothbrush and avoided his own gaze with the raccoon rings.

In the dream, it always happened the same way: they were at the clay pits. The bike ride had already happened. The smell of the clay pits walled off the rest of the world. It bricked away the summer. And Somers and Hugo tossed rocks into the pits, and they teamed up and rolled one big mother of a rock right up to the edge, and the ground crumbled, as though the earth wanted to swallow them up too, and they skittered backward, laughing as the stone thundered to the bottom of the pit, and they congratulated each other on being badass for the accomplishment of rolling a rock into a pit.

And then Mikey bayed. A dog-like noise, that's what it was. Maybe more dog-like in the dream than it had ever been in real life. Not a word or even a cry. Baying. And he pointed down the length of Market Street, and in the dream, Somers wanted to say no. He wanted to say this was a mistake. He wanted to get on his bike and pedal. He wanted to slide to the edge of the pit, to that crumbling edge of dirt, and keep sliding, to fall, to end up with broken legs at the bottom of a hole. But he couldn't. In the dream, he did the same thing every time: he looked up, and he saw Emery Hazard.

In the dream, the hate was so real. It was visceral. An internal-organs kind of hatred, deep in the bowels, and like everything else in Somers's life, it was subjected to the same degree of perfect-boy pressure. He hated Emery Hazard for being different. He hated him for being a faggot. He hated him because Emery Hazard scared him—terrified him, although that fear was buried so deep that Somers wouldn't recognize it for what it was until years later.

Awake, with the toothbrush a sharp pain now, with the blue spume of toothpaste turning pink at the edges as Somers bit harder on the plastic and felt it bite back in return, he could be sensible. He could be motherfucking sensible about the whole thing. He could look back on that day, he could say he was a kid, just a stupid kid with a lot of baggage, and he could admit that he'd been a scared, repressed queer boy who hadn't known how to handle those facts. He could even appreciate—in the mirror, that foamy mouth parted into a brief rictus—the irony of his childhood: that both Emery Hazard and Mikey Grames had been, in their own ways, frighteningly different; that they had been mirrors of each other; and that Somers had been drawn to both of them for that very reason. He could acknowledge all of that without looking too closely at his reflection, without having to see his own eyes.

But in the dream, none of that self-awareness existed. In the dream, he hated Emery Hazard more than he had hated anyone in his entire life. Somers was a friendly guy. His whole life he'd been good at making friends. Even with the weird kids. Even with the losers. That was one of the perks of being the golden boy; you could be friends with anyone, at no risk of loss of social status. Hell, people actually liked you more if you went out of your way to chum it up with the losers. But Emery Hazard was different. Emery Hazard opened up a gaping red hole inside Somers, and he wanted to hurt him, he wanted to hurt him so badly that Hazard would go away and then Somers wouldn't have to face that aching hole inside himself.

In the dream, the hatred boiled on the surface. And underneath the surface, fear. And in the dream, every time, every goddamn time, he followed Mikey while Mikey followed Hazard. He ran when Mikey ran, and Mikey ran when Hazard ran. And when they caught him, he kicked Hazard, and he hit him, and he spat on him. In the dream, he could feel bone and sinew in the skinny boy's wrist as he pinned his arm. He could feel the flex of muscle—not much muscle, because Hazard was just a string bean back then—and he could feel the boy's fear, could feel the sweat slicking his skin, and it felt good. It felt good to be powerful. And it felt good to touch him like this. To have control of him like this. He still remembered the surge of pleasure, the white-foam cresting pleasure, as Mikey dug the knife into Hazard's stomach. One red line spilling blood down his pale, hairless stomach. Hazard grunted, but he didn't cry out, and that made Somers want to hurt him more. And then Mikey cut another line. And this time Hazard wheezed, and he was crying now, but he still wasn't making the noises Somers wanted to hear. And then the third line. Somers had never heard anyone breathe the way Emery Hazard breathed right then. He was sucking down air, and he still sounded like he was strangling.

Then Hugo's face turned the color of sour milk, and he let go of Hazard's other arm, and he jetted. The dream lasted only a few minutes longer. It lasted just long enough for Mikey to take a step back, confusion on his thick, dumb face. It lasted just long enough for Hazard's scarecrow eyes to cut to Somers, and for Somers to stand there, suddenly sick to his stomach. It lasted, that dream, just long enough for Somers to hear again the same thoughts he had heard all those years ago: his fear of letting go, his fear of Mikey, and the words, *It's him or me, him or me, it's got to be him because it's him or me, oh Christ if Mikey figures it out, oh Christ, it's got to be him, it's got to be him, it's got to be because if Mikey*—

Somers spat out the bloodied froth of toothpaste, and he met his own eyes with their black raccoon rings, and then he brought his fist down on the ceramic sink, one, two, three, and the head of the toothbrush snapped and the piece of molded plastic and nylon bristles shot towards the tub and pinged off the tile. For a moment, standing there was all Somers could do, just stand there and breathe, and he looked rabid with the bloodied spume sticking to the corners of his mouth, with his breathing rapid and shallow, and his eyes like he'd gotten two knockout punches overnight.

"Fuck, fuck, fuck, fuck, fuck."

And then he hit the sink again, and the rest of the toothbrush slithered out of his hand and tinkled against the drain plug.

He rinsed his mouth with cold water until he couldn't see any more blood, and he threw away the toothbrush, and he washed his face. It was a dream. It was the past. Yesterday, all the shit that had happened, the strain of an impossible case, the photographs, that was why he was dreaming that kind of shit again. Plus the run-in with Mikey at the fair. And then Hollace showing up out of nowhere. And Jesus Christ, it made sense that he'd have some sort of dream about the old days. It really did. It made perfect sense. But he had to keep washing his face because his eyes were red and stinging.

The rap at the door came while he was drying his face. "Did you fall in?" Hazard asked.

Somers took a moment longer, his face buried in the fluffy cotton, and he was back in college for a moment, back in college, reading Faulkner, and he could almost hear it, could almost hear the professor saying—

—*the past is never dead*—

The knock came again. "John? Are you all right?"

Somers dropped the towel and opened the door.

"What's—"

He stretched up on tiptoes, kissed Hazard's cheek, and swatted his butt. "Hurry up. We've got a murderer to catch."

As he moved into the kitchen, he cast a backward glance and saw Hazard staring at him.

"I'm the one who needs to hurry?" Hazard muttered.

"I heard that."

Hazard gave him one of those almost-invisible Emery Hazard smiles before he shut the bathroom door, and then Somers slumped on the kitchen counter. He'd forgotten about Faulkner. He just wished he could forget about that damn dream.

CHAPTER FOURTEEN

JULY 3
TUESDAY
10:29 AM

THEY DROVE TOGETHER in Hazard's VW Jetta. The car, once cherry-red, had faded to a pinkish white in most places, and the transmission sounded like rocks in a tumbler, especially when Hazard shifted past third. Worst, in Somers's opinion, was how small the car was. Some days, that was the car's best feature. Some days, it was nice to have Hazard's hand bump up against his knee every time the dark-haired man shifted. But today it was the worst feature. Hazard seemed to fill every available inch of the car with his shoulders, and his knuckles rasped against Somers's knee every fifteen seconds. Brake. Shift. Rasp. Gas. Shift. Rasp. Brake. It could drive a guy crazy.

When they reached the station, Hazard went to unbuckle his belt.

"Hold on. Before we go in there, let's make a plan."

"What kind of plan? We're solving a case."

"We're solving a case, sure, but we can't even tell people what we're trying to figure out. Christ, I'm not even sure I know what we're trying to figure out."

"Are you ok?"

"Yeah, of course."

"No. You look . . . tired. And you tossed a lot last night. This morning, technically, but you sounded like you weren't sleeping."

"I slept fine."

"You talked a little."

"What?" Somers settled his hands on his knees and tried to keep his fingers relaxed. "I don't talk in my sleep."

"You did last night."

"I don't talk in my sleep, Ree."

"Don't you want to know what you said?"

"My breakfast order? An egg sandwich?"

"You kept saying you were sorry."

"Fuck me."

"What?"

"Nothing. I just remembered something."

"What's going on with you today?" Hazard's fine, dark brows stitched together. "You really look like you need more sleep."

"Ree, I'm a big boy. I can take care of myself. Let's talk about the case. Last night, what happened with Kjar—are we going to take a position on who the other guy was?"

"You mean, was the other guy Hollace?"

"Right."

Hazard studied him for a moment, and worry was written in broad strokes across his features. When he spoke, though, his voice was clinical. "For now, I think we assume they're connected. It seems like too much of a coincidence that Newton would have two murder-related surprises in one day. The shooting at the station, that took him by surprise."

"And he sounded pretty surprised last night, at least, the little we heard from him." Somers thought for a moment. "So we work them as the same case? I don't know. There's something off about the whole thing. If Hollace was already planning on having Kjar kill Newton last night, why take the added risk of a public shooting? The MOs seem different. Hollace wanted us to see him. Hell, he wanted us to follow him. And sure as hell wanted everyone to know he was smarter. Last night, though, whoever ran that thing with Kjar, that was some sneaky, underhanded stuff."

Hazard's brows had knitted together more tightly, his whole face a thundercloud.

"And don't tell me I'm overthinking this," Somers said. "Yes, you're right: two surprises yesterday do seem like coincidence. And maybe you're right: maybe they're related. Maybe they have the same cause. Maybe not. But they sure as hell have two very different minds behind them, and I don't get the feeling that they're working together."

"You're right."

"And don't tell me—wait. What?"

"You're right. They aren't the same. In fact, as you said, they're almost opposites. Someone who likes to work in the shadows. And Hollace, who wants approval, recognition, praise."

"One of them might try again. Hell, both of them might try to get him in the hospital."

"Christ," Hazard said. "We'll be lucky if Cravens even puts a token officer there. As far as she's concerned, as far as anyone is concerned, Kjar is dead and there's no reason to believe anyone else is involved. Goddamnit."

"Would it really be the worst thing in the world if he doesn't make it?"

Hazard made a sour face.

"So what's our plan?" Somers asked.

"Our plan is to work the case the way we always do."

It was strange, entering the station that day. One of the front doors was boarded up with plywood, and a few stray pearls of glass sparkled in the morning light. Inside, the floor had been scrubbed, but Murray's blood stained the grout, and eventually, Somers knew, the department would have to pay to have the tilework redone. Stranger still, though, was seeing George Orear at the front desk. Orear, a fussy little man with precision-combed black hair, sat where Jim Murray had been for the last twenty years. The rest of the station's front desk seemed the same: Gina Rands was there, wrangling two of her red-headed children, and Somers could guess that she was going to complain about dog droppings in Truant Park the way she did every other week; Kristi Meyers was there, a busty woman pushing forty, who had doubtless invented another problem with her neighbors, her standard ploy for luring Officer Foley out to her house so she could press her advances on him; even old Mr. Brewer was there, and he'd seemed old even when Somers was a boy, and God only knew what he was going to complain about, although to judge by the rack of deer antlers he had propped next to his seat, it was going to be interesting. These were the kinds of problems that Murray had dealt with, day in and day out, for decades. Seeing the station's lobby with its passel of crazies drove home, even more than the bloodstained grout, Murray's absence.

At their desks in the bullpen, Somers and Hazard found preliminary reports from Newton's house. They read in silence; Hazard chewed a pencil, and he bent so far over the packet that a lock of his long, dark hair tumbled out of its part and across his forehead. Somers tried to read, but he found it difficult to focus. So he looked at Emery Hazard instead. He wore a simple blue button-up, but it fit well across his shoulders. As always, without regard for the heat, he wore a dark sports jacket, and it fit well across his shoulders too. He even had a tie in a neat double Windsor. All very proper, all very respectable. And then there was that curl of long, dark hair across his forehead, and that made Somers want to mess up every inch of Hazard's proper and respectable attire. Mess it up and leave the big man red-faced and sweaty.

"Are you done reading?"

"What? Oh. I got distracted." Yes, Somers was thinking. Red-faced and sweaty and—and crying out Somers's name.

"Thinking about the case?"

"Sure," he said absently, still thinking about hooking his finger under Hazard's tie and drawing it down.

Hazard glanced up, his scarecrow eyes narrowed. "Thinking about what?"

"Like you said: the case."

"So you saw that they found Ted Kjar's fingerprints on the window frame?"

"Yep."

"And you saw that the knife Kjar used, it matches a weapon reported stolen from Osage Beach last month."

"Right. We'll have to check that out."

"And you saw that they interviewed someone in the Haverford who said he saw Dracula running through the halls?"

"Yeah. I mean, shit. They probably saw you and got confused."

"Fuck you. You didn't read this."

"Fine. I told you: I got distracted. But the fingerprints—"

"That was all bullshit. No fingerprints. No knife. No Dracula."

"What about—"

"Somers, there's nothing here. Nothing that takes us anywhere significant."

Rubbing at his eyes, Somers nodded. "Ok. Nothing on the car?"

"No."

"Nobody saw it?"

"Nobody that's been willing to tell us anything."

"And the ladder?"

"Ace Hardware sells them. And Home Depot. And Farm and Home Supply."

"So it looks just like it's supposed to look: like Kjar fell back into drugs, his mind snapped, he took off for a few days, came back, and attacked Newton."

"Yes. But that's damned inconvenient for us."

"Autopsy?"

"Not yet. It hasn't even been twelve hours. If this new ME is anything like Kamp, I might kill him."

Somers nodded; Dr. Kamp, although once a brilliant neurosurgeon, had never been an effective ME. He had come back to Wahredua after a prestigious career, but age had taken its toll, and he had fallen into heavy drinking. During Somers and Hazard's last case, someone had broken into the ME's office and beaten the doctor severely. He had, a few weeks later, officially retired. Somers realized he didn't know anything about the new ME, but he figured he couldn't be much worse than Kamp.

"If you did kill him," Somers said, "I could explain to the jury that it was justified."

Hazard cocked his head, his scarecrow eyes suddenly burning like autumn sunlight.

"What?" Somers said.

"You're my boyfriend."

"I am? God, I've got awful taste."

"You know me."

"Sometimes I wonder about that."

"Are you going to be an asshole or are you going to work with me?"

"Like you said: I'm your boyfriend. Do I really have a choice?"

"Somers."

Grinning, Somers said, "You think we should start by talking to Ted Kjar's wife. I think it's a great idea."

"Then why are you being such a dick?"

"Because you are very fun to rile up."

CHAPTER FIFTEEN

JULY 3
TUESDAY
11:11 AM

THEODORE AND JOSEPHINE KJAR lived in one of Wahredua's enclaves of middle-class prosperity, a neighborhood in the southeast quarter of the city that aspired to the prestige of the bluffs without quite managing to achieve it. Their house was new, especially for Wahredua: maybe thirty years old, a mixture of siding and brick with well-maintained tuck-pointing, and both the house and the yard showed signs of care and prosperity. Fat-headed sunflowers filled a bed near the door, while neat lines of boxwood marked the edge of the porch. It even smelled like a middle-class neighborhood: the fresh linen scent of laundry venting, the perfume of the rosebushes in the next yard, and Hazard would be damned if he couldn't smell a pie baking. In the yard, a red-and-white sign announced that the house was for sale.

When Somers knocked, footsteps moved behind the door, and then silence.

"Mrs. Kjar," Somers said.

"Go away."

"Mrs. Kjar, my name is Detective Somerset. I'm with the Wahredua PD."

More shuffling came from within, and then the door opened a crack, and a bloodshot eye stared out at them. "I want to see your badges."

They displayed them.

"No, I want the numbers."

They held out the badges again, and then the door shut. For the next five minutes, Hazard studied the house. There was no sign of movement within, and he heard nothing to indicate that Josephine Kjar—or whoever had answered the door—might have tried to make a break for it out the back door. The sun pounded down, hotter even than yesterday if that were possible, and sweat dampened Hazard's hairline.

"You're going to burn."

Hazard gave Somers a glance.

"You're going to fry, actually. Cook. Sear. Sizzle."

"I'm fine."

"You're white."

"I wear sunscreen when I go for a run."

"I wear sunscreen. You wear an asbestos suit."

"You don't like the color of my skin."

"God, you're making me sound like a racist."

"You think I should go tanning."

"I never said that."

"When I go to the beach, I get tan."

"Sure."

"I've been working all summer. We both have. I just haven't had much time outside."

"Right. I know. But maybe you should stand up here, under the porch. You know because you're so fair."

"Fair? I'm not a fucking maiden, Somers."

"Right, right."

"Maybe I'll get a little color if I stay here."

"You will. You'll get red. Sizzle, remember?"

"Fine. I'll—I don't know. I'll get a different sunscreen."

"Ree, I wasn't saying—"

The door opened again, all the way this time. The woman who stood behind the storm door was tall and thin and toned. She looked like the kind of woman who did Pilates, who owned yoga pants, and who could probably beat the shit out of any guy stupid enough to get in the way of her Zumba-kickboxing. She had long, ashen hair, and her red-rimmed eyes made it an easy guess who she was.

"I'm Jo Kjar," she said, opening the door. "I'm sorry about that. It's just—well, things have been so strange."

"We'd like to talk to you about your husband," Somers said.

She started crying then; silently, yes, but crying nonetheless, with the tears streaming down her cheeks. "Yes," she managed to say. "Please, come in."

They followed her into a well-furnished living room. Everything in the space spoke of good income and good taste: minimalist wood-carvings, a few understated paintings, and a sofa and chairs with clean, modern lines. When they sat, she retrieved a box of Kleenex from the coffee table, and then she clicked the remote. Before the television winked out, Hazard saw a local news program on the screen. He checked his watch.

"It's a recording," she said, wiping at her eyes. "From this morning. I recorded all of them. Isn't that stupid? But I'm doing it again with the noon broadcasts. And I'll do it again with the six o'clock ones. It's so silly. Whatever they have to say, it's only going to make things worse. But I have to know. I have to." She wiped at her eyes again, and then she broke out with a single, harsh sob before she pulled herself together again.

"Mrs. Kjar," Somers said, "your husband—"

"I know. I know. Two officers came by this morning. They were nice. Foley and—the other one had a foreign name, I'm sorry. I don't know. But they told me. He's—he's dead. And he attacked the mayor." The last she sped through, as though if she slowed down she might not be able to finish.

Nodding, Somers said, "We need to talk to you about him. I know it will be difficult. I'll do my best to make this as easy as I can, but no matter what, it's going to be difficult. And I'm sorry about that."

She nodded, pressing the tissue against her cheek as though she were holding her face together.

"Tell us about your husband."

"Oh God," she said, dissolving into tears again. It took her a few minutes and several more tissues before she could speak, and when she did, it was in short, jerky sentences. "He was a good man. A good man. He told me he had a problem. I—I knew he had a problem. But he never did anything wrong. Never. Not anything. He never even returned a library book late. And he won awards." Her voice pitched into a wail at the end of this, as though somehow the awards were the tipping point, the thing that made the rest of it unbearable.

"Had you noticed any changes in his behavior lately?"

"Well, yes. But only because he was under so much stress."

"Stress?"

"From the downsizing." She stared at them, and a hint of surprise crept into her voice. "At InnovateMidwest? That's where Ted worked until—oh, I don't know. March, I think. Being out of a job is a terrible stress, especially for men. I read about it in Good Housekeeping. Men identify with their jobs. Did you know that losing a job makes a man twice as likely to suffer mental illness?"

"Did Ted have a history of mental illness?"

"You heard about that, I guess. Or you found a file somewhere."

"About what?"

"You know about the time he was in the hospital. That was a long time ago, Officer. I know that it was for rehab; I know that. But he wasn't getting any treatment for his depression. Then he went on Prozac, and he was fine. He did Narconon. He was fine. He really was fine."

"But stressed."

"Yes, of course. I mean he was very stressed some days. We've been—we had been frugal with our money, but we weren't ready to retire. I even thought about taking part-time work. You know. Secretarial. Something like that. But Ted didn't want that, and I didn't push it because I thought it might make him feel worse. He was convinced he was going to find another job, and in the meanwhile, he had his book."

"Tell me—" Hazard began.

Somers cut him off. "Anything else you noticed? I'm asking about his behavior, Mrs. Kjar."

Her eyes shifted toward the sliding glass door.

"Mrs. Kjar, if there's something we need to know, now is the time to tell us."

"He was fine. Oh, God, he said he was fine. He'd been working on his book. It was keeping his spirits up, you understand. He'd even picked up some accounting work on the side. Just a few odd jobs that he did from home—I saw him working on those papers, really going at it a few times. And he did day trips for research. Things were good, right up until—right up until—"

"Right up until they weren't."

"I don't know what happened. I went to the ATM to get twenty dollars for Connor Johansen, the boy who cuts the lawn, and our checking was empty. I tried our savings. That was empty too. And I came home and waited for Ted and drank a bottle of wine. I was terrified. I thought we'd had our identities stolen. I kept telling myself that's what had happened, but part of me knew. Part of me was thinking about the nights he stayed up working on his book. All night. He never slowed down, never seemed to get tired. Part of me was thinking about the way he would smell sometimes. Something like plastic. And body odor, like he'd forgotten to bathe." She looked at her empty hands as though wishing she had a wine glass again. "He didn't come home that night. At some point, I guess I figured it out."

"He didn't come home ever again?"

"No, he was back a few days later. But by then he wasn't hiding it anymore. He started, well, raving. I guess that's the best word. I asked about the money. He shouted about crimes. And injustices. I pressed him about the house, were we going to lose the house? He left again. Someone—someone called me that time. They told me they saw him passed out at the end of Jefferson Street. When he came home the next time, I locked the door and waited for him to go away."

"You were frightened," Somers said.

"I started going to my sister's. Or the library. Or the mall. I'd spend all day out of the house just so I didn't have to see this happening. It's a sickness. Addiction, it's a sickness. But he'd been fine for so long. And he'd never touched the stuff, not once, since we got married. He's a good man. He was a good man. Ted was always very passionate; people would laugh if they heard me say that, but just take a look at his projects. Nobody does work like that unless they're passionate. And I kept telling myself it was a sickness, and he'd get better if he could just let it run its course. I kept telling myself that until I came home one day. I wasn't even trying to be quiet. I wasn't being a sneak. I just—came home. That's all. I walked in the door, and I heard Ted upstairs, I heard him talking, and he was ranting again. Shouting."

"What was he shouting about?"

"I don't know. I could hear him, but I couldn't make out the words. And when I went upstairs to check on him, he hung up the phone, and he yelled at me. He told me to—to quit being a sneaky bitch. I saw the pipe. That's what they call it, right? The pipe he was smoking that stuff with." A single tear squeezed out of one eye and rolled down her cheek, and her hand with the tissue lay limp in her lap. "I told him I wasn't going to stay and be spoken to that way. I told him he could go buy drugs and shoot up and do whatever he wanted and I didn't care. I told him the bank had been calling. I told him I knew he was a liar. I told him we were losing the house. And I told him I didn't care if he died. I told him I never wanted to see him again, not after what he'd done to our family." She wiped her eyes. "He didn't come back."

"When was this?"

"June 15th."

"He'd been missing for two weeks?"

"He texted me and said he'd gone to get help. I assumed that meant treatment. I assumed I wouldn't hear from him for a few days. But then it was a week, and I started calling around, trying to find out where he'd gone. I still loved him. Do you think that's crazy? Someone can hurt you and hurt you and somehow you just keep on loving them. That's crazy; that really is crazy when you think about it. And then it was two weeks, and the sheriff's men, the deputies, I guess you'd call them, they came around asking about Ted, and I told them, and I tried texting Ted and I tried calling him and—and nothing.

"They told me he'd attacked the mayor in a bathroom, and I kind of laughed. I thought it was a joke. But I felt so sick inside I couldn't believe I was laughing, and I didn't know how to stop. And they left and didn't ask me anything else because—because I was laughing, I think. Oh God. Oh God oh God oh God." She suddenly seemed to remember the tissue, pressing it to her face, not really wiping but just pressing, and she took a shuddering breath. "I checked the phone records, you know. I was smart enough to do that. Just a minute." She stepped over to an escritoire, opened a drawer, and removed a folded document. Holding it out to Somers, she said, "He called the FBI office in St. Louis eight times. You know how well that went. And he called the State's Attorney General three times. Officer, if I'd known my husband was sick, really sick like that—" She stopped, hung up on her own words and staring at them, hoping for a lifeline.

As usual, Somers knew exactly what to say. "Mrs. Kjar, we're not sure your husband was ill. We're not sure of anything except that you loved him and were trying to help him."

"But what I said to him. What I said about leaving, about him dying—"

"No, you shouldn't think like that. Whatever happened to your husband, it didn't have anything to do with that. I can promise you."

For the first time since they had stepped into the house, Hazard glimpsed something like hope in the woman's eyes. "Thank you. Those other men, the ones who asked me about all this, they weren't nearly as kind."

Hazard didn't doubt that; Patrick Foley was a lot of things, but he wasn't a shoulder to cry on.

"Mrs. Kjar," Somers said, "what do you know about your husband's relationship with his employer?"

"With Jack? Jack Philipeau? I think they got along all right; I don't think Jack wanted to let him go even with the downsizing."

"Jack was his immediate supervisor?"

"Yes, he was in charge of the accounting department."

"I was referring to Mayor Sherman Newton. What kind of relationship did he have with your husband?"

"None. I don't even know if they'd ever spoken. Maybe a few words in passing, but I don't even think the mayor interviewed Ted when he was hired. Jack did all that."

"Did your husband talk about the mayor? Did he mention him at all?"

Shaking her head, Jo said, "Never. You probably think that's a lie, but I wouldn't lie. Not now. Not when it can't help—" She scrunched up her whole face, and a tremor ran through her. "Not when it can't help Ted anymore. He never talked about the mayor. I don't even know if he ever said his name. Maybe during the last election, but if he did, it was only in passing. We voted for Mr. Newton."

"So when your husband, as you said, 'ranted,' the mayor didn't come up?"

"No. I told you, he didn't say anything specific. Just . . . just things about crimes. About innocent people being hurt."

"You said you requested your phone records."

"That's right."

"Did your husband have a cell phone?"

"Yes, he did."

"Do you know where it is?"

"No. And before you ask, Officer, I've tried using that find my device program. The app. Whatever you call it. I've tried it. And all it will tell me is that the phone is off, and then it shows me the last location where it was on."

"Where?"

"A gas station. I checked the times. That seemed like the right thing to do, so I checked, and that was the same time he texted me, telling me he was going to get help. I think he must have been filling up the car before he left town."

"What did he drive?"

"A Honda Accord."

"Year?"

"I don't know. It's newer. Maybe five years old. Maybe a little more."

"All right. Could you show us that gas station on the app? That's another place for us to start."

"Yes. But I can tell you, those other guys didn't seem nearly as interested in all this."

"I'm sorry they gave you that impression," Somers said with a soft smile.

"Oh, that's not even your department, is it? You don't need to apologize. Let me see here." She retrieved her phone and tapped at the screen, and after a minute she held it out for their inspection.

"The Kum-n-Go on Prescott," Somers said, letting his eyes slide to Hazard's. Hazard knew what Somers was saying. That was the same gas station where, according to Newton, Kjar had confronted him. The last place anyone had seen Kjar before he disappeared and no one could find him, not even the Sheriff's Department. "Thank you, Mrs. Kjar."

"I can pull up the call history on the computer. I don't need his phone to do that; I can pull it up right now if you'd like."

"That would be very helpful."

"You two really seem like you know what you're doing. Not like those first two."

Somers gave her the same soft smile. "We're going to do our best to find out what happened."

"I wish the other two had said something like that. They were very serious. Almost angry. And it's not any fault of mine."

"Of course not."

"Mrs. Kjar," Hazard said, "can we see Ted's office? Did he have an office?"

"What? Office? Yes, I suppose so. Here, I'll show you where it is, and then I'll print off the call history while we're there."

She led them down a hallway and into a small study that had probably originally been designed as a bedroom. The closet's folding doors stood open to allow space for filing cabinets, and a plain but functional computer desk butted up against the only window. The computer itself looked like a workhorse instead of the typical, lackluster home PC that Hazard had expected. Perhaps that was because of the side work that Kjar occasionally brought home. Or perhaps he liked video games. Or he liked streaming high-end porn. It was a crap shoot.

"Now I'll just log on—" Jo Kjar swiped the mouse back and forth and tapped the keyboard. "There. Give me just a minute. Feel free to look around."

Somers, raising an eyebrow at Hazard, shrugged. Hazard ignored him. He moved to stand next to Jo Kjar, examining the desk. A T-Mobile bill sat on the desk, the payment coupon partially torn along the perforated line. A mug that read, WORLD'S BEST DAD held an assortment of pens and pencils. Under Jo's hand, the mousepad displayed some sort of spaceship in flight.

"Is that a Tie Fighter?" Somers asked.

Jo Kjar smiled absently as she opened a web browser. "You know your *Star Wars*, Officer. Ted loved *Star Wars*."

In the desk drawers, Hazard found paperclips, binder clips, rubber bands wrapped in a ball, a pad of fluorescent pink sticky notes, stationery from Bridget Halls, Realtor, a box of Nutri-Grain bars (strawberry), and twelve folders labeled with the months of the year. January through June held copies of the major bills that Ted had paid in that month, including credit card and bank statements. The Kjars were comfortably well off, or had been until recently. In March, withdrawals appeared with growing regularity, draining first the checking account and then the savings. Cash withdrawals every time. Money to feed a drug habit. Or a pattern that was meant to look like that.

Next, Hazard checked the filing cabinets. The top cabinet held previous years' tax returns, warranty cards, manuals for different household appliances, various paperwork pertaining to insurance programs, and a single hanging folder stuffed with golf scorecards. Ted Kjar never did very well, but apparently he liked keeping track.

The bottom filing cabinet was stuffed with the research for Kjar's book and printed copies of each chapter. The working title, according to the header, was *World War II in Dore County: 1941-1945*. The first chapter was on daily life, and Hazard was surprised—and thrilled—

to discover authentic ration cards, original photographs, draft paperwork, newspaper clippings, and even a handwritten recipe book for Victory Gardens. It was a treasure trove of historical artifacts, and it was sitting in the dinky filing cabinet of an accountant-slash-amateur historian. There was a chapter on industrial development and the Missouri Pacific rail lines, complete with original blueprints and train schedules. There was a chapter on agriculture, and Kjar had placed at the front of this chapter a photograph from the 1942 Missouri State Fair when a two-headed calf from Wahredua won a special blue ribbon. There was even a chapter on local politics, and Hazard took his time with this one, flipping carefully through the pages and scanning for anything that might seem significant, but aside from Kjar's detailed documentation of an affair between city council member Arthur Little and a woman the *Courier* called "an elegant mulatto who is also an accomplished songstress," he found nothing of interest.

When he had finished, he rocked back on his heels, studying the cabinet. Something was wrong; he knew it; his brain knew it. But he couldn't put his finger on it. He was remembering the Dore County Library on a dark January evening, and he knew something was wrong.

"What?" Somers said. The blond man held a sheaf of documents, probably the call history, and he and Jo Kjar were both watching Hazard.

"I'm not sure. Mrs. Kjar, you said Ted was actively working on this book?"

"That's right. He'd spend days on it. Going out for fieldwork. As you saw, he collected some gems. I always thought he would have been better served to choose a topic with broader appeal; Ted really had a gift for research, and he could have written a knock-out book. But he loved the town. And he caught a bug for the World War II era, and that's all he would work on."

"He read a chapter at the library a few months ago."

"Before he was laid off, yes. That was still when he was riding high, it seems to me now, and he was excited to share what he'd been working on."

"Which chapter was that?"

Somers was eyeing his partner with unalloyed curiosity now.

Jo Kjar shook her head. "Let me think. Is this important?"

"I'm curious."

"Well, in January, I remember he was doing a lot of driving on the weekends, and I only remember because he slid off the road in a snowstorm while he was driving to do some research and we had a terrible fight about it when he came home. I said it was silly to waste his life doing that kind of research. And he said what he always said."

"What was that?"

"Oh, goodness. Some quote. Something he was always quoting."

"Faulkner?" Somers said, his eyes suddenly sharp, and Hazard felt a flash of surprise.

Jo Kjar hemmed and said, "Could be. Let me—it really was his mantra, you know. I think he had it around here. Hold on." She stepped out of the room, and her steps clicked down the hardwood.

"What's going on?" Somers said.

"I don't know."

"A history book?"

"I said I don't know, Somers. But something is weird in here."

"Yeah. This guy was crazy." Somers put up a hand. "I'm not saying he was schizophrenic, but you heard her: it sounds like he was cracking up."

"He was an accountant."

"Yeah, I know, they're all a little crazy, but—"

"No, she said he was doing work on the side. After he got laid off. Where is it?"

"Back with the client."

"No."

"Maybe he took it with him to therapy. Accountants are crazy."

"No, Somers. This guy kept the scorecard from every time he hit the links. He kept the manual for his goddamn weed-eater, and he penciled in the relevant details on the warranty card in case he lost the manual. If he was doing work for a client, if he was getting paid, he'd have some kind of paper record here. A copy of a paid invoice. Something."

Somers cocked his head, about to say something, but Jo's heels clicked back towards them, and he shrugged.

"Here it is," she said, holding out an index card. "He'd pinned it above the calendar. He said it helped him focus. 'Hegel remarks somewhere that all great world-historic facts and personages appear, so to speak, twice. He forgot to add: the first time as tragedy, the second time as farce.'" Jo made a face. "He minored in history and he never really shook it."

"That's a quote from Hegel?"

"No," Hazard said, and he was surprised that his lips were numb. It was surprising they could feel numb when his heart was pumping a mile a minute. "That's a quote from Marx. *Der achtzehnte Brumaire des Louis Napoleon.*"

Jo handed the card towards him as though he had won a prize. "You must have minored in history too."

"He didn't," Somers said. "He just loves documentaries."

Hazard barely heard him. He took the card, folded it, and slid it into his pocket. "What chapter did he read at the library, Mrs. Kjar? I was there. I should remember, but I don't."

"Well, he was traveling in January. And when he went off the road, he was going somewhere—where was it? Ozark. Ozark, Missouri. Oh, God, we really had a blow-up about that. I asked why he was going to Ozark in the middle of winter. It's not a place to visit any time of year, but especially not in winter. It's so small it makes Wahredua look like Las Vegas. But he had to go down there, he said. Something about a building there. It had been built—well, I suppose it had been built during World War II."

"The Works Progress Administration."

"Yes. That was it. Yes, exactly. He probably traveled more for that chapter than any of the others. I said to him, 'Ted, it's a book about Dore County. Why do you have to keep leaving?' And he would just say, 'Research.' That's all."

"That chapter's not here."

"Oh, I'm sure it is. He was working on it exclusively after the downsizing."

"It's not here, Mrs. Kjar."

Her hands twisted, and she peered over Hazard's frame as though she could see through the filing cabinet and discern the chapter's location. "But it has to be. He always kept a hard copy of the manuscript on file. He'd print out everything he wrote at the end of the day."

"Where are his customer invoices?"

"Excuse me?"

"You said he did a few odd accounting jobs after he was laid off. Where would he keep records of that?"

"I don't know. I—I assumed he had them in the filing cabinet."

"How about the files for that kind of work?"

"Well, it was mostly on the computer. He rarely had to bring home paperwork. But I don't know—"

"May I?" Hazard dropped into the chair and began searching through the computer, starting in Kjar's email, which had been scrupulously cleaned—perhaps even suspiciously cleaned—and then the recent downloads. He checked the recycle bin. All of them were empty, as though Kjar had never used the computer before.

"That's odd," Somers said. "Check My Documents."

Empty.

"Something's not right," Somers said.

"Mrs. Kjar," Hazard said, "could we take this?"

"The computer? I don't see why—"

"It's important. We'll give you an evidence receipt for it, and you'll be able to get it back at the end of the investigation." Hazard didn't tell her that it might be a long time, a very long time, before she got it back. If this case went the way he was starting to think, she would probably be better off just buying a new one.

"Yes, I suppose. Although I have to say, those other men—"

"Thank you."

In a matter of minutes, Hazard and Somers disconnected the relevant cables, and they removed the machine to the Jetta. After a few more minutes with Jo Kjar, it became clear that they had reached an end to their interview. Hazard barely heard the final courtesies. He was thinking about *Der achtzehnte Brumaire des Louis Napoleon*, which he had read in translation as *The Eighteenth Brumaire of Louis*

Napoleon. He was thinking about Marx and history repeating itself. First as tragedy, then as farce. But what was the tragedy here? And for fuck's sake, what was the farce going to look like? And Hazard was thinking, too, about the other famous quote from *Der achtzehnte Brumaire des Louis Napoleon*: Men make their own history, but they do not make it as they please. And his heart was still going a mile a minute.

"Thank you, Officers," she said as she walked with them to the door.

Hazard was so caught up in his thoughts—

—*first as tragedy*—

—that he barely heard himself respond. "Detectives, Mrs. Kjar. We're detectives."

That rankled her; she drew herself up, squared her shoulders, and said, "Well, I really don't know how I'm supposed to keep it all straight. The ones who came the first time kept insisting that I call them agents. And then the ones this morning wanted to be officers. And now you have to be detectives. I don't really see what it matters."

"It matters because—"

"Agents?" Somers said. "What do you mean? Who came here?"

"Oh, two days ago. Three, maybe."

"Who, Mrs. Kjar?"

"The men. The ones I've been telling you about, the ones who didn't really seem to care about Ted." She stared at them, her expression expectant and then slowly morphing into disbelief. "The ones from the FBI."

CHAPTER SIXTEEN

JULY 3
TUESDAY
12:20 PM

JO KJAR COULD TELL THEM nothing else: not the names of the agents, not the exact day they had come, not even her best guess at what they had wanted besides Ted. That's all they had asked about: where was Ted, where might he have gone, had he left anything with her or with a trusted friend, on and on. Jo told this with a morbid lack of interest, as though she had suddenly reached an emotional tipping point and could no longer muster the necessary emotional energy. They left her, then, and Hazard was unsurprised to see her press the tissue to her face again, numbly trying to hold herself together.

In the Jetta, the A/C whined pathetically and did about as much good cooling them down as spit on the breeze. Hazard waited while Somers dialed the FBI field office in St. Louis. The blond man spoke quietly into the phone, navigating a web of secretaries and receptionists and bureaucrats with the same ease and grace that he did just about everything. When he finished, he thanked the person he was speaking to and disconnected the call.

"The FBI doesn't have any ongoing investigations on Ted Kjar. At least, nothing they're willing to admit to local law enforcement." Somers sighed, turning the phone in his hands. "They also say that they don't have any agents in the area right now."

"That they're willing to admit to local law enforcement."

"Let's get the computer to the station," Somers said with a shrug. "We'll see if we can track down these mystery FBI agents another way."

"To the apartment."

Somers's eyebrows went up, but he nodded. "All right. What happened in there?"

"I don't know."

"I'm asking about you. Your face went white when you heard that quote, the Marx one."

"I don't know." Hazard shifted too hard, and the transmission clanked, guttered, and then the Jetta died. They rolled towards the next stop sign, and Hazard swore and reached for the key in the ignition.

"Hold on," Somers said, wrapping his hand around Hazard's. "What was it?"

"It was just strange. I haven't thought about that quote in years."

"Ree."

"That's it."

The Jetta's windshield seemed to magnify the sun, and the inside of the car cooked like a sauna.

"But you think it might be more than that, right? You think it has something to do with that book, the one Kjar was writing."

"I think it's weird that it disappeared. Not just the hard copy, Somers. The computer files too."

"What does a book about World War II have to do with Mayor Newton? Or with Ted Kjar, or with Hollace, or any of it?"

First as tragedy.

"I don't know. If I knew that, we wouldn't be baking in this piece of shit."

"Why is Hollace Walker here?"

"To kill the mayor."

"Why is he really here, Ree?"

"I don't know. Revenge? Money? I've got no idea."

"Where do you think he is?"

"I don't know."

With a suddenness that disturbed Hazard, Somers released his hand and dropped back against the seat. Somewhere inside the frame, plastic popped, and the seat fell back into its lowest recline. Somers stared up at the ceiling, and then he started to laugh.

"Are you all right?"

"Mild whiplash. I'll be fine. Ree, this thing about Hollace . . ."

"What?"

"Nothing."

"What is it?"

"No, I just didn't sleep well, and I'm tired, and I'm not thinking straight. Let's go. Start the car before we broil alive."

"Is there something you want to say?"

First as tragedy.

Men make their own history, but they do not make it as they please.

This little pussy is going to get it.

"No," Somers said, kicking out his legs and putting his hands behind his head. "This is kind of like a steam room. I might fall asleep."

Hazard cranked the ignition, and the Jetta sputtered and coughed and jerked back to life, and they headed back to the apartment. After dropping off the computer, they returned to the car.

"The Kum-n-Go?" Hazard said.

"I think so. It's the last place anyone saw Kjar before the attack."

"No, the mayor claims he saw him at Riverside Burgers."

"Ok. This is the last place someone else might have seen him. There might even be security footage."

"Let's see if that's true."

The Kum-n-Go on Prescott was a shabby, two-pump affair with a convenience mart about the same size as a pack of gum. The whole thing looked ready to go under a bulldozer, especially in contrast to the renovated storefronts on either side. Someone had decided to jazz up the convenience mart by hanging neon signs along the street-side window, with alluring messages like *ADULT ADULT ADULT* and *LIQUOR BEER WINE* and *WE GOT SMOKES*.

"I know where we're coming on our anniversary," Somers said, leaning up from the permanently-reclined seat.

"I feel like I'm going to get herpes just looking at that place."

"Shush," Somers said. "Save some romance for when we're off duty."

Inside the convenience mart, they found that the neon signs had advertised correctly: smut mags in paper covers lined a shelf at the back, above two more shelves containing flavored lubes and condoms. Coolers took up another wall with the aforementioned alcohol, and behind the bulletproof glass, tobacco in various forms was available. The proprietor of the Kum-n-Go looked like he might have started his existence inside the convenience mart and would probably end there too: he was a heavyset, middle-aged man with a poor comb-over, and the patch on his mechanic's shirt said David.

"You two are the queers," was apparently the store's standard greeting.

"Detective Somerset. This is Detective Hazard."

"I know."

"We're looking for footage from your security cameras from approximately two weeks ago."

"Can't help you."

"Excuse me?"

"Can't. Help. You." The bell jingled, and David's gaze flicked to the door. "I've got a customer."

He sure did. He also looked like his tongue was about to fall out of his mouth because the customer was a girl who couldn't have been over twenty, wearing cut-off shorts that barely passed her pelvis and a sports bra. The bra looked like it had a hell of a lot of work to do; the girl had some significant assets, and David was clearly interested in those assets. So interested, in fact, he really might lose that tongue.

"Sorry," Somers said in his best Somers voice, one hundred percent your buddy from next door. "Just a few questions and we'll be out of your hair. Could you tell me why you can't help us? Is there a problem with the cameras?"

"I've got a customer."

"She's looking at nuts," Hazard said, which was true to a certain extent since the girl was examining packs of trail mix. "Answer the question."

"Who the fuck—"

"We'll be fast," Somers said. "Tell me the problem."

"The problem is that these cameras are on a twenty-four-hour cycle. The problem is that you want something from two weeks ago. The problem is that two weeks is a lot longer than twenty-four hours. And the problem is that you two might want to munch each other's asses, but I'm trying to run a business."

"You're trying to look at that girl's breasts," Hazard said.

"Be right back," Somers said in a low voice. He drifted back to the rack of snacks, and in that some low, friendly voice, struck up a conversation with the girl. Hazard couldn't hear what he was saying, but he heard the peal of girlish laughter that followed, and he assumed that he was supposed to keep this fat pervert occupied.

"Are you familiar with Missouri statutes on obstructing a police investigation?" Hazard said.

David glared through the bulletproof glass.

"Section 575.030, I think, is the relevant one. It goes something like this: a person commits the crime of hindering prosecution if he prevents or obstructs—"

"I'm not doing shit. I don't have the video."

Another girlish giggle came from the snack rack.

"It's a class D felony."

"I don't have it. That's not a felony. Not having a video, that's not a felony."

"It'll be interesting to see if the county prosecutor agrees. I don't suppose you'll be able to keep working here if you have a class D felony on your record, but I don't know. Unless—are you the owner? Boy, that'll make keeping your liquor license a lot more difficult."

"I don't fucking have it. If you want to—"

"David," Somers said, breaking in smoothly, his voice that hundred-percent buddy voice still. "David, this is Brenda. Brenda, I want you to meet David. David here, he's an important guy."

This news came as a shock to Hazard. And, judging by appearances, to David as well.

"David, you're the owner here, aren't you?"

David stared at Somers, dumbstruck. And then his gaze shifted, minutely, to Brenda.

"David?"

"Ye—yes."

"See, Brenda. David's a guy you'd probably like to know. He can do you all sorts of favors. I bet if you had trouble with your car, he could help you. Or if you needed him to order something special, he could do that. He's probably got buddies. You know, these guys, they usually have a good network. He might even be able to give you a discount. That's why you might want to know David."

Brenda giggled again, and she did, perfunctorily, bat her eyes at David, but most of her attention was on Somers.

"And he's important in other ways, too. David, I was just telling Brenda that you're helping with an active police investigation. Go on. Tell her more."

A brick-red flush rose in David's cheeks, and he coughed and muttered something.

"What's that?" Brenda said, leaning towards the glass. Then, to Somers, "Is he really?"

"Oh, definitely. David might have seen a kidnapping."

"I didn't—well, the video. It's gone. Like I said."

Disappointment clouded over Brenda's face.

"But," David said. "But I think I know what you're talking about. You're talking about that thing with the mayor, aren't you?"

Somers, with a rather obvious sideways glance at Brenda, put a finger to his lips.

"Look, the video's gone. But they got a copy of it. You can get it from them."

"Who?" Hazard asked.

"I told you he was important," Somers said.

"Yeah," Brenda asked, eyes wide. "Who'd you give it to?"

"Those deputies. They came by a couple weeks ago and got it. The same night, they came and picked it up. And I'll tell you something else." David squirmed on his stool, and some of his comb-over worked its way loose and spilled over his forehead, but he was so excited he didn't notice. "I'll tell you something they don't know.

They didn't listen to me. They didn't even ask me. They just wanted the video. Not like you guys. They didn't even think I might have something important to tell them."

Brenda's eyes darted to Somers, and Somers nodded at David. Brenda returned her rapt attention to the clerk, which judging by how deeply he was flushing, might have been the single best moment of his life.

"I saw that truck. The one he got into. It was down the block, so the camera didn't pick it up. But I saw it. And I saw him get into it."

Hazard's phone buzzed, and he drew it out, intending to silence it. When he saw the number, though, he hesitated.

"You saw it?" Brenda was looking between David and Somers again, as though watching an intense tennis match. "What was it? What happened?"

"Just a pickup truck. Just a brown pickup truck."

"Did you get the plates?" Brenda asked, almost jumping out of her cut-offs in excitement. "That's what the cops always need, right? You need the plates."

"That's right," Somers said.

"I didn't."

"Oh." Brenda sank back in disappointment.

"But," David said, squirming on his stool again, "I know whose truck it is."

Hazard thumbed the call to accept it.

"Detective Hazard?"

"Speaking."

"This is Sheriff Engels. We met, to a degree, at the fair yesterday."

"Whose?" Brenda asked, almost climbing the glass partition in excitement.

"Mikey Grames," David sat, settling back onto his stool with the air of a man who has just delivered the ultimate bombshell.

Brenda gasped. Then, looking at Somers, "Who?"

"What do you want, Sheriff?" Hazard asked, but he could barely hear himself because Mikey Grames's name was flashing inside his head, as bright as those neon signs that read ADULT ADULT ADULT

175

in the store window. Only this wasn't saying ADULT. It was more like DANGER. DANGER DANGER DANGER. Mikey Grames.

"Well, Detective, I've got some information I think you'd like to hear. It's about this case you're working."

"All right."

"I think we should talk in person. You'd better bring your partner."

"Sheriff," Hazard said, catching Somers's eyes and jerking his head towards the door. "We were already on our way."

CHAPTER SEVENTEEN

JULY 3
TUESDAY
12:59 PM

IN THE JETTA'S PASSENGER SEAT, Somers reclined—by necessity, since the seat had finally broken, rather than by choice—and studied the ripped fabric that hung from the car's ceiling. The heat was oppressive, even with the Jetta's A/C giving a few licks of cool air now and then. And the sun, at this time of day, reached a knife-like incandescence, cleaving the day in half. But Somers's mind wasn't on the broken seat or the torn fabric or the heat or the supremely white sun. It was on Mikey Grames.

Faulkner, too, because he couldn't quite shake Faulkner. Or, more accurately, he couldn't quite shake the idea that there was something about Faulkner, something from that class on Southern Gothic literature, that kept trying to rise to the conscious level of his mind. All he could think, though, was that Hazard would laugh if he ever knew Somers had taken a class on Southern Gothic literature.

Mikey Grames. Jesus, it was like a sign. Somers was a religious man, but he didn't particularly care for the idea of a deity who played with human lives the way a three-year-old might play with action figures. Somers was more of the watchmaker line, thinking God had wound everything up and left men and women to do their best. And maybe he got involved sometimes. Maybe he cared and still stuck his hand in for the big stuff. But this kind of thing, with Mikey at the state fair, with Hollace showing up out of the blue, with the dreams starting all over again—this kind of stuff was another order entirely. It felt Greek, really. Like a Greek tragedy. And Hazard would laugh at that too.

First as tragedy. Those were the words, right? The ones from Marx, the ones that had left Hazard looking like he'd had some bad dairy. Yes, tragedy. Marx hadn't been talking about Greek tragedy, he hadn't been talking about *Oedipus* or anything like that, but that's where the words went inside Somers's head. First as tragedy.

Because how could Mikey Grames be involved in all of this? How was that fair? That was the word that kept surfacing. Fair. It wasn't fair. Somers had left Wahredua. He'd gone to college. He'd grown up. He'd become a better man—or at least he'd made a fair shot at it. Even Emery Hazard, who had more reason than anyone else to hate Somers, seemed to accept that he had changed. At least, that's what Somers had believed until he had seen those photographs. And then Mikey at the fair, and Hollace, and suddenly it felt like they'd gone back in time, like maybe nothing had changed, and that scared the shit out of John-Henry Somerset.

"Comfortable?" Hazard asked.

"I need a pillow." Somers realized the car had stopped. How long had they been sitting here? A minute? Two? Five? "Sorry. I was thinking."

"About Mikey."

"He's a real piece of shit."

"Sure."

"You really think he's involved in this?"

"That's what Brenda's new friend David told us."

"But what do you think?"

"I think I need to get that seat repaired. You sound like you've got all your blood rushing to your head. Let's go."

They were at Wahredua's city center, a few blocks of public buildings on Jefferson Street. Most of the buildings were from the sixties and seventies, and their appearance betrayed their age: the windows had yellowed, and the lines of the buildings were low and long and flat, and everything from the metal trim to the doors to the walkways looked like it had been done on the cheap and fast. It was towards one of these buildings, the longest of them, that they directed their steps.

"He didn't say what he wanted?"

"Just that he wants to talk. And that he's got information."

"But he didn't tell you anything else?"

Hazard shook his head.

"If he's anything like Bingham, I'm done. I'm moving. I don't think I can stand anything like that again."

Hazard shook his head again. Somers didn't need to elaborate; in several of their previous cases, they had butted heads with Dore County's former sheriff, whose corruption had infected the county for decades and had ultimately led to a conspiracy among his victims and, eventually, his murder. Sheriff Engels, who had been elected by a narrow margin against several other candidates, was a dark horse for Somers. In the last few months, Somers hadn't heard anything bad about Engels. But he hadn't heard anything good either, and that said something.

A deputy at the front desk buzzed on the intercom, and Engels's voice came through, asking for them to be sent back. The Sheriff's Department reminded Somers of the police station in most ways: their custodial staff used the same cleaner—something purchased in bulk by the county government, no doubt—and there was the same burnt-coffee smell, the same hum of the Xerox machine, even the same kinds of voices—the gruff, masculine bravado that only ever shifted a few degrees in either direction. But it was different, too. A lot of the deputies had left—or been asked to leave—after the extent of Sheriff Bingham's corruption came to light, and the faces here, for the most part, were fresh and young. There was also, it looked like, a serious backlog of paperwork that they hadn't caught up with. So, maybe it shouldn't have been a surprise that it had taken this long for the sheriff to do something about Ted Kjar.

The sheriff's office was a small room at the back of the building, and it had changed with the arrival of the new sheriff. Bingham's walls had been decorated with plaques and awards, with commendations—many of them issued by his own department—and with other symbols of power and prestige. These had been stripped from the walls, and in their place, Engels had made only two concessions to ornamentation: the first was a dartboard, a rather substantial piece with doors that could be closed and with built-in racks for the darts. Two red darts were buried in the bullseye, and the third plugged a narrow span in the triple ring under the twenty. The black darts were still racked. The other adornment was a high-gloss poster for the Columbia City Ballet Company, and it showed a muscular boy in revealing tights raising a waifish girl over his head. It was, Somers thought, perhaps the last thing he expected.

Engels, an older man who had already sailed past fifty, had trim white mustaches and thick, silver hair. Pomade glistened on top of that silver hair and in its simple, swept-back part. He looked like a relic from another time, which wasn't necessarily a bad thing. When he leaned over the desk to shake their hands, Somers caught a whiff of Gray Flannel, and he decided he might like Engels after all.

"Detectives," he said when they were seated. "Thank you for coming over here."

"You have video footage we'd like to see," Hazard said. "From the Kum-n-Go. Mayor Newton told us he asked you to look into an encounter with Ted Kjar."

"That's right. We've got it, and you can have it, although I'm not sure it'll do you much good."

"Why's that?" Somers asked.

"It's a low-resolution footage; you can make out the mayor's car, and I suppose you can tell that the mayor is one of the men in the video, but if the other man is Ted Kjar, that's only because I'm taking the mayor's word for it. I don't like that."

Somers tried to hide the surge of surprise. "That's an interesting thing to say."

Engels watched them. From the hallway, a voice shouted, "I swear to Christ, that pig had titties the size of tin cans." And then laughter ran up and down the corridor, and it trickled off slowly, and then the only noise was the creak of Engels's chair as he shifted his weight, and he still hadn't said anything.

"I don't know much about you, Sheriff," Somers said. "You came out of nowhere for the election, but I remember you had some serious credentials."

"You were a deputy," Hazard said, his scarecrow eyes fastened to the man in front of them. "And a soldier. You served in the first Iraq War. And then twenty-two years in Cape Girardeau County. And then retirement. A pension. And now this."

"A Marine, actually." Engels adjusted his belt. "I've heard a lot about the two of you. This day has been coming, and I wasn't sure I'd like it. I've asked about you. I hear the same things, more or less."

"What's that?" Somers said.

"That you're good at this work."

"I'm sure they said a lot more than that."

"People say all sorts of things, Detectives. You probably know this already, but the real trick isn't getting people to talk. It's figuring out what matters."

"Do you have a problem with us?" Hazard said.

"I don't know."

"The last sheriff did."

Somers groaned, and to his surprise, Engels laughed. "They said you were a bastard. But they said you were a smart bastard."

"Did they say I was a faggot?"

For the first time since Hazard and Somers had sat, Engels's eyes betrayed a hint of emotion. "I don't have much use for that word."

"Why? You don't like faggots?"

"Detective, you can say whatever you want outside of this office, but if I hear that word one more time, I'll ask you to leave."

The look of shock on Hazard's face was almost comical, although the dark-haired man masked it quickly.

"Why did you want to talk to us, Sheriff?" Somers said. "You told my partner you have information; is it something that can't be shared over the phone?"

Again, Engels rocked in the chair, and the metal squeaked, and footsteps pattered up and down the hallway, and somewhere, maybe the next room, a microwave dinged. "My sheriff, when I was first getting started, he said something to me once. It was a bad time for the department. A really bad time. They'd cleaned out over half the deputies, and the ones that were still there weren't worth a pinch of salt. I was one of the new hires, and I started to wonder: were these the best ones? These were the ones they decided to keep? Because believe me, some of those deputies I wouldn't have trusted to staff the night desk at the Red Roof Inn. And I started getting angry about it because I had some experience in the military and I had some brains and I was junior to a bunch of rednecks who didn't have the sense to lick a stamp. So I asked my sheriff one day." He smiled, and the smile propped up the trim white mustaches and made him look ten years younger. "I marched right into his office. I put my badge on his desk. And I demanded to know why in the hell he had kept these deputies. You know what he told me?"

"He sent the other ones to the Red Roof Inn," Hazard said, baring his teeth.

Engels laughed. "No. He said that the ones who had trouble, the ones he had to watch, were the good ones and the bad ones. The ones in the middle never caused anybody trouble."

"That's the stupidest bullshit I've ever heard."

"Maybe," Engels said, lacing his hands over his belly. "I'm not saying it's true everywhere. I'm not saying it's the only guiding light. But there's some truth to it, I think. After all these years, watching a lot of different men and women put on the uniform, I believe there's something to it. And as I said: I'd heard about you two. You solve hard cases. Impossible cases. You do damn fine work. But being that good, it makes you different. And if you're different, you start to think you're special. And that's when a cop or a deputy starts to go bad: when he thinks he's special."

Somers stared at the sheriff, and he was thinking of the deal he had made to keep blackmail from sticking to Hazard. He was thinking about their off-the-books investigation into who had shot his father. He was thinking of the dozen different ways and times they had bent—or broken—rules in order to close a case. He knew that, up to a point, the sheriff was right. But what Somers didn't know is if he would have done anything differently.

"That's all?" Hazard said.

"That's all. I just wanted to look you in the eyes and take your measure."

"You got it."

"I did, Detective. I did."

"I'd like that video footage. And whatever other information you have."

Engels nodded. "The truck, the one that your shooter used? It belonged to Carl Trauffer. It was stolen about a week ago. A little more, actually."

"We know that."

"I thought you did. Well, one of my deputies picked up a lady for possession, and this lady decided she might share some information in hopes of softening the county prosecutor's heart."

Somers leaned forward. "Someone saw that truck after it was stolen?"

"Yes, Detective Somerset. Someone did. From June 27 until June 30, it was parked outside the Yorgenson trailers."

"How sure is this?"

"She was certain. She was, I think, indulging in her own supply, otherwise she might not have said anything. When she sobered up, she stopped talking, and she was terrified. I think she knows that she made a big mistake in releasing that information."

"Or she's an excellent actress," Hazard said.

"Perhaps."

"All right," Hazard said, rising. "The footage?"

"I'll have one of my deputies provide you with a copy; we digitized it as soon as we took possession of the tape." He buzzed on the intercom and issued the order.

"Thank you," Somers said.

"My pleasure. If there's anything else I can do to help, please let me know."

Hazard, being Hazard, took the sheriff's hand, grimaced, and said nothing.

As they followed the sheriff to the door, Somers tipped his head toward the ballet poster. "Your daughter?"

A small smile creased Engels's mouth. "My son, actually. That's him right there."

In spite of his best efforts, Somers felt his eyebrow rise.

"It's all right," Engels said, laughing. "Most people react a lot worse. A couple of my deputies just about swallowed their tongues when I told them."

"It's still that kind of place," Hazard said.

"Maybe." Engels hesitated. "Detective Hazard, I don't like to be overly familiar, but I will tell you something personal, and then I'd like to ask you for a favor."

Hazard's scarecrow eyes could have burned through sheet metal.

"My son and his husband are not eager to come here for the holiday. Our town has a . . . reputation. I'm afraid this has become a point of unhappiness between us, and I don't like that."

Hazard, when he spoke, had no emotion in his voice. "And the favor?"

"I wonder if you and your partner wouldn't mind having a meal with my son and son-in-law."

"Having lunch with the only queer police in the city, that's going to make your son feel better?"

"Damn it," Somers said. "Ree—"

"It might. You've got a reputation too. I've told my son about you. And about Detective Somerset. I think it would do him some good to meet both of you and to know that things do change. Slowly, maybe, but they do change."

And there it was again, at the back of Somers's mind, that little bubble: Faulkner. There was something about this, something so close to the tip of his tongue—

"I'll think about it."

"Thank you."

"Sheriff," Somers said, "did you send deputies to talk to Josephine Kjar?"

"Yes. After the incident at the Kum-n-Go. I sent some men around to see if Ted was holed up at home. They talked to her, tried to find out if she had any idea what was going on. That was two weeks ago, though."

"Any reason they would have gone back? Followed up?"

"I can ask."

"Any reason they would have identified themselves as federal agents?" Hazard said.

"What do you mean?"

"Jo Kjar told us that FBI agents stopped by her house," Somers said. "She told us that they were interested in Ted's location, but they didn't give away much else about why they wanted to talk to him."

"I see."

"Do you know why FBI agents would want to talk to Ted Kjar?" Hazard said.

Engels stroked his mustaches with both thumbs, his eyes distant and fixed on the Columbia City Ballet Company. "I surely do not."

"We called the St. Louis field office," Hazard said. "No open investigation on Kjar. No agents in the area."

"Or so they say."

Somers nodded. "Did your deputies pick up anything else about Kjar? Anything strange? Why someone might be interested in him?"

"Aside from all this?"

"Maybe not aside from it," Somers said. "But maybe running alongside it."

Engels and Hazard shot him sharp glances. Identically sharp, in fact, and the dual expressions made Somers fight a laugh.

"What do you mean by that?" Engels said.

Hazard had the same question in his face, and he looked frustrated that Engels had beaten him to it.

"I don't know," Somers said. "I just—it feels like it's here. Like it's right under our feet."

"You boys fish?"

Somers nodded. "A little."

Hazard shrugged. "Probably less than he does."

"Well," Engels said, thumbing his mustaches again, his eyes distant once more. "When you fish, you've got to stand real still. Especially once you get out in the water. And some water, no matter how good you try to read it, some water has currents that run deep. I think if you boys are going to keep fishing, you'd better stand really still and see just what kind of currents are running."

Nodding, Somers shook the sheriff's hand. They left, emerging from the Sheriff's Department into the swampy heat and the smell of scorched asphalt and diesel exhaust. Somers wiped his forehead. It was going to be hell riding in Hazard's car, especially if they were driving all the way out to the Yorgenson trailers. Maybe Swinney and Lender would offer up their department vehicle. Or maybe Somers could borrow a car from his parents. From anybody, for that matter, who had a car with a working air conditioner.

"Ree, I'm going to call—"

Hazard snagged his arm and pulled him into an embrace, and then a kiss, and then his scruff rasped along Somers's jaw and Hazard brought his mouth to Somers's ear. "Kiss me one more time, and then look at that Camaro. The one idling against the curb."

"Just one more time?"

"Stop screwing around."

Somers kissed him—and it was a damn good kiss; he could tell by the way Hazard whined a little, his head rolling to one side to expose his neck, his whole body thrumming like Somers had strummed an E on the bassline. When Somers broke away, he turned to the street, tugging Hazard along behind him. A deputy passed them, his eyes about as wide as brass cymbals, and Somers gave him a mock salute.

"Ignore him," Hazard said, his voice still raw with desire.

"I am." But Somers wasn't ignoring the smoke-colored Camaro that idled against the far side of the street, its nose poked up behind a fire hydrant. The windows were tinted, and Somers was careful not to stare directly at the car. Hazard had clearly wanted Somers to notice the vehicle without drawing attention to it. "All right," Somers added in a low voice as they approached the Jetta. "What about it?"

"It pulled up right when we got here."

"All right."

"And it's been sitting here the whole time we were inside. Idling. On a day this hot."

"All right. Let's see if our new buddy wants to go to the Yorgenson trailers too."

Hazard cocked an eyebrow. "That's our plan?"

"What did you want to do?"

"Work on Kjar's computer."

"That can wait. If Engels already released his snitch, she might go back to the trailers and let them know she spilled the beans. I want to get down there before they have a chance to clean anything up."

Nodding, Hazard climbed into the Jetta. Somers grimaced as he lay back into the permanently reclining seat; the torn fabric on the Jetta's ceiling filled his vision. Magnified by the windshield, the summer sun raised the temperature to an unbearable level, and Somers cranked down the window.

"We're buying you a car."

"This one is paid off."

"It's been paid off since Jimmy Carter was president."

"No, not quite. I think it was—"

"Ree, we're getting you a car. A new car. With a seat that works."

"I can tie that seat in place. It'll be good as new."

"With a seat that works. And with air conditioning."

"We're halfway through summer, I don't really think—"

"With air conditioning. And one that's big enough that you're not copping a feel every time you shift." Somers blew out a breath and put his hands behind his head. "As soon as this case is done."

The tires thumped underneath them, and then Hazard's huge hand slid up the inside of Somers's thigh, into the vee between his legs, and gave a playful—and then a second, more suggestive—squeeze.

"No teasing," Somers said, knocking away the touch.

"Just shifting. If I got a new car, I might not make mistakes like that."

"For the love of God. I might literally boil alive in here."

"To boil you have to be in a liquid—"

At that point, Somers stopped listening. The tires thumped out another block, and then another, and then Somers propped himself up and craned to look behind them.

And there it was: sleek and low to the ground, the Camaro streamed after them like smoke trailing a fire.

"Looks like we've got company," Somers said.

CHAPTER EIGHTEEN

JULY 3
TUESDAY
1:31 PM

"LET HIM FOLLOW US," Hazard said; he glanced once in the mirror and then returned his attention to the road.

Somers, on the other hand, kept his attention firmly fixed on the Camaro. As they left the city behind and the roads opened up, the gray car dropped back. For a good twenty or thirty miles, the roads were a fairly straight shot; the Camaro didn't need to keep close. "We don't have to. We could stop. Make something out of this."

"If we stop, he shoots right past us and pretends he was never following us."

"Maybe. Or maybe he stops too, and you get to use those big muscles to knock somebody around."

Hazard flushed and rocked his shoulders a little; he was a very smart man, and he was a very cynical man, but Somers had noticed that he wasn't immune to a little flattery.

"I want to see what happens if we just keep going," Hazard said.

"All right."

"This trailer park—"

"It's not a trailer park." Somers dropped back into the seat at full recline. Air streamed into the car now that they were moving: muggy, humid air, thick with the smell of green vegetation and what Somers suspected was the Jetta's slow leak of gasoline.

"The sheriff called these the Yorgenson trailers. What is it? A family piece of land with some double-wides?"

"No. Yorgenson is a big ranching business. I guess it's family-owned, but it's family-owned on a major scale. Like, they own and run most of the ranching in the southern part of the state, and that's more than you'd think."

"I grew up here. I know about ranching."

Somers wiped sweat from his forehead, reached up, and ruffled Hazard's hair. "But you didn't know about Yorgenson."

"That's their name?"

"Yeah. But like I said, it's really a corporation at this point. And they own all this land for running cattle. I think they have sheep and horses too; they move them around depending on rainfall and what they think the best use is. I got stopped once, about fifteen miles up Route 62. Sheep. A whole herd of them."

"Flock."

"Yeah, that's what I thought. Fucking sheep."

"No, they're a flock. Not a herd."

Somers tugged on the long, loosely curling hair at the back of Hazard's head.

"Ow." He glanced down. "Oh. You were joking."

"I'm so funny."

"It's just—"

"I know, I know. I've got this amazing body, so you assume I'm just for show. Anyway, a whole herd—"

"Flock."

"—of sheep, and I had something to do that day, so I was going to back up, take a different way, but they were behind me too. Hundreds of them. I sat there for probably, I don't know, twenty minutes. One of them was just dropping poop as he walked, right across the road, and of course I had to drive through it. I smelled it all the way to Jeff City."

"That's some sheep shit."

Somers laughed and tugged on that dark curl again. "See? You're funny too."

"The trailers?"

"Oh, right. Well, Yorgenson bought up a bunch of land in the southwest corner of the county. A few hundred acres that jutted up against what they already owned, and I think Don Freidman owned it, and he had already died, and his kids just wanted to be rid of it. So they sold it."

"You're telling me, what? These are squatters?"

"Yep. It's kind of an extended family situation. There are a few different last names, but they're all related to the one in charge, an older guy named Mikelson. Erl Mikelson. I think the family has a standing cell in the county jail. The men tag in and out, keeping the cot warm, and sometimes the women take a turn too. Drunk and disorderly. Assault. Indecent exposure. One of them, one of Mikelson's boys, is at Eastern Correctional for second-degree murder. It should have been first—that's what I understood anyway, this was while you and I were at college—but he was such a raving lunatic that nobody believed he could have planned anything."

Hazard shifted his hands along the wheel; the Jetta's familiar clanking and grinding marked their passage between long fields of soy and wheat and corn, broken by tree-lines and, less frequently by densely wooded stretches. From time to time, that overwhelming green smell that entered through the window would change, suddenly crisp and cool as they passed through shade, or carrying the scent of crushed pine needles.

"Are we talking about Ozark Volunteers?"

"Probably."

Somers closed his eyes. The Ozark Volunteers. That was never good. Wahredua's home-cooked version of the Neo-Nazis, the Ozark Volunteers—more fully known as the Supreme Justification of God in the Ozark Citizen Volunteers—were an extremist right-wing group: religious and conservative fanatics who hated the government and just about anybody who was different from them. In Wahredua, for a long time, that had meant Emery Hazard, the only gay boy. Now, after Wahredua's growth and change, it meant a lot more: all the people of different races and cultures who had come to the city as it had evolved. And now that also meant John-Henry Somerset was on their list. It didn't terrify him, but he had the good sense not to go poking his nose into the little enclaves of white power that still dotted the county.

Or, Somers thought as the shadows of leaves and branches scurried across the inside of his eyelids, on most days he had that much sense. Today, not so much. Today, they were driving straight into the open arms of Jesus—or, if he couldn't be there, the arms of his self-appointed custodians in Dore County.

"If they're squatters," Hazard said, "let's call the sheriff. Let's have him arrest them for trespassing, and we'll see if they're any more eager to talk when we've got them sitting in the county jail."

"That's the problem. I don't think Sheriff Bingham ever pushed the issue much, but I know after the second-degree murder went down, he went out there and tried to haul them off the Yorgenson land. Yorgenson money means a big deal, and I guess the company had finally reached the end of their rope. Bingham, for all his faults, wasn't going to let campaign donations dry up because he hadn't taken care of a trailer-lot full of inbred morons."

"So why are they still there?"

"The whole thing is still tied up in court somehow. Mikelson, the old one, Erl, has some sort of document that he claims Don Freidman gave him. It signs over about a hundred acres of land to Mikelson and his clan."

"That sounds like a bunch of bullshit."

"I'm sure it is. I'm also sure it's Dore County, and a lot of things, including civil suits, still don't move the way they do in the rest of the world. The Yorgenson Corporation will take them apart in court eventually, but it's taking a lot longer than anyone thought it would, and until it's resolved, there they are."

"That really sounds like a bunch of bullshit."

Somers grinned, opening his eyes to the tattered cloth ceiling, and said, "And that's why we love our hometown."

"What about this sheriff?"

"What do you mean?"

"Engels is different from Bingham, don't you think?"

"So far. It's hard to know for sure, but he gave one hell of a good first impression."

"I don't like him."

"Of course you don't."

Bristling, Hazard looked down at Somers, a furrow digging deep between his brows.

Somers laughed and patted his shoulder. "You don't like hardly anyone, Ree. It's not that big of a surprise. And you definitely don't like people in authority. And you really definitely super-duper don't like anybody that acts like they might be smarter than you. Or even as smart as you. So, yeah, I can see why you don't like him."

The furrow dug a little deeper. The tires thrummed. Hazard's scarecrow eyes darted to the road and back to Somers. "I think you're smart."

This one sent Somers over the top, and he laughed so hard he had to wipe his eyes.

Hazard, his shoulders climbing almost to his ears, hunched at the wheel. "I don't see what's so funny."

"No, that was very sweet. And I know you meant it. Thank you. It just sounded funny the way it came out. From what the sheriff said, it doesn't sound like he trusts the mayor much. Maybe not at all. The way he described that video footage, how he said he couldn't tell who it was without taking someone's word for it, that sounded like he already thinks the mayor might be trying to pull something."

"He'd be stupid to trust the mayor, and I don't think he's stupid. But I don't like him because he thinks we're dirty, Somers."

For several moments, Somers considered his response. The jigsaw fields of corn and soy and wheat dropped away behind them, and lines of old oak and maple and sweetgum ran up against the road, their branches latticing the sunlight. The open window brought the cooler air now, the crushed acorn smell, and moss and dark, damp soil hidden away from the summer heat. They were going now to a wilder place. A place shrouded from the full light of day. Somers had read too many books in college. He had read, to be precise, too many novels. And symbolism had wormed its way into his head. And he didn't like this, driving into the shadows.

"I don't think he still thinks we're dirty," was all he said, though. "I think he wanted to meet us. See for himself. And I don't think he would have said the things he did, especially that bit at the end, if he hadn't made up his mind that we were more or less toeing the line."

Hazard's shoulders dropped. He reached over, his big hand cupping Somers's knee. He didn't squeeze or stroke or fool around; he just cupped his knee, and that, too, was something new over the last few months. Emery Hazard wasn't a man of public displays, and everything he did was, to a certain degree, calculated. Somers had told him that he liked to be touched, though, and Hazard had definitely taken that message to heart.

"More or less?"

"If we're honest with each other, yes. More or less. I've gone up to the line a few times, Ree. On these really hard cases, on the ones that don't make any sense, I know I have. With my father, especially. I'm not saying we're dirty. But what we've done—I guess I didn't know that about myself, not until the last year. I didn't know how far I'd go to protect the people I love." His fingers tightened around the hard tendon and muscle and bone of Hazard's wrist.

Hazard nodded slowly, his gaze fixed on the windshield and the road and the oak and maple and sweetgum and somewhere out there, the horizon. And that was all. No answer. Not even a squeeze of the knee. Just that sun-dusted silence. Was he thinking about his answer? Was he thinking the lengths to which he would go to protect someone he loved? Was he thinking, Somers wanted to know— needed to know—about the night he had fought against a man with a knife, about the deep cuts and lacerations that had taken away much of the use of his arm, as he fought to protect Somers's daughter? Was he thinking that sometimes the price to protect someone you loved was too high, that he had paid too high of a price, that he was tired, maybe, of paying that price? And then Somers thought of the dream. And he remembered holding Emery Hazard's wrist, the way he was holding it now, feeling sweat-slick skin over flexing muscle as the teenager fought to free himself, while Mikey Grames brought the knife down his chest in a red line. And Somers remembered the noises Hazard had made, and the hate Somers had felt, and the fear, and the sickening, ricochet thought: *It's him or me.* They never talked about that day. But it was there, between them: the first knife that had touched Emery Hazard had been because of Somers. And then, all those years later, the second knife had been because of Somers too, and what had happened to his arm, and—

First as tragedy.

And Faulkner, too. And then he thought, Jesus Christ what the fuck does Faulkner have to do with it?

"Ree, I need to say something to you. About the photographs, about all of this, I—"

But Somers's phone rang. He drew it from his pocket, saw Swinney's name, and put it to his ear. And it was easier, it was so much easier, to talk to Swinney.

"Hey. How's it going?"

"I've been thinking about your case."

"Did you solve it?"

Swinney didn't laugh. She didn't even come close to laughing. Instead, her breathing quickened, and across the line the background noise shifted, altered, and then dwindled. In the relative quiet, her breathing was much louder. Or maybe she really was breathing louder. And faster. Lots faster. Like she'd just run a marathon. Or like she had a gun pressing up under her jaw.

"Swinney?"

"This is a mess. This is a fucking mess."

"What's going on? What's wrong?"

Hazard glanced over, his scarecrow eyes suddenly sharp as scythes. Somers shook his head to indicate he didn't know.

Swinney's frantic breaths continued for another twenty or thirty seconds. "It's not your fault. I know that. But, Jesus, Somers. Right now. Right now it really feels like your fucking fault. Before you—no. That's not really right. It's not you. It's him. It's his fault."

"Hazard's?"

"Before that big old horsefucker came down here, things were fine. You were fine. You were happy. Your life was good."

No, Somers wanted to say. No, I hadn't been happy. Not for a very long time.

"And mine too. And everybody's. Before he came down here, things were simple. None of these weird cases you guys keep catching. None of the shit, the backstabbing political shit. None of the dirt."

"Is this about Lender?"

"You know where I am?"

"Huh?"

"Do you know where I am?"

"The station?"

"I'm sitting on a shitter in the ladies' room." If Swinney heard the ironic juxtaposition of her vocabulary, she didn't acknowledge it. "Just me, thank God. If Cravens had to pee or Carmichael was on her period, hell, I'd be sitting in a broom closet. I'm in here because I need to talk to you. And because I can't fucking trust my fucking partner of the last eight fucking years. That's why I've got this fifty-year-old porcelain freezing my ass."

This had been coming for the last six months; Somers knew that. But it was a damn inconvenient time for it. Last November, Somers and Hazard had suspected that Albert Lender, Swinney's partner, had betrayed them to the mayor and helped the mayor plan their deaths. Then, only a month later, Swinney revealed to them that Lender had murdered a suspect in custody in order to hide the identity of the real killer. That revelation had cost Swinney dearly; it had destroyed her partnership with Lender, but because they didn't have enough evidence to bring Lender down, she had been forced to continue working with him. The toll had shown over the months in her haggard expression, the dark hollows under her eyes, and the tension felt by everyone between the two detectives. It had been building to a breaking point. And now, Somers realized, something had broken.

"Tell me what's going on," he said.

"I think I've got something. I'm going to have something; I know I will. I—I've been following him, all right? Do you understand what I'm saying? Over the last few months, I've been following him. And something big is going down. Something so big that it's got him about to pop. I knew something wasn't right, not the way Cravens took that call, not the way she tried to play it off. And he knew it too. As soon as I hang up I'm going back out to the bullpen. He's going to give me some bullshit excuse. Maybe in an hour. Maybe in fifteen minutes. I know he will. And I'm going to follow him." Her voice thinned, and the last word was a squeak barely recognizable as a word. Somers's heart was thumping now, and that was the only noise in his ears. Then, her voice twisting as she tried to get it under control, Swinney said, "I'm going to get him. That motherfucker has been laughing at me this whole time, thinking he's so much smarter than me, going behind my back and laughing, motherfucking laughing at me. But I'm the one laughing now."

But she didn't sound like she was laughing. She sounded like she was crying, alone, on an outdated toilet. And she sounded desperate.

"All right," Somers said. "We can meet you. We'll come back—"

"No. Fuck. Nothing out of the ordinary. Listen, where we met last time, remember?"

"Sure."

"Ok. But tonight."

"What time?"

Her hesitation surprised Somers; she had been resolute up until now, and she had had a plan. But something had suddenly changed.

"Eleven," she said. "Did you hear me?"

"Yeah, all right. Eleven."

"Bring that horsefucker if you have to."

"Swinney, are you sure you're all right? We can drive back now."

On the other end of the call, Swinney made a honking noise, and Somers could visualize the ragged trumpet of toilet paper as she blew her nose. "Eleven. And don't be late."

"We won't. Swinney, one more thing."

"I'm sitting on a cold shitter. What?"

"Anything new happening?"

"Jesus Christ. New? Did you hear everything I just said? Have you even been listening?"

"I know, I know. I'm asking more generally. Especially out in the county. Anything with Yorgenson Agro or the trailers out on their land?"

"Mikelson and the rest of them?"

"Sure. Or anything else that comes to mind. Anything with the Volunteers."

"You know Mikelson and his brood are frequent flyers at the county jail, right? I think the deputies pick up one of them at least every week."

"I was telling Hazard about that."

"It's possible they're cooking out there. Doesn't matter how many we lock up—or, for that matter, how many labs blow up. By the time we've swept up one mess, there's another dozen of them out there just getting started." Swinney's complaints weren't new to Somers, but he still felt a pang of sympathy. Swinney and her partner dealt with illegal drug activity, especially the production and sale of methamphetamines. The police cooperated with the Sheriff's Department, but for all intents and purposes, Swinney and Lender had to cover a hell of a lot of ground without a lot of backup. And, as much as any two individuals could, they'd done a decent job—at least, as far as Somers could tell. Now, though, he realized that he didn't actually have any proof of that. Swinney and Lender worked hard, yes. And they regularly busted dealers and shut down makeshift labs. But did that really mean anything? Who else had purchased Albert Lender's loyalty? Had he steered Swinney carefully away from major operations, while still appearing to be effective and engaged in his job?

Swinney was still speaking, saying, "They could haul a trailer onto a new spot of land pretty easily, and it's not that hard to set up a cookshop once you've got the space. God knows those cows or whatever the hell Yorgenson is ranching out there these days aren't going to call it in." Suddenly Swinney's breathing quickened. "Damn those sons of bitches."

"What?"

"I'm not sure. I've got an idea, but . . ."

"Swinney, what?"

"I'll tell you tonight. I have to check something first. Eleven, all right?"

"Eleven."

The line disconnected, and Somers set the phone in his lap. Turning his face to Hazard, he met those scarecrow eyes. "Well, she says they could be cooking out there."

"What's at eleven?"

"She wants to meet." Somers filled his partner in on the conversation, ending with the realization that had come to him while talking to Hazard. "Ree, it's always nickel-and-dime stuff, what she and Lender find. I mean, I never really thought about it. I guess I always took it for granted: we're a small county, and we're tucked up in the middle of God's armpit, so I thought it made sense that we'd just have a bunch of toothless morons cooking up meth for local use."

"But you think there might be something more."

"I don't know. Swinney didn't say anything like that; she was just so upset about Lender. But what she said about him, the little bit I could understand: she said she followed him, and she said he'd been laughing at her. That sounds like he's been deceiving her, right? Tricking her?"

"We know he's lied to her before. Manipulated her. Used her."

"But she already knew about those, same as us. She figured out something new today. And the only serious cases they work, the only sustained stuff, is all about drug production, and then, I don't know, something just clicked."

"Intuition."

"Don't say it like that."

"Distribution."

"What? Are we playing a new game? Emery Hazard shouts out individual words?"

"I'm saying, think about distribution. If you're right and if whatever Swinney discovered about Lender is tied to their primary responsibility of dealing with drug-related cases in the county and if Lender has somehow been obscuring the presence of a larger manufacturer, well, those are a lot of ifs, and that's a lot of supposition."

"Thank God I've got my intuition."

To Somers's delight, Hazard flashed one of those tiny, near-invisible Emery Hazard smiles before saying, "If all of that's true, then the next question is: how are they distributing this product?"

"Biker gangs."

Hazard rolled his eyes.

"What? Maybe."

"Maybe. I won't rule it out. But there's something that would make a lot more sense: a local organization that is deeply entrenched, with a wide-spreading network that is, in some places, almost invisible, with political aspirations, a deep mistrust of the government and of law enforcement, a history of violent refusal to obey local ordinances, and undoubtedly a need for regular cash infusions."

"Undoubtedly? Now who's making suppositions?"

Hazard threw him the bird before saying. "Well?"

"Yeah, it makes sense. If there's drug manufacturing happening on a local scale, the most likely organization to be working it or controlling it or distributing it is the Ozark Volunteers."

"But Swinney and Lender have never gone after them?"

"I don't know. I mean, I don't have my nose in their case files, so it's possible."

"Don't do that."

Somers grimaced. "Fine. You're right: I'm pretty sure they've never seriously sniffed anywhere near the Ozark Volunteers' collective hairy ass. And if they had, I'm pretty sure I would have heard about it. They've got enough clout that the shit would have really started to fly."

"And Naomi would have talked to you."

"Dear God, Ree. Don't make me do this."

"You know you have to."

"I do not. I most definitely do not."

Hazard shrugged, his attention locked on the asphalt peeling away beneath their tires.

"And you know what, Ree? I'm going to tell you why not: she's a grade-A bitch. That's number one. She ruined my marriage. That's number two. She twisted the knife with those goddamn divorce papers. That's number three. She's a fucking lunatic. That's number four. She's—"

"All right. You don't have to call her. We'll figure this out some other way."

Here, along this stretch of the state highway, the oaks pressed so close to the road that their roots rumpled the gravel stretch of shoulder, and the hot, green, summer smell of their leaves mixed with the cooler scents of shade and bare earth that the breeze carried from deeper among the trees. The Jetta whined, its engine straining to carry them fifty-five miles an hour along state roads, and the tires gave a steady whomp-whomp that was making Somers's blood pressure rise.

"Fine." He grabbed his phone and unlocked the screen.

"You don't have to—"

"Ree, shut up. Just shut up because I'm pissed right now and you know I'm pissed and I just need you to shut up for a minute." Tapping on her contact, he put the phone to his ear. "This is exactly what you wanted, and don't pretend it isn't."

Hazard at least had the good grace to look embarrassed.

The call went to voicemail, and Somers spoke brusquely, asking Naomi to call him back as soon as possible. He didn't expect his ex-sister-in-law to do that; if anything, he expected she would only call if she had a way to screw with him. But Hazard was right: Naomi was their only solid contact with the Ozark Volunteers' nebulous membership, and she was high-ranking, and most important of all, she loved trying to ruin Somers's life. So the odds were good that she would talk to them. And that she would be really nasty about it.

"Why hasn't anybody else thought of this?" Hazard said in the ensuing silence.

"Because nobody else, thank Christ, is related to Naomi. At least, God, I hope not."

"No, why hasn't anybody else wondered about the extent of the drug problem in the county? Why hasn't anyone followed up on Lender and Swinney?"

"You know why, Ree. It's the same reasons as always: we're a small department; we're a small town; we're a small county. Lender and Swinney have been here for ages, and they do good work, at least on the surface. But you know the rest of it too: if we're right, if Lender's been masking a major drug operation for years, then there's a lot of money behind it. And that money isn't going just into Lender's pocket."

"Cravens?"

Sighing, Somers let his shoulders fall. "I don't know. Maybe. Probably, I guess."

"And the former sheriff. Maybe the new one. Health inspectors, possibly, or DSS representatives, even Forest Service rangers, anybody that might have a legitimate reason to go into Ozark Volunteer land and see something they shouldn't see. Of course, it would be more efficient to cut it off from the top—" Hazard drew in a short, sharp breath.

Somers's head shot up. "Now that's interesting."

"This shit with Kjar. You think it's really about something else?"

"Let's find out why the man who shot at the mayor had his stolen truck at the Yorgenson trailers. Maybe that will give us an answer."

They drove the remaining miles with only the sound of the air rushing through the open window and the thump of the Jetta's tires and the whine of the engine struggling to carry them faster. Instead of a legitimate road, a pair of dirt ruts torn into a grassy strip provided the only access to the Yorgenson trailers. Hazard slowed as they approached the turn-off. Somers's eyes skipped toward the trees. He didn't know what to expect at the trailers, but the weight of the .40 caliber he carried was heavy in his mind.

Hazard's muttered swearing drew Somers's eyes to the rearview mirror, and Somers, propped on one elbow, glanced behind them. The smoke-colored Camaro had vanished. And Somers guessed that wasn't a good thing.

CHAPTER NINETEEN

JULY 3
TUESDAY
2:00 PM

SEVERAL HUNDRED YARDS of dense trees hid the Yorgenson trailers from the state highway. Hazard guided the Jetta along the rutted track, the car bouncing and jostling, the open windows letting in air heavy and moist with earth, with cottonwood fuzz, with decay. Maybe a rabbit, part of his brain thought. Maybe a squirrel. A groundhog. A wild cat. Something dead, the summer heat spoiling it, cooking it low and slow into a soupy mess. Ahead, the curtain of oak and elm and maple parted, and the trailers came into view.

But even as the Jetta rocked towards the trailers, even as part of Hazard's mind processed the smell of something dead and rotting, most of his attention was still on the smoke-colored Camaro that had disappeared.

"Maybe the driver has a friend out here," Somers said. "Just driving this way for fun."

"He was following us. He wasn't out here to visit a friend."

The trailers were dismally ugly. They were an older generation of prefabricated housing, before a lot of the most pressing problems had been identified and, to different degrees, addressed: on the closest trailer, a utility panel hung open to reveal a propane-powered water heater, the hookup lines rusted and the blue flame flickering behind an open panel. The owner had stacked firewood right below the tank, in violation of common sense and probably any number of codes, and dead brush piled against the aluminum siding. On another trailer, steelwork around the windows rusted in long, dripping gouts down the aluminum siding. The third trailer, sitting higher than the others on cinder block pillars, showed signs of rot around the door, where the laminate coating peeled away from bloated, dissolving engineered wood underneath. This last trailer wore two flamingos on either side of the door, the molded plastic x'ed in place with duct tape.

But what Hazard didn't see, in spite of the flamingos and the rotting wood and the cinder block and the blue pilot light bowing in the afternoon breeze, was any sign that people were here.

"Where are the cars?" Somers said.

Hazard stopped the Jetta; the engine died with a whine and a shudder, and then everything was quiet. Hazard popped open the door and listened. Branches creaked, and somewhere farther off, something skittered and knocked against wood. A terrified animal sprinting for safety, Hazard thought, but the sound had gotten his pulse pounding.

"No birds," Somers whispered.

No. No birds. Hazard studied the trailers again. The windows were dark. No curtains offered any chance at privacy, but the sun was high enough that the shadows inside the trailers hid anyone that might be inside. Beyond the trailers, the land opened up, a rocky scree swelling up into acres and acres of open pasture. Prime land for ranching, Hazard thought. But no cattle. No horses. No sheep. Nothing.

"Fuck this," Hazard said.

Somers, nodding slowly, said, "Let's get the hell out of here."

Hazard turned the key. The Jetta whined and clanked and then gasped and settled back to rest.

"What's that mean?" Somers said.

"It's fine."

Hazard turned the key again, pumping the gas. Out of the corner of his eye, he caught a gleam of sunlight, and he glanced up. The windows inside the trailers had gone dark again, but there had been something. The sun, a part of his brain thought hopefully. Just the sun. But he stomped harder on the gas, cranking the key. The Jetta just sputtered.

"If I die because you're too cheap—"

The roar of the motor startled Hazard, and the noise was so close and so sudden that for a moment, he thought the Jetta had come alive. His hand dropped to the gear shift, and he drove home the clutch, and only then did he realize the Jetta's dash was still dark and he heard Somers shouting, "Get the fuck out, get the fuck out of the car," and the blond man shoved him towards the door.

Hazard stumbled in the direction Somers had shoved him, making it a handful of yards before the first sounds of shooting penetrated his consciousness. Ahead of him, a bullet ripped away bark, exposing the pine's white pulp. The smell of sap washed over Hazard, so thick he could barely breathe. A second bullet rustled a branch, and pinecones rained down, pattering off Hazard's head and shoulders. Then he reached the pine and ducked behind it, his heartbeat hammering in his ears.

Somers.

Hazard glanced back at the Jetta, and for a moment, he saw nothing. Then, much farther than Hazard had expected, he glimpsed Somers in the curtain of oaks that ran toward the highway. The blond had his .40 caliber Glock in his hands, and he was pressed up against a tree. His eyes met Hazard's and then cut towards the trailers.

Hazard followed his partner's gaze. A big diesel truck, a Silverado with a flatbed, roared around the side of the farthest trailer. That had been the sound Hazard had heard—not the Jetta finally coming to life, but this big old beast. Somers must have seen it first, and he had correctly predicted what was about to happen. As Hazard watched from his momentary shelter, the Silverado plowed into the Jetta. The little cherry-red VW crumpled like a tin can in a machine press. Without even slowing down, the truck smashed the Jetta clear of the rutted track and shot towards the state highway.

Two more things happened then. Another shot rang out, and then the Silverado swerved, crashing into one of the massive oaks lining the dirt road. The truck rattled, its engine humming, but nobody moved inside it.

That shot, Hazard realized, had come from the highway. And the other shots had come from the trailers. He looked for Somers again, found his partner, and saw the same realization in his eyes. They were pinned down. Two groups of shooters: one inside the trailers; one moving in from the highway. Hazard and Somers stuck between them.

Hazard studied his surroundings. He had to move, and he had to act fast before either group of shooters refocused their attention. Reaching Somers now seemed like an impossibility; Hazard would have to cross the cleared track, running between the Jetta's wreckage and the Silverado. While the two ruined vehicles would provide limited cover, Hazard would also have to give up the protection of the tree line, and he would be stepping into a shooting gallery. Somers seemed to realize the same thing; the blond man was scouring his surroundings, his features set in frustration.

If they separated, though—Hazard thought again of the Haverford and its darkness and those islands of light and the tripwire at the end and the flare of the muzzle and the thought, however, fleeting, that Somers was dead.

He realized that he had found Somers again, and he was staring at him. Somers was staring back. And then Somers turned and darted deeper into the trees, and Hazard swore.

All right. He had to do something. First, though, he took a breath and made himself think. Two groups of shooters: the trailers, and the highway. They weren't working together, to judge by the Silverado's fate. That meant that somehow Hazard had walked into the middle of a battle. Or, to put it more accurately, he had arrived right before the battle had started.

Two groups of shooters, and Hazard needed to get behind substantial cover before he got shot. Getting to the road wouldn't be any help; even if he made it past the shooters, whoever was attacking from that side would be able to run him down. The trailers—well, the trailers wouldn't be the best cover, but they'd be better than nothing. All Hazard needed was a distraction.

Then he smiled.

He feinted towards the Jetta, then doubled back, sprinting. Shots rang out, and Hazard hoped that his trick had bought him the few precious seconds that he needed. He cleared a pair of oaks and skirted a sweetgum, its prickly balls rolling underfoot. Then, he saw it: the leftmost trailer was now lined up dead ahead of him. He took in a breath, smelled that dead thing liquefying in the summer heat, felt that poisonous stench fill up his lungs like porcupine quills, and lined up his shot.

The first bullet went wide, and he had to take a breath and corral his fear for Somers. The second shot went true. It struck the dead brush at the base of the trailer. The bullet threw off sparks, and for a moment, he thought he'd gotten it. But the sparks died down, and Hazard swore and ducked behind the pine again. Another fusillade rang out; Hazard crouched, wincing as a bullet struck inches above his head and sprayed splinters down onto his neck. For what felt like an eternity, the firing continued. And then it was over.

Hazard crabbed sideways until he cleared the pine, and then he lined up and fired again. Another hit. The dead brush quivered, and sparks flew up from the shot, but still nothing. Hazard swore again. Knees aching, he readied himself to duck behind the pine again.

Only some dumb bastard opened fire on the woodpile. He must have seen the brush twitching and assumed that someone was hiding inside it. And whoever this guy was, he had a hell of a lot of ammo because he poured shot after shot into the brush and the stacked, seasoned wood.

This time, there were plenty of sparks. And some of them caught in the dry, dead leaves. They licked their way across good-quality firewood, and then they licked higher. Smoke trailed up, twitched as a current caught it, and danced east. With a satisfied grunt, Hazard scooted back to his position and waited.

Two more rounds of fire were exchanged. Hazard peeked around the tree. Yes, the blaze was really going now—the perfect source of fuel, and those idiots at the highway had done him the favor of setting it alight. The flames lapped up the side of the trailer now. The utility panel, still hanging open, quivered once. The blue flame of the pilot light quivered too, a kind of a vicious anticipation, as though it somehow knew what was coming. A normal propane tank had safety features to prevent this kind of thing from happening, a pressure release valve, but with everything rusted shut—

The tank exploded. The blast threw up a jet of flame, and shrapnel from the exploding tank ripped open the side of the trailer. The sound from the blast clapped hard against Hazard, and he ran towards the noise. The supply of propane must have been good because when the smoke shifted, Hazard saw that one full wall had been ripped away, revealing a grungy bathroom and a bed with Scooby Doo sheets pulled down and a TV room with a ten-point buck mounted on the wall and a kitchen, singed linoleum wagging up where the trailer's frame had ripped free. A man with a hunting rifle sagged over the sink, blood masking his face. He lifted the rifle. His movements were slow and dazed, and Hazard had already closed most of the distance. Hazard brought up the Smith & Wesson, fired once, twice, and the rifle fell from the man's hands. It clattered to the edge of the trailer, and its weight pinned the linoleum back into place. Then Hazard snatched up the rifle and kept running.

Three shots to the brush near the propane tank. Two shots to the dead man in the trailer. That left only one more cartridge in the .38. Hazard juggled the rifle; it was a Remington, a bolt action, and he guessed the magazine held three cartridges total. Maybe four. So if Hazard were very, very lucky, and that bastard in the trailer hadn't taken any shots, he had four cartridges. That seemed too good to be true, though.

Circling the ruined trailer, Hazard found cover behind two plastic water barrels and knelt. His ears were ringing from the gunfire, and for a moment, he could hear nothing. No movement came from the road. Then gunshots flashed inside the next trailer, the one with the gouts of rust, and Hazard worked the bolt and settled the rifle's stock against his shoulder. A moment later, muzzle flashes sparked again, and then the trailer's door flew open. Stumbling backward, a man hit the porch railing and tumbled over to lie still on the ground.

Hazard breathed out, steadying his aim. Pain jangled up his bad arm.

Then Somers appeared, squatting in the trailer's doorway and scanning towards the road.

"For fuck's sake," Hazard muttered. Then, louder, "What the hell are you doing?"

An easy grin lit up Somers's face when he caught sight of Hazard. He jerked a thumb at the trailer "I'm thinking of buying one. For us, you know. Want to see what it looks like inside?"

"Already did." Hazard dipped his head toward the trailer he had just ripped open. "Not interested."

Somers opened his mouth to respond, but a shot pinged against the trailer's aluminum siding, and he retreated.

"All right?" Hazard called.

From inside the trailer, Somers shouted back, "I changed my mind. I don't think I'm going to buy one. I don't like the neighbors."

Hazard shook his head, bracing his hands as best he could; relief and adrenaline were a powerful mix, and he knew the shakes would be coming soon. They weren't out of this yet, either.

"John."

"I know. I'll cover you."

Hazard waited, but Somers didn't return to the door. A moment later, though, a screen popped out of a small window at the front of the trailer, and three shots went off. Hazard took the opportunity and ran. He sprinted between the trailers until he reached the rear of the one that Somers was using. The shots cut off. Hazard took up a spot alongside the trailer, watching in case anyone decided to press the sudden opening, but nothing moved in the line of trees. A moment later, the trailer's rear door slammed open, and Somers took the steps two at a time.

"Well," he said, crouching next to Hazard. "This is a shit-show."

"Two groups. We got caught in the middle."

Somers's exaggerated eye-roll almost made Hazard blush. Almost.

"That trailer," Somers said, nodding at the one with the flamingos, "has a nice cook-shop set up. It also has an older fellow. Really unpleasant. Had a mind to put a few holes in me."

"I guess Erl Mikelson isn't going to be bothering the sheriff's deputies anymore?"

Somers shook his head. "What the hell happened over there?"

"Oh. I blew up that trailer."

"You blew it up?"

"Um, with a little help."

A bullet whizzed, and the trailer's porch light exploded in a shower of glass.

"Let's talk about it later. How the hell are we getting out of here?"

"Pasture."

"You want to run into an open pasture?"

"Ree, these guys aren't marksmen. We do it smart, and we do it together, but yes: that's about the only direction that isn't closed off. If we go any other way, we'll run straight into them—or we'll run into the state highway, which is the same thing in this case."

A bullet punched into the barrel where Hazard had been hiding a moment before, and water arced out. In the tree line, shapes moved, and Hazard realized that without Mikelson and his group returning fire, the attackers had decided to begin their approach.

"I'll cover you," Hazard said. "Go."

"Ree—"

"Go."

Somers sprinted towards the swell of ground, and Hazard lined up his shot. His bad arm throbbed. On his next exhale, he squeezed the trigger, and the stock kicked hard. Someone in the tree line went down.

"Come on," Somers called.

Breathe in. Breathe out. This time, the pain was worse, a kind of shimmering electricity from wrist to shoulder, but he steadied himself. Hazard was ready for the kick. Another of those shapes behind the screen of oaks dropped. If Hazard were lucky, like Jesus-walking-on-water lucky, he had two more cartridges in the rifle. And never in his life had he been lucky.

Well, except with Somers.

Hazard threw the rifle over his shoulder and ran. Somers, waiting for him where the pasture crested, fell into place at his side, and they ran out into the wide, open prairie. Two shots came after them, but Hazard only heard the gunfire, and he didn't know where the bullets had gone. After the first frantic dash, they settled into a more sustainable pace. Maybe a half mile east, cottonwoods grew along a creek, and the water flashed patches of sunlight back at the sky. That would be their first destination: the only cover in sight, and it might take them somewhere they could get help.

That was when Hazard heard the engines. The growling thrum was distant but growing closer, and he risked a look over his shoulder. When he stumbled, Somers caught his arm, but Hazard didn't break his glance.

Two big trucks were bouncing up the rocky slope, coming straight towards the open pasture. Scree spun under their tires, spitting out clouds of dust, but in another minute or two they would reach the relatively flat grassland. It might be a bouncy, uncomfortable ride, but it wouldn't be a hard one. Two trucks like those would cover the distance easily, quickly. And they'd catch Hazard and Somers before they made it another hundred yards.

"For the love of God," Somers muttered, grabbing Hazard's arm to steady him. "Pay attention. If you twist your ankle—"

"Keep running," Hazard said, dropping the rifle into the crook of his arm. "I can scare them, slow them down. Maybe I'll even hit one." Maybe, he thought with wild fantasy, maybe he would kill one driver, and that truck would swerve into the other truck's path, and then both trucks would be out of commission. Maybe they'd both explode, like something in one of those stupid action movies Somers liked to watch. Maybe in half an hour, Hazard would be safely on his way back to Wahredua.

But all of that was just a kid's dream, he knew. He might get off a shot. If he were lucky, Jesus-lucky, and he had two cartridges left, then he'd get off two shots. And if he were really lucky, then maybe he'd even hit one of the drivers. But the reality, Hazard knew, was that they would just mow him down. They wouldn't even slow; those trucks would go over him like he was nothing but a bump in the road.

"Will you quit it," Somers panted, "with this martyr complex? Now run, goddamnit."

Hazard was going to argue, but that's when the thunder started. At least, it felt like thunder: an enormous concussive force that shook Hazard. But it wasn't thunder. The sky was clear and blue and shining. The trembling came from the ground, like an earthquake threatening to toss Hazard head over heels. He staggered, and again Somers caught him, and pain lanced up Hazard's bad arm. Then, blinking tears from his eyes, he saw it: cattle.

A whole herd of cattle was racing across his and Somers's path. Hazard wasn't sure if it had been the gunshots that had startled the herd and set it to flight, or if it was the noise of the trucks, or the explosion, or if it had been something else entirely. All he knew was that hundreds of cows were running at a diagonal to him. And that was only the tip of the herd; it grew wider. Wide enough to swallow up the space where Hazard and Somers were running. Thousands of pounds, tens of thousands of pounds of flesh and hooves and bone. If Hazard and Somers were caught in the stampede, even somewhere towards the fringe, they would die. And it would be a brutal, painful death as they were trampled.

"The creek," Somers chanted; it had the sound of a mantra, as though Somers could summon it into being by repeating its name. But the creek was still almost a quarter mile away, and Hazard's arm had turned to fire, and the cattle were moving fast.

Maybe. Maybe. If they ran full out, if they were lucky, if neither of them—

Hazard saw it a moment before it happened. Somers ran with easy, loping grace. The lines of his body were perfect, fluid, made for this. And then a clod of earth puffed up in front of them—a bullet, part of Hazard's mind said—and Somers jagged right, and there was a gopher hole. Hazard could see it, as big as his wrist, maybe bigger, and he saw Somers's foot coming down. He reached for his partner, but his arm was too stiff, too slow. Instead of catching Somers's arm, he caught fingerfuls of sleeve, and the fabric went stiff and ripped free of Hazard's weakened grip as Somers fell.

The blond man hit the ground at full speed. He rolled three times and then skidded another four or five feet. Faster than Hazard could have expected, the blond man sat up. A bloody rash opened one side of his face from temple to jaw, and dirt smudged the bridge of his nose and his forehead, but he scrambled up.

"Your ankle—"

"Fine," Somers said, but he took a step and would have fallen if Hazard hadn't caught him, this time with his good arm. "I'm fine," Somers wheezed, his face the color of the sun-bleached grass. "Let's go. I'll shake it off, I'll—"

On the next step, though, he folded again, and Hazard had to fumble to keep him from falling.

The roar of the trucks was loud. The thunder of the herd shook its way up Hazard's legs. He hauled Somers upright, met his eyes, and said, "I need both hands."

His pain must have been worse than he was letting on because he just nodded, his face that same burned-out white, and panted for breath.

Hazard turned. His bad arm was ringing like a fire alarm, now, a metallic shriek that ran all the way to his elbow, but he forced himself to lift the Remington, to set in place, and to hold still. But he couldn't do that last part. He couldn't hold still. He could smell the torn stalks of the indiangrass and Somers's coppery blood and the exhaust from the diesel engines. His arm shook like a leaf in a strong wind. Against his shoulder, the stock rocked back and forth. Hazard bit the inside of his mouth, and now he was tasting the coppery blood, tasting his own blood, but he still couldn't hold his arm steady. He'd have to shoot like this, with the herd's stampede like a thunder in his ears, with the guttural growl of the diesel, and something else, a whine buzzing at the edge of his hearing. It was so ridiculous, so out of place, that Hazard almost laughed. It was like a mosquito. Or a string trimmer. Or—

"Fuck me backward," Somers said, his hand clutching Hazard's shoulder and spinning him.

Rocketing towards them across the waves of indiangrass, his frame bent taut and low, came Jonny Moraes on an ATV.

"Fuck me backward," Hazard echoed, and his arm hurt so badly that he had to drop the rifle against his shoulder and sag.

The herd was still coming. The two diesel engines still growled towards them. But Jonny Moraes reached them first, his dark eyes unreadable as he pulled up in front of them, and the ATV didn't sound like a mosquito anymore. It sounded like a dog at the fence.

"If I have to shoot you," Somers said, breaking the tension between them, "it's going to really ruin my day."

Moraes grinned and jerked his head at the ATV's rear seat. "Want a ride?"

In a wash of bovine flesh, the tip of the herd poured between Hazard and the two trucks. Glass glinted off the windshields. Then one of the trucks swung around, and the driver side window rolled down. A face emerged from the cab. The figure peeled off a ski mask and stared at Hazard. The distance swallowed up the stumps of brown teeth, but Hazard recognized him anyway: Mikey put a hand to his mouth, whooped something that was lost in the noise of the stampede, and then drove back the way he had come.

CHAPTER TWENTY

JULY 3
TUESDAY
2:57 PM

Their escape on the ATV, juxtaposed with the rest of the afternoon, seemed banal in comparison. Moraes drove them east and south, following the stands of cottonwood and the silty reflections of the creek and the damp earth printed with deer tracks and the tiny prints of rabbits and foxes and, in one spot, the markings of a wild dog, maybe a wolf. Hazard wrapped his arm around Somers, holding the blond man tight against him. His partner's face was still bleached with pain, and Somers rocked with every bounce that the ATV took. Hazard's bad arm ached, but it was tolerable. Anything was tolerable. Anything up to and including having his balls knocked off by this ATV was tolerable as long as Somers was all right.

Behind them, the herd of cattle disappeared into the yellow folds of indiangrass, and eventually even the roar of the two diesel trucks vanished. Moraes didn't stop the ATV until they had rolled beneath a pair of leaning willows. The branches curtained behind them, and then, when the motor stopped, the only noise was their breathing, and the click of the engine cooling, and the creek rippling.

Moraes climbed down, but he hadn't managed to turn before Somers had the big .40 caliber Glock trained on him. Even with his face washed out by pain, Somers looked deadly serious. "I meant what I said about shooting you."

"I just saved your life."

"Very conveniently," Hazard said. "Hands up."

Slowly, deliberately, Moraes raised his hands.

"Will you do it?" Somers asked.

Nodding, Hazard slid down from the ATV. Moraes flashed him an angry look, but Hazard ignored him, and he took the pistol from Moraes's holster. Then he retreated to stand next to Somers.

"All right," Somers said. "Tell us."

"I was following you."

"Why?"

"Because you think I had something to do with what happened to the mayor." Moraes's dark eyes sparked, and his hands closed into fists. "I didn't. I did my job."

"Not very well," Hazard said. "Either you're a traitor or you're incompetent. Which one is worse?"

"I'm incompetent? I just pulled your ass out of the fire. You walked right in there. Walked into the lion's den, lay down, and put your heads in his mouth. How does that sound for incompetent?"

"We were handling it."

"Mother. Fucker."

"We were—"

"We were in trouble," Somers said. "And we either have the worst luck around, or somebody wanted to be sure we got stuck in the middle of that."

For the first time, Moraes looked uncertain. "In the middle of what?"

"You first," Somers said. "From the beginning."

"I want my gun."

"From the beginning."

"Can I put my arms down?"

"Sure," Hazard said with a shrug. "If you want to get shot."

Moraes shook his head, but he kept his hands up. "Like I said: I was following you. I borrowed my buddy's Camaro. It's nice. It doesn't look like a cop's car. You guys thought I had something to do with the mayor's shooting, and that stuck with me. I didn't like it. I didn't like—I didn't like that it was you two that thought it. You're smart. You get people, you get the ones you're after. And I didn't like that you were after me."

"Where did you start following us?"

"At the station."

Shock flickered inside Hazard. He had seen the Camaro outside the Sheriff's Department, but that had been hours after they left the station.

Moraes must have seen something on Hazard's face because he smirked. "When did you finally notice?"

"We're asking the questions," Hazard said.

"At the Sheriff's Department," Somers said.

With a shrug, Moraes said, "Not bad. I thought you wouldn't spot me until we left town, and by then it would be too late."

"What did you see?" Somers said.

"I saw the two of you doing your job." A smirk creased his mouth. "And making out."

"Was anybody else following us?" Hazard said, fighting the heat in his cheeks.

Moraes hesitated, then shook his head. "Not that I noticed."

"And?" Somers said.

"And what?"

"What did you decide?"

Again, Moraes hesitated.

"Come on," Somers said. "You can tell us that story about the injustice of it all, how you didn't like that we considered you might be in on what happened at the mayor's house, all of that. But that's bullshit, right?"

"It's not bullshit."

"It's not the whole truth."

Hazard felt something click into place. "You thought we were in on it?"

A flush worked its way under Moraes's dark skin. "That's not crazy, all right? Everybody knows you two play fast and loose sometimes. Everybody knows you've got beef with the mayor. I like you. Both of you. But you're both—I don't know. Wild, I guess."

"Give him back his gun," Somers said.

"Not yet," Hazard said. "What about the rest of it?"

"You came down here. I dropped back; there's not a lot of turn-offs, and I figured in case you hadn't seen me yet, I didn't want to stick to your bumper. I had gone about two miles past the Yorgenson trailers when I realized I'd lost you. I should have realized it earlier. Those big trucks, they were parked across the turn-off, and they had a lot of guys. I saw them, but I thought it was just hunters. Some sort of shit like that. Then dispatch radioed about officers under fire, and I realized it had to be the two of you, so I spun around and ditched the car."

"You went on foot?"

"I wasn't going to drive up. For all I knew, those redneck sons of bitches would shoot me just for looking at them. I'm parked—" He craned his neck, his arms still above him, and shrugged. "God, I don't know. I'm all turned around. But I went the last quarter mile or so on foot. I didn't have a siren, and I sure as hell wasn't going to play Lone Ranger."

"You could have waited for someone else to show up," Somers said. "When I called this in, dispatch said they'd send everyone they could. You just needed to wait."

"No," Hazard said. "He couldn't sit around and wait. He had to get in there and see. He had to catch us in the act."

"Do you blame me? Look me in the eyes and tell me that. Would you have done it differently?"

Hazard shrugged. "Keep telling it."

"The guys in the truck were shooting into the trees, but a few of them were already down, and the rest really didn't look like their hearts were in it. I tried to get a look at the guys in the trucks, but they all had masks on. Even in this heat. And no tags on the trucks, either, so that's a dead end. I was going to get closer, but then there was an explosion, and this fire shot straight up into the sky—"

Somers shot a glance at Hazard, and Hazard, for some reason he couldn't explain, suddenly felt his cheeks heat.

"—and then, a few minutes later, the shooting stopped. I saw the two of you pinned down behind that trailer. And then I saw you take off for the pasture, and I knew that was going to be a hot mess, so I thought I'd try to help. I squeezed off a couple of shots just to put Jesus in those guys. Most of them got their tails up and ran, but I saw a truck go after you." He shook his head and glanced back the way they'd come. "I didn't think about the cows. Cattle. Whatever you call them. Those shots got them really riled up,"

"And you just happened to have an ATV?" Hazard said.

"No. Erl Mikelson had six of them. They were parked on the far side of his trailer, the one with the meth lab inside. I grabbed the keys." Moraes grinned his blindingly white grin. "All of them. I took off after you. I went the back way, though; I didn't want one of those guys plugging me. And now here we are: your asses are well and truly saved thanks to me, and I'm standing here like a jackass because you're still pointing my gun at me."

"Give it back to him," Somers said.

With a grunt, Hazard proffered the pistol, and Moraes holstered it. He shook out his arms, as though making a point of his irritation, and said, "Whoever's at the Yorgenson trailers, they're going to want to talk to you. Let's get you back there."

"Just a second," Hazard said. "You saw what we saw."

"What?"

"You saw what we saw."

"What do you mean?"

"You saw two groups of people shooting at each other."

"Yeah."

"And you saw Mikelson's cookware."

"Yeah, I had to go in there for the ATV keys—what's going on?"

"What do you think is going on?"

For a long moment, Moraes was quiet. Then, in a low voice, he said, "You think this has something to do with the mayor?"

"I just want to hear your thoughts."

"Tell me why you came down here."

Hazard shook his head.

With a sigh, Somers said, "The sheriff has a source who saw that white truck, the shooter's truck, parked at the Yorgenson trailers. We came down to ask some questions. Instead, we walked into a—"

"Stop," Hazard said. "I want to hear what he thinks happened."

Again, Moraes studied them. The creek continued to ripple, and the breeze stirred the curtain of willows, and the air smelled like pollen and sweat and the hot vinyl seat covers on the ATV. Somers, no longer worried about Moraes, slumped on the ATV. Pain still leached the color from him, but the road-rash on his face had slowed its bleeding, and his tropical-blue eyes were alert.

"All right," Moraes said. "If we're following the dotted line." He paused, letting it hang like a question.

Hazard shrugged again.

"That truck goes missing. Stolen, right? And then it's here for a few days. And then it shows up in Wahredua, and the guy using it tries to kill Newton and that leads you right into a trapped building. There's a meth lab here, so it looks like Mikelson has a problem with the mayor, decides to eliminate him, and fails."

"And the rest of it?"

"You mean Kjar?"

Hazard shrugged again.

"I don't know. Maybe Kjar was working for Mikelson. I heard he was a drug addict, so maybe he owed him money. Maybe he was—Christ, I honestly don't know. What did you learn at his house?"

Somers opened his mouth, but Hazard shook his head.

"All right," Moraes said, "well fuck you too. The rest of it? The rest of it, this stuff today, this looks like war."

"War?"

"Territory dispute. Something like that. Mikelson's little gang of meth heads gets put down, hard, by a rival gang. But I don't really know. I can't do this kind of shit without information, so instead of letting me guess while my ass is hanging in the wind, just tell me what's going on."

"That's what it looks like to me too," Hazard said. "A meth maker tries to kill the mayor and, at the same time, lure the cops into a trap. Then he's eliminated by a rival dealer."

Somers, his eyes shockingly blue in his white face, cocked his head. "And, in the process, Mikelson is conveniently unable to explain to what extent he was involved in the attack on the mayor. Our lead suspect is dead. Most of his group is dead. Almost like someone wanted things that way." He shook his head, touched his temple, and his fingers came away red. He studied the bloody digits for a moment before saying. "All of it sounds like a nice little cover-up except for Kjar."

"A cover-up," Moraes said, eyeing each of them in turn. "That's some paranoid shit."

"Paranoid is the tip of the iceberg with this guy," Somers said, blowing a kiss to Hazard.

CHAPTER TWENTY-ONE

JULY 3
TUESDAY
6:03 PM

THE NEXT FEW HOURS were a waste, as far as Somers was concerned. Moraes drove him and Hazard back to the Yorgenson trailers, where they answered the same questions over and over again from different deputies and, in a separate round, from Hoffmeister and Lloyd, two of the Wahredua PD's finest. The questions couldn't turn up anything substantial, though, because Somers and Hazard didn't have anything substantial. Or rather, Somers didn't have anything. He wasn't sure about Hazard.

The heat grew worse as the afternoon drew on, and the pounding in Somers's head that had begun with his fall worsened. His ankle had stopped twingeing after he got up and moving, but his head—he had to close his eyes, even during some of the questions, because it was so bad. It wasn't a headache so much as it was something else, though. A light. That's what it felt like. This bright, scintillating point of light stabbing at the back of his eyes. Headaches didn't feel like that. Nothing in the Christ-loving world felt like that, and the pain made him so nauseous that Somers had to crawl away from Hoffmeister in the middle of questioning and throw up at the edge of the rutted track that led to the Yorgenson trailers. He had to crawl because of his leg, of course, but also because of that light spearing through his brain.

Hoffmeister kept trying to ask questions after that, and Somers lay in the weeds, listening. From time to time he would open his eyes, and he could focus on one thing, only one, a bluebell growing just past the tip of his nose. And the bluebell would swell to enormous proportions, and the nausea would climb the back of Somers's throat, and the light widened like an event horizon, and then he would snap his eyes shut. And after a while, Hoffmeister stopped asking questions.

Then steps came back, and Somers opened his eyes, and brown wingtips were there bending the bluebell to one side.

"I can fucking see that he's not fucking doing well," a familiar voice said. "If you hadn't been wasting my fucking time with your fucking questions, he might be doing a lot fucking better. No. Don't open your fucking mouth. I'll take care of him."

Big arms looped under Somers's shoulders and knees, and he rose into the air. He smelled Hazard's sweat and his pomade, and he buried his face in his chest. The light at the back of his head was fracturing, thousands of little lights now stabbing through the gray matter inside his skull.

"Shush," Hazard said, and Somers knew, just from the way Hazard walked, that it was hell on Hazard's arm to carry him, and that in spite of that pain Hazard was going slow, trying not to jostle Somers. "You've got a concussion, I think."

"My head."

"Yeah, that's where most concussions are."

A door clicked, and after an awkward jumble, Somers found himself stretched out on vinyl upholstery. The back of a cop car. But at least this one didn't smell like vomit and stale take-out. Then something cool and damp touched his forehead, and then again, and again. Always cool. And some of those spears of light drifted away, and Somers felt good enough to reach up, even with his eyes closed, and wrap his hand around Hazard's wrist. The fine, dark hairs on the back of Hazard's arm tickled his palm, and the hand slowed its movements, dabbing more gently at Somers's forehead now.

With that light stabbing the back of his brain, Somers didn't even realize he was talking out loud, not at first. The words were just running through him, through his brain and out his mouth, and so it wasn't even really talking. It was more like . . . like water. Like cool water dabbed against his forehead and trickling down his face. It was like that, just a trickle of words.

"I held your wrist like this before."

"I remember. We got out the ropes that night." Hazard's voice had an amused rumble. "You were very . . . attentive."

"No. Before."

"You've grabbed my wrist a lot of times."

"It wasn't even summer, not yet. But it was so hot. And everything smelled like mulch until everything smelled like clay."

Hazard's hand had frozen, the damp cloth fixed in one spot.

"I held your wrist. I held it. I was so afraid, and I—I did it. I did what he said. I held your wrist."

"John." The cool, wet cloth shifted once.

"I could feel your muscles. Just like now. When you move your hand, when you rotate your hand, I can feel it." His thumb ran over straining tendons. "Like this. Like now. And you were trying so hard, but there were three of us. And I was so afraid. It was either you or me. I'm such a fuckup, Ree. It was either you or me and I—"

"I don't want to talk about this." Hazard's weight shifted, and the car creaked under him, but Somers held on.

"You hate me."

"I don't hate you."

"I know." Somers leaned into Hazard's hand; the rag fell away, and Hazard's big mitt cupped Somers's face, and Somers knew he was crying but he couldn't feel the tears because his head had become this massive puncture hole, a black space where that light had stabbed straight through him and left nothing in its place. "You love me. But you hate me. That's—that's just how it is, right? You love me, here, now. Right?" He nuzzled into Hazard's hand. "Ree?"

"Yes." The word came up from a gravel pit. "I love you. John, you've got a concussion. Don't—"

"But you hate me too. You hate me. You're always going to hate me because of the past, it's still here." Somers opened his eyes, and that blade of light sharpened and carved deeper into him, and he shut his eyes and reached out blindly, his hand groping across Hazard's chest. "It's here. It's here, and it never goes away, just like Mikey won't ever go away, just like Hollace won't go away, just like the dreams. Oh fuck. Oh fuck me, Ree. Fuck me. I thought the dreams would go away. I thought the dreams—"

"Take a breath. Just take a breath. I'm going to let go of you now. I've got to get the keys so I can drive you to the hospital."

"No," Somers said, nosing into Hazard's hand again, his fingers tightening around his wrist. He said that again, no, over and over again, but that was all he could get out now. The pain had gotten too intense. It fanned brighter and brighter, and then Somers couldn't even say no anymore. But he knew if Hazard let go, if he let go now, it was over. Because what Somers was saying was truth: the past never went away. The past was always there, in the blood, in the bone, in the flesh. In the scars they carried.

"The past is dead and gone, John. Just let go of me for a second. I've got to get the keys. Shush, John. It's all right."

But it wasn't all right. And Hazard was wrong. Or maybe he was lying because he was kind and good and wanted Somers to feel better. Because the truth, Somers knew, was that the past wasn't dead. The past—

—Faulkner—

—wasn't even past.

"John, I'm going to take your hand off me now. Can you nod so I know you understand me? I'm going to get the keys, and I'm going to drive you to the hospital. John. Are you with me?"

"Yeah."

Hazard pried Somers's fingers loose, and Somers let his hand fall to rest on the rubber floor mats, and he felt crumbs and dust bunnies and broken bits of twigs, an old gum wrapper, all the things carried by shoes into the car now brushing his hand. From outside came shouting—Hazard's voice—and then answering shouts, and then more of Hazard again. Then the car dipped, the support creaking under new weight, and the engine turned over, and the door clapped shut, and they rolled away.

"Twenty minutes," Hazard said. "Half an hour, tops. Just hold on."

The rest of the afternoon disintegrated into fractal memories: disjointed variations of the same memory, of rocking in the back seat of the cruiser, of his hand bouncing against the rubber mat, of a blast of air conditioning, and then rocking into the vinyl again. He remembered even less of the hospital, just the vague sense of Hazard carrying him, and then long patches of time that blurred, the same honey color as the walls, and machines, and beeping, and then, eventually, finally, cool darkness, and he could drift, and his head didn't hurt anymore.

When he woke, he couldn't see anything, and for a panicked moment Somers thought he had gone blind. He had read about those kinds of things, about head injuries that somehow knocked lose an essential optic connection, and maybe that had happened. That fall, the way he had hit the ground—

But then his eyes adjusted, and he took in the double room with its empty second bed, and the curtains with ducks printed along the hem, and the grayish halo of a sodium vapor lamp outside the window, smudged between the glass and the curtain. It was night, Somers realized. Jesus, how long had he been out?

Hazard had patched together two chairs and stretched out, and his long legs hung off the end. His eyes were closed, but when Somers shifted and swung his legs off the bed, Hazard said, "Not on your fucking life."

"Oh. You're awake."

"So are you."

"I thought you weren't supposed to let people with concussions sleep."

"They checked on you. Woke you up to make sure you could wake up. They thought about sending you home." Hazard's tone made it clear how he felt about that idea, and it explained why Somers was still in the hospital.

"Does that hurt your neck? Lying like that, I mean. Do you want a pillow?"

Hazard didn't answer.

"It looks like it does."

"Why the fuck didn't you say something?"

And terror prickled deep in Somers's bowels, and he wasn't sure why. Say something? Had he said something? He had . . . the memory, although that wasn't the right word, that he had said something. Something very stupid. Or very important. He wasn't sure which. Maybe both.

"I thought it was just a headache."

"Just a headache."

"Yeah, you know. I hit my head. A headache. That's all."

"Oh. So you've had that kind of headache before."

"Well—"

"The kind where you can't even stand you're so sick. The kind that leaves you crawling into the weeds to throw up."

"There was a bluebell."

"What?"

"It wasn't just weeds. There was a bluebell."

"A fucking bluebell. Perfect. Fucking perfect. If you ever scare me like that again, John, I will shave your ass and use it for a jack-o-lantern."

"Oh yeah?"

"Don't smile. Don't make some goddamn joke about how you might like that."

"I was going to say that you might like that."

Then, to Somers's relief, one of Emery Hazard's shadow smiles darted across his face, and he sat up and fixed Somers with a straight-on look. "Yes. I might. I really might."

"Ree, did I say something? I keep feeling like I—"

Something on Hazard's face stopped him. It wasn't an expression that Somers could read, and that was frightening.

"What? What did I say?"

"Just your usual bullshit." He rolled those massive shoulders and stood. "I've got to go."

"What?"

"I've got to go. I want to run something down before we lose any more time."

"All right." Somers dragged himself to the edge of the bed. "I'll just grab my shoes, and—"

"Not a chance. Not a fucking chance in the world. If you try to leave, I will handcuff you to this bed. I already told the nurses." This time, the shadow smile lingered a heartbeat longer. "And I told them they could do whatever they wanted to you while I was gone."

"Ree, you can't go by yourself. Hollace is out there, and maybe somebody else—"

"I'm just going on a drive. I promise: nothing dangerous."

But that wasn't true, and Somers didn't know why he knew it, and he didn't know how he knew it, but he knew it. He knew it deep in his gut, he knew it the way he might have known he'd swallowed glass: this piercing, invisible obstruction below his stomach that felt like it might rip him apart.

"This is stupid," was all he could say though. "I'm fine. I can go with you, I can watch your back."

"No. I want you here. I want you getting better. Because I intend to make sure you know how very happy I am that we're both still alive."

The words were playful. The tone was playful. But something was off. Something raised Somers's hackles, and again he found himself trawling the black spot in his memory. Had he said something? He felt sure he had. But what? And why was Hazard acting so strangely?

"I'll be back later tonight," Hazard continued. "As soon as I'm done, I'll come back and fill you in."

"Take Moraes."

"That shit for brains? After he damn near let us get shot to pieces and then decided to play rodeo star on a stolen ATV?"

"He saved our—"

"He's probably knee-deep in reports, Somers, from that mess we left at the Yorgenson trailers. Christ, do you know they found two guys out there? Two guys who got run down by those damn cows. That could have been us. That mess was so bad we would still be filling out reports and answering questions and letting Hoffmeister and Lloyd poke around our assholes if you hadn't passed out."

"I didn't pass out. And I'm fine. My head only hurts a little."

"You are a fucking terrible liar."

"Ree—"

Hazard just gave him one of those invisible smiles and jangled the cuffs he kept in his jacket.

"I don't like this," Somers said, dropping back against the mattress.

"I'll be back."

"You sound like the Terminator."

"Just get some rest, ok?"

"Ree, what's wrong? Did I—"

—say—

"—do something?"

"Yeah, you got a concussion. Be back soon."

And with that bullshit answer, Hazard left, and the whole thing was as weird as any encounter Somers had ever had with his boyfriend. He settled back against the pillow, letting his eyes shut. The headache drummed now, a rolling, steady thrum, which was better, anyway, than the white-hot carving knife he had felt earlier. He took a breath, and then another. Whatever it was with Hazard, they could fix it. Somers had done stupid shit before. So had Hazard. And they always fixed it. As long as it wasn't—

—*first as tragedy*—

—the old stuff, as long as they kept that stuff in the rearview mirror, they could keep building, repairing, patching up, no matter how bad things got. So he took a breath. And another. And he wondered why he smelled sour sweat and chewing tobacco and something worse, something rotting.

He opened his eyes, and he realized three things:

He hadn't heard the door.

He didn't have his gun.

Mikey Grames was in the room.

CHAPTER TWENTY-TWO

JULY 3
TUESDAY
7:51 PM

IN THE HOSPITAL PARKING LOT, the streetlights hummed, and tires whispered against the asphalt, and the air smelled like sun-hot tar. Sweat already dampened Hazard's collar, and only some of that was from the summer evening.

Why Hollace Walker? Why was Hollace here now? And what did he have to do with anything that was going on with Kjar and this subterranean drug war? Hollace was nothing. A nobody. His father was a local professor who had all but disowned Hollace at birth, and his mother had led a hard, rough life raising a mixed-race child as a single mother in small-town Missouri. Hollace wasn't money or power or prestige. He wasn't even, for what it was worth, really even a local anymore. Hazard guessed Hollace hadn't been back in town for a long time, maybe not even since he had left after high school.

So why was he here now? The photographs seemed to be part of the answer. Hollace had tried to scare Hazard into staying out of the events that were transpiring. And the shoot-out earlier that afternoon was another part of the answer: Hollace was involved, somehow, in the drug war. What did that mean? Hazard wasn't entirely sure, but he was starting to sketch the outline. Hollace must have been working with a drug dealer. With a cartel, more likely. And when they had decided to move in on the Ozark Volunteers' territory, Hollace had been the obvious choice—not just because he knew the town but also because he might be able to keep the cops off his back. He might be able to scare them. That must have been Hollace's reason for sending the pictures: to threaten Hazard into steering clear. Or was there something else? Why Jeff? Why those pictures, with their glimpses of a story that raised Hazard's hackles? Why the hint that there was more there, maybe a great deal more, than what Hazard thought he had known?

Hazard didn't have any answers. He also didn't have a car, and that pissed him off to no end. The Jetta had been running just fine. Sure, there had been a few times that it was slow to start, and a couple of weeks before, the transmission had made that really horrible noise, but on the whole, it was a fine car. A paid-off car. And it had character. Or, rather, it used to have character. Now it was a crumpled piece of metal that was probably already being dragged to a salvage yard.

At that point, Hazard knew he had options: he could call his insurance company; he could book a rental; he could check with Cravens about a temporary loan from the motor pool; he could even just go ahead and buy something, although he'd get a bitch of an interest rate and probably a shit-poor price if he went at it last minute like this.

Instead, though, he did none of those things. He dialed a number that he kept in his phone without Somers's knowledge.

This time, the call connected on the first ring. "What?"

"You heard he's in the hospital?"

"I heard it was a concussion." Glennworth Somerset's voice betrayed none of the concern a father might feel for his son, but Hazard had long since stopped expecting anything paternal from Glenn. "Has something changed?"

"No."

"Then why are you calling me?"

"I need a car."

"I'm not Hertz."

"I also need to talk to you."

"This may surprise you, Detective Hazard, but I don't need to talk to you. And I certainly don't want to talk to you. Good night."

"This is an important question. An in-person question. Traditionally, you're supposed to ask the father's blessing first."

In the call's background, electric feedback hissed for a few seconds, and then Glenn said, "You're joking."

"Fifteen minutes. Wahredua Regional's parking lot. Bring something you don't mind letting me use for a few days."

"Even if I agree to see you, you can't possibly believe I'll give you my blessing, not after—"

"Fifteen minutes, Glenn."

Hazard dropped the call, and he walked to the end of the parking lot, where one of the streetlights stuttered a cone of light and where the next fifteen yards of asphalt lay in darkness. Back here, someone had been drinking. Shards of glass pebbled the darkness, glinting like stars when the light stuttered, and amidst those stars, like flat and oblong nebulae, crushed beer cans marked someone's grief or celebration. Some of those cans were Bud Lite, which was what Somers drank—when he drank, now, which was less often— and it was those cans, it was those damn cans, that ripped off the bandage.

They had been in Hoffmeister's patrol car, and Somers had been lying on the back seat, and it was obvious that he was hurting, really hurting, and that he needed a doctor. But he wouldn't let go. He grabbed on to Hazard's arm and he wouldn't let go. No, Hazard thought with a shiver, even though the heat prickled under his arms and sweat pasted the cotton undershirt to his ribs. No, not his arm. Somers hadn't been clinging to Hazard's arm. He had been gripping his wrist.

And then he had said it. He had gone and motherfucking said it, the one thing Hazard had never wanted him to say, the one thing he had never wanted to hear. Somers had gone and talked about all of it: Mikey and the knife and holding Hazard's wrist and the helplessness and the cut and the blood and the smell of clay. Fuck him for that, Hazard wanted to shout. Fuck him for remembering that smell, the smell of the clay pits, smothering Hazard as he twisted and tried to pull free. Fuck him for remembering that, and fuck him for saying it, and fuck him for the worst of it, for pointing out that here they were all these years later, that nothing had really changed: Somers still had a hold on Hazard's wrist; Somers still ran the show; Somers was the one who could decide, today or tomorrow or whenever, that he was going to let go, and then it would be over, no matter what Hazard wanted.

With a low cry, Hazard kicked the biggest chunk of glass, and it jittered across the asphalt and kissed the curb, and when it rocked back, the light stuttered across it, and the torn paper S that was all that remained of the Smirnoff label stared right back at Hazard. S. S for Somers. And then he let out another of those low cries—just a breath, really, just a sharp exhalation of breath, so low that nobody in the world would ever hear it—and he kicked another piece of glass, and then a flattened can, and then another. He whammed them like hockey pucks, trying to catch that first, big chunk of glass, trying to flip it over or knock it into the darkness so that he wouldn't have to stare at that motherfucking S anymore.

First as tragedy, then as farce. And it had been tragedy, that first time. They had been kids. They had been scared, both of them—Hazard knew that about Somers, he understood it now in a way he hadn't understood twenty years before. It had been a tragedy because neither of them had been able to stop it. But this, whatever this was between them, the way it was heading—this was going to end the same way. It was like crashing into a bridge abutment at a hundred miles an hour, somehow dusting yourself off, and then doing it again. The first time, sure, it was really sad. The second time was a fucking joke, and that joke was on you.

He tried to slow down: his kicking, his breathing, his thinking. He tried to slow all of it down. But he kept letting out those low, sharp grunts, and his throat was raw from them, and he wanted to stop and he couldn't and that made it all worse.

The whole of it lasted five minutes, maybe, and when it ended, he stood with hands on knees, shaking, as though he'd just run a marathon. Then he combed back his hair, and he wiped his forehead and his cheeks and his nose, and he took long, controlled breaths and blew them back out again. That S, that motherfucking grinning piece of shit glass with the Smirnoff S, was still there, still staring back at him, and so Hazard moved away from it, following the asphalt, his knees threatening to buckle on every other step.

The car slid into the parking lot like something liquid. It was an Aston Martin DB5, which Hazard recognized from a pair of documentaries he had watched and—unfortunately—from that James Bond movie that Somers had made him see. When the car pulled up next to Hazard, the window went down, and Hazard found himself staring into all-too-familiar Somerset eyes. Tropical blue eyes. Cold, furious eyes.

Glenn Somerset wasn't his son, though, and age and injury had robbed him of whatever vitality he might have carried into middle age. Earlier that year, when Hazard had come face to face with Glenn for the first time since high school, Glenn Somerset had been a stout man, his dark hair quickly graying, his second chin wobbling when he turned his head too quickly. He had been the quintessentially successful WASP, with the body type to prove it. That same night, though, Glenn had been shot in the gut, and although he had survived, the wound had taken its toll. Tonight, in the stuttering glow of the sodium lamp, he looked feral and goblinish, his cheeks sunken, his eyes dug deep into his face, his flesh shriveled over his frame.

"I'll drive," Hazard said.

Glenn left the car idling and stepped out of the car, but he kept his body between Hazard and the door. "If you have any idea that you're going to ask my son to marry—"

"I absolutely am going to ask him," Hazard said. "Move."

"You're out of your mind. You're out of your damn mind. My son—"

"Is the best goddamn thing in the universe. I know. And if he's stupid enough to stay near me, I'm going to marry him. Move before I dump your ass on the ground and take the car."

"I won't allow it."

"He's thirty-five, you old bitch. You can't cut off his allowance anymore."

Hazard had seen hate plenty of times in his life, but what he saw in Glenn Somerset's blue eyes made him hesitate. It was a degree of fury approaching insanity, and Glenn tensed his shrunken, goblin body as though he might launch himself at Hazard and tear at his face.

"I don't think you have much to worry about, though," Hazard said, allowing an icy smirk to touch the corners of his mouth. "Your son isn't stupid, and it's just a matter of time before he figures it out."

Suspicion and—yes, there it was—hope damped the fire in Glenn's eyes. "Figures what out?"

"That nothing ever changes. Does it, Glenn?"

"Not a fucking thing."

"Then move."

They might have stayed that way for another minute or another twenty years, but then a group emerged from the hospital, laughing and talking, drunk with happiness and good cheer and maybe something out of the same bottles that had ended up in this back corner of the lot. The sound jolted Glenn, and he scurried around the car and dove into the passenger seat as though afraid Hazard might leave him.

Hazard shifted the Aston Martin into gear, letting it ease forward, testing it as though it were a wild thing at the end of a leash. The car had guts. Jesus, it had more than guts. It had a caged, ferocious intensity, and for a moment, Hazard forgot about everything except what it might feel like to open this car up, to let it off the leash, to hold the damned tiger by the tail and just see where the hell they ended up. He wasn't a car guy, not by any means, but Jesus damn.

"All right," he said, and it was more for himself than for Glenn. He punched the gas, and the Aston Martin leaped forward, streaking out into the night like a bead of water on glass.

"I absolutely will not—"

"Listen, we've got something more important going on. What do you know about all this?"

"You're very sloppy with your pronouns."

"You don't like my fucking pronouns? How about this: what do you know about Ted Kjar attempting to kill the mayor?"

"Nothing."

"What do you know about the shooting at the station yesterday?"

"Nothing."

"Your son is in a hospital bed—"

"We've discussed this. He has a concussion. He had one playing football. He'll be fine."

"He might not be. Whoever set this up, they wanted us there. They wanted us in that house when Kjar attacked the mayor. Not just me. Your son. At the very least, they wanted to ruin our careers. I'm guessing they wouldn't mind if a hell of a lot worse happened to us."

"What you've dragged my son—"

"Either you help me and you help your son, or you tell me, right now, that you really never gave a damn about him."

Instead of the Jetta's whining, clanking groans, the Aston Martin was almost silent. It was a whisper, less than a whisper, the sound of silk sliding over skin, a goddamn sexy sound as it stroked along Wahredua's streets. The car even smelled sexy, damn it: leather, and a hint of something else, something high-priced, maybe sandalwood.

"I was telling the truth," Glenn Somerset said, but his voice had taken on a new caution, as though he were picking rocks to cross a rushing river. "I don't know anything about what happened at the mayor's house. I also don't know anything about the shooting."

"But?"

"But I can make certain guesses. I can infer. I also—" He smiled, and on his wasted, kobold features, the effect was gruesome. "I also know something about history."

History, Hazard thought, his heart suddenly racing faster than the Aston Martin. Like Ted Kjar's book. Local history.

"All right. Let's hear it."

"No."

"What?"

"I want something from you. Quid pro quo, Detective."

"You want me to leave your son alone."

"God, if only such a thing were possible. I would be better off asking you to make him leave you alone, but I'm not even sure you could do that. My son seems blind to your more detrimental qualities."

"What do you want?"

"I want a favor."

"A favor? What is this, some sort of *Godfather* bullshit?"

"Well?"

"Fine. Let's hear your favor."

"I have your word?"

"Tell me the goddamn favor, already."

"No. I'll ask you in a minute. What do you know about InnovateMidwest, Detective?"

"What?" Hazard stared out the windshield, studying the dusk as they left the town behind them. Fields of weeds and wheatgrass and sedge spread around them, dotted here and there with wildflowers that had survived summer's heat. The last of the falling sun burned everything orange, and darkness was rushing in fast. "Nothing. I mean, not much. It's nominally a real estate investment firm, or something along those lines. They buy up property. In theory they're going to flip it, some bullshit about urban renewal, but I've noticed that they usually do nothing. Usually, they let the vacant properties drag down real estate values and then buy up the surrounding lots, and on and on."

"More or less true. They have some larger projects in mind. Subdivisions. A country club with a golf course. That little dry run they call Cairndow. He changed the name of that place so many times, Scottish names, English names, country club names, and it turned a profit every time. Maybe even a water park. Did you know I'm an investor?"

"I guessed."

"And did you know that InnovateMidwest has turned a profit every year since it was founded in 1995?"

"You say that like it's a bad thing."

"Oh no, Detective. It's a very good thing. I appreciate a solid investment, and InnovateMidwest has been exactly that: solid. Unshakably solid."

"I don't—"

"You know, most new businesses operate at a loss for their first few years. Some operate at a loss for much longer."

"But an investment firm couldn't do that."

"Not for that long, no. But especially in the first few years, acquiring property and infrastructure, it would be understandable. In fact, it would be expected."

Ahead, Hazard spotted the turn for the Somerset house, which sat off on its own, a private island of wealth and privilege. He slowed the Aston Martin, but his thoughts kept racing. "But they turned a profit."

"Every year. Every single year."

"How?"

"That's an excellent question, Detective. One that I never cared to ask. Do you know why?"

"Because you didn't want to know the answer."

"Exactly. I learned that lesson very young. I only ask questions that I want an answer to, and I didn't care where the money was coming from, only that the investment was, as I said, solid."

"But you have an idea."

"I do."

"And you're going to tell me."

"Why don't you tell me, Detective?"

"Some more of that quid pro quo?"

"If you like."

Hazard turned onto the private road that led back to the Somerset house; the Aston Martin glided onto the blacktop, still smooth as silk. "Somers and I are convinced that there's drug money behind this. In fact, there might even be a drug war. We thought the Ozark Volunteers were the ones cooking and moving product. What you're suggesting, though, is that InnovateMidwest is a front for drug money?"

"You can do better than that, Detective. My son thinks you're very smart."

"Fuck you."

"You're being reductive."

"Fuck—" Then it hit. "Fuck me. You mean it's the Ozark Volunteers and InnovateMidwest? They're both part of it?"

"Why not?"

Why not? That was an excellent question. InnovateMidwest was an excellent way to launder money: it would have been relatively easy to fabricate rental agreements on unused or underused properties and then to funnel the cash in as profit. It would also explain, from the firm's earliest years, its sustained growth and success. The local cops and deputies would be relatively easy to control, as Lender had proven, and if drug enforcement agencies started sniffing around, the Ozark Volunteers were the ones taking the risk of cooking and moving the product. And then Hazard thought of Jo Kjar telling them that her husband had been doing accounting work at home, and he thought of Ted Kjar winning a local accounting professionals' award, and he thought maybe Ted Kjar had been a little too good at his job and started asking questions. That still didn't explain why Ted had attacked the mayor, but it seemed to be part of the puzzle.

"We're in the goddamn middle of a goddamn drug war," Hazard said, for a moment forgetting Glenn Somerset's presence.

"What makes you say that?"

Shaking himself, shaking off the trance of logic and analysis, Hazard said, "Today, we got caught in a shootout. I'm guessing somebody is trying to move in on this territory. They're going to take out the producers, but they're also going to take out the mayor, because he's supporting them, and anybody else they think is in their way."

"Possibly." Glenn said the word so clinically, with such a lack of interest, that his disagreement was obvious.

"What do you think is happening?"

"What have you done since arriving in Wahredua, Detective?"

"What do you mean?"

"What have you accomplished?"

"If this is something about me queering your son, ask him sometime about his college days."

A sneer tucked up the corner of Glenn's mouth. "You're always so crude. You're always on the attack. Consider my question and answer it appropriately."

Perhaps a hundred yards farther down the blacktop, the Somerset home rose, a sprawl of shadow as the last daylight ended. There were no lights on, not anywhere, and for a moment, Hazard could see the house empty and abandoned, rotting from the inside out, like the Bordello he remembered from childhood.

"I've done my job. I've put away murderers. I've also done a lot I never realized was detective work, like answering that call when Elaine Dupre fell down her steps, or investigating competing allegations about goat-rape, or trying to deduce which kid is dumping in the public sandbox. Real Sherlock Holmes-level stuff."

Glenn's mouth was still tucked up in its sneer. "You have destabilized, over the last nine months, various forms of regional power that have held sway for thirty years. You removed an important local detective. You exposed the sheriff's son as an incestuous rapist and murderer. That, in turn, led to the sheriff's murder, and your investigation revealed a cabal of prominent citizens with dark secrets of their own. You even—" A smile ghosted over those gremlin features. "—solved the murder of Jesus Christ. And what do you think you've accomplished?"

"Judging by how frequently people get killed around here? Not much."

"You have weakened the mayor. You have deprived him of important local support, and you have forced him to use up valuable resources—both tangible and otherwise—to deal with the fallout of your investigations. You have made him vulnerable. Just as you did with the sheriff. And what happens, Detective, when the oppressed suddenly realize that the tyrant is not invulnerable?"

"They rise up," Hazard said, thinking of Sheriff Bingham lying on the sand, the top of his head taken off by a high-powered rifle. "You're saying this is exclusively about the mayor?" He took a breath, slowing the Aston Martin as they approached the wrought-iron gates at the edge of the Somerset property. "And that means what I saw today, that skirmish at the Yorgenson trailers, that wasn't about a new group moving in on this territory."

"What if I were to tell you that I personally witnessed a confrontation between Mayor Newton and someone you and my son know very well? Naomi Malsho is a formidable woman, and based on the argument I witnessed at Big Biscuit, she and the mayor have reached an end to civil discourse."

"What happened? What did she say?"

"I don't know. I wasn't invited to sit with them. Whatever influence or position I had, your work in this town has put an end to that. I just happened to be sitting in the diner when they were there. Purest coincidence."

"And you didn't hear anything?"

"No, nothing specific. Although if I were the mayor, and if Naomi Malsho had looked at me the way she was looking at him, I would have bought a new life insurance policy."

"You're suggesting that Naomi Malsho isn't content with whatever arrangement she had with the mayor."

Glenn peered out the window into the fields of darkened indiangrass. His reflection in the passenger window was ghastly, hollowed out by the glass into something from a nightmare. He caught Hazard's eyes in the reflection and grinned, and that smile looked so much like Somers's, so much like the smile Somers wore when he knew something Hazard didn't, that Hazard whipped his head back forward and focused on the keeping the car on the road. "I think," Glenn said, "that Naomi has always been ambitious, and she has a habit of capitalizing on the weaknesses of others. She didn't make it to the top of the Ozark Volunteers by batting her eyelashes."

"So a faction of the Ozark Volunteers has decided that maybe they're tired of taking all the risk and letting the mayor get fat. Maybe they're going to keep the money and take him out of the picture. And they're killing whoever doesn't go along with them." Hazard frowned. "But the white truck was at the Yorgenson trailers. So that means the Yorgenson group was trying to kill the mayor, and the group that attacked were, what? Loyalists?"

"Redcoats," Glenn said drily.

It was a troubling theory, and more troubling because it had the ring of truth. Hazard knew Naomi Malsho, the de facto leader of the Ozark Volunteers, and she was as ruthless and intelligent as Glenn claimed. She wasn't the type to sit back, take the risks, and let somebody else profit. And she wasn't above murder; she had engineered convenient deaths before. But it didn't explain Hollace. And Hazard forced himself to remember that Glenn Somerset didn't know everything. He might even be wrong.

Hazard pulled to a stop at the gates. Glenn gave him the code, and Hazard punched it into the box, and the gates rattled open. The Aston Martin glided to the front steps, and they stopped, and only the purr of the engine was between them now.

Glenn Somerset popped open the door and sat there, his ravaged features fixed on Hazard.

"Well? Ask your damn favor."

"Were you serious, earlier?"

"I said I'd do it, so just tell me what it is."

"No. What you said about my son."

"Yes. I meant it. If he's still around, I'm going to—"

"No, the rest of it."

Hazard heard his own words, louder than the Aston Martin's gentle rumble. *He's the best goddamn thing in the universe.* "Yes."

"If you really believe that, then here's the favor I want: think about this. Think very carefully about who you are and what you are, Detective Hazard. I'm not talking about your sexuality. I'm talking about you. Think about that, and then consider whether you're the kind of person my son deserves to spend the rest of his life with."

Hazard's wrapped around the steering wheel. The tips of his fingers buzzed with trapped blood.

"Detective?"

"All right."

"You understand—"

"Goddamn perfectly. Get out."

Glenn Somerset left, then, and he shut the door quietly, and he stood there, inches from the Aston Martin, watching. Hazard knew what the man was waiting for, and he didn't want to give it to him, but that buzzing in his fingertips had spread, and it had taken up residence inside his head, and so he punched the gas and shifted and the Aston Martin squealed and raked sideways and then spun forward with the stink of burnt rubber. He shot through the gates without even considering whether or not they were still open, and then he was flying, really flying, the Aston Martin off its leash now, skidding as he turned onto the state highway, the tires shrilling again in protest.

Consider whether you're the kind of person my son deserves to spend the rest of his life with.

Deserve? No, Somers didn't deserve that. Hell, nobody deserved that. But—

The kind of person my son deserves.

Then the buzzing had made its way from his fingertips to his head to his heart, and Hazard had to fight to keep the road in focus ahead of him. He had to fight, too, to turn his thoughts somewhere else. Outside, night had fallen, and the world came to him like slides passing through a projector: measured strips of asphalt and yellow paint; the sandy flutter of a nightjar suspended in the headlights; the liquid gleam of eyes at the side of the road. A deer perhaps. The smell of the car, the rich leathery smell, overpowered him now, and he felt sick. He needed fresh air, but when he rolled down the window, all he smelled was shit, and so he rolled it back up and drove another ten miles until he was clear of the mink farm on this side of the city.

Through these carefully spliced moments, he drove to Smithfield. His hands knew where he was going before his head knew, and when his head knew, he groaned. He was going to the Bordello. And a strange fear suddenly gripped Hazard, a fear of Hollace Walker, and it had nothing to do with drugs or murder or the mayor. It had to do with the past, as though Hollace were trapped in one of those pieces of Victorian fiction where a long-forgotten figure returns to reveal a terrible secret. And Hazard didn't know what the secret was, didn't know what it could be. He only knew that it was there, inside him, alongside the memory of Hollace telling him, *You either burn or you get burned*, alongside the memory of Mary Heintzelman in the cafeteria repeating Hollace's words after he fell:

Did they see? And whatever this secret was, it would reveal the truth about Emery Hazard, that ultimate, final truth that he had tried so hard to ignore, the truth that Glenn Somerset had dragged into the cool glow of the Aston Martin's interior lighting.

Hazard was so lost in those thoughts that he barely noticed the sunset happening ahead of him, a dusty red above the roofs of Smithfield. His route took him past the Haverford, where blue plastic tarps covered the ruined façade and a sign read *Condemned No Trespassing*, and it wasn't until he turned two blocks north of the Bordello that he realized the time, and that the sun had already set, and that he wasn't seeing a haze of light reflected in pollutants along the horizon. He was seeing the Bordello. It was on fire.

CHAPTER TWENTY-THREE

JULY 3
TUESDAY
7:51 PM

IN THE HOSPITAL ROOM, Somers's first instinct was to reach for his gun, but it was gone. His eyes met Mikey's, and then he lunged for the call button. Mikey was faster. Even hollowed out by methamphetamines, Mikey was still faster. They grappled for a moment, the plastic casing slick in Somers's hands, and then Mikey reared back and punched Somers.

The punch, all on its own, was decent. It cracked Somers's head back, and half his vision clouded with stars. But it wasn't some kind of wonder knock-out punch. No, what got Somers was the headache, which came ringing back as soon as the blow landed. It was like snowglare, that shearingly white pain, and he lost his grip on the call button and he lost his grip on the bed frame and he came within an inch of losing his grip on his stomach. For the next minute, all he could do was breathe.

But breathing turned his stomach too. Every lungful brought that sour sweat smell, like Mikey hadn't showered in days and his clothes were stiff as cardboard, and every breath brought the decomposing stench of those brown stubs in his mouth. The only thing that kept Somers from sicking up in a plastic bin was the chewing tobacco smell; it was harsh, but not unpleasant. Maybe Mikey knew this because when he sat in the chair that Hazard had left only minutes before, he broke off a plug of chew and went to work on it.

"Don't yell. Something really bad's going to happen if you yell."

Massaging his eye—it would be black and blue, and Jesus, Hazard was going to ask questions—Somers studied the man in front of him. The worst of the pain drew back, and Somers tried to take in the details. The last he had seen, Mikey had been working a pitching game at the county fair. He'd gotten in a fight with Hazard. He'd set to work saying all the things he'd used to say in high school, and he'd added some new ones. But he'd just been . . . Mikey. Pathetic, really. Aggravating, yes. A hate-filled sack of shit, yes. But pathetic. Just a shell of a human being, really, excavated by drug use and addiction and hard living.

"You just hit an officer of the law, Mikey. That's a class B felony, and it's got mandatory—"

Somers saw the second punch coming; Mikey only threw from his shoulder, and he telegraphed it as clear as day. He knocked the punch aside. Mikey got up then. He pushed back the lank, straw-colored hair, shook out a shower of dandruff, and puckered his mouth into an ugly little anus. Then he swung again. This one, too, was all shoulder, and it was basically written in skywriting letters, but Somers was in a hospital bed, and his head was killing him, and Mikey just kept swinging. Some of the blows landed, and they rocked him hard enough that Mikey was able to close, grab a handful of Somers's short hair, and pin him to the mattress. Then he opened his mouth and hocked a brown loogie in Somers's face.

The slime and snot and spit and chewing tobacco was warm on the bridge of Somers's nose, spattered across his eye, and up to his hairline. It was particulate too—grainy with the flecks of tobacco that Mikey was working on.

"Don't yell," Mikey said again, ripping hard at Somers's hair. "And don't wipe that off."

Somers opened his mouth, but Mikey tore at his hair hard again.

"Don't yell, you stupid little pussy, or something bad's going to happen to your little girl. Nod so I know you understand me."

Evie.

The thought was paralyzing, and Mikey gave another vicious jerk to Somers's hair, this time ripping out a chunk. Somers felt the blood warm on his scalp, and he felt the eye-watering pain, but all of that might be happening to someone else. He could only think about Evie.

"What—"

The slap, when it came, was hard but casual. The way some old bastard might smack a dog's nose with a newspaper. "You talk when I want you to talk." Mikey's breathing had quickened. His sallow features flushed now, and those dead-dog eyes brightened. They weren't alive. Jesus Christ, not even close to alive. But they were bright like Venus in the motherfucking sky.

"I like you like this," Mikey said, loosing his grip, studying Somers's face. Then he looked at his hand, where blood pasted blond hair to his fingers. "I like my spit on your face. I'm going to like it when I cum on your face. I'm going to like it when your blood and my cum and my spit, when that's the only thing you're wearing. I'm going to like it so much I might even give you a bath with a second load. And then I'll send that picture to your boyfriend."

Evie. Focus on Evie. Did this bastard have her? Had he already hurt her? Somers fought the rising panic. No, no. He had said something bad would happen. Not that it had already happened. Oh fuck that was a sophistical shit argument, the whole thing based on Mikey's tenuous grasp of grammar.

"Yeah. If I'd known back in high school you had a pussy between your legs, I wouldn't have wasted my time going after Emery Hazard. I would have done you like we did Jeff, all of us taking turns, using that boy's holes the way he always wanted them to be used. I would have done worse to you. I hated you. Did you ever have any fucking idea how much I hated you?"

"Not we. You. You did that to Jeff."

Another slap, and Somers thought he felt a tooth loose in his jaw.

"I hated you so fucking much." Mikey considered him for a minute, and then he hocked up another loogie and leaned over Somers and he let the spit and tobacco drop, hang, suspended by a long line of spittle, before it smacked, hot and wet, against Somers's mouth. "Don't wipe it off."

Somers was shaking. He'd never known a feeling like this. Never, in his entire life, had he known anything close. Hatred, yes. So much hatred it was like an ocean behind a boy's twig dam. But that wasn't the worst of it. The worst was—

—the warm, rotting tobacco taste on his lips, and the smell of Mikey's spit, and the violation of it all—

—the knowledge that he was helpless. John-Henry Somerset, rich boy, golden boy, detective, was helpless.

For now. For this motherfucking moment. And as soon as Evie was safe—

"You always thought you were better than me. I knew it. Everybody knew it. Everybody wondered why a pretty rich boy hung out with Mikey Grames. I wondered about it. I figured you were doing it to make your daddy angry. Or you were doing it because you were really one sick son of a bitch. But you weren't doing it because you liked me; even I knew that much." Mikey settled back into the seat. His voice turned contemplative. "I guess everybody's got it pretty much figured out now, though. You were desperate for somebody to plug that hole between your legs, and you were terrified somebody would find out you were a cock-hungry whore, so you did whatever you could to hide yourself. How am I doing? You can answer me."

Somers raised an arm to wipe the loogie from his lips, and Mikey clucked and shook his head. Grimacing—he could taste him, he could taste this motherfucker, taste his snot and his spit—Somers dropped his arm and said, "You're right."

"Really? That's kind of a shame. That's the story all you faggots want to hear, isn't it? That anybody who was mean to you, anybody that ever said boo, they were just cock-hungry too, and too afraid to show it. Isn't that right? I bet you've thought that about me sometimes. I bet you've thought maybe I was just a scared little faggot. How am I doing?"

No, Somers wanted to say. No, he'd never thought Mikey was gay. He'd thought Mikey was insane. He'd thought Mikey was a psychopath, even as a kid, and he'd thought the world would be a better place if somebody took Mikey behind a barn and put a bullet between his eyes. What he said, though, was, "You sound like you really enjoyed getting your dick inside Jeff."

That got to him. Color rushed into Mikey's face, and he sprang out of the chair and landed three hard slaps: one-two-three. There was nothing controlled about him now; he looked like he'd lost his shit and didn't have an icicle's chance in hell of finding it.

"You are such a fucking faggot," he said, breathing heavily now, the tooth-rot like a brown cloud between them. "You're such a little bitch, and you say bitchy little things. The kind of things that send a real clear message to the world. The kind of things that tell people you need a man in charge of you. You need a man in your mouth, in your pussy, and then back in your mouth again. You need a man because you're a little faggot bitch with no self-control." His pupils had exploded now, and his breath whistled through the words. "If I didn't have a job to do—" He wrestled with that; the struggle of it was obvious in his face, and Somers realized that he was on the edge of something very much like what had happened to Jeff Langham all those years ago. One wrong move, one wrong word, and whatever self-control Mikey still had would snap, and they would fight, and one of them would die, and Evie might be the one who paid the price.

So Somers did what he was best at: he read the room, he read Mikey, and he gave the sick son of a bitch what he wanted. Somers dropped his head, tucked his shoulders, and curled arms and legs inwards. If he'd had a tail, he would have tucked it between his legs, but other than that he sent just about every submissive sign he knew, and he prayed that it wouldn't be exactly what sent Mikey over the edge. He guessed, though, that it wouldn't. He had known Mikey for a long time, and he knew how Mikey worked. Mikey had hated Hazard. He had gone after Hazard—

—the knife, the blood, the flexing tension in Hazard's wrist as he struggled—

—but Hazard had always taken it. Quietly. Furiously. But he had taken it. Jeff, though. Jeff had talked back. And he had talked back. And he had started giving it back. And that meant, in Mikey's world, that Jeff was a little faggot bitch who needed a man in charge of him, and that had ended with Jeff putting a shotgun between his teeth.

How much time passed, Somers never knew. It felt like an eternity, but only in the moment. Afterward, it was hard to recall if it had lasted ten seconds or twenty or maybe just one or two. Then Mikey made a strangled noise, and his hands clutched at the chrome bed rail, and Somers realized it was killing Mikey, almost literally, not to do what he wanted to do. And that, in some ways, was more terrifying than anything else because Somers had no idea what—or who—could exert that kind of control over Mikey.

Then the strangling noise cut off, and Mikey delivered another of those cold slaps, and he dropped back into the chair.

"Maybe there's some hope for you," he said, but his breath was still whistling, and red still cut deep vees into his cheeks. "Maybe I could keep a pussy like you around." He tossed something onto the bed. "Look at it."

Somers retrieved the phone. It wasn't Mikey's—or, better said, Mikey had never had the money for a phone like this, the most recent model, probably a thousand dollars easily. Someone had given this to him. And on the screen, a video waited. Somers thumbed the play icon.

There was sound, and somehow that made it worse: the squeak of the merry-go-round, Evie's high, excited laughter, her repeated cries of "Go, go, go," the rumble of a big Dodge Ram rolling up the side street. The sound made it real. The video was simple. Straightforward. Innocent, almost, except that it wasn't innocent at all. Somers forced himself to think: the video had been taken recently. He could tell because there were Fourth of July decorations in the windows of Evie's preschool. And it had been taken in the morning; the shadows told him that much. But Monday morning, Somers had taken Evie to the fair with Hazard. That seemed a hundred years ago, but it had only been yesterday. So this was—from today? From this morning?

"Do you understand? Or do I need to give you a lesson?"

"Where is she?"

"Well, God bless, you gaping raw pussy. She's with her mom. You remember? That woman you weren't man enough for? You couldn't get your little cock to do anything for her, so she left you for a real man? And before you get any ideas, there's somebody there, somebody waiting right outside. Just to make sure you don't do anything stupid." Mikey laughed, and another wave of that rotting stink crested. "You know, I never would have thought of this if not for that fuck-up a few months ago. Remember that guy? The one that got into your place and cut up your pussy boy because he was trying to get to your daughter?"

Somers barely heard him, barely heard the reference to Rex Kolosik. His heartbeat took up his whole body. He remembered Edgar Allen Poe. He had read Poe, hadn't he, in high school? Or maybe in college. Definitely in college because ignorant fucks in high school didn't read Poe, and Somers was being painfully reminded of exactly the kind of ignorant fuck he'd been in high school. So he'd read Poe in college. And he remembered the story, the one about the heart. The beating heart. And that's the kind of heartbeat Somers felt, that kind right there, the kind that could move the floor, the kind that could shake him to pieces. Hell, it could shake the whole building to pieces.

"Do you understand?"

Think. Think. He had to think. He had to think quickly because all of this was spiraling out of control. Mikey had someone watching Cora's house. That meant Mikey was working with someone. And that meant, Somers guessed, that it wasn't Mikey calling the shots. Mikey was mean. And he had a peculiarly insightful cunning, a type of cunning that helped him see the weak spots in any armor. But he wasn't smart, not the kind of smart to plan this—this shit, whatever it was.

Somers swiped at the screen and pulled up the contacts. They were blank. Of course.

"What the fuck do you think you're doing?"

"Putting my phone number here. My personal number." And he did, but as he tapped the numbers, he turned the phone away from Mikey by degrees. "Whatever you want, I'll give it to you. If you want money, Mikey, I've got money. My father's got money. I can get you some tonight, I can get you whatever you want."

He saw, on Mikey's face, the effect of his words. Those sallow, decimated features relaxed, and the harsh red lines in his cheeks eased. Mikey liked this behavior. He liked fawning and groveling and begging. It was probably close to mainlining for a son of a bitch like him, and Somers intended to give him exactly what he wanted.

So he groveled. He kept talking as he tapped at the screen, barely hearing the words coming out of his mouth as he dismissed the contacts and opened the phone's settings. Please, he was thinking—and he was saying it, too, "Please don't hurt her, please, I'll do whatever you want," but inside he was thinking, *Please, please be the idiot, the royal fucking idiot I know you are, please.* General setting. Location. Advanced. Location sharing. Toggle to ON. And there it was, proof that Mikey was a fucking idiot so royal he should have had a crown: no password protection. The toggled slid to ON. Then Somers tapped share with contacts. Toggle to ON. Choose a contact. Yes, there was only one. One fucking contact in the whole phone. Tap, tap, tap. And done.

Somers couldn't let himself sigh. He couldn't let himself breathe out in relief, or sag against the mattress, or close his eyes. Part of that was because he couldn't give Mikey any sign that he'd accomplished what he wanted. But part of it was that he didn't feel relief. Not even a trace of it. Getting the phone's location was a step towards a solution, but it was one step, and a hell of a lot could still go wrong.

"For the fucking love of Christ," Mikey said, grinning now, and it was so ugly on him, that fucking smile, so ugly the way his lips were scabbed and picked and split and chapped, drawn back over the rotten stumps of teeth, that Somers felt sick again. "You really are a pussy, aren't you? The way people talk, you're supposed to be a big shit. You're supposed to be a man. They're wrong, aren't they?"

Somers turned the phone, holding it out to him, but Mikey ignored it.

"I asked you a question."

Down the hall, a woman laughed, and the sound was so sudden and so genuinely pleasant that it sounded horrendous. Then casters squealed along the linoleum outside the door, and a man said something in a gruff voice, and the woman pealed laughter again, and the casters squeaked away from Somers's room.

Another of those cold, disciplinary slaps. "I asked you something."

"Yes."

"Yes, what?"

"Yes, they're wrong."

"You're not a man."

"No."

"What are you?" His lips, picked down to raw patches of shiny red skin, puckered like an anus again.

"I'm a faggot."

"You already knew you were a faggot. What did I teach you tonight?"

"I'm a pussy faggot bitch."

"And what do you need?"

The urge to cry came so suddenly and so painfully that Somers couldn't quite believe it. It wasn't any one thing: it wasn't the things Somers was being forced to say, it wasn't the pain in his head or the aftereffects of Mikey's blows, it wasn't even, not entirely, Evie. Part of it had to do with memory. Part of it had to do with that specific memory, with the smell of the clay pits, with the feel of Hazard's wrist turning in Somers's grip, with the rigid lines of tendon and bone flexing against Somers's palm. He had done this, Somers knew. He had done this to the person he loved the most in the whole world. He had done this thing, and he could never undo it, and that was why he wanted to cry.

First as tragedy.

He didn't cry; that was a close call, but it was important because Somers knew it could have launched Mikey in a dangerous new direction. "I need a real man in charge of me."

"You do. And you need a real cock in that hole. In both your holes."

Somers could still smell the clay like it was there, in the room, instead of all those years in the past.

"Say it."

"I do. I need a real cock in both my holes."

"I should have known what kind of pussy-boy you'd be," Mikey said, rising and collecting the phone. "I'm going to tell you three things, and I want you to understand them, and if you do, you might live long enough to find somebody that can plug you really well and keep a stray bitch like you in line. The first thing is that you're going to turn everything you've got on Kjar over to me. All of it. You're going to forget about that old, fat bitch who thinks she's in charge. You're going to run everything past me first. And then you're going to bring back whatever you get. That's the end of it. Do you understand that?"

"Yes."

"Good. The second: your little girl is on the line until our business is done. If you think you're smarter than me, you go ahead and try to move her or hide her or send her away. But if she's not with her mom or at preschool, I'm going to assume you're not following through on our deal, and I'll take steps. I want you to know something: I won't kill her. That's stupid. You know how much a little girl that age, a little white girl, you know how much she would go for? The things they do to those kids, well, I figure you don't want that happening to your little girl. Now, do you understand that?"

"Yes," Somers said, and his jaw cracked.

"I want you to listen really carefully to this part. You can still have a life, or as much as a life as a pussy-faggot like you can have. You can have your little girl. You can even stay here, and you can play at being a detective, and you can get that pension down the line. But you've got to make a choice."

And suddenly the earthy, iron-tang smell of the clay was so strong, so present, that Somers thought the floor had opened up, that one of those shadow-clogged pits had caved open beneath his bed. He knew what Mikey was going to say because he'd been thinking it himself all those years ago.

"It's him or you," Mikey said. "I'm going to call you." He wagged the phone. "I'm going to give you a place and a time. And you're going to make sure he's there. If he's not, well, we're going to find out how much that little cutie of yours can bring on the open market. Do you understand me?"

Somers reached for the brushed-chrome rail. He didn't know what he was going to do, but he knew he needed to be on his feet. The punch came faster than he expected, and this time both his eyes cascaded with stars, and he had to fight not to slip into the darkness between those drifting points of light.

"Do you understand?"

"Yeah."

"Don't get stupid on me. You almost got stupid. You wouldn't want me to do anything to that little girl. I know you wouldn't." He paused, as though considering something. "You ever wonder why we've never had DEA down here? You ever wonder why the FBI doesn't poke their nose in? You ever think about that? Because I think you should. I think you should turn that over really carefully before you make any phone calls you might regret."

Shaking the stars from his vision, Somers managed to sit again, and he cleared his eyes well enough to lock onto Mikey's face. He knew, then, what he was going to do to Mikey. He was going to hit him the same way Mikey had been hitting Somers. He was going to hit him and hit him and hit him. He was going to wear gloves so his hands would last longer, and he was going to keep hitting until there wasn't enough left of Mikey's face to fill a crack pipe.

"Don't get that look," Mikey said with a laugh. "I'm doing you a favor. You can still have a life, right? And tell you what, I'll throw in something extra for old times' sake. When he's out of the picture, if you start feeling an itch down in your puss, just give me a call. I'll slap on some contacts and come right over. I'll fuck you from behind, and when you look back and stare into my eyes, you might even think it's him again. For a gaping cunt like you, that's as big a favor as you can get." Mikey waited, and as the surreal moment dragged on, Somers realized he was waiting for a thank you. Disgust in his face, Mikey shook his head and said, "Keep your phone on; I want to wrap this up tonight."

CHAPTER TWENTY-FOUR

JULY 3
TUESDAY
8:20 PM

IN FRONT OF EMERY HAZARD, the Bordello was burning. The crumbling Victorian ruin blazed up towards the sky. It might have been a funeral pyre for the old matron. The flames licked and leaped along the wood, tonguing the gingerbread finishes and the scrollwork, and already Hazard had seen two gouts of fire shoot up from the roof. The whole building was lost; that much was obvious. It was also obvious, to Hazard at least, that someone had made sure the building would be lost. Someone had used plenty of accelerant just in case; the odor of gasoline still hung in the air, mixing with the billowing smoke. He thought for a moment of Lady Mabbe, whom he had met inside the Bordello nine months ago, and he felt a pang of loss. He hoped she hadn't been inside.

    He had parked the Aston Martin and left the vehicle at the curb with the half-formed plan of entering the building to see if Hollace was still inside. The heat, however, beat him back, and even on the opposite curb, the intensity of the fire left the air thin and hard to breathe. Having called the fire in, now all Hazard could do was watch.

    Watch, yes. And think. Because Hazard knew that he had been right. He didn't have any proof. He didn't have any evidence. Logic and analysis were useless. But his gut told him he was right: Hollace had been here. And someone else had been looking for Hollace. Someone else had figured it out first. Who?

The first possibility, he thought as he retreated behind the Aston Martin's body, his hair stirring in the fire-stoked wind, was the Ozark Volunteers. Enraged by the attack on their territory, they might have struck back.

The second possibility was one that Hazard liked even less, although he had to acknowledge it. This was the possibility that Hollace himself had set the fire. The only motivation Hazard could think of was that Hollace was intending to fake his own death, but that only postponed the question: why? To trick Hazard into believing he was dead? Or to trick someone else—someone he was trying to hide from? Did he want Hazard as a witness, corroborating the fiction of Hollace's death by placing Hazard at the scene of the fire? That seemed unlikely; Hollace couldn't have predicted that Hazard would be here.

The third possibility was that the mayor had somehow managed this. Hazard didn't think the old man was conscious, let alone capable of ordering a hit, but he couldn't rule it out completely.

From the curb, Hazard ran through his thoughts one last time and made a decision: he needed more information. Situated on Smithfield's edge, only a few blocks from where Mississippi divided the failing neighborhood from its more prosperous surroundings, the Bordello was a landmark not simply because of its notorious history as Wahredua's only ever publicly acknowledged brothel but also as a site for street prostitution well into the present. As Hazard glanced up and down the cross streets, though, he saw sun-thinned plastic bags and trampled receipts and what looked like a sanitary napkin and a gutted Adidas running shoe with the sole slipping out a long gash on its side. He saw brick row-houses with slumping porches, an abandoned lot wrapped in wire fencing, windows broken from the inside so their glass fell in constellations on the street. He saw a sodium lamp on its side, still flickering feebly through some miracle of engineering. But he didn't see a single goddamn hooker.

They might have cleared out because of the fire and because they expected, rightly, that law enforcement would eventually arrive with the fire department. But this was Smithfield, and neither the fire department nor the police would be rapid in their response. That wasn't a fact that Hazard liked, but it was a fact nonetheless. Besides that, though, was a simpler, more elemental fact: streetwalkers, just like everybody else, were human. And most people liked to see a fire, especially a roof-leaper like this one.

So where had they gone? There should have been at least a few of them clustered together, watching and talking and pointing. But the street was empty. Not a cat. Not a dog. Not even a rat, and some days Hazard guessed there were more rats than people in Smithfield. The fire hissed and snapped, and then somewhere inside the Bordello a joist snapped and the building groaned and sagged, and fire jetted up at the stars. But Hazard might as well have been standing on the moon for all the company he had. A shiver tingled between his shoulder blades.

All right, so the ladies had already cleared out. And they either cleared out because they were scared—gunshots, maybe—or because someone told them to—a pimp, or someone else, someone they feared enough to obey. If it had been gunshots, that was something Hazard needed to know. And if they had been told—well, that was something Hazard needed to know too. With a groan, he checked the .38 under his arm, gave the cross streets one last glance, and started walking.

He went deeper into Smithfield, away from the Bordello and Mississippi Street and the old oak where, frightened to death, a young Emery Hazard had once climbed and hidden with the boy Hollace Walker. Deeper into Smithfield was the only direction that made sense. If he headed towards Mississippi, he'd only end up walking out of Smithfield, and he was sure the street girls hadn't gone that direction. Following the other road, the one that ran at right angles to the Bordello, would have carried Hazard along Smithfield's border, keeping parallel with Mississippi Street's dividing line. While one or two of the girls might have gone that way, Hazard doubted most of them had. Human instinct, when you were afraid, was to get somewhere safe. Safe, yes, but they would still need to work too. Police and fire would stick as close to Smithfield's periphery as possible, so there was a decent chance the blocks closest to the border would see cop traffic, and the girls wouldn't want to work there. He put Mississippi at his back and went into the dark warren.

There were no stars. It took him time to realize that, almost a full block, and then he saw the gauzy light of the sodium lamps burning through the haze and realized why there weren't any stars: the Bordello's smoke hung a pall over the night. And there were no lights in the windows. He had been in Smithfield before, but few times at night, and the difference could be measured in the windows. If people lived in the buildings surrounding Hazard, they intended to give no sign of it. Once he caught the lightspeed-warp glow of a television, but otherwise, the windows gave back nothing. Either the people living here had hung heavy blackout curtains, or they had learned to go to bed with the sun. Ten blocks south of here, warm yellow light would be blazing, turning windows into shadow-shows of life. Here, though, there was only the dead window-faces, and the taste of electrical wire burning, and the charcoal-dust glow of the sodium lamps in the smoke.

Two blocks further, on the steps of a river-stone church with tarnished brass lettering that read Emmanuel Lutheran and, hanging in the front door, a smaller sign that read Please Join Us for Worship at Our New Location, Hazard found the first girl. She was Hispanic, she was a bottle blonde, and she was so young she probably still couldn't even go to the prom. When she saw Hazard, she smiled, but it had about as much feeling in it as if she'd peeled it off a tube of Crest. She kept smiling as he approached, and then Hazard realized she was too young to make him for a cop. She'd figure it out. Probably before the end of the month, she'd know goddamn well. And that was worse than all the rest of it, even worse than thinking about the fact that she was never going to have some pimply boy feel her up at the prom.

"Hey," she said, rolling her shoulder awkwardly. She wore a cropped top and a mini-skirt, and she was showing enough breast and leg to start a riot inside Emmanuel Lutheran.

"Evening."

"You're cute," she said, giggling into her hand. "Fifty dollars. Twenty for a blow job."

"Twenty dollars?"

"Well, yeah."

"Last time it was twenty cents," Hazard said, thinking of all those years ago and the woman with the purple leotard pinched between her legs.

"No way. Nobody blows for twenty cents."

"Maybe it was a charity case."

"You talk really funny." She drew herself up, crossing her arms over her breast, and her brown eyes took him in again. "And you don't even look at my tits."

"My boyfriend would be angry if I did."

"Your—well, what do you want? I'm not one of those, I mean I don't have a—" She made a fumbling gesture at the front of her skirt.

"I want to ask you—"

"Oh no." The voice was loud and angry and it carried half a block as easily as it might have carried half a mile. "Oh no you don't. Leave that child alone."

The woman coming up the street had the same peroxide-blond hair as the girl, but she also had an enormous feather boa, a rhinestone-studded bustier, and a pair of leather panties that bit deeply into her fleshy thighs. Judging by the bulge at the front of those panties, Hazard assumed this woman was exactly what the poor girl had been talking about.

"He's a cop, Marita. Don't say another word. Officer, we were just standing here minding our own business. That's all. There's nothing to see here."

"At half-past eight? With the Bordello burning to the ground? On a dark block?"

"It's our business. We can mind it however we please."

"In front of Emmanuel Lutheran?"

"Jesus doesn't mind. He's got better things to do. He's probably in Vegas eating ass."

That, Hazard thought, was perhaps the most genuinely interesting theological point he'd heard in his entire life.

"I wanted to ask—"

"We've got nothing to say. Isn't that right, Marita?" The woman grabbed the girl's arm and tugged.

"If I wanted her for solicitation, I could have her. That's not why I'm here."

"You aren't even looking at her tits. Or mine." With an almost comically grandiose flash of intuition, her electric-blue eyeshadow exaggerating every blink, the woman said, "Oh. You want some of this." She tugged at the package in the front of her leather panties. "Sweetie, if that's what you want, you've got to do some talking. If this is some kind of entrapment—"

"Oh for fuck's sake. I don't want to have sex with either of you, no matter what parts you've got. I want information."

"Like—" That electric-blue eyeshadow jumped again. "Like what we do? You want to know what guys like? You want to hear about it, that kind of stuff? Because I can tell you some stories. There's another uniform boy that comes down here for me special, and he always pretends it's just an accident, it's just this one time, and he always pretends he doesn't want—" another tug at her bulge "—but once we get going, once he's behind me, he starts reaching around. You'd think it was the goddamn Titanic and he was holding for dear life."

Marita giggled into her hand again.

"I absolutely do not—" Someone from the station? Another cop who came down here to grab some dick and pretend he wanted pussy? To be honest, Hazard kind of did want to know, but he clamped down on the urge. "I do not want that kind of information. I want to know about the Bordello."

"Go on, Marita. Go mind your business up on my spot."

"Harry said I wasn't supposed to work corners yet, just this—"

"It's a better spot, child. Just go on. I'll talk to Harry."

The girl gave Hazard one last appraising glance and then darted up the block. At the corner, she took up her pose again, ass and breasts thrust towards the street in what looked like painful contortionism. The woman stayed, hands on her hips, tugging the rhinestone bustier down over her surgically-massive breasts.

"You're the gay one."

"That's what I like to be called."

She smiled, to Hazard's surprise, and some of the tension went out of her face. Without the rigid lines, Hazard could see her age now, even hidden to some extent by the makeup she wore. She looked very tired, like she'd seen the world go around too many times to believe in anything besides Jesus eating ass in Vegas.

"She should be in school."

"She's got six younger brothers, and her mom OD'd last week."

"I can call DSS. I won't drag you into it."

"She doesn't want DSS. She doesn't want them split up. And don't tell me there's a chance they'll be together. There are seven of them, and there's nobody that'll take seven, not all together. You're mandated, right?"

"That's right. Doesn't really matter what she wants. I have to tell somebody about her."

"But if you do, I'm not telling you anything."

"I might arrest you for that."

She snorted. "A few days with meals, air conditioning, and I'm not working on my feet—or on my back. Maybe a couple of nice ladies in there with me, ladies who know how to treat a girl. Slap on the cuffs, Officer."

"Detective. Detective Emery Hazard." He didn't know why he told her his first name; it came out, and it felt right when he did.

"Kandy. With a K."

"Do they really?"

"Do they really what?"

"Put you in with the women."

"Thank God most men can't see past a pair of bouncies." She rocked on her heels to demonstrate. "One time a guy, I guess he was a queer, figured it out, and they didn't have a good goddamn idea what to do. Put me all by myself. That was Kansas, though."

"What do you know about the Bordello?"

"I want you to say it. Say you won't call anybody down on that girl."

"Not a chance. She's a child. She shouldn't be doing this. She shouldn't have to."

"All right," Kandy said, rocking on her heels and again exhibiting her bouncies. "I didn't see anything."

"Plenty of girls work the Bordello. I'll just keep asking." He took a handful of steps down the next block."

"Plenty of girls work the Bordello, sure," Kandy called after him. "And when those guys showed up and started shooting, they all scrammed because they don't have the balls God gave a puppy."

"But not you," Hazard said, turning back to her.

"Not me."

"I'm not making that deal."

"I guess it's a good thing I didn't see anything." But as Hazard put his back to her again, she added, "Good thing I didn't see anything like those men who rolled up on the Bordello about five minutes before it caught on fire. Or anything like that phone the guy threw out the window. Good thing I didn't hear anything either. Didn't hear gunshots, for example. If I'd heard something like that, I'd have to tell a cop. Didn't hear a man say something about Emery Hazard."

Hazard marched back to stand in front of her. Kandy must have glimpsed something in his expression because she tugged hastily at the bustier again, and the rhinestones gleamed like star-drops in the weak light. She stayed right where she was, though, and after a minute she managed to look him in the eyes.

"Fine," Hazard said. "A deal. I don't say anything official. Not yet. But I get that girl a job, a real one. And she starts going to the St. Margaret Food Pantry, and she gets those kids into the county health center when they need it, and if I catch her working a corner again, then I call it in."

Kandy considered this. She dug out a juul and drew on it sharply, and then she tapped it against her palm and studied him. "You think she's innocent or something like that?"

"Innocence is a bullshit reason for anything. I think she's young and she's still got a chance."

"All right."

"All right?"

"Yeah."

"Tell me how everything went down."

"Do you know him? Hollace?"

Hazard fought to keep the surprise from his expression. "I do."

"Then you know what he was like: crazy. And you know—"

"No, I don't know that."

"Jesus, I only knew him from seeing him a few times and I knew that. He was . . . I don't know. He was not nice. I mean, when he got back here, he kicked Phineas and the Lady out of the Bordello, and they had been living there for twenty years probably. They're old, and Hollace didn't blink at throwing them out on the street. Phineas went back once—he's old, I think he's got that dementia, or whatever they call it, because he forgets just about everything. When Hollace came back, he really laid into him. Left him on the stairs, I guess. I wasn't around for it, but I haven't seen Phineas since."

"He beat up an old man?"

She dragged on the juul again, and when she exhaled, the vapor had a bubblegum scent. "He might have killed him. There's still blood on the steps; you can see it if you look. But that's not really the point. The point is he's a crazy son of a bitch. Or was a crazy one."

"Did he hurt anyone else?"

"After that thing with Phineas, he was gone for a while. Then he'd come back and work like the devil. He'd come outside every once in a while and talk. That's how I learned his name. He never wanted anything. He probably doesn't need to pay for it; he's got those eyes, those pretty green eyes. But you never know with guys like that. Sometimes they want something they're too afraid to ask for, so they pay and they get mean about it."

"How long?"

"A week. Two weeks."

"He's been in town for two weeks?"

"Something like that. But he wasn't here most of the time."

"And then something changed?"

"And then—well, he came back. Early this morning, really early. Still basically last night, and I was out working. At first I thought he was using. I didn't really read him as a junkie; he didn't have that vibe. But I'd already been wondering about him. It's pretty strange shit for a decent-looking guy to roll into town, move into that old shit hole, and spend his days doing nothing at all. I thought maybe he was running from something. Or I thought maybe he was a junkie and hadn't used up his stash, but that seemed like a long shot. He just didn't seem like the type. But it was the only thing that made sense."

"Why did you think he was using?"

With a laugh, Kandy exhaled another bubblegum cloud. "Why? Because he was out of his goddamn mind. Crazy, like I told you. He drove up and he was screaming. But not like he was in pain. He was—I don't know. Angry. Even that's not right. You ever seen somebody really cranked on meth? Or coked out of their minds? That hyperactive paranoid bullshit, and they start talking about how microwaves are a government conspiracy to control our brains, or how the Girl Scouts are spying on them, or how they're being followed by grocery store bag boys."

"Substance-induced psychotic disorder. Cocaine, amphetamines, and methamphetamines are all known to induce that. Lots of persecutory delusions."

"That sounds about right. Well, it was like that. He was screaming, 'Coming after me? Coming after me? In my own fucking house, he's going to put a knife in my back and come after me? No way. No fucking way.' He was on the porch, pacing back and forth like that, louder and louder. 'They're coming, they're coming. Fine then, let 'em come.' We could hear him, the girls and I, out on the street. And then Janaya, who's always got to be a smart ass, yelled back at the house, 'They're not coming yet, but they will be when I'm done with them.' And he came down off the porch." She said the words slowly and distinctly, as though they expressed something impossible to conceive. "He came down, and he walked right over to her, and he started to beat the shit out of her. His eyes. Those pretty green eyes. He looked like he was seeing something else, like he was on another planet. It took all the rest of us to get him off her, and Janaya crawled—crawled, goddamn it, because she couldn't stand up—crawled away from him as fast as she could, and me and a couple of the girls got Hollace back inside. He went wild then. He said he was getting his gun. He said he wasn't going to let him have all the fun. That's when I left." Kandy paused. She studied the juul, as though considering giving it one more shot, and then she tucked it down the front of the bustier and said, "Janaya can't walk, you know. She's got her knee puffed up so big it looks like a marshmallow."

"Tell me about tonight."

"Those guys rolled up, and the girls ran."

"But not you."

"The Bordello's my walk. I earned that. I wasn't going to let some coke-head run me off." Then, to Hazard's surprise, Kandy sniffed and wiped the corners of her eyes. "But he wasn't a coke-head, was he? Because I saw those other guys go inside. And I heard the shots. And now the whole place is on fire, and that means Hollace wasn't using, was he? He wasn't just—what'd you say? Paranoid?"

"Persecutory delusions," Hazard said, but his mind was moving faster than that, skimming over analysis, and it was hard to keep his focus on the conversation. "What were the other guys like?"

"I don't know. Tough guys."

"White? Black? Asian? Old? Young? Fat? Thin?"

"Tough guys. White trash. They weren't fat, but some of them had beer guts. Not young, but that's hard to say. A lot of those guys look older than they are because of the shit they do."

"Did they say anything?"

Kandy shook her head.

"They just walked into the Bordello?"

A nod.

"And then?"

"He wasn't a coke-head," Kandy said. "He was right. They were coming for him. I heard shots. I was going to go, but then the window broke, and—" A car turned at the intersection, and Kandy huddled into the shadows of Emmanuel Lutheran. The behavior would have been suspicious on almost anyone, but on a girl who walked the streets for a living, it made Hazard hesitate. For all her bravado,

Kandy was scared. Scared for her own life, for some reason. She was still talking, saying, "I don't even know what to tell Janaya; she'll probably be happy they got him, I guess. Because of her knee."

"Who came out? Did anyone come back out?"

"Not while I was still around."

Hazard's mind branched and forked, considering possibilities. Hollace might be dead. Probably was dead. And, to judge from what Kandy told Hazard, Hollace had known he was in danger. So why stay?

"You said something about a phone. He threw it out the window?"

"I want two hundred dollars."

Hazard stared at her. "I don't have two hundred dollars."

"You're a cop, aren't you? You're supposed to pay snitches."

"I don't have—"

"You're good for it. I know you are. Two hundred dollars. I'll even give—" Kandy's eyes flicked sideways with mental math, "—forty to Janaya. For her knee."

"Fine. I'll get you the money. Now tell me about the phone."

Kandy locked eyes with him for a moment, and then she nodded and reached deep into the bustier. Drawing out a phone, she held it towards Hazard.

"He threw it out the window," she said, "And he shouted down at me. He said, 'Give that phone to Emery Hazard.' I didn't know who you were, didn't know how I was supposed to find you. And then I heard him scream, and I ran."

CHAPTER TWENTY-FIVE

JULY 3
TUESDAY
8:20 PM

SOMERS MANAGED TO get out of bed. His head was still bitching at him, but the slow, cold drip of Mikey's loogies was worse than any headache. That cold, wet slime was awful. The feel of it, yes. But the smell was worse, the same stench as Mikey's rotting teeth. And the flecks of tobacco, those were worse too—their rough grit. But worst was the taste, as though Somers had kissed Mikey.

I'll fuck you from behind, and when you look back and stare into my eyes, you might even think it's him again.

He made it to the toilet in the small bathroom and vomited. Then he washed his face in the sink, and he washed his mouth too, working soapy fingers deep, scrubbing around his teeth. As a child, he had hated having his mouth washed out. His mother had done that; she had thought it a particularly fitting punishment for vulgarity. And in Grace Elaine Somerset's book, swearing wasn't the only kind of vulgarity. Anything Somers said that sounded common or street or low-brow had to be scrubbed out of his mouth, and he thought about that as his nails bumped along the ridges of his teeth, and he thought what his mother would have done if she had suspected he'd have a dick in his mouth one day. She might have gone out and bought Borax. She might have just cried. She might have called up Mikey and asked him to straighten out his friend.

Thinking like that wasn't helping anything, but it was hard to shove the thoughts away. When Somers couldn't taste anything except the liquid soap and its faint chemical perfume, he rinsed his mouth and washed his face one last time and looked in the mirror. Tissue was already puffing up around both eyes, and tomorrow and the day after, they'd be some real beauties, but those were the only signs of what had happened.

"Spit washes off." Somers didn't even realize he'd said it out loud, but it seemed profound, and he touched the bridge of his nose, his cheekbone, his lips, as though he might feel the residue. His fingers were shaking.

Evie. That brought him out of the worst of it. He had to see about Evie, then he could worry about the rest of it, then he could worry about Hazard—

—you might even think it's him again—

—and then he could deal with Mikey. He dried his hands and dabbed at his face with the paper towel, but this hurt too much and he gave it up. Then, water beading in his hairline and running down the cut of his jaw, he found his phone.

On the screen, a notification said, *A location has been shared with you.* Somers dismissed it for the moment, but inside he was thinking, Damn right, damn right it's been shared with me, damn fucking right. He found Cora's number, and then he paused with his thumb on her name.

Mikey had warned him. Mikey had told him not to change Evie's schedule at all. Her mom and preschool, that's what Mikey had said. Someone was there, right now, watching the house. Someone was there, and if Somers called, if Cora took Evie and got in the car and ran, something would happen. She'd have a flat. Or she'd be run off the road. Or she might just disappear, and one day, someone would find her. Dead. Raped and dead. But they wouldn't find Evie, oh Jesus Christ, he said let's see how much she'll bring on the open market, oh Christ, not Evie, so they wouldn't find her.

It was one of the hardest things Somers had ever done, but he scrolled past Cora's name. His contacts flew up under his fingers. Names. Tens. Dozens. Maybe hundreds. People he had known his whole life, most of them. And none of them could help him when he needed them.

Except one. He pressed, and Hazard's name flashed on the screen.

When Hazard answered, his voice was tight with excitement. "You won't believe what's happening over here."

"Where are you?"

"Smithfield. What's wrong?"

"You've been gone—" Somers hesitated. Not long, the rational part of his brain knew. Not long at all. Maybe an hour. A little more.

Hazard's voice had dropped when he spoke again. "John, what's going on?"

What Somers wasn't going to do—what he knew wouldn't help anything—was tell him over the phone. He just needed Hazard to come pick him up. In fact, it might be better not to tell him at all because soon, tonight, Mikey was going to call, and he was going to say a place and a time, and if Hazard wasn't there—

—how much that little cutie of yours can bring on the open market—

"John?"

"I'm fine. A little shaken. Mikey was here." He had to clench his jaw, then, to keep from falling apart.

"Mikey Grames? What the hell happened? I'm on my way, John, but I need you to keep talking. What happened? Are you hurt?"

"I'm fine. I mean, he roughed me up a little, but I'm fine. I just— I need to get out of here. I need to work."

Over the line came the sound of a car door shutting, and then Hazard saying, "What the fuck was Mikey Grames there for?"

"He told me he was taking over the investigation."

Hazard let off a string of swears. "What?"

"He said we bring everything to him first."

"And you told him to fuck himself."

Somers leaned his forehead against his fist.

"What's going on, John? You're not telling me something, and you're scaring me."

That last part, which was perhaps the rawest, most vulnerable Emery Hazard had ever been in the years Somers had known him, broke the dam. Somers tried to stop. He wanted to stop. But he heard himself say, "They're going to hurt Evie."

For a long moment, the only noise was the hum of the fluorescent lights, and a long way off, the sound of the elevator dinging. Then, in an eerily calm voice, Hazard said, "I'm going to kill that goat-fucking son of a bitch."

"Ree."

"I am. I'm going to kill him tonight. John, go over to Cora's. Stay there until you hear from me."

"Ree."

"No. I don't care anymore. That piece of shit threatened her? He threatened Evie? Well, that's it. I'm going to cut him into a million pieces, and fucking good luck solving that murder."

"Ree, for fuck's sake, will you listen to me? He's got someone there. At the house already. If I call, if I show up, if I do anything, he pulls the trigger."

But not literally. No, it would be worse. But Somers wouldn't let Hazard know that. He couldn't tell him that much; he didn't entirely know what it would do to the big man, but he knew it would carry him over a cliff and he wouldn't come back.

Hazard's breathing, ragged, came across the line. And when he spoke, it was with a bewildered helplessness that was almost childlike. "John, what am I supposed to do?"

"What are we supposed to do, Ree. We. And right now, we don't do anything."

"Fuck this case, though. We're done with this case. If it's about Evie—"

"Don't talk bullshit. You're not good at it, and you know better than that. We're still working this case. And we're going to figure out what to do about Evie and Mikey and all the rest of it. But we've got to do it right or everything will go to shit. Mikey wants something, and I think I can use that against him."

"Something more than for us to hand over the case? What?"

Somers cursed himself inwardly; he hadn't meant to discuss this. "Nothing, never mind."

"What? Money? I don't have much, but we'll—"

"Don't worry about it. I'm going to give him what he wants."

"If it'll get him off our backs, you should give it to him, John. Even if it only buys us another day to plan. Jesus, how much does he want? I can call my parents; they've got some savings."

"Just drop it, all right? I'll make sure he gets what he wants."

"Yeah. All right." But Hazard didn't sound convinced.

I'll fuck you from behind, and when you look back and stare into my eyes, you might even think it's him again.

Somers fought off a shiver. "How fast can you get here?"

"Pretty damn fast. I've got the Aston Martin."

"How the hell did you—never mind. I'll be waiting outside."

"John."

"Yeah?"

"It's going to be ok."

Somers's heartbeat was counting the milliseconds now, but all he said was, "I'll be outside."

When the Aston Martin rolled up, Somers felt a flicker of anger. His father had always treasured his cars; they were one of his most visible status symbols, and although Somers had been given a very nice car to drive when he was a teenager, he had never been allowed to touch the Aston Martin—and there had always been an Aston Martin in the garage, a parade of models over the years, of which the Aston Martin was only the latest. He slid into the car, the upholstery soft, the air smelling like leather and sandalwood and Emery Hazard, and he let out a breath like he'd been underwater.

"Jesus Christ. Your eyes."

Somers stopped Hazard's hand before he could touch the puffy skin.

Hazard met his gaze. "I'm going to kill him, John."

"We've got a little over two hours before we need to meet Swinney. I want to get some work done."

"At the station?"

Somers shook his head. "No. Things feel off."

"You think there's someone dirty? Someone besides Lender, I mean?"

"I don't know what I think. But I don't want to go to the station."

"St. Taffy's?"

The cop bar would be loud, Somers knew. At this time of night, and the night before a federal holiday especially. That was a good thing. For the most part, the sight lines in the bar were decent, which meant that although they would see people they knew, which wasn't ideal, St. Taffy's would also be a public space, relatively safe, and it would be hard for someone to overhear their conversation. He nodded.

After all those years of driving that old clunker, Hazard handled the Aston Martin like he was made for it. They sped across the city; Wahredua's orange sodium lights blurred past them, and the storefront windows, dark now, rippled like black water. When Hazard wasn't shifting, he kept his hand on Somers's knee, and his grip was tight and possessive. And that only made Somers feel worse about what he was going to do. What he was going to have to do to save his daughter.

It would be a betrayal. Somers knew that. And he knew betrayal was about the worst thing you could to anyone, and it was definitely the worst thing he could do to Hazard. It would shatter everything Somers had built with the man he loved. And if Mikey hadn't done anything else but that, it would have been enough to make Somers hate him until the end of time.

Inside, the bar was as loud as Somers had expected. St. Taffy's had a gleaming concrete floor, a well-stocked bar, and a massive 4K television hanging above the bottles. Tonight, it was a Cardinals game, and normally Somers would have taken a seat in the front part of the bar and enjoyed watching it. Instead, though, he followed Hazard to the back of the bar, behind the pool table. No one was playing pool, thank God, and nobody had claimed the last row of tables. Somers took a stool, and when the waitress came, he ordered a Bud Lite and ignored the look Hazard gave him. Hazard ordered Diet Coke, and he ordered them each a hamburger even when Somers shook his head.

"You need to eat something."

"Tell me what happened."

So Hazard did; Somers listened with growing amazement to the details and suggestions that his father had made, the possibility that the Ozark Volunteers were attempting to break off from the mayor's control, and Naomi's role in all of it.

When Hazard had finished, all he said was, "Now you."

So Somers told him. Not all of it. Not the worst of it. He left out the spit, and the tiny grains of tobacco in phlegm, and the things Mikey had said—

—I'll fuck you from behind—

—and the real threat to Evie. He left out, too, the other thing Mikey wanted.

"All right," Hazard said. "So we go scout out Cora's house right now."

"He's got someone—"

"We park a block away. Or ten blocks away. Or we can walk from here if it'll make you feel better. We kill the son of a bitch who's sitting outside, and you take Evie and Cora away from here while I go start taking Mikey apart piece by piece."

"And what if there are two guys? What if there are three? What if there's a chain of them, each one watching another, in case we try anything?"

"Mikey's not that smart. And he doesn't have unlimited resources."

"No. But whoever's doing this, Hollace, whoever it is, he's a hell of a lot smarter than Mikey. You know I'm right, Ree."

"I also know that doing what Mikey asks, giving him the case, that's not going to be enough. Let's say we do what he asks: we turn over what we've got on Kjar. Fine. The whole thing is over, for all I care. But after that, Mikey—or whoever is doing this—he's got a cop in his pocket. Two cops, actually. And so the next time he wants to do something, he's got us dancing at the end of a line for him. And the time after that. And the time after that."

"I know."

"It doesn't sound like you do. It sounds like you're scared and you're honestly thinking about giving this motherfucker what he wants."

Somers laughed in spite of himself. "You don't have any idea what you're talking about."

"Why? Because Evie's not my daughter. Bullshit. She's mine."

"No. Not that. I didn't mean—"

"Then what?"

Again, Somers laughed, and he rubbed his eyes, and the puffy skin seemed hot enough to burn his fingers. "Oh for fuck's sake, I don't even know what I'm trying to say."

"Yes, you do." Hazard's scarecrow eyes had taken on a dangerously inquisitive focus. "There's something else. Something you're not telling me."

"There isn't."

"What is it? What does he want?"

"Nothing. I told you, didn't I? I told you the whole fucking thing."

"You're getting angry. You're not looking at me. You're talking differently than you normally do. You're lying."

"Just drop it, Ree. Whatever you think, I'm telling you everything. Can we drop it?"

Their burgers came then, with patties almost as big as the plate, the meat seared golden and crisped on the edges, and the smell of onion sharp and fresh. Hazard got another Coke. Somers asked for a Bud Lite, and Hazard talked over him, ordering him a Sprite.

"I can have another beer."

"Take a bite."

"I'm not going to get wasted tonight. I can't. But I need—I just need to unwind, all right?"

"Take a bite."

"I'm not hungry."

"Take a bite, John."

Snatching up the burger, Somers tore off a mouthful, chewed once, twice, and then swallowed. The food lumped in his throat, and he had to chug Sprite to force it down, and then he glared at Hazard. "Happy?"

But the taste of the meat, the fat, the onion, the tomato—suddenly he realized he was hungry. Starving. And he took another bite, chewing more carefully, and another.

Hazard ate too. And between bites, he said, "If you think we can't take care of this ourselves, we should call the FBI. This is exactly the kind of thing they handle."

"We can't. Mikey basically told me that whoever's running this show, he's got juice inside federal agencies. That's why the DEA and the FBI have never followed the trail of drugs back to Dore County."

"She."

Slurping on the Sprite—empty, now, and the straw sputtering at the bottom—Somers said, "What?"

"She has juice. Naomi."

"I don't know. I don't think Naomi would do this; not to her niece."

"Really? She had her own people murdered to try to win a political war."

"I'm telling you, she wouldn't. Not Evie."

"That's a problem because it blows a hole in your dad's theory. If Naomi's not behind this, though, then we've got a bigger problem. Anyway, even if you're right and it's not Naomi, Mikey was wrong. Or lying."

"That's not a risk—"

"I'm not saying we should call. I'm saying Mikey either didn't know what he was talking about or he was lying. I agree; it's too much of a gamble to risk a call. But think about it: we know the FBI have been here. They interviewed Jo Kjar."

"Or somebody impersonating FBI agents did."

"Fair." Hazard chewed more slowly. Hamburger juice ran down his chin, a glistening line through his scruff, and Somers wiped it away with a napkin. Hazard blinked; he looked like he hadn't even realized he was still eating. "What about the sheriff?"

"You don't like the sheriff."

"No. I don't. But I feel like we're running out of options."

"The sheriff isn't an option. The other cops aren't an option. Ree, my dad basically told you what we'd already suspected: people have been covering up for the drug manufacturing here for years, and nobody knows how deep that goes."

"Engels is new."

"Engels is, but a lot of the Sheriff's Department isn't."

"What about—"

"Ree, I'm going to handle this. I promise."

Hazard laid down the remaining crust of burger. "What exactly does that mean?"

"I'm going to handle it. That's all it means. Let's talk about Hollace."

"I'm not done—"

"Ree, Hollace might be the link between the two threads we're trying to draw together."

His face grim, Hazard bit the end off his crust. "Go on."

"There's some sort of battle going on for control of the drug industry in the county, right?"

"That's what it looks like."

"And you told me that Hollace thought someone was after him. He kept talking about someone coming after him. And from what you told me, they found him. He's dead because of whatever he knew. So what did he know?"

"All he left was this phone." Hazard set it on the table between them. It was a smartphone, but an older model, the aluminum case scratched and cracks webbing the glass.

"What's on it?"

"Let's find out."

Hazard pressed the power button, and after a moment, the screen flashed to life. It worked its way through a series of loading screens, and then it showed a series of apps.

"No passcode," Somers said.

"He wanted me to have it."

"But he wasn't sure you'd get it. Why didn't he put a passcode on it? Something you could have guessed, but something to keep it safe in case it didn't get straight to you."

"I don't know."

"Why didn't he text you the information? Or call you?"

"I don't know."

"What's on the phone?"

"I don't know, Somers. I just turned it on." Hazard angled the screen so they could both study it more closely. There were three apps: one for phone calls; one for text messages; and the camera. Hazard checked the phone app. Empty. The messaging app was empty. But the camera had a single, saved recording in the gallery.

The video framed Hollace's face, and the background was dingy: torn and stained wallpaper, wires hanging from broken light fixtures; a doorway that opened onto a larger space, beyond which the details became indistinct. Afternoon light, low and golden, backlit Hollace. He seemed distracted, his attention fixed away from the camera as he turned in a circle. The background behind him spun and swam: more of that filthy wallpaper, peeling wainscoting, a window grimed so thickly that the light coming through looked orange. Then the doorway came into view again—he had completed a full circle, Somers realized—and something silver flashed at the base of the frame. Hollace redirected the camera, his attention moving to the lens, and began to speak.

"Emery, you hate me, man. You can hate me. That's all right. You blow my fucking mind, man. Running out of the station like that. Running straight at me. My fucking mind, man. Blown. And then in the Haverford, I thought for sure—" In the distance, something thumped. It was a low noise, barely audible on the phone's speakers, but it was familiar. Something about that noise sent a chill through Somers.

"What was that—" Somers began to ask. Noise. What was that noise?

But Hazard cut him off. "It's the Bordello. Listen."

"They're here," Hollace said. "Fuck me, they're here. I'm going to leave this with someone, Emery. I think it'll get to you. I hope it will. Because I'm not going to be the first person they kill, not for this shit, but I hope I'm the last. I never should have trusted Mikey Grames. Never. Goddamn lunatic is too greedy for his own good."

He laughed, the sound shrill, and then, in the background, there was another of those dull thumps that sent a shiver through Somers. Somers knew that noise, but it was like something in a nightmare, something he couldn't quite place. And then it came to him. The shotgun had sounded like that at the Haverford. "Fuck, Hugo bit it because he was stupid, but I'm not stupid."

"Hugo?" Somers said.

Hazard's pale skin had lost its remaining color, and a shudder ran through him, shaking the phone and its video.

"What is he talking about?" Somers asked.

So pale he was blue at the lips, Hazard shook his head.

"I wish I could have told you the whole thing," Hollace said. "I wish I could have seen your face when I did. But I tried to play a long game, and I got burned. You either burn or you get burned. That's this whole fucking world."

Another of those low thumps came, this time much closer, and Hollace flinched. Now Somers could hear footsteps on the video—not running, not quite, but quick and determined.

The camera swept away, and the speakers rustled with the sound of Hollace's clothing, and then the camera swept up again, taking in Hollace's face one last time, his eyes wide, the emerald green ringed with white terror. Hollace threw an elbow off screen, and glass shattered—the window, Somers realized, that dirty window—and fresh, clean, evening light poured in. It was golden over Hollace's face, and it made him look, for a moment, young again.

"Somebody should have told you this a long time ago," Hollace said. "I'm glad I'm the one that gets to, though." He drew a breath, and a little smile quirked his lips; the sunlight was so fierce that it looked like it might wash him away. "Jeff didn't commit suicide, Emery. He was murdered. And I'm telling you so you'll do me a favor and put a bullet in Mikey Grames."

Then a gunshot exploded, and the camera jerked to the side, and the video went dark.

CHAPTER TWENTY-SIX

JULY 3
TUESDAY
9:51 PM

HAZARD LAID DOWN THE PHONE. He eyed the Diet Coke he'd been drinking, and then he waved down the boy who'd been bringing them drinks, and he asked for a Guinness, and he sat back on the stool. He was tired. His back ached. That was an old man thing, having a backache like this. But that made sense because Hazard felt old. Thirty-five, barely, but he felt ancient. The television blared organ music as a camera panned across the green swath inside Busch Stadium, and St. Taffy's buzzed with happy voices, and glass clinked on glass, and the smell of fried onions came from the kitchen, along with the dark, roasted wheat smell of the Guinness, and he realized that at some point the boy had brought the beer, and he drank. When he set down the glass, Somers was watching him.

"You didn't finish your burger," Hazard said.

"I don't think I can. Head's hurting."

"Are you going to be sick?"

A slight smile tugged at Somers's mouth. "I'll be all right."

Any moment now, Somers would say something. He'd ask Hazard how he was feeling. He'd ask what Hazard was thinking. And Hazard didn't know what he'd say. He couldn't tell the truth. He couldn't say that his insides were buzzing, a neutral, meaningless kind of buzz that sounded like the hubbub of voices inside St. Taffy's. He couldn't say, Well, Somers, thanks for asking, but all I'm feeling is this weird buzzing. He couldn't tell Somers that he didn't feel anything, really. He didn't think anything. Except that his back ached. And he was tired.

Somers's hand clutched Hazard's once, tightly, and then slid up to squeeze his wrist, and then slid up again, his fingers warm as they tucked inside Hazard's sleeve and printed themselves against the inside of Hazard's arm. It was the way you might grab someone who was falling, and you were afraid they might slip out of your grasp.

"I can meet Swinney myself."

Hazard shook his head.

On the television, someone must have gotten a good hit because cheers went up through the televised crowd, and a second wave of cheers rippled through the bar. It snapped that tenuous buzz of conversation, and a sick, fever flush ran up inside Hazard. The burnt-wheat taste of the Guinness turned foul on his tongue, and he pushed his stool back and stumbled into the men's room. It smelled like the men's room at any decent-sized bar: air fresheners, piss, the smoke from a stolen cigarette, and something that Hazard thought of as wet paper towels. He made it to the sink, and he spat down the drain. Resting his forehead on the glass, he relished the brief chill, and then he spat again and wiped the mirror and washed his hands.

Somers had ordered him another Guinness, not that Hazard was going to drink it. He didn't feel like he could eat or drink anything, let alone Guinness. The taste of the last one was still festering, and Hazard inched the beer towards the center of the table.

"You can ask," Hazard said. "I'm not going to break."

"I didn't know Jeff very well. He wrestled, right?"

Hazard nodded.

"I really only remember one thing." Somers stopped, and purple lines ran across his cheekbones, and he shook his head. "One other thing, I mean. Not that night. Something else. I remember I was carrying gear for football. I'd screwed something up, and Bing was making me tote gear as punishment, and I was probably halfway to the field when I dropped it. All of it. And Jeff was walking past me, and he stopped and picked it up, asked if I wanted help getting it out to the field. That was it. I mean, I'd talked shit about him. I'd watched

Mikey go after him. I'd even been there for some of it. But he helped me pick up the gear, and he offered to carry it. That says a lot about him, doesn't it?"

Hazard nodded again, but he was barely hearing Somers. Three words blazed in the front of his mind like bonfires a mile high: Not that night. That's how Somers had said it. Not that night. Not the night that Mikey and Hugo had found Jeff. Somers had been with them, but he had left. He didn't want any part in what they were doing. And what they did—what Mikey told Hazard they had done—was rape Jeff. Rape him and beat him and humiliate him. What they'd done to him had been so bad that he had driven out to the bluffs, taken his dad's gun from the back, and opened a hole in his head. And, in doing that, he had opened a hole in Emery Hazard too. A hole that had never closed, not in all these years, not even after coming back here, not even after finding Somers. Inside, Hazard, buried at the bottom of that hole, a clock was still stuck with both hands at midnight. Stuck and silent and still. Never ticking forward another minute. Never again. No future, not for Emery Hazard.

What had been so awful about it, what had cut so deeply into Hazard, was that Jeff had abandoned him. It had hurt in a way Hazard had never known something could hurt. Hazard had come back here, in part, to know what had happened. He had come back hoping to make things right. And in some ways, he had done this: he had confronted Mikey Grames, he had made peace with himself, and he had fallen in love, real love, with John-Henry Somerset.

Except here was this recording from Hollace. And Hollace said that Jeff hadn't killed himself. He had been murdered. And if he'd been murdered, then he hadn't abandoned Hazard. He'd been taken. He'd been ripped away. And Hazard knew he would be angry. He knew, later, the anger would scud in like thunderclouds. But right then he was . . . numb. He'd heard about this, read about it, in shock victims. There wasn't even any pain. Just those clear thoughts: Jeff hadn't left—he had been taken.

"What do you think?" Hazard said.

"I think you might want a different partner for this."

"Don't be stupid."

"Ree, I was involved. At some level, I was part of it. You should have someone with you who—"

"Cut it out. Right now. And tell me what you think."

The razored purple lines darkened on Somers's cheekbones, but he nodded. "I have reservations."

"I'm not getting another partner, so you can sing a different song or shut the fuck up."

"That's not what I meant. I have my reservations about what Hollace said. It . . . it might not be true, Ree."

"You heard him: he was terrified, and he knew he was most likely about to die. Why would he lie?"

"That's a great question."

"Then give me your great fucking answer since you're so smart."

"The thing about Mikey—"

"No, I'm really curious. Hollace was desperate to give me this message. It was the last thing he did before he died. But you're clever enough to see through that elaborate charade, so let's hear the rest of it. Why'd he do this?"

Somers lifted his chin as though the last part had been a slap. Another cheer ran through the bar—something on that motherfucking game—but Somers didn't break eye contact. "I deserve better than that."

For a moment, Hazard tried to hold Somers's eyes, and then he dropped his gaze and ran a hand through his hair. "Fuck. All right. Yeah, you do."

"Another thing to question is what he said about Hugo. Hugo Perry wasn't murdered. He died in a car accident."

"He died," Hazard corrected, "because a train hit his car dead-on. He was drunk, parked right on the tracks, and it was night. You remember what you told me? You said there were pieces of him scattered for fifty miles."

"It was a bad accident."

"It's a damn convenient way to make sure there's no autopsy."

Frustration tightened Somers's features. "You know what I remember about Hollace? Back from high school, I mean. You know what he was?"

"He was like me: he was an outcast because he had a black father and because he was poor."

"Maybe. There's some truth to that; people around here aren't very accepting."

"Oh, really?"

"Don't be snide. You were different, but you weren't like Hollace."

"I was the town faggot."

"You had self-respect."

Hazard was so surprised by this that he glanced at Somers; the other man's tropical blue stare fixed him in place, and Hazard groped blindly across the table for his beer, his fingers trailing through rings of condensation and a soggy scrap of lettuce and thumbing over a stack of Sweet'n Low. When he found the beer, he drank deeply, but he still couldn't break Somers's gaze.

"No matter what shit we did to you, you took it. And you came back. And you didn't make a thing out of it. That was what made you scary, you know? And that was what made people . . . I don't know. That was what made them realize how shitty it was. Jeff wouldn't take it. He didn't have to, really; everybody liked Jeff, even after he came out."

"Not everyone."

The blush in Somers's cheeks was the color of heartsblood now, but his voice remained level. "No, not everyone. But enough people liked him that he didn't have to put up with Mikey's crap, and he talked back and gave Mikey shit, and that made Mikey furious. But it also normalized everything. Guys giving each other shit and fighting, everybody's familiar with that. But people torturing the shit out of a scrawny boy and he doesn't say anything, not a word, just keeps coming back, that's strange. And scary."

"Not scary enough to keep Mikey away."

"Mikey is psychotic." Somers's hand lifted a fraction, as though he might touch his face where Mikey had hit him, but then he recovered and lowered it again. "My point is about Hollace, though: Hollace didn't keep quiet like you did. Hollace would take shit and grin and ask for more. Hollace was skeevy."

"What the hell does that mean?"

"It means there was always something off with Hollace. Hollace would smile. He'd grin, and it was the creepiest grin I've ever seen. No matter what we did to him, no matter how much we made fun of him or called him names or gave him shit, he'd have this huge grin on his face. It was like a clown's smile, sometimes. Or like a serial killer. I didn't know shit about criminal psychology back then, but I knew something was off with him. Everything was a mask, and if I looked close enough, I could see where the mask really didn't fit too well. We'd call him the worst possible shit and he'd just grin and nod like it was the best joke he'd ever heard, and he'd come back for more. It was kind of sad, kind of like a dog you hit but he keeps coming back. And that meant he was fun to keep around because you do just about whatever you wanted to him, and he'd be there again the next day."

"Christ, you were a real piece of work back then."

"I was." Somers grinned. "I still am. One time—well, lots of times, really—we made him get cocaine for us. Did I tell you about this before?"

"Bits and pieces."

"He got it at the Haverford. At least, that's what he told us, and I don't think he was lying about that. Somebody's always dealing there, and it's just the kind of thing Hollace would do."

"Getting into it. That's what he called it. Getting into trouble."

"I was going to say acting like a fucking moron. Hollace was smart enough. And he always had those complicated plans. One time, he walked us through this huge scheme to use a model train set to run a video camera through the vents at school just to get some shots of the girls' locker room. Hollace had it all figured out: how much track it would take, how to run the power, how to time the camera so it got pictures at the right places. I mean, that's smart stuff. But it's also so complicated it's stupid. And it wasn't necessary; if you wanted to see a naked girl, you could buy a magazine from the Gas-Up out on Route 17. They never carded anybody in their lives."

"He didn't want to do that, though," Hazard said. It was easier now, with this conversation, to focus his thoughts. Easier to keep his mind from wandering into that black ocean where everything having to do with Jeff had foundered and sunk. And more about Hollace was coming back to him. "Hollace just wanted to impress people. He . . . he took me out to the Bordello one time and told me to steal something. He said it would make people think I was cool. And when I did, he switched it and said he'd done it. That's the kind of guy he was; he wanted people to be in awe of him."

Did they see?

"That jewelry? That pin or whatever it was?"

"You remember that? A brooch, yes. How the hell do you remember?"

"Because it was cool. You did that?"

"I just said I did."

"Yeah, but—you? Emery Hazard? Skinny, scrawny, scarecrow Emery Hazard?"

"Fuck you."

Somers grinned, and it was like someone had loosened a screw, and Hazard actually felt himself relax, the line of his spine slackening.

"What I was trying to tell you," Somers said, "was about the coke. The Haverford."

"So tell me. You're the one that went off topic."

"The first few times, he'd bring it to the party, and everybody treated him like a king. Some of the football guys, the real idiots, started calling him Holla. And Hollace loved it. Just like you said: he wanted to impress. He acted like he was dangerous, like he had secrets. And then, after a while, it wasn't cool anymore. Because even though Hollace was bringing coke, he was still Hollace, and most people could tell there was something creepy under the mask. And a few more times, all his posturing, all his attitude, it started to get old. Rubbed a lot of the guys raw. Do you remember Simon Pacheski? A real asshole, but he was pretty hot stuff in high school."

"He was hot, huh?"

"You know what I mean. Anyway, one time, Simon tried talking to this girl that Hollace liked. And Hollace and Simon had been buddies up until then, as much as anybody was buddies with

Hollace. But Hollace, he wanted this girl. She was from, Christ, I don't know. Osage Beach. Or Jeff City. She wasn't local, and Hollace probably thought this was his chance to score, and then Simon swooped in."

"So what happened?"

"What was that phrase you said he used?"

"Getting into it."

"He really got into it that night. He put something in that girl's drink. Nobody saw him do it, but we all know that's what happened. And then, when Simon took her on a drive—"

"To fuck in the back of his pickup."

"—Hollace called the police. They stopped Simon because someone had reported date rape, and sure enough, the girl was drugged out of her damn mind."

"What happened to Simon?"

"He hadn't done anything yet; he told the cops he was just driving her home. But it took a lot for his parents to hush it up, and I don't know if you remember, but he basically moved away from Wahredua as soon as he graduated."

"You're saying Hollace did all of that just because Simon hit on a girl Hollace had only talked to once?"

"And it was about as fucking stupid an idea as you can come by. I mean, it was clever, and it just about ruined Simon's life, but it was stupid because Simon liked Hollace all right. If Hollace had told him to back off, he probably would have. And it was stupid because everybody knew what had happened."

"No. You assume you know. You don't have any proof."

"Ree—"

"No, that's important. You know it's important. You don't have anything you could put in front of a jury."

"I know: I don't have any proof. It was sixteen, seventeen years ago, and I didn't have any proof back then. But you know, too, that sometimes you know what happened even when you don't have any proof to back it up."

"So what are you saying? You're saying that Hollace is behind all of this? We already knew that."

"You know he's involved. But?"

"What do you mean, but?"

"There's more. Go on and say it."

Hazard sat back. The kitchen door swung open, and the smell of hot frying oil swept into the room. A woman three tables away roared with laughter; her nails had an iridescent, peacock shine, and she was flexing them now as she laughed through her story, miming something—claws, most likely, although the gesture also reminded Hazard of someone grabbing on to something. Clutching. Hanging on for dear life. Amen, Hazard thought. A-fucking-men.

But what? That's what Somers wanted to know. He was still looking at Hazard, and Hazard could feel the scrutiny behind the question. But what? But Hollace had been the closest thing that Hazard had had to a friend. Hollace hadn't been a friend, not really. He certainly hadn't been a good friend. But he had been there when nobody else wanted anything to do with Hazard. He had been there when Jeff had vanished, when that black tide had foamed in and drowned Hazard's whole world.

"I don't know what you want me to say."

Somers sighed. "He wants to manipulate you."

"Into doing what? Investigating a twenty-year-old suicide? Murdering Mikey Grames?"

"What he said about Jeff and Mikey, he knew exactly what he was doing. All he had to do was wind you up and point you in the right direction, and now you're going to do what he wants you to do."

"He's dead."

"That doesn't mean he didn't want something. Maybe he just wanted to send you after Mikey, kill him for being a backstabbing son of a bitch. Maybe it's something else."

"Maybe, maybe, maybe. That's a lot of goddamn maybes."

"Here's another: maybe he just wanted to hurt you one last time. That was Hollace in high school. He'd buddy up to you, convince you he was your friend, and then shit on you just because he thought it would make him look cool. Or maybe he wants your attention off this case; Christ, maybe he was a company man even when he was about to die, so he was trying to stick to his mission. That's what Mikey wanted; he wanted us to stop looking into the attacks on the mayor."

Somers's phrasing shot a depth charge into Hazard, and his head snapped up. "No."

"I was there, Ree. That bastard threatened our little girl, and he said if I didn't—" Somers stopped; he seemed to adjust what he'd been about to say, and he continued, "If I didn't stop looking into this stuff, he'd do something horrible to her."

"But that's not what he said."

"I think I'd know. I was there, all right? There's not anything else he wanted, so just drop it."

Shaking his head—there was something peculiar about Somers's denial, something that tugged at Hazard's attention—Hazard said, "No, he didn't say stop looking into the attacks on the mayor. He said hand over the stuff on Ted Kjar."

"That's what I'm—" Somers paused. "Damn. I'm such an idiot."

"Why only Ted Kjar? Why is that what Mikey cares about?"

"Because that's the part that matters." Hazard rocked the tall glass of Guinness, staring into the brown slosh, his heart suddenly pattering. "Why? Why does that part matter?"

Somers started to say something, and then he swore. "It's ten to eleven."

"What?"

"Swinney. We're supposed to meet her in ten minutes."

They left cash on the table and hurried out of St. Taffy's, but Hazard's mind kept going back to the points they had established: Hollace Walker had been involved in this mess; he was trying to manipulate Hazard; and he wanted Jeff's death to be at the front of Hazard's mind. In contrast to that complicated chain of events was the starkness of Mikey's threat: drop everything that had to do with Ted Kjar. Hazard didn't know where the two connected, but he didn't need to know, not to make the decision that mattered. No matter what, he was going to figure it out, all of it: Ted Kjar, the mayor, Hollace, and Mikey Grames. And Jeff, too. And, most importantly, he was going to make sure nothing happened to Evie while he did it.

CHAPTER TWENTY-SEVEN

JULY 3
TUESDAY
11:01 PM

HALF A YEAR EARLIER, Somers and Hazard had come to Smithfield to meet with Detective Liz Swinney. Their meeting, in a vacant storefront deep in the worst part of the city, had revealed important facts about the case they were investigating. It had also shed light on Swinney's knowledge that her partner, Al Lender, was crooked—and the dilemma Swinney faced with that knowledge. Since then, Swinney had worn thinner and thinner, stretched in two directions by loyalty to her partner and loyalty to the force. Somers didn't envy her; his partner before Hazard had been a criminal, and the echoes of that lingered.

This street looked like any other in Smithfield: brown paper bags keeling over when the wind dropped; sunburnt weeds choking the storm drain; a name tag that read Tits McGee slapped onto a parking meter; and the shrinking brown light of a lone sodium lamp, struggling against the pink-and-blue neon of the stores along this block. A wing-and-seafood joint, a dollar store, a payday loan office. The Church of the Three-Day Nazarene had boarded up its windows since the last time Somers had been here, but Mystique, the beauty parlor next door, was still open, and a very tall drag queen sashayed into the street as Hazard parked the Aston Martin. The queen stopped long enough to give the car a long look, and then she cocked her hips and blew them a kiss. Hazard killed the engine, and the queen stayed in the middle of the street, watching until the Aston Martin's lights turned off. Then, with an irritated swish of her hips, she plunged into the shrinking brown light, her wig gleaming.

"Never say I don't take you anywhere interesting," Somers said.

"We might as well shoot a signal flare," Hazard said, thumping the Aston Martin's wheel. "Driving this, we might as well light a bonfire and send smoke signals."

"Lucky for us, nobody knows how to read smoke signals." Somers unbuckled his belt and reached for the door.

"I'll stay here. With the car."

"Are you scared?"

"I'm not scared. But if somebody decides to boost—"

"If someone steals this damn thing, it'll teach my father right for trusting you to drive it. I want you in there. Whatever Swinney has, you need to hear it from her."

Hazard moaned and whined, but he left the Aston Martin and followed Somers. The storefront beyond the dollar market was abandoned; kraft paper blocked out the windows and the reinforced glass door, and someone had tagged the length of wall with the informational supplement: Goyo Sucks Ass. Apprehension tingled at the base of Somers's neck; he remembered what Hazard had said the last time they'd met Swinney here.

"She chose a spot where she can put a bullet in our heads and nobody will find us for weeks."

Hazard stopped. Behind them, the door of the wing-and-seafood joint jingled, and the night air blossomed with pepper and vinegar and Tabasco. A group of men emerged, laughing, shoving each other, their attention turned in the other direction as they headed away from Hazard and Somers. But Somers realized, as they left, that he had a grip on the Glock holstered at the small of his back, and he drew it now and let out a shaky breath.

"You think she might—" Hazard asked.

Somers shook his head. "I have no idea."

"This is a fucking joke. When this is over, I'm taking early retirement."

"You want me to go first?"

"Don't be an idiot."

Hazard tugged on the door, and it opened as it had all those months before, exposing the darkened, abandoned storefront. The smell, at least, had stayed the same: wet carpet and dog and old socks. Somers breathed slowly. That kind of smell came from the long abuse of the elements and from animals that had taken up residence. That's all it was, he told himself. But Somers noticed that Hazard had drawn his Smith & Wesson .38, and he held it high, ready to drop and fire.

The darkness was the same. The smell was the same. The whirr of his heartbeat was the same. But something was different, and Somers's mouth had dried up as they shuffled into the darkness. Something raised the hairs on the back of his neck. Something tightened the skin from the center of his chest all the way down to his groin. His next breath came out in a stutter.

Ahead of him, Hazard stopped. The darkness hid everything but the broad outlines of movement, but Somers could tell that Hazard had turned back to him, was facing him, waiting for an explanation.

Pop pop, Somers thought, frozen by the realization. Two shots in the darkness. That's all it would take. And then they'd be dead, rotting in the July heat until the stink grew so foul that the authorities were called, and then their bodies would be found here. Two shots in the darkness. Maybe, maybe, Somers would see the muzzle flare. But probably not. Probably the bullet would cleave his skull, and this dog-and-sock darkness would pour through the hole of splintered bone, and that would be the end. Darkness like wet carpet and dog and dirty socks. And Mikey would do—

—how much that little cutie of yours can bring on the open market—

—whatever he wanted to Evie. There wouldn't be anyone to stop him. Cora would be lucky if she survived; she was tough, and she was smart, but she wasn't trained to handle anything like Mikey or the people he worked with. Mikey would—

Hazard's hand found his arm, tightened, the grip painful but steady.

"Swinney," Somers breathed.

There was no response except, distantly, the jingle of the wing shop's door, and then Hazard squeezed his arm once in acknowledgment. The last time they had come, Swinney had been waiting for them here, in the front room's darkness, and she had guided them back to the storeroom. But tonight, they were alone in the stinking shadows. That's what had set Somers's nerves jittering. Where was Swinney?

He breathed out, steadying himself. Maybe she just trusted them to find their way back to the storeroom. Maybe she was so worked up about whatever she had to tell them that she wasn't thinking clearly. Maybe she had just forgotten how they had done this last time, or maybe she didn't think it mattered. But Somers thought it did matter. Somers thought it mattered a lot. And his pulse rang in his ears.

With his free hand, he reached up and squeezed Hazard's wrist. He felt that familiar flex of tendon and muscle and bone, and for a moment, he was back in that alley near the clay pits, and then Hazard released him and moved towards the storeroom. They walked as quietly as they could across the damp, unraveling carpet, and they only had about five yards of ground to cover, but it felt longer. A hundred yards, maybe. A full football field. And it felt like they had to cover all that ground on their hands and knees, Jesus, that's what it felt like it was so goddamn far.

Hazard stopped at the storeroom door, taking up position just to one side. Somers moved behind him, adjusting his grip on the Glock 22, his thumb skipping along the polymer frame. One heartbeat. Breathe. Two heartbeats. Breathe. Last time, though, the door had been open.

Two shots in the darkness. Pop pop.

Three heartbeats. Breathe.

For whatever it mattered, Hazard probably tried to open the door quietly, but it was an old building, empty and neglected for unknown years, and humid weather and fluctuating temperatures had warped and rotted the particle board, had rusted the hinges, had turned the door brittle and the metal stiff. The knob rattled. It probably saved their lives.

The first shot exploded through the door, blowing a hole in the dry-rotted wood, but in the darkness, Somers's perception of it had nothing to do with sight. Instead, Somers heard a soft bark, and then the crack of the wood, and the humid fetor rippled as air shifted from the force of the gunshot, and splinters pin-cushioned his hand and lower arm. Hazard grunted. All of that happened at the same time, and Somers's mind put it together immediately, visualizing the shot and the hole in the door and understanding that, had Hazard not taken the precaution of standing to one side, he would be dead or dying right then.

As those realizations flashed through Somers's head, Hazard's strong hand found the back of his neck and dragged him to the ground. The next shot, with its soft bark, hit the drywall just above them, where they had been standing a moment before. The bullet punched through the plaster, and chips of drywall rained down on Somers, plinking against the Glock's polymer, stinging the back of Somers's neck, pattering his back like pea-sized hail.

Somers rolled right, towards the door, and came up on one elbow. He fired the first shot blind, called himself fucked, and took the next one more carefully. He aimed against the angle of the first shot, calibrating as best he could where the shooter might be standing. Hazard was shooting too; the muzzle of his .38 flashed once, twice, thrice. Another shot from the storeroom blew out more of the drywall, and then Hazard was cursing.

"Ree?" Somers shouted over the ringing in his ears. The gun inside the storeroom had been muffled, but Somers's Glock and Hazard's Smith & Wesson had thunderclapped inside the confined space, and Somers struggled to hear anything.

Hazard waved at him, the gesture barely defined by the shrinking brown light from the street, but it was enough. Somers, still firing, scrambled to his feet and kicked open the door. He kept shooting, and each shot strobed, giving instantaneous glimpses of the room and then shuttering it again. Somers had only impressions, snatches of the room that his mind could process before the darkness unfurled again: a rack of shelving against one wall; the patina of an old waffle iron; the bulb bare and dangling like a hangman's noose;

the blue-flowered linoleum; the door to the alley; and beyond, framed by the door, a swatch of alley, the brick glazed milky white by the security light.

Somers crossed the room. He stumbled once, his foot catching on something giving yet firm. Old carpet, his brain said. A rolled-up carpet. He caught himself and kept going. At the door, he paused, readied himself, and then risked a glance.

Nothing. Just the security light painting the brick, and broken asphalt, and a dumpster, and under the dumpster, a tom with a notched ear. The tom, crouched and ready to pounce, laid his ears back and hissed at Somers.

The shooter was gone.

Over the ringing in his ears, Somers heard Hazard shouting, and he shouldered the alley door shut and dropped the deadbolt and then stumbled back across the darkened storeroom. His feet found that soft pile in the center of the room, and his brain said carpet again, but acid boiled in Somers's stomach and he had to grit his teeth to keep walking because he was sure, he was a hundred percent sure, that it wasn't carpet. He stopped. His hand fished the air until the string brushed his palm, and he jerked. Weak fluorescent light pulsed, blinding Somers for a moment before his eyes adjusted. And he had been right. It wasn't a pile of carpet that he'd stepped on twice. It was Liz Swinney.

CHAPTER TWENTY-EIGHT

JULY 3
TUESDAY
11:08 PM

SOMERS PRESSED TWO FINGERS to the carotid artery, just to be sure, and he found that she was soft and warm and still and dead. He hadn't really needed to check, but he'd done it because Liz Swinney deserved to have everything done right. She had been shot twice in the chest; her white blouse was stained with blood, and more blood spilled across the blue-flower linoleum. One of the bullets had taken her in the center of the chest, and it had snapped off one of the buttons on her blouse. Somers fought the urge to reach out and close the gaping fabric. She deserved that, too, but this was a crime scene.

From the front room, Hazard shouted again, and Somers went back to him. Hazard had produced a flashlight, and he was playing it back and forth over the ground. In the light's backwash, Hazard's eyes were red and slitted, and tears leaked down the sides of his face.

"Ree," Somers shouted over the thunder still clashing in his ears. "Are you all right?"

Hazard nodded, but he raised one hand to his eyes, careful not to touch them. "Water," he shouted back.

Digging the keys from Hazard's pocket, Somers jogged back to the Aston Martin. Adrenaline leaked out of him now. His legs turned rubbery, and he felt like he was bouncing more than running. Bouncing on a bad suspension. Every bounce came down harder, like he was sinking into the sidewalk. Swinney was dead, he thought, and his hands shook a little as he got the Aston Martin open, and he dug around in the car until he found a bottle of water. In the summer's heat, it felt the same temperature as—

—Swinney, dead, soft, still warm—

—as his own skin, and when he dashed off the cap and drank, it was like drinking nothing. Just a swig, that's all he took, just one drink of nothing, and then he bounced back to Hazard on his rubbery legs.

The big man was sitting, head back, eyes still streaming tears. When Somers touched his arm, he passed the flashlight, and Somers took it in his teeth. With one hand, he peeled back Hazard's eyelids, and with the other he poured the water. Hazard tried to blink, and he swore, and then water rushed into his mouth carrying the detritus from his eye. He gargled and stopped swearing. When the water ran out, Hazard shook himself like a dog, and then he hung his head between his knees, spitting onto the soggy carpet, his long, dark hair plastered against his scalp. Somers crushed the plastic bottle and pocketed it; this was—or would be—a crime scene, and until they knew how it played out, there was no reason to take unnecessary risks. The thought was so ridiculous that he laughed.

"I don't see what's so funny," Hazard said, spitting again and wiping his mouth. When he raised his head, his eyes were red, but they were open. With the flashlight flooding his face, his pupils contracted, leaving only the glitter of scarecrow gold, and locks of his dark hair curled across his pale forehead. He was beautiful. Just so damn beautiful. With a growl, he swatted the flashlight away. "Mind pointing that somewhere else?"

"Ree, Swinney's dead. Come here."

He helped Hazard up, and together they moved back into the storeroom. It was worse seeing her this way a second time. More of the details crowded into Somers's attention: one heel slipping free from her flat, arms spread wide as though to cushion her fall, her face already unnatural as death massaged her features.

"Lender," Hazard said, squatting next to her.

"Maybe."

"What do you see?"

"She got shot twice. In the chest."

"And?"

"This isn't a game, Ree. Just tell me."

"I already told you: Lender killed her. You didn't believe me."

Grunting, Somers settled into a squat next to Swinney. He still wanted to reach over and tug the fabric closed. Not for decency's sake. Swinney would have laughed about something like that. But because Swinney had been careful about things like that: about her clothes and her shoes and her hair. She'd probably had to buzz her hair every other week to keep it that short, but she also had that single, long, reddish-blond lock in front, and that probably took a lot of work to maintain that look.

What had Hazard seen that was making him so sure? Somers examined her face again. There was no rictus, no frozen mask of surprise or terror. She was dead, and the electric currents driving the muscles in her face had stilled, and the only expression she wore was what might have passed for slack stupor, as though she were a particularly dim cousin from the country. But she hadn't been slack. And she'd never been stupid. And she deserved better than this.

The wounds, Somers decided. Whatever Hazard had seen, it had to be something with the wounds. He narrowed his attention, taking in the two shots that had ended Swinney's life. The cotton blouse had split in jagged x-shaped tears. It was difficult to tell anything about the wound itself; the torn flesh was visible under the blood, but no details, nothing that might give away the killer's identity. She deserved better. She deserved so much better. She had put up with male bullshit her entire career, and she had been trying to help them, and she had been a good cop, and she deserved better. Somers leaned closer, reaching for the gaping fabric, but Hazard caught his arm. The dark-haired man didn't say anything; he just stopped him.

There. Right there, where the fabric over her chest had split when the bullet tore through the button and into her body. The cotton had shredded. That was just like what had happened where the other bullet had gone in. But this wound had a difference. The fabric here, drawn tight and fastened by the button, had peeled back when she had been shot. And because it had unfurled, opening away from the wound, it had escaped the worst of the blood. The cotton at the edge was still white. But not completely. An oily smudge marked the fabric in a perfect quarter circle. Somers looked at the rest of the torn cotton for confirmation, but the blood hid the telltale marking. It would show up in the forensic analysis if anyone bothered to look for it, and it was only chance, only luck, that it showed up here.

"You're telling me that stuff," he indicated the smudge, "that's bullet wipe?"

Hazard nodded; he still hadn't released his arm.

Somers studied the body again. Most tests to determine the distance of a shooter took into consideration the physical attributes of the wound and the presence of gunpowder particulates on skin and clothing. In this shitty storefront, though, with a weak fluorescent light and no equipment and Swinney's body still covered in blood, it was impossible for either detective to make that kind of determination. But the bullet wipe—by some miracle, it had escaped the blood, and it was there, as plain as day. And bullet wipe meant that the shooter had been standing very close when he had fired.

"She let him get close to her."

Nodding, Hazard released Somers's arm and stood.

"Why would she let him get close to her? She knew he was dirty. She knew he had killed before." Somers stood too, wiping palms on his trousers, and shook his head. "She wasn't stupid. She was out here, the middle of the night, the middle of nowhere, trying to meet us in secret. Lender shows up. Why the fuck would she let him get close to her? And he didn't sneak up on her, Ree."

"No. Not much chance of sneaking up on her, not in a place like this." Hazard stepped carefully around the body, his attention moving from the alley door to the shelving with its waffle irons and toasters and black-and-white TVs the size of a case of Bud Lite, and then to the door that led to the front of the store.

"What?"

Planting himself in front of the door that led to the front, Hazard mimed drawing a gun and pointed his finger at Somers. "What do you do?"

"Shoot you."

"I've already got my gun out."

"If I'm smart, so do I."

"Do you see her gun?"

Somers swore and glanced down. Swinney's holster was empty.

"What do you do?"

"Damn it, Ree, I don't know."

"I just walked in with a gun. You weren't expecting me. You know I'm dirty."

"I shoot you."

"She didn't shoot him, though, so think of something else."

Somers allowed himself a frustrated yowl and scrubbed fingers through his hair. "I—I walk away. I move backward. That's what just about anybody does when they're looking down a gun. It's instinct, I guess. Get away from danger. But he didn't shoot her in the back, Ree."

"People usually keep their eyes on the danger while they move away from it. That's instinct too; keeping danger in sight, locking eyes with a predator, that kind of thing." Hazard waited, and then he blew smoke from his finger-gun and said, "So?"

"Sew a goddamn button. What?"

"Move backward."

Shaking his head, Somers paced back while Hazard advanced. It took only a handful of paces for Somers to reach the alley door, and he reached back, his eyes still fixed on Hazard, trying to unlock it.

"Boom. You're dead."

"But she didn't die here."

"No. She didn't." Hazard holstered the finger-gun and looked annoying self-satisfied.

Somers glanced at Swinney, where she lay on the floor, and said, "You're telling me she panicked? She couldn't even keep her calm long enough to try to make it to the door? Instead she—what? She backed up until she hit that rack of toasters and then let Lender kill her?"

"Swinney never seemed like the kind who would panic."

"Right. So your whole theory goes down the drain."

"That was your theory."

"What?"

"That was your theory. I never said she panicked."

For a long moment, Somers fought the urge to throttle his partner. Then, drawing in another breath, he tried to take in the scene with fresh eyes. Swinney had been watching the front; she knew the alley door was locked, and she was waiting for Hazard and Somers to arrive. She wasn't stupid, so she probably had her gun out because she knew her information was sensitive and because she guessed someone might try to silence her. She might have even guessed it would be Lender. But when Lender shows up, he has enough of an advantage that she doesn't get off the first shot. Or—or she just couldn't pull the trigger. She had worked with Lender for a long time. Maybe she couldn't, when it came time. She just couldn't. So instead, she tried to get away from the danger, moves towards—towards the goddamn toaster ovens.

Then it hit. "She wasn't trying to get away."

"I don't think so," Hazard said, stepping past Swinney's body to the long shelving unit. He opened a waffle iron, shook it, and then set it back down with a frown. "Let's see why she cared so much about kitchen appliances."

Joining him, Somers loosened the crumb drawer on a toaster. Antique crumbs dusted his hand, but there was no incriminating evidence. Then he pried the plastic case from an old, six-inch television. Nothing there, either. Together, they worked their way down the shelves. Hazard disassembled a quesadilla press. Somers broke the glass on a pizza oven. They each, separately, discovered Easy Bake Ovens, but when Hazard lifted his, a mouse squeaked and darted away, and Hazard swore and dropped the Easy Bake, and inside the plastic housing the bulb shattered.

"Don't say a fucking word," Hazard muttered as he reached for the toy oven again.

It was Somers who found them, tucked into the grease drawer of a Dinky Donut home fryer. Rancid oil soaked the papers' edges turning them translucent in the fluorescent light. Somers studied the top page, passed the second to Hazard, and tried to figure out what he was seeing.

It was an employment record. A truncated one, and considering its subject, the reason for the redaction was obvious. The paper highlighted only a few relevant details about Bruce Schaming, Special Agent for the Federal Bureau of Investigation: his age (forty-two), his years of service (twelve), his field office assignment (St. Louis), and his assignment to the Criminal, Cyber, Response, and Services branch. When Somers had finished, he passed his sheet to Hazard and took the other. It was almost identical, only this information was for Steven Graham, age fifty-five, years of service nineteen. Both documents had grainy black-and-white photographs. Schaming was Latino, and he looked a lot younger than forty-two. Graham was white, and he looked every year of fifty-five.

"These aren't official records," Somers said. "Not even close. These look like someone copied and pasted the information and printed them on an inkjet at home."

"That sounds right." Hazard's voice was distracted, and his eyes were fixed on the page, although he didn't seem to see anything.

"Why did Swinney have these? What did she want us to see? Are these the agents that talked to Jo Kjar? Or are these the guys who were pretending to be agents? What's this stuff supposed to mean?"

Hazard shook his head.

In the distance, sirens blared, and Somers hesitated. Then, taking the page from Hazard, he folded it with his own and pocketed them. He met Hazard's eyes. "Nothing about Lender."

"That son of a bitch—"

"Nothing about him. Nothing about the papers. None of it. Jesus, if we weren't driving a car that everybody would recognize for a hundred miles, I'd say we should leave. Right now."

Hazard's scarecrow eyes flickered with thought, and then he nodded.

Somers sighed and moved towards the storefront, intent on being outside and visible before the first cops arrived on the scene. The store was dark, and someone had obviously called 911 to report the shooting. Somers didn't want to die because a cop rushed into a darkened building and made a mistake. And—this bothered him more—he didn't want to give a dirty cop an easy excuse to put a few holes in him and Hazard.

At the door, though, he stopped and looked back at Liz Swinney, her heel slipping free from its flat, her red-gold hair lusterless in the tremulous fluorescent light.

"We're going to get that fucking bastard," Hazard said, squeezing Somers's shoulder.

Somers nodded. But Swinney still deserved better.

CHAPTER TWENTY-NINE

JULY 4
WEDNESDAY
1:12 AM

THEY WAITED. IT SEEMED most of the last two days had been waiting, and as they waited, Somers's headache swelled. It had been quiet for a long time; he attributed this to a series of emergencies that had pumped adrenaline and endorphins through him: Mikey, and then Somers's realization that he would have to betray Hazard, and now the shootout and Swinney's death. But the last of that adrenaline had dripped out of him, and the headache had gone nova behind his left eye, filling half his field of vision with pulses of starlight that whited out everything else.

They were separated. They told their stories. The other cops asked questions, and on their faces—when the starlight dimmed enough for Somers to make out their features—he saw something new. Or maybe it wasn't really new, but he was seeing it for the first time. He saw the same thing he had seen in Sheriff Engels's face: suspicion. Hoffmeister and Lloyd and Norman and Gross, even big old dumb Patrick Foley, they all looked like they'd worked the same bullshit over a game of cards and reached a conclusion. They looked at Somers like he was dirty. Like he and Hazard both were dirty. And that hurt worse than a supernova behind his left eye.

When Cravens finally reached him, she looked awful. Her skin was gray, and in the harsh cross lighting of the patrol car headlights, a mustache of delicate silver hairs threw shadows on her upper lip.

For a long time she stood there, strapped in place by the cross lights, and then she took off her hat and settled it over her fist and worked her hand in it, trying to puff it up.

"What's happening in this town, Detective?"

Somers shook his head.

"Why were you here?"

"Detective Swinney said she had information for us regarding our investigation. She said she would only meet us here, at this time."

Cravens shook her head slowly. Her fingers popped against the inside of her hat, and it made Somers think of a puppeteer's hand. Right then, he guessed, Martha Cravens would have been happy as a puppet. She would have been happy dancing on strings if she didn't have to deal with this mess anymore.

"Is there anyone who can corroborate that?"

"No, Chief."

"Where's Detective Lender?"

Somers weighed this question. It was hard with that star exploding behind his eye, but he gave it his best, and then he said, "I don't know. But I think that says something. Don't you?"

Cravens might have been a statue except for those fingers, restlessly flexing under the blue cotton. "Do I need to take your badge until this is over?"

"No, Chief."

"I don't know, John-Henry. I really don't know anymore. Whatever this is, it's not small-town stuff now. And I'm a small-town cop. We all are. I ought to take your badge until this is over." She went truly still then, the fingers inside the hat curling up like spider's legs, stiff and dead. "Only aim to do your duty," she said, echoing the quote she had spoken in her office two days before. "Hal Edgcomb is having a good laugh at me now."

With careful, unnatural movements, she perched the hat on her head and marched back to the storefront where Liz Swinney had died.

Sometime later, Hazard and Somers were allowed to leave, and they drove back to the Crofter's Mark in silence. They parked underground, where the air was still hot from the day, viscous with the Midwest humidity, stiff as river mud in the enclosed space. They rode the elevator to the fourth floor; from the mirrored walls, a thousand different John-Henry Somersets looked back, and a thousand different Emery Hazards. Somers ignored his own reflection. That poor bastard was fucked a million ways from Sunday. He looked, instead, at the spectral Hazards, with their red-rimmed eyes and their long dark hair curling over their foreheads and their huge shoulders still strong and true.

Another shootout. Another brush with death. And they were both alive. Swinney was dead, God rest her, God help her, she was dead, and there was nothing Somers could do about that. But he was alive. And the man he loved was alive. And Somers knew that after tonight, after what he was going to do to Emery Hazard, the man he loved might be gone, and so tonight had to be tonight, but it also had to be an eternity of all the other nights they might not have together. It had to be John-Henry Somerset's last chance, however he could, to make up for all the things he had done wrong. In the elevator's mirrored coffin, he could smell the clay again, smell it overpowering the summer smells of mulch and honeysuckle and hot tar. Somers was hard, so hard it ached, and he pressed himself against Hazard, enjoying the painful throb between his legs as he magnified the pressure there.

"Fuck," Hazard breathed between kisses. "Fuck, I thought—" They kissed again, stumbling back against the silvered glass, Somers so hard he thought he might pop right there, just grinding against his boyfriend's leg in an elevator like a goddamn teenager. "Fuck yeah," Hazard huffed. "Fuck yeah." His strong fingers grabbed a shock of Somers's hair, bending him back an inch, kissing him harder. Then Hazard retreated, his scarecrow eyes like polished chips of the hottest sunset in July. "Your head. I didn't want to—"

Somers kissed him. The elevator dinged.

His breath sheared ragged, Hazard managed to say, "Tonight, what happened, if you don't want to—"

Behind Somers, the doors rattled open. He kissed Hazard again, more insistently, driving his tongue into Hazard's mouth as he humped the big man's leg. "I want you to fuck me," Somers said, pulling back long enough to meet those scarecrow eyes.

The elevator dinged again. The doors rattled once more. Hazard wheeled Somers around and caught the doors with his heel. They stayed there for a moment, foreheads together, and Somers heard himself breathing like he'd run a mile or ten.

"I want you to fuck me. Like last night. Just fuck me, all right? Hard."

Grabbing two handfuls of Somers's shirt, Hazard tugged so hard he actually lifted Somers off his feet, and together they stumbled into the hall. Somers walked Hazard backward towards the apartment. His hands moved non-stop: Hazard's belt, his fly, the buttons on his shirt. When Hazard broke away from Somers's mouth long enough to look at the door and jam the key home, Somers sucked on his neck, his teeth dragging lightly over the skin in the way he knew Hazard liked, and the big man shuddered so hard that Somers thought he might have gotten off right there.

"You're a fucking maniac," Hazard muttered, elbowing the door open, staggering back into the apartment as his trousers dropped.

Somers grabbed the bulge under the dark-haired man's boxer-briefs. Hard as a goddamn rock still. He squeezed, and Hazard's breath whooshed out, and he steadied himself against the counter, his knees opening reflexively. "Do that again," he panted, "and you're not going to get fucked, blondie."

By then, Somers was past thinking. He wanted to be past everything. He wanted to be past the pain in his head. He wanted to be past the humiliation he had suffered at Mikey's hands. He wanted to be past the terror he felt for Evie. And most of all he wanted to be past the past, past the guilt, past the knowledge that he had hurt the one he loved and could never undo that hurt. He wanted all of this, but he wasn't getting it. He might not be thinking, not with his dick like a fucking titanium rod, but he was still hurting, and he was so tired of hurting.

"Fuck me," he whispered, nuzzling into Hazard's shoulder as he undid the rest of the buttons. He stripped away the big man's shirt, trailing kisses over his chest, the fine dark hairs on Hazard's chest bristling against his tongue. "Fuck me, Ree. Fuck me so hard I can't walk tomorrow. Fuck me so I bleed on your cock tonight."

Hazard's hand caught another shock of hair. He had gone still, and when he spoke, the heat had gone out of his voice. "What?"

"Just fuck me." His teeth closed lightly around one of Hazard's nipples; the big man moaned and bucked reflexively, and Somers's tightened his teeth, biting to the point where he knew it would hurt, but it would be a hurt that drove Hazard wild.

To Somers's surprise, though, Hazard tightened his grip and turned Somers's head up. "What's going on?"

"I want you to fuck me."

"What you said, about bleeding."

Somers was losing him. He was losing what he needed tonight: the hardest, roughest fuck he'd ever had from Hazard. Not just like the other night; the other night had been raw and brutal and primal, each of them responding to terror and violence. But tonight, tonight had to be even more than that. Tonight had to pay for everything.

"It was stupid," Somers said. Hooking his arms around Hazard's neck, he marched them towards the bedroom. He kissed Hazard again, hard, his tongue forcing its way between Hazard's teeth. "Just dirty talk. Just trying something out."

"John—"

But he suckled on Hazard's collarbone again, biting the delicate skin so deep it would bruise, and he felt Hazard thrust against him, his fingers spasming in Somers's hair hard enough to hurt. Yes, that was what Somers wanted. Yes, that kind of mindless hurt. Because Hazard wouldn't do it on purpose. He walked around day by day like a thunderstorm about to crack open, but deep down, he was just a fluffy white cloud. He wouldn't hurt Somers, not unless Somers drove him to it. And he was going to do it. He was going to push every button he knew until Hazard couldn't see, couldn't breathe, couldn't think, could only fuck, and then, then maybe he'd do it in a way that let Somers pay for what he'd done wrong all those years ago.

When they reached the bed, Somers stripped out of his own clothes while Hazard tugged off his underwear. The big man took a step to the nightstand, but Somers grabbed his hand and pulled him onto the bed. On his knees, Somers stared over his shoulder, letting heat flow into his gaze. He knew how he would look: lips puffy, cheeks flushed, eyes liquid with sex. And he knew Emery Hazard couldn't resist that look.

"Fuck me, Ree. Right now."

Hazard climbed up behind him, arms going around Somers's chest, his weight on Somers's back enough to make Somers grunt. His mouth tickled Somers's ear, his tongue tracing the cartilage, and then he whispered. "Not like this. Not tonight. I want to look into your eyes."

Wrapping his own hand around Hazard's, Somers guided it to his hair. "Then you can twist my head around when you're balls deep. See how you make me feel."

Hazard kissed his cheek. He kissed his jaw. He kissed the lines of his shoulder. He kissed across Somers's upper back, the heavy scruff rasping like sandpaper and sending electric jolts between Somers's legs. Somers could hear his own breathing, could hear the neediness in it.

"Ree, just fuck me already."

No answer. Only a line of kisses trailing down his spine, and then Hazard's mouth returned to the other side of Somers's face, starting the same path.

"Just fuck me. Just fucking fuck me, please. I need you. I need you inside me right now, Ree."

Both arms wrapped tight around Somers again, and Hazard whispered in his ear, "Not like this. Not tonight."

Not tonight. Somers wanted to scream. Any other night, a million other nights, and Hazard would have already been halfway done with the job by now. Any other night, Hazard would have given Somers the best sex of his life without even thinking about it. But tonight, of all possible nights, tonight Emery Hazard wanted to be tender. Somers bottled up the scream. Somers bottled it up along with everything else, and the ache in his stomach, the sick feeling, grew. Why couldn't Hazard just give him what he wanted? Just this one time, why couldn't he?

"Fine," Somers said. He wiggled loose from Hazard's grip, dropped on his back, and pulled his knees to his chest. "Now fuck me. Now you can see my eyes, so just fuck me."

Hazard loomed over him. From the bedside lamp, light ballooned towards the ceiling, and that same light picked out the edges of Hazard's form: the individual grains of stubble, the puffy tip of one nipple, the hard scallops of his abdomen, the rigid line of his dick. His hands moved to the inside of Somers's legs, widening them, and he bent over Somers, leaning down for a kiss. Somers turned his head to the side, squeezing his eyes shut.

"Just fuck me, please." Like he was ordering in the line at Burger King. Like that. Jesus, what was wrong with him? What had been wrong with him his entire life?

Hazard kissed his cheek, and Somers could feel the wetness on Hazard's face.

"John—"

"Here. I'll show you how."

He grabbed Hazard's dick, tugging him forward.

"Hold on," Hazard mumbled, and the dark-haired man seemed almost embarrassed. Crabbing across the bed on his knees, he fumbled in the drawer where they kept the lube.

"No. I don't want that. I just want you to—"

"Fuck you. I know. I'm not deaf. What the fuck is going on with you?"

Wrapping his legs around Hazard's torso, Somers hoisted himself up, catching Hazard's face when he tried to turn, kissing him, kissing harder, kissing until he felt the tremor of lust run through the big man.

"I want you to fuck me. Just like this."

Instead, he felt Hazard's hand, cold with lube, slide between his legs.

"I don't—"

"I don't fucking care," Hazard said, and with heart-stopping ease, he shoved Somers backward and went to work. Somers kicked at him, once, and tried to scrabble away. He was past thinking. Past anything close to reason. He only knew that he wanted one thing, one simple thing, and that was for Hazard to fuck him and hurt him and break him, and now, for some mind-bending reason Somers couldn't understand, Hazard refused to give him what he wanted. Their struggle went on another minute, maybe two, and Somers was painfully aware of how hard he was, of his breath, of the air anchored in his chest and being hitched out of him by centimeters.

When Hazard entered him, it pinged once, not even really an ache or a flash, more like a blip on a radar, and then Somers was lost. They were both frantic. They were both beyond anything but the mindlessness of this moment. As always when Hazard was inside him, Somers felt himself lifted on a white wave, hurtling higher and higher, leaving body and brain behind. His face was wet, but not with sweat. Hazard thumbed away the tears and kept driving into him, his face a pale mask of fury and desire and fear. And when the wave crested and broke, Somers was clutching at Hazard's wrist, holding on for dear life, and then the smell of clay came rushing back in, and the feel of those muscles and tendons and bones in Hazard's wrist was so familiar, so horribly familiar, that Somers was crying even harder—crying so hard he was shaking.

Hazard scooped him up, holding him against his chest, one lube-sticky hand parting Somers's hair. He didn't shush him or rock him. He just held him, tightly, as though he were holding all the pieces together and to slacken now would allow Somers to tumble into a pile of parts.

At some point, Hazard turned off the lamp, and the ballooning light shrank and folded and disappeared, and the moon-glow of the city dusted panels of the bedroom: a stretch of floor; Somers's side of the bed; Hazard's bad arm, crooked at his side.

"Fuck me," Somers whispered, his fingers light on the bandage. "Did I hurt your arm? I didn't even—Jesus, I'm such a fuck-up."

"It's fine."

"The way I was grabbing you—"

"It's fine." Something rumbled in Hazard's chest, the vibrations communicating themselves through skin and into Somers, and then Hazard said, "Are you?"

"What?"

"John, what is going on? You're upset about Evie. Ok. You're terrified. I get it. So am I. We've been shot at. Christ, you've been shot. And Swinney—" His breathing deepened. "Tonight, this, I've never—you've never—"

On wobbly legs, Somers got to his feet. Now, when it didn't matter anymore, he could feel pain. A little. Hazard, the big dumb brute, had been gentle as always; if anything, it had been Somers who had managed to hurt himself with all his stupidity.

"Hey, I want to talk about this."

"It was nothing. I don't know. I just—just a fuck, Ree. I just needed a fuck."

He stared back at the dark-haired man. Believe me, he thought. That's all Somers needed right then. Just believe me for right now, for this minute, and that'll be enough.

"That's bullshit. The last time, that was a fuck. That was both of us reacting to almost dying and the fact that you'd just about taken a shotgun to the face. That still meant something, John. It meant we were alive. Tonight—come on, I don't even know what tonight was. What I did to you—"

"You did what you're good at."

Pain flashed across Hazard's face, disappearing almost instantly. He gathered handfuls of the bedding, pooling it in his lap. The cotton rustled, and the pad of Somers's foot whispered on the bare boards as he swept it back and forth, and from the street, even at this late hour, bright, drunken voices warbled up through the darkness.

"I need to wash up," Somers said.

"Yeah. Sure."

In the bathroom, the light was too bright. Somers cleaned himself, scrubbed his face, and then crossed his arms over the sink and let his forehead rest there, the ceramic cool, the water still flowing. It sounded like a miniature river. Miniature, but loud enough that, for a few minutes, Somers didn't have to hear anything from the bedroom. He didn't have to hear Hazard rearranging the bedding, that horrible empty sound of cotton shifting against cotton, which was really just another, more awful form of silence. Somers had screwed this up. He knew that. He had wanted to give Hazard one thing, one last thing: a hate fuck, a revenge fuck, something to pay for the past. And Somers had screwed it up. Then he turned off the water.

Drawing clothes from the dresser, he slipped into jeans and a t-shirt, his eyes playing tag with Hazard's, never quite meeting. "I've got to run out."

"All right."

"Won't be long."

Hazard rolled over, his back to Somers, and tugged the sheet up to his neck.

Scooping up his phone and keys and wallet, Somers backed towards the door.

"I'll see you in the morning, Ree."

Outside, someone laughed again. Drunks. Drunk people walking home from St. Taffy's. And Somers wanted to go downstairs, line them up, and smash their teeth against the curb.

"Night, Ree."

He stopped at the apartment door. His phone vibrated, and Somers didn't recognize the number. He glanced back at the bedroom: silent and dark. And then he stepped into the hall, shut the door, and answered.

"Bring your pussy boy to the Maycomb Packing building. Twenty minutes."

The call disconnected.

And this next part, this was the real betrayal. Somers keyed in a message and sent it, and almost a full minute later, his phone rang. When he answered, he spoke four clear words.

"We need to meet."

CHAPTER THIRTY

JULY 4
WEDNESDAY
2:42 AM

NAOMI MALSHO ARRIVED in a late model Mercedes, the kind that had probably cost more than the house Somers had lived in with Cora. She had been Somers's sister-in-law; his wife's sister. When she got out of the car, she looked like what she was: expensive, beautiful, and dangerous. She wore yoga pants and a workout shirt, her dark hair was pulled back in a bun, and she carried a massive Desert Eagle Mark XIX at her side. A gun that big looked like it could shoot through a bank vault and leave enough wiggle room for you to squeeze inside.

On the corner of an abandoned Smithfield gas station, Somers checked the street again. Still empty. The lot was dark; someone had shot out the sodium lamps a long time ago because no glass littered the weeds and gravel. Naomi checked the street in both directions too. And then, as though to make her point clear, she drew the Desert Eagle.

"I've got, I don't know, five minutes. This has to be fast."

"You said it was about Evie."

"If you want to come after me, come after me. If you want to put a bullet in my head, you can do it right now. But this stuff with Evie, you're going too far, Naomi. I never thought you'd do something like this. Not to Evie. Not to your sister's daughter."

"What are you talking about?"

"Mikey didn't tell you?"

Naomi's delicate features remained impassive, but the Desert Eagle gave a tiny jump. "Tell me what?"

"That he's got somebody tracking Evie. Taking pictures. Ready to pick her up. If you want us to pause the stuff with Ted Kjar, all right, we can talk about that. But not like this. Not when you're holding Evie's life over my head. And not when it comes down to Emery—"

"Tell me everything from the beginning." She shivered; even in summer, maybe yoga pants weren't warm enough for a two-AM meeting.

Something clicked, and Somers said, "You didn't send Mikey?"

"Are you talking about Mikey Grames?"

"He showed up in the hospital. Told me if I didn't drop this stuff about Kjar, he'd sell Evie into one of those child sex rings." He checked his phone. "I've got like three minutes, Naomi. You didn't do this?"

Her face froze with indecision.

"Naomi!"

"No."

"The Kjar case?"

"It means nothing to me."

"Evie?"

"Give me some credit, John-Henry. I wouldn't hurt my niece."

"Who do you have that's smart and capable? Somebody you'd trust to get to Cora's house and get rid of the piece of shit that's sitting outside. There might be more than one of them out there."

The indecision melted away from her, and she holstered the massive pistol. Moving towards the Mercedes, she drew out her phone, then stopped and looked back.

"You know what Mikey's involved in?"

"You tell me."

"I'm not sure. I think it has something to do with the meth manufacturing in the area. Where are you meeting him?"

"I'm not worried about me. I'm worried about—"

"I'll take care of Cora and Evie. Where are you meeting him?" She shook her phone at Somers. "Quickly, John-Henry."

"The Maycomb Packing building in—Christ, I've got to go."

"Go."

"Evie—"

"Trust me: those guys are going to wish they'd never met Mikey Grames. Evie and Cora won't miss a minute of sleep; that's a promise."

Nodding, Somers dropped into the Aston Martin and put it into gear. He launched down the choppy asphalt, skidding around two corners before he brought his pulse under control. Evie and Cora were going to be safe. That was what mattered. Hazard was going to be safe. That was what mattered. And if Somers did everything right over the next five minutes, somebody would need a microscope and a hell of a lot of superglue to put Mikey's face back together, and that was what mattered.

He slowed the Aston Martin long enough to check his phone and to spot Mikey's position: not in the Maycomb Packing building, but in the one next to it. The little shit was trying to play it smart. Or to play it safe. He probably had a couple of good old boys tucked up high in Maycomb Packing, ready to put a few rifle rounds in Hazard and Somers as soon as they walked inside, but he was going to stay safe in the building next door. Somers's lips peeled back. It wasn't a grin. It was more like a dog about to bite. But it felt really damn good.

He took the rest of the distance quietly, and he left the Aston Martin two blocks back and ran on foot. He was down to the last thirty seconds or so before he reached the deadline Mikey had set. That was ok. Thirty seconds was going to be enough.

When he got Mikey, he was going to take his time. The thought was darkly luminous inside Somers, ecliptic, like a black hole fringed with fire. He was going to force Mikey back to the Aston Martin. He was going to cuff him. He was going to drive him out to the clay pits—abandoned now, and abandoned was good because it meant they would be alone. Alone with the summer, the mulch, the honeysuckle. Alone with that motherfucking clay plugging Somers's nose. And then, when they were there, Somers was going to take his time. He was going to teach Mikey Grames. That thought, in particular, was crystal clear for Somers. Teaching. This was about teaching that piece of shit. Teaching him intimately how he had made Hazard feel, how he had made Somers feel, how he had made other people feel. And when Somers was done teaching—and he was going to take his time, a long time—he was going to hit Mikey in the face. And then again. And again. Until that face was like a Jack-o-lantern two weeks after Halloween. Christ dammit, he'd forgotten the gloves. If he wanted to work on him that long, he was going to need gloves. Somers held back a sigh as he trotted down the block. He'd have to pick some up after he got Mikey back to the clay pits.

Somers checked his phone again. The red pin marking Mikey's location hadn't moved. Still inside the building next to Maycomb Packing. Time was up. Any minute now, Mikey would be calling with more threats, with more demands, with more of his bullshit. Somers eyed the building. Maycomb Packing was a refrigerated warehouse from the 1960s, the glass-block windows squinting back like thick spectacles. Next to it was the garage that had serviced the Maycomb trucks. Three bay doors were rolled down on the front—permanently, to judge by the rust caking the frames—and the windows here had plywood backing. A pair of doors bracketed the service bays, and Mikey's pin showed that he was behind the door on the right.

Still running, Somers cut left, shearing off the angle of his approach to gain a few precious seconds. Mikey was still inside that building. He was probably making phone calls, trying to figure out where Somers and Hazard were, why they hadn't shown up. He was probably calling the guys he had watching Evie and Cora. Maybe he was just checking, maybe just making sure that Somers hadn't tried anything. Or maybe he was giving the order: take the little girl, kill the woman. Somers's stomach dropped like someone had thrown wide a trapdoor. What if Somers was making a mistake? What if Naomi wasn't fast enough, or her guys weren't good enough, or something went wrong? What if Mikey did exactly what he'd threatened, and those bastards took Evie, and she got sold to—

He had reached the left-hand door, and he stopped. No more of that. He couldn't risk it. He had to focus on this moment, right now. But a second doubt wormed at him. What if this were another one of those games? What if this were a bluff or a blind or a decoy or whatever the hell you called it? What if Mikey had suspected Somers would never bring Hazard, and right now, men with guns were stalking the fourth-floor hallway of the Crofter's Mark, putting their shoulders to the door, splitting the wood around the lock. Hazard would be smart. He'd hole up in the bedroom, call 911. But he'd be one man, and they'd have planned the whole thing out.

Enough. Enough, Somers told himself. He reached out to check the door, and his hand shook. Just a little, but that was bad. Thinking like this, afraid like this, he was in a bad headspace. He needed the focus he had felt only moments before: that violent, blacklight vision of what he was going to do to Mikey.

The latch lifted. Somers pushed, but the wood had swelled over the decades, and the door stuck. Huddling against the door, Somers rocked into it. With a squeal, the wood grated inwards and stopped. Somers studied it again. A quarter of an inch. He needed to move it another quarter inch, maybe less. But that squeal had been louder than he liked. Had Mikey heard? Had he been staring at his phone, furious, confused as to why his goons at Cora's house weren't answering—they're dead, you motherfucker, Somers wanted to say, they're dead and my daughter is safe—and he had heard the wood squeak?

Summer humidity choked Somers. The air, thick and sticky, wrapped him like raw wool. A bead of sweat trickled down his back, tickling between his shoulder blades; just one bead there. But sweat swamped his underarms. He could smell that sweat. Smell his own fear.

Still nothing from inside. Maybe Mikey hadn't heard. Maybe he'd been shouting at a subordinate. Maybe he'd been listening to the line ringing, waiting for Somers to pick up so he could issue another ultimatum. But he wasn't going to have a chance. Somers wouldn't give him another chance. Now, right now, this was going to end.

As quietly as he could, Somers dropped his weight against the door. This time, it popped free without a sound. The air smelled like hot wood. A strand of cobweb glued itself to Somers's cheek. He took the first step into the garage, into darkness, tasting forty years' worth of motor oil and gasoline and antifreeze with every breath. Traps, his mind said. At the Haverford, there were traps, so be careful. For a moment, Somers stood in the darkness, listening, allowing his eyes to adjust.

Light from the sodium lamps outlined the plywood-backed windows. It wasn't much, but it was enough, as Somers's eyes adjusted, to give him a sense of the place. It was one open room, although the floor was divided by the three service bays, and a shadowed break in the windows at the back corner likely marked the manager's office or the bathroom or a supply closet. A little more light came through the door he had just entered—outlining him, Somers realized—but it allowed him to see an old grease gun and a rack on casters full of lead-acid car batteries. Why nobody had scavenged those, Somers didn't know. He hooked the door with his elbow and shut it behind him.

Still nothing. No voices. No movement. But the phone said that Mikey Grames was here. Somers inched forward. With every movement, he awaited the subtle tension of a wire. He remembered that from the Haverford: like a cobweb, he thought, his free hand scrubbing at the strand still glued to his cheek. It had been like stepping into a cobweb. The wire had been strung so that it hit high on his shin, and it had held for a heartbeat before the force of Somers's passage triggered it. And then the shotgun had flared, and the scattershot fireworks lit up his side. He was waiting for that again. Waiting to cross one of those trip wires. And then he'd be dead, and he'd never get to hear Hazard tell him how stupid he was, what a fuckup he was.

And still nothing. Not a goddamn sound. Somers's sweat slicked the Glock's polymer grip, but he didn't dare release it, not even long enough to dry his hand on his jeans. Maybe Mikey had been smarter than Somers. Maybe he'd figured out that Somers was tracking his location. Somers's breath quickened. Adrenaline dizzied him;

blackness ate at the corners of his vision. Where was Mikey? Where the fuck was he?

At the center service bay, Somers froze. To his left, the service pit opened up like a black hole. But it wasn't black. Not entirely. Somewhere down there, where a mechanic would stand under the trucks, working on them with the extra space that the service pit afforded, something glowed. It was a faint blue color. An electric blue. Like the light of a phone.

Somers's heartbeat thundered in his ears. He held for a moment. His thoughts zagged: it was a trap; it wasn't. Taking a long minute, he scanned the garage again, and he still saw nothing, and he heard nothing. He squatted at the edge of the pit. The machine grease smell was stronger here. And something else, too. Iron. Or copper. Something metallic.

It was a phone. From here, he could see that much. And it looked like the phone that Mikey had shown him in the hospital. Somers let one sneaker drift over the edge of the pit. He'd drop down there. He'd see—

No. Fuck no. Whatever this was, something wasn't right. Somers stood, his back to the wall, and scooted towards the door. The whole thing had gone wrong. All that mattered was that Evie was safe. The rest of it, Mikey, all of it, could wait. He'd go back. He'd tell Hazard. He'd tell him all of it. And Hazard would yell. He'd probably throw things. Hell, he'd probably break something big and expensive. One of those big feet would probably go right through the TV. But when he calmed down in a day or a month or a year, he'd say something that was grudgingly approving. Something like, *I can't believe you did the smart thing. I thought you were just a dumb blond*. Something like that. A grin ghosted on Somers's face as he side-stepped towards the door. He was going to apologize. He was going to explain everything. And then they'd come at this from the right angle, working it together.

Somers caught the latch, tugged, and the sticky Midwestern night poured in around him, full of crickets and watery starlight and a rotting-grass smell, like wet clippings left too long on the ground.

Someone kicked him in the back of the knee. Somers went down. He caught himself in the doorframe, but his wrist hit the wood wrong, and his fingers popped open. The Glock shot out of his hand, cracked against stubbly weeds, and disappeared into the dark.

For a moment, Somers had a single thought: get the gun. Then the door slammed inward, knocking him against the frame. His head cracked against wood. The door came in again, propelled with tremendous force, and then again. Somers fell forward, his head ringing, and tried to drag himself clear. He tasted metal. And dirt. And the world fuzzed around him. The gun. Get the gun.

Then a small cold ring of metal pressed against the back of his neck, and Mikey said, "Just stop. Stop right there before I have to do something that's no fun."

CHAPTER THIRTY-ONE

JULY 4
WEDNESDAY
7:02 AM

AT FOUR IN THE MORNING, Hazard was pissed. He lay in bed, the grey satin light from the street ruffling above him, and got angry. What the fuck had happened tonight? And why the fuck had it happened?

At five, he was worried and called. Somers's voicemail picked up, and then Hazard was pissed again.

At six, he was afraid. He didn't like that word. He dodged it and smacked it away, but it kept coming back. And there was the feeling, too. That feeling in his gut, something worming through him, gnawing holes in his intestines, and it made him sick and it hurt and it was enough to drive somebody out of his mind. By six, he was boxed in and didn't have anywhere left to go, and he had to admit that he was afraid. He called Somers again, voicemail again, and he was afraid. And angry. And worried. But the fear crusted over everything else, thick and waxy.

He walked a full circuit of the apartment, naked, his bare feet padding out a staccato. A full circuit. A full goddamn circuit, one shoulder to the wall, as though he were a bloodhound that had lost the damn scent. And then, when he got back to their bedroom, he stood there and stared at the boarded-up window. It seemed unreal that the day before, or the day before that, or whenever it had been, that they had been tangled up in each other against that window while Hollace Walker lined up a shot. It seemed like a lifetime ago.

"Where are you?" He said it out loud, and he knew that was what crazy people did, but he was crazy. Somers had made him crazy. Love made him crazy, and there wasn't a damn thing he could do about it now. His voice sounded like rusty sheet metal inside a compactor. "Where the fuck are you, you selfish fucking piece of shit?"

And that helped. A little. But he walked another circuit. A whole other circuit, like a goddamn dog. And the thing at his heels, the thing that wouldn't leave him alone and chased him out of bed and chased him through the rooms of their small apartment, the thing that was biting big chunks out of his ass, was the fact that Emery Hazard, because he was a proud, arrogant, conceited, self-righteous son of a bitch, hadn't asked his boyfriend where he was going.

How hard would that have been? How hard would it have been, when Somers said he needed to go out, to say, where? Where are you going? Why? What's going on? Do you need help? Instead, though, Hazard had sulked in bed like a child. Jesus, he'd even pulled up the sheets. He should have put his head under the covers, and that would have rounded out the whole thing perfectly.

Another part of him, though, argued back: but Somers had hurt you. He'd wanted sex, yes, but it had been more than that. Somers had been—well, Hazard didn't know what, exactly. That was part of the problem. He hadn't known what Somers wanted. But he had known that whatever it was, it wasn't Hazard. Somers had wanted something else, and Hazard had just been—had just been a convenient dick. Something at hand, so to speak. And that, even more than the strange things Somers had said—make me bleed, what the hell did that mean?—even more than the way Somers had cried when Hazard was inside him, even more than at the end, the way he had clutched Hazard's wrist, and all of the sudden Hazard had been sixteen again, with Somers pinning him to the wall while Mikey cut into his belly, more than all of that, the worst part had been knowing that whatever Somers wanted out of that fuck, it wasn't Emery Hazard. And Jesus Christ, he thought with disgust as he found himself staring at the gray rectangle of window again, if that isn't the most pathetic thing in the whole world.

At seven, he was afraid and worried and pissed and couldn't stand it any longer. Hazard showered. He made himself stand there, the hot water drumming against his shoulders, the steam spun like cotton candy in the air. He shaved, and his hands shook, and instead of the stubble now he wore two cuts on his cheek. He tried to make himself eat, but after five minutes of staring into the milk and Cheerios, he dumped the mess down the sink and ran the disposal. Then he called Cora.

"Emery? What's going on?" From the other line, Evie's warble interrupted, and Cora said something to the little girl, and then she came back. "God, is John-Henry all right?"

"He's not with you?"

"No, of course not. Is he all right?"

"Yeah, yeah. I just thought—he said he had something to do, and I thought maybe he was going to help you with something."

"No. I thought I might have to call the plumber the other day; the sink was clogged. Then I thought how silly it was, and I decided I could fix it myself, and—"

"He's not there, though? You didn't call him?"

"No. Emery—"

"Are you and Evie all right?"

"Of course we are. But we're going to be late for school if we don't hurry, isn't that right, miss? She's decided she has to be the one to put on her shoes. All by herself. She says Reeree taught her."

"Oh Christ. I'm sorry."

Cora laughed. "Don't be silly. Nine times out of ten, it's adorable. It's just when we're already late for school—the power went out last night, and it reset the clocks."

"You're sure you're all right?"

"Emery, what's going on?"

"Nothing. If you see him, though, will you call me?"

"John-Henry?" Cora's voice hushed. "Emery, is everything all right between you? I know it's not my business, and you can tell me not to pry. But I don't mind talking about it; really, I don't. Is he—" The hesitation was so strong Hazard could almost see her biting her lip. "Is he drinking again?"

"Fuck me," Hazard said. He hadn't thought about that. It hadn't even occurred to him.

"Language," Cora said weakly.

"Sorry. I don't know. I don't think so. But I don't know. We had a fight. Or he was having a fight with me and I didn't know about what. And then he said he had something to do, and he left."

From the street, twin horns blared simultaneously, and a man with a cigarette-burned voice shouted obscenities about someone's mother. Hazard's hand twitched at the blinds. Light stabbed in, vanished, stabbed again. He had to make himself drop his hand.

"He likes a place—he liked a place over in the old rail services part of town. The Hammer? The Screwdriver? I think that was it."

"Yeah."

"He comes back, Emery. He always comes back."

"I've got to get to work."

"He'll get it out of his system."

"I'm late."

"Evie sends kisses."

He disconnected the call, twitched the blinds once more, and that fucking light stabbed at him again. The light lanced something inside of him, and all the worry oozed out. Behind, it left red, inflamed anger. Somers was drinking. He was out on a fucking bender. He wasn't an alcoholic, not really, but he was the next best thing: a coward who hid inside a bottle when things got bad. No, that wasn't even really it. It wasn't just when things got bad. When things got bad, most things, Somers could stand up and take it on the chin and then hit back harder than about anyone Hazard knew.

No, Somers started drinking when he felt like he wasn't appreciated. It made him sound like a Hollywood diva, but there it was: that had been his explanation when he and Hazard had first been partnered. That's why Somers's marriage had fallen apart; and now he was out there, doing it again.

And what exactly the fuck did he have to feel unappreciated about? Hazard looped the cord to the blinds around his fist. What exactly had made Somers feel like Emery Hazard didn't appreciate him, didn't appreciate every hour with him, every moment with him?

He looped the cord around again. What exactly made Somers doubt, even for an instant, that he was the most important thing that had ever crossed Hazard's path by sunlight or moonlight or starlight or darklight? Another loop. His fingers puffed, pallid and purple with the tinge of trapped blood. What had it been? That Hazard wouldn't fuck him bloody? That Hazard hadn't stopped him when he walked out the door? What? Hazard deserved to know that much. What should Hazard have done differently?

First as tragedy, then as farce.

And it was a farce. This whole fucking thing was a farce. Somers daring to act like this, daring to go out drinking, and he might be out there right now, he might be—

—fucking some other guy—

—with a clatter, the blinds ripped away, and light crashed through the window.

Hazard left the tangled blinds on the floor, soaking in the overabundant sunlight. He left the apartment. He left every goddamn fucking thought about Somers and his fucking selfishness behind. And he went to work.

CHAPTER THIRTY-TWO

JULY 4
WEDNESDAY
7:57 AM

HAZARD COULDN'T STAND the thought of going to the station. When he found the underground parking empty, the Aston Martin gone, he decided to walk. But not to the station. If he walked to the station, he would go inside. If he went inside, he would end up at his desk in the bullpen. If he sat at his desk in the bullpen, somebody—Norman, probably—would say something. Somebody would have seen Somers at one of the dives out on Mississippi. Somebody—goddamn it, Hazard was sure it would be Norman—would talk about Somers sloppy drunk. And then Hazard would have to break Norman's nose.

So instead of the station, he walked north and west. Even in the morning, the temperature bumped higher and higher. The smell of gasoline and two-stroke engine oil smothered everything else; on the next block, Hazard found its source: a lawnmower tipped on its side, leaking oil across the sidewalk, a cloud of gasoline almost visible above it. Hazard checked his pockets. No lighter. And that was the story of his life. He checked the cross streets, looking for a convenience store, a lumber yard, anywhere he might find a pack of matches. Blowing this lawnmower to hell, that would make him feel better. Blowing anything to hell would make him feel better. But he didn't see anything, not even a telephone booth, and he kept walking.

The Newton Funeral Home didn't look like much; it certainly didn't look like it held anything besides lithograph prints and silk flowers. But at the back of the building, behind a reinforced door, the county medical examiner had his small office. Dr. Kamp might not be working as medical examiner anymore, not after being assaulted a few months earlier, but Hazard knew that the county had retained a provisional examiner until a more permanent decision could be made. And the provisional examiner, Hazard hoped, might have found something during Ted Kjar's autopsy that would nudge the investigation forward.

Hazard moved quickly through the building, through the fog of air freshener and the fainter smell of ammonia, to the reinforced door at the back. He punched in the code, 1-2-3-4, and shoved. The door buzzed, but it didn't move, not as much as an inch. He tried again: 1-2-3-4. Nothing. Just that damn buzz.

With a fist, Hazard hammered on the door. It took a minute before the door rattled, and then it opened an inch, and a dark eye looked out.

"I told you I don't have time for this. If you need something, go bother those detectives."

"I need—"

"Yes, I'm sure you do. Go tell it to Hazard or Somerset."

The door slammed shut.

Hazard raised his fist, thought about it for a moment, and hammered again. He kept hammering for another full minute before the door opened a crack.

That dark eye narrowed with anger. "I told you: whatever it is, take it to Detective Hazard or Detective Somerset. It won't hurt either of them to lift a finger for a chance, and—"

"I'm Hazard. Open the door."

"I'm sorry?"

"Open the fucking door."

"Did you—" The dark eye twitched. "Detective Hazard?"

"Open the door."

"Yes. Of course."

The door shut and opened again, this time all the way. Hazard pushed in, shouldering the door and ignoring the woof of exasperated breath. But he stopped when he saw the ME's lab.

It had changed. Hazard hadn't been inside for months, not since Kamp had left, and he couldn't believe how different the place looked. Although the fundamentals remained the same—the black-and-white tile, the chipped porcelain of the autopsy table, and the stainless-steel cadaver drawers—everything had changed. Someone had scrubbed the grime from the tile and eradicated the rust from the beneath the chipped enamel. Even Kamp's desk, nothing more than plywood over two sawhorses, was gone, and in its place stood a simple steel work table.

"I'm not ready to see you."

Hazard spun to face the speaker. She was tall, no longer young but not quite into the badlands, and she had a painful thinness. Like piano wire, Hazard thought. Piano wire at the end of the board, thin and pulled so tight she'd was likely to snap. The dark eyes, though, made up for a lot of the rest, and right then, they were tight with displeasure.

"When I'm ready, I'll send over my report, and then I'll be happy to talk to you. Until then—"

"No, you won't."

She took shallow breaths, and her cheeks pinkened. "Excuse—"

"No. You won't ever want to talk to me. And I don't care if you're done. You're taking too long, and I—"

"I'm taking too long? Detective Hazard, if you don't like—"

"What do you have on Ted Kjar?"

"If you don't like how I—"

"What do you have?"

She took a deep breath. "If you have something to say about my work—"

"Yes. I do. I want to know what you have on Ted Kjar, and the sooner you tell me, the sooner I'll leave you alone."

She quivered for a moment, piano wire ready to snap, and then she said, "You're an asshole."

"Ted Kjar."

"Everyone says you're an asshole."

Hazard grunted, turned to the desk, and grabbed a stack of files.

"Don't you dare." She slapped the folders out of his hand. "Where's the other one? They told me the other one is the only reason you're still on the force."

"The reason I'm still on the force," Hazard said, snatching up the files again, "is because I close cases. And I want to close the case on Ted Kjar. And that means I need you to tell me what you've got, unless—" He eyed her, taking in her bushy hair, the straight lines of her Kmart clothes, the men's sneakers. "Unless your undergraduate at Vassar didn't prepare you adequately for medical school and you've got nothing to report."

Pink darkened to rose in her cheeks, and her nails curled into her palms. "Bryn Mawr."

"Medical school?"

"Columbia."

"And?"

She blinked, and her nails fell out of fists. "And what?"

"And do you have enough medical training to tell me anything useful about Ted Kjar?"

She wrestled the files away from Hazard, tossing several back onto the work table before folding one open. "He died because someone shot him in the back."

"I know. I shot him."

"Then what do you want, Detective Hazard?"

"Whatever you've got."

"I've got nothing else. You can see yourself out, Detective."

"Toxicology."

"I told you: I've got nothing else."

Hazard stared at her. She was lying. He was sure of that. Not because he had Somers's skill at understanding people but because the file she held contained dozens of pages. Too many pages for her to know nothing more than the fact that Kjar had been shot. And she wasn't going to tell him; that much was obvious too.

He reached for the file, and she put it behind her back.

No. No, he wasn't getting that file unless he knocked out a few of her teeth. That didn't sound too bad to Hazard, but he guessed it might shorten his time on the Wahredua PD substantially.

So that made things simple: he'd come back later. Only someone had changed the door code, so he'd have to break into the lab. He'd take the file and—

And he wouldn't have to do any of this if Somers were here. Somers would smile and bat those golden eyelashes and this woman would probably forget her two-semester sequence on the History of Feminism at Bryn Mawr and want nothing more than for Somers to club her over the head and drag her back to his cave.

"Is that all, Detective Hazard?"

If Somers were here. That was as far as he could get. If Somers were here. And that, more than anything else, hurt because it showed how much things had changed. Somers had become part of his life, and now, with him gone, it was like—

"Detective Hazard?"

He forced himself to meet those dark eyes. What would Somers do? Oh, he'd bat those dark gold lashes. He'd smile. He'd say something witty and flirty, something charged with so much sex that one extra atom would cause an explosion. But he'd also be kind.

"I'm sorry."

"What?"

"I shouldn't have come in here like that. I shouldn't have spoken to you the way that I did."

Outside, distantly, a bottle rocket popped, and the woman jumped. It was the Fourth of July, Hazard realized. He had known the date, of course, but the significance had escaped him until now.

"I'm acting poorly because I'm upset. And I'm upset for personal reasons. John—" He stopped. "I shouldn't have taken it out on you. I'm sorry."

"Apology accepted." Some of that piano-wire tension eased, and she held out a hand. "I'm Denice Boyer."

"Dr. Boyer. I'm sorry we met this way. And I'm sorry about the rest of it." Hazard pumped her hand once and made a beeline for the door.

335

"Detective Hazard."

He halted at the door.

"There is something. If you have a minute." The pink in her cheeks had softened. Carnation pink. It did a hell of a lot for her, especially alongside those eyes.

What would Somers do now? Hazard tried for a smile, even though it felt like dragging sand from the bottom of Lake Palmerston, and said, "Thank you."

They sat on folding chairs, the file spread on the desk. Dr. Boyer turned the pages, and she spoke to the paper instead of to Hazard, her voice low as though she were telling a secret. "I told you the truth, Detective. Up to a point, I mean. Officially, the cause of death is catastrophic injury to the heart caused by gunshot wounds."

"My shots."

"Yes." The page trembled between her fingers, and she let it flutter to rest and then smoothed it. "What you described, Mr. Kjar's behavior, his attack on the mayor—it was very odd. I read all the reports, including your statement and Detective Somerset's. I did the autopsy. There are a few irregularities, and I'll tell you about those, but—" Her hand smoothed the page again and again.

"Dr. Boyer?"

"I moved here from Denver. Did you know that? Probably. Everyone says you're really excellent at this work. But have you been to Denver?"

"Once."

"It's a city. Do you know what I mean?"

Hazard nodded.

"That's what I was used to: city life. I had the same apartment for seven years, and I never met my neighbors. Not once. That's my fault, I know, but I'm just saying, I never met them. And then I left. Personal reasons. An ex, back in Denver. He was—he worked for the county too. The same office. And when I ended things, he made my life difficult. He told stories. He had pictures. And I know I could have taken it to court and I probably would have won, but I just couldn't. I—" She flushed, and Hazard was starting to suspect that various shades of pink were her permanent color. "I loved him. And when something like that ends, it's like someone's gone to work on your insides with a razor blade and a vacuum cleaner. Do you know what I mean?"

Hazard couldn't speak. He couldn't even nod.

"Of course you don't," she said with an empty little laugh. "What I mean, though, is that it just wasn't worth the fight. I didn't want to be there, not after everything, so I took this job."

Another bottle rocket popped outside the funeral home, and then there was the long, whistling cry of another, larger rocket, and the frazzled concussion at the end.

"Dr. Boyer, why are you working on the Fourth of July?"

"Small towns are different." She took a breath, and with a gesture that looked remarkably final, she smoothed the page one last time. "I was shopping at the Kroger, and a woman came up to me. She was sobbing even before she started talking. And she told me her name was Josephine Kjar, and she begged me to find out what had happened to her husband. Nothing like that had ever happened to me. Nothing. Everyone that I'd ever stood over at the slab, they were all strangers. Even after I'd cut them open and emptied them out, even after I knew everything their bodies could tell me—things they never even knew themselves—even after that, they were still strangers. But now . . ." She shrugged, and her eyes came to rest on one of the refrigerated drawers.

"What did you do?"

"Nothing that will stand up in court, I'm afraid. Nothing illegal, I don't think, but the results aren't something you can put in front of a jury."

Hazard ran through the normal process in a post-mortem examination, but his mind skipped back, like someone flicking the needle on a record player, the same words over and over again: *with a razor blade and a vacuum cleaner*. Yes, he thought. Yes. Cut up and bleeding and empty. Yes, that was exactly how it felt.

"During the autopsy, I found a few irregularities, which I've mentioned. Abrasions on the arms and legs. These corresponded with injection sites, bruising, and damage to veins. It seemed possible that Ted Kjar was simply a novice at mainlining drugs, and that in his efforts to locate a good vein, he had given himself those minor abrasions. Of course, that didn't match what anyone had said about Ted Kjar. The story I kept hearing was that he had a history of drug use. I suppose he might have been out of practice, but something felt off."

"You were doing your own investigation?"

"A few phone calls. To Mrs. Kjar and to other people who knew Mr. Kjar. I am the medical examiner, Detective. Nobody seemed to think it was strange."

"They ought to have. Our last medical examiner couldn't pull his head out of a bottle long enough to breathe."

"The irregularities," Dr. Boyer said with a smile, "didn't end there. I wanted to know more, especially about those signs of injections. Normally—and, more importantly, officially—toxicology tests are conducted in the Highway Patrol labs in Springfield. I sent off all the samples. Standard procedure. It might be months before you hear anything; longer if you want DNA."

"In a high-profile case, like this one, with the mayor, it might be less."

"It might be. But not by much. Four weeks, minimum. And I lay in bed that first night, telling myself that the mayor was alive and that four weeks really wasn't that long, and by all accounts Ted Kjar had just gone crazy. It didn't matter. She had come up to me. Walked right up to me. And she had asked me to help." She bit her lip and shivered.

Somers would know what to say. Somers would have a joke. Something to break the tension. "Just wait until she asks you to water her plants," Hazard said. It was stupid; it wasn't anywhere as good as what Somers would have said.

But it worked. Dr. Boyer laughed, the sound cracked but alive. "Yes, I suppose that's the real risk of a small town. Everyone needs a favor."

"Like me."

"No, Detective. This isn't a favor for you. This is the only decent thing I could do, and I'm glad I did it."

"You ran the tests?"

"They're not terribly complicated. I did the equivalent of a standard drug test. You know, the kind that many employers use. Pee in a cup. That kind of thing. The results are almost immediate."

"And?"

"And he lit up like a Christmas tree, Detective. Marijuana, cocaine, amphetamines, methamphetamines, barbiturates, ketamine. The window isn't that big, Detective. Ted Kjar was loaded with a wide variety of drugs in the days before his death."

Hazard shook his head. "Cocaine, yes. Amphetamines, meth, yes. He was an addict, and he was acting crazy. And—" His conversation with Kandy came back to him. Substance-induced psychotic disorder. "That makes sense, I suppose. It explains his behavior at the end, the violence, the paranoia. But the rest of it? All those downers? That doesn't fit. He didn't act dopey at all. No one ever described anything that might suggest he was using that class of drug."

Dr. Boyer's remarkable eyes fixed Hazard. "I thought the same thing, Detective. Exactly the same thing. And then, as I thought about it, I wondered if Ted Kjar wasn't the one deciding what he used."

Hazard nodded slowly. "Then who the hell was?"

CHAPTER THIRTY-THREE

JULY 4
WEDNESDAY
8:41 AM

Hazard walked without paying any attention to where he was going. He knew it was hot; the sun baked the back of his jacket, and sweat snugged the cotton up under his arms. He knew Fourth of July celebrations were going to pick up steam in the next hour with a parade down Market Street, which meant the station would empty and he might have a chance at getting some work done. He knew, too, that what he had just learned, what Dr. Boyer had revealed, had changed the case drastically. He wasn't sure how, not yet. But he knew it was important.

But all of those realizations spun through his head like gossamer. He could see them. He could recognize them. But the moment he reached out for one, it melted away. Somers would know what to do next. That cropped up again and again: Somers would know what to do next. Hazard, who always had a plan, who always knew the next step to take, suddenly found himself walking without any plan at all, and he sure as hell didn't know where his steps were going to stop.

He walked like that for a long time. And part of it was about Somers. And part of it was about the case. And part it was about being tired, tired in a way that went back farther than one sleepless night. He couldn't put his finger on it until, as though of their own accord, his feet stopped, and he looked up, and he knew where he was. Then it made sense. Then he knew why he'd been so tired for so long, and why that exhaustion had swept back over him again, and why it was with him now, under the summer sun. It was Hollace's last words, delivered in the video he had left for Hazard: *Jeff didn't commit suicide.*

The Langham house occupied a corner lot in one of Wahredua's oldest middle-class neighborhoods. Jeff had never cared about money; that had been a good thing since Emery Hazard had been a poor boy. But Jeff's parents had always been well to do. His father was a dentist. His mother, a hygienist who worked with her husband. The house, a two-story with clapboard siding and crisp white paint, looked like the house every boy wanted to grow up in. Hazard had been inside once. Jeff had invited him while his parents were out, and they'd gone up to Jeff's room, where he'd knocked out the toe kick under a built-in bookshelf and produced a bag of weed, and they'd smoked and fucked all afternoon.

But he'd only been inside that once. It had scared him, as a boy, the thought of meeting Jeff's parents. It had scared him because it had been too much like spitting in God's eye: meeting Jeff's parents, that was something you did in a real relationship, and Hazard knew that what he had was too perfect. It was a dream. If he had gone through that door, if he had shaken Dr. Langham's hand and complimented Mrs. Langham on her chicken pot pie, that dream would have ended. And the thing was, Hazard thought, that it had ended anyway. It had ended with Jeff beaten and tortured. It had ended—

—*Jeff didn't commit suicide*—

—with a hole in the back of Jeff's head. And now Hazard wondered what might have been different if he'd gone inside and shaken a hand and eaten a bite of chicken pot pie.

Whatever he was doing here now, it wasn't going to help. It wouldn't bring Jeff back. It wouldn't make Somers miraculously appear. It wouldn't help Hazard feel any better, and it felt small and shabby for him even to think it might. Jeff was dead, and that was the end of it. The last pieces of the puzzle, the questions that had driven Hazard back to Wahredua, had been answered. He knew what he hadn't known twenty years ago: he knew why Jeff had killed himself.

Except.

That one word buzzed around his head with a mosquito whine. Except for the photographs. Except for Hollace's last words. Except for that final statement: Jeff didn't commit suicide. He was murdered. Why? That was the first question, the one at the surface, that one that troubled Hazard the most. Why had Hollace told him that? Why bring back the worst thing that had ever happened in Hazard's life? Why lay it down on the autopsy table, slit it open, and spill out its guts all over again? To turn Hazard on Mikey, as a final act of revenge? To torture Hazard one last time?

Heat prickled Hazard's forehead; not sweat, this time, but the feeling of pink skin just two degrees below sunburn. It barely registered. Right now, he could leave. He could walk away from all this. He could ignore that last message from Hollace. In fact, he should ignore it. It had been too convenient, the way it had reached Hazard. It had been too dramatic. It had been intended to do exactly what it was doing: blow out the bolts anchoring Hazard so that he'd drift away. Whatever else Hollace had intended, if he had sent that message with any intent of restoring justice, it had been secondary. Hazard knew, analytically, that much.

His gut didn't know anything of the sort, though. He was here. He had come here, not even thinking about it because deep down, he needed to know. Because he had come back to this place, come back to where the first boy he loved had been taken from him, because he needed to know the truth. He thought he had done that. But inside him, the clock measuring out his life was still stuck, both hands jutting up at midnight. And now—

He took the first step onto the Langhams' lawn, the grass crisp from the heat, crunching under his feet as though it were frosted rather than early July. And now that he was walking, his steps were carrying him backward, carrying him into the abyss. And abyss was the right word: this wasn't a scraping, sliding drift into darkness. This was a plunge. At that first step onto the brittle, summer-yellow spears of grass, he had plunged into the darkness.

Because after Jeff's death, that's where he had gone. Into the darkness. The ground had opened up beneath him, and the boy known as Emery Hazard had vanished. Even now, all these years later, he didn't really remember those first weeks. There were shards of time sharp enough to cut. His cheeks gritty with salt tracks; his eyes inflamed; his mother's hand like creek water on the back of his neck. And the droning cries of the cicadas storming against his window. And sleep. Not the sleep itself, which was even deeper and darker than the despair into which he'd fallen, but its cusp: the ragged edge when he started to wake and the pain sawed at him again. He had gone to school most of that time, although he didn't remember much. But one thing, one little thing that he had shoved away, came back to him now. As the Langhams' house grew with every step, as sun-dry grass splintered under his wingtips, he remembered another afternoon, standing by the dumpsters behind the school, the wind rattling the cyclone fence. He had escaped here because being inside, being in class, where Jeff had sat just a few seats away, was too much. Mikey had been there. And Mikey hadn't said anything at first; he had just stretched out his legs, heels resting on the empty seat where Jeff should have been, and he'd said, "Fuck yeah, that's nice."

Hazard had run out of the room. He didn't know if the teacher noticed; he didn't care if the teacher sent him to the principal or to detention or, for that matter, to the moon. All he could think about was that seat, that empty seat, and Mikey's filthy high-tops resting one on top of the other, heel on toe, and the way Mikey said, "Fuck yeah, that's nice." And he'd been out there five minutes, maybe ten, sucking in breathfuls of the spoiled fruit and wet milk cartons, long enough for Hollace to show up. This came back to Hazard with shocking clarity; he hadn't thought about any of this in so long. But Hollace had been there with the burnt remainder of a joint, probably the last quarter, and he'd lit it and toked up and passed the joint to Hazard. It wasn't the first time Hazard had smoked pot; it wouldn't be the last. But it hit him hard, so hard that panic sank claws deep into him, and he suddenly felt like someone was watching, someone who meant to do to him what had been done to Jeff. And right then, with Hazard's heart stuttering, with the smell of yesterday's Swedish meatballs gagging him from the dumpster, Hollace said something as he took back the ash-heavy joint. He said, "He wasn't smart about it, you know? He shouldn't have told him, you know?" He drew so deeply on the joint that ash flaked away and the tip glowed cherry. "You're not going to say anything, you know? Because it'll happen to you, too. You know?"

In the paranoiac haze of the weed, the words had made perfect sense. Hazard knew what Hollace was talking about: he was talking about Mikey, and how Jeff always talked back, how Jeff wouldn't just take their shit and be quiet. And Hollace was talking, too, about the high school principal, Mr. Eggington, and what might happen if Hazard said anything about the weed. He was talking about Hazard being queer, too, and what would happen if he made a fuss. All of those things, Hollace wrapped them up in those three interrogatives. It had made sense, at the time, if only because Hazard had been sure, between the drug and the grief, that he had been marked for something terrible

Only now, as his wingtips clacked on the Langhams' front porch, Hazard wasn't sure. He wasn't sure about any of it. If what Hollace said was the truth, if Jeff hadn't killed himself, then what had Hollace been talking about near the dumpsters behind school? Not the weed; in hindsight, that much was obvious. And not Hazard's sexuality, either. By then, everyone knew that Hazard was gay. So, who had Hollace been talking about when he said, "He shouldn't have told him, you know?" Not Mikey; Mikey had beaten and raped Jeff, but he hadn't killed him.

So who had? The photographs that Hollace had sent showed Jeff walking into the sunset after being beaten; where had he gone?

Lost in his thoughts, Hazard didn't remember knocking, but the door swung open, and a woman stood there, her shoulders hunched, her bobbed hair a chestnut color that, at her age, wasn't anywhere close to natural. Lorena Langham had lost her only son; Hazard vaguely remembered that Jeff had sisters, older and younger, but he hadn't known them, and after Jeff died, Hazard hadn't wanted to know them. In her drooping posture, he saw the effect that Jeff's death had on her, even all these years later. He saw it, too, in her eyes, and in the way she looked at him.

And he realized he didn't have a damn thing to say.

"Yes?" she said.

From deeper in the house, a man asked, "What are you doing over there? Did someone knock? I didn't hear anyone—" The man who came into view was most certainly Rick Langham. He looked like Jeff: the same patrician nose, the same widow's peak, the same jawline, although softened by age and the middle age sprawl. He fastened a look on Hazard and said, "What the hell do you think you're doing here? You've got a lot of nerve showing up like this."

"My name's Emery Hazard."

"Oh for Christ's sake, Lorena, shut the door."

"You know who I am?"

"You're goddamn right we know. Now get off the porch; we didn't ask for any of this."

"I need to talk to you."

"Shut the door." Rick leaned past Lorena, swatting at the door with one hand, but his wife had a firm grip. "You don't have any right, you know. You can't just show up like this."

Shaking his head, Hazard said, "I—I've got to talk to you about Jeff. You know who I am, and you know why I'm here, and I've got to talk to you."

"Listen to me, you son of a bitch." Red plumed in Rick's cheeks. "You don't get that right. You don't get anything close to it. Because of you, my son—"

Lorena squeezed his hand, and Rick Langham cut off with a sound like steam escaping. Eighteen years, they'd been waiting to say something like this. Eighteen years of hatred boiling up, trapped, with nowhere to go. Hazard squared his shoulders and lifted his chin.

"You're right. Because of me."

Rick screamed then, his hands tearing at his hair, and he turned and plunged into the house. Lorena stayed. She looked rooted; an earthquake might have toppled her, but not much else. Her fingers, where they touched the wood, whitened with pressure, and then she would try to relax, and blood would pink the tips again, and then emotion would surge into her face and the tips would blanch.

"Why are you here?"

"I should have come. When it happened, I should have come. But I couldn't. I don't know what else to tell you. I'm sorry about that, though, and I'm sorry it's taken me so long to come here. And I'm sorry for what happened to your son because of me."

A tear spilled down one of her cheeks, and she knuckled it away, and with what looked like a great deal of effort, she pried her hand from the door. "Why don't you come in?"

"Dr. Langham?"

She shrugged, and that shrug had eighteen years in it. Without another word, she turned and walked deeper into the house. Hazard followed. Lavender and vanilla filled the air, so sweet it was cloying, and the furniture in the front rooms had an old-fashioned, Victorian look to them: striped damask, bulky wood frames, every piece of furniture looking like it was meant for perfect posture—and if you tried anything else, you'd break your back.

The kitchen, however, had a homey touch, and Hazard sat at a trestle table and listened to water splash in the kettle, the hiss of gas, and the clink of spoons on china. Lorena left the tea service by the stove and sat opposite Hazard, her wrinkled hands folded on the table.

"He doesn't mean that. Neither of us does. Not in any way that counts. What happened to Jeff, that wasn't your fault. I've thought about it all these years, and I know that. But it doesn't mean I can stop feeling it. I look at you, and I keep feeling it. I'm sorry for that. I don't know what to do about it."

"It was my fault. If I hadn't done what I did, he'd be here."

"What did you do?"

Hazard shifted; the wood pinched the fabric of his trousers, and for a moment he was trapped, pinned by her gaze. "I dated him. I made him come out. And I—I wasn't with him. When they went after him, I wasn't there."

"We should have told you a long time ago. We should have talked to you when it happened. That would have been the right thing to do, the responsible thing to do. The adult thing to do. You were a boy, barely more than a child; we were grown up. Or at least, we were old enough that we should have been grown up. But even when you're an adult, sometimes the right thing to do seems impossible. Sometimes there's so much pain that you can't do the thing you know is right. Sometimes you can't even admit that a thing is right until the opportunity is gone, and then all you're left with is regrets."

Like Somers, Hazard thought. Like Somers disappearing, and I let him go even though I should have said something, even though I should have talked to him. He worked on the trapped fabric, trying to free himself. He wanted out of this house. He wanted the hot July air, the smell of road tar melting, the shiny sunburn prickle on his face. Anything but this room and the hiss of the gas jets and the woman whose life he had ruined.

"Have you had someone die?" she asked. The kettle rumbled behind her; in the corner of Hazard's vision, the cobalt gas wicked against the copper. "Someone you love, really love?"

"Yes." Jeff. I had Jeff die.

"It's a strange thing. It takes everyone differently. You know Rick is a hunter, don't you? Of course you do. Well, he blamed himself for a while. And for a while, the police had the . . . the one that Jeff used. It was always in the back of the truck, you know. Rick says you never know when the perfect shot will come along." She paused, as though both of them could taste the irony slicking the surface of that statement. "The police had it, and then, one day, they didn't. It was just there again, racked up against the window, as though it had never left. It was like something out of a story; part of that's because Rick never told me, and so I discovered it all by myself, but part of it's because of what it was: the thing that had killed my son. It was like something in a fairy tale, something cursed. I could throw it away, give it away, drop it in the river, and I knew it would come back. It would be there, racked up against the window." She went silent; they sat there until the kettle whistled, and then she moved with slow, heavy steps to the stove, and she poured the water into the pot, and a cloud of chamomile stunk up the kitchen.

Carrying the tea service to the table, she said, "Rick went hunting. Even when it wasn't in season, he'd go. Mostly for duck, but quail and geese and partridge. Whatever he could shoot, really. I suppose I shouldn't tell you that." She lowered the tray, lowered herself, and lowered her eyes to him. Their gaze was flat like the ancient earth, so flat Hazard felt he could skate right off them into nothing. "You being a policeman and all. I suppose he was poaching, technically."

"I don't—" Hazard had to clear his throat. "I don't care about ducks."

"He always took the gun. That same one. For ten years. And then, one day, it was gone."

And that was all. She poured the tea, set Hazard's in front of him, and turned the sugar spoon in his direction.

"What about you?"

"I slept in his bedroom. I slept just about anywhere, and I slept just about as much as I could. I think Rick would have divorced me or packed me off if he thought he could manage it. I didn't share a bed with him for a long time after Jeff died. Every night, I'd go into Jeff's room, and I'd shut the door behind me, and I could smell his hair on the pillow." A smile wrinkled the flesh around her eyes, but the smile was flat too. "After a while, I started spraying his cologne. Smells fade, you know."

"Drakkar Noir."

Surprise put the first spark of life in her face that Hazard had seen since arriving. "Yes, that was it."

Hazard dragged his spoon along the teacup's rim, and it chimed. Drakkar Noir. He remembered that smell. He remembered pressing his face against Jeff's bare chest, remembered the tickle of wiry hair against his nose, remembered Jeff's arms crisscrossing his back.

"One night, I was going through Jeff's drawers. He'd only been gone a week, but it felt like forever. We'd had the wake, the service, the funeral. My baby was in the ground. It had only been a week, and I thought if every week was like the last one, I'd lose my mind. I—well, I knew someone had hurt Jeff. Before he died, I mean. And I was convinced it had been more than that. I didn't believe my baby could do a thing like that, could put cold steel between his—" She choked, although her face remained smooth. "Between his teeth. I wasn't going to believe that. And so I started going through his stuff. I knew if I could find something, anything, that told me who had hurt Jeff, I'd know who had killed him. That's a very silly way of thinking, of course. I know that now. But at the time, it was all I had."

She looked at Hazard, sipping her tea, her eyes asking something.

He nodded.

"In a shoebox in his closet, I found what he'd been planning. I found a note. And I found razor blades. And the note said that he was tired of living a lie, and that he was sick of hating himself, and that this way was better than shaming the rest of us with the truth. That's the word he used. Shaming. As though—as though I cared about something so small." She sipped her tea again. Her eyes roved the ceiling, as though she were trying to divine something in the paint. "I knew, right then, that my boy had killed himself. I knew he had been sick. Not because he was gay but because his brain wasn't giving him enough of whatever chemical he needed. And I knew one other thing." Her eyes cut to Hazard.

"When?"

"Pardon me?"

"When did he write that note?"

"I've heard about you. No one will say anything to my face; there's still too much shame—there's that word again. But when I'm under the dryer at Brianne's, and the other girls are talking, I hear things. A lot of it is about the Somerset boy, of course. Most of them say you ought to have your hand smacked for taking the best cookie out of the jar, and most of them have their noses up in the air. But for some of them, well, some of them are happy for you. And I suppose I'm happy for you. Up here." She tapped her temple. "And they say you're a good detective. I know that much from the *Courier*. And that's the kind of question I wondered if you'd ask."

"When did he write it?"

"He wrote it the spring of his sophomore year."

Hazard had to close his eyes. His fingers tightened on the tiny teaspoon until he felt the chrome-plated metal heat to the temperature of his body until it seemed to vanish from his grip.

May. They had started dating in May.

He opened his eyes.

"Thank you for saving my son's life."

"I didn't—"

"You did. You didn't make him come out, and you didn't make him date you. Those were his choices. But you saved his life. And that's the only thing I care about."

Hazard shook his head; the movement felt slow and exaggerated, like a boxer reeling from a punch. "You said you knew he—"

"I knew he killed himself. I knew when I saw that note. He already had it in his mind, and when those people hurt him, that brought it back. I read a lot about it, and that's what I learned. For some people, it doesn't go away. It's just a clock running out. But you—you gave him time. You gave him time not even he thought he had. That means a lot to me, Detective Hazard. And I wish I'd told you that eighteen years ago. I didn't. And I'm sorry about that."

Emery Hazard's major accomplishment in the next moment wasn't the fact that he managed to keep quiet; it wasn't that he managed not to overturn the table and stomp the teapot into shards; it wasn't, even, that he managed to meet Lorena Langham with dry eyes. It was solely and singularly the fact that he managed to let go of the teaspoon. When he uncramped his fingers from around the thin metal, he was back in control of himself, and he packaged up the storm in his chest and set it aside, to be dealt with later.

"Mrs. Langham, I need to talk to you about Jeff's death. I don't think it was a suicide."

"That's it." Rick exploded from around the corner, as though he'd been hiding and waiting—which, in fact, Hazard assumed he had been doing. "I knew that's what this was about. I knew it. You piece of shit. You giant, selfish, walking piece of shit. It's not enough for you, is it? It's not enough that you got to ruin our lives once." He lunged across the distance, grabbing Hazard's jacket, trying to yank him out of the seat—the fabric of Hazard's trousers tore—and then realizing too late that Hazard weighed too much for him to lift. His face purpled, and he leaned down. Spittle flecked Hazard's face as the man spoke. "It wasn't enough to ruin our lives, to drag Jeff down, to put us through—to put us through hell, all right? That wasn't enough for you. No. You're back. And whatever you want, you're not going to get it from us. This is some kind of power play. Just like the other guy. This is some kind of scheme. Well, I don't care who you are. I don't care if you grew up here. I don't care—" Here, his voice warbled, and for a moment Rick seemed about to dissolve. "I don't care what you were to my son. You want to drag this family through the mud, and I'll tell you exactly what I told that bastard you sent here first."

"Rick," Lorena said.

"I don't know what you're talking about," Hazard said.

"I'm talking about you, you—you fucking faggot."

"Rick! That's enough!"

"Let go of me, Dr. Langham. Right now. I'll talk about this, but you've got to let go of me."

"Rick, let him go. Just let go."

"No. No, I won't. I'm going to do what I should have done. I'm going to stop you. I'm going to protect my family." Rick was trembling now, as though Hazard were the one holding him instead of the other way around and had given him a good hard shake. With one hand, he reached for his pocket.

The movements were so slow, so sloppy, that Hazard could read them in advance, as though Rick were following the dotted lines in a coloring book. With his good hand, Hazard smacked the gun out of Rick's grip. It thudded against the floor, and Hazard dropped his foot on it, his eyes cutting hard at Lorena.

She just sighed and, with surprising calm, raised both hands.

"That was stupid, Dr. Langham." Hazard prized the man's hand from his jacket and shoved; Rick stumbled back. His hip cracked against the counter, and the kettle clanged, empty, onto its side. "You're not going to do anything stupid again, are you?"

Still trembling, Rick shook his head and then buried his face in his hands. He was crying.

"Mrs. Langham?"

"I'm sorry. I told you grief makes us act very differently."

"Grief might, but this is something else." Hazard scooped up the gun—a little .22 that was barely more than a peashooter—and pocketed it. "What's going on?"

Lorena looked at her husband with something like pity; it was the second emotion she had showed since Hazard had entered the home. "Do you want to tell him?"

Rick was sobbing now; Hazard couldn't even tell if he had heard his wife speak.

"You're not the first one to come around," she said, her wrinkled hands cupping her tea again. A fresh wave of chamomile hit Hazard, and he swallowed a gag. "Another man was here a few weeks ago. He asked a lot of questions about Jeff. And about his death. Offensive questions. When he came back the second time, he . . . he made a scene. He said things that left us both very upset. He scared us, Detective Hazard."

But it wasn't fear that Hazard was seeing in Rick Langham's shaking shoulders. It was guilt, or something damn close to it.

"Who?" Hazard asked, although he thought he already knew.

"Ted Kjar."

CHAPTER THIRTY-FOUR

JULY 4
WEDNESDAY
8:41 AM

SOMERS KNEW WHERE HE WAS, but he wasn't ready to admit it. Instead, he sagged in the chair. The ropes kept him from sliding to the ground, and he was grateful for that; the carpet, gray-green and shiny from decades of traffic, didn't look like anything he wanted to touch.

He knew, from the sunlight that squeezed past the plywood, that it was morning. And not early morning either; the light was strong and full-bodied, which meant that it was mid-morning. Eight. Maybe nine. So he'd been here—what? Five hours? Six?

They'd been bad, those five hours. Really bad. But not as bad as they could have been. The cramped apartment was hot, and sweat slicked Somers's scalp. In occasional bursts, when the beads of sweat grew heavy enough, they ran down his neck, and when those drops of sweat glided into one of the cuts, it burned like hell. He could smell his sweat. He could smell the flop-sweat, in particular, and it smelled like his own fear and helplessness. He could smell cigarette smoke and another odor, like overheated electrical equipment, and both of those came from Mikey Grames, who was sitting in the chair opposite Somers, a Marlboro between his lips.

"You could make this a lot easier."

Somers gave one weary shake of his head.

"I'm not asking you for much."

Somers blinked; or rather, he meant to blink, but as soon as the lids were down, his eyes shuttered, and he was drifting away, too tired even for fear to keep him awake.

An ember of pain, just above his knee, dragged him back, and now he smelled burning denim and singed hair, and when he opened his eyes, he saw the hole in his jeans. Mikey flicked ash away from the tip of his cigarette, but he kept it near Somers's leg.

"I'm talking to you."

"You killed Hollace."

"Did pussyboy cry about that? Emery's always played tough, but scratch him, and every goddamn time you'll find a little bitch under the surface. Did he tell you Hollace was his only friend? Did he tell you Hollace made him feel better? Did he tell you Hollace kept him from slitting his wrists?"

"How did it go down? He wanted to work with you, and you shot him in the back?"

"I didn't really want to kill him, you know. He's like a dog in a fight. You might not like the dog. You might not want to be left alone with the dog—not unless you're holding its leash. But put him in a pit, let him go, and he's a lot of fun to watch. And the things he wanted to do to Emery, well, I was going to enjoy that." Mikey wedged the Marlboro between his lips, drew hard on it, and said, "For a detective, he was one stupid piece of shit as a kid. He never wondered why I could always find him so easily. Never wondered why I knew where he was going to be. Never even thought about it, I guess. You know why?"

"Because he's a good guy. He's loyal. He's not a backstabbing piece of shit like you."

"He's loyal." Mikey weighed this, tilting his head. "Yeah, he is. Hollace just wanted me to like him. You too. You remember him hanging around, desperate for attention." He sucked on the cigarette again, flashing a grin around the butt. "That day I got to cut on Emery, that was Hollace. That day we went after the Langham faggot, that was Hollace."

Somers shifted in his seat, trying to pull himself upright. This was the longest Mikey had talked. Until now, it had been a different routine: question, cut, question, cut. Questions, of all things, about Ted Kjar. Somers knew he had a certain amount of willpower, and a part of him was proud that he'd held out against answering Mikey's questions so long, but he also knew, in a quiet corner of his brain, that Mikey hadn't really worked on him that hard. Cutting wasn't pleasant, but it sure as hell wasn't as bad as things could get. So why was Mikey holding back?

As though Mikey had sensed the train of Somers's thoughts, he flicked the burning stub of cigarette onto Somers's chest, where it smoldered against his shirt, the cotton darkening, threads splitting under the heat, until Somers contorted his body hard enough to dislodge the stub and send it tumbling down onto the shiny carpet. Smirking, Mikey stood and picked up something on a table, his back to Somers as he assembled it.

"He knows you're involved in this," Somers said, but his breaths came faster now. What was Mikey doing? It looked like aluminum. Several pieces of it, in fact, which Mikey was now fitting together. "He's not stupid. Neither of us is."

Mike, his back to Somers, froze. And then he started to laugh. It wasn't a particularly nice sound, but it was honest, and it came from his gut, and something inside Somers shriveled and blackened and blew away on a cold wind when he heard that laugh. "You know, Naomi can be a real bitch sometimes, but when she's right, she's right. She said you were just stupid enough to try something like this. Hell, after I talked to her, I didn't even mind pulling my guys back from your little girl. Because when she's right, she's right. And she was right about something really important: you're not the one I need to twist titties on. I just need you to start twisting Emery's."

In that rush of fear, Somers let himself face the facts. He knew where he was. He recognized the smell of microwave cookery, of Salisbury steak; he recognized the prickly stink of bad weed; he recognized the smell of decades of body oil and dirt and smoke absorbed into every inch of fabric. And he knew what that meant.

He was inside the Haverford, where two cops had been killed. He was inside the Haverford, where Hollace Walker, after trying to shoot the mayor, had led them into a maze of booby traps that had almost killed Somers. He was inside the Haverford, inside Hollace's maze, and no one knew he was here. No one except, maybe, Naomi. And she had helped put him here.

"Why don't you explain it?" Somers said, hearing the panting in his own voice and hating it. "Why don't you tell me why you're doing this, why you killed Hollace, why you're helping Naomi, why you used Ted Kjar, all of it? Why don't you tell me?"

"For the fucking love of God," Mikey muttered, shaking his head. "If Emery's as stupid as you, I don't even know why I'm bothering with this shit." He stepped aside, revealing a tripod stand for his phone, which now faced Somers. "Now, I want Emery to be motivated. Really motivated. And John-Henry, you're the fire I'm about to light under his ass." He tapped out another Marlboro, lit it, and the ember glowed like Venus in the night sky. But the knife in his hand—a new knife, a bigger knife that Somers hadn't seen yet— glowed brighter. A lot brighter. "I'm going to get you ready for showtime, baby. We want you to look just right. And do me a favor, will you? Don't hold back. I want to hear you scream."

CHAPTER THIRTY-FIVE

JULY 4
WEDNESDAY
9:29 AM

HAZARD SAT THERE in the Langhams' kitchen, trying to process what he had just heard. One part of his mind was focused on the details of the surroundings, taking in possible threats: Lorena Langham still held her cup of tea; she might throw that at his head, to distract him. Rick stood against the counter, one hand pressed to his hip, still sobbing, but a minute ago he had pulled a gun on Hazard. That gun was now in Hazard's pocket, but it didn't mean Rick wouldn't try something again.

But even as his brain catalogued those possibilities, most of his mind was elsewhere. Most of his mind was grappling with one gargantuan question: why had Ted Kjar come here, asking about Jeff's death? For a sudden, vertiginous moment, Hazard felt like he was peering over a cliff, glimpsing the truth. There was something here, something that linked Jeff's death, almost twenty years old, with everything happening now. But what?

Jeff didn't kill himself. He was murdered.

First as tragedy.

Dragging himself back into the present, Hazard looked first at Lorena and then at Rick. "Tell me everything."

Rick was still crying quietly, and he massaged his hip, his posture that of a toddler after a tumble, taking the whole thing as a personal affront. But Lorena looked at Hazard, her face still smooth, her eyes flat enough to sail off the edge of the world.

"We were hoping you would—"

"No. I want to hear all of it from the beginning."

After a moment, she nodded. "Mr. Kjar came a few weeks ago. He—we didn't know each other. Not well. Certainly not well enough for him to drop by unannounced. But he explained that he was working on that book he was writing, and he said that he wanted to ask us a few questions about the town. I'm not stupid, Detective. I assumed he really wanted to talk about Jeff, but—" Her wrinkled hands flexed once, as though a galvanic current ran through them. "But it had been so long. When Jeff died, I couldn't talk to anyone. I didn't want to talk to anyone. But it's been so long, and I wanted to talk. Part of me, anyway, wanted to tell all of it. The truth."

The truth, Hazard thought, and the words throbbed like a migraine. The truth. She wanted to tell the truth. And suddenly, horribly, he wanted to laugh, and he had to bite the inside of his cheek. What the fuck was the truth in a town like this?

His eyes shot towards Rick, and Lorena read his question and answered, "He was at work. It was the middle of the day, and I thought that was a little odd, but I knew Mr. Kjar was passionate about the book. I had some half-formed explanation in my head that he was using his vacation days to work on it. I didn't know until later that he was no longer working. I didn't know a great deal, it turns out. I think Jo had something to do with that; it's a small town, and she must have worked hard to keep word from spreading about Ted's situation."

She had switched from Mr. Kjar to Ted, Hazard noticed. Pity? Complicity? What had prompted that lapse?

"When he came inside, I made tea, and we sat and talked. Little things at first. What it had been like, growing up here. Rick and I are both from the area, you know, but I grew up in Wahredua proper. Rick was what we used to call a corn-boy." She smiled briefly at this, but the smile was just as empty as the rest of her face. "I kept waiting for the first question. I had heard so many different ways of trying to introduce the topic. People would pause, and their expressions would get serious, and they would say something like, 'Lorena, I just want to tell you how sorry I am.' Or they'd say, 'Have you ever considered talking to someone?' Had I ever considered it?" She laughed, her fingers tightening around the teacup until they were white, and Hazard waited for the cup to shatter. "All those vapid expressions, but people come back to them again and again. Not an ounce of originality."

"But?" Hazard asked.

"But Ted Kjar wanted to know if I liked camping."

Hazard's eyebrows shot up.

"I know," Lorena said. "I thought the same thing. I told him I didn't really like to camp. I hadn't done it since I was a girl, when First Methodist ran a summer camp on the north side of Lake Palmerston, and I only did it once. I got poison ivy on the inside of my elbow so bad that I couldn't bend it for a week. Ted didn't care about Lake Palmerston or Bible camp or poison ivy. He asked about Jeff. And then he asked about the rest of the family. And he kept asking about day trips, hiking, picnics. Where did we go when we wanted to be with nature? Rick, will you get the picture?"

Rick had stopped sobbing; his eyes red, he nodded and drifted towards the back of the house.

"And the rest of it, too, please."

Another nod.

Lorena's fingers were still white against the teacup, the skin tight over bone. "I answered his questions, but I thought they were silly, and the longer he went on, the more upset I began to feel. He'd skipped work—that's what I thought anyway—for this silly book. He was taking up my time. But all he wanted to ask about was camping and nature preserves and state forest and if any of our friends owned cabins. Finally I couldn't stand it anymore. I said, 'Mr. Kjar, I don't feel like I'm helping you very much, and I have to finish the laundry'—that part was a shameless lie, I'm afraid—and since I can't help you, I think I'd better get back to work.' And he sat there, staring at me, and then he reached into his pocket and showed me this."

Rick had returned, carrying a brown cardboard box, from which he withdrew a photograph. He placed it in Lorena's hand, and a shudder ran through him as he did, as though it had transferred something foul by his touch. Lorena studied it for a moment. Her face contracted, her attention drawn towards a single point: the photograph.

What was it? Something gruesome, Hazard guessed based on the way Rick had tried to shake it off. A picture from the murder scene? Something that showed Jeff's body before the mortician got to work on him, bone slivering his hair, the back of his head a raw fissure. And there would be something that everyone else had missed, Hazard knew. Some sort of forensic detail that would reveal, in hindsight that Jeff's death hadn't been a suicide. It had been murder.

Lorena let out a breath, turned the photograph over, and passed it to Hazard. He felt a flicker of doubt. She had just told him that she still believed Jeff had killed himself. She had told him that, in fact, to comfort him. So whatever was in the picture—

No matter how much Hazard might have prepared himself, he never would have been ready for it. There he was: Jeff. The first boy Hazard had ever loved. Jeff, with his compact, muscular frame, his eyes dancing happily, his hair short and mussed. He wore a smirk, and Hazard had seen that expression on Jeff's face. It was his fucking around smirk. It was the way Jeff smiled when he was about to twist open the top of Hazard's jeans and slide his hand past the elastic waistband of Hazard's underwear and touch him. Just a touch. Just teasing. Because they were both sixteen and primed to go off like firehoses.

Jeff, alive, happy, smiling. No graphic depiction of the violence he had suffered at the end. No horrifying reminder of how he had died. Nothing at all. It had been taken on a bright, sunny day, and the location for the picture explained Ted Kjar's line of questioning. In the photograph, Jeff leaned against the wall of an old log cabin. Thick chinking, reddish-brown with dust, showed between the logs, whose wood had grayed with the passing of long years. Behind Jeff and the cabin, a sliver of stone-strewn earth showed, tassels of blue sky hanging between a pair of beech trees, and something else.

Pulling the picture closer, Hazard tried to make it out. A sign, he thought, but the print was too small to read.

He turned the photograph in his hands. The paper was stiff, almost brittle, and the same rust-colored dust had stained the back. There was no handwriting, nothing to indicate where it had been taken or developed, but Hazard could tell that the picture was old. In one corner, a few drops of water distorted the image and the paper, but other than that, the paper had survived the last twenty years relatively well.

But that was all. No smoking gun—literal or figurative. Nothing that could explain where Ted Kjar had gotten this photo or why it mattered.

"Do you know where he is?" Hazard asked.

Lorena shook her head. "I, that is, we thought you might."

"No."

"It wasn't taken long before he passed. I can tell you that much. He still had those clothes in the hamper; I saw them after the funeral."

Hazard laid down the photograph. He was afraid his grip, which tightened at Lorena's words, might tear the old paper. He thought about taking the teaspoon again, letting himself vent his anger on the chrome-plated metal, but he pushed away the cup instead. Right now, he needed to break something serious. Something substantial. Tearing a photograph, bending a spoon, that was kiddie shit. He needed to knock down the Empire State Building.

"You don't recognize the place?"

"That's what Ted asked me too. I don't."

"Neither do I," Rick said, his voice sounding like it had gone through a wood-chopper.

"And we don't know who might have taken the picture, either."

"But you thought I might have."

She nodded at Hazard.

"I didn't take the picture. I don't know the place. Did Kjar tell you where he got this?"

"No. After he showed it to me, he became agitated."

"He was crazy," Rick said. "The whole town knows it now. A drug addict. He was out of his mind, Lorena. He almost killed the mayor. He'd been out of a job for months, doing God knows what, and then he came here. He came into our house, stirring up shit. He kept saying that this was important. That it could change everything. That he finally could prove it? Prove what? Prove that our son killed himself. Thanks, but no thanks. We don't need that stupid photograph. We don't need a reminder about what happened to my son. But you let him come in here. You wanted to talk. You acted like such a goddamn fool, and now everybody's going to know that too."

Lorena's gaze remained rigidly fixed on Hazard

"I want you to leave," Rick said, jabbing a finger at Hazard. Then, wheeling around, he stomped out of the room.

When his crashing footsteps faded, Lorena shook her head. As though nothing had happened, she said, "Ted became very upset. Worked up, I guess. He kept talking in circles."

"About Jeff?"

"No. Nothing I could understand. Saying, 'This is it, this is it, the son of a bitch can't walk away from this.' Things like that. 'They can't cover up for him now.' That was another. It all sounded, well, crazy. I mean, Jeff died all those years ago. He killed himself. What could one picture of him mean?"

"You didn't ask."

For a moment, the strain in Lorena's face was incredible, as though some internal pressure threatened to rip open the fault lines. And then she shook her head. "I didn't want to know. I was scared. I was scared of him. And I was scared of the rest of it."

The rest of it. The truth. Hazard resisted the urge to bend that teaspoon into a pretzel.

"He was scaring me, so I asked him to leave. And he did."

"But he left you the photograph?"

"No. That came later. With the rest of it." She gathered the teacups, carried the tray to the sink, and stood there a moment, staring out into the backyard, where thirty yards of grass divided her from the closest neighbor. Whatever she saw, she was somewhere else, Hazard knew. She was somewhere a long way off. She was alone, where no one could help her, just like everyone who walks into the past. Inside that labyrinth, everyone was alone with their own private monsters.

"Jeff was so independent." She said it as though it were an explanation. "He didn't need us the way some of his sisters did. He was always so mature, always so grown up. He'd get phone calls here and talk just like an adult. He'd even want privacy, and he'd drag the phone into his room and shut the door, and I was . . . charmed. You can love your children so much that everything is charming." Her eyes came up, lost in that labyrinth. "What was I missing?"

"Mrs. Langham, could I see Jeff's room?"

She started, and the cups rattled across the tray. One spilled over the edge, and it shattered at the bottom of the sink with a crack.

"Yes," she said. "I'm sorry."

"Sorry?"

She shook her head, smiled numbly, and waved at the stairs.

Hazard took them two at a time. The grain of wood in the banister chafed his fingers. One time. One time he had come up these stairs, and that day, he had felt like he was flying up them. Just once, with Jeff's battered high-tops on the stairs ahead of him, Jeff's ass right ahead of him, Hazard reaching out once, daring to squeeze that ass right here, in Jeff's house, and Jeff had just laughed and spun around and pulled Hazard down on top of him, and they had made out on the stairs, made out so hard that Jeff had kicked off his high-tops and worked his fingers inside the waistband of Hazard's jeans, stroked him until Hazard shivered and bit Jeff's neck. And then he'd laughed again and tugged him up the stairs and into the room.

A floorboard creaked as Hazard followed the memory, and he had to close his eyes for a moment because Jeff's room hadn't changed. Tacked to the far wall, on a poster for *Aladdin Sane*, David Bowie looked at the ground, lightning jagging down his face. The rolltop desk was open, the way it had been the one time Hazard had been here, displaying the Compaq computer where Jeff had pulled up a blank word processor document and typed *I LOve You*, just to show off, and Hazard had laughed because Jeff couldn't type worth a damn. He'd bought the computer with his own money; that struck Hazard now, and he wasn't sure why he'd never wondered about that before. The computer, the weed, the CDs, the clothes. But no job. The battered black high-tops were next to the bed, one upright, the other on its side, like Jeff might be back any minute to straighten them.

Hazard moved past all of it to the built-in shelves, and he worked his thumb behind the toe kick and it snapped free. Maybe a note. Maybe another photo. Maybe a telephone number on a scrap of paper. Instead, though, there was only a baggie that had yellowed and thinned as the plastic broke down; inside, the weed looked like wood shavings.

The toe kick pinched his finger when he shoved it back into place; it left a long white crease along his thumb, and Hazard sucked on it as he made his way back to the kitchen.

Lorena Langham looked up at him with something like hope, and Hazard shook his head.

She collected the brown cardboard box from the table and said, "Let me walk you out. You should take that picture."

Hazard slid it into a pocket and followed her to the door.

"Rick's right, you know."

"I'm sorry?"

"I shouldn't have talked to him. Ted, I mean. He was sick, wasn't he? And he came here, and I was . . . I was ready to talk. I wanted to talk. All these years, and I thought I was finally going to get to tell someone. Isn't that strange? My son's death, and I wanted to talk about it."

"That's not strange."

"But it is. Because now it's my story. Whatever Jeff might have told people, he can't tell them anymore. Now it's mine. It's all about me." Her lips quirked in a bitter smile. "Rick was right: I acted like a fool. It's just—it's just that we carry it for so long, don't we? I do, at any rate. I've carried it for so long. So long, maybe, that I don't know how to set it down anymore." She laughed, then, like someone who's fallen down the stairs and just realized her neck isn't broken. She passed him the box. "Detective?"

"Yes?"

"It's not your story, either."

He pressed the box to his chest. Cardboard bent, and its papery smell rushed up at him.

"I'm saying that as a kindness to you. Maybe both of us can just put this away, now. I hope I can. I know you should. It's not yours; it's time for you to tell your own story."

He struggled for a moment. The cardboard twisted in his arms, and he thought the flaps at the bottom might split and spill out whatever it held. He didn't remember moving, but he realized he was outside, staring at Lorena Langham through the storm door, her eyes already lost again in the labyrinth. Heat swamped him, dragging on his clothes, licking along his cheek like a hot dog's tongue. Then Lorena closed the door, and he was alone. Alone, too, in his own labyrinth.

He walked two blocks to a small park, a handful of acres set on a neighborhood street. The air smelled like rancid barbeque from one of the grills, and it smelled like the sun, and it smelled like the dust warmed by the sun. He sat there, his face prickling and cooking like bologna on a griddle. A red stripe ran along the curb ahead of him, and that made him think of Jeff too: of Jeff parking the truck snug up along red, laughing when Hazard warned him, and laughing again when they came back and he found the ticket on the dash. And Hazard remembered Jeff shredding the yellow carbon copy into the gutter, and Jeff laughing again, and Jeff saying that his friend would take care of it.

A sparrow fluttered down, pecked at something in the sidewalk, and hopped once toward Hazard. He stared back at it. His fingers found the cardboard flaps, the corrugated edges sawing the inside of his hands. The chemical treatment of the cardboard rushed up, blocking out the ancient barbeque smell for a moment.

Inside were pages. A stack of eight-and-a-half by eleven pages, a printed manuscript. And photographs. Cabins. Trails. Picnic shelters. A bridge. A limestone courthouse.

In spite of the heat, a shiver ran up Hazard's spine. This was the missing chapter of Ted Kjar's book, the one that had been removed from his home. He bent back the box's flap and saw the postage. Sent from Ted Kjar on June 15 to Rick and Lorena Langham. The photograph of Jeff, Hazard realized, had been sent with this chapter—at least a hundred manuscript pages about the Works Progress Administration in Dore County.

And what the hell, he wondered as he wiped sweat from his forehead, was so important about that?

CHAPTER THIRTY-SIX

JULY 4
WEDNESDAY
9:50 AM

THE TIP OF THE PLIERS slid deeper under Somers' fingernail, and then, with a twist, the nail popped free. Blood pooled on the stinging nailbed, a dark crimson lacquer that flooded over the steel for a moment. Somers managed not to cry out, but he made a whumping noise deep in his chest, and his legs tried to kick—tried, because they were tied tightly to the chair.

Mikey breathed out slowly, as though performing brain surgery, and drew back the tool. He studied Somers for a moment. He cocked his head. His eyes crinkled at the corners. Then he ripped off another nail.

Somers groaned through clenched teeth.

"I knew you were a pussy," Mikey said, wiping the pliers clean on Somers's leg. "You always acted like a tough guy, especially when you hung out with us, but I knew. I mean, what the hell—they're just fingernails. What are you going to do when I really get started? I bet you cry like a little girl."

Mikey's breathing was faster now. His pupils dilated. The pliers rested on their nose, drilling into Somers's leg with slow turns. Mikey didn't even seem to be aware of what he was doing; his gaze was fixed on Somers.

"This is what you always wanted," Somers said. Part of his brain—the rational part, the part that made decisions, the part that had trained and studied and worked to make him a damn good cop—knew that he needed to talk and get Mikey talking back. The intuitive part of him sensed, too, that Mikey was bursting at the seams with old hatred. That intuitive part of Somers recognized, in a way he couldn't fully put into words, the dark mirror of Emery Hazard that stood in front of him, and Somers felt a flicker of hope. The same deep, geological veins of alienation and hatred and powerlessness ran through both men, but where they had driven Hazard to become a stronger person, a better person, they had pushed Mikey towards this. And Somers felt hope, yes, definitely hope, because he guessed that Mikey, unlike Hazard, had never learned to take back the power that had been stripped from him in high school.

"You wanted this, right?" Somers asked again. "You think this makes up for the rest of it, for all the shit you took back in the day?" He laughed, just one single, rusty croak, and said, "You're so fucking pathetic, aren't you, Mikey? Jesus, you still stink just like you did back then. What? Your daddy never taught you to wash under your arms? Oh, fuck, man. That's really insensitive. You didn't have a dad, did you? Just some guy that dropped a load in your mom and moved on."

Mikey's breath tightened like a coil. The pliers cracked against his jaw, and Somers did cry out this time, a low sound as he bent at the waist as far as the ropes would allow.

"You—" Mikey's voice was thick and wild. "You can't talk to me like that. You can't. You stupid faggot. You stupid pussy. I'm going to cut off your balls. I'm going to cut off your cock, and then you won't have anything left for Emery to play with. Maybe I'll cut you a nice little pussy down there, and if you don't bleed out, he'll have another place he can stick it to you."

Somers heard the words, but they cracked across the surface of his mind like stones skipping off ice. Most of him, almost all of him, was pain. After the first cry, though, he breathed through it, and the red haze faded, and he tried to string Mikey's words into order. The future. That was what stood out most clearly. Mikey was talking about a future, some kind of future Somers might have with Hazard.

And that meant that Mikey didn't mean to kill him. Or—and this realization closed around Somers's heart like a fist—or Mikey wanted Somers to believe he had a future. But that didn't seem right. Mikey was angry. He was furious, beyond the point of reason, and Somers guessed that Mikey had unintentionally given himself away.

"You fucking. Selfish. Bastard." Mikey sawed the blade back and forth. "You always thought you were hot stuff. You always thought you were better than everyone else. You always. Thought. You. Were. Better. Than. Me." He gave the blade a final, vicious jerk, and Somers let out another bark of pain. He couldn't help it, and he hated that he couldn't help it, but that intuitive part of his brain knew that it was for the best. Some of the insanity in Mikey's eyes sharpened; he liked hearing Somers cry out in pain. But he also relaxed, his breath softening, his shoulders loosening, his fingers peeling back from the pliers.

Somers sucked in a breath, met Mikey's eyes, and said, "I am better than you. I always was."

Mikey's lips peeled back over his teeth. "You want me to do something stupid. You think you can get me to use this on you. You think you can get me to end it fast."

"You always do something stupid, Mikey. I'm just trying to hurry you along."

Those lips peeled back even further.

"Nice try, John-Henry." He wrenched the blade free, and red staticked over Somers vision. "I got a job. I'm good at that job. I don't have to swallow shit anymore."

"Why are your teeth so brown, then?"

To Somers's surprise, Mikey laughed. "Goddamnit. I forgot. I forgot you're always like this. Does he get off on it, having you dump on him? Does he like this cocky-boy routine?"

"I only talk like this to pieces of shit who threaten little girls."

"Of course he does. He boned up every time you went after him in high school, didn't he? He liked it, you hurting him, you taking control of him. And he still likes it." Mikey cocked his head. "Let's show him what you're really like under all that swagger.

Collecting the pliers, Mikey left, and a clatter from the room beyond told Somers that he hadn't gone far. Somers fought a wave of dizziness. For the moment, though, that didn't matter. What mattered was this place and getting out of here alive. Somers wasn't sure how much time had passed since Mikey had taken him from the garage. Hours. Four? Five? Six? Had Hazard realized that something was wrong? Yes, Somers thought. Hazard would have worried. He would have called around. He would have figured out that Somers wasn't at his parents', wasn't with Cora, and then Hazard would have done what he did best: he would have winnowed the possibilities and started tracking Somers. That should have been a nice thought, a reassuring thought, but it wasn't. It wasn't reassuring at all because Somers knew he was inside the Haverford.

Inside the Haverford, where Hollace had set up a labyrinth of traps designed to kill anyone who came looking for him. The tripwires that Somers and Hazard had run into the last time they came here were only the beginning. Somers knew this because he could see, from where he was tied up, the last line of defense: two shotguns trained on the apartment's front door, their barrels sawn to maximize scatter, and a fireman's axe suspended and primed to swing down, hitting at chest height on the average man. At the window, a bouquet of grenades hung, ready to explode if anyone came through the glass; that one scared Somers more than the shotguns because it meant Mikey wasn't afraid of dying himself.

And then there were the train tracks: they ran along the apartment's wall, disappearing through a hole cut into the plaster. Somers remembered Hollace's plan, all those years ago, to send a model train through the vents in the girls' locker room. Somers wasn't sure what Hollace had planned to do with the train, but he doubted it was to snap a few pics of girls in their bras. Somers pictured the model train jetting along those tracks, silently propelled by their electric current, carrying a load of C-4 down the hallway while Hollace watched a closed-circuit camera, detonating when Hazard reached the top of the stairs. Boom. Just like that, it wouldn't matter how smart Hazard was or how well he did at evading the rest of the traps. Something like that would vaporize him, and Hazard would never have a chance.

And the worst part was that Hollace was dead, and now Mikey was safe behind the traps. Mikey would never have been smart enough to rig up something like this on his own, but he was plenty smart enough to take advantage of what Hollace had provided.

That was why Somers wasn't reassured, not at all, by the fact that Hazard was coming for him. Hazard was smart. No; Hazard was brilliant. And he was strong and determined and dangerous. There wasn't anyone in the world Somers trusted more. But this place was a nightmare, and even Hazard couldn't make it through Hollace's defenses. Not alive.

All of that meant one thing: Somers had to get out of here.

From the other room, Mikey was still moving around, the sound of his steps carrying clearly, along with muttered speech to himself and the occasional sound of objects shifting. He was looking for something. Again, Somers found himself wondering what Mikey's job was. It had something to do with the drug trade; that much, at least, he felt certain of. All of this went back to the meth production in Dore County. Hollace, Somers guessed, had been working for someone outside the area. Another organization that wanted to move into the area. A competitor that wanted to eliminate the Ozark Volunteers. And Hollace was their local boy. He was the inside man. He had come here, and he had tried to kill the mayor. When that had failed, he had waged war on the Volunteers. What Somers didn't understand, though, was why Hollace had approached Mikey, and why Mikey had turned around and betrayed Hollace.

Somers didn't know. He didn't care, at the moment. He just needed to get out. He scanned the room. When the Haverford had been built, this room had obviously been intended as the main social area—the structure was old enough that it might have even been called a parlor or a sitting room. Even though Smithfield had always been a poor area of Wahredua, the Haverford had, at some point, been a semi-prestigious building, and its residents would have required the equivalent of a sitting room.

This room, located at the front of the apartment unit, might have once served that purpose, but since Hollace had taken control of it, it had been transformed into a workshop. The traps on the apartment's front door added a layer of security, but they weren't the main focus of the room—even the model train track, vanishing into that shadowy excavation in the wall, wasn't the main focus. The main focus was the workbench, which took up the longest wall. Rigged together out of two-by-fours and plywood, the workbench sagged, and the plywood splintered along its edges. Hollace had piled a bizarre miscellany of equipment on the bench: plastic two-liter bottles, shop rags, an ancient tin can of kerosene, a spool of heavy-gauge wire, a decapitated Ken doll, compact balls of newspaper, an eyeglass kit, wadded-up masking tape, a yellow Bic lighter, a drill with a long black cord snaking down to its foot pedal, and much, much more.

Studying the workbench, Somers saw several possible ways. The steak knives would be the best option for cutting himself free, but the reality was that it would take time to saw through the ropes, and Somers didn't think Mikey would be gone that long. He might be able to start a fire—Christ, if there really was kerosene in that tin, then he could get a decent blaze going—but that wouldn't help him escape. He could even try to pedal the drill, but the most likely outcome of that would put the bit right through Somers's wrist or arm.

That left, as far as Somers was concerned, only one decent option. With another glance at the door that led deeper into the apartment—Mikey was speaking in full sentences now, his tone even, as though he were reciting—Somers threw his weight forward. Mikey had tied Somers to the chair, and he'd done a good job of it. Somers could hardly move. But hardly wasn't the same as not at all, and Somers rocked back and forth, building momentum with those tiny movements. Rope hissed across his arms, his chest, his ankle, millimeters of friction building into hot lines. And then, so suddenly that Somers almost fell, the back of the chair lifted off the ground.

With his feet bound to the chair, Somers couldn't do more than a fumbling, awkward hop. He—and the chair—launched forward. Somers made it farther than he had hoped. The chair hit first, at an angle, and the force of the fall shook the chair's frame. Wood squealed. For a moment, Somers hoped that the chair might break—an arm might come free, and he would be able to work himself loose. But the old, heavy chair held, and Somers fell onto his side.

The whole process was noisy. There wasn't anything to do about that. Somers lay there, his heartbeat whooshing in his ears, and listened. For a moment, he couldn't hear anything else. His back was to the door, and for all he knew, Mikey was standing there, staring at him. Maybe Mikey was holding those pliers. Maybe Mikey was thinking about doing something more permanent than popping off Somers's fingernails.

Somers forced himself to breathe, letting the rush of his heartbeat slow, and then, there it was: that schoolboy-recital voice in the other room as Mikey continued speaking. Thank God, Somers thought, and the rush of hope was so sudden that it stung. Thank God.

His hands were tied to the arms of the chair, and he couldn't move them much. But Somers had good aim, and he also had a fair bit of luck, and he had landed where he had wanted to land—his fingers just inches from the old-fashioned drill's pedal. Squirming, twisting, contorting, Somers managed to drag himself those final few inches. His hand brushed the pedal. Then, with one last, straining effort, he got a grip and tugged.

The black cord swung closer, and Somers gripped that next. He pulled. In his mind, he saw the drill sliding to the edge of the bench, falling, its tip biting into Somers's chest or belly and puncturing an organ. There wasn't anything to do about that possibility, though, so Somers just looped the cord around his fingers, and then looped it again, and then again. As he gathered up the cord, the drill scraped across the plywood. Metal and glass rattled; the plastic two-liters gave off hollow, drumming noises. Somers twisted the cord again. And again. The Bic lighter fell first, its yellow plastic striking the old wooden floor with a crisp crack. Then, the two-liters came down, and they tumbled everywhere with those same hollow bongs. Then a wad of newspaper. Above Somers, the drill hung on the edge of the plywood. Come on, Somers thought. Come on. Come on, you piece of shit, I saw you up there, so come on!

He wrapped another length of cord around his hand. The drill jerked sideways. For a moment, Somers thought it might stay where it was, and then it flipped sideways and fell. This time, the noise was loud: a clash of metal and wood. The drill bit skated along the floor, digging deep into the boards. There was no way that Mikey had missed that.

Despair tightened fingers around Somers's throat. The drill had fallen. Just the drill. And—

Then he saw it. A small plastic case. The eyeglass repair kit. Somers rocked and twisted, inching the chair forward. His fingers prickled; they felt stiff now, puffy, and Somers realized that the strange angle and the rope had cut off too much blood, and his hand was falling asleep. He worked his numb fingers at the clasp. He just needed to open the eyeglass case. His fingers were slow. His nail skipped along the smooth plastic edge. Please, Somers thought. Please, God. Please, please, please. Then he managed to catch an opening, and he thumbed the lid up.

He grabbed the smallest screwdriver and, twisting his hand, buried it in the nylon rope wrapped around the arm of the chair. Some of the metal gleamed; if Mikey looked closely, he would see it. But Somers didn't have time to worry about that. Footsteps came behind him, and he fumbled again, catching hold of the yellow Bic. His thumb rolled the striker, the movement stiff and partial, and the lighter sparked and died. Somers tried again. This time, more sparks; they singed the back of his hand. He thumbed the lighter again, and a tiny flame with a blue eye sprang up. Somers rolled the flame inward, toward the ropes around his wrist. Heat and pain registered. Then Mikey's foot connected with Somers's hand, and the lighter clicked off the corner of the workbench, and Somers let out a grunt.

"What's going on?" Mikey asked, squatting over Somers, his face upside-down and enormous in Somers's vision. "I leave you alone for two minutes, and look what you do." He stretched across Somers and collected the lighter, turning it in display like some sort of TV showcase. "Is this what you were playing with?" His thumb ran smoothly over the striker, and that blue-eyed flame danced again. Mikey let it die. Then he struck it up again. "This little guy? Is this what you wanted?" The lighter swallowed up the flame again. "I'm talking to you."

Somers stared at the workbench and set his jaw.

"I thought I was being nice. I thought I'd give you back to Emery in one piece—more or less. But maybe that's not the right idea." Mikey stood so abruptly that Somers felt dizzy. The toe of Mikey's boot dug into Somers's back. "You don't respect me because I'm being too soft." Then the kick came, hard and low, and Somers howled in spite of his best efforts. "So I'd like to hear you say it. I'd like to hear you tell me that you respect me." Another kick, and Somers hated the noise he made, hated how he tried to twist away, hated the tidal wave that came over him, the desire to say exactly what Mikey wanted. "Tell me you respect me, John-Henry. Tell me why you respect me."

"Fuck you."

The next kicks were savage, delivered in an insane fury, and Somers didn't know how long it went on. He tried to curl into a ball, only the ropes wouldn't let him, and so he jerked and quivered and thrashed, and the kicks kept coming. When they ended, Somers could still hear himself shouting, and it was a long time before he had enough control of himself to wire his jaw shut, and even then he grunted and moaned behind his closed teeth.

With surprising strength, Mikey righted the chair. He was breathing heavily now, and his eyes were wide and empty, as though they'd been scrubbed clean from the inside. "Tell me."

Somers gasped air through gritted teeth.

Mikey kept his eyes on Somers, but he flipped the lighter in his hand, and then he flipped it again. He shot past Somers, and something metal clunked on the workbench, and then Mikey stood in front of Somers again, the open tin of kerosene in his hand.

"Tell me."

"Fuck you."

For a moment, Mikey's eyes were so wide and empty that they were like plate-glass windows looking out on Shit Mountain. Then his hand jerked, and oily-sweet kerosene splashed across Somers's legs.

"Tell me."

"You want me to respect you?" Somers said, panting. "Give me a reason. Not this kiddy bullshit."

"A reason? You're the reason. Got you tied, got you cut, got you just where I want you. A reason? Hollace-fucking-Walker is a reason. I killed that stupid black bastard. He spent his whole life thinking he was smarter than me, and I'm the one that tricked him into leaving his safe haven here. I'm the one that got him scared out of the nest. I'm the one that moved in, and now I'm high and dry, and when Hollace ran off to his backup, when he ran off to the Bordello, the boys I sent after him made sure there wasn't enough left for a shit-stain in your boyfriend's panties. That's a fucking reason."

Mikey's arm stuttered like a man having a fit. Kerosene licked Somers's chest, his arms, his jaw. He could taste it where it stippled his lips, dizzying, a thicker-than-gasoline taste. When the tin was empty, Mikey pitched the tin overhand, and it rang out against the wall, and he brought up the hand with the lighter.

"Tell me you respect me."

"All right," Somers said, shoulders dropping. He didn't have to mime fear; fear was about the only thing he had left, fear of the yellow Bic, of the blue-eyed flame, of the whoosh of igniting vapor and the heat and the light and the smoke. "Look, you're smarter than we are. You—you played us like fucking idiots, all right?"

Mikey eased back, a smirk tugging at the fine lines around his mouth.

"You killed Hollace. You got me. And you're going to get Hazard. So, yeah, I respect that."

"I killed Hollace."

"Yeah. You killed him."

"That motherfucker thought he was so smart. All he wanted was a truck. Just a white truck. Something invisible, he said. So I got him a truck. He still remembered who calls the shots in Wahredua." Mikey turned the Bic in his hands. "He thought he was so smart. Didn't he?"

"Hollace always thought he was smarter than everyone."

"He did. The stupid mixed piece of shit. He did think he was smarter than everyone. But you know what? Sometimes he had a good idea. And when he drove off in the truck, I started wondering why he'd come back. I wondered why he was here all over again. I wondered why he needed an invisible truck." A grin sliced Mikey's mouth wide open. "And after he picked up the truck, I followed him. I followed him back here. I saw how he went in through the fire escape. I saw how he came out again with a big rifle. And I decided maybe Hollace knew something I needed to know."

"So you waited until he came back. And you tried to kill him."

"I did kill him." Mikey's words came out with so much force that spit flecked Somers's cheek. "The little chickenshit ran, but I found him again. Tracked him down to that old whorehouse he always talked about. And you know what I did?"

"Christ, Mikey. I know already. You killed him. Trust me, I'm not going to forget." Somers felt a tingle down his spine. The urge to cause trouble. To poke this white trash moron in a sore spot. How had Hazard said it? To *get into it*. "Yeah, you really did a good job with Hollace. You can tell that one to all your buddies. You'll still be telling it when you're old, right? That's your big win, the time you got Hollace Walker."

The Bic flitted between Mikey's fingers. He drew his lower lip between brown, rotting teeth. It was embarrassing, now that Somers saw it, how desperate Mikey was for approval. Had he always been this way? Somers guessed so; Mikey had simply mistaken fear for approval, and hatred for approval, and silence for approval.

"You don't even know half of it."

"The fuck I don't."

"You don't. You and Emery, you think you're so smart. You don't even know half. Not even a quarter of it."

Somers rolled his eyes.

"You don't know about the FBI."

"We know."

"You don't know all of it, though. You don't."

"Mikey, I already told you. I respect you. That thing with Hollace, you made your point. You don't have to tell me a story."

"What story? What fucking story? I'm telling the truth. Those two, those g-men, the mayor knew all about them. When they came down here, when they started poking around again, he knew. He told me. You know who he trusted to take care of it? Me." He tapped the lighter against his chest. "I took some boys over to the Deluxe Drive-in. Once the feds were asleep, we went in. Newton just wanted a bullet in the head for those guys, but I'm smart. I like an opportunity. And those two didn't even grab their guns. So I decided to have a little fun. I decided to ask them some questions. Some hard questions. That was the fun part. And if they told me something I wanted to know, if they told me something that gave me an angle on Newton, well, that was going to be good too. So I worked them over. Let me tell you, those guys can't take a punch. The younger one, that dark-skinned little fucker, he started squealing. His partner had *it*. He didn't know anything about *it*, he just knew that his partner had *it*, that *it* was important. Little fucker sold him out after the first punch. We looked around. Couldn't find it. The old guy, he was a lot tougher, wouldn't give it up." Mikey shrugged, the gesture almost philosophical. "I thought maybe I'd get another run at them, so I took them with me. Then I had to take care of my business with Erl out at the trailers, and I saw it. Perfect opportunity. Pin the bodies right there on Erl, nobody comes back looking at me. Those little fuckers gave me the slip, though. Got right out of the truck while I was taking care of business. By the time I realized, those cattle were running them down. But no biggie, same thing: problem solved."

"Except they didn't die. They're in the hospital. They're alive. And you didn't get what they were hiding."

Shoulders drawn back, chin high, Mikey let the Bic drop to his side. "Doesn't matter now, does it? I've got you."

Somers blinked, trying to process the one-sided conversation. *I've got you.* What had the FBI agents had brought with them? A file on the mayor? And what did the last part mean?

Before Somers could decide what Mikey might have meant, the other man puffed out his chest and said, "You don't want to mess around with me, John-Henry. You don't."

"Yeah, I get it. You're a man. You're the man. But this, whatever you're doing, it doesn't have to go like this, Mikey." Somers tried to put something earnest in his voice, something genuine, something other than what he really felt: that yellow, licking fear, and the desire to put a bullet in Mikey's head. "We can help you. Emery and I. We can do a lot to help you."

"Help me?" Mikey laughed. He tucked the Bic into his pocket. "What do you think you're doing? Of course you're going to help me. That's the whole reason I'm keeping you around. That's the whole reason your pussyboy is still alive. That's why Hollace had to go because he thought he could get you to do what he wanted." He leaned forward, patting Somers on the cheek, and Somers had to fight the urge to snap at his hand, maybe take a finger or two. Mikey's pats had a wet, slapping sound where his hand found kerosene. "But he forgot. He was away too long, and he forgot that around here, I'm the one who says jump. Isn't that right?" He slapped again. "Jump, John-Henry. Jump." One more of those wet slaps, Somers's cheek hot, the stink of kerosene in his nose, the taste of it slick in his mouth.

Mikey grinned. "Now, I promised I'd get you ready for showtime. And I did. Let's make Emery a movie."

He adjusted the phone on the tripod and pressed something, and it beeped as the recording began. Then he picked up the pair of pliers.

CHAPTER THIRTY-SEVEN

JULY 4
WEDNESDAY
11:59 AM

BACK IN THE APARTMENT, Hazard bent over Somers's laptop, clicking and searching and clicking again. On the coffee table, he had set up Ted Kjar's computer, and next to the monitor he stacked the printout of Kjar's manuscript chapter and the handful of photographs. On top, he left the picture of Jeff standing outside the cabin.

Somers was still gone.

Hazard reeled himself back from that thought. He lifted the picture of Jeff, and it was like lifting stones from the bottom of the Grand Rivere: pressure weighed down the photograph, making it a hundred times heavier than it ought to have been. He slid a magnifying glass over the image, studying it. He had done this a half dozen times already. Under magnification, a few details in the photograph became clear: Jeff's shirt, untucked; the top of his jeans, unbuttoned; and the sign. It was a new sign, stamped metal, and its white-on-green letters said simply Cairndow. But the magnifying glass didn't reveal anything else, and aside from the untucked shirt and the unbuttoned jeans and the Cupid mole showing above the line of cotton—

—and that look in his eyes, and the cocked smile, and the flush, the way he'd looked when he was still pulling himself together after Hazard had made him come to pieces—

—and the sign, Hazard had no clues. A search for Cairndow turned up results for a coastal town in the Scottish highlands, but Jeff had never been out of the state, much less out of the country. Everything in the first few pages of search results had to do with that town: recommended itineraries, bed and breakfasts, a stagecoach inn. Hazard even used the street view feature of Google Maps, scouring areas around Cairndow, but the stark Scottish landscape looked nothing like the background of Jeff's photograph. And after another minute, Hazard shook the photograph loose, the paper sticky under his touch, and watched it feather down to land on the pile.

Somers was still gone.

Hazard reeled himself back again. Cairndow. Where the hell was Jeff? Why had this picture been so important to Kjar? And—this was the question boiling like hot tar—why did Jeff look like he had been royally, majestically fucked not fifteen minutes before that picture?

Turning to Kjar's computer, Hazard examined the progress bar displayed on the monitor. It had been a fairly simple thing to search for a recovery program, something that would restore files that had been removed from the computer's recycle bin. Hazard had paid the thirty dollars, downloaded the program, and started it. In ten minutes, maybe fifteen, he'd have fresh copies of everything deleted in the last week from Kjar's computer. Another box ticked on the progress bar, and Hazard flexed his hands with frustration.

Somers was still gone.

Again, Hazard dragged himself back. He focused on the case. He was close to putting it all together. He was close to having the answer. And somehow, he knew, it all fit together: Jeff's death, Ted Kjar's attack on Mayor Newton, Hollace's return and the struggle for control of the local drug trade. Shutting his eyes, Hazard tried to trace the threads again. Mayor Newton's connection to the manufacture and sale of methamphetamines was clear to Hazard, even if Hazard didn't have hard proof. Equally clear was the role of the Ozark Volunteers in the drug business. From what Hazard had seen and from what he could guess, Hollace had come here either to disrupt the Ozark Volunteers' business or to kill the mayor—in fact, it seemed likely that he had been sent here to do both. And finally, Ted

Kjar had lost his job at InnovateMidwest, shown increasingly paranoid, erratic behavior, and attacked Newton in his home, almost killing the mayor and, in the process, dying himself. And Ted Kjar and Hollace both pointed back to Jeff Langham's death, almost twenty years ago.

With a long, slow breath, Hazard shook his head. And that was where everything went to shit. If it were just drugs, it would all be simple enough: a vicious battle for control, with Mayor Newton and the Ozark Volunteers entrenched and fighting back against Hollace and whatever new cartel he represented. But where did Ted Kjar come into this? And how could a twenty-year-old suicide—

—murder—

—have anything to do with what was happening now?

And Somers was still fucking gone. The thought propelled Hazard out of his seat. He tried to wind himself back, but he couldn't, and his paces ate up the room back and forth. Somers was still gone. He was still out there, still sleeping one off, or maybe shacked up with somebody. Maybe he'd gotten black-out drunk and gone home with a girl. Or a guy. Maybe he'd gotten in an accident. Maybe he was bleeding out in the Aston Martin's wreckage. Hazard took a shuddering breath, grabbed handfuls of his hair, and yanked hard enough that his eyes stung. Maybe, just maybe, Somers was in a puddle of his own piss somewhere. Maybe that's all it was. Maybe he was just nursing a really bad hangover.

But the faster Hazard walked, the harder his feet thumped the floorboards, the harder it was to convince himself. Because the reality was that even if Hazard believed the very worst, even if Somers had gone out and drunk himself into oblivion and then fucked his way through a whole—

—fraternity—

—sorority house, even if Hazard admitted that this was possible, that he knew some part of Somers could do these things because Somers had done them in the past, then the rest of the truth was that Somers would never abandon his family, or his partner, or his case. He might fuck up. Hell, Somers seemed to have a knack for self-obliterating fuckups. But he would always come back, and it was almost noon, and Somers was still gone, and Hazard knew that meant something was wrong.

Snatching up his phone, Hazard dialed, and the call went to voicemail. He hesitated. His breath felt furry in his throat. And when the beep came across the line, he said, "I just need to know you're ok. Will you call me?" His thumb squeaked along the aluminum, and he said, "Please?"

Then he tossed the phone back on the table. A tremor had started in his shoulders, and he paced the room twice more before he flopped onto the sofa, staring at the photograph of Jeff.

Ok, he said to himself. Think. You're so goddamn smart, so think. You think you're so goddamn smart, so do this one thing, figure out this one thing, and then you can pat yourself on the back. And if you figure this out, Somers will be all right, and he'll call you, and he'll tell you he got a flat or he lost his phone or he had amnesia like this is some kind of goddamn soap opera, but he'll be ok, and everything will be over.

But his injured arm throbbed, and he knew Somers didn't have amnesia, hadn't just dropped his phone in the toilet, none of those things. Hazard's arm hurt like hell today, and he had one wild thought that Somers had left because of his arm, or because Hazard hadn't solved the case fast enough, or because—

Enough, he told himself. Enough, enough. You're so goddamn smart, you think you're so goddamn smart, so think.

Like a man dealing cards, he spread out the photographs that had accompanied Kjar's manuscript. They hadn't changed since the first time he saw them: several old log cabins; trails and trailhead markers; brick picnic shelters. A bridge built from river stones. And a limestone courthouse. These pictures were obviously meant to accompany the chapter that Kjar had been writing for his local history of Dore County. And a brief skim of the chapter had allowed Hazard to identify the buildings and trailheads and cabins as projects carried out under the aegis of the Works Progress Administration, which was exactly what the chapter covered.

To that point, everything made sense. The only problem was that the photograph with Jeff, with the old log cabin and its thick chinking and the reddish dust, didn't match anything in the chapter. And when Hazard searched online for Cairndow, or Cairndow cabin, or Cairndow park, or Cairndow Works Progress, he came up with absolutely nothing. Well, nothing except for all that Scottish stuff.

He was butting heads with a brick wall, and he knew it, so he scrubbed at his face. All right, he told himself. All right, you've tried that a few times and it's not working, so come at it from another angle. He searched for Ted Kjar Cairndow. Nothing. Then he tried Hollace Walker Cairndow. Nothing. He tried Ozark Volunteers Cairndow. More nothing. He tried Naomi Malsho, Mimi Malsho, Sherman Newton, Wahredua, Dore County, and various permutations, all with Cairndow. Nothing. Then he started looking at online slang dictionaries, drug-use forums, anywhere that Cairndow might have some secret significance. Aside from a couple of Greek boys on a gap year trying to score weed in the Scottish Highlands, he found nothing.

But the more he typed the word, the more it rang in his inner ear, the more convinced he was that he had heard it before. Cairndow. Where had he heard it? Who might have mentioned it to him, and why?

A ping from Kjar's computer interrupted his thoughts. Hazard glanced at the monitor; the recovery program had finished. Clicking and scrolling, Hazard examined the files that had been restored. The majority of them were drafts of Kjar's manuscript. Someone—perhaps Kjar, perhaps someone else—had deleted those files. Why? Because they were important, but Hazard already knew that. That was why Kjar had sent his copy of the chapter to the Langhams, along with the photographs he had collected. Hazard opened the chapter on the local Works Progress Administration, and he skimmed it, looking for changes, alterations, updates—anything that might tell him why the file had been deleted, or what Kjar had discovered. Everything he saw, though, looked identical to the printed copy that Hazard already had.

Hazard closed the document and looked at the rest of the recovered files. They were PDF files, and when he clicked on them, he saw that they were scanned images. Financial statements, Hazard realized. InnovateMidwest's financial statements from last year. They had turned a substantial profit, he saw. These documents would have been closely guarded by a privately held firm like InnovateMidwest. Why had Kjar gone to the trouble of scanning them? To sell them to a rival? Was this some kind of corporate espionage gone bad?

Before Hazard could follow the thought, his phone buzzed, and he snatched it up.

"Hazard," he said, waiting to hear Somers's voice at the other end, all his anger evaporating in an instant.

"Uh, Detective?"

"Foley? What's wrong?"

The redheaded cop's voice lowered. "Somers with you?"

"No. Is he with you?"

"What? No. I tried to call him. I thought—listen, something's weird over here. Chief isn't answering her phone, and I thought about John-Henry, but he's not answering either, and he always said you . . . Christ."

"What's happening?"

"I was on duty at the hospital. Those two guys, the ones that got caught in the stampede."

Hazard's mind flashed to Swinney's corpse, to the flickering fluorescent light, and the crumpled paper records for two FBI agents.

"Are you still there?"

"He just showed up. He was . . . he was acting really strange. Told me to get out of there. Got right up in my face. He was spitting. Like a goddamn cartoon." Foley's voice sounded dazed. "I finally left because I swear to God, I thought he might, well, I don't know. He had his hand on his gun, Hazard. I'm not a chickenshit, but goddamn if I don't feel like one. So I left and tried calling Cravens, and then Somers, and—"

"Who?"

"Detective Lender. He's in there right now."

CHAPTER THIRTY-EIGHT

JULY 4
WEDNESDAY
12:46 PM

IT TOOK HAZARD TOO LONG to get to Wahredua Regional. Somers had vanished with the Aston Martin, and the Jetta was destroyed, and, for that matter, so was the Interceptor. In the end, Hazard had to jog a handful of blocks to the station, borrow a patrol car, and drive to the hospital while sitting on superheated vinyl upholstery, surrounded by the smell of drying puke.

At Wahredua Regional, Hazard ran. He ran down hallways painted lime-green, mustard-brown, and hideous shades of ochre. His mind ran faster. When he reached the end of this hall, what would he find? Two dead FBI agents? Would Lender just shoot them? No, that seemed sloppy, even for Lender. Maybe a ventilator would be turned off. Or maybe he would have pushed a drug, a bubble of air, something through the IV line. Would he take a risk like that after sending Foley away? At this point in the game, when everyone had all their cards on the table, maybe it didn't matter anymore. Lender had killed his own partner. He had shot Swinney and left her to die in an abandoned storefront in Smithfield. And if someone sent Lender to kill these agents, he would do it, regardless of Foley or Hazard or anyone else.

Near the end of the next hallway, a chair waited outside a room, with two paper cups of coffee on the floor next to the chair and a rolled up magazine slowly peeling open, a woman's face showing on the cover, and the single word *Jugs*. Foley's chair, and Foley's coffee, and Foley's jerk-off rag. So where was Foley?

Hazard slowed his steps. He pulled the .38 from its holster under his arm, and he held the gun low at his side, hoping it would be discreet. At the doorway, he listened for a moment and heard quiet breathing, the rustle of clothing, and then, in a weary voice, "You can come in."

Raising the gun, Hazard stepped around the corner.

Albert Lender sat in a molded plastic chair, his shoulders slumped, his hands hanging off his knees, and he looked like shit. Gone was the squirrelly accountant type. Lender still wore the thick, yellow plastic frames, and he still wore his enormous, bristling gray mustache, and he still wore a suit like a CPA might have worn back in 1972, but he didn't look like the same man. His eyes were hollowed, his cheeks shadowed, and those hands, hanging off his knees, trembled with palsy. Hazard didn't see a gun, but he kept the .38 steady on Lender.

From one of the beds came a soft moan, and Hazard risked a glance. Under the bandages and cuts and bruises, the men didn't look much like the pictures that Swinney had provided. They had been trampled by a stampede of cattle; that thought rang out clearly in Hazard's mind, and he thought of the Yorgenson trailers, set out on Yorgenson land where they ran cattle all year. One of the men—older, white, the one that Swinney's information had named Graham—was either asleep or unconscious. Judging by the thick bandages around his head and the chart labeled John Doe #1—God, not a drop of imagination in this whole damn county—Hazard guessed he had never woken up. The other man, with Latino features under the layers of sterilized cotton, had to be Bruce Schaming. And Bruce's dark eyes were bulging, and he was moaning around an improvised gag of medical packing gauze and an electrical cord.

Hazard gave Schaming a cool, clinical assessment and then returned his attention to Lender. "What now?"

"These guys don't look too good, do they, Detective Hazard? They look like they might not make it. Maybe not even through the day."

"You're going to kill them? Like you killed Swinney, you backstabbing motherfucker?"

Lender's hands twitched, and then they flopped against his knees again.

"Say it. I want to hear you say it. I want to hear you say you killed her." The .38 might as well have been a soap bubble; it floated up in Hazard's hand to the level of Lender's head. "Right now."

Lender's jaw cracked. "I liked her." He worked his lips silently, and his jaw cracked again, and he said, "Are you arresting me? Are you going to shoot me? Because what you said, you can't prove it, and if you shoot me, you're the one that'll pay for it."

"I don't give any fucks about paying for it. You deserve it. That's all that matters."

"Where's Somers?"

"Shut your fucking mouth."

"Did they get him?"

"I said shut your fucking mouth."

Lender nodded slowly. His hands spidered down his shins, tugging at the trousers, trying to smooth out forty years of creases set by cheap dry cleaning. "This has gone to hell about a million ways from Sunday. It was supposed to be easy. Not simple; it wasn't ever going to be simple. But it was supposed to be easy and quiet and done. And now—" He grinned, and it was like a skull grinning. "Now it's all fireworks. Isn't that a mess?"

"Why don't you tell me about it? Why don't you tell me what was supposed to be easy, and why don't you tell me why it wasn't?"

Lender snorted. He stood, suddenly, and Hazard fought the reflex to squeeze off a shot. Sweat prickled under his arms; he could smell his own fear, mixing with the stink from the bedpans, mixing with industrial disinfectant, mixing with the damp mustiness of bodies that have only been cleaned by sponge baths. If he shot Lender now, he would smell gunpowder. He would smell the visceral gassiness of body cavities blown open. The .38 slipped up another inch.

"It wasn't easy because you and Somers get your teeth into everything like a pair of dogs." Lender wiped his forehead, although the skin looked fever-dry. "I told him you two wouldn't let it go. I warned him. But he's the same way: gets his teeth into something and won't let go."

"You're talking about the mayor. That's what this is? Something he planned?"

Lender studied the two men in the hospital beds. He pushed back his suitcoat, exposing the Sig holstered at his side. Hazard adjusted his aim, ready to fire if Lender so much as touched the butt of the gun. Then, shaking his head, Lender let the coat drop.

"Killing feds, that's just stupid. He's gotten stupid about this whole thing, and I'm not stupid enough to keep following." Lender moved towards the door, ignoring Hazard's gun, and he cast a backward glance at Schaming. "Make sure you take out that gag, Detective. You wouldn't want people asking awkward questions."

"Stop right there, you son of a bitch."

"Or you'll shoot me?" Lender paused. Those huge glasses magnified his eyes, warping them so that they looked cartoonish. "Have you ever shot anyone like that? In cold blood? Because you'll have to shoot me if you want to stop me."

"I will. I'll blow out your knee if you take another step."

Lender took a stride into the hallway. Hazard grimaced, and the .38's muzzle dipped, but he didn't fire.

"We're a lot alike, Hazard."

"Fuck you."

"We are. We both know that life isn't black and white. We both know there are hard choices to make." Some emotion Hazard couldn't read wiped Lender's face blank, and he said, "I made my hard choice, Hazard. And fuck me for making it."

He waited a moment longer. His leg was turned awkwardly, as though he were presenting it as a target, but he didn't say anything else, didn't do anything else. And then, when that moment had ticked by, he walked down the hallway.

Jamming the .38 into its holster, Hazard fought the urge to go after him. Yes, he knew Lender had killed Swinney. Yes, he knew Lender had done a lot more: killed a suspect in custody, leaked information, lied to Hazard and Somers in order to lure them into a trap. But Lender was right about one thing: Hazard couldn't prove any of it; at least, he couldn't prove it in any way that mattered. And so he had to stand there and let the bastard walk away.

But under the smoggy anger, two truths clicked into place for Hazard. He had suspected, and now Lender had confirmed, that the mayor had set these events in motion. And, more importantly, something had gone wrong. Terribly wrong. Part of that, as Lender said, was that Hazard and Somers hadn't swallowed the show that had been performed for their benefit. They hadn't been content to believe that Ted Kjar, crazy and vindictive, had broken into the mayor's home and tried to kill him. But Hazard thought something else had gone wrong too. The arrival of Hollace and this new criminal force in the area? Or something else? Something deeper?

A pleading grunt from the bed drew Hazard's attention, and he unwound the electrical cord. Schaming spat gauze onto the floor, made an O of his mouth, and tongued chapped lips. "Water."

Hazard spotted the lengths of cord that had been used to tie Schaming's hands, and he undid those as well, and then he poured water from the plastic pitcher and handed Schaming a cup. The thin plastic crinkled between Schaming's shaking hands, and some of the water spilled through the stubble on his jaw, but he managed to drink most of it. When he'd finished, he let the cup fall, and Hazard realized this man was exhausted and hurting and probably very, very confused about what was happening.

Hazard displayed his badge. "Emery Hazard. I'm a detective with the Wahredua Police Department."

Schaming nodded. He flopped back on the pillow; under his olive complexion, he looked washed out. "I know. We read all about you and the other one, your partner. Somerset. Damn." He rubbed at his mouth. "That stuff really dries you out. I've heard of cottonmouth, but this is something else entirely. Who was that?"

"Albert Lender. Detective."

"Yeah, I know the name."

"You know my name. You know my partner's name. And you know Lender's name. You're sitting in a hospital bed, and you just about had a dirty cop put a bullet between your eyes, and you're not acting very surprised. Why don't you tell me what's going on?"

"I was asleep. When he came in here, when he got that gauze in my mouth, I was asleep. In case you were wondering. You'd think I learned my lesson from last time, but a guy's got to sleep sometime."

Hazard shook his head. "All of it. From the beginning."

Schaming shifted under the thin sheets. The hospital gown rode up almost to his chin, and for a moment he looked childlike in spite of his age and stubble and the weariness in his eyes. He glanced at Graham and sighed. "I wish I knew. Honestly." He put up both hands. "I'm not giving you a line here, I'm just saying, I wish I knew. I guess I ought to be giving you some kind of hard-ass Bureau crap, right?"

"All of it." Hazard settled himself in Lender's seat, pitching his body towards Schaming. "From the beginning."

Schaming shook his head. "I'll tell you what I can, but I'm being honest: this was Graham's show. Honestly, it was more like an obsession. We're not even supposed to be here. This isn't an active investigation. It's not even an inactive investigation. He asked me to take two personal days and drive down here because—because he can't let it go."

"Slow down and tell it from the beginning."

"Right. All right. Graham and I work white collar stuff. I was an accountant before this. Did you know people did that? Some of the other guys, they had coding jobs. Some of them were grad students. I mean, you think FBI agent means some hard-ass who used to work Compton, and sometimes it does, but sometimes it means a guy who used to do the books at PricewaterhouseCoopers."

Hazard nodded and rolled a finger.

"Right, right. So Graham's been doing this a lot longer than I have. And he's worked a lot of cases. White collar doesn't always sound bad, but a lot of the times, it's the little guy who ends up getting hurt. Corporate fraud trickles down, you know? And Graham cared about that. A lot. He's getting close to mandatory retirement, and he's been getting . . . restless." Schaming rubbed his eyes.

"Frantic might be a better word. Or crazy. And there was one case that he couldn't let go."

"InnovateMidwest."

"You know about that?"

"It's your story."

"Yeah, InnovateMidwest. That's the one he couldn't let go of. He said he knew there was something wrong. He said he had proof. That's all he would tell me, but I've worked with Graham for a long time, and he's never lied to me. He's lied to his wife. He's lied to his kids. He lies to the hookers he picks up. But he doesn't lie to me, and when he said he had proof, I believed him."

"If he had proof, why isn't this an official investigation? Why are you down here in a hospital bed, taking personal days so nobody asks where you are?"

"It's my story, right? That's what you said." Schaming grabbed the cup again, the plastic crinkling under his grip, and shook it in Hazard's direction. Hazard filled it, and Schaming drank, and the whole thing felt like one big buy for time.

"You're going to tell me eventually," Hazard said. "Keep drinking like that and you'll piss yourself before you finish the story."

"I pissed myself when that first cow went over me," Schaming said, rocking in the bed, one hand fingering a spot low on his waist. "Graham told me somebody stalled the investigation. It was, I don't know, twelve years ago, fifteen, maybe longer."

"Corporate fraud?"

"That's what Graham said. He said that's where it started anyway. And he said he dug around deeper. He said this guy, the one he was trying to get, he's into all sorts of weird shit. He said this guy would go across state lines for all sorts of things: gambling, prostitution, drugs. He said if it was that bad fifteen years ago, it was only going to be worse now, and he said we could do a lot of good."

"Who's your guy?"

Schaming's eyes darted to the window. The July-blue sky held nothing. At the horizon, a scattering of trees stuck up like dark quills.

He seemed to realize something, and he was trying to hide the worry creeping into his face. "Look, this isn't really—"

"It's Sherman Newton. Is that right?"

Shaking his head, Schaming said, "It's a small town." In one hand, he still held the cup, but the other hand was creeping across the sheets towards the call button. "I'm not trying to put you in a difficult situation."

"You can push that," Hazard said, eyeing the button. "But if I wanted you dead, I'd have left Lender to do what he came here to do. You push that, and a nurse will come in here, and they'll fuss over you, and that'll be the end of this conversation. And next time Lender comes back, I might not be here."

Schaming looked at the button, and then he jerked his eyes away, as though embarrassed. It looked like it cost him a lot to meet Hazard's gaze.

"You're telling me that fifteen years ago, the FBI knew that Sherman Newton was involved in some degree of fraud. They suspected that he was connected to regional, maybe national drug trafficking, sex work, and gambling. And they didn't do anything."

"Well, fuck, man. I'm telling you that one guy thought he had proof of that stuff. I wasn't there; I'm telling you what Graham told me."

"But you believed him."

"Yeah. Enough to come down here, anyway." Schaming pressed his free hand to the thick plaster around one leg—the cast came to the hip, Hazard realized. "Didn't know I was going to get trampled to death."

"How?"

"These guys broke into my room. They were fast. I mean, Christ, I was in a new place, and this was just some favor for Graham. It wasn't anything serious. I'd taken a couple of pills to sleep; I didn't even know what was happening before they had me tied up." His mouth made that parched O again, and he ran his tongue around his lips before saying, "I'm an accountant, all right?"

Hazard nodded. FBI screening and training was rigorous. But training was one thing and being out in the field was another. Some guys talked the talk and walked the walk right up until it was real, and Hazard wondered if Schaming really had taken sleeping pills, or if the pills had made any difference, or if Schaming had just frozen the first time he was taken by surprise.

"And?"

"And they beat the shit out of me. Out of Graham too."

"What kind of guys?"

"What? Guys. Just guys. They were wearing masks. I don't know."

"White guys? Black guys? Mexican guys? Mafia? Cartel?"

"I don't know, man. White guys, I guess. Yeah. They were white. And I was too busy to be noticing—"

"How?"

Schaming's mouth snapped into a tight line. "What the hell are you saying?"

"How were you busy? Were you knitting? Were you making lemonade? Were you sorting through your old underwear?"

"Fuck you, all right?"

"What were you doing?"

"I was getting my ass beat. They ripped that room apart, and the whole time they were asking questions. And no, I didn't tell them anything. You don't have to fucking ask."

"What were they asking?"

"Just bullshit questions. I don't even remember."

"You don't remember, but you know they were bullshit?"

"I don't remember. And anyway, it doesn't matter. I didn't tell them a single thing."

Hazard shook his head; he guessed that Schaming might have told them anything they wanted to know, but he also guessed that Schaming hadn't known what they wanted to find out. "What were they looking for?"

"I don't know."

"Did you hide something in your room?"

"Look, this was a favor. For Graham. Just drive down here with him, watch his back, help him make everything look official in case anybody asked questions. That was it. I was supposed to be home by now, not in a fucking hospital room."

"Did Graham hide something in his room?"

"I don't know. I don't even know what they wanted."

They wanted whatever Graham had; that much was obvious to Hazard. Instead of saying this, though, he asked, "And then?"

"And then they dragged us out to the middle of nowhere. This shitty little compound of trailers. And they started shooting. And the other guys were shooting back. Graham got the door open, and we ran. I mean we just started running, just like that, while they were all still shooting at each other. I was sure they were going to come after us. And they did." Schaming grimaced. "Them and about a million cows. A fucking stampede. And you know how the rest of it went: the cows got us first."

Hazard nodded, letting Schaming founder in the memory, and then asked, "How does someone stop an FBI investigation? Who does Newton have under his thumb in the FBI?"

"It's not that simple, buddy. Somebody pulled Graham off that investigation. Who knows why? Fifteen years ago, that was only a couple of years after 9/11. A lot of things changed after 9/11. The Bureau was trying to find its footing still, trying to figure out the best way to go after terrorists. White collar stuff, unless they were funneling money to Al-Qaeda, that didn't mean beans."

"Does Graham think that's what happened?"

"No." Schaming blew out a sharp breath. "And don't ask me if he's right. I don't know. I don't—I don't really want to know. I'm an accountant, all right? I got a gun. I got sprayed with mace. But I'm just an accountant, and I'm not supposed to be dragged out of my motel room by guys in masks, tied up, and left to get crushed to death when a herd of cattle runs over me."

Hazard ignored him, his mind turning over what he had heard so far. The thought of Newton having an inside man at the FBI, someone powerful enough to stop an investigation into InnovateMidwest, was troubling. No, it was more than troubling. It was terrifying. With that kind of reach and power, it wouldn't be hard for Newton to crush Hazard and Somers. If the mayor recovered from being stabbed, and if Hazard's investigation took him where he thought it was leading, then he might face someone more powerful than he had realized.

But the more he thought about it, the more he forced himself to consider the matter logically, the less certain he was that Newton was as powerful as Schaming's story made him sound. Newton, as far as Hazard could tell, didn't have that kind of pull. If he had, he would have used it before. No, Newton was a big fish in a small pond: powerful in Wahredua, powerful in Dore County, but his power waned within a few hundred miles.

That didn't mean, however, that Graham's story was a lie. Newton didn't need to have an inside man at the FBI. All Newton needed was a friend who had a friend who had a friend. Newton applied a little pressure, or he greased a few palms, and then a few more palms were greased, and on down the row until, under the convenient excuse of a new anti-terrorism program or a shift in Bureau resources or whatever they had told Graham, the investigation into InnovateMidwest was shelved. Not permanently; Hazard was sure they had promised Graham that it was only a temporary hold. But weeks had turned into months had turned into years, and no one had ever taken the case back off the shelf. Until Graham got old. Until Graham got close to mandatory retirement. Until Graham dragged his partner down here, into central Missouri, and kicked the hornets' nest. And then—

"All right," Hazard said. "Tell me the rest of it."

Schaming was staring at him, his dark eyes bugging, but Hazard rolled his finger again and Schaming said, "We came down here."

"And you did something stupid."

"Fuck you, all right? Fuck you, and fuck this shitty little town, and fuck this shitty little hospital." Schaming jerked upright in bed, his hand shooting towards the call button. "I'm calling this in. I'm calling the whole fucking thing in. I don't need some small town dick with a badge telling me—"

"Tell me the rest of it," Hazard said, rising out of his seat and clapping both hands down on the chrome rail. "Then you can pitch a fit and call your boss and tell him what a shit-show you and your partner made of a local investigation. But first you're going to tell me the rest of it."

"I ought to—"

"Right now. Right fucking now. All of it. Or I'll rip that call button off its cord and I'll tie you up the way I found you and I'll see if Lender's still in the parking lot."

The plastic cup crumpled in Schaming's grip. "The Bureau's going to bury you. We'll bury you."

"Yeah, you and all your fed buddies. But first, you're going to tell me."

It might have gone either way, but Hazard dropped back into his seat, and Schaming let out a nervous breath.

"We came down here. We got rooms at the Deluxe Drive-in. Separate rooms. I told Graham I wasn't putting up with his old-man farts if I was taking personal days to come down here, and he paid for the rooms. Then Graham drove us out of town. Out to some piece of land."

"Where?"

"I don't know. I wasn't driving."

Hazard shook his head. This was his luck: to get the shittiest agent the Bureau had ever produced. "A name? Landmarks? Anything you remember?"

"It was pretty dry. Rocky. I mean, not really anything to see. There was this old cabin, and there was a trail that had mostly washed out, although—"

"What?"

"The trail was washed out, but I could see where it kept going."

"No. The cabin."

"Yeah."

"Did it have a name?"

Schaming was staring at him as though he were crazy.

"A sign," Hazard said. "Did it have a sign, anything like that?"

"No. It was just a cabin."

Hazard couldn't stay seated; he got to his feet and paced. At his side, his bad arm throbbed as it swung with his steps, and that throbbing moved into his head, pulsing in time with his thoughts.

The FBI had come here. A white-collar fraud case into InnovateMidwest, fifteen years old. And the first thing that Graham did, the first thing he did when picking up a case that was fifteen years old, was drive out to the middle of nowhere. Only—Hazard's heart thudded so hard it felt like it was packed with lead shot—only it wasn't the middle of nowhere, not exactly. There was a cabin there.

Somers would have laughed. Somers would have pointed out that Hazard was being irrational. Somers would have grinned and said something about how Hazard was always so proud of being logical, and here he was, jumping to conclusions. The vision of Somers, laughing and grinning and rubbing Hazard just the right amount of wrong, was so strong and so clear that it lodged deep in Hazard's chest, making it hard to breathe.

But the fact was that Hazard couldn't stop himself. He couldn't keep himself from associating the two things: the cabin that Schaming had seen, and the cabin with

—Jeff, cheeks flushed, smirking, the top of his jeans unbuttoned, the Cupid mole above the elastic of his boxers—

—the sign for Cairndow. And what Hazard could confide to the ghost of Somers, even if he couldn't admit it to anyone else, was that he knew that he was right. He knew the two were connected. He knew that he was on to something. And he knew it the way he had known he loved Somers, at some gut level, at a place deeper and more primitive and much, much more important than logic, he knew. And when he saw Somers, he was going to tell him, and he would let Somers laugh and rib him and all of it, and he wouldn't even mind because he would have Somers back again.

As thoughts cascaded through him, Hazard realized he was shaking: part nervous energy, part excitement, and part the bone-deep weariness of almost no sleep over the last few days. He spun towards Schaming; the olive-skinned man reared back, as though he had seen something in Hazard's face that startled him. Or frightened him.

"Where? Where was this cabin?"

"I don't know. I wasn't—"

"Which way were you driving? North? East? West?"

"What about south?"

"Jesus Christ. South is the fucking river. Which way?"

"I wasn't driving." Schaming said it with offended dignity, but he hunched his shoulders, and his cheeks were red.

"Did you drive over the railroad tracks?"

"I don't remember. No. No, we didn't."

"Did you drive through a trailer park? Or through a really rough part of town?"

Schaming rolled his shoulders.

"Did you pass the Tegula plant? And if you ask me what that is, I'll knock out your fucking brains, because it's the only plant in the area."

"No."

"Did you go past the college? Lots of new development. Fancy brick buildings, lots of stucco, everything looking less than twenty years old."

"No."

"Did you drive past a bunch of old warehouses, buildings that look like they're from the 1920s, a movie theater that's—"

"Yeah. Yeah, we passed this old movie theater, only now it looks like it's some sort of club."

Hazard let out a shredded breath. They'd gone east. That wasn't much, but it was something, and he could start looking. He shot towards the door.

"Hey," Schaming called after him. "Hey, what about that other guy, what about Lender—"

As Hazard reached the hospital parking lot, a wave of wet, summer heat crashed over him, and his phone buzzed. He jerked it out, so intent on his thoughts that he barely realized what he was doing. In his mind, he had some half-formulated idea that it was Somers, calling to apologize, and that Hazard would have to explain everything—explain it slowly, explain it in order, explain it so that Somers would see the same connection Hazard saw—and then stopped when he saw that it wasn't a phone call but a message from an unknown number.

He swiped open the message.

HI!
Buzz. Another message showed up.
EMERY HAZARD.
Buzz.
YOU FUCKING FAGGOT.
Buzz. Buzz.
GIVE ME WHAT I WANT.

And then a video loaded, and Hazard tapped the play icon, and he felt cold, cold in spite of the heat swaddling him. The video jerked, as though someone were settling the camera into place, and then it cleared, and Hazard stared at Somers. The camera closed tightly around Somers's face. Hazard shivered; he was so cold, so goddamn cold, that he blew out a breath and was surprised it didn't fog the air. He had to stay focused. He had to think. Those were the only thoughts he could articulate.

Someone had beaten the shit out of Somers. One of Somers's eyes was puffy, so swollen that Hazard doubted the blond man could see anything out of it. His cheek had split over the cheekbone, and blood fringed the crisp line of his jaw. A ball gag held his mouth, and Somers's teeth bit clean lines into the rubber. Where his lips had split, they left tiny streamers of blood down his chin.

All of that was bad. All of that was enough to shoot fireworks up inside Hazard's head, to blast away any other thought. But Somers's eyes. Those eyes were full of a desperation Hazard had never seen before. Turquoise blue shimmered under a sea of tears. Somers jerked his head away, as though trying to pull back from something, and then a flush burned up his face, and he screamed through the gag. Something moved in the background, and then a pair of pliers swam into view in front of the camera, holding the fingernail that had just been ripped from Somers's hand.

Hazard could hear his own breath whistling. The thick, humid heat collared him, left him barely enough air to stay on his feet, but he was shivering so hard that the phone slipped out of his hand like a bar of soap and Hazard caught it and stared.

He had Somers. He was hurting Somers. And there was no doubt in Hazard's mind who he was. Mikey Grames. Mikey, that sick son of a bitch. It wasn't enough that he had tormented Hazard through high school. It wasn't enough that he had beaten and sodomized Jeff. It wasn't enough that he had gone into the hospital, had humiliated Somers and threatened Evie. Now this. Now he had Somers, had taken him somewhere, and was torturing him. Hazard's fingers spasmed around the phone, and he was shaking, he was shaking so hard he had to sink onto one of the cement benches at the emergency pull-up, and a few scattered neurons wondered if he was having a stroke.

The video ended, but it didn't matter. Hazard could still hear that scream. He could still hear Somers's screaming, the noise muffled by the gag and worse because of that, worse because Mikey had even taken away Somers's voice. The phone buzzed again. Hazard stared at the new message; his eyes blurred the blue bubble. He blinked. He scrubbed at his eyes. He pulled in a breath, and he tasted old cigarettes and diesel exhaust and Juicy Fruit gum bubbling on the hot asphalt. Buzz.

I WANT PROOF.

Hazard typed back, *Prppf og what?* He figured that much was a miracle, considering how his hands were trembling.

Buzz. Buzz.

A cry-laughing emoji came back, followed by *HAHAHAHAHA.*

Buzz. Buzz. Buzz. Buzz.

PROOF THAT SHERMAN NEWTON KILLED YOUR FUCKTOY. TONIGHT. MIDNIGHT. WAIT FOR A LOCATION.

CHAPTER THIRTY-NINE

JULY 4
WEDNESDAY
1:22 PM

IT WAS THE SMELL that was getting to Somers more than anything else. More than the pain. The pain was low on his list. It had been—he could think this much with hindsight and perspective—relatively minor, all things considered. The pain, the torture, the cutting, the hitting, it could have been worse. It could have been so much worse. Instead of fingernails, Mikey could have taken fingers. Instead of boxing at Somers's face, Mikey could have worked him over with a hammer. Instead of cutting on him in little jagging slashes, Mikey could have popped out eyes, severed tendons, cut away muscle.

So it wasn't the pain that was getting to Somers, although every inch of him was hell. It wasn't even the fact that, at the end, he had screamed. Everybody screamed. Push anybody far enough, long enough, hard enough, and they'd scream. And Somers dared anybody to keep quiet while they were having their last remaining nails ripped out. Well, Hazard could probably do it. Hazard was so damn quiet he could probably keep silent through Chinese water torture. But anybody else would scream, and Somers didn't really care that Mikey had gotten him to howl.

No, it was the smell, and not the kerosene that Mikey had splashed on Somers. It was the smell of his piss, the fact that in the middle of the torture, when Mikey was digging the pliers under another nail, Somers's bladder had spilled like a cheap canteen, completely out of his control, just a hot rush along the inside of his thigh, pooling under him, running off the chair in a tinkling fountain. That smell, that fucking smell, that bothered Somers. The helplessness of it. And the stink of it. And the childish shame. And the way Mikey had laughed, wide-eyed and genuinely, pleasantly surprised.

"Don't tell me," he said when he finished laughing, and he leaned back, eyeing the wet patch of carpet. "You and your boy are into raunch. What do they call it? Water games? That's it, right? That's what you're into? Jesus-fuck-me-over. You're just a little piss pig at heart." And then he started taking pictures.

When Mikey left, Somers dozed. It wasn't sleep. It wasn't even close to sleep. It was more like drifting, like his mind had come unmoored and the current was carrying it. Minutes would go dark, shuttering down around him, and then he would blink and jerk upright, trying to remember where he was for an instant before the pain and the ropes and the smell, that goddamn smell, reminded him. And then, other times, memories would flash like an old photographer's bulb, glaringly vivid: Hazard curling an arm around him as they stood at the window, watching the sunset; Evie, newborn and tiny and squalling; dinner with Cora, God, so many years ago, still in high school, and she had her hair long and she had her mother's earrings like moondrops. And then, reality would jerk him back.

He wasn't sure how long Mikey had been gone, but he could hear the man in the other room, could hear plastic click on plastic, could hear water, could hear steps. And music. It took Somers a moment to realize what the low sound really was: Mikey was humming. "It's Raining Men." That fucker. That motherfucker. And the jauntiness of Mikey's music, the sheer pleasure in it, was worse than anything else, and Somers's face heated, and his eyes stung, and worse than the hitting, worse than the cutting, worse than the screaming, worse than the piss, this, Mikey's singing, this made him want to curl up and cry.

"Hallelujah," Mikey crooned in time with his own internal radio.

Somers dragged his mind away from the song, away from Mikey's mockery, away from the fury that glowed like smelting along his veins. As carefully as he could, Somers probed the ropes binding his arm to the chair. For a moment, he felt nothing but nylon, and his heart stuttered. Then, his fingers found the tiny steel tip of the eyeglass screwdriver, wedged between strands of rope, still hidden.

The gambit with the lighter had worked. Somers had wanted Mikey to catch him; when he had fallen in the chair, he had known that Mikey would catch him, and so it was important to make Mikey think that he had gotten one over on Somers. And, Somers reminded himself with something that sounded, even to him, like desperation, it had worked. Mikey hadn't noticed the tiny screwdriver tucked between the ropes and the chair's arm. Somers toyed with the screwdriver. How long would Mikey be in the other room? Long enough for Somers to work on the ropes? It killed Somers, but the reality was, he didn't think so. And he didn't dare risk it. He wouldn't get the screwdriver out until he knew he was alone, until he knew he had time to work, uninterrupted time. Or—because Somers had to admit that he didn't know if he would get that much time—or if this went on too much longer and Mikey didn't leave, he would just have to risk it. Better to risk it than let Hazard walk into this maze of booby-traps.

Footsteps moved towards Somers, and he straightened his fingers along the arm of the chair. No need to give Mikey any clue that Somers had a secret weapon. No need to make him suspect that Somers still had a nugget of hope still buried. Somers let his head sag. He tried to look like he was drifting again, but he wasn't: he was there, and he was waiting.

"Drink up."

Mikey jerked Somers's chin, and the mouth of a plastic bottle chittered against Somers's teeth.

"Drink, pig."

In spite of himself, Somers swallowed. It was water. That was all; he had expected piss. He had expected, maybe, something even worse. But it was just water. He swallowed another mouthful. He didn't want to meet Mikey's eyes. Piss pig.

"That's right," Mikey said, tipping the bottle, his fingers fastened to Somers's jaw. "You're going to piss yourself again. On camera. He'll like that, won't he?"

Heat scorched Somers's cheeks again, but something in Mikey's voice rang false. Somers glanced up at the other man; those dead-dog eyes were locked on Somers. No, that wasn't quite right, Somers realized. Not on Somers. On the bottle.

And Somers thought of Simon Pacheski, who had driven away from a party with the girl Hollace liked, and so Hollace had doped the girl's drink.

And Somers thought of the model train track running away into the plaster cavern.

And he realized the traps weren't the only thing Hollace had left.

Somers tried to twist away from the bottle, but Mikey's fingers bit into his cheeks, and the plastic crinkled against his teeth. The best he could do was refuse to swallow, and the water flooded his mouth and spilled out between split lips. Somers felt a faint, chemical sting that plain water shouldn't have had. Or was that his imagination?

With a muttered swear, Mikey eased the bottle down, stopping the flow into Somers's mouth. "I said drink. I want your bladder full so you can piss a few gallons for your boy."

But there it was again: that false note. This time when Somers glanced at Mikey, he saw frustration in the man's expression.

"I can make you." Mikey grinned, and it hollowed out his cheeks and flattened the humor in his eyes.

Somers shook his head. Lips throbbing—imagination? or was there really something in the water?—he said, "I'm not what you said. That thing you said, I don't do that."

With a mocking sound of concern, Mikey threaded fingers through Somers's hair, "Well, fuck me sideways. My little piss pig is embarrassed. Now listen, pig: there's no judgment here. You like what you like. I don't care about that. So drink up, and maybe the next time you piss yourself, you'll be at home, with Emery plowing you. That'd be nice, right? Home on your rubber sheets, pissing yourself like a pig."

He jabbed the bottle at Somers's mouth again, and Somers clamped his lips shut. He felt a flash of pain, and fresh warmth on his chin told him that his lips had split again. Mikey gave a few more experimental thrusts with the bottle. He had moved closer to Somers, his fingers still combing blond hair, and Somers noticed, now, the tweaker's erection. "Fuck me," Mikey said, talking almost to himself, his fingers tightening Somers's hair until tears came to the blond man's eyes, "but I could make you. I could. And I think I will."

He forced Somers's head back, pried open his jaw, and shoved in the bottle. Before Somers could spit, he pinched Somers's nostrils, and clamped a hand around the bottle's neck, squeezing until Somers's teeth crimped the plastic.

Somers thrashed. He twisted his head as best he could. He tried to knock over the chair. But Mikey had strength and position and leverage, and as the seconds ticked by, Somers's lungs began to burn. Don't swallow, he told himself. Don't swallow because it's not about watching you pee yourself, it's not about that at all, it's going to be like Simon all over again, only you'll be the one who's drugged, you'll be the one blacking out, and there won't be anyone to warn Hazard. Don't swallow. Don't you dare fucking swallow. Don't you dare swallow because if you do, Hazard will die, and—

And then instinct and reflex, coded into him at the most primitive level, took over, and his throat opened, and he swallowed, and when his mouth was clear he gasped for air. He took in too much water, but he got air, and then he was coughing, his lungs spasming as they tried to force out the water. Mikey rocked him forward, pounded on his back, and after a minute, when it was obvious Somers wasn't going to throw up, hit Somers across the back of the head as hard as he could.

The blow exploded like black snow in front of Somers's vision. He didn't lose consciousness, not quite. He was aware of movement, the feeling that he was falling—although that might have been just from the blow—and the squeal of wood on wood, and then ammonia in his nose, and feathers. Thousands of feathers on his face, his arms, his hands. And he thought maybe he was dead. Maybe they were angel feathers. Angels carrying him. But that wasn't right because nobody had ever told him angels smelled like ammonia.

Some of the darkness faded, but not all of it, and it took Somers time to realize why: he was in a closet. And the feathers weren't feathers; they were clothing, old and prickling and clinging to his sweaty face. The ammonia smell: mothballs. He swallowed a laugh. So much for angels.

Already, he could feel the effects of whatever Mikey had put in the water. Invisible strings pulled him down, down, towards a deeper darkness than the closet and its prickly, abandoned clothes. How much time did he have before it took full effect? Minutes? Somers curled his fingers over the arm of the chair. He found only braided nylon. The screwdriver had fallen out. It had slipped free of the ropes when Mikey had dragged him into the closet, and it was lying there, on the floor, probably only a few feet away—and completely out of reach. Then his index finger brushed molded plastic, and Somers let out a jittering sigh that was, by any other name, a sob. He gripped the handle between his first two fingers and began sawing with the screwdriver's flat blade.

For the first time in days, luck was on his side. The flat head of the screwdriver frayed the nylon fibers, and as they split, their ends tickled Somers's hand. His head swam. Enormous purple flashes struck like lightning, and Somers caught himself sagging, tipping forward, his hand relaxing. Only a jolt of terror and luck and an athlete's conditioned reflexes allowed him to catch the screwdriver before it slipped away.

Somers drew a deep breath and kept sawing. Stay awake, he told himself. Stay awake, motherfucker, stay awake, don't you dare close your eyes—

—a brilliant flash of purple, and then the darkness, and his head didn't hurt anymore, nothing hurt anymore—

—he came up gasping like a man breaking pitch-black waters. No, no, no. Don't do it. Don't fall asleep. Don't close your eyes. Don't even—don't even think about it. He didn't even know what he was telling himself, didn't even know what the words meant anymore, but he could feel their intensity. And more of the fibers were splitting now, severed by the screwdriver, unraveling into the darkness to dance like spider legs.

And then, wrenching his wrist to the side, the last of the rope fell away. Somers dropped the screwdriver in his lap, pinching it between his thighs, and shoved two fingers down his throat. The effect was immediate: he puked. He puked like he hadn't puked since his first year at college, when he'd been thinking about pledging and he'd drunk eighty-proof vodka with two junior-classmen until he fell off a porch. It all went into his lap, flooding him like the piss had, only this was worse. Once it started, once the stink got in his nose, he just kept puking. The hot, watery bile and the chunks of whatever his last meal had been soaked his clothes.

After a while, nothing more came up. The dizziness, the heavy sandiness to his eyes, the precipitous edge of the darkness—they stayed where they were. Not any worse. But not any better either. His body had already absorbed some of the drug; Somers would have to fight it until it wore off.

But now, at least, he had a chance.

Fishing the screwdriver out of the puddled vomit, Somers sawed at the ropes on his other hand.

CHAPTER FORTY

JULY 4
WEDNESDAY
1:22 PM

HAZARD HAD READ ABOUT SOLAR WINDS. He had read about the continuous flow of charged particles through space, an invisible stream of electrons and protons and alpha particles blasting across the galaxy. Right then, he felt as if that dark, invisible wind were rushing against him: as though it were streaming through him, disrupting signals, turning him into a static-hiss version of himself, a scrambled black-and-white image of who he normally was. It lasted maybe five seconds, maybe ten, that feeling of being hammered by solar wind, of disintegrating from the inside out. And then it was over. And then Hazard's hands were still, and his breath rolled like the tide, and he tapped two letters into the phone: *Ok*.

There was no response, but then, there was no need for a response. Hazard knew everything he needed to know: Mikey had Somers, and he was going to torture him, probably kill him, if Hazard didn't come up with proof that Sherman Newton had murdered Jeff all those years ago.

The other Emery Hazard, the one he had been fifteen minutes before, would have wondered about the strangeness of it all. He would have wondered how Mikey, as stupid a son of a bitch as had ever shat on God's green earth, had gotten the drop on Somers. He would have wondered why Mikey, who had been so insistent about taking control of the investigation into Ted Kjar's death, now wanted information on Jeff's murder. He would have wondered at Mikey's obsession with Kjar.

But that Emery Hazard was gone as of thirty seconds ago. The solar wind had shredded him and left behind this fuzzy, staticky copy. And this Hazard, the one whose hands were still, this Hazard didn't care about any of that. He cared about three things: getting the proof about Newton; trading it for Somers; and then taking Mikey apart with a hacksaw. Alive.

Hazard took a deep breath and then walked towards the patrol car he had borrowed. At one in the afternoon, the parking lot became an oven, and the asphalt radiated enough heat to cook Hazard's soles. The air remained swampy, though: heavy with moisture and a green, vegetative note that reminded Hazard of sour mulch. As he walked, his mind turned more quickly. The horror and shock of—

—Somers tied up, tortured, screaming into that rubber gag where his teeth made fine white lines—

—the video was fading, fading, gone, and in its place came clarity. The last message, the one asking for proof linking the mayor to Jeff's death, that held an extra piece of information, beyond what Hazard had realized. If Hazard needed confirmation that Mikey was behind this, it was right there in front of him: your fucktoy. That's what Mikey had called Jeff—how long ago? two days? three? when Hazard had run into Mikey at the county fair—and it couldn't be coincidence that Mikey used it again in the message. He was rubbing salt in the wound. He was reminding Hazard who was in charge.

But he wouldn't be in charge for much longer, Hazard thought, popping open the patrol car's door and sliding onto hot vinyl. In a few hours, Mikey Grames wouldn't be in charge of anything. In a few hours, when Somers was safe, Hazard would take Mikey out to the clay pits, abandoned now for years. And Hazard would tie Mikey down. He'd use chains, heavy gauge stuff, and he'd drive the spikes deep so there wasn't any chance of Mikey getting away. And then Hazard would see what kind of noises Mikey made when Hazard butchered him like a chicken. He'd start, Hazard thought as he twisted the key in the ignition, with the legs. There were good, solid bones in the legs, and if Hazard tied off the arteries correctly, he could spend a long time with Mikey. A really long time.

He drove first to the Deluxe Drive-in. It was a three-story walkup, the exterior corridors all exposed to the elements, and the doors peeling to expose battered particle board underneath. The whole thing looked like it had been built in 1977 and had been meant to last no longer than a year. Somehow, even with the cement pitching sharply underfoot and the all-purpose carpet disintegrating in the sun, it had lasted this long. Hazard just needed it to last one day longer.

From the parking lot, he studied the Deluxe Drive-in's façade. Parked at one end of the third-floor corridor was a room service cart: mop and broom and bucket on one end, soap and shampoo and conditioner, towels, trash can. A mobile all-in-one service stop. But there was no one in sight. Hazard counted out two more minutes. He checked his watch. It was past check-out. And it was before check-in. So somebody had parked the cart up there on purpose, but they hadn't put it away for the day yet. That meant there was a resupply closet up there. Maybe even there was a storeroom where the cart was locked up at night.

Two guys come in from out of town. They want two rooms. They're going to be staying for the weekend—that's what Graham told Schaming, anyway. The Deluxe Drive-in, however, was more likely to rent rooms by the hour than rooms by the day. Rooms by the minute, maybe. And people who rented rooms by the minute wanted rooms on the ground floor. They wanted in and out. They wanted minimal time out in the open. So no desk clerk with any brains would give Schaming and Graham prime rooms, not when they could make a lot more renting them out over and over again to people who just needed a place to screw for sixty minutes or less.

That left the second and third floors. Had Graham requested privacy? Maybe. Hazard didn't know the man, but it would have made sense: Graham was here unofficially, and he was here to investigate the mayor. He would have wanted to keep his presence quiet. And, more importantly, no one had heard the break-ins. That meant that Schaming and Graham hadn't had neighbors. And since the Deluxe Drive-in didn't look like it was overflowing with guests, that meant the clerk had probably put them on the third floor, saving the second floor for ordinary travelers who didn't make a fuss about having some privacy.

Third floor, then. And since the storeroom was up there, and the cart was up there, why not make life a little easier and put them in the rooms at the end? Everybody gets what they want: Schaming and Graham get peace and quiet; the clerk gets happy customers; and whoever's doing room service can clean up the rooms right next to the supply closet. Human laziness trumped just about everything except human greed.

Hazard took the stairs two at a time, and when he reached the exterior corridor on the third floor, he trotted to the end. Up here, a faint breeze plucked at the room service cart's trash bag, and the rustling plastic was the only noise. Hazard studied the two doors at the end. At first glance, there was nothing strange about them except the Do Not Disturb hangers. Kneeling, Hazard inspected more closely. Hairline cracks showed in the jamb around the strike plate. Hazard settled five fingertips on the door and nudged it. The door swung open, and wood and the brass strike plate tumbled free of the jamb.

Well, Schaming was telling the truth in part. And whoever had attacked them—Mikey, Hazard assumed—had done a decent job of making sure no one at the Deluxe Drive-in realized there had been a break-in. Not right away. Those Do Not Disturb hangers did a lot of the work; the rest was human laziness.

Inside, the room was as Schaming had said: torn to shit. Hazard moved through the space quickly, aware that time was passing for Somers and that he needed to hurry. Drawers had been pulled free, their faces ripped off to expose hinges and rolling tracks. The mirror lay in splinters across the countertop. Someone had hammered the shower curtain rod out of the wall, obviously to inspect it for contraband. Holes had been knocked in the walls. The bathroom door had been kicked through in places, exposing the hollow core. Whatever Mikey—or the mayor—thought that Graham had, they wanted it bad.

The second room was in a similar state. Hazard moved through it just as quickly. Then he returned to the exterior corridor and leaned on the railing, breathing in the hot air that smelled like soap from the cart and, more faintly, bleach. Below him, the asphalt shimmered like an oasis.

Whatever Mikey had been looking for, he hadn't found it. And Hazard wasn't sure he could find it either. If Graham had hidden it, he had hidden it well, and the only person who might be able to retrieve it would be Graham. Hazard was smart, but he wasn't all-knowing, and the more time Hazard took, the more Somers would suffer.

Still, Hazard forced himself to think through it all one more time, just in case. If he were Graham, coming down here to reopen, unofficially, an investigation into one of the town's most powerful men, and if he really did have some kind of proof that Newton had committed a crime, then he must have wanted security. He must have wanted a guarantee, a backup plan in case things went wrong. But the backup plan couldn't be the Bureau; Graham was older now, at the edge of retirement, and he'd already seen his case quashed once. He wouldn't be willing to risk that again.

Some other guarantee. Something to make sure that the evidence didn't disappear if a very bad accident happened to Graham.

Hazard took the stairs two at a time down, but instead of heading to the car, he went into the motel office. It was a small room with a divider. Bulletproof glass and a turnstile told a story about the Deluxe Drive-in. Hazard rapped on the glass.

The guy who answered was probably in his thirties, his hair thinning and combed over in a part that started at his ear. "Twenty dollars by the hour."

"What about a day?"

"Thirty. But you'll have to take the second floor."

"The guys who rented those third-floor rooms."

"What about them?"

Hazard produced his badge and pressed it against the glass. "Tell me about them."

"Come on, man."

Hazard clinked the badge against the glass again.

"What's there to tell? They rented rooms for the weekend, but the older guy paid extra, cash, so I'd hold the rooms for the rest of the week. They never even come out. They must be like bunnies. Maybe they go out to eat or something, but otherwise, they must be a couple of jackrabbits."

"What did the older guy give you?"

"Like, how much? Two hundred."

"No. What did he give you?"

The guy frowned, and the wrinkles ran all the way up under his combover. "Like, what bills? I don't know. Twenties. Maybe a fifty. We don't take anything bigger than a fifty."

"Bullshit me one more time and I'll find a way around that glass."

"I don't even know what you're asking."

"What did he give you?"

"Nothing. Cash. That was it."

Hazard tapped steadily on the glass with his badge, measuring the beat to his words. "Here's how this is going to go: either you give me what he gave you, or we make this official. And then I'll have to file a report about minors engaging in illicit activities on the premises. And I'll have to file a report about sex trafficking on the premises. And I'll have to make a report about the sale and possibly manufacture of drugs on the premises."

The guy with his hair parted right above his ear mouthed each significant word as Hazard said it: *minors, trafficking, manufacture, drugs*. He took each word like a punch. "No way. That's not even true, man. None of that stuff, we don't have any of it at the Deluxe."

"I think you do. But I guess we'll have to see what an official investigation turns up. We might even have to shut this place down for a while. Six weeks should do it."

Six weeks, the guy mouthed.

"He still didn't give you anything?"

"It's just an envelope. I mean, he asked me to put it in the safe, and I said sure, even though we don't have a safe. But I kept it for him because he gave me fifty bucks. It's just an envelope."

Hazard rolled his hand.

"He asked me to hold onto it for him."

"Yeah. And now I'm asking you to get it. And I have a badge."

The balding guy scurried into the back. When he returned, he held a manila envelope that he passed through the turnstile.

"He gave me fifty bucks to hold onto it."

"If you wanted money, you shouldn't have passed it through already. And you really shouldn't try to extort a cop." Hazard rapped the edge of his badge on the glass one last time and left. In the car, he checked the envelope: a flash drive. On the front of the envelope was scribbled an address in St. Louis. That was it.

The patrol car roared to life, and Hazard drove back to the apartment. As he drove, he put the flash drive out of his mind for the moment and thought. All the jams, all the kinks, all the disruptions to Hazard's thinking had burned off in the intensity of this new state. He only had three things to worry about, and he was going to deal with them in order. First: link Sherman Newton to Jeff's murder.

The connection was already there, Hazard knew. He had known there was something, some link, between the mayor and Jeff because of the package Ted Kjar had sent to the Langhams and that picture of Jeff standing outside a cabin. But now, after speaking to Schaming in the hospital, Hazard knew that Jeff's death was tied up in the recent events. It was more than a tragedy from the past. It was more, even, than a killer's successful ploy to pass off a murder as a suicide. Jeff's death had to do with things today, right now. And Hazard felt like he had the first thread on how it connected.

Ted Kjar was that thread. Ted Kjar was the link. The FBI agents had come here, following up on a cold case—but a white-collar case, a corporate fraud case. And Hollace had come here, with his gang war, and told Hazard that Jeff's death hadn't been a suicide. But only Ted Kjar had links to both. Ted Kjar had been an accountant. Ted Kjar had been an employee at InnovateMidwest, conducting internal audits. He had been a good accountant. Until now, Hazard had assumed that Ted had somehow run afoul of the mayor in two separate ways: first, by uncovering some sort of illegal dealing within InnovateMidwest and threatening to expose it; then, in a bizarre coincidence, by uncovering some truth about Jeff during his research for his book. But that didn't make sense, Hazard realized. It was too much coincidence. What if, instead, Kjar's forensic accounting had led him to the truth about Jeff's death?

Hazard grimaced as he pulled into the Crofter's Mark parking garage. If Somers were here, he'd push back on Hazard's theory. He'd say something about how that was still a huge coincidence. He'd say that it wasn't really any better than Hazard's original explanation that Ted Kjar had somehow separately uncovered two separate conspiracies. And, Hazard felt a hint of a smile crack the edges of his mouth, Somers would point out that since Hazard wasn't a trained accountant, they'd need an expert to comb through all of InnovateMidwest's paperwork if they wanted to have a hope of finding what Kjar had found. And then, indulging in his general preference for pushing every single one of Hazard's buttons, Somers would have said something stupid, something like, *It might as well have been the other way. Maybe Kjar was doing research for his book and—*

Hazard braked so hard that the cruiser's tires screeched, and George Larsen, from 3C, stopped in the middle of the parking garage and glared. Hazard barely saw him.

For fuck's sake.

Even when Somers was absent, even when he was tied up and being tortured and God only knew how far away, he was still an inescapable asshole. And he was right.

Somers—it barely mattered now that Hazard had imagined the whole conversation—Somers was right. Going through the finances, going through all of that, that was the wrong way. That was a dead end. And Ted Kjar had known it. He hadn't sent extensive financial records and a detailed paper trail to the Langham household. What had he sent?

Hazard's smile was so cold he thought it might have frosted the glass. Kjar had sent his book. Chapter four. The missing manuscript. And he had sent it to the family of a boy who had been murdered as insurance so that in case he died, there would be a way for someone else to follow the trail back to Newton.

Why hadn't Kjar included a note or a letter? Why hadn't he explained what he had discovered? Why hadn't he gone to the police? Hazard didn't know, but he remembered Jo Kjar telling them about interrupted phone calls, and Ted's increasing paranoia, and his inexplicable disappearances. He swore at himself, loudly, and hammered the dash. Hazard had missed the most important, the most obvious fact about the whole case, the one that explained Kjar's erratic behavior and the convoluted course of this case: Mayor Newton had been telling the truth.

At their first and only meeting with the mayor, Newton had provided Hazard and Somers with documentation about Ted Kjar's mental health. It had all seemed too convenient: from the beginning, Hazard had suspected that the documents were the first steps in Mayor Newton's plan to invalidate anything Ted Kjar might reveal. After Kjar's death, Hazard had wondered if those documents had been the groundwork for Ted Kjar's murder. It was a great deal easier, after all, to believe that Ted Kjar had broken into the mayor's house and attacked him, only to be fatally wounded by a protective detail of police, if Ted Kjar was certifiably crazy. In Hazard's opinion, it had all been much too convenient.

But—and here Hazard felt that tingling awareness of what Somers might have said—what if both things were true? What if Ted Kjar really had been using drugs and been mentally ill, and Newton had used that to discredit him and to frame him for his own murder? What if Kjar's break had been triggered not only by drugs but also by escalating confrontations with Newton about corporate fraud and a decades-old murder? It would explain so much; most importantly, it would explain why Kjar hadn't taken his discoveries to the local police. Instead, he had tried to work through the FBI, but his increasing paranoia had made him unstable, and it seemed that no one had taken his claims seriously.

And then Mayor Newton had decided to eliminate Ted Kjar. Hazard remembered what he had learned at the ME's office: Dr. Boyer had run drug tests, and Kjar had tested positive for uppers and downers. Someone had kidnapped Kjar. Hazard thought of the Kum-n-Go, the last night anyone had seen Kjar before he disappeared, and the clerk telling them that Mikey had driven past in his truck. Somehow Mikey had convinced Kjar to get in. Mikey had doped him, sedated him, and hidden him until the mayor had acquired a protective detail. Then, shot up with coke and crystal, Kjar had been turned loose on the mayor.

That, Hazard realized, was where things had gone wrong for Sherman Newton. Mikey had been helping him, and then Mikey had betrayed him. Hazard could still hear the mayor's shocked words in those few moments before he broke down the door. *What are you doing? No. You can't*—Those words were really the only clue Hazard had, but they were enough. The plan was for Kjar to appear to be attacking the mayor, and then for Hazard and Somers to break in and kill him. Instead, Kjar very nearly succeeded at taking the mayor's life.

And what about the rest of it? What about everything with Ted Kjar? Was he looking for a way to keep the mayor from retaliating? There were threads Hazard couldn't line up. His explanation, he knew, wasn't perfect. But it was the closest he'd come to something coherent since Chief Cravens had called him into her office.

Seated in the living room, Hazard booted up Ted Kjar's computer and inserted the flash drive. There was a single large video file, which he opened, and it began to play. The shot was poor quality, and the camera showed a cramped room with a TV, a bed, and a single lamp. Crepe myrtle patterned the teal wallpaper, which was pulling back from the upper right corner.

As Hazard watched, the grainy black-and-white footage flickered, and a door slammed shut. The shift in the camera's picture and the sound came so close together that Hazard realized the camera must have been embedded in the wall. Hidden. And recording something that was supposed to be a secret.

A man wandered into the room and sat on the bed, his face toward the camera. He was middle-aged, his donut of graying hair frizzy on one side, his stomach filling out the white dress shirt that he wore. The camera shook again, and the door closed again, and two more people came into the room.

One walked across the camera's field, but his height put his head out of the frame. The other walked more slowly. A girl. Naked. She couldn't have been more than twelve. Maybe, maybe at the outside, thirteen. And she wore a Halloween mask, the rubberized kind, that looked like a knock-off Molly Ringwald.

There was no subtlety. No pretense. The balding man drew a wad of cash from his pocket and passed it to the standing man, and the standing man left.

Hazard fast-forwarded when he couldn't stand it anymore.

There were hours of footage. There were businessmen in middle age. There were old men, so old Hazard half-expected to see a heart attack. There were young men. One, Hazard thought he recognized as a minor athlete, a wide receiver who had played for the Chiefs in the 1990s and had gotten an extra fifteen minutes of fame when rumors started flying about his frequent trips to Thailand. There were girls who wore scarves, who wore mirrored glasses, who wore masks like the knock-off Molly Ringwald. There were so many girls, and all of them barely more than children.

There were more boys. The athlete, the one from the Chiefs, liked to spank them. There was a businessman who liked to tie them up. There were boys who painted their faces. There were boys who wore cowboy hats tipped low and bandanas tied high. There was one boy who wore a rubberized Halloween mask, and if the first girl's had been a knock-off Molly Ringwald, this was a knock-off Jonathan Taylor Thomas. The message wasn't subtle at all: this was the boy next door, but the boy next door you could fuck.

And Hazard's hands tingled when he saw that boy with the mask. His breathing seemed to shift into neutral; nothing in, nothing out. He leaned forward, nose brushing the screen, and looked for that Cupid-shaped mole. The boy in the JTT mask showed up a lot. One guy, one of the older guys, made the boy ride him and call him daddy. The old man's hands wrapped tight around the boy's hips. Was it there? Was that a smudge on the camera, was it a bruise, was it a shadow? Was it the Cupid mole that marked Jeff low on his waist?

Hazard finished his fast-forward viewing of the footage. He rewatched the parts with the boy, and then, halfway through the old man asking to be called daddy, Hazard lurched into the bathroom and bent over the toilet. His stomach heaved like a giant fist was crushing it, but nothing came out. He heaved again. Nothing. And then he wiped his forehead and spat and wiped his cheeks and spat and wiped his eyes and spat and flushed and went back to the computer.

He turned off the video; he couldn't watch anymore. This was what Graham had: a video that showed someone—presumably Sherman Newton—trafficking minors for sex. The faces of the clients were visible. That was, perhaps, maybe the whole point; blackmail was a lot more profitable than a one-night stand, no matter how much Newton was charging. But the problem was that Newton's face didn't show in the recording. And all the kids—the ones who might testify, the ones who had been the victims, the ones that Graham might otherwise have tracked down and asked for help—had their faces hidden.

Like the boy in the Jonathan Taylor Thomas mask. The one who might have had a mole on his hip just like Jeff.

The video was something, but it wasn't enough. For a moment, Hazard allowed himself to wonder: how had Graham acquired the video? How long had he possessed it? Possibilities ran through Hazard's mind. Had Newton—because Hazard was convinced that the man in the video was the mayor, even if he couldn't see his face—been betrayed by an accomplice? Or had a third party filmed everything and, under duress, turned over the material to the FBI? Or had it been someone else, some middleman with no real role? A tech guy paid by Newton to convert the video to a digital format? Christ, how many possibilities were there?

Hazard went back to the bathroom and washed his face. Then he returned to the computer and looked through Ted Kjar's recovered files. He could still smell the summer heat on him, in the toasted smell of his wool trousers, in the sweat slicking his hair, but it contrasted now with the cool rush of air conditioning. His stomach rumbled; he wasn't sure when he had last eaten. He pushed those thoughts away to focus on the task in front of him. He needed to find something that linked Newton to Jeff. His best chance seemed the cabin. And Ted

Kjar had believed that the necessary information was in the chapter of his history that he had mailed to the Langhams.

Only Cairndow didn't show up in that chapter. Not anywhere. Hazard read through it again, and then, just to be sure, he opened the digital file, recovered from Kjar's computer, and ran a search. Nothing. Nothing even remotely resembling Cairndow.

Hazard scrolled through the recovered files again. He wanted to dive into the financial records, but he resisted. Kjar had put the spotlight on this manuscript, on the history of the Works Progress Administration in Dore County in the early 1940s. Only Cairndow wasn't listed in any of the Works Progress Administration projects. It sounded like—

With a shiver, Hazard fell back into memory: the glow of the Aston Martin's interior, and Glenn Somerset's dispirited voice as he said, *He changed the name of that place so many times, Scottish names, English names, country club names, and it turned a profit every time.*

He changed the name.

So it wouldn't be listed as Cairndow. Maybe it was never listed as Cairndow. Or maybe it was listed once, in that snowfall of financial records, as Cairndow. But it had been something else first.

On the computer, Hazard pulled up Google Maps. Then he worked his way through Ted Kjar's manuscript, dropping pins for every WPA project mentioned: the Ozark Courthouse, Fort Winston, the Wyatt Earp Ranger station, on and on, a total of fourteen projects until he had turned the last page of the printout and could study the map before him. Then, zooming in, he marked the county into quadrants. He eliminated both western quadrants immediately; Schaming had given enough information that Hazard knew the FBI were interested in a property east of Wahredua. The northeast quadrant held two WPA sites: the Beaumont-Jefferson Loop, a sixteen-mile trail through heavily wooded country; and the Cropper Memorial Pavilion at a local state park. It was possible that the cabin was located on the Loop, but for the moment, Hazard dismissed the northeast quadrant.

That left only the southwest quadrant, which had four WPA projects on record: the Arrowrock Trailhead; the Old County jail;

Ulysses S. Grant High School; and Camp Winnipeg. The jail and the high school Hazard ignored. A quick search turned up six cabins built by the WPA at Camp Winnipeg, but a Google Image search showed a green, riverside backdrop, nothing like the rough hardscratch in the photograph of Jeff. That left only the Arrowrock Trailhead. Hazard keyed the name into Google. He had to dig to the third page of Google results, but there it was: the Arrowrock Trailhead, located on private property, not accessible to hikers.

Private property.

For the first time that day, a white, phosphorous-fire hope burned inside Hazard. This was it. He was sure this was it. Nothing on the Google search indicated who owned that private property, but with a little more sifting, Hazard found an address for the Arrowrock property: 1722 Missouri Highway 29. He plugged that address into Google, and swore, grinning, at the result.

Lewis and Clark Estates, Luxury Homes in the Heart of the Ozarks, a McEnnis Brothers' Development.

Hazard knew he could drive out there, follow that curving state highway, park right at 1722 Missouri Highway 29, and find nothing. Maybe—just maybe—he'd see a billboard, some sort of publicity announcing a neighborhood. But he wouldn't find any houses. He'd find trees. Acres and acres of trees and scrub breaking up into rocky Ozark hills. There wasn't a subdivision out there. There wasn't goddamn anything out there. Except maybe an old WPA cabin at a forgotten trailhead.

But somebody wanted people to think the land was being developed. Or that it would be, soon. Hazard opened up the most recent financial statements for InnovateMidwest. Buried in the documents, he found leasing agreements for a property called Lewis Estates located at the same address. He opened up the previous year's documents; nothing called Lewis Estates. At the same property address, though, there was a contract for a cash-rent agricultural lease of land at 1722 Missouri Highway 29. And the year before that, copper rights at 1722 Missouri Highway 29 were sold for a sizeable sum—they figured for a substantial amount, in fact, of InnovateMidwest's profit that year. He jumped back ten years. And there it was, listed at 1722 Missouri Highway 29, for 1998, 1999, and 2000: Cairndow Apartments.

Seeing that name snapped the wire running from Hazard's skull to his backbone, and he slumped against the couch. Here it was, an answer to the question Glenn Somerset hadn't been able to ask: how did InnovateMidwest make a profit? How, year after year, from its very beginnings all the way through one of the worst recessions in U.S. history, did Sherman Newton squeeze money out of the air? Simple, Hazard thought as he opened another year. Newton made up deals and funneled his drug money through his real estate investment firm. It hadn't taken a genius to uncover the deception, although it was a testament to Newton's influence—and to an ungodly amount of bribes—that Newton had managed to pull off his scheme for so long.

This was what Ted Kjar had uncovered. How? Hazard wasn't sure anyone would ever know. Had Ted just been slightly more diligent than previous internal auditors? Had he noticed the recurring addresses, questioned how one property could serve, year after year, for mineral rights and agricultural leases and the promise of a burgeoning luxury subdivision? Or had it been that cabin? In his mind, Hazard envisioned Kjar out on another of his long drives, the ones that had bothered his wife, Jo, so much, searching out every WPA site in the county. Had he driven along 29, looking for the Arrowrock Trailhead? Something in Hazard's gut told him that this was the case. Kjar had been out, diligently following up on his passion project, just a little local history. And he had stumbled onto a money laundering operation, as well as decades' of corporate fraud, when he noticed something simple: the McEnnis billboard, perhaps. Something that made him think twice, the next time he looked at the InnovateMidwest records, about the truth of the words in front of him.

Hazard stood up, stretching. His back cracked. His bad arm twinged like a banjo after a bluegrass festival. His stomach, though, was what took up most of his attention: his stomach heaved, and Hazard realized he was starving. He took unsteady steps into the kitchen, found bread and corned beef and sauerkraut, no Swiss, but what the hell, and made himself a poor man's Reuben sandwich. It tasted like shit; he kept hearing that gagged scream, kept seeing Somers's teeth whitening the rubber ball. But he ate it. All of it. Because he needed fuel. Because he was going to finish this. Tonight. And then he was going to take his time teaching Mikey a lesson.

As he chewed, swallowed, chewed, swallowed, Hazard faced a nagging truth: he had found Cairndow. He had figured out—although he would need time and experts to prove it—what Ted Kjar had discovered. But he hadn't figured out anything that connected Newton to Jeff's death. His teeth working meat and bread into a slurry, Hazard let his gaze unfocus, let his mind spin. He knew, already, what the connection was. He knew. He knew it was true because it hurt so much. He could hear, the way he had heard it almost twenty years ago, Jeff bragging that he didn't need protection. He could hear Jeff talking big, the way he always talked big: about how he was going to move to New York, go to Columbia, about how he had a friend who could help him pay for it. He could hear the thump of Jeff kicking the tires on his dad's borrowed pickup, laughing when Hazard pointed out the red curb, tearing up the ticket when they came back. That was the most vivid part: Jeff's blunt, strong fingers shredding the paper, the tiny squares fluttering into the gutter and pasting themselves against the hot summer sludge at the bottom. His friend would take care of it. His friend.

His friend, Sherman Newton. Jeff had never said the name, but now it was all too clear who he had meant. There was more. There was a barbed-wire truth coiled around those thoughts, but Hazard couldn't go the rest of the way. At some point, the conclusions became too sharp, too dreadful, and he turned away.

His friend. Just leave it at that: friend.

Somehow, Ted Kjar had discovered a connection between Jeff and the mayor. But how? Hazard returned to the sofa, sandwich in one hand, and wiped fingers clean on his trousers. He picked up the photograph, fanning it, as though this were some exotic print fresh out of the developing bath. Nothing changed, of course; chemicals had fixed the image to paper a long time ago. Twenty years ago. Jeff, his cocksure smile, his blown-out expression, the top button of his jeans undone. Even now, all these years later, Hazard thought he knew what Jeff had smelled like when the picture was taken: dusty, sweaty, and still sticky with sex.

Just a friend.

And then his gaze shifted past Jeff to the old WPA cabin with the thick chinking between the logs, all of it stained reddish-brown from the dust. Sliding the picture into a pocket, Hazard chewed the last two bites of his sandwich and dusted crumbs onto the floor. Then he headed for the cruiser in the parking garage. He felt, all of the sudden, in the mood for a house. Maybe something developed by the McEnnis Brothers.

CHAPTER FORTY-ONE

JULY 4
WEDNESDAY
2:14 PM

THE DRUGS SWALLOWED UP Somers before he could get himself free, and he woke, sometime later, with his head throbbing and purple enameling the inside of his eyelids. He blinked into the darkness, and he breathed, and after a few minutes his head cleared a little. Then he set to work freeing himself. By the time Somers sawed through the rope on his other hand, he noticed that the vomit puddled in his lap had cooled. It was some kind of mercy, he guessed. Yes, it was cold. Yes, it stank. But the stink covered up the smell of his pee. This smell, acidic and bilious, made him gag, but at least it wasn't the same shameful, broken funk of pissing his pants. And it wasn't the kerosene, either. So at least there was some small mercy to the vomit.

With both hands free, Somers untied the ropes binding his legs to the chair, and he pulled each knee to his chest in turn, stretching. It felt so good, so goddamn good after all those hours, that his eyes teared up. Then he popped his neck and back, and then he elbowed aside the hanging clothes still prickling his face, and he bent forward to examine the closet door. Just a simple round knob. Somers touched it; the metal was warmer than he expected, and it clinked once. He rocked it, testing for a lock.

It turned. Somers let out a breath. He let the door wobble open a crack. Fresh air—relatively fresh, anyway—nosed into the closet. Light slashed across Somers's fingers. His heart had picked up in his chest, and he drew in air slowly, trying to calm himself so he could listen.

Everything was quiet. Everything except his heart, anyway. His heart was going a mile a minute. And Somers wondered if it could possibly be as loud as it sounded in his ears. What was he missing? Christ, that heartbeat was so loud that, for all he knew, Mikey could be on the other side of the door playing the trombone and Somers might not hear him. After another moment, Somers nudged the door open. A hinge creaked. That was a loud noise. That was a hundred times louder than his heartbeat. He froze, hand on the knob. If he heard footsteps, he'd pull the door shut, loop the ropes around his wrists—once, just enough to pass a quick glance—and hope that he could put the screwdriver in Mikey's eye before things got any worse.

But no footsteps came down the hall, and no voices raised in alarm, and after another minute of sitting and listening and cursing that mambo-level heartbeat, Somers eased the door open another inch. He got to his feet and shuffled out into the hall. Even after stretching, his muscles were stiff, and he took mincing steps, grimacing as everything in his body pulled and ached and throbbed. When he was free of the closet, he shut the door behind him.

Somers felt ancient. Only some of that had to do with his muscles, though. The rest of it had to do with the last twenty-four hours. They had been some of the longest hours of his life. Two points of comparison came to mind: the night Evie had been born, all those hours of counting the time between contractions, walking, tracking down ice chips, massaging Cora's feet (so puffed up with retained water that they looked a little like elephant feet, which he made the mistake of telling her and, as a result, got a bloody nose), checking the dilation, and then getting up to walk some more. That night had been an eternity.

And the other night, the only other night that had lasted as long as this one, had been a Sunday night last October when Somers had lain awake, watching minutes drag by on the clock, and thought about meeting his new partner: Emery Hazard. That night, all those months ago, had been long enough for a lifetime. Somers had walked himself through everything he remembered about Hazard. He'd paced every memory forward and backward. He'd dragged up to the light every horrible thing he'd done to Hazard. And he'd made himself a promise that night, at the end of it all, when he had faced the worst things that he'd done. He had promised himself that he would make things right with Emery Hazard.

Somers checked the hallway. In one direction, it ended in a closed door. At the other end, the hall opened onto a larger room, where the relative brightness told Somers a window looked out on the bright July day. From that direction came a whir-whir-whir, and the rattle of a copper pull chain. That was the direction Somers had come from, towards the front of the apartment. He took a step and hesitated.

In the front room, where Mikey had tortured him, Somers had observed a number of traps. All of them had been designed to kill anyone who tried to come into the apartment. It was possible that there were more traps. It was possible that Hollace had rigged the whole apartment before Mikey killed him, turning it into a maze of death and destruction. What would happen if Somers opened the door at the end of his hallway? Would a sawed-off shotgun put a few more pellets into him? Would an axe swing down and cave open his chest? Would a chandelier of grenades explode like roadside snappers?

Somers hobbled away from the door, towards the whir from the next room. He stopped at the end of the hallway. The room itself was nothing remarkable: the same thin carpet shiny from years of heavy traffic; the same chipped plaster walls; the same crumbling molding. But the windows were remarkable. Hollace—or someone—had boarded over them, and bright July sunlight haloed the plywood. Attached to the plywood in a zigzagging series of hooks was a line of grenades. It was impossible to tell without close study, but Somers guessed there wasn't any way to pry off the plywood without triggering at least one of the grenades. He let out a breath. So much for the windows.

He turned, his steps slow and careful as he approached the front of the apartment. He paused, listened, and heard only the steady whirring of a fan. Nothing that sounded like a person. Nothing that sounded like Mikey was inside that room, waiting for Somers with a grin on his face. For a moment, that possibility was so real that Somers actually trembled. Could Mikey have planned all this? Could Mikey have allowed him to get the screwdriver? Had he wanted this, just as part of some sick game, so that Somers would have hope burning like a live coal in his chest? Somers didn't let himself stay and think about it. He swept around the corner and into the front room.

He was alone. The same work tables lined the walls, covered with the same crap that Somers had seen before. He found a wrench, a big one, as long as his arm, buried under a sheet of tin, and he picked it up. The tin sheets shrieked against each other, and Somers winced, but he still felt better with a weapon in hand.

In this room, kerosene fumes thickened the air—Mikey had splashed the fuel everywhere, and Somers's head spun. At the apartment's front door, the axe and the tripwires still waited for the first person to try to breach the apartment. Somers might be able to disarm them and escape that way. Or he might not. What if Mikey had locked the door? What if Somers missed something, another trap? No, he wasn't ready to take that risk. Not yet. Better, first, to see if there was anything that might help him.

From where he stood, Somers could see through the archway into a small kitchen with peeling cornflower linoleum and gusseted curtains that had, at some point, probably been yellow. They were now the color of grime; not gray, not exactly, but a spectrum of stains and smears. That was where Mikey had gone earlier. That was where he had been talking. And that was where he had gotten the water and the pills.

Somers edged through the front room, keeping clear of the traps, scanning the work tables for anything he might have missed the first time, and listening. Listening desperately. As he reached the archway, he concluded that the lighter—the one that he had made a grab for, his sleight-of-hand to distract Hollace—was gone. That was too bad. As a last resort, Somers might have to burn the damn building down.

He lingered a moment outside the archway, heard nothing, and ducked into the kitchen. At the same moment, he heard, deeper in the apartment, a door open, and then voices.

Shit.

The kitchen was small and galley-style, with a counter, sink, refrigerator, and oven running the length of the room and leaving space for a small, two-person table near a window at the back. This window was boarded shut, and Somers gave up on it after a moment's examination. With enough time, he might be able to pry off the boards, but not with two people in the apartment.

The counter was bare. The cabinets mounted above the sink held a can of Ajax, an egg timer, and a discarded piece of wood trim. The oven was empty, and it was gas. Somers stood for a moment, his hand on the oven's dial. The voices were coming closer. He set the egg timer for two minutes. Grabbing one of the chairs—stainless-steel legs, peeling vinyl seat, a mustard color that hadn't been mass-produced since 1978—he flipped it around, holding it by the back, and realized he looked like a cartoon lion tamer. He wanted to grin. He couldn't manage one. But later, when he told Hazard about this—

The voices had moved into the front room. Somers crept closer to the archway. Would they come into the kitchen on their own? Or would the timer bring them running?

"That little faggot," Mikey was saying, the words louder and louder as he moved towards the kitchen, "won't have any idea what hit him."

The Haverford's ancient floor creaked under Mikey's steps. Somers tightened his grip on the wrench; the cast metal bit into his palm. The weight, he thought, was enough to crack a skull. Swing any old thing hard enough and you can crack a skull. That's what he kept telling himself, anyway.

"Get the one from the closet," Mikey was saying. "I want another video of the faggot before we—"

Somers never knew which happened first: if Mikey saw him, and then stopped speaking, or if Somers swung and simply didn't hear the rest of what Mikey was saying. Mikey's eyes went wide, and he tried to duck, but the wrench hit him at a speed Somers guessed was somewhere over sixty miles an hour. The stainless steel opened a gash down his scalp, splitting open hair and skin, and blood washed over Somers's hand and dotted his face. After a drunken, sideways step, Mikey hip-checked the counter and fell.

No one shouted. No one screamed.

Mikey might have been dead. He might have been alive. Somers dropped the chair, patted his pockets, and found the phone. Then he got back to his feet. The other guy, the one Mikey had been talking to, might come back at any time. Somers's heart purred in his chest like the Aston Martin. He could feel that heartbeat everywhere: in his eyes, in his neck, in the painful throb of every wound, right down to his fingertips. He adjusted his grip on the chair, settled himself again, and tried to breathe. Adrenaline worked through him like a cocktail, this splinteringly prismatic sense of energy, like there were a hundred different Somers and they were all wired to run and hit and fight and fuck.

The egg timer went off.

From deeper in the house, the other man shouted. It sounded like a question. Then, another shout, angrier. Footsteps on the plasticized carpet. "That fucking faggot is gone—"

This time, even with adrenaline burning him up like fire on a cheap fuse, Somers knew exactly what happened: the guy shouted, "God fucking damn it, are you all right?" and then he walked right through a trip wire. One of the shotguns whumped, the noise so loud it made Somers start, and the man screamed.

Somers darted into the apartment's front room. A black man with trim gray stubble lay on the floor. Buckshot had dissolved one side of his torso; the shredded remains of a white t-shirt, now scarlet, drooped over the man's collapsed ribcage. Now, looking at the extent of the damage, Somers knew that the man hadn't just tripped one wire; he had gotten both, and both of the shotguns had hit him. Somers jerked his eyes away from the wound. He had come within a few inches of looking just like that man, and it had been Hazard's quick mind that had saved him.

The man wheezed. Blood burbled around his lips, and single bubble with a cotton candy hue swelled grotesquely before it popped, and then he was still and silent. In the air, the reek of gunpowder overpowered everything else, and Somers breathed it in greedily. It was the cleanest thing he'd ever smelled in his life.

On the worktable closest, one of the men had set a pistol, and Somers dropped the chair and grabbed the gun. It was a 9mm Beretta. He checked the magazine. Ten rounds. Somers took a careful step, and then another, and then he realized that he was alive, that he had a gun, and that the whole building hadn't exploded. That was a miracle. And he wanted to get out of this place before he ran out of miracles.

But first, he had to warn Hazard.

That was when the chair cracked across his back. The steel legs hit like police batons, and pain exploded across Somers's neck and back. He dropped sideways, losing his grip on the phone, and rolled. He had the Beretta tight, and he brought it up as he came onto his side.

The chair swept through the air. Two steel legs snapped against his forearm, and everything went numb to the wrist. Carried by the force of the blow, his arm flew out to the right, and the Beretta tore away from his tingling fingers. It thunked against the wall, spun, and disappeared under the worktable.

Mikey stood over Somers, bringing the chair up again. His face, masked in blood, twisted into an expression of fury.

"You dirty little piss pig," Mikey said. A strip of scalp hung down where the wrench had split the side of his head, and the bloody scrap of flesh and hair bobbed as Mikey talked. "You dirty little cockgobbling piss pig. I'm going to—"

Somers wasn't interested in hearing what Mikey was going to do. He surged up onto his knees, planted a foot, and charged into the drug-wasted man. Mikey brought the chair down, and it glanced across Somers's back, but the angle was wrong, and Mikey had been surprised, and it didn't do much more than a bad hit in football.

His shoulder crunched as he collided with Mikey. He felt the give of muscle and tissue as he drove his weight, focused at the point of his shoulder, into Mikey's diaphragm, and then he felt something tear. He didn't feel the rush of breath; it must have happened, but

Somers was distracted by that flopping strip of hair and skin, which tickled the side of his face. His momentum carried them back two steps, where Mikey slammed into the wall. Plaster caved under his weight, and white dust puffed up around them.

Dropping the chair, Mikey grabbed Somers's ears and started to pull. The pain was excruciating, and the instinctive, animal-fear of having his ears ripped away was so intense that Somers forgot everything else for a moment. He found himself grappling with Mikey, wrestling to keep the other man from peeling his ears away from his skull.

Then, with a brutal efficiency that surprised Somers, Mikey reared back and cracked his forehead down, aiming at the bridge of Somers's nose.

Luck, more than anything else, saved Somers. Part of it was the fact that, at the last moment, Mikey let go of Somers's ears. Part of it was that Somers recognized, just below the level of conscious thought, what Mikey was about to do. And part of it was that Somers still had decent reflexes, even all these years after he'd stopped playing ball. He brought his own head down, and he took the headbutt on the dome of his forehead rather than on the nose, and that, he would realize later, saved his life.

At the time, though, it hurt like the seven hells. Skin parted, and blood poured down Somers's face. For a moment, he and Mikey were free of each other, and Somers staggered back. Wiping at his face, trying to clear his vision, Somers saw the drill too late. He twisted, but Mikey punched the old tool forward, and the bit chewed open the side of Somers's arm. Luck, again. Luck because Mikey was in the wrong position to operate the foot pedal, and so the drill bit wasn't spinning, even if it did still cut like a bitch.

Mikey brought the drill back, obviously intending to finish the job. Somers gave the worktable a quick, desperate glance. Scotch tape and newspaper and—

He snagged the spool of heavy-gauge wire, slid his hand inside, and brought it up like a shield. The drill bit skipped off the steel. Fury contorted Mikey's face.

"You faggot," he was screaming, any semblance of rational thought vanished. He swung the drill like a sword now. No finesse. No tactic. Just the blind, insane need to hurt. Several times the drill went wide. When Somers parried with the spool, the drill bit struck and skidded along it. Then Somers kicked in and caught Mikey's knee.

The distraction lasted only an instant, but Somers took advantage. With his free hand, he grabbed the dangling strip of scalp and hair that hung from the side of Mikey's head and pulled. In his entire life, even when he was old and gray, Somers would never forget the peculiarly greasy feel of the raw underbelly of the flesh, the bristle of Mikey's hair, the blood gumming against his hand. It would come back to him, for decades, in nightmares of his own face being ripped away.

In the moment, though, Somers could spare the sensation no thought. He grabbed, pulled, and watched a quarter-inch strip of Mikey's face peel away from temple to jaw. Years ago, when Somers had bought his first house with Cora, they had peeled marigold-print wallpaper from three of the six rooms, and the sensation was something like that.

Mikey screamed, dropping the drill, and tried to turn away. The movement only made things worse as more flesh ripped away. He dropped, and Somers released the too-slick strip of skin, scrubbing his hands on his clothes. For a moment, Somers thought Mikey might have passed out: the man was on the floor, silent, flattened against the worktable.

And then Somers realized that Mikey wasn't screaming—that in some burst of insanity or hate or fury, Mikey had moved beyond pain, and he was now searching for the fallen Beretta.

It was time to run. Somers jinked toward the door, scooping up the fallen phone as he went. Ahead of him, the axe still hung, ready to chop deep into the chest of the first person through the door. Picking up his speed, Somers jumped, grabbed the axe with his free hand, and pulled as hard as he could as he fell. The axe tore free from its temporary rig, swung into the force of Somers's fall, and almost took off his foot. With another ragged breath, Somers yanked open the door. It swung easily, too easily, and for a moment he envisioned a shotgun waiting for him, right at the level of his chest, and the spread of buckshot shredding him from neck to crotch.

But outside, there was only darkness: thick, total darkness. No electric lights. No windows. Nothing. Somers glanced back. Mikey, his ruined face looking even more monstrous in the dusty light of the apartment, came up onto his knees, the Beretta in his bloody fist. Somers plunged into the darkness.

He was free. He was free. He was in a funhouse full of booby-traps with a madman behind him, but he was free. And he had a phone, and he had the axe, and the Haverford was a maze of twists and turns. All Somers had to do was follow the intersecting corridors cutting one way and then another, and in a matter of minutes he would have lost Mikey. Temporarily, maybe. But Somers only needed a few minutes. A few minutes to call Hazard, and then time to plant himself deep in the darkness and wait, the axe held high, until Mikey—

Behind him, the Beretta barked, and it was like a horse kicked Somers in the back of the thigh. He felt himself lifted from the force of it, and he came down unsteadily on the next step, and then, when he tried another step, his leg gave way. He caught himself on the wall, the axe blade scraping up plaster in dinner-plate-sized flakes. Another shot rang out, and a chunk of wall next to Somers's head vanished, as though something inside it had taken an enormous bite.

In spite of the pain in his leg, Somers managed to keep going. Not running, Christ, not even close to running. But he could take a step, use the axe as a crutch, and drag his wounded leg. And he was in the darkness, he realized as his heart tried to crack open his chest. He was in the darkness, which was the only reason he was still alive, because otherwise those shots would have gone into his back, and he'd be dead.

The open door of the apartment was a yellow spot the size of a silver dollar behind Somers, and from that yellow spot came shouting. "I'm going to find you, you piss pig. I'm going to find you, and I'm going to put this drill up your ass, and I'm going to see how much you like it when I turn your little pucker into ground beef. I'm going to leave you alive for it, too. I'm going to show Emery. I'm going to show him what's left of you, while you're still alive, and I'm going to make him fuck you before I put a bullet in his head. I'm going to make him fuck your shredded asshole, and you'll probably still love it. I'm going to—"

Keep yelling, Somers thought, exhaustion sweeping over him. Keep yelling so I know where you are, back at the apartment, afraid of coming into the darkness to meet me. He focused on the hallway. It was impossible to see anything, the shadows were so thick, but he remembered the layout of the Haverford from before.

The Haverford was laid out like a game of tic-tac-toe, but with row after row of succeeding squares. At least, that was the closest Somers could come to visualizing the floorplan: three primary hallways that ran the length of the building, and then intersecting hallways at regular intervals, chopping up the Haverford into cramped, lightless apartments. The last time he had been here, ancient electroliers had hung at the intersections, producing shimmering bubbles of light in the dank darkness. Now, though, the electroliers were dark too. Or gone—Hollace and Mikey might have removed them. Either way, blackness had swallowed the Haverford, and it hid any number of pitfalls and dangers.

Those dangers, though, didn't matter right then. For the moment, the only thing that mattered was getting to the next intersection, where Somers could jag right and disappear into the maze of hallways, losing Mikey in the dark. Limping, dragging his injured leg, his breath stinging like he was breathing in cinders, Somers visualized the intersection ahead of him. He couldn't see it, in the dark, but he drew its outline in his mind as the goal line. Just keep moving. Just keep moving, keep moving, keep dragging that goddamn leg, just keep going because that son of a bitch is coming.

Somers glanced back. Nothing. Just the emptiness of the Haverford's artificial night. He turned his attention towards the intersection. How far could it be? Ten yards? Fifteen? He wasn't sprinting, by any means, but if the Olympics ever held an event for a guy who'd been tied up, beaten, and shot, he thought he stood a pretty good chance at gold. The pain had settled into a throb that flared with each step. The smell of vomit wafted up when he sucked in those stinging breaths. Ten yards. It couldn't be any farther than ten yards. He counted off the invisible distance in his head, estimating as best he could. One yard. Two. Three—

Instead of vision, it was some other sense that alerted him: partially sound, the way the noise of his dragging steps changed; partially something else, an awareness of proximity that he couldn't pin to anything in particular. He slowed, stretched out his hand, and touched plywood.

A full sheet of plywood. He limped to the right. The scratch of wood continued under his fingers. A seam, and then the plywood began again. Somers bit the inside of his cheek. His fingers curled hard enough to make the raw nailbeds ache. A wall. Hollace had built a goddamn wall right across the hallway. Somers had walked into a dead end.

Dragging in a breath that sounded close to a sob, Somers turned. He'd go back. Go the other way, loop around. He just had to—

He just had to hurry.

But when he turned, where the yellow scab of light marked the apartment he had just escaped, the blue-white pinprick of a flashlight bobbed in the darkness. And it was coming toward him.

CHAPTER FORTY-TWO

JULY 4
WEDNESDAY
2:14 PM

ARROWROCK TRAILHEAD, which had at different points also been Cairndow and Lewis and Clark Estates and any number of other names and lies, sat at the end of an overgrown dirt road off Highway 29. The patrol car rocked and bounced along the deep ruts. On either side, weeds and tall, heavy stalks of indiangrass snaked along the glass, hissing warnings. Branches clattered at the windows, scraping, stalling when they caught the rubber seals like desperately clutching fingers. Like someone afraid of being left. Or—this last thought echoed inside Hazard like a bell under a great dome—like someone holding him back, trying to keep him from running into a burning building.

The thoughts were fanciful. He knew that. They skimmed the surface of his mind, hardly even there. Most of him was still in that staticky, buzzing state where nothing seemed to matter except finding answers, finding Somers, and finding Mikey. But those fanciful—silly, really, even ridiculous—thoughts kept coming, skating across the icy crust of thoughts just long enough to distract him and then disappearing again. He blamed this on Somers. He'd never had these kinds of thoughts before—

—falling in love with—

—Somers.

Over the course of a half hour, the brush and trees thinned, and the road sloped upward, and the ground became rocky, exposing dusty, rust-colored earth underneath. The July sky clarified and intensified into a blue that made Hazard's eyes water. Then, with a suddenness that surprised him, Hazard followed the dirt road around a small, crumbling bluff and saw the cabin.

He knew, in that moment, he was right. It was the cabin from the photograph. It was the cabin that Jeff had stood in front of, with his hair mussed and his eyes bright and his just-got-fucked smile. Hazard rolled the cruiser to a stop, got out, and aching weariness made him stumble and grip the door. The cruiser's hot metal burned a rectangle along the inside of his hand, and Hazard focused on the pain, swam into it until the world became sharp and crisp again. Then he set off toward the cabin, loose stones cracking away under his steps.

Twenty years had passed since that photograph, and those twenty years had left their mark: the cabin slumped to the right, as though shrugging—or warding off a blow; one shutter had been ripped free, exposing teeth of broken glass. In several places, some small animal—a vole, a mouse, a rat, something—had tunneled through the chinking, peppering the bottom of the cabin with small, dark holes. The door, when Hazard touched it, swung open. No lock. No rusty hinges. No wobble. Like it had been waiting for him, all these years, and that was a fanciful idea too, but it skated closer this time, a little too close, and sweat slicked Hazard's palms.

The first thing he noticed inside were the animal smells: old, dried scat; the faintest hint of lingering corruption from a snake that had crawled inside and died probably a year or two before. Dust whirled up from the open door. The shaft of July light, full of dense particles, looked atomic or subatomic, its own spinning universe. It was a simple, two-room unit, and the dividing wall didn't reach the ceiling. In the first room, a simple Shaker-style table stood with four chairs; cabinets lined a wall, the toe kick flapping out like a tongue; and a sink—cold water only—faced the broken window. Glass sparkled like ice at the bottom of the stainless-steel basin. The next room held four bunks. Only one still held a mattress, and it had been split down the length, where cotton batting clouded up, its tips stiff and brown with dust.

This was where Jeff had come with Sherman Newton. To have sex? To make love? That second version was so much worse. Hazard tried to imagine the mayor twenty years ago, but all he came up with was liver spots and a trembling jaw and Lectric Shave. And this was where Ted Kjar had come, too. He had come investigating corporate fraud. But he had left—Hazard spun, taking in the gutted mattress, the ice-shine of broken glass, the wagging toe kick—he had left with some kind of connection between Mayor Newton and a boy who had died almost twenty years ago.

How was that possible? There was nothing that Hazard could see that might signify anything important. Nothing except that photograph of Jeff, smiling, cocky, so recently sexed, standing in front of the cabin. Hazard's best guess was that Kjar had come here, looking for answers about InnovateMidwest's property dealings, and found that picture. But Newton wouldn't have been careless enough to leave a picture—no matter how innocuous to the passing glance—sitting in this cabin for twenty years. If Newton had killed Jeff, and Hazard was increasingly sure this was true, then he would have made every effort to destroy any evidence of a link between the two of them.

The more Hazard thought about it, the more troubled he was by the photograph. Why had Newton taken it? Because he was infatuated with an attractive, engaging boy. Even though it was dangerous for him to have a photo, he wanted it. Jerk-off material, maybe. Or maybe just—maybe just a trophy. Or maybe something else. Whatever the reason, Newton must have known it was a risk to take a photograph of the boy he was fucking and then to hang on to it.

But people made stupid mistakes like that all the time. Politicians, in particular, made stupid mistakes like that all the time. Politicians seemed especially vulnerable to the syndrome of thinking they were the exception: they were smarter, they were cleverer, they were better planners. Politicians got caught all the time for incriminating texts and tweets and, yes, pictures. So it made sense, in a way, that Newton had made a mistake and either not cared or thought himself immune to its effects.

All of that made sense, except for the murder. After the murder, Newton must have been frantic to obliterate any trace of a connection to Jeff. It was possible, although unlikely, that Newton was either sadistic enough or foolish enough to keep his trophies after killing the boy, but Hazard doubted it. Beyond that, though, Newton certainly wouldn't have been stupid enough to leave the photograph here, in a cabin that was moderately remote but completely unsecured.

So why bring the photograph here at all? Why had it ever been inside this cabin? If Newton had wanted a trophy, why hadn't he developed the photograph himself and kept it somewhere no one would find it? An out-of-town Fotomat or a private dark room. Then a safe deposit box.

Dropping into one of the Shaker-style chairs, Hazard groped toward an answer. He knew it was here, in this place, the answer he was looking for. He breathed in lungfuls of the dust: huge globes of pollen, tiny crystals of reddish-brown dirt, gauzy spores, all drifting in the shatteringly hot columns of July sun. Here. For some reason, Newton had brought the picture here. He had taken the picture here because this was his secret meeting place with Jeff; that made sense, or it made enough sense. But why bring it back? Another sunny afternoon, stealing away from the town to drive up here, his heart beating with a mixture of excitement and lust and the taboo, stolen pleasure of seeing a boy barely halfway through high school—

Jeff. Hazard's head came up. In front of him, the doorway was a blazing rectangle, so bright he had to squint against it. He smelled the lingering decay of the dead snake. Down the hill, the wind raked the indiangrass into lines, and the rush of the stalks rubbing together blended into another hiss. Jeff had been here. That was why Newton had brought the photograph: to give it to Jeff.

The realization flashed so brightly that Hazard shrank away from it. Until now, he had assumed that the relationship had been predatory, ephebophilic, coercive. He had imagined—inarticulately, indistinctly—dark rooms and threats and force to compel Jeff into a sexual relationship. But this sudden thought, that Mayor Newton had brought the photograph here to give to Jeff, uprooted everything. What if the interest had been mutual? Hazard got up from the chair. His knees buckled again, and he fell into the Shaker table, and the wood groaned. In the last day, ever since Hollace had revealed that Jeff's death might not have been a suicide, Hazard had feared that in those few months that he and Jeff had been dating, Jeff had been the secret victim of abuse that had culminated in his death. But what if—that huge, shining rectangle of the door blurred, swept sideways—what if Jeff had been cheating?

The rational part of Hazard's mind, the adult part of his mind, clamored in a shrill, insistent voice that teenagers weren't physiologically and mentally developed enough to enter into a consenting relationship with an adult. Legally—Hazard shuddered, and the movement bumped the Shaker table, and its legs clattered against the poured concrete floor. Legally, Jeff had been only a year away from the age of consent. Maybe less. Maybe eight months. Maybe six. So it didn't matter that the rational part of Hazard's mind insisted, louder and louder, that Jeff was the victim no matter what he thought, that Jeff had deserved to be protected from an adult who had twisted his mind and convinced him they were in love. None of that mattered. The part of Emery Hazard that was still sixteen years old, that part of him had crashed up against this new truth and broken.

It took a few moments. Then Hazard straightened his knees, forcing himself away from the Shaker table. The wood clattered again, but he didn't really hear it. He blinked, and the blurred outline of the doorway clarified and straightened. He took a breath and tasted death, the old rot of the snake that had crawled in here to die. And he tried to think.

Newton had brought the photograph here. He had shown it to Jeff. But he wasn't stupid. He must have set conditions. You can see it, but you can't keep it. Maybe later. When you're older. When this is legal. Something like that. He might have felt indulgent, like he knew he shouldn't be giving Jeff the picture but a few minutes wouldn't hurt.

But Jeff—Jeff had never been willing to settle for anything less than what he wanted. How had Somers put it? Jeff wouldn't just be quiet and take it. Jeff fought back, and when fighting back didn't work, Jeff tried to find a way around the rules. And he would have found a way to keep the photographs, maybe squirreling them away one at a time, slowly, so Newton didn't realize any were missing. In the end, Jeff would have gotten his own way. Like that parking ticket he tore up. Or sneaking out of the house to see Hazard. Or the weed in his room, hidden—

Hazard's gaze snapped to the cabinets.

The weed he kept hidden behind the toe kick of his bookcase.

From where Hazard stood, the toe kick stuck out like a wagging tongue. He got to his knees, grabbed the wood, and hauled it back. The wood curved, bent, and then, somewhere, it began to splinter. Hazard ignored the warning noises. He dug out his phone, turned on the light, and swept it back and forth. From the opposite wall, a coin of yellow light flashed back at him—one of the many holes that animals had dug through the chinking. Hazard swept the light again, and then he saw them: a loose stack of photographs, fanned across the concrete. As Hazard watched, a gust of air entered the gap in the chinking, and one of the photographs lifted and fluttered, ready to take off. And then he understood: time and humidity and the passage of animals had bent back the toe kick. The wind entering through the chinking had pushed one of the loose photographs into the center of the room. It had lain there for who knows how long before Ted Kjar showed up, curious about a property that had been bought and sold and rented a hundred times over, inflating profits on a balance sheet that no one wanted to look at too closely, and he had found the photograph. Maybe, Hazard realized, he had found more—photographs too painful to show to the Langham family.

He reached under the cabinets and swept the prints into the light. And he studied them for a moment, the naked bodies, the twined limbs, the achingly familiar slopes and shadows of Jeff's body laid bare against Newton's frame, middle-aged even back then and already sagging and grotesque against Jeff's. In many of the photographs, their faces were fully visible. In many of the photographs, it was clear from the sweat and the flush and the lack of clothes what they'd been doing. In many of the photographs, the background showed crepe myrtle patterning teal wallpaper.

In one photograph, Jeff lay on a bed, his legs spread, exposing himself to Newton and the camera. Jeff's head was propped on a pillow, and he stared into the lens with smirking bravado. Between his teeth he held a rubberized mask. The kind they sold on Halloween. A knock-off of the boy next door. The photographs trembled in Hazard's hands, and he wondered if Jeff had been just about to put on the mask or just about to take it off. Then he gathered the pictures together, lined up the edges, and tapped them like a deck of cards so they'd fall into place. He squeezed his eyes shut. He might have stayed that way forever, but he had what he needed: proof that Newton had been fucking Jeff Langham. Proof that Newton had been pimping him out.

On the floor where Hazard knelt, he saw something else. Something caught in the toe kick. He plucked it, surprised at the thickness and texture of the paper—not a photograph. And then he turned it over and saw a blushing red crepe myrtle against teal. His eyes went to the wall behind the bed. Then he stood and moved to the wall with the door, and he ran his hands over it until he found the hole where the camera had been hidden, and then he knew. It had been here. It had all happened right here. He had the proof he needed.

And with that proof came a dark knowledge, like the negative to the photographs he was seeing: Jeff beaten and bruised and bleeding, sodomized by Mikey and Hugo, dragging himself along the streets of Wahredua in the night. Only Jeff hadn't gone home. He hadn't climbed into his father's truck, where a shotgun hung in the rack in the rear window all four seasons. He hadn't driven out to the bluffs that overlooked the Grand Rivere, with Wahredua spread out below him like embers in old ashes. He hadn't wrapped his lips around the slick barrel and waited for the despair to crest.

He had gone—where? City Hall? Newton's home? In pain, afraid, having endured violations of his body and his mind, Jeff must have turned to his friend. To the one who had promised to get him into Columbia and help with tuition. To the one who had fixed the parking ticket. To the one who had—the brilliant rectangle of July light burned against Hazard's closed eyelids—in the heat of some amorous exchange, probably said that he loved Jeff, that he would do anything for Jeff. And so when the world had gone red and vicious, Jeff had dragged himself through those dark streets until he stood in front of his friend, Sherman Newton. And Sherman Newton had known, at that moment, that he was in danger. That his whole life was at risk of coming apart because this boy, this stupid boy, had taken such a stupid, stupid risk. And at that point, Hazard guessed, Jeff had ceased being a hot boy that Newton enjoyed fucking and pimping and had become, instead, a problem to be solved. And Newton had solved him. Permanently.

How much time had passed, Hazard didn't know. He opened his eyes. The sun had shifted. Maybe a few inches, maybe less, but the light soaked him now, threatening to boil him in his clothes. Sweat snaked the nape of his neck and disappeared into his collar. He got to his feet, groggy, wondering if he had heat stroke and if the world would flare up and vanish in a snap of magnesium-white light.

But he didn't pass out. He made it to the cruiser, the photographs crumpled against his chest, and he ran the A/C. On his phone, he found the most recent text message from Mikey, and he tapped out a reply: *I've got something for you.*

He waited. The engine rumbled, and the A/C kicked a little higher, and the sweat on his forehead hesitated instead of falling faster. He was still waiting. Was this part of Mikey's game? Making him wait because he knew it was the best torture he could inflict? Hazard shifted the car into gear, made a three-point turn, and let the car trundle towards the hill. With his free hand, he flipped over the photographs until all he could see was the yellowing paper on their backs. He didn't need to see the images, not ever again. He'd be seeing them forever.

And then the phone jumped in his lap, and Hazard pumped the brake.

Ree, don't come. It's a trap.

CHAPTER FORTY-THREE

JULY 4
WEDNESDAY
2:41 PM

AT THE DOOR to the apartment that Somers had just evacuated, a white pinpoint of light bobbed. A flashlight, he realized, and that meant that Mikey was coming to find him. The plywood scraped Somers's back and shoulders; the improvised wall had put him at a dead end.

Then the phone blazed in Somers's hand, lighting up like a neutron star and chirping. Somers shoved the phone behind him and threw himself to the ground. Two shots rang out, loud enough to daze Somers, but he dragged himself along the floor. The muzzle flashes left wandering red dots in Somers's vision.

"John-Henry," Mikey said, laughing. "I'm coming."

Somers ran his hands along the wall. It was rough construction, improvised as a blockade and not the result of serious craftsmanship. How solid was it? He shoved at the base of the plywood. It flexed.

Thank God for composite materials.

Rolling onto his back, Somers drew his good leg up to his chest and then drove the heel straight into the plywood. A long crack ran through the wood. He pulled back again and kicked. This time, the plywood folded—although not all the way. It clung stubbornly together.

"You're not going anywhere, you little piss pig."

The axe.

Somers wanted to laugh. He wanted to cry. He was holding on to the fireman's axe with manic strength, but he had forgotten about it in his panic. Getting onto his knees, he chopped at the swinging section of particle board. The blows were crude and aimed blindly in the pitchy shadows, but enough of them went true that the length of wood clipped free and fell.

The darkness behind Somers was complete except for the swinging pendulum of the flashlight.

"You can't kick your way through a wall, you dumb fuck."

No, Somers thought, wanting to laugh again hysterically. No, but you can chop your way through. Chop, chop, chop. And he threw himself on his stomach, slid the axe under the wall, and dragged himself forward.

He had created the opening in the dark, without an accurate sense of its size, and when his shoulders scraped the splintered plywood, another bubble of panic swelled in his throat. Scrabbling forward, Somers dug his fingers into the Haverford's filthy carpet and pulled. Tacks and carpet staples whined and popped free, and the splintered wood slashed open Somers's arms and neck and back, but after another moment, he was through. He collected the axe, used it to balance himself and gain his feet, and staggered to the right, into the first intersection.

Another gunshot exploded behind him, and then Mikey was screaming, "You stupid motherfucker. You'll be lucky if you make it ten feet out there. Go on and try, you faggot. Go on and try!"

Somers stopped against the next wall. His neck and shoulders stung with a hundred tiny scratches, and his chest was a fireball. But he was alive. And after a few more shouts, Mikey stomped off in the other direction, and Somers realized, like a man kicking up from the bottom of the sea and finally, just finally breaking to air, that he was out. Not all the way. Not even close. But he was out.

He was out, but he was also in total darkness, in the center of Hollace's maze of traps. That meant that, a few steps in any direction, death might be waiting for him. He needed light. He needed—

The phone. He dug it out of his pocket and stared at the screen. For the second time in the last few minutes, he fought the urge to laugh. There, on the screen, Hazard's name glowed out at him. Emery Hazard. Emery Hazard was texting this goddamn phone, and all he could say was, *I've got the proof.*

Proof?

Somers scrolled up through the messages, reading the all-caps texts that Mikey had sent earlier demanding proof that Sherman Newton had killed—

—*your fucktoy*—

—Jeff Langham. A chill clamped down on Somers, squashing some of that fireball in his chest. This was what they wanted? Blackmail material? He wasn't sure, not yet, that he understood completely. Mikey had wanted to control the investigation. Why? Somers's thoughts had a buzzing lightness to them, like mosquitos on a summer night; it was hard to think, hard to come anywhere close to thought when it would have been so much easier to drop, right there on the filthy carpet, and sleep for a hundred years. Why? He forced himself towards the question. Why would Mikey want to control the investigation into the attack on the mayor?

Because, Somers thought with a shaky smile, Mikey wanted something. Something had changed. Hollace and Mikey had started working together—or maybe they'd been working together the whole time, and they changed their plan. All of the sudden, they didn't want the mayor dead. Instead, they wanted him under their thumb. Whose idea had that been? Somers let out a shuddering breath that he barely recognized as his own; adrenaline was wicking off him, leaving him sick to his stomach and trembling and exhausted. Hollace, he decided. Hollace was the smarter of the two, even if he hadn't changed much since high school. And Hollace had always been a manipulative son-of-a-bitch. Hollace had sent the pictures to Hazard. Hollace had tried to threaten Hazard into steering clear of the investigation. And Hollace had known that Jeff Langham had been murdered. He'd taken those photographs and used them not just to threaten Hazard. He'd planned on using them to blackmail the mayor. And, as a backup plan, he'd used them to prime the pump with Hazard. To get Hazard well and truly worked up about Jeff's death just in case things went wrong. And when they did go wrong,

Hollace had pulled the trigger, and now Hazard was shooting forward, doing exactly what Hollace had wanted.

And Mikey? The answer came to Somers clearly. Mikey must have decided he liked the blackmail plan so much that he killed Hollace. But without Hollace's original photographs, now Mikey needed proof of his own.

From somewhere down the hall, a door clapped open, and something boomed hollowly. Somers jumped. Leaning on the fireman's axe like a cane, he swiped at the phone and sent a single message back to Hazard: *Ree, don't come. It's a trap.* Then he turned on the phone's flashlight and swept the beam back and forth. The phone buzzed in his hand, then again, and then again. Somers focused on his surroundings: the flattened, greasy carpet; the plaster, one portion chewed on a diagonal, as though a toddler had really gone to town on it; the dull reflected light of the electrolier's brass finish. The air still smelled like gunpowder; Somers's shirt stuck to him when he moved, and he hated to think of the combination of fluids in the cotton weave.

The phone buzzed again. Again, Somers ignored it. How to get out? Mikey had been trying to scare him—

—*You'll be lucky if you make it ten feet*—

—but that didn't mean there weren't serious dangers to consider. To his left, the hallway continued the length of the building. To the right, he could follow the branching corridor to another intersection. Best, for now, to change up his path. He followed the hall to his right, running the light over everything, probing the floor with the axe's haft, taking slow steps, ready to throw himself to the side if he brushed a tripwire.

With an intensity that surprised Somers, the phone buzzed steadily in his hand. He let out a swear. A phone call. The dumb bastard was calling him. He couldn't take a hint. He couldn't just accept Somers's word that things were dangerous, that he needed to stay away. He'd just keep calling and calling with that unbearable stubbornness until—

"What the hell are you doing?"

"You're all right? Christ. Tell me you're all right."

"I'm fine. I'm trying to escape. But instead I'm having a very irritating phone call."

Hazard's next few sharp breaths dotted out a line of Morse code, and there was so much relief in that sound, so much goddamn love, that Somers felt some of his frustration easing.

"Thank God. I just—Somers, how bad are you—"

"Ree, I can't talk. I'm still trying to get the hell out of here, and for all I know, Hollace put up cameras and mics before Mikey killed him. The place is trapped to hell, and I've got to focus and get out of here or Mikey will catch up. He's not just going to pull off my fingernails next time." Somers breathed out and wished he could laugh. "Hollace even got a train set up. A goddamn train. Didn't have a new idea in twenty years."

Hazard's voice was strained when he spoke again. "Mikey?"

"Yeah. He's using this place—"

"I'm coming."

"No. I don't want you—"

"I'll be at the Haverford in fifteen minutes. Ten. Just hole up for ten minutes."

"I didn't say I was—"

"Oh Christ, Somers, I'm not an idiot. Ten minutes. Eight if I don't kill any pedestrians."

He wasn't joking, Somers realized.

"Ree, I don't want you to come. Call the station; get everybody out here, but don't let them come inside. I'm going to work my way out, and then we'll sit and wait for him. At some point, he'll try to rabbit, and we'll have him. But coming in here—even you, Ree—it's suicide."

"Eight minutes."

"Call the station. Just do this for me, all right?"

"If you'd read any of those goddamn texts I was just sending you, you'd know that I already called the station. They've got everybody out. Even pulled George Orear off the front desk. Two different bomb threats: one to City Hall, another to the County Fair. They don't even have anybody answering phones at the station; I finally called Moraes on his cell."

455

Hope melted. "Ree." Somers stopped. That sounded so pathetic, so fucking pathetic, that he wouldn't let himself go on like that. He firmed up his voice. "Ree, I'm ordering you not to come. I'm senior partner, and I'm ordering you."

Another line of those short, dotted breaths. "Eight minutes."

"Goddamnit, Ree—"

"I love you."

The call disconnected. Somers stared at the phone, at its blue rectangle of light, and didn't know whether to call Hazard back and rip him a new asshole or tell him he loved him too or both. After another agonizing moment, Somers swung the light back the way he had come. At the edge of its watery beam, the hole in the plywood wall was visible.

Hazard was coming here. In spite of Somers's best efforts, Hazard was coming. And that meant he was going to walk into Hollace's maze. He was going headfirst into the danger that Somers was trying to keep him away from, and nothing Somers could do would stop him. That was what was so fucking annoying about Hazard. That's what was so goddamn wonderful.

And the only thing to do for it now, the only option Hazard had left him, was for Somers to keep the big brute alive. For a moment, though, he couldn't do it. He couldn't go back, not to the stink of his piss, not to the burn of kerosene in his eyes, not to the helplessness and the humiliation and the agony. He couldn't, even though he could see, in his mind's eye, the path of shotguns and grenades and tripwires that Hazard would follow. Somers couldn't do it because he was just so damn afraid.

But he took a deep breath. And with a clarity that he always dreaded in his dreams, he smelled the clay pits again, and he smelled summer, and he remembered the flex and force of Emery Hazard's skinny wrist in the vise of his hand. The rest of it too: Evie, and nights that they lay together, and that white wave carrying Somers to its crest, and the friction-burns of Hazard's stubble on Somers's shoulders when he kissed the hollow there.

With a sigh, Somers took his first step. The first step was the hardest, and after that, he limped as best he could. He squatted at the plywood wall, peered through the hole, and held his breath. That ugly yellow eye of light still marked the open door to the apartment. No sound besides the frantic murmur of blood in his ears. Dropping onto his stomach, Somers shoved the axe through the hole and dragged himself back toward the nightmare room where he had been tortured.

All of this for that jackass Neanderthal, he thought as he dragged himself upright. God help him if he ever forgets my birthday.

CHAPTER FORTY-FOUR

JULY 4
WEDNESDAY
2:59 PM

HAZARD NEVER COULD REMEMBER the drive back from the Arrowrock Trailhead. Somers told him—later, much later—that Hazard had said something about killing pedestrians, and they had both laughed, but for two nights after that, Hazard stayed up looking through old traffic reports, wondering if he had, indeed, killed someone. His memory remained a blank: up until the end of that phone call, his recollection was as clear as ever; then there was nothing until he reached the Haverford. No gray fog. No hissing static of partial memory. Nothing. A perfect snip and splice.

In the few days since the explosion, the Haverford already looked to be falling in on itself. Signs in the windows proclaimed the building condemned—either the speedy work of someone in the city housing office, eager to get rid of an old problem or a lie on Mikey's part to keep anyone from entering. Where the explosion had ripped away brick, huge tarps flapped in the breeze, offering a modicum of shelter from the elements. The building looked like it had undergone the kind of subterranean collapse that Hazard often associated with the faces of the ancient: a caving-in of everything vital, leaving only the framework.

He circled the building once in the patrol car. His blood was up. The front of his brain was clamoring about all the things he was going to do to Mikey when he got him. Lots of things that required time, plenty of time, and a dull razor. But on the second pass, Hazard's eyes fell on the back door, where Hollace had set a trap that had almost taken Somers's life. And then Somers's message came back: *Ree, don't come. It's a trap.*

For the first time since speaking with Somers, the full meaning of those words hit Hazard. During their conversation, Hazard had held the vague idea that Somers meant Mikey was waiting for him—possibly with backup. But now, with some of the shock of speaking to Somers wearing off, the full meaning emerged. It was a trap, the whole building. Hollace had turned the Haverford into a maze of death, just as he had the last time Hazard had been here.

But Hazard barely heard the thought. He didn't have time for that. Somers was in there. Somers was cut and hurt and bleeding. And if Mikey got a hold of Somers again, he wouldn't just pluck out his fingernails. He'd kill him. He'd butcher him. He'd—

Hazard wrapped his fingers around the steering wheel until the molded plastic creaked. Then he pumped the brake, let the patrol car crawl to a stop under a fire escape, and killed the engine.

He needed a plan. He tried to set his mind in motion. What he wanted, more than anything else at the moment, was clarity. Logic. Reason. Analysis. All the things that he prided himself on, the things that made him strong when other people were weak.

But every time he tried to sink into that icy rationality, something interrupted him: the smell of Somers's hair after they'd been in the sun; those Caribbean blue eyes turned up at him before a kiss; the way Somers spun Evie in the center of their small living room; the sound of his breathing while he slept. Those things barreled through Hazard's thoughts and left holes the size of semis.

And then another memory came flapping out of the darkness: sitting in a living room that smelled like cigarette smoke and fried hot dogs, a mammoth console TV with faux-walnut paneling occupying the floor in front of him, the molded plastic grip of a red-and-grey gun in one hand. On the screen, a pixelated duck swept up out of the grass, and Hazard's hand spasmed, his finger slamming down the trigger as he tracked the duck—and its frantic quacking—across the screen. And then it was gone, and a brown-skinned boy rolled on the ground and laughed because Hazard had never gotten a duck, not once, no matter how many times he played the game. Hollace wouldn't even try; he just liked to watch and laugh as Hazard grew more and more frustrated.

It had been years later—after Jeff's death, after the day he had seen Somers in the locker room with steam curling off golden skin, after high school and Wahredua had closed behind Hazard like chapters in a book he'd kicked across the room, after all that—that Hazard had realized why he'd always lost at the game. He'd been in college, then, walking the four blocks to the laundromat, and he'd passed a rent-to-own furniture store, and in the front window they'd set up a flimsy particle-board TV stand and a sofa that looked like it had more scratch than an alley full of toms. And maybe in some odd nostalgic kick—the days of Nintendo were long past—someone had set up the game system and strung the long cord from the box to the gray and plastic gun.

The gun at Hollace's house had never had a cord. It hadn't been the first mystery Hazard had solved, and he recognized the familiar rush of understanding as pieces clicked together. There had been no cord. And that meant that Hazard had been playing with a broken gun. And Hollace had known—Hollace had known the whole time. That had been the joke, of course: to watch the dumb faggot play at a game he never had a chance of winning. And now, laughing silently, Hazard realized another thing. Hollace's mother had never had the money to buy a Nintendo. Christ, he should have realized that from the start. Another lie Hollace had told; another lie Hazard had swallowed. Hollace had probably fished the damn thing out of the junkyard.

Hot July sunlight prismed across the cruiser's hood, bouncing up into Hazard's eyes, and he blinked. That was the kind of game Hollace always wanted to play, the rigged game, the one that only Hollace could win. That was how Mikey played too, even if Mikey's style was different. Mikey wanted muscle and numbers to make every game go his way, but in the end, it came down to the same thing: he only played when he thought he'd win.

And that's what Hazard was walking into now, he realized. He was walking into a rigged game. Somers had warned him about the traps. But Somers had said something else. The train. That story about the train, about running it through the vents with a camcorder to peep at the girls in the locker room. Somers had said—

Somers had said that Hollace hadn't had a new idea in twenty years.

Clarity washed over Hazard. He was sitting in a hot car, the air pasted to his skin, sweat packing his shirt up under his arms, but the sudden thought was ice-cold and clear. What did Hazard know about Hollace? The train. The drugged drink. Calling in false reports of crimes—Mikey had borrowed that one already by drawing out Wahredua's PD to the boardwalk and City Hall. That was the last, clearest thought. Not just Hollace's love of *getting into it*, the phrase that had carried him into so much trouble as a kid. But Mary Heintzelman, eyes wide and crying in the lunchroom as she reported Hollace's words after he'd fallen in the stairwell, with his confetti poppers tied like tripwires: *Did they see?*

And suddenly, a fresh picture of Hollace came together in Hazard's mind. No longer was he the poor, mixed-race boy whose father had abandoned him. No longer was he Hazard's fellow outcast. For the first time, Hazard felt like he saw the real Hollace: the petty manipulator, the boy who felt every social sting and who wanted to pay them back a hundred times over. The boy who envied the same people he despised. A pitiless creature who had lured Hazard into trusting him and then used that trust to feel powerful— used it to hurt Hazard, to embarrass him, and to feel, maybe for the only time in his life, better than someone else. The monster who had watched Jeff beaten and abused, who had watched Jeff drag himself to help, and who had watched Jeff murdered. Who had photographed all of it. Who had mailed those photos, one by one, to Hazard.

The glare off the hood stung Hazard's eyes. The heat swamped him. He kicked open the patrol car's door and emerged into the smell of piss and sun-hot, fermenting garbage. Broken beer bottles clinked underfoot.

How do you win a rigged game, Hazard asked himself as he stared up the Haverford's brick lines.

By breaking the rules.

Where did Mikey want him to go? All the most obvious points would be certain death: the main entrances and emergency exits would be trapped. Side doors, service pull-ups, and ground floor windows, Hazard guessed, would also be closely guarded. The explosions a few days before had emptied the Haverford, and that meant the only constraints to their protection measures were time and money. Hollace, bankrolled by whatever criminal element he represented, probably had plenty of money. So it all came down to time. With the sun singeing the pink skin on his face, Hazard could feel the seconds ticking away from him. Hollace and Mikey, no matter how well they planned and prepared, couldn't have trapped everything. They would have worked their way from the ground floor to the roof, beginning with major access points and then, in triage, working their way—

And Hazard stopped. Because he was doing it: he was playing the game. He was playing it, in fact, exactly the way they wanted him to play it. He was trying to outsmart them, and he was trying to outmaneuver them. But they had drawn up the rules, and that meant he was going to lose, no matter how hard he tried.

Better, instead, to play his own game.

Abandoning the patrol car for a moment, Hazard hoisted himself onto the lip of the closest dumpster, propped himself on his good elbow, and scanned. Nothing that would do what he wanted. He moved to the next dumpster, dragged himself up again, and there it was, right on top, like a gift from God. Hazard hauled the old microwave to the dumpster's lip. It was hard, especially with his bad arm not responding. The goddamn thing weighed a ton; it was ancient, probably one of the earliest models, and the size of a small house. Instead of trying to lift it, he just tipped it over the edge and let it crash to the alley floor. Then he got a decent grip with his good arm, bent his knees, and lifted what felt like a goddamn mountain.

By the time he got the microwave into the patrol car, he had sweated through every inch of clothing, but he knew he had what he wanted. He keyed the car, drove around the Haverford again, and parked in front of the building, the nose of the patrol car aimed like a missile at the crumpled brick façade. Then, with the car idling in drive, Hazard set the parking brake and got out. He lugged the microwave from the backseat, his bad arm singing like a bitch from all the strain, and wedged it in the driver side footwell, the corner of the behemoth raised just above the gas pedal.

Sweat slid along salty tracks around Hazard's eyes. He checked the steering wheel. He checked the gear shift. He blinked furiously and ran his sleeve over his forehead and shook back his dark, wet hair. This was it. He popped the parking brake. Still idling, the patrol car lurched forward and began rolling. Hazard kept up with it for a couple of feet and then released the microwave. It hit the gas pedal like somebody was trying to shoot the moon.

The patrol car launched forward. The engine growled. The tires squeaked on the asphalt, and the burnt rubber smell made Hazard wrinkle his nose and take a few steps back. The car, a Ford Crown Victoria, probably needed about nine seconds to go from zero to sixty. That was Hazard's best guess, anyway. The Crown Vic didn't get its full nine seconds, but it got enough, and when it crashed into the Haverford, it hit plenty hard enough.

The patrol car speared straight through the plywood barriers across the Haverford's front. Reddish-orange dust billowed into the air. Metal screeched as brick clawed the Crown Vic's paneling. One of the car's tires caught the rope securing the largest tarp, and the plastic sheet stretched taut and then ripped in staccato stretches before the largest section tore free and whipped after the car, pulled along in its wake. The Crown Vic punched deeper into the building; supports already weakened by the explosion gave way, and as Hazard watched, a third of the Haverford's front wall collapsed. Then portions of the floor and interior walls pulled away as the destruction spread. Rubble avalanched into the hole that the Crown Vic had dug, burying the car and laying out a scree-covered slope that climbed to the ripped-open walls of second- and third-floor apartments that now faced the street when, moments before, they had been so deep within the building that they had lacked any windows.

Hazard waited. He wasn't a smoker, but he wished right then that he had a cigarette. The sun hammered at him, and he could feel the faint sting of sunburn starting up again on his cheeks and forehead. Maybe a goddamn lemonade instead. Or a Coke. Or anything with ice in it. Dust spilled up into the air, and Hazard could taste it, the hot brick powder of it. Through the dust, where brick had fallen away to expose structural supports, sunlight picked out the shapes of gray squares duct-taped to the girders. He didn't like the look of those gray squares, and he'd give it another minute before—

A second series of explosions rocked through the building as the bricks of C-4 detonated in a series of ear-jarring booms. Shards of metal pinged against the asphalt; one skipped, spun across the blacktop, and hit Hazard's shoe so hard that a sharp edge buried itself in the wingtip's heel. The thunder lingered, and Hazard shook his head to try to clear the sound. Then there was nothing except the occasional shift of the debris as brick and rebar settled.

Now that, Hazard thought as he moved towards the scree-covered slope, was definitely not in the rules.

CHAPTER FORTY-FIVE

JULY 4
WEDNESDAY
3:10 PM

IN HIS MIND, Somers had envisioned his plan of action: hustling down the Haverford's hallway, disarming tripwires, pulling down shotguns, deactivating the clusters of grenades that hung near windows and stairwells. The reality—as had been the case too often lately—fell short of the plan.

He was too slow. His leg, his whole leg, turned to fire when he moved, and even propping himself up on the fireman's axe, the best Somers could do was a slow hobble. The bullet hadn't hit an artery, thank God. It hadn't—as far as Somers could tell—hit bone. But it still hurt like hell, and the muscle was damaged, and he had to stop in the hall to tear up strips of his shirt and bandage the wound because blood had filled his shoe and his toes were swimming in it.

Another part of it was the fatigue that pulled on him like gravity. And part of it was the smell when he reached the doorway to the apartment, and the memory. Piss, vomit, kerosene. And now shit. That last smell came from the dead man, sawn in half by the sprays of buckshot. For a long time, Somers couldn't enter that room again. He just held on to the doorframe, legs trembling, and tried and tried and tried and failed. And then, like a switch, he remembered the clay pits, and that was enough for him to move again.

The first order of business was to clear a way for Hazard to enter the apartment. On the phone, Hazard had said that he would be there in eight minutes. Somers wasn't sure where Hazard was, but he guessed that his partner was underestimating how long it would take him to reach the Haverford. So Somers gave himself a total of fifteen minutes before he needed to call and tell Hazard how to get into the building safely. He'd already wasted five of those minutes limping down the hallway and lingering, like a coward, in the door.

Ten minutes. He had ten minutes to figure this out.

Ignoring the dead man, Somers worked his way through the apartment. There was no sign of Mikey. He was, Somers hoped, out in the Haverford's darkness, searching for him. All the more reason for Somers to hurry.

It was a corner apartment; the door at the back, which Somers hadn't risked opening during his escape, led to a bedroom with a window that opened onto a fire escape. There was other stuff in this room: a computer with two monitors, a small safe bolted to the floor, a closet door braced with an abandoned Keds. But Somers's focus was on the window and, beyond it, the fire escape. This was how Mikey and the other man had entered the apartment. The only problem, Somers now saw, was that they had made sure no one followed them: a cluster of grenades, strung up like a hand of bananas, now protected this window. The windows on the other side of the apartment were protected in the same way, but this window was more important because of the fire escape. The rusty skeleton might have looked like it was about to peel away from the building, but it was still a shot at getting out of this place. And if Somers could escape, he could call Hazard, and then Hazard wouldn't have to come inside.

The trap on the window was simple enough, but that didn't make it any less dangerous. Someone—presumably Hollace—had tied loops of wire around each grenade's safety pin. Then, the wires ran together, looped under the window frame through a metal eyelet, and ran up to the top of the lower sash. If someone climbed the fire escape, reached this window, and opened it, the wires would snap out the safety pins, and the grenades would detonate as the intruder came through the window. It wasn't a perfect security measure—if someone broke the window instead, and climbed through without raising the sash, the grenades wouldn't do anything. But to do that, they'd have to break the window, making enough noise—at least, this is what Somers assumed—that Mikey or one of his tough guys would hear, and they'd come running.

Just standing this close to the grenades chilled Somers. He understood the trap. He knew the mechanics of it. And he was fairly sure that he could simply loosen the bundle of wires from the lower sash and nothing would happen. After all, the grenades needed their safety pins pulled before they would detonate.

But if he was wrong, even if he was only partially wrong, even if only one of the grenades went off, he'd be dead. Metal shrapnel would slice him apart. That would be the end for Somers. And, most likely, for Hazard.

Somers shook out his hands. He was running out of time; Hazard would be here any minute now. Somers needed to be out of the building, needed to call Hazard and tell him he was outside, to keep the big man from risking his life. He blew out hard enough to empty his lungs, pulled in fresh air, and gave the set-up one last look.

Simple. It was simple. The wires had been braided around a nail on the edge of the sash, invisible to someone who glanced in from the outside. Then electrical tape had been wrapped around the braid, securing it from slipping or sliding loose. So first the tape. Then the wires. And then Somers could take a real breath. If he messed up, though. If he fumbled. If that wire gave the tiniest jerk upward and one of those safety pins popped free—

God, Jesus, Joseph, and Mary. He reached for the tape, tried to get the edge of it under his thumbnail, and then he stopped. Because he didn't have a nail. Not a damn one. Mikey had made sure of that. And he couldn't just chop the wires with the axe; that would put enough pressure on them to knock at least one of the pins loose.

What was he supposed to do?

No. Thinking that way wasn't going to help. What would Hazard do? Besides all the brooding and thundering and stomping around, what would Somers's dark-haired partner do? He'd be smart. He'd go one step further. He'd see what Somers was missing. But what? That was the problem; Somers knew Hazard would figure out a better way of handling this. But Somers wasn't Hazard. He couldn't just miraculously come up with whatever insight Hazard might have. He couldn't just pretend he was smarter. He didn't have the same gifts as Hazard. He had to work with what he had. But he didn't have anything but a bunch of bloody fingertips because Mikey had ripped his nails out with a pair of—

Yes. The thought buzzed so hard up Somers that, for a moment, he was terrified his hand had slipped and tugged on the wire.

Yes, he had to work with what he had.

He limped back to the front room. What did he have, besides a bullet in the leg and his mauled fingers and a fireman's axe? He didn't smile, but he felt a kind of grim amusement as he surveyed the worktable with its assortment of tools. The drill. The crumpled newsprint. A spool of heavy gauge wire. And the pliers.

The pliers that Mikey had used, working the tip under each nail, twisting, forcing the nail up from its bed, exposing raw, bleeding flesh to the stinging air. And, a bit below the plier's jaws, as with so many pairs of pliers, an added convenience: wire cutters.

This time, he did laugh. He scooped up the pliers, and he thought about Hazard's face when he told him that he'd tried to see the world the way Emery Hazard did. It would give Hazard a big head, telling him about this. He'd be unbearable for a week or two, that smug expression on his face. And it would be worth it. Hazard could have a big head for the rest of the year, for all it mattered.

Returning to the back bedroom, Somers eyed the tangle of wire again. He could do this. Slowly, carefully, without putting pressure on the bundle of wires, he could do this. He eased the cutters around the bundle of wire, an inch down from the knot of electrical tape. Then, eyes on the taut length, he closed his fist around the pliers' grip. The cutters bit into the wires. One by one, they snapped with faint, whining pops. And then they were all severed, and the bundle of grenades plummeted. Somers caught it and lowered it the rest of the way. Gently. Then he sagged against the glass, his whole body flushed and prickling. He had done it.

Then he started to laugh. He turned and put his elbow through the glass, and shining teeth rang out across the fire escape. As easy as that. All the work with the pliers, with the frantic disarming of the trap, all of it for nothing. He could have just broken the glass. Mikey wasn't around to hear—

Something exploded.

CHAPTER FORTY-SIX

JULY 4
WEDNESDAY
3:21 PM

THE SCREE-COVERED SLOPE glittered with shards of glass. Broken bones of rebar jutted out of the rubble. By the time Hazard reached the Haverford's third floor, where a joist stuck into the air, the debris had slashed his hands in a dozen places. Worse, though, was the white-hot star of pain in his bad arm. Dragging that microwave around had been a dumb-shit idea. This, though, pulling himself up the shifting, sliding wreckage, had been worse. It had put too much strain on the arm. In the back of his head floated the fear that this time, the damage would be permanent. But Hazard ignored that fear. He could ignore it because, for the most part, he was just so goddamn angry.

Gripping the snapped-off joist with his good hand, Hazard scrambled the last few feet and threw himself onto the sagging edge of the third floor. He hit it at the waist, and he balanced there until he got enough breath back to drag himself the rest of the way. When he'd gotten to his feet, he stopped. Something wasn't right. He shuffled backward until his shoulders hit the remaining wall, and then he looked down the hallway, scanned left, past an apartment cracked open to expose its insides like a dollhouse: the chipped white porcelain of a bathroom, a beaded curtain, a plaid sofa with one arm ripped and then bandaged with an Evict Tricky Dick bumper sticker that had probably been there forty years. Past the apartment to the hallway that ran on the far side of the Haverford, all of it laid bare because the walls and floor had fallen away. And then Hazard saw what was wrong.

The last time, the Haverford had been a dark warren: corridors intersecting at regular intervals, and the only light glittering like lacquered ladybug shells. To some extent, this was still true of the far side of the building: daylight entered where the Haverford's brick had fallen away, but deeper in the building, darkness smudged out Hazard's vision. On Hazard's side of the building, in contrast, light streamed through dirty windows. The effect was sharp, bright squares. Anything moving in front of those squares would be outlined. Hell, anything moving in front of those windows would be target practice. And Hazard thought of mechanical ducks waddling the width of the shooting gallery, their yellow wooden forms backlit by incandescent bulbs.

He glanced at the ruined section of the building and saw his confirmation: the stairwells, visible in parts where the walls had fallen, were boarded up. Hollace and Mikey hadn't foreseen Hazard's destruction of the Haverford. In their plan, even if he had somehow penetrated the building and evaded the first line of defense, he would have been forced to climb to this side of the building. And as he moved along this side of the building, past the windows, he would become a target. A perfect target. Waddling like a goddamn duck in a shooting gallery.

But he was a target here, too, standing against the bold daylight. Loping as fast as he could, Hazard raced down the hall toward the closest patch of shadow. A shot rang out. Chips of brick exploded behind him, and he felt one of them—maybe more—tug at his trouser leg. A second shot rang out, and one of the windows burst outward. Each shard gathered sunlight and blinked it back at Hazard, blinding him. A third shot rang out—he couldn't see where it hit, not through the sudden dazzle. Then shadow swallowed him, and he slumped against the plaster, sucking in air.

The gunshots still rang in his ears, but Hazard could make out the sound of laughter. And he knew who it was. Mikey had always laughed that way. In high school, he laughed that way when he knocked Hazard's books out of his hands. He laughed that way when he plugged the locker room toilet with Hazard's clothes. He laughed that way, a dumb, redneck huck-huck, as the tip of his pocket knife cut three lines into Hazard's chest. And now he was laughing close enough that Hazard could hear him even over the rush of blood in his ears.

"You dumb faggot."

Another shot rang out. The window frame buckled, and splinters darted like long shadows through the sunlight. Hazard hunkered in the darkness, scanning the building. If he could get deeper into the building, he might be able to lose Mikey. This part of the Haverford had been destroyed, but much of the building still stood, and the hallways formed a maze that Hazard could use to his advantage. If he wasn't killed by whatever traps Hollace had set. If he wasn't picked off by Mikey when an open window traced his silhouette. If he managed to survive, he could run.

Brick dust clouded the air, and when he breathed, he tasted the baked clay. Yes, he could run. He could leave Somers—oh, sure, he'd tell himself he was only being logical. He was only being prudent. He was only being rational. He could run, and he could tell himself that he was running to get help. He was running for backup. But the bald truth, the butt-ugly truth, was that he would just be running, the way he had run all those years ago when Hugo Perry's face went cottage cheese and Mikey and Somers couldn't hold him anymore. That day at the clay pits, Hazard had run. And twenty years later, he had come back. And that clock inside him, with its hands twinned at midnight, would never tick again if he kept running. If he ran—

"You've got more guts than I thought. More fucking guts by a ton." Mikey's voice came from the far side of the building, echoing weirdly along the hallway. "You came right here. You came right for me like you weren't scared. That's something."

Keep talking, Hazard thought. The voice was moving closer to him, and that meant that Mikey was moving to a new position. A better angle, most likely, from which he could hit Hazard. Keep talking, motherfucker.

"It's because of him. Is that it?" Mikey laughed, huck-huck. "You know, I wondered about you when you came back. That day you went after me in the Casey's. You cost me my job, faggot. I didn't like that. Do you remember that day?"

Hazard did. He remembered dragging Mikey, shoving him, threatening him, demanding answers. The truth: all about how Mikey and Hugo had sexually assaulted Jeff, had raped him, and how Jeff had gone and put a gun between his teeth. Only that hadn't been the truth. Not entirely.

"I asked you a question, faggot."

"You said he killed himself."

Instinct told Hazard to move, and as soon as the words left his mouth, he threw himself forward. Sunlight ringed him with a corona for a moment, and then he hit the next patch of blackness. A gun boomed. Glass pattered on the carpet, throwing double and triple and quadrupled slashes of light on the wall.

"You do remember," Mikey said casually, as though they were really just having a conversation and this wasn't a goddamn shooting gallery. "I thought you'd kill me that day. You should have killed me. But you didn't. And when I told you what I did to your fucktoy, when I told you how I broke your fucktoy and made him my fucktoy, when I told you that and you didn't even touch me, you know what?"

Blood gummed Hazard's hands; the nicks and slices from the debris stung as he worked his fingers around the grip of his .38 and drew a bead on the closest hallway.

"I asked you a question, faggot."

"Fuck you."

A shadow moved. Hazard fired. Once, twice, the adrenaline squeezing out that second shot even though Hazard's brain already knew that he was shooting at nothing. Gunsmoke filled Hazard's nose and mouth, obliterating the taste of everything else. When the ringing in his ears slowed, he could hear Mikey's huck-huck-huck.

"I really thought that fucktoy had killed himself. I mean, I had my cock in that boy every which way from Sunday. I broke his nose, I think. Broke some of his teeth because the little fucker tried to bite me. Hugo really liked choking, and I let him go at the fucktoy as hard as he wanted. Probably gave the little fucktoy brain damage. It was pretty clear when they found him with the back of his head blown off: the little fucktoy killed himself. You still haven't answered my question."

The shadow moved again, deep in the hallway, and Hazard's hand jumped. He didn't pull the trigger. Not quite. But he came close, and he knew—this thought floated, lucid and slow above the hot chaos that had taken over his brain—that Mikey was testing him. Playing with him.

"You know what I realized when I told you all that the first time and you didn't do anything but shove me around? Do you, faggot? I want to hear you tell me what I realized."

"I'm not going to kill you."

Huck-huck bounced down the darkness. "I'm supposed to come out and give myself up?"

"Oh fuck that. I'm telling you I won't kill you, Mikey, because I want you to know I'm going to keep you alive. I'm going to keep you alive for a long time. With modern medicine, with antibiotics, I bet I could keep you alive for twenty years. You think about that. Twenty years of me snipping off pieces. Twenty years of me flaying skin. Twenty years of me doing whatever I want to you. And I've had a long time to think about what I want to do to you."

"Now see, that's exactly what I'm talking about. You know what a real guy's supposed to sound like. Hell, you even do a decent job talking like one. I bet when you've got your new little fucktoy in bed, when it's just the two of you, you can say stuff like that and get his little cock buzzing."

A shot cracked the air, and the bullet burned a line across Hazard's shoulder before burying itself in the wall. White plaster blew out like steam. Hazard pumped out two more shots, and he used the time to bolt to the next patch of darkness. He was almost lined up with the hallway now. The darkness was thick. Thick, yes. But not perfect. And when Mikey moved—

—his brain screamed a warning, but it might as well have been a fly buzzing around his head—

—Hazard would put two holes in him, head and chest, and that would be the end of it.

"This is just like you." Mikey's voice twisted out of the darkness, seeming to come from all sides. Hazard scanned the corridor to his right, and then set his gaze on the intersecting hallway. "Just like you. You think you're so smart." The voice moved closer, but in the Haverford's shadows, it was impossible to tell where it was coming from. "You think you're so strong." Mikey was closer. Much closer.

Something twitched in the shadows ahead. Yes. Grim satisfaction heated Hazard's chest. There he was, the smug little bastard. Lurking behind a stack of cardboard boxes. Hazard inched forward, trusting the darkness to hide him for a few feet until he could hit Mikey on the first shot. Movement came again. It was a gun, Hazard realized. The tip of a gun, just visible past the edge of the uppermost box, and it was waving as though Mikey were exhausted. Or terrified.

That warning was screaming again, louder than ever, telling Hazard to get back, to reconsider, to think.

But Hazard couldn't. He was past thinking. Thinking hadn't gotten him anywhere in twenty years. That fire inside him was hotter than magnesium, hotter than fission, hotter than fusion. That fire was burning up everything else. He was so close now. Mikey was just a few feet away. Mikey, who had hit and cut and tortured Somers. Mikey, who had broken Jeff. Mikey, who had carved those shiny lines into Hazard's chest. He was just a few feet away, and all Hazard had to do was reach him. He was so tired of the cold demands of logic and reason. He just wanted to burn the world down.

Something brushed carpet, and Hazard risked another glance to his right. Nothing there either. He had moved too deep into the brick building, and aside from where the windows punched out squares in the darkness, he could see nothing. He took another step forward, and then another, and then he was close enough.

"But you know what I realized about you, that day I told you how I took Jeff Langham and made him my cocksucking little bitch?"

Too late, Hazard realized the voice was coming from his right. Too late, he realized what he was seeing ahead of him. And then the warning his brain had been screaming—
—it's a maze, the whole building is a maze, and he can come at you from any side, and that gun is cardboard, you're looking at a cardboard cutout just like one of those goddamn ducks in the shooting gallery, and he's coming—
—reached him. He spun, rising, and there was Mikey. His face was twisted with manic glee, and he swung the rifle like a club. Hazard brought up his .38—his good arm—but too slowly. The rifle cracked high on his forearm, and pain burst like a star, and Hazard's fingers opened. The .38 clunked on the carpet; Hazard barely noticed. The lower length of his forearm sagged, and the broken bone tented skin and cotton. The pain was so great that Hazard lowered his arm without even meaning too. The rifle came back, cracked against Hazard's forehead, and he dropped like the .38.
"I realized," Mikey was saying, his voice distant and crumbling, as though it were coming up from those clay pits twenty years ago. "You aren't strong. You're just a lonely, pathetic faggot like all the rest of them."
Then the rifle came down again, and everything went dark.

CHAPTER FORTY-SEVEN

JULY 4
WEDNESDAY
3:21 PM

THE EXPLOSION SHOOK THE BUILDING, and Somers knew that he had made a mistake: he had snipped the wrong wire, had pulled too hard, had somehow dislodged one of the safety pins. The Haverford's floor bucked once, rocking Somers forward, and then it dropped. Stumbling back, Somers had just enough presence of mind to drop the bundle of wires and catch himself on the window frame. A second, lesser shock ran through the structure, and the floor sagged another few inches, and then Somers let out a wild laugh. It took a moment to realize that he was still alive. Then his brain caught up with reality. Something had definitely exploded, but it hadn't been the grenades, and he was—somehow, miraculously—still alive. It sounded like the explosion came from behind him, towards the front of the Haverford. The floor now sloped in that direction, putting Somers at an angle. One of the computer monitors toppled forward, and the closet door swung open.

From inside the closet, a train rolled out. The model looked like something a hobbyist could pick up at a specialty store: a decent size, with real metal parts instead of cheap plastic, and obviously meant to run on a track with an electric current. It was strapped with gray bricks of molding clay on each side. Only they weren't gray bricks. From what Somers knew about Hollace and about this goddamn insane asylum, the stuff that looked like molding clay was probably

C-4. The train picked up speed, chugging towards Somers, and he danced one step to the side. Then he pictured the train colliding with the wall, and the C-4 triggering—was that how it worked? Somers wasn't sure—and he dropped to his knees and caught the engine car by its nose. His fingers trembled on the miniature cowcatcher. Jesus Christ, if he never saw an explosive again, he'd be a happy man.

Voices from the computer caught Somers's attention, and he glanced up. When the explosion had shaken the building, it must have woken the computer from its sleep because now a picture showed on the monitor. Eight pictures, actually: four rows of two squares, each showing a live video feed from somewhere inside the Haverford. Three of the boxes hissed with static. Several others showed green-hued night-vision shots of various hallways inside the Haverford. And the last showed Emery Hazard.

Hazard stood in a hallway with huge windows open to let in daylight. When he crossed those beams, the sun picked him out in a perfect target. When he darted into the shadows, it was harder to see him, but the infrared camera still picked him up in a blaze of orange and yellow. He and Mikey were shouting back and forth. The sound of Mikey's voice made Somers's gut clench, like he might shit himself, and he had to force himself to breathe.

Where was the camera? Where was this happening? Somers scooped up the engine car with its blocks of C-4, carrying it like it was glass, and stumbled up the sagging floor to the computer. He worked the mouse, clicking, scrolling, but there wasn't anything to help him. The label just read Camera 8. That meant nothing to Somers.

His eyes moved back to the camera feed as Mikey swung the rifle like a club. Somers barked a warning, feeling like a kid shouting at a cinema screen, feeling stupid and helpless as Mikey swung again, and then again, and Hazard dropped out of the video feed like someone had opened a trapdoor.

Somers sucked in a shaky breath, and when he let it out, it sounded like a bark again. Helpless. He was helpless. He was so goddamn helpless that it was going to get Hazard killed. A flush worked its way through Somers, and his skin prickled and itched like he'd rolled in stinging nettles. Helpless, fucking helpless, fucking—

He had to shut down the thoughts carefully. And it was hard. So much of what Somers did came to him naturally. So much of what he did was instinct. He was good at just about everything—it sounded cocky, but it was true, and he knew it was true. But this—this kind of rigid self-mastery—this was totally foreign. Somers never needed to shut himself down; usually, he just needed to do what came naturally, and things worked out all right.

But a clinical part of his mind knew that if he continued this way, if he let fear and helplessness swamp him, Hazard really would die. So he had to shut this down, and it was hard. Harder than he could have guessed. And it made him think of all the ways Hazard had done this, all the self-control, all the willpower it had taken for the big man to come back to this town, to work with Somers those first few weeks, to do all the things that were unnatural and scary and hard.

As a kind of stormlight-clarity descended on Somers, he realized he wasn't helpless. Not entirely. What would Hazard do? Hazard would use his brain.

Camera 8.

8 meant that they had at least eight cameras. Somers's lips trembled on the edge of a smile. Good job, Sher-fucking-lock. Eight cameras. And how did people number things? Well, normally—God, let it be normally—in order. Bottom to top. Top to bottom. So eight was either at the top of the Haverford, or it was at the bottom.

Top.

Ok.

Where on the top floor? Somers knew he was on the top floor as well. He studied the camera feed. Mikey, hunched at the waist, was dragging Hazard off screen, their silhouettes like charcoal rubbings as they moved in front of the July light.

The windows. The windows on Somers's side of the building were boarded up. His heart began to pound. That meant Hazard and Mikey were on the opposite side of the Haverford. And—another glance at the video—they were moving away from the front of the building. That was where the explosion had occurred; the damage was visible in the camera feed, crumbling plaster and exposed brick and a live wire sparking and dancing.

And that meant Somers knew where they were, and he knew where they were going. And all of the sudden—years later, he would repeat the same thing: that he didn't know how the idea came, that it was luck or fate or God, he'd leave it up to somebody else to decide—he saw the tunnel. The tunnel at the front of this apartment, the tunnel that Mikey and Hollace had cut into the wall with the track and the electric current that would carry a model train through the walls. A train like the one Somers cradled against his chest. An engine car with enough C-4 to blow out a good section of the Haverford's top floor.

In Somers's mind, the Haverford's floor plan unfurled, and he saw the train tracks navigating the cramped space between the walls. To get to the apartment—and Somers knew that Mikey was coming back, he knew that Mikey wanted to give Hazard the same special treatment, he knew that Mikey wanted to make it last, finally fulfilling the childhood fantasies of ripping and burning and cutting—Mikey would have to bring Hazard along the outer wall. Yes, there were two approaches to the corner apartment, but Mikey and Hollace had walled off one hallway—the one that Somers had hacked through to escape.

That stormlight clarity, like the sky when curtains of rain parted, made it easy to see everything. It was like seeing the future. Mikey would be tired; he'd been up almost as long as Somers, and he'd been in two fights, and now he was dragging Hazard's rather sizeable ass. That meant that Mikey wouldn't be scrambling over barricades or hauling Hazard under plywood walls. Mikey was going to take the path of least resistance. He was going to come straight down the open corridor. And he was going to walk right past the train.

The only question, for Somers at least, was how to kill Mikey without hurting Hazard. He didn't like the answer. The answer was that he would have to kill Mikey up close. And that meant he couldn't use the train as a weapon; no matter how carefully Somers tried to shape the charge—and since he didn't have a good goddamn of an idea of what he was doing, it wouldn't be very carefully—any blast that would kill Mikey would also kill Hazard.

But the blast didn't have to kill Mikey. It just had to distract him.

Somers checked the closet and found a detonator for the C-4. Then he moved to the tunnel Hollace had cut into the Haverford's walls. Somers lay the engine car on the track and peeled off the C-4 brick on the side that faced the Haverford's interior. This portion he carried to the worktable and set down as gently as he could. He had the vague idea that C-4 was stable and wouldn't go off from being bumped, but he didn't want to test it.

Then Somers went back to the track. He found the meter that controlled the electric current, and he nudged it just over the line. The engine car crept forward. Somers killed the current and checked the camera feed in the back room. His wounded leg was really burning now, but he ignored it. Three of the cameras were busted, and Somers couldn't find Hazard or Mikey on the other five. He let out a sigh. It was going to be a gamble. He checked his gut and didn't feel anything one way or the other. Then he spun the needle just over the line again, watched the engine carefully inch towards the tunnel, and left the apartment.

He walked straight into the darkness, following the same course as the train would. So many things could go wrong. If Mikey took too long, the train might be too far down the wall when Somers triggered it, and Mikey would recover quickly from the distant explosion. If the train moved faster or slower than Somers had gauged, then it would present similar problems. If Mikey changed his mind and took another route, or if he spotted Somers by some twist of bad luck, or if he put a bullet in Hazard as soon he suspected something was wrong—

On Somers's left, a custodial closet offered a small place, darker even than the pitchy darkness of the hallway, and in the darkness, he let his head rock forward against the painted wood of the door. Ammonia drifted up, and when he moved his foot, his shoe splashed in something, and another cloud of ammonia wafted past him. His eyes stung. He might have been crying; he wasn't sure, and he didn't dare raise his hand to his cheeks to find out. If he knew he was crying, if he had to face that, he might really lose it, and then he wouldn't be any help to anyone. He blew out a breath, and then another, and he listened.

It came sooner than he expected.

Footsteps padded down the hall in uneven stretches, interspersed with the whisper of something heavy being dragged over carpet. Light hit the custodial door, shining a white band through the gap at the base. The puddled ammonia glistened, and tiny waves crashed outward as Somers flexed his foot. He rotated the axe a quarter-turn in his hand. How far had the train come? If he detonated it now, it might be too early. Or too late. And it sounded like Mikey was still far enough down the hall that he might have time to recover before Somers reached him. Keep moving. Keep moving you dumb piece of shit, keep moving. Keep your ass moving.

And then, another uneven step, and the carpet's low whisper.

Somers listened to their approach. He should have planned this better. He should have done something else. Anything else. Anything but this stupid idea that was going to get him killed, get Hazard killed, get both of them—

A footstep scuffed carpet. Somers's heartbeat shot up. He thumbed the detonator and waited for the crash. It would be loud, and if he were lucky, there might even be some light and heat, and—

The explosion roared so loudly that Somers's hearing turned to a white hiss. Light—reddish-orange—flowed past the custodial closet, filling the space with upside-down shadows and carrying with it a smell like burning wood and plaster and something chemical that Somers assumed was the C-4 itself. The Haverford shuddered, and then the floor canted down. The sudden shift smacked Somers's face against the door, and ammonia whorled around his sneakers and into the filthy carpeting.

I blew up a building. That was the only coherent thought in Somers's head for a moment. And then, slightly clearer, Thank God I only used half. Then he thought of Hazard, and he dropped the detonator and threw open the door. Staggering out into the hallway, his leg burning, Somers brought up the axe and scanned for Mikey.

He paused, though, and for an instant, he forgot about Mikey and even about Hazard. Ahead of him, the explosion had ripped a hole in the side of the Haverford. Around the jagged edges, brick teeth hung loose; one swayed in the currents of hot air. Worse, though, was how the floor sagged: Somers could see where the explosion had sheared through a load-bearing wall as well as several joists. A second hole had opened in the floor, and pieces of brick and plaster spilled onto the level below.

Hazard lay there, at the edge of that drop, his face pale under a mask of blood. The gash along his forehead looked bad. Really bad. More cuts, smaller, covered his arms, and pieces of plaster and brick had sliced his shirt open and left bloody slashes across his chest. Somers's stomach dropped. And he felt—almost sleepy. That wasn't quite the right word, but it came close to this feeling of having everything inside him swaddled and packed away, leaving an oddly clear and distant view of the scene before him.

He found Mikey, his lips peeled back over rotting brown stumps, crawling away from the collapsing section of floor. The shrapnel had hit Mikey harder; something had punched a hole through Mikey's cheek, and a broken tooth peeped out when the flap of flesh fell. The long strip that Somers had ripped from Mikey's face was now black with clotted blood and dirt. Brick and plaster had ripped through Mikey's jeans, and he was bleeding. Bleeding enough, in fact, that the shrapnel might have gotten an artery. Somers limped towards him. He wasn't going to let Mikey die of blood loss. This piece of shit was going to die with four inches of steel buried in his brain. The pain in Somers's leg flashed like a distant flight beacon. The axe blade came up. The axe was red, the whole thing except a silver crescent at the edge, and that singular realization made Somers happier than anything in his life except his daughter and Emery Hazard.

Mikey scuttled sideways on hands and knees, shouting something, begging. Begging, Somers thought. The little bastard was begging. After a lifetime of listening to other people beg, after a lifetime of getting off on it, now Mikey was begging. Somers couldn't hear the words, not over the rushing white noise that the explosion had left in his ears, but he saw Mikey's split and scabbed lips flapping, he saw the bloody gums, he saw the thick, tobacco-stained tongue like a flag. If the axe went through Mikey's head hard enough, Somers wondered — at the right angle, it would have to be at the right angle — would it cut out his tongue? There was only one way to find out.

As Somers swung, Mikey squealed and rolled his back against the wall. One of the tall man's legs kicked out. His heel caught Somers's bad leg, and the sudden rush of pain sent Somers staggering. The swing of the axe went wide, and the blade buried itself in the wall.

Somers was still falling. He held on to the axe, trying to right himself, but the blaze of pain ran straight from his leg to his head, and he was on the edge of total exhaustion. He landed hard on a knee — his bad leg — and the second wave of pain was worse than the first. All he could do was clutch at the axe, hanging on to the edge of consciousness by his fingernails, and try not to fall the rest of the way.

And then, so quickly and forcefully that Somers never had a chance, the axe was ripped from his hands. He blinked through the black snowstorm, trying to see what was happening.

Mikey.

Mikey had the axe.

Mikey, his tongue probing the hole in his cheek, tasting his own blood where severed flesh flopped grotesquely against his jaw.

The axe came up.

The axe came down.

CHAPTER FORTY-EIGHT

JULY 4
WEDNESDAY
3:32 PM

HAZARD HAD BEEN AWAKE. The pain clustered in his head, a white fractal that kept changing shape. But he had been awake. And then there had been noise, so much noise that for a moment, he thought the world had ended. Something had hurt him. Cuts and bruises, something that socked him on the jaw and doubled that twisting fractal in his head. And then static in his ears.

He had to open his eyes. That was the hardest part, opening his eyes. For a moment he couldn't, and in spite of the red glow through his eyelids, Hazard thought he might have died. And then the dried blood gumming his lids gave way, and his eyes opened, and he stared up into a haze of smoke and John-Henry Somerset limping forward with an axe.

"John."

Only it didn't come out John. It came out like a rabbit turd in his mouth, tiny and foul and making him want to vomit. Hazard rocked onto his side, and the floor sagged. He couldn't hear it—that static charge in his ears swallowed up everything else—but he could feel the vibrations of wood splintering underneath him. Even through the pain clustering inside his head, he knew what that meant: the building was structurally damaged, and the floor was giving way.

Hazard flopped onto his side in time to see Somers bring the axe down toward Mikey's head. Mikey was gibbering—no sound, again, not through that white roar of noise—but his lips moved frantically over the brown slime that passed for his teeth. A long strip of flesh was missing from Mikey's face, the effect horrible, as though he were wearing a rubberized Halloween mask. And the look there, the terror, the helplessness, the desperate plea to stop, were familiar to Hazard. He had felt those same things before. He had felt them, in fact, when he had stood face to face with Mikey, and then Hazard had been the one to beg. He had begged, and Mikey had kept hitting, had kept spitting, had kept cutting no matter what Hazard said.

For a moment, time seemed to pause. The axe cut a gleaming arc. Mikey's lips peeled back in rabid fear. And Hazard waited. Inside himself, below the sting of fresh lacerations, below the throbbing white mass of a concussion, he waited for something. Some sort of realization. Some sort of closure. He waited to find himself suddenly feeling pity for Mikey. Or to find himself flooded with forgiveness like arctic water. Or to find himself balanced, at peace, finally understanding all those years of torture and abuse. He waited for that clock, the one with its hands locked at midnight, to tick forward, finally, and count out a future for Emery Hazard.

And then Mikey kicked out, and Somers stumbled and went down hard on one knee. Mikey flung himself at the axe, tugging on it. It looked like Somers was trying to hold on, and it also looked like Somers didn't have a damn chance. He was in too much pain. His face had lost all color, and he rocked slightly, as though he were keeping upright against a strong gale.

Hazard realized, then, that he didn't have understanding, and he didn't have forgiveness, and he didn't have pity for Mikey. He never would. What the bastard had done to him—and to Jeff, and to Somers, and to who knew how many others—was beyond those things. At least, it was beyond those things for Hazard. He didn't even have the desire for pity or forgiveness, not as far as Mikey was concerned.

But Hazard did have an opportunity for payback. And payback was one goddamn interesting bitch.

Hazard got to his knees as the axe came free from the wall. He got to his feet as Mikey ripped the haft from Somers's hands. He got the first step as Mikey pulled the axe back. Something—movement glimpsed from the corner of his eye, a rush of air, maybe even the vibrations in the toppling floor—alerted Mikey, and his gaze cut towards Hazard. The axe started to come down. But by then it was too late for Mikey.

Hazard hit him before the axe had dropped a quarter of its distance, and the two men barreled backward and into the plaster. Pain rolled up Hazard's broken arm. It didn't mean anything. Mikey punched out, using the axe haft as a lever, trying to force Hazard back. Hazard was beyond any of that, though. This was twenty years in the coming. This was for the skinny boy with the scars on his chest that Mikey had tortured. This was for Jeff. He got his working hand around Mikey's fingers and twisted. Bone popped and broke. Mikey screamed, and Hazard couldn't hear him, but he could smell the foulness of those rotting teeth, and he could feel the scream feather the stubble on his cheek.

He broke Mikey's other hand. The pain was intense; using his injured arm like this, forcing it to serve him, was like clutching a live coal. That was distant, though. The axe dropped, and Hazard ignored it. He didn't want an axe. He was beyond tools. He was beyond everything, really. The world had faded. The Haverford with its shattered plaster and its crumbling brick and its sagging floor had retreated. For all that it mattered to Hazard, they could have been a hundred thousand years in the past, grappling in the darkness of a cave. He brought his head forward, hard, and butted Mikey in the nose. Cartilage crumpled. The tall, skinny meth-head folded like fresh newsprint. Hazard punched, and he felt rib give way under the first blow. Hazard had lost a lot of strength, his arm screamed when he threw the punch, but it was worth it. Mikey had always been mostly a showman: a lot of dog and pony, a lot of razzle-dazzle. And now, after twenty years, the reality was a disappointment. The skinny little tweaker was already a dead man. Hazard knew. And he knew that Mikey knew it. He hit again. Hazard's arm lit up like a string of Black Cat fireworks, but it was worth it. Mikey gagged, and the wash of fetid breath made Hazard bare his teeth with excitement.

Then Mikey had a knife in his broken hand.

For Hazard, the world fractured. One part of it continued to move fast. And another part, a part inside him, moved slow. That inner part remembered the darkness of the apartment, and the gray scum of light on a knife, and the blade biting deep into Hazard's arm, over and over again, as he was helpless.

In the fast part of the world, Hazard's body moved by instinct and, maybe more importantly, by fear. He didn't even have time to process what was happening. There was that inner psychic trail that led back to the apartment and to Rex Kolosik and a knife stabbing down at him, and there was everything else: his hand, his bad arm, jerking up with speed and strength that Hazard hadn't had since his injury. He clamped low on Mikey's arm, almost at the wrist, as the switchblade swung open. And by that point, it was over. Hazard shoved, and the knife slid into Mikey's gut, the point drilling up under his ribcage.

Mikey shuddered. He would have fallen if not for the knife, and one of his hands found Hazard's chest and tugged, his broken fingers writhing across Hazard's shirt, slipping between the buttons, pulling on them in a grotesque mockery of a lover. Then he shuddered again. His eyes were huge. His jaw hung like a ventriloquist's dummy. Decay wafted off the brown stumps of teeth. Hazard saw death in the man who had haunted him, and he waited for the clock, that horrible frozen clock, to start.

Then Mikey charged. Later, Hazard was never sure if it was intentional. He wondered. Late at night, when he carded Somers's short blond hair with his fingers, he would wonder if Mikey had been just fucked up enough to go kamikaze. To try to take them both out at the same time.

The charge took Hazard by surprise. Worse, it took him off balance. Mikey plowed into him, and the force of the rush knocked Hazard backward. Mikey plunged past him, his own momentum carrying him over the edge of the broken floor and into the gaping darkness. Hazard snatched at the wall. His fingers scraped up plaster and a scrim of wallpaper. For a moment, he might have steadied himself, but that was his broken arm, and the shattered length of the forearm flopped, and his fingers were weak and loose. And then he fell into darkness.

CHAPTER FORTY-NINE

JULY 4
WEDNESDAY
3:34 PM

SOMERS LAY THERE, his leg burning with pain, as Mikey raised the axe. The silver crescent glittered. An inrush of air, following the backward trajectory of the axe, parted the clouding dust. For a moment, Somers could see Mikey's face clearly: hate and exhilaration pumped red into those features, and Mikey looked like he was still half-drunk with the realization that he had managed to stay alive a few moments longer. At the top of its arc, the axe was a long, blood-red shaft in Mikey's hands. And then the crescent edge sliced down.

Pain paralyzed Somers, and the animal part of his brain cowered and waited for death. But the blade didn't find flesh. Instead, Mikey's head snapped left, and his eyes widened, he tried to turn the axe's momentum to the side. Like a cartoon superhero flying in from the side of the screen, Hazard crashed into Mikey, and both men slammed into the plaster, laths snapping under their weight. They struggled for a moment, Hazard's weight and strength giving him an advantage over skinny, tweaked-out Mikey. A temporary advantage, part of Somers's mind calculated. Very temporary. Because Hazard had a serious head injury. His arm had never fully healed. He had taken Mikey by surprise, but how long would that advantage last?

Not long. The tiny, primitive part of Somers's mind told him to run. Or, if he couldn't run, to crawl. To drag himself away from the brawling men as fast as he could. Because it didn't matter that he loved Hazard. It didn't matter that Hazard was fighting to save them both. Nothing mattered except Somers living another day, breathing another breath, scraping another inch forward under the sun.

Fuck that, Somers thought.

Then, out loud, he screamed it: "Fuck that!" Fuck anyone and anything that thought it could get between him and Hazard. He rolled onto his side, on his uninjured leg, and managed to get up on one knee. Fuck anything that tried to get between them. Fuck this world. Fuck this town. Fuck his parents. Fuck Hazard's parents. Fuck Mikey Grames. Fuck—goddamn fuck it to the lowest fucking hell—evolution. Somers shoved off the floor, caught himself on a broken lath, and dragged himself upright. His leg was a column of fire. He was shaking. His whole body was shaking. How much farther could he go?

A step. He could take another step for Hazard.

And another.

And another.

Neither man heard him. The axe had fallen to the floor, and Hazard had done something to Mikey's hands. The tweaker had them curled against his chest, cradling them. Mikey's face was a bloody mess; his nose didn't look anything like a nose anymore. It was just a flat triangle hanging off his face. With drunken disbelief, Somers took in the scene fully: Hazard was winning. With his head banged to hell, with a bad arm, with nothing but guts and a good right hook, he was winning.

Then Mikey had a knife. Somers barely saw it, barely had time to process what he was seeing, but Hazard saw it. Hazard reacted so quickly that Somers didn't even realize, not at first, what he had seen: Hazard's injured arm jerked up, his hand forked Mikey's wrist, and then he drove the knife into Mikey's gut.

That was the end of it. All those years, all of it come down to this, and Mikey was finally dead. Still standing—he was wobbling there, staring at Hazard, his eyes full of shock—but he was dead. He'd be down and on the ground and he'd be dead in—

Mikey charged.

Insanity brightened Mikey's curdled expression. It lit him up like moonlight. He coiled against the wall and launched forward, and he hit Hazard—whether by bad luck or fate or skill—at exactly the worst possible moment. Hazard stumbled, carried backward by Mikey's rush. The big, dark-haired man tried to spin clear. Mikey's sprint carried him toward the gaping darkness in the floor, and between one instant and the next, Mikey disappeared. The black maw swallowed him. And Mikey didn't scream. Didn't make a sound. Somers's skin pebbled with horror at the silence of Mikey's dying fall.

Hazard stepped back again, still trying to catch his balance. His bad arm swung out. His nails stripped ribbons of plaster from the wall. For a moment, he seemed to catch himself. And then his hand spasmed, and he lurched forward into the hole that Somers had blasted in the Haverford's floor. Hazard fell.

Somers scooped up the axe. His leg was a bonfire, but it was miles off, and it gave just enough light for him to see. He swung the blade, and it bit deep into the wall. Plaster exploded out, the dust like something swept off a tombstone, and the teeth of broken laths snapped out. Then the axe caught. It held fast. Somers gripped the haft and slid, letting his momentum carry him down the sagging floor. When he reached the end of the haft, he gripped tight, and the force almost pulled his arm from his shoulder. But he held. And he swung out over the blackness that had swallowed up Emery Hazard.

And there, clutching at the splintered tip of a joist, was a big, pale hand dusted with dark hair. The fingers trembled, on the verge of a spasm that would send him plummeting into oblivion.

Somers swung to the end of his reach. He caught Emery Hazard. And he held him by the wrist.

CHAPTER FIFTY

JULY 4
WEDNESDAY
9:51 PM

THE HOSPITAL GAVE them a shared room.

After everything else—after Somers dragging him out of the pit, after their slow escape from the maze of traps, after the poking and prodding with doctors, after the hours of talking to Cravens—it was the room that almost did Hazard in. Somers insisted that they share a hospital room. Of course. And one of the nurses, a tiny little thing with hair like she'd been kissed by a blow dryer, kept giggling and blushing until another nurse, this one matronly, sent her to change a bedpan or whatever the hell she was supposed to be doing.

It was a long time until they were finally alone, with the lights low, and every breath Hazard took laced with liniment and salve and something that wasn't a taste, something that was a feeling, a cottony cloud in his head from whatever they'd given him. Outside, one last sullen red fissure ran along the horizon. It was almost night. The sodium lamps had popped on over the last half hour. Something big and black, an owl, maybe, swept through the light, tunneled through the darkness, and emerged again, its wings flapping slowly.

"This is ridiculous," Somers said, plucking at the hospital gown, and then plucking at the bedding, and then snapping a finger against the chrome rail so that it chimed.

Hazard closed his eyes and tried not to answer. But after a moment: "It's one night."

"That's not the problem. I asked for a king-size bed."

"They don't make hospital beds in king. Or queen."

"I bet they do."

"They don't."

"I bet they do, Ree. For big people."

"Big people?"

"Yeah. I mean, bigger than you. Although, not much bigger. I mean, the way you went after that cafeteria icebox cake they brought you, you're catching up." Somers clicked his tongue. "Hey, there's an idea. Maybe we get you a few more pieces of that cake, and they'll have to give you a bigger bed. For medical reasons."

Hazard's eyes snapped open, and Somers was grinning at him.

"Hi."

"Go to sleep, will you?" And without waiting for an answer, Hazard closed his eyes again.

It didn't help, though. When he closed his eyes, nightmares kaleidoscoped through his head: that video of Somers being tortured; the sound of his screams; the photographs of Jeff and the mayor, naked and tangled together; Hollace's dying message. He tried to banish these, and in their place came something worse. He had been stupid. He had been arrogant and stupid, and it had almost cost Somers his life.

Worst, though, was the end: following Mikey's lure, letting hate and anger get the best of him, and then the crack of the rifle as it broke his forearm, and the clunk and darkness as it hit his head. His arm, now wrapped in plaster, throbbed at the memory. And then, Hazard thought, what was truly unforgivable was that he'd done it again. He'd tried his hardest to stop Mikey. He'd done everything he could. And in the end, he'd failed. Mikey had been the one to kill Mikey — he'd run himself right out over that broken floor, and he'd fallen four stories to his death. And he would have taken Hazard with him if Somers hadn't been there.

In spite of Hazard's best efforts, he found his eyes open again, and he stared at the cast around his arm. Black Sharpie already stained the length of the cast. Huge block letters read *John-Henry Somerset was here. Have a great summer.* Like he was signing a goddamn yearbook. Or writing a buddy from camp. Have a great summer. What the hell went on in that blond head sometimes?

"Are you ready to admit you were wrong?" Somers's voice had gone rough and low.

Hazard ignored him, his attention on the plaster.

"I just want to hear you say it. I just want to hear you say you were wrong. Then we can move forward."

Hazard wanted to say it. He needed to say it. And he would say it, soon. But—but Christ, it hurt to hear Somers say that. Even though Somers was right, it hurt like hell. And Hazard had to drop his head and blink to clear his eyes.

The hospital bed squeaked, and Somers's feet landed heavily on the linoleum. His cane rang out against the chrome, and then Somers grunted and pushed himself up. His steps were slow and shuffling and interspersed with asthmatic breathing that Hazard knew, even if the limp was real, was fake. He knew, too, that Somers was putting on a show. Somers was trying to take out some of the sting. Somers was trying to make him laugh.

But there wasn't anything to laugh about. For Emery Hazard, who had worked his whole life to be right, who had trained himself to think, to use his brain, to reason things through, it was bad enough to be wrong. Even worse, though, was having Somers call him out like this. A lot worse. It stabbed straight to the heart of Emery Hazard, past all his defenses. It hurt him more than he knew he could be hurt.

Somers's dragging steps stopped at the edge of Hazard's bed. His fingers, smooth and golden, cupped Hazard's chin. He was gentle. Christ, why did he have to be gentle? If he yelled, if he threw a chair, if he knocked Hazard around—

—with a belt, chased him around the apartment with a belt just to get a hard-on—

—that would be one thing. But this, being kind, being gentle, being funny to try to ease the worst of it, this was so much more awful.

Somers's touch was gentle, yes. But firm. And he forced Hazard's head up. Hazard stared into blue eyes he had fantasized about since childhood: tropical blue, and darker and bluer the deeper he went. Somers's thumb trembled on the side of Hazard's neck, just under his jaw, the way a bird's broken wing might tremble.

"Ree."

"Fuck, I know. I'll—I'll say it, all right? Just—Somers, don't make me. Not tonight."

For a moment, Hazard thought Somers might take pity on him. He thought Somers might relent. Then the trembling thumb pressed tight, and Somers said, "You told me you'd never wipe my ass."

Hazard swallowed his own spit and started to cough. "What?"

"You told me you'd never wipe my ass. We talked about this, remember? You told me you'd break my arms for some reason and then I'd have to hire somebody to wipe my ass, and I said we were roommates, so the least you could do was help me out, and you said—"

"What are you talking about? Wiping your ass? Somers, what I did—"

"You said not even with sandpaper. Not even with a sandblaster. And I want you to admit you're wrong because if you don't—" Somers cocked his head at the cast, and then at Hazard's other arm, still injured and without its full use. "—you're going to have a long, dry, itchy, chafing time. Smelly too."

The cottony feeling from the opioids made Hazard smack dry lips and blink. "What?"

"You have to say you're wrong." Somers pronounced each word slowly. "And then I'll wipe your ass for you."

"I don't need you to—I can wipe my own—why are we talking about my ass?"

"I've always liked your ass. I have a personal interest in keeping it in mint condition."

"Somers, what I did today—I failed. I failed you. I almost got us both killed, and the only reason we're alive is because you're amazing enough to salvage even my fuck-ups."

Somers raised his knee to the bed and hesitated. He squinted at Hazard. "My johnny's open in back."

"What?"

"The hospital gown. It hangs open in back."

"I thought I was the one who got hit in the head."

"Technically, we both did. I had a concussion yesterday. Or the day before. Or whenever it was."

"What are you talking about?"

As Somers shifted weight to his knee, the mattress dimpled under his weight. He grabbed the chrome rail of Hazard's bed and grunted as he moved his injured leg. "I'd like to cuddle with you."

"Ok."

"And I'm warning you: my johnny is open in back. Don't take advantage."

"Take advantage?"

"I want you to try really hard and be a gentleman."

"Christ, how hard did you get hit?"

Hazard tried to sound grumpy, but it was difficult with Somers clambering over him, knees cracking against Hazard's shins, hands messing up the sheets, feet tangling in the blanket scrunched at the end of the bed. Somers flipped and flopped and turned over no less than a dozen times, like a dog trying to find the perfect spot, and then he curled up against Hazard's side, his face buried in Hazard's chest.

With his broken arm, Hazard reached up and parted the short blond hair. The cast bonked Somers's head.

"Ouch."

"Sorry."

"This is why I wanted a king-sized hospital bed."

"They don't—"

"Ree, what would have happened today? If you hadn't come for me?"

"You would have escaped. You already had a phone, and you were already on your way out. The only reason you stayed was because I was too stupid to listen to you."

"Maybe. Or maybe I would have walked right into one of those tripwires the way I did last time we were at the Haverford. Or I might have lost too much blood and passed out in the hallway. Or I might have come around a corner and found Mikey looking down the barrel of a gun. I might have gotten out on my own. But I probably wouldn't have."

"If I had listened—"

"Who knows what would have happened? I don't. And you don't. I'm the one who went off on his own, Ree. I'm the one that didn't trust you enough—" Somers's voice caught, and he dug his face deeper into Hazard's chest. "I'm the one that fucked up and left. If I'd stayed and talked to you, if I'd told you what I was doing, if I hadn't been so afraid, things would have been better."

He was crying, his tears sizzling through the hospital gown that Hazard wore. Hazard tried stroking Somers's hair and only ended up clubbing him again, and then Somers hiccupped and tried to laugh and it was a little bit better. They lay that way for a while. A TV hung in the corner of the room, and the forecast called for highs in the 90s and plenty of humidity, and that meant that summer was going to be the same as always.

Drying his cheeks with the heel of his hand, Somers propped himself up and caught Hazard's eyes again. "Tell me about it."

And Hazard did. He told Somers about Ted Kjar's chapter on the WPA. He told Somers about the property out on Route 29. He told Somers about what had happened, the whole conspiracy of chance events that had led to Ted Kjar's discovery: the internal audit, the old cabin, a mouse or a snake or a vole that had opened a hole in the chinking, and a stray breeze that had brushed an incriminating photograph out onto the bare cement floor. He tried to tell Somers about the other photographs, the ones with two bodies twined together, but he couldn't. That part of the story swept through his mind like the owl he had seen in the parking lot, tunneling into the darkness between dustings of light. Somers rubbed his chest; from the look on his face, he had figured it out on his own.

"So Kjar puts enough of the clues together to decide that Mayor Newton was involved with Jeff. And he suspects that Mayor Newton kills Jeff—to silence him, or to keep their relationship from becoming public knowledge. What did he do next? Confront Newton? Why not take it directly to the police or the FBI?"

"Maybe he did. If he tried the police, what do you think happened?"

Somers shook his head slowly. "If he took it to Lender, I can buy it. But Cravens? The rest of them? You think everybody was in on it?"

"No. That wouldn't be practical. Or, most likely, possible. I bet Kjar was careful. He took it to someone he trusted. Maybe he even took to Cravens. But what did he have? Some pictures? And Kjar was already using again. He was just a junkie with a crazy story."

"They could have gotten Newton for statutory rape, Ree."

"Maybe. They were old pictures. They'd been exposed to the elements. They'd been discovered under bizarre conditions. And the mayor's got a long reach."

"That's what you think happened? They weren't being bribed to keep their mouths shut. They're just cowards, and they weren't going to stick out their necks for something that didn't feel solid?"

Hazard shrugged.

"That's bullshit."

"I think he did try the FBI. That might have even been what drew Graham and Schaming here. They went to Kjar's house, remember? But they were doing this as a side job, and Kjar had already disappeared by then."

"He'd gone off the grid. Probably so high or stoned or whatever that he didn't even know how to get home."

"Why?"

"He was an addict."

"But why ketamine? Why the barbiturates? What was that all about?"

"He liked uppers and downers."

Hazard shook his head. "Your father said something about what happens when a predator looks weak. Is that what happened here? Kjar attacked the mayor; he didn't succeed in killing him, but he made him vulnerable. And then what? Mikey decided he wanted some of the action? He decided he wanted more than what Hollace was going to give him?"

"Why didn't Mikey just blackmail Newton in the first place? He's lived here the whole time. He's gotten in some bad scrapes. He could have been gathering evidence, building enough of a file to keep the mayor in line. Instead, he waited until the last minute, and then he sent you to dig up the proof that he needed. Why did he wait so long to play that trump card?"

"Because he didn't know."

Somers dropped his hand. "Of course he knew. He told you he wanted proof that the mayor killed Jeff."

"Yes. But he didn't know before, oh, a few days ago. Until Hollace told him." Outside, in the parking lot, the owl ghosted through the light again. Hazard wet his lips. "A long time ago, after Jeff died, Hollace said something to me. He said, 'He shouldn't have told him.' Jeff. He was talking about Jeff. And I thought he meant Mikey, I thought he meant Jeff shouldn't have talked back to Mikey, shouldn't have said something to Mikey. But it wasn't that." The owl flapped its wings once and glided into the darkness. Gone. Swallowed up. "He knew. And Hollace thought I knew too, and he was warning me to keep my mouth shut."

"He was always following us around," Somers said. His hand rubbed a circle on Hazard's chest, friction building into a glow. "He was always there, wanting to be part of it even though we never let him." His fingers curled, pinching skin, and Somers didn't seem to realize. "That day, Ree. That fucking day. The day out by the pits, when I—"

"It's all right."

"It's not all right. If I'd done something, if I'd stopped it right then, if I'd been anything but a coward, a scared little chicken shit, if I'd—"

"It's all right, John."

"It's not all right." He shook his head, and tears spattered the hospital sheet. "It's not all right, Ree. What I did to you, all those times, it led to this. It led to Jeff hiding. It led to him and Newton. It led to—"

"John."

"Just don't say it, all right? Just don't say it, Ree." He pushed himself up. "I thought we could leave it behind. I thought we could get beyond it somehow, I don't know, because I love you, because I need you. I need you so goddamn much I don't even know how to say it. But we can't, Ree. It's here. All that shit, it's still here between us, still here, and it follows us. The past isn't past, you know? That's what Faulkner says. It's not dead. It's not past. It's not. It's always here."

First as tragedy, Hazard thought. And it was true. What had come first in his life was tragedy. And the aftershocks had followed him here, to this night under scratchy hospital sheets. Inside himself, Hazard reached the edge of a dusty span of light, and darkness lay ahead. Thought winged him forward into that darkness. The past had carried him to this point, to the injuries he carried, to the scars that would never fade, to grief that couldn't be buried. But it had led, too, to the man beside him, the man he loved. It had led to John-Henry Somerset.

He started to laugh.

At first, Somers stared at him. Then Somers reared back, and red fired up in his cheeks, and he planted a hand on Hazard's chest to gain a little more distance. "What?"

Hazard kept laughing. It just rolled out of him. He never laughed like this, but now he did, and it just kept coming.

"What's so funny?"

"That quote," Hazard said, gasping for air as more laughter swept through him. "That quote's so goddamn stupid." And he dissolved into laughter again.

For another moment, Somers stayed where he was, fingers splayed against Hazard's chest as though he might push clear. And then a smile tugged at his lips. He didn't laugh. But the smile got bigger. And he slugged Hazard high in the chest. Not hard, but not soft either.

"Don't laugh at me."

"I'm not laughing at you." Hazard got both arms around the blond man, although the movements were awkward and slow, and pulled Somers against him. His lips found Somers's neck. And then his cheek. And then his mouth. And then their foreheads were together, and Hazard swam deep in those turquoise eyes. Deep. Deep where the blue became almost black. And he said, "Do you have any idea how much I need you too?"

Somers shook his head a fraction.

"And not just to wipe my ass."

"Ree."

"It's all right, John. It's going to be all right." But he wasn't sure. He didn't know, not the way he usually knew. Inside, where a piece of his life had stopped ticking forward all those years ago, there was only stillness. He kissed Somers again. Stillness. And then he kissed him again. Stillness. And Somers turned his head, and his blond stubble sparked along Hazard's neck, and the johnny slipped and exposed the curling dark script over Somers's lines of lean muscle. And there was lust and excitement and an erection hard enough to drill to China, but there was also that stillness inside Emery Hazard.

"Ree," Somers said, drawing his lower lip between his teeth, a blush flooding his cheeks as he turned down his eyes. "Do you — would you?"

Hazard tugged on the folds of the johnny and slid his hands back until he heard the noise in Somers's throat that he liked so much. Fireworks lit up the sky. Their boom rattled the window. For a moment, the owl was visible again in blue and red shadows. And the hospital bed rattled, but not because of the fireworks.

Fuck me so I bleed on your cock.

Somers's breath rasped in his throat. He pawed at Hazard's chest, a whimper building in his throat.

Fuck me so I bleed.

Shivering, Hazard dropped the johnny and let it fall back into place. He kissed Somers's neck; his lips felt dry.

"Ree?"

"Sorry. My arm, you know? Both arms."

Somers stared at him; fireworks exploded again, pocketing his eyes in red and blue, and he looked a long way off. Then he nodded. "Yeah. Of course." He raised himself and scooted towards the edge of the bed.

"You can stay. Snuggle, like you said."

"No. We should get some rest."

CHAPTER FIFTY-ONE

JULY 5
THURSDAY
3:41 PM

THE NEXT DAY, Hazard and Somers had two visitors. The first was Chief Cravens, who came and sat and was silent for a minute. The only noise was the squeak of vinyl when she shifted. Sweeping long gray hair over her shoulder, she looked first at Somers and then at Hazard.

"There are going to be a lot of questions."

Hazard nodded. He glanced at Somers and was glad to see that the blond man kept his expression neutral.

"Questions about what?" Somers asked.

"About a dead man at the bottom of the Haverford. About a patrol car buried in the building's rubble. About two cops with a grudge."

"You think that's what this was about?"

"Detective Hazard, I'll tell you what I saw. I assigned you and your partner as part of a protective detail for the mayor. During that duty, you shot and killed a man who almost murdered the mayor. To that point, your actions are commendable. Then—" Cravens's eyes settled on something in the middle ground, and Hazard realized she was hiding something. He looked at Somers for a clue, and Somers shook his head slowly. "Then you and your partner essentially disappeared. I told you I wanted information on Ted Kjar. I told you we needed an airtight explanation for why he attacked the mayor. I told you that this was important, that it was your only priority. And instead, what do I get? Instead, I get my two best detectives acting like vigilantes. John-Henry, you were kidnapped. Abducted. Tortured. And Emery, you didn't call for help. Instead, you—"

"That's not fair," Somers burst out. "He didn't know. Not at first."

"That's enough," Cravens said.

"And when he did, when I finally got in touch with him—"

"That's enough."

"—he tried to get backup. You were all too busy running around town, chasing imaginary explosives, just like Mikey wanted you to."

Cravens drew in a breath. Her cheeks had shiny red circles. "Are you finished?"

"What were we supposed to do?" Somers said. He was flushed too, the red staining his collarbone and the hollow of his neck. "Should he have left me there, let Mikey work on me some more?" He displayed his bandaged fingertips. "Should he have sat on his thumb while he waited for the rest of you to realize you were digging around the boardwalk for nothing? Should he have walked away from the only piece of evidence—" Somers paled so suddenly that he looked sick, and his eyes cut to Hazard.

"What evidence?"

Hazard met Cravens's stare.

"What evidence, Detective?"

"A few different things." He wet his lips. He didn't like to gamble, but he'd done a lot of thinking in the sleepless hours after the Haverford. He was ready to toss the dice. "A video that someone sent to the FBI."

Cravens flinched.

Hazard's next breath was easier because he'd already won. The rest was just the details. "I wondered how Special Agent Graham got possession of a video showing boys and girls being pimped out. At first, I thought maybe someone had filmed Mayor Newton and intended to blackmail him and the johns. But that didn't make sense because Mayor Newton was the one doing the filming. I found what remained of his . . . set in a cabin. So Newton filmed everything, and

I'm guessing he blackmailed every john he caught on tape. He was very careful not to show his face. And I started wondering: how? How could something like that make its way to the FBI?"

To her credit, Cravens managed to meet his gaze. The corner of her left eye twitched like Morse code. "What are you saying, Detective?"

"That was a long time ago. Before you were made chief, I bet. And what I remember is that Martha Cravens was tough as balls. The first female detective on Wahredua's PD. A good one; she had to be a good one because she had to get past all that old-boys bullshit."

"What are you saying?"

"I bet if I pulled some of the files from '97, '98, '99, I'd see that you were looking into sex work. I bet I'd find cases that you closed. And cases that you didn't. Cases that kept you awake at night. And I bet you kept looking. You were good; you had to be so damn good. And you weren't going to let kids get whored out, not in your town. Not if you could stop it."

Her voice sounded like gravel in a tin pan. "What are you saying, Emery?"

"Whoever found that video, they knew they couldn't use it. Not here. Not with Edgcomb as chief. It wouldn't have any legs; it would disappear. She must have thought it would be better to send it somewhere else. To make sure somebody else knew about it. Somebody who might be able to do something."

Cravens might have nodded. Or it might have been a tremor. Her eyes were wet and clear like rainwater. "This video you found, you said it doesn't show the mayor's face? It could have been anybody. So there you have it. If somebody found it . . ." She shrugged and opened her hands.

"It doesn't show his face. But it couldn't have been anybody; we both know that."

She said nothing.

"But I wonder why things didn't change when a new chief took the job. The chief reports to the mayor. She serves at his discretion."

Color came into Cravens's cheeks, and her breath rattled. When she spoke, it was with hollow authority. "That's interesting speculation, Detective. But I'm afraid it's just that: speculation. I'm more interested in how Mikey Grames got involved in all of this." Her voice gained strength. "That's what I'm asking myself. That's what everyone's asking me. Even the mayor. The man can't breathe off a ventilator, he can't practically string together a coherent sentence because he's on so many pain pills, but he made it clear what he wanted to know. Why Grames? What did he have to do with this?"

Hazard could feel Somers's eyes on him. He focused on Cravens, on the grim line of her mouth, on the knowledge in her eyes.

"I won't play this game."

"Ree, don't—Chief, he's just upset. He's been through a lot. We both have."

"No. It's not that. I'm not playing this game. You know."

Cravens's flush darkened to scarlet. "I don't know what you're—"

"You didn't know all of it, but you knew enough. And you let it happen."

"Ree, just stop it, all right? Drop it. Chief, he's on pain pills, and he's hurt, and we've both seen the butthole of hell, and—"

"Am I supposed to understand that you think I have some special knowledge about this case? That you think I know something about Grames or Kjar or the mayor that might have bearing on your investigation and that I concealed that information? That's a very serious thing to suggest, Detective Hazard. I want you to be very clear with your next words."

"You knew."

"Ree, for fuck's sake—listen, Chief, just let me—"

Cravens pushed out of the chair. It squeaked like a dog fart, and it was the only noise in the room except for her ragged breathing. Then she slashed one hand through the air and said, "You're both suspended. There will be an investigation starting with the shooting of Ted Kjar—"

"I thought I was provisionally cleared," Hazard said. Something nuclear was happening at the center of his chest, but it didn't have anything to do with Cravens. Or not directly, anyway. It had to do with the fear in Somers's face, the fear that Hazard saw at an angle, out of the corner of his eye. And it had to do with Cravens, indirectly, because she was causing that fear. She was taking away Somers's job, and that was enough to start fission sparking under Hazard's ribcage.

"The investigation will start with the shooting of Ted Kjar and include the death of Detective Swinney—"

"Fuck you."

"—and the deaths of Michael Grames and Hollace Walker."

He locked gazes with Cravens. Her voice was angry. Her posture was angry. The cross of her arms across her chest was angry. But in her eyes, he saw something else. Something gray and scuttling and brittle, and he thought he would need Somers to tell him what it was.

"I'll collect your badges from the hospital staff; I assume they're with your belongings."

She walked to the door, and Hazard spoke. "You know that plaque you talked about? The one your chief had in his office."

Her shoulders stiffened.

"That quote about doing your duty and failure?"

Her hand closed over the knob.

"That's bullshit. And you know it's bullshit. And you didn't do your duty or even come close. I hope I'm being very clear with what I'm saying."

The door slammed shut and rattled the wall so hard that a four-process poster of Your Growing Body fell.

Somers shook his head and dropped back against the hospital bed.

"John—"

"You can't just play the game, Ree? Not once?" And then he rolled away from Hazard and put an arm over his eyes.

Hazard waited for the moment life would tick forward again, but it was still frozen. That clock inside him still had both hands shooting up at midnight. Outside, in the afternoon light, there was no owl and no blacked-out strips of night. Just broken asphalt.

Their second visitor came an hour after Cravens. Albert Lender looked like he'd died and been left in a swimming pool. It was that bad, the general effect of decomposition, like he was a man coming apart at every stitch. His face was puffy, his eyes raccooned with illness or fatigue or something else, something deeper, and his left arm had developed a shake that made Lender look late-eighties instead of late-forties. He slunk through the door and stayed there, as far away from them as he could.

"Somers, get my gun."

Somers didn't get Hazard's gun. But he did roll over and peel back his arm and study Lender.

"You look like shit."

Lender nodded. He traced under his eyes with his fingertips, and then he sagged. "Can I—" He cleared his throat, and some of the rust came off. "Can I talk to you?"

"Sure," Hazard said. "You can talk to us. And then you can walk out that door, find yourself a nice, quiet spot, and put a bullet through the roof of your mouth."

Groaning, Somers put his arm back over his eyes.

Hazard felt a pang of guilt. He nodded at the chair, and Lender sank into it. The vinyl squeaked again.

"I just—I had to tell someone. I had to talk to someone."

"No. What you had to do was keep your partner safe. What you had to do was watch her back. What you had to do was your job." Hazard shook his head. "Instead, you did what you did."

Lender started to cry. With tears running down his cheeks, he bent forward and sobbed silently.

"Stop that, you fucking crybaby. You put those bullets in her. You shot Swinney. And you killed her. You don't get to cry about that."

"I didn't mean for it to go that far." He was still crying, but the words had a forced, mechanical quality, as though Lender had rehearsed them. He probably had rehearsed them, Hazard thought, if not to use today than to use on himself, as a kind of self-hypnosis, a reassurance that he was still a good guy deep down. "I never meant for it to be like that. Especially not—especially not that. I never wanted anything like that. It was just little things. And I needed—I needed help sometimes. Just little things, but it made a big difference for me. And—" He cut off, his jaw sagging, his eyes staring out at the shitty stretch of asphalt.

"And then it wasn't just little things anymore," Somers said softly, sitting up now, his gaze fixed on Lender. "And then it wasn't even big things anymore. Then, one night, it was you and Swinney, alone in that cramped storeroom. And you had to make a decision."

"She wouldn't let it go. She just kept talking. She kept going in circles, about you, about Kjar, about the FBI. Those goddamn FBI. I'd listened to her talk on and off for all those years, and I knew when she was just talking to talk. And she was doing it. She was talking just to take up time, and you guys were coming, and I knew if I didn't do something, she'd—" His jaw sagged again. He was seeing something else. That storeroom, maybe, and the look on Swinney's face when her partner shot her. Hazard hoped that was the only thing Lender saw, waking or sleeping, for the rest of his life. "I need to know what to do. I need someone to tell me what to do so it's over."

"Tell Cravens," Hazard said. "Better yet, tell the county prosecutor. Tell somebody when you've got a dozen witnesses in the room, and hand over everything you've got on the mayor, and let them put you in a cell until they can find time to execute you. That's what you can do. And it might be the only good thing you do in your whole goddamn life."

Lender blinked, as though suddenly aware of Hazard, and he had a strangely hurt look in his eyes. "I'm a cop. I put away bad guys. Swinney and I, and before Swinney, I—I put away a lot of them. Meth dealers. Meth cooks. And before that, I worked a chunk of Smithfield. I did a lot of good."

"You're a fucking joke. You're a hypocrite, and you're so dirty you couldn't touch a lump of dog shit without making it smell worse. If you're not going to confess, then you might as well go put that bullet where I told you."

Dropping forward, Lender started to cry again. "Please, I just want to know how to make it right. I can help you guys. I can—I can make some of it go away. The stuff with Mikey, I can make it all right. And Cravens will have to let it go then. I can do that much. Put you guys back where you should be, and then you'll keep doing what you're doing. And that'll be because of me. That'll be something good I can do, one last good thing."

"Because of you?" Somers's voice was so cold that Hazard didn't recognize it. He had to look at his partner, see his mouth moving, to believe that the tones of horrible, frigid disgust were the man he loved speaking. "The things we do, you want some part of that? Not a chance, Al. Not ever. Get out of here. Get lost. Go lose yourself somewhere we'll never find you, you understand? Find a way to spend your life that might clean up some of the shit you've left for the rest of us."

The tremor in Lender's arm had grown worse; he clutched it across his chest and lurched to his feet. With two staggering steps, he reached the door and threw himself into the hallway.

"I thought we were supposed to play the game," Hazard said when the door had swung shut.

Somers grunted. "Don't push me right now." Then the blond man swung his legs over the edge of the bed and inched forward. Propping himself on the cane, Somers eased weight onto his injured leg. Then he shuffled to the cabinets, opened them, and poked around with the end of the cane.

"What the hell are you doing?

With another grunt, Somers raised the cane. From its end hung Hazard's trousers. Somers waved them in his direction. "Getting dressed."

"You heard Cravens." Somers's head disappeared into the cabinet, and he threw Hazard's shirt over his shoulder. A shoe followed.

"What? We're running before she realizes we have our badges in those cabinets?" The second shoe flew at Hazard's head and he caught it.

Somers emerged from the cabinet and fixed Hazard with a long look. "No, dummy. The mayor's doped up on painkillers, but he's talking."

It took Hazard one long, painful heartbeat. Then he grabbed the trousers.

"And if you think I'm working your zipper," Somers grumbled from inside the cabinet, "you're out of your damn mind."

CHAPTER FIFTY-TWO

JULY 5
THURSDAY
7:19 PM

THEY DROVE FIRST to the mayor's house. Somers kept asking why; Hazard didn't answer. He just thought. And thought and thought. Not about Cravens or Lender or any of the rest of it. About Sherman Newton. About Ted Kjar. About fire, and glass breaking, and the whoosh of the chemical extinguisher as it powdered the room. And about Jeff Langham, of course.

At the house, Somers had to help Hazard down the slope—his injured arms made it difficult to balance, so he leaned on Somers's arm and felt eighty. When they'd reached the bottom, the grass was long, whispering against Hazard's stained Nikes. It was dry. No one had watered it in days. Not since Sherman Newton had been stabbed in his bedroom. Hazard tried to remember it as it had looked that night: still wet, the water lacquered with moonlight everywhere except where someone had walked. Someone who had come to the house after Moraes had turned on the sprinklers, but before Hazard and Somers had inspected the grounds. Squeezing his eyes shut, Hazard thought. He remembered standing in the doorway. He remembered the dull throb in the heel of his hand where the Smith & Wesson had kicked. He remembered the ashy chemical drift from the extinguisher settling on him. And the chime, the ringing metallic chime of metal on glass as Somers—

"It's a summer night," Somers grumbled as they reached the back of the house. "This place shouldn't be giving me the creeps."

"They taped up the window." Hazard pointed to Newton's bedroom window, where opaque plastic provided a temporary barrier.

"The goddamn creeps. Can you at least tell me why we're here?"

"We're here because we've missed something."

"Ree, we didn't miss anything. We did good work. You did great work."

"The mayor opened his window."

"What?"

"That night. That's what Moraes told us: he heard something, and he went to investigate, and the window was open."

"Yeah. And he made the mayor close the window. And then, an hour later, Ted Kjar broke the glass. He crawled into the house and stabbed Newton. End of story."

"There was a fire."

"Are you ok?"

"And I was breaking down the door. What did you do?"

Somers screwed up one eye. "I was the one who hit his head. What's your excuse?"

"God damn it, Somers. What did you do?"

"I went to the Jetta. I got the extinguisher you kept there because that car was basically an engine fire waiting to happen. I came back and used the ladder because I knew you were trying to break down the door."

"And?"

"Come on, what's this about?"

"And you saw the broken window. You saw the fire. You saw me shoot Kjar."

"Don't start with that. If you start beating yourself up, I'm not going to wipe your ass."

"And you put out the fire, and you crawled through the window. Right?"

"Yes. You have a flawless memory. You are oh-so-brilliant." Somers ran his free hand through his hair. "Can we go before this place gives me more nightmares?"

"Why didn't you get cut?"

"What?"

"You crawled through a broken window. Why didn't you get cut?"

"Kjar—"

"I'm not asking about Kjar. I'm asking about you."

"I knocked out some of the broken glass. With the extinguisher; I used the canister to knock out the shards that were loose. Then I crawled through. What does this have to do with Kjar?"

"Can you get up on the roof?"

"Call Moraes."

"You're young and spry. Can you get up there?"

"I'm older than you. And I got shot in the ass."

"John."

One of Somers's patented smiles blazed out, and he swatted Hazard's butt. "You know I love to show off for you."

Without waiting for an answer, he limped over to the house. An aluminum ladder still lay alongside the foundation, and Somers maneuvered it awkwardly into place. The clunk rang out down the quiet street. Then he climbed, and it was obviously difficult for him. But he did it. And when he got to the level of the roof, he braced himself against it with both hands, panting.

"You ok?"

"Fine."

"You're pretty red in the face."

"God damn."

"Do you want to come down? Maybe I can ask Moraes to—"

"You goddamn will not. Why'd I get up here? What am I supposed to be looking for?"

"You'll see it."

"You're always so smart. It's not fun. You could have told me back at the hospital. You could have told me—fuck me sideways."

"I did tell you to fuck me sideways. Once. And you said I was too big to go across the bed that direction."

Somers reached into the gutter. The shard of glass was as big as his hand, and it flashed orange in the sunlight. "There's glass in the gutter up there. Looks like most of the window"

Satisfaction made a tight knot in Hazard's gut.

"Ree," Somers let the glass drop, and it tinkled against the other shards. "The glass is outside. Almost all of it. That means someone broke it from the inside. The force of the blow knocked the pieces out, onto the roof, where they slid and the gutter caught them."

"That's because Ted Kjar was already inside. Mikey drove him over here while Moraes was still on duty. They put up the ladder, Kjar climbed to the window—probably so doped he didn't know what he was doing—and they stuffed him somewhere. The closet, I guess. Then Mikey took down the ladder, drove away, and when Moraes came to check, all he saw was Newton enjoying the night air."

"Hey. Ree. It's us."

"What?" He blinked up at Somers, shook himself like a wet dog, and asked again, "What?"

"The whole thing. The ladder. Coming early and then coming again. That's about us. Cravens was insistent about us taking the third shift. That's the most dangerous shift, right? That's when the attack is most likely to take place. And, conveniently enough, that's when the attack does take place. We're right here. We're sitting in the hallway outside his room when Kjar attacks."

Calculations were taking place behind Hazard's eyes, and he nodded. "But they had to be sure. Things can go wrong. Timing can be off. Maybe the neighbors are outside having a barbeque. Or maybe there's a car idling up the block. So they set up everything in advance and made sure they had a chance in case there were delays. They made sure we were in the house."

Somers climbed down the ladder; when he reached Hazard, red patched his cheeks. "What if it wasn't Kjar that broke the glass from the inside?"

"Newton? You think he did it?"

"The glass breaks. We react. You kick down the door and you see Ted Kjar with a knife. And what do you do?"

Hazard's breathing had altered. Deepened.

"What do you do, Ree?"

"I shoot the motherfucker."

"Any cop would have done it. Any cop would have done it, Ree, but you—"

"He knew. He knew how I'd react when I saw the knife. He fucking knew. He used me. That son of a bitch—" His breath hitched. His whole chest hitched like someone had tied a knot around his heart and yanked once. "Why the fuck would he do that?"

"Because he's a son of a bitch like you said."

"No. Why take that kind of risk? He might die. Whatever he wanted to do that night, was it worth being stabbed multiple times?"

"I don't think that was the plan. I don't think that was the plan at all. Think about it. We heard the glass break. He's got our attention now. He goes back to the bed, and he and Kjar are going to do a little stage-acting. He wants it to look like Kjar is attacking him with a knife, and he wants you to see Kjar attacking him with a knife."

"And Kjar is out of his mind on drugs. He probably didn't even know what was happening."

"Mikey," Somers said. "He told the mayor that Kjar would be stoned. Out of his mind. Totally passive. All the mayor had to do was put a knife in Kjar's hand and shout for help. You'd break down the door and do the rest."

Hazard was shaking his head.

"But something went wrong," Somers said.

"What do you mean?"

"Pretend you're Newton. Pretend a noise wakes you up. The breaking glass, let's say. And pretend there's an intruder."

"That's not what happened, Somers."

"But that's what he wanted us to think happened. Are you pretending?"

"What's your point?"

"Are you pretending?"

"What's the damn point?"

521

"What do you say?"

"What?"

Somers gripped Hazard's arm. "What do you say? When you're waking up out of a sound sleep, when you realize someone is in your bedroom, when you're scared. What do you say?"

"How the hell should I know?"

Shaking him, Somers said, "What do you say?"

"Get the fuck off me."

"Ree."

"Help, I guess. Or maybe, who is that. Or, get out." Then he drew in a sharp breath, and his eyes flashed to Somers.

With a nod, Somers said, "You don't say, 'What are you doing?' You don't say, 'No. You can't.'"

"Jesus Christ."

Somers nodded again.

"Jesus fucking Christ."

Somers gave Hazard's good arm one last squeeze. "The mayor planned the whole thing. Something went wrong, but he planned the whole thing."

"He wanted to kill Ted Kjar."

"No, Ree. He wanted you to kill him. Kjar must have taken the pictures and confronted the mayor. Newton wasn't going to go quietly. He fired Kjar. He started setting everything in motion to make Kjar the suspect. And then, when it was time, he had Mikey pick up Kjar and drug him to keep him docile until they needed him."

"And the mayor must have set the fire." Hazard's breath was coming faster now; his cheeks felt hectic. "A fire makes everything else secondary. Maybe we would have been able to take Kjar's body with us; maybe not. But the crime scene burns down. If the mayor's lucky, we can't get Kjar's body, and so a lot of valuable forensic evidence is damaged. Everybody's looking at crazy Ted Kjar, who broke into the mayor's house, tried to kill him, tried to burn the place down. It would have worked, except Mikey had another idea."

"Once they had us in place," Somers said, pushing back his hair with one strong hand, "two perfect idiots, Mikey pumped Kjar full of everything he could think of. Mikey must have been shooting him up with every upper he could get his hands on. As soon as the downers started to wear off, Kjar had some kind of psychotic break. The mayor shouted. You kicked down the door. The rest of it played out the way Mikey wanted. Newton wanted a sham; Mikey gave him the real thing."

"But the mayor survived. Mikey must have realized that he'd screwed up. He must have realized the mayor would hunt him down when he recovered. Even if it was a mistake, Mikey must have known that much. He wasn't going to be alive much longer."

"That's why he went after me and Evie. Hollace told him what had happened with Jeff. It was the perfect solution: Mikey could blackmail the mayor, save his own skin, and still get a cut of the drug money moving through Dore County. Mikey just needed to kill Hollace, take me as leverage, and get you to provide him with the proof."

"The mayor's plan with Ted," Hazard said. "It might have worked. If Mikey hadn't double-crossed him, it probably would have worked."

"Best way to do your killing: get someone else to do it for you."

Hazard nodded slowly.

"Ree."

"We're going to see him."

"Ree, that's a bad idea."

"Right now."

Somers bitched and moaned and dug in his heels. Then they drove to Columbia. An orange sun dropped like the Times Square Ball on New Year's Eve; inside the Aston Martin, even with the visors down and the air blasting, Hazard sweated and shaded his eyes. Summer evenings were long, and the sun still had plenty of sky to drop, but already the world floated in a peachy haze. And when the sun did crack against the horizon, Hazard thought, when it finally did crack and disappear, would it be like the Times Square Ball? He wasn't stupid; he knew there wouldn't be music and fireworks and dancing. But the rest of it—would it be a new year? Would that part of Emery Hazard's life that had stalled all those years ago, would the hands on that clock finally shudder forward?

University Hospital was the only Level 1 trauma center in mid-Missouri. It was one of the best in the state. It was, of course, where they had Life-Flighted Mayor Newton when he had been stabbed, and it was here that he was making his recovery. Hazard's hands trembled, and he wrapped them around his knees. He hadn't played baseball much as a boy, and almost never as an adult, but there was something about the way his knees fit into his hands that reminded him of a ball socked home in a mitt. There was something steadying about it.

Next to Hazard, Somers drove quickly but carefully. The Aston Martin flowed through traffic, even as they entered Columbia and the streets grew more crowded. The blond man looked like he'd been through hell: dressed in bloodstained clothes, his face black-and-blue, each finger puffy with cotton at the tip where the nails had been ripped free. But he was smiling that typical Somers smile, and his eyes were distant and they were that perfect blue. That was Somers. Nothing kept him down long.

Hazard's thoughts turned black again. Would it be as simple as pulling a plug? That was the expression, but Hazard doubted it would be that easy. There would be backups. Failsafes. Doubtless there would be some sort of alarm to alert nurses and doctors. Hazard shivered; sweat trailed down the hollows of his temples, and one drop wicked left and stung his eye. He blinked. The shivering was getting worse, but all he could do was clutch harder at his knees. He visualized it, walking himself through scenarios. He would have to disconnect as many pieces of support as possible. And he would have to barricade the door. And he would have to trick Somers into leaving; Hazard wasn't going to drag the man he loved into this. It would probably be a murder charge.

But it would be worth it. Because Jeff deserved this. Jeff deserved justice. And Hazard deserved it too; he deserved a chance to lay down this burden. He deserved rest, even if it was broken by nightmares he had made. He would do this for all the boys who had been beaten, who had been shot, who had been dragged behind cars, who had been killed because they were different and because someone else was stronger. He would do this because now, finally, he was the one who was stronger. And at the end of it all, when the rust on the gears cracked and dusted away and that part of Hazard's life clicked into motion and he had a future again, it would be worth it. Even if it was a future spent behind bars. Even if it was a future without Somers.

He didn't know if he believed that bullshit, not that bullshit at the end especially. Somers drove lazily, one cotton-tipped hand at twelve on the wheel, the other ruffling his short blond hair. Hazard was shaking enough to fall apart, and holding on to his knees wasn't helping anymore. There wasn't anything solid enough to hold on to. He could hold on to the Rock of Gibraltar, and he'd still be shaking so hard he'd probably pull the damn thing down on top of him. Nothing in the world could—

Somers caught his hand, peeled it away from his knee, and wrapped his own around it.

Hazard wasn't shaking anymore.

University Hospital was made up of tan buildings and, shouldering over them like a younger brother that has grown too tall, a newer, glass and steel structure. They parked, and they walked through the slow boil of Midwestern heat, their clothes pasted to them, the asphalt frying their soles. It was a long, tortuous walk through corridors and up elevators and past a gauntlet of nurses, and when they finally reached the room, an older man in a blue uniform sat at the door, a newspaper folded over his leg. He stopped them, and he listened, and after seeing their badges and squawking into his radio and waiting for a response, he nodded and waved them into the room.

The last tension eased out of Hazard. Each breath came easily. Life buoyed him up. This was it. In a few minutes, everything would be over, and—

—Somers, dear God, Somers—

—life would start again.

The mayor had aged decades since the night of the attack. Shrunken, wasted, nothing more than old sticks tied with sinew, he lay with his eyes closed. An oxygen cannula hung from Newton's ears, and a tangle of wires and tubes ran beneath his hospital gown.

Hazard tried to trace them. Would removing a single one be enough? He wanted to laugh. He felt like he was floating, that's how goddamn good he felt, like he could float right out of this building. And why was he so caught up on the tubes? All he had to do was get Somers out of the room, block the door, and pick up a pillow. He'd make sure that was the end of it.

Newton's eyes flicked open. They were dark and hard and small, swallowed by puffy folds of flesh. He coughed, and one feeble hand hooked the air. Picking up the water pitcher, Somers poured a small amount and offered Newton the cup. He drank, smacked his lips, and studied them. The liver spots, Hazard noticed, had darkened, or the mayor's flesh was paler now, and they looked like someone had gone to town on Newton's face with a hole punch.

"Detectives," he said, and his voice was cracked and rough. "Thank you."

Those two words punctured Hazard's buoyancy. He shot out of the chair. "You motherfucker—"

With one arm, Somers caught Hazard, and he used the other to brace himself against the bed. "Sit down, Ree."

"I know, you old bastard. I know all of it."

"Ree, be quiet."

"I know you set up Ted Kjar—"

"Ree, for the love of Christ."

"I know you set him up so I'd kill him. I know you tried to have us killed, back when I was new here. I know—"

"Sit down," Somers said, shoving Hazard so hard that his knees hit the chair and he fell into the seat. "And shut up."

The door opened, and the old cop peered in. By the way he stood, Hazard knew he had one hand on his service weapon, even though the door hid most of his body. "Everything all right?"

Somers looked at Hazard. Hazard looked at Somers. And then Hazard looked at Newton.

With that wrinkled claw, Newton made the same hooking motion as before, and Hazard waited for the cop to draw and start firing or, best case, to pull out his cuffs. But after a moment, he realized Newton was trying to wave the cop away, and after another moment, the old cop seemed to understand as well. He nodded, eyed each of them again, and let the door swing shut.

"Can you do this?" Somers asked.

Hazard jerked his chin in a savage yes.

"Can you hold yourself together for this?"

Another fierce nod.

Somers pursed his lips, shook his head, and scrubbed at his hair. "You're a terrible liar."

"Maybe you should go."

Casting an eye at Newton, Somers shook his head. "Ree."

"You should go, John. Just answer a phone call. Hit the head. Take a smoke break."

Somers chucked Hazard on the chin. Tears made his eyes crystalline, and when he spoke, his voice was thick. "I don't smoke, you big, dumb Neanderthal."

"Yes," Newton croaked. His eyes glittered in those thick, fleshy pouches. "Go."

"Ree, I didn't come all this way so you could do something stupid. I came here so we could get a confession. Look at him; he's drugged out of his mind."

"Go," Newton said again.

"Get him talking. Get him on tape. Even if he's drugged, even if the confession isn't worth shit in court, it'll mean something. It'll be the end of him. Sometimes you pull one thread, and the whole thing falls apart. This is it."

"Go, John-Henry. Go take your smoke break." Newton struggled to grasp a plastic control, and the bed hummed, propping him up. Even that small effort left red puddling his cheeks. His breath hissed. "Leave me to talk to your faggot."

"We aren't going to talk," Hazard said.

Newton's lips quirked, and at first, the gesture was so spasmodic, so frighteningly intense, that he thought Newton was having a stroke. He waited for the lips to fall still and unresponsive, but they continued to crawl back from his teeth. And that was when Hazard realized the mayor was smiling.

"Go, John." Hazard planted one hand on Somers's and pushed, gently. He could still be gentle. For another minute, with the man he loved, he could still be gentle. "Please go."

"No. I'm not leaving, not unless we leave together. We can just talk to him, Ree. We came here for answers."

"John."

Confusion and hurt showed in Somers's face.

"Go," Hazard said with another gentle push.

"You're crazy. You're not thinking right. You're out of your head, that's what this is. You're out of your own head because the Emery I know wouldn't do this, wouldn't even be thinking about it."

"You don't know me. You never did."

"Bullshit. That's bullshit." He punched Hazard then, hard, high in the shoulder. "You son of a bitch. You stupid selfish goddamn son of a bitch. You don't get to do this. You don't get to be selfish like this. You and I, we're together. You're mine. I'm yours. That's what you said, Ree. Those are your words. And if you do this, you're doing it for you. Because you don't care about us enough not to do it." Somers hesitated, pulling his lower lip between his teeth, and he must have seen on Hazard's face the truth: that the words hurt Hazard; that they were killing words. And that they weren't enough. "You're a better man than this. You're better than he is."

The door opened, and the old cop was there again, hand hidden behind the door and doubtless resting comfortably on his service weapon. "What's all this shouting? What's going on?"

"My partner's upset," Hazard said. And he knew, now, why the cop was there. The universe was lining up: it was opening itself for him, rearranging everything to clear a path between Hazard and Newton. It was drawing the two men together like the only two coordinates that mattered, and Hazard heard, dimly, his third-grade teacher Mrs. Shelton explaining that the shortest distance between any two points was a line. "He needs some air."

"I'm not upset. I'm not going anywhere, not on your fucking life. Don't touch me—don't. Get your hand off me."

But the old cop was good at his job, and, more importantly, he had his hand on the service weapon—visibly now, the old revolver in plain sight.

"I'm not—Jesus Christ, Ree, just think about this."

The cop hesitated at the door, giving the mayor a long, hard look. Again, Newton crooked his hand, and the cop hustled Somers out of the room. The door clicked shut. A machine beeped. And it beeped again. And it beeped. And a fan whirred to life.

"You arranged to have me kill Ted Kjar."

Propped up by the hospital bed, Newton was barely able to hold up his head; it wobbled on the end of his neck, sinuous, serpentine, like a cobra called up from a basket. His eyes were hard as asphalt chips. He blinked once.

"You tried to have me killed. Somers too."

Another blink.

"You had Lender kill Swinney."

Nothing this time.

"You—you touched Jeff."

Newton's puckered lips moved soundlessly. And then, the front of the sentence clipped, "I fucked him. I fucked him every week. Twice a week. Three times." His head wobbled. "Do you have a recorder?"

"You fucked him."

"Did you have him first?" The lips petaled together like a horrible, rotting flower, and then they opened again. "I've thought about that. He was so tight. And so eager. He'd never tell me when I hurt him." Newton's eyelids drifted down and then snapped up. "And I hurt him. He liked that I hurt him, I think. Did you?"

An invisible fist closed around Hazard's throat. His voice squeaked out. "I loved him."

"But I fucked him first." The eyelids drifted down again. "I can see it in your face. Whatever you did, I did it first. Whatever he whispered in your ear, he heard it from me. Did you like how he used his mouth? His tongue?" His eyelids snapped up again, exposing those chips of asphalt. "I taught him that."

"You killed him. You killed him. The only good thing in my entire life, and you took him away." That invisible fist closed tighter. Hazard sucked air, but it was like drawing on a straw. Black nibbled the edges of his vision. "Mikey hurt him. Hugo hurt him. But what you did to him—"

Sherman Newton, mayor of Wahredua, settled his head against the bed, and his eyelids rolled up and down like windshield wipers. "He was bleeding. Not just his face. All of him. His little rosebud, torn open and bleeding. And I made him kneel on the carpet and let me fuck him like that. He cried and cried." The desiccated tip of Newton's tongue slathered his upper lip. It was like running sandpaper over roadkill. "I think he knew, by then. I think he knew what he deserved. He wanted me to love him, but a nasty boy like that—a nasty boy like that just needs Daddy's cock. Nobody loves a nasty boy like that."

"I loved him." Blackness chewed Hazard's vision down to tunnels. "I did. And he deserved more. He deserved to be held in my arms." Hazard's fingers curled around the chair, and the wood frame groaned. "He deserved to be protected."

"Coming to me," Newton mumbled, his eyes fluttering now like a man in a last, extreme fight against sleep. "Coming to my house. Waving his bleeding little rosebud like a flag for the whole world to see. Right there, on the front porch. Can't have that. Daddy can't have that. Daddy can't, not his bad boy, not his boy, bad—"

The rest of it was swallowed up by the shrill pitchiness in Hazard's ear. It wasn't a noise, not exactly. It was like a cicada song, so loud that it obliterated everything else. He slid his chair under the door handle, wedging it shut, and staggered across the room. He yanked the pillow from under Newton's head. The old man's skull bounced against the bed. Once, twice, Hazard fluffed the pillow, and then he leaned forward, settling the cotton case against Newton's face and leaning forward. He didn't need two good arms, not for this. He didn't need anything anymore. Nothing. And that was good because he was going to prison for this—if they didn't execute him. Nothing. He would have nothing. No sunlight, no air, no owls darting through gossamer light blanketing the night. And that was fine. He could lose all of it and if it meant justice for Jeff, if it meant that stopped clock would tick a new minute into Hazard's life, if it meant he could have some kind of future, even if it was short and blank and nothing at all, even if it meant no Somers—

No Somers. Not ever again. Not the boy, golden and perfect with steam curling up from his shoulders, that he had dreamed about and feared in high school. Not the man, golden and perfect, he had come back to. Not the dumb jokes. Not the teasing. Not the harassment. Not the smell of his hair and his sweat and that crushed-amber-and-salt cologne he wore. Not the slip and grit of his skin under Hazard's hand, not the dark lines on his chest, not the invisible tickling of hair under his navel. Not his mouth. Not his kisses. Not his heart.

He couldn't let go, though. All that hate. All those years of hating that had channeled him here, like stormwater forced along a drain, and it had to come out somewhere, it had to end somewhere. He couldn't let go of the damn pillow, even though his cheeks were hot and wet, even though he was shaking, even though a deep, visceral ache ran from neck to crotch like he was being ripped in half. He couldn't let go.

Somers.

John-Henry.

John. And the words on his chest in black calligraphy.

Learn to do well; seek judgment.

Hazard thought of the FBI video, the photographs from the cabin, the scrap of wallpaper that Newton had tried to remove. Justice felt far away. Justice might not work; it had been so long ago, and the evidence wasn't perfect, and it would be so easy for Newton to slip away. So much easier to take the pillow and end it now. So much better to let all that hatred and rage finally have vent.

Seek judgment.

For Somers, he could at least try.

Hazard turned. He didn't know where he was going, just that he had to turn or he'd do something he could never come back from. He staggered and fell. He knocked into a bulky piece of equipment, and it glided away on casters. He kept falling. He hit the wall, and his ass punched through the drywall, and Hazard sagged, no longer able to keep his footing. He sat there for a moment. One part of his mind was painfully aware of the mayor's ragged breathing. Still alive. The old bastard was still alive. And another part was painfully aware of his position, of how ridiculous he looked with his ass buried in plaster and him halfway to a squat like he'd been frozen taking the most ridiculous shit ever.

Then, fingers aching, he felt his hands come back to him, and the pillow fell, rolled off his shoe, and lay on the linoleum.

Newton's eyes, hazy, maybe even unconscious, locked onto him. Hazard dragged himself free of the wall; gypsum dust and fragments of plaster snowed down around his feet. He could taste it on the air, that fresh-construction smell, so much better than the closed-up sickness that hung around Newton. With a few painful, hobbling steps, he reached the door, wrestled the chair free, and stepped into the corridor.

Somers stood a few yards away under a wall sconce, a cylinder of light bathing his face as he shook his head and spoke into his phone. "You wanted to do something good, all right? So goddamn it, get up here and do something good. No. I don't want your fucking excuses, I want you to—Ree? Christ, Ree." The phone swung down to his side, and a tinny voice bleated once more, and Somers stepped towards Hazard. He walked like a man picking out his moves on a tightrope. "What—"

The old cop elbowed past Hazard and harrumphed. "What the hell did you get up to? Mr. Mayor?" His voice rose, the way the elderly often speak to the elderly, with a kind of condescending simpatico. "Mr. Mayor, are you all right? Well, you just go back to sleep then if you're tired."

Somers crashed into Hazard, arms wrapping tight, his face buried in Hazard's neck. Then, almost as quickly as he had come, Somers pulled away, slipping into the hospital room. He wiped at his face, where silver shine marked both cheeks, and then he wiped again and shook his head. Then he smiled. Then he wiped his eyes, and his smile got bigger, and he had to scrub his whole face with his sleeve. And he buried his face in his elbow and his whole body shook.

"John," Hazard said. He cupped the man's neck with one hand, his thumb running whorls through the short blond hair. "John, I'm sorry, I didn't—I wasn't thinking. Don't cry, all right? Listen, you can do whatever you want, say whatever you want, you can yell at me for the rest of our lives, just goddamn rip me apart, but don't cry, all right?"

Somers shook again, his face still hidden, and then Hazard felt a wave of suspicion.

"John?"

Shaking his head, Somers drew back his arm, obviously trying to compose his face, but another wave of laughter rolled through him. The old cop was staring at them in horror. Newton was staring at them with drunken, clouded interest. And Hazard suddenly had a horrible feeling of disorientation, the sense that this had all been a dream, that he was naked, that there was something he hadn't even—

"Your ass," Somers said again before breaking into giggles. He had to wipe at his face, and repressed laughter shook him so hard that he stumbled and caught himself on the chair.

"What?"

"Your ass. You big old fat ass. You broke the hospital with your ass."

The goddamn lunatic laughed so hard that Hazard had to take the keys, and he laughed for the whole first hour of the drive. And then he started bawling, and Hazard had to pull over and cradle Somers against his chest while sobs tore the blond man apart. It might have gone on like that forever, except thunder cracked the thick, humid air. No rain, but that crack of thunder set everything in motion: Somers wiped his face, and he kissed Hazard—short, bird-like pecks, and after every kiss he drew back and studied Hazard's face. And after three or four of those kisses he put the heels of his hands against his eyes and started shaking again.

"Ree, can you just tell me? Just tell me already."

"Tell you what?"

Somers stayed that way another minute, as though he couldn't stand to see Hazard. Then he dropped his hands, and the flesh around his eyes was still red and puffy from the healing wounds.

Hazard looked at him, waiting for something. For that feeling to wash through him: that everything was all right, that everything would be all right because he had Somers in his life.

But Somers was on the other side of the Aston Martin, and it might as well have been the other side of the moon.

And inside Hazard, both hands on the clock were still locked at midnight.

CHAPTER FIFTY-THREE

JULY 5
THURSDAY
11:39 PM

IN THEIR BEDROOM, Hazard lay awake. The gray wash of citylight, bright where a street lamp poked its head closest to the window, crawled with the shadows of moths. They had showered. Separately. They had dressed for bed. Silently. They had lain in the darkness. Distantly, no matter how the light tried to paste them together.

Hazard stood. The smoke-light lit him up, but it was a kind of dead light. The scar on his stomach wasn't even visible. The stiff dark hairs had grown up, choked it like weeds. If someone saw him in this light, Hazard thought, meeting his wavering shadow in the window glass, they might think he was whole. His bare feet scuffed the floor, and he found his filthy clothes, and he went through the pockets until his fingers brushed paper. He tried looking at the photograph in the dead light from the city, but it was a gray smear.

The darkness was deeper in the apartment's front room, and he sat on the sofa, elbows on knees. On the coffee table, his phone waited. He picked it up, unlocked the screen, and saw the waiting voicemail. Pressing the phone to his ear, Hazard listened.

It was Johnny Moraes talking low. "Three things, really quickly before I decide I'm fucking myself over. The chief is cutting you guys out of the loop. The mayor's dead—somebody shot him in his hospital room. And Hoffmeister and Lloyd just found Albert Lender. He was parked at the back of the station lot. It looks like he blew his own brains out." Moraes's voice went silent, and something scraped across the microphone, and then the voicemail ended.

Hazard listened to the message again. Then he deleted it.

His big feet padded through the darkness; he found gym shorts and a tank top—anything else was too damn hard with the cast and his injured arm—and at the apartment door, he slid into his shoes. From the rest of the apartment, only silence. He ran his fingertip along the photograph's edge. The paper was fuzzed and soft there. He wanted to do this next part alone. He slid back the chain on the door. He checked the Aston Martin's keys in his pocket. He'd be back in an hour, maybe less.

That was why he didn't understand how he found himself in their room, instead of going down the elevator, with the bed sinking under his weight, his hand at the small of Somers's back. The blond man's eyes flicked open, bright and sleepless in the gray surf of citylight.

"How long have you been awake?"

"Since the bed got cold."

Hazard ran his fingers up the bumps of Somers's spine. The blond man shivered; his chest pebbled, and maybe he really was cold. Or maybe it was Hazard's touch. Or maybe it was something else.

"Whatever it is, you can go do it. Whatever you need to do."

Hazard had something on his tongue, something snippy, something about how Somers would find a way to follow him and make sure he didn't do anything stupid. But what he said was, "I don't think I can."

Somers blinked. His turquoise eyes were still vivid, and they were the only spot of color in the whole world right then. He rolled onto his back, and Hazard's hand slid over the notched muscles of his abdomen, and he slid his fingers through Hazard's and squeezed once. "Let me get dressed."

They drove together in the Aston Martin, with the glow of the dash making it feel like they were swimming through the night. They followed the river out of town, and when they turned onto a gravel road, the overgrown weeds whispered like rain against the undercarriage. The moon, low, peered over the bluff ahead. They passed the Bouche farm, the abandoned silo gaping open at the sky, and they kept driving until they reached the straggle of cottonwoods at the edge of the bluffs. They rolled to a stop, killed the engine, and the river murmured and splashed below them. From here, the trees choked out the moon, and the river rushed past them, glossy and black. The air tasted like mud and the dust stirred up from the gravel.

Hazard walked along the bluff, and Somers's steps crunched the stones behind him. Ahead, the cottonwoods opened where some of the bluff had given way. Hazard stopped there. A breeze picked up, washing over bare arms and shoulders, and he was surprised that he could shiver in July. A moment later, heat washed over him as Somers slid an arm around his waist. The touch was tentative, and a moment later, Somers asked, "Is this ok? Do you want me to wait in the car?"

Hazard didn't answer. He couldn't answer right then. He just slung an arm around Somers. He had come here, less than a year ago, with Nico. He had thought, then, that he had moved forward, that life would go on, that he was free of the past. He had thought he had understood what had happened to Jeff. His slipped his hand into his pocket and brought out the photograph. Jeff, his hair tousled, his eyes bright, his shirt untucked, his jeans low on his waist. Jeff beautiful and happy and a stranger. That was the truth: Hazard had never really known him.

It had been so easy to trap Jeff in amber, to try to preserve him, the perfect glowing memory of him. It had been easy because Jeff had been his first love, because they had been young, because it had ended before they could fight, because of the suicide. The truth was harder; it mixed in his mouth like mortar, gritty and viscous. The truth was that Jeff hadn't been perfect. He had been young and foolish. He had liked that men liked him. Everybody liked Jeff; and Jeff had liked being liked. He had liked money for sex. He had liked Hazard, but he had liked Newton too, and he had liked being young and beautiful and desired. He had been a kid, a kid who had made mistakes. And it was so much easier to forgive when Hazard thought about it like that.

537

He pulled free of Somers, took the photograph in both hands, and tore it into strips. He tore the strips into pieces. Behind him, the wind kicked up again, brushing the indiangrass forward, the heavy stalks rustling. Hazard cupped his hand towards the wind, and the scraps of paper stirred, levitated, and shot away from him. For a moment he could see them in the air, glittering with moonlight, and then they were gone. He shivered again; even with Somers against him, he was cold.

Had it mattered, choosing justice over vengeance? Hazard didn't know. Legally, yes; Hazard was glad not to be facing a murder charge. In that sense, at least, it had made a difference. But he thought it had meant more than that. For him, anyway. And he didn't want to linger or think about it any longer. He ruffled Somers's hair and slipped free of the blond man's hold and started back to the car.

When they were back in the car, with the blue light from the dash picking out the lines around Somers's eyes, Hazard said, "The mayor's dead."

Somers's chest bucked with a sudden intake of breath, and he looked ready to say something. Then he scrubbed both hands down his face and looked at Hazard. All Hazard could see was Somers in the hospital, speaking into his phone, his face shot through with rage.

"Lender's dead too. He shot himself."

The blond man's voice was dry and unsteady. "I guess Lender finally couldn't take it anymore. Must have been driven by guilt. I bet it was killing Swinney; I bet that pushed him over the edge."

"John."

Heat rushed into Somers's cheeks.

"The sheriff said he thought we were dirty. Or that we might be dirty. That we were the kind most likely to get dirty."

"Well, we're not. We're not even close to dirty." But now Somers couldn't meet his eyes.

Hazard shifted the car into reverse. Indiangrass butted at the windows.

"All right. I called Lender." Somers opened his mouth, ready to say something else, and hesitated.

For a moment, Hazard felt everything between them balanced on a knife's edge. If Somers said what Hazard was waiting for—if he said something like, *I did it for you, I did it because of what he did to you, I did it because I didn't want you to have to do it*—it would be over between them. Maybe not immediately, but it would be over.

Instead, Somers shook his head. "I thought you were going to do something stupid. I told him he could take the heat for it. I told him it was one good thing he could do with his life. But you didn't, Ree. You didn't do it. But I never said—I never told him to—" Somers's chest bucked again. "I'll tell Cravens in the morning."

"No."

"No?"

"No."

"Ree, if you—"

"I said no, John. No goddamn way. Not a chance. Nothing we had would ever have stuck to him. He never would have even seen the inside of a courtroom. This, what happened with Lender, at least it was justice." But he felt like he was speaking lines in a play.

They drove in silence, and in that silence, Hazard could hear the stillness of that part of himself frozen at midnight. There was one last burst of rage, a leftover Fourth of July light show. It wasn't fair. He was done with all of it, done with Jeff, done with Mikey, done with everything from his past. He had come here, back to this shit town, to find a way to get that part of his life ticking forward again. Then the fireworks turned to cinders. Then the cinders died. And then it was just a cold, dark July silence inside Emery Hazard, and he realized those hands twinned at midnight were broken, not frozen. He realized that he was broken. And just like that, he was too tired to care anymore.

CHAPTER FIFTY-FOUR

JULY 6
FRIDAY
9:11 AM

CRAVENS WAS IN HER OFFICE when Hazard got to the station. Nobody stopped him as he walked into the building. Orear, who now occupied Murray's spot, didn't even look up from his paper. Carmichael waved as she walked towards the break room, but she didn't stop to talk. Thank God. A wave of energy was carrying Hazard, and it was going to shatter whatever it crashed into first.

The door opened and shut silently. The air was still, and it smelled like fresh linen. Cravens had dusted since the last time Hazard had been in here; the pictures of her nieces and nephews had all shuffled a little to the left, and the shelves had a fresh gleam. She looked up from her computer, and her hands froze on the keyboard for half a second before she said, "You're suspended."

Hazard took a seat. He touched his pocket, felt the reassuring solidity of what he carried there, and looked at the chief.

"Go home, Emery."

"There wasn't any justice for Jeff."

"Is that one of your cases? Don't worry; Moraes and Foley are filling in for you, and they'll work it."

"It's not one of my cases. I'm talking about Jeff Langham. Sherman Newton killed him when he was sixteen. Newton made it look like a suicide."

This time, Cravens's hands froze and stayed frozen.

"He confessed, in a way."

"He was medicated—"

"There are photographs. There's the wallpaper. There's the video."

Cravens didn't flinch. Her shoulders squared up, and she let her hands settle in her lap, and she turned her full attention on Hazard.

"I know it was you. I can't prove it. But I know. You knew nobody would touch it while Edgcomb was chief. He would just make it disappear. So you sent it to Graham; he was already investigating the mayor for fraud. You might not be able to see the mayor's face, but you're not stupid, and neither is Graham. You both knew what you had. You just needed a way to make the connection solid. And then Graham's investigation got shelved, and he got pulled to work on something else. But he didn't forget. What's on that tape, nobody could forget. That's why Graham came back. Not because of white-collar fraud. That's not the kind of thing a guy carries around his whole career. But kids. The things they made those kids do. He remembered that, and he came back."

"I don't know what you're talking about." Her voice was brittle and high. "You're talking about wallpaper. About a poor kid that killed himself almost twenty years ago. You're not making any sense."

"Don't do that."

She bit her lip.

"Sheriff Engels told me that the really good cops and the really bad cops are the ones most likely to go dirty. I still don't know if I agree with that. He thought Somers and I were dirty. Or I guess he thought we might be."

"I'm going to tell you right now that you should stop talking before you say anything to incriminate yourself. During the investigation into your recent behavior—"

"No. We're done with that. All of it. Right now, I just want you to listen. I think he was right in a way. When you're good at the job, when you care about the job, it eats you up. The wins are never big enough because you're always winning after somebody else lost. And if you're good, you start to see the ones who get away. And you start to wonder if any of it matters. How can it matter? A guy kills his girlfriend, and I put him away. The girl's still dead, though. And that guy gets to keep on breathing." Hazard stopped. He had to stop. The pain in his chest was too great.

"And?" Cravens said, shifting to look at the wooden top of the desk, her hands outlining the blotter. "How do you deal with that, Emery? You've been a cop how long? Ten years? Twelve? And a detective maybe half that? Less? How do you deal with it after twenty years? After thirty years? How do you deal with it when Lloyd Rebarchek, so stupid he peed uphill—literally—while he was working a stakeout, spent seven hours in his own piss, gets bumped up to detective before you because his dad and Edgcomb's dad have hunted together since high school?"

This was why, Hazard realized. Somers asked him why he couldn't play the game. Part of it, he knew, was that he was arrogant. Part of it was that he was too detached, conditioned to be antisocial. But part of it was this, something he couldn't name but that he could taste in the air, a kind of cancerous hunger in Cravens. It was a hunger that led to compromise after compromise—a thousand backroom deals with the devil, a thousand petty betrayals of truth and honor. None of them was a fatal sin. But you died from a thousand cuts just as well as you died from a blow to the heart. Lender was proof of that. Cravens was proof of that.

"But Rebarchek got out a year after that," Hazard said. "And you got to be detective. Then you got to be chief. And Newton got away with everything because you covered up for him. You covered up the old stuff, everything you knew about, and you made sure he stayed squeaky clean after that. You even helped him out with this big plan. You set up me and Somers. You were the one who insisted we take third watch. You made sure we were there. You made sure I was the one who put a bullet into Ted Kjar."

Cravens rolled back in her chair; the casters squeaked on the anti-static mat. She hunched at the waist, her eyes fixed on him, the posture of a feral animal backed into a corner. This was it, Hazard realized. This was the chance to see if Sheriff Engels was right about good cops and bad cops. Hazard knew which buttons to push. It was like some sort of sixth sense had activated for him and he knew—a hundred percent, guaranteed—what to say. That he had talked to Graham, and that the FBI had figured out, years ago, who had sent the video. That Hazard had proof. That if Cravens didn't put him and Somers back in rotation, the investigation totally dropped, that he would send everything to the press and let the new mayor decide if it was worth keeping her as chief. It would work. Another day, another place, another situation, it might not. But here, it would work perfectly; Hazard felt it in his bones. All he had to do was open his mouth. And it would be the next step down a dark staircase. And Hazard knew that whatever he told himself, he would never come back if he did.

He checked his pocket.

He knew, too, there was another way.

"You were a very good detective."

Cravens blinked, and her lips pursed. Not quite as feral now. A bit confused, perhaps. Suspecting a trap.

"You are a good chief. Not when it came to Newton, but when it comes to the rest of it. This is your chance to be a great one. Newton is dead. Lender is dead. You've got a clean shop, and you've got good cops, and you can do great work. You can bring justice to a town that hasn't had it for a long time. That's what you wanted, and now you can have it."

The casters chirped as she inched closer to the desk. Her eyes were rainwater again, and she blinked rapidly. Her breaths huffed, but when she spoke, her voice was hard. "I can't just put you back, Detective Hazard. I can't. There are too many questions. Too many things that went wrong. Too many problems. You and Detective Somerset are good cops. You'll come through all right—maybe a slap on the wrist, maybe, worst case, you get knocked back to patrol for a while. But you'll come through. And what you said, we'll do it together: we'll make this place better."

Hazard touched his pocket once more. Then he drew out his badge and shook his head. "There is one other way."

CHAPTER FIFTY-FIVE

JULY 6
FRIDAY
10:31 AM

HAZARD FOUND SOMERS at the park, pushing Evie in a swing. Already, the sun baked the air. Evie's cheeks were red, and sweat glistened at Somers's hairline. When Hazard reached them, Somers pecked at Hazard's cheek, fumbled the swing, and Evie skewed sideways. Hazard caught the chains, steadied her, and gave another push.

"Let's try that again."

Somers grinned, but uncertainty was written all over his face. He gave another quick peck.

Gaze focused on Somers, Hazard gave Evie another push, enough to keep her swinging for a minute, and wrapped both arms around Somers. "Try a little harder."

"Ree—"

"All right, I will." And he kissed Somers on the mouth, with just enough tongue that he felt Somers melt and harden against him in equal measure. When Hazard pulled back, he saw confusion in Somers's face. Confusion and fear.

"You were gone this morning. I thought—I don't know what I thought. I was worried."

Hazard jerked his head at Evie, who was shrieking with delight as the swing carried her. "No preschool?"

"Not today."

"Really?"

"Yeah." Somers smiled, but he was still eying Hazard with that same look of confusion and fear. "I was thinking about something else. Somebody else."

"Really?"

"He's pretty much the only thing I think about except for her."

Hazard raised an eyebrow. "Really?"

"Look, Ree, I've been thinking about last night. About all of it. What I did—"

"You didn't do anything. You didn't make Lender take money. You didn't send Lender to that meeting with Swinney. You didn't put him in a room with Sherman Newton. And you sure as hell didn't put a gun in his hand."

"Ree, I called him. I—"

"You called him because you were afraid for me. Maybe because you were afraid of me. And you said it because—" Hazard's voice thickened. "Because you love me."

"Yeah."

Evie squawked as the swing slowed, and Somers turned to give her another push.

Hazard slipped behind him, arms tightening around Somers's chest, and spoke low into the blond man's ear. "I love you. More than anything else in the world, I love you. And I'm also pretty goddamn good at figuring things out, and I figure you didn't do anything wrong. Lender did what he did. That's all."

Somers shook in Hazard's arms, twisting his head away, but Hazard didn't let him go.

"I fucked up, Ree. I really fucked up. Can you let go? I just—Ree, let go, will you?"

"Keep struggling like that and you're going to hurt my arm."

Relaxing against Hazard, Somers said, "That's a cheap move."

"I like you right where you are." For a moment, Hazard let his chin rest on Somers's shoulder, and he noticed the way Somers's body vibrated at his touch. "Are you all right?"

"Yeah. I mean, I don't like what I did. But I don't—I don't think it was bad, not completely. Can you feel shitty about something, but not a hundred percent?"

Hazard kissed him where his neck met his shoulder, and Somers trembled again.

Then Hazard pulled something from his pocket and pressed it to Somers's shirt.

Somers stared down at it. He fingered the badge. "What did you—"

"I talked to Cravens. You're back. No investigation. No discipline. Whenever you're physically fit, you'll be back catching cases."

Spinning fast enough to break Hazard's grip, Somers planted both hands on Hazard's chest. "I'm back?"

"John—"

"What about you?"

"John—"

"What about you, Ree?"

"John—"

"You selfish piece of shit. You didn't even ask me."

"John—"

"You didn't even talk to me. You didn't even let me know in advance. You just walked in there like goddamn Emery fucking Hazard, just did what you wanted to do, just did what you decided without any consideration for anyone. Is that about it? What else did you do? Are you going to be arrested? Am I supposed to wait while you serve time? What did Cravens want besides your badge?"

"John—"

"No, I don't even want to know." Evie's swing had stalled, and she was squalling now, her plump legs kicking the air. "You selfish motherfucker, you can't do stuff like this. You don't get to do things like this, not to me. You—"

"John, I can't. I can't do it anymore. I—"

"Just fuck off, Emery. Just fuck off for a while, all right?"

And Somers scooped up Evie, who was working herself into a royal fit, and marched towards the car.

Hazard followed him. At the edge of the park, he stopped, shielding his eyes against July sunlight, to read a banner that had been strung across Lafayette Street.

Special Election for Mayor: Vote Naomi Malsho. She's Got Your Back!

CHAPTER FIFTY-SIX

JULY 6
FRIDAY
7:42 PM

FOR HAZARD, THE REST of that day was hell. He followed Somers home. Somers wouldn't talk to him. He drove with Somers to the store. Somers wouldn't talk to him. He trailed Somers down the diaper aisle, ignoring the stares from the other Piggly-Wiggly customers, and Somers still wouldn't talk to him. The only hiccup in Somers's silence came when Hazard couldn't get his sneakers off, not with both arms injured, and Somers just grunted and told him to sit. When Hazard flopped onto the sofa, Somers knelt, peeled off the sneakers, and tossed them in the closet. And then he said, "If you'd stop tying your damn laces so tight, you wouldn't have so much trouble."

Yes, the rest of that day was hell. They orbited each other. Somers would take Evie into the spare bedroom to play. If Hazard followed, Somers would leave. Not right away. Not with any visible emotion. But after a few minutes, he would leave, and most of the time, he took Evie with him. Hazard couldn't watch TV; it felt like an intrusion. He couldn't read; his mind whirled too much. He couldn't leave and walk for the same reason he couldn't sleep: because if Somers was out of sight for too long, he might disappear forever.

So Hazard cleaned. He'd developed a good routine over the years, with Alec, with Billy, a routine that kept him moving and busy and visible. It was important to be visible. It was important that Alec or Billy—

—or Somers—

—see Hazard working, see him sweating, see him suffering. They needed to know he was being punished, that he was punishing himself. And then, eventually, if he went hard enough and long enough, they'd relent.

He started in the bathroom, dusting Ajax in the tub, wetting a sponge, and scrubbing. His broken arm was out of the question, so he worked the sponge with his bad arm. Pain flashed up as soon as he began. It kept going, getting hotter and brighter, and Hazard just dug in deeper. He was going to make this tub gleam. He was going to make it shine.

After the tub, the tiled wall.

After the wall, the toilet.

After the toilet, the sink.

His arm was agony from shoulder to hand. Cracks opened between his fingers as he let the sponge drop; Ajax was hell on bare skin, and the chemical burns were raw. After stretching his back, Hazard shuttled the bathmat and the trash can and the toilet brush out of the bathroom. He eyed the tile. And the grout. Especially the grout. He shook out more Ajax, wet the sponge again, and got on his knees.

Footsteps moved through the apartment, coming closer to the bathroom. Hazard's heart pumped faster. Good. Somers would see. Somers would see him on his knees, would see his hand blistered from that damn Ajax, would see him scrubbing the grout, and then Somers would know. He'd know Hazard was sorry. He'd know Hazard loved him. Hazard knew enough about relationships to know that his plan would work: if he'd just humiliate himself enough, abase himself enough, Somers would eventually let the past be the past.

The footsteps slapped the bare wood, stopping behind Hazard. And then they moved into the bathroom. Hazard's heart thumped to the top of his chest. Somers's smell mixed with the Ajax. There was a whisper as the door glided shut.

"Give me that."

"What?"

"Don't act stupid. Give me that."

Hazard bent forward, hoping it looked like his attention was focused on the sponge, the tile, the goddamn grout, anything but what he was really focused on: John-Henry Somerset, who was the center of the world, the only thing in the whole universe worth paying attention to. "I'm in the middle of something."

"You're in the middle of fucking up your hand. Give it to me." Somers leaned over him, grabbed the sponge, and threw it in the tub.

"I wasn't finished."

"Yes, you were. You goddamn fucking were finished, Ree. Get up." Grabbing Hazard's wrist, Somers pulled him to his feet. He hit the faucet so hard, Hazard expected the handle to fly off. Then he shoved Hazard's hand into the water; it foamed, and amidst the blue Ajax bubbles, pink splashed the porcelain.

"I'm just—"

"I know what you're doing. God and Jesus Christ, Ree." He pumped soap into Hazard's hand and wiped the cleaner away. Then he thrust it under the water again. This time, there was more of the pink splashes. After a minute of letting the water run, Somers held up Hazard's hand for inspection. He grunted. Then, patting it dry with a towel, he said, "I couldn't put a bandage on those even if I wanted to."

"It's fine."

"It's not fine, Ree. Every time I turn around, it's—" He dropped the towel and sighed. "No more of this crazy self-destructive bullshit, all right?"

"I wasn't—"

"Don't. Don't lie to me. You lie to me, and I'll goddamn tie you up and put you to bed right now. Do you understand me?"

For the first time since the park, anger burned off the thick fog in Hazard's head. He met Somers's eyes silently.

"Do you understand me?"

"Yes, goddamn it."

Somers rotated Hazard's wrist. In a softer voice, he asked, "How's your arm?"

It took a moment for Hazard to work out the word. "Hurts."

"Your hand?"

"Hurts."

"You deserve it, you big idiot. No more of this. I catch you with a sponge or a mop or a bottle of Windex, and I'll damn well shove it up your ass. And not in a kinky way, you perv." He stretched his hand flat on Hazard's chest, and Hazard couldn't tell if it was to push him away or to gather a handful of his shirt and draw him in. In the end, it was neither; he swung open the door and left, saying, "Watch a goddamn documentary and leave me the hell alone for a while."

"I was trying to leave you alone," Hazard grumbled to himself.

"You were not," Somers's voice came from the other room. "And if you say that again, I really will tie you up and put you to bed."

After that, Hazard watched a documentary. He didn't even know what it was. It could have been anything. It could have been that one he'd picked up the week before at the library, the one on chemistry. *Nobel and the Noble Gases.* Or maybe it was the one about the woman who escaped from the Japanese theater cult: *Saying No to Noh.* It could have been anything. Nothing. It could have been black glass. It could have been goddamn static like what had played inside Hazard for the last few days. All he saw was twenty-four hours on repeat.

When the sun got in his eyes, he realized it was getting late. In the spare bedroom, Somers was talking low to Evie. Singing. He was singing, and Hazard had never heard him sing before, hadn't known that Somers had a sweet, husky tenor. Hazard hunched on the sofa because that sound hurt so much that it was physical. It scared him because he didn't know if anything had hurt him that much. Not losing Billy. Not losing Alec, for God's sake. Not even Jeff, not his death, not even learning the truth about him. None of it had come close. They were pinpricks. They were paper cuts. This, listening to this and knowing he'd lost it for good, this was somebody sawing straight up through Hazard's breastbone, ready to kick in his chest and rip out his heart.

He got to his feet and made it to the door. He dragged his sneakers out of the closet and saw that they were tied. Loose, floppy bunny ears. Tied just right so that Hazard could shove his feet in, walk around without them falling off, and kick them off when he got home. Hazard never used loose, floppy bunny ears. In his whole life, Hazard hadn't tied laces like that. And that left only one option: at some point, Somers had tied them. And that little fact tickled the detective part of Hazard's brain. The part of his brain that he had trained and coached and strengthened, the part of his brain that reveled in the cool rush of logic and analysis, of seeing the pieces fall into place, that part of his brain stirred and tried to wake.

Hazard wanted to ignore it. He wanted to put on the shoes, open the door, and walk out of the apartment. He wanted to leave before the pain got too big for him and he couldn't handle it anymore.

But Somers had tied his shoes. He'd tied the laces. At some point after helping Hazard take them off, at some point after snapping at him, at some point during the afternoon, Somers had walked to the closet and pulled out the shoes and done the laces just right. Why?

So Hazard could leave? Or because, even when he was angry, Somers was still trying to take care of him?

Fuck, fuck, fuck, fuck.

Leaving was easy. It would be easy to walk out. It would be easy to chalk this up as just another failure. It would be easy, down the road, to say that this was inevitable. It was never going to work out—that's what he'd tell people. He'd say something about how they were too different, about how they'd had such a shitty past, how people never really change. He'd pat himself on the back and feel like a martyr. He could even tell them how ungrateful Somers was, how he'd tied the shoes and all but shoved Hazard out the door. They'd like that. The pretty boys would coo and pet his shoulders and tell him he deserved better.

And just like that, everything clicked and settled. Maybe there was someone better out there. Maybe there was someone easier. Maybe there was someone who fit Hazard in a way Somers didn't. Maybe that person was out there, and he wouldn't have to carry around the past, wouldn't have to worry about what would claw its way back into their lives.

But Emery Hazard doubted it. And even if there was someone better, Hazard didn't want him. He wanted the guy who told him he was being a dick. He wanted the guy who tied his laces so he wouldn't fall. He wanted the guy who'd lived through the past, seen the worst of the past, and still kept coming. He wanted Somers.

So he kicked the shoes back into the closet, and he went to sit on the sofa.

Silence came from the spare bedroom. And then the door opened, and Somers slipped into the living room. Dusk turned everything to copper. It picked out motes of dust in the air. It threw stark shadows against the wall. It painted Somers from head to toe. He raked fingers through his hair, crossed the room, and settled on the coffee table facing Hazard. He ran fingers through his hair again, this time with a little shake at the end, and he spoke towards the carpet.

"I'm going to quit too."

The words were so surprising that all of Hazard's planned speeches disappeared. "What the fuck are you talking about?"

"I'm talking about doing the only thing that's right. We're partners. What we did, we did together." He swallowed, his Adam's apple making a painful-looking jump in his throat. "All of it except that phone call. That was me. If anyone's leaving, it's me."

"What the fuck," Hazard said again, pausing because he wasn't even really sure what he was hearing, "are you talking about?"

"I understand what you did. Going in there, taking the heat, letting Cravens pile shit on you. And in exchange, I get to go back. I understand, Ree." He flattened his hands over his eyes. "Christ, I love you for it, even if it does make me want to knock some sense into you." He wiped hard, his hands gliding down the planes of his face, the tear tracks smeared and glistening. "But I'm not going to let it go this way. You're a better detective. You're the best detective. Period. The best I've ever met. You're the one that's going to stay on the force. I'm going in there tomorrow morning, and I'm going to tell Cravens exactly what happened, and if she doesn't like it, I'm going to scream to every paper I can find exactly what I know about this town and what's been happening here." A hint of the old Somers surfaced in his smirk. "I think she'll see reason. She'd damn well better; she's going to need you."

"John." Hazard paused. He was still trying to figure out where everything had changed. "Baby—"

Somers hiccupped, the sound somewhere between a laugh and a sob. "Baby? Have you ever called me that before?"

"Baby—"

"I like that. I like hearing you call me that."

"Baby, you're being a goddamn moron."

Pink scudded along Somers's cheekbones. For a moment, anger tightened the corners of his eyes, and then he laughed. A real, big, full laugh. And he wiped his eyes again—hard again—and said, "All right. That's not what I thought you'd say."

"What did you think I'd say?"

The pink deepened to red. "I thought—I don't know, Ree. I thought you'd see reason. What you're doing doesn't make any sense. You're the best—"

"Drop that bullshit right now. John, I quit today because I wanted to quit. I needed to. I had to, I think."

A full minute ticked past. Hazard's pulse beat in his throat. It beat behind his left eye. He thought maybe something was wrong inside him, maybe a coronary, maybe a stroke. He reached out, his pulse so thick in his throat he could barely breathe, and caught Somers's hand.

"You wanted to quit?"

"I guess."

"You guess? You went in there, you threw down your badge, you made some kind of bargain to get me my job, and you guess?"

"I don't know. It's like something's broken inside me. It's like something stopped."

"Ree—"

"I thought finding out about Jeff, I thought that would make things better. I thought that was why I came back here."

"Ree, you're not broken."

Hazard shook his head.

"Listen, Ree, you're upset. What we've been through, what you've been through, Christ, I can't even imagine. You need some time. You need to step away. I get it. But you don't need to quit. You're too good at this. You're so good you—you have a responsibility to do this."

Hazard shook his head harder. "I thought something would change. Inside me, I mean. I thought I'd get to the truth, I thought I'd finally understand, and I thought I'd change. I thought this thing inside me, whatever it is, this broken thing would finally be fixed. I thought I could move forward with my life."

"You can move forward with your life. You can. With me, with Evie."

"I know. God, I know. Thank you for saying that. Thank you so goddamn much because it's the only thing—" Hazard shivered so hard that the sofa groaned. "I did it, John. All the things I set out to do when I came back here. I did them: I found the truth about Jeff, I found out who was responsible, and he got justice. Don't look away from me. He did. That son of a bitch got what he deserved. But nothing changed. Inside me, everything stayed the way it was. And I realized all those things I came back for, all the reasons that brought me home again, they didn't mean shit."

"It's me, right?" Somers was crying now and not trying to hide it. He dashed his arm under his nose and honked. "It's me, that's what you're trying to say? You can't—you can't get past it, what I did to you. You couldn't forgive Mikey, right? So why should you forgive me? That's ok. I can't ask that of you. That's not fair for me to ask that. You can hate me, Ree. You can hate me every day for the rest of your life. I deserve it. But don't leave me, all right? Please don't leave me."

It was like a flash had gone off, one of those old-fashioned photograph flashes that lit up like lightning and hazed the air with smoke. Hazard could barely see. Dazzled. That was the word for it.

"For fuck's sake," he breathed. And then his hand closed around Somers's, and he pulled. Somers resisted for a moment, but Hazard kept pulling, and the blond man slid forward and landed in Hazard's lap. He brushed at the blond man's face, at the platinum tracks of tears, and Somers jerked his head away. Hazard stroked his cheek again. He stroked the short blond hair. He stroked the spot on Somers's neck that he knew Somers liked. He stroked the line of his jaw. And by then, some of the shaking had left Somers, and when Hazard ran his thumb along the wet lines on his face, Somers didn't pull away. "For fuck's sake, I love you John-Henry Somerset. You. The one right here, right now. You want me to say I forgive you? I forgive you. Everything. Anything. It's gone. I love you. I love you, John. That's all. That's all I can say, and I'm going to keep saying it until—"

Somers turned his head so suddenly that his kiss caught Hazard mid-speech. It was a tender, hesitant kiss. And then it grew. It blossomed into something hot. Somers's hand slid across Hazard's chest, past the collar of his shirt, his fingers running through the stiff, short black hair like a wildfire. Somers broke the kiss; he pulled back. Hazard's mouth was sand; his lips ached like the worst stone-bruise of his life. He wanted more.

Looking into Somers's eyes, Hazard heard again, *Fuck me so I bleed.*

Somers turned his head away, red flooding into his cheeks. He struggled to plant his feet, and he shimmied backward, trying to get off Hazard's lap. "I know you don't want to—I know you don't want me like that, not after the way I acted last time. I shouldn't have thought—"

Hazard caught the hem of Somers's shirt and tugged. Somers squirmed and shimmied, and the shirt fell on the floor. Hazard let his hands fall on Somers's chest. His thumb and forefinger compassed one of Somers's nipples. He squeezed, just hard enough that the bud puffed tenderly, and Somers moaned and spread his legs. His eyes blackened, the pupils swallowing the turquoise. Hazard squeezed again, harder, and Somers groaned again and found his wrist, clamping down, the message clear: he wanted more. This time, Hazard used both hands, and Somers humped the air, his face twisted in a mask of pain and pleasure.

The blond man slid forward, his dick hard and tenting his jeans, and he rutted against Hazard's stomach. One of his hands came up, mussing Hazard's hair, fingers twining through the locks. He forced Hazard's head back as he ground himself against Hazard's body. Hazard blinked through the dusting of hair in his eyes, meeting Somers's gaze. He let his hand rove down, over the rippled muscles in Somers's stomach, to the hard length of Somers's erection. He palmed it through the denim, and Somers grunted and thrust into his hand.

"Please," Somers whimpered, his hand tightening with need, tightening until Hazard's hair pulled painfully and tears stung the corners of his eyes. Somers didn't seem to notice. He rocked against Hazard's touch, his whole body shaking. "Please, Ree. Please."

Hazard twisted the button, let the jeans pop open. He massaged Somers's abdomen with the heel of his hand, applying pressure just above the band of Somers's boxers, where golden blond fur peeked above the elastic. Hazard pressed hard. And then harder. Somers cried out sharply and bucked.

"My cock, Ree. For the love of fuck, you fucking tease, get your hand on my cock."

With a grin, Hazard rolled his hips, spilling Somers onto the sofa. In one efficient movement, he stripped Somers of boxers and jeans, leaving the blond man naked on the sofa. Hazard knelt over him, and Somers reached up, his hand snaking through the opening in Hazard's athletic shorts, his fingers slipping through the Y in Hazard's boxers, his touch like lightning on Hazard's dick. He felt himself pulse, and Somers's eyes widened as he rubbed the wet across the sensitive head, and Hazard roared.

"Fuck me," Somers breathed.

Fuck me so I bleed on your cock.

"Fuck me because I'm yours. Fuck me like I'm yours, Ree. I'm yours, yours, I'm only yours, so please, for the love of God, fuck me."

Growling, Hazard brought up his knees, forcing Somers's legs back and towards his chest, exposing the blond man. Hazard adjusted his weight, trying to balance himself on his forearms so he could reach down. He shifted. Pain flashed up first his bad arm, and as Hazard jerked back at the sensation, he planted his broken arm, and the second wave of pain was so intense that he toppled sideways, planting his face in the sofa.

"Christ, Ree. Christ. Are you—are you all right?" Somers helped him up.

"Fuck this fucking cast and fuck my fucking arms." Hazard wobbled. He couldn't support himself on both arms. He couldn't even push himself upright. "John—I can't, I mean, it's not that I don't want to, but—"

Laughing, Somers swung himself across Hazard's body, straddling him. His hand laced around Hazard's dick, pumping once, and Somers smirked.

"Looks like I'll have to do all the hard work." His grin was so hot it was smoking. "As usual."

The sex was slow and awkward and tender. Somers set the pace, and he had a devilish way of bringing Hazard closer and closer without giving him any relief. Hazard felt himself winding tighter and tighter. His injured hands clasped at Somers's hips, trying to force him to go faster, demanding, insisting, but Somers would just laugh and push his hands away and take control again. That tightness coiled at the center of Hazard's chest. He could visualize it compressing there, coiled like a spring. Everything else was darkness. Everything except Somers's perfect body sliding onto Hazard's, everything except that coiled kinetic explosion at the center of Hazard's chest.

"I love you," Somers murmured, rocking faster. "I love you." Faster. "I love you."

"I—" Hazard tried to say, and then he bucked up into Somers, and the coil of kinetic energy in his chest exploded, and the world whited out.

They lay there like that, together for the first time since—

Together, really together, for the first time. Ever.

And when Somers drifted off, Hazard stroked the blond hair lightly, not wanting to wake him, not wanting to stop touching him. He was surprised to find himself thinking of the future. They'd find a small house, a fixer-upper. They'd have a yard, and Evie would have a swing, and maybe Hazard would plant a garden. Hazard would keep Evie at home with him; no need for a preschool or sitters. When the time came, he'd walk her to school. They'd have to make sure they had three bedrooms because in the shadows Hazard thought he saw a little boy. And Somers would work; he'd have to. He was too good of a cop not to keep working. And when the tough cases came—well, Emery Hazard still loved logic and reason and analysis, and maybe Somers would want to talk things over at home, at night, after the kids were in bed. Get a new perspective. Yes, Hazard thought, and he felt part of himself unspooling, turning, gliding forward towards this future. Yes, it was a future. It was his future. Maybe not all of it. But some of it would be his. Emery Hazard had a future. And inside him, for the first time since he had come back to this town, the frozen clock ticked one hand past midnight.

THE RATIONAL FACULTY

Hazard and Somers's adventures continue in their next set of books: A Union of Swords. Keep reading for a preview of *The Rational Faculty*, the next Hazard and Somerset story.

CHAPTER ONE

OCTOBER 30
TUESDAY
6:00 AM

EMERY HAZARD LIKED MORNINGS the best. In the morning, the world still made sense.

Like this morning.

He was up at six, rolling out of bed while his boyfriend, John-Henry Somerset, smacked the alarm and limped toward the shower. Somers's leg had almost fully healed from the gunshot, but it was still stiff in the mornings. Hazard made a mental note to see if Somers was still doing his exercises; he guessed that his boyfriend was getting lazy. Hazard, who had taken a broken arm away from their last case together, counted himself lucky: with physical therapy, he was back to his full range of motion, and he was building strength quickly. He'd hit the weights again today. Maybe, today, he'd get back to his old max.

This quick account of injuries and recovery ran through his head as he stumbled through the hallways of their new home. The move had been sudden, unexpected. A part of Hazard could recognize that both of them had been desperate for some sort of change, some sense of control. A way to stop the freefall their lives had entered after the Fourth of July nightmare with Mikey Grames. A part of him recognized, in the creaking floors and in the peeling wallpaper and in the endless list of updates and repairs, their shared, panicked need for a fresh start.

In the kitchen, he set the coffee maker to work. Then he got out the frying pan, the eggs, the bacon, the spinach, an onion. While rashers of bacon fried, he chopped, cracked shells, whisked. He rescued the bacon, only partially burned, and he started the omelet. From the fridge, he retrieved milk and orange juice, and then he set the table. The omelet slid free of the pan as Somers came into the kitchen.

"Morning."

"Morning."

Dressed for work—a simple gray suit, a dress shirt with a blue windowpane design—Somers looked as beautiful as always: the blue in the shirt set off the blue in his eyes, the gray complemented the golden hue of his skin. He looked like the boy Hazard had loved and feared in high school—the boy who had terrorized Hazard. But he was better now. Maturity and kindness and humor had softened the lines that had been too painfully perfect when they were teenagers. He sat, hands in his lap, staring at the omelet and the bacon and the glass of milk and the glass of juice.

"Damn," Hazard said, rising from his seat. "Coffee."

"I'll get it."

"I'm already up."

He poured a travel mug of coffee, fetched cream and sugar, and set it at Somers's elbow. He stayed there, standing behind Somers, and then he set his hands on Somers's shoulders.

Somers still sat with his hands in his lap. He was still staring at the plate.

"It's a spinach omelet," Hazard said.

Somers twisted to face Hazard.

"We'll go back to oatmeal in a few weeks," Hazard said. "But I wanted to see how you felt with a little more protein in the mornings."

"Ree, we talked about this."

"I lost track of the bacon for a minute. That's why it burned."

Somers watched Hazard's face, still twisted around so they could see each other.

"You're going to be late for work if you don't eat."

"Ree."

"I just need to get a new routine with the omelet. The bacon won't burn next time."

"I don't care about the bacon. Bacon is bacon. It's delicious no matter what you do to it."

Hazard saw the struggle in Somers's face, but he refused to surrender. Refused to make this easy for Somers when nobody had made it easy for Hazard.

"You like omelets," Hazard said.

"We sat down and we talked about this."

"You like spinach omelets. You've ordered them three times when we've gone to Big Biscuit."

Somers stared at him. Helpless.

Gently, Hazard turned him back toward the table. He ran his fingers over Somers's collar, adjusting it, making sure it sat properly.

"You're going to be late," Hazard said again.

And then, shoulders slumping slightly, Somers ate. Hazard collected another mug from the cabinet, poured himself coffee, and sipped at it—black—at the table.

"This is really good," Somers said between bites.

Hazard grunted, watching his boyfriend over the rim of his mug, but also looking out somewhere else, somewhere beyond the kitchen.

"Thank you," Somers said.

"I'm going to pick up some goat cheese."

"You don't have to do that."

"It'll be better with goat cheese."

Somers paused. Then he collected a rasher of bacon, folding it with his fingers, back and forth. He looked up from the plate, but not quite all the way. "What are you going to do today?"

"I'm going to pick up some goat cheese."

"I'll get it on the way home."

"You might have a big case. You might get caught up at work. You might be there all night."

"Fat chance. I'll be lucky if Cravens ever puts me back to work."

With a shrug, Hazard said, "She will. She'll have to."

"If she sends me out to the college again, I'm going to quit. Anything would be better than knocking on doors in a dorm, pretending I give a hoot about kids smoking weed."

Hazard just sipped at his coffee again.

"Shit," Somers said, with a worried look. "That's not what I meant."

"I know."

"Your situation, it's bullshit. I didn't mean for it to sound like anything else."

"I know, John."

"This is ridiculous. Ree, let me talk to Cravens. We'll come up with a plan, a way to get you back to work."

Carefully—Hazard was finding, these days, that he had to be more and more careful, or else things happened like the back window, like the rototiller, like the closet door—he set down his coffee. He reached over, tugged Somers's sleeve down so that it showed past the cuff of his suit jacket, and squeezed Somers's hand once. Somers tried to hang on, but Hazard was already rising, collecting the plate with the half-eaten omelet.

"You're going to be late." He studied the plate. "Tomorrow, we'll try it without spinach. Goat cheese and chives, maybe."

"Please don't talk about the damn omelet. The omelet was fine. It was perfect. I don't want to talk about the omelet."

Hazard scraped the remaining food into the garbage and carried the dishes to the sink. Through the window, he could see daylight raking across the backyard, picking out blades of grass in crisp lines. Funny how morning worked: dawn made it look like everything had already started, but the sun didn't break the horizon until much later. Mornings could be tricky that way.

"I'll get groceries on the way home," Somers said, still standing awkwardly at the table when Hazard turned back, fidgeting with a button on his sleeve. "I don't want you to have to do all that stuff. I can do my part too."

Carefully, carefully. "And what am I supposed to do instead?"

Somers grinned, and it was like a light going on in the room. He crossed to stand in front of Hazard. Then he reached up and tugged on a long lock of dark hair. Three months of dark hair, the loose wave spilling past Hazard's jaw if Hazard forgot to push it behind his ears or tie it.

"This," Somers said, and then he kissed Hazard. "Or this." He tugged on the three month's growth of beard.

"Ow."

"I like the mountain man vibe, I really do. It's a nice Grizzly Adams look."

"But you'd like me better if I shaved and cut my hair."

"I didn't say that."

"You think I'd look better, then."

"Oh, sweetheart, I'm not stupid enough to walk into that one either."

Hazard felt a smile, a real smile, start. "You're going to be late."

"Maybe I don't mind being late. What's the big rush?"

"I'm looking forward to my goodbye kiss."

Hazard had meant it as fun, an easy flirt. He was surprised at the stillness in Somers's blue eyes, at the way Somers tilted his head, and then at the slow, gentle kiss that followed. Hazard's pulse pounded in his throat when they broke apart. He felt sick low in his stomach.

"I love you," Somers said.

"I love you too."

"When you're ready to talk, I'm ready."

"Talk about what?"

Somers looked like he was trying to smile, but he just shook his head. "I'm getting groceries on the way home, ok? I am."

Hazard raised his hands in surrender. "Don't forget the trunk or treat."

"Shit. Thank you. Ok, I'll get candy too."

"And one of the pumpkin buckets for her to put her candy in."

"Right. Where do you get one of those?"

"Are you sure you don't want me to go?"

"No way. I'm a grown man. I can find a child's pumpkin bucket." Then Somers did smile. "I think."

"And the utility room. Do you need anything for the sink?"

Somers blinked. "The sink?"

"It's leaking. The sink in the utility room. It's leaking. I told you about it."

"Shit."

"I mentioned it a few days ago."

"Shit, I know. I'm sorry."

"I'll figure it out. I bet there's a tutorial online. A video, probably."

"No way. Not a chance." Somers planted a hand on Hazard's chest. "I've got one tiny skill set that makes me useful around here, and I don't want you stealing my glory."

"It'll probably take fifteen minutes."

"Fine. I'll do it. And it'll only take me ten."

Hazard rolled his eyes, but Somers's grin was infectious, and he found it hard to pull away from the second goodbye kiss.

A few minutes later, after collecting keys and wallet, Somers was gone. Hazard stayed in the kitchen, sipping the rest of his coffee at the sink. For a while, standing there, he counted blades of grass cut out by the sun. He kept the lights on as long as he could. He made plans for the day, the week, the month. A hundred things to do. A million things to do.

And then, after a while, he couldn't do any of it. He turned off the lights in the kitchen. He poured his coffee down the sink.

In the morning, with Somers there to anchor him, Hazard still felt like he could navigate the world. In the morning, Hazard had things to do: things that mattered, things that meant something. He could wake up when Somers woke up. He could make breakfast. He could estimate macros—fat, protein, carbs—and plug them into a mental calculation related to Somers's body type, and he could think about the best meals he could feed Somers, the best way to keep him lean and healthy and strong and satisfied. That was what Somers didn't understand, of course. Somers didn't seem to understand anything, which made sense: Somers had other things to do with his life. Real things.

The days Evie spent with them stretched out the morning, made a few more hours pass easily. Somers's daughter—no, Hazard corrected: their daughter—had just turned three, and she split time between Somers and Cora, her mother. When she was at Somers and Hazard's house, Hazard could hold it together a few more hours: he could plan games and puzzles, he could launder her stuffed animals, he could pack a lunch and think about strawberries versus blueberries, the chance of listeria on deli ham. But then she would go to preschool, or back to Cora's, and Hazard would be here again. In the dark.

Of course, the dark was an exaggeration. Hyperbole. A ridiculous description of the situation. Hazard could stand here with the lights off and see perfectly fine with the sun coming in the windows. Hell, for that matter, he could close his eyes and find his way through the house. He spent his whole day here. Every day. Twenty-three hours. Twenty-four if he was lucky. He knew that it was thirty-seven steps to get from his bed to the kitchen—fifty steps if you counted the stairs. He knew that it was twenty-one steps from the kitchen to the trash cans. Or nineteen steps to the recycling bin. The longest distance possible in the house—in his mind, the image of a tiger pacing—was seventy-four steps: from the far corner of the storage room in the basement, up to the kitchen, across the house, upstairs again, and into Evie's bedroom at the front of the house. He had measured this several times. Several times, he had stood there, face against the mullioned glass, considering the fall. The rhododendrons grew thickly below the window. He had concluded that, at most, he might break a leg.

Once, only once, he had not been paying attention, and Somers had come home and found him sitting in the dark. And since then, Hazard had been careful to keep his ear tuned to the sound of movement, steps. He had started to suspect that Somers might come home unannounced again, a sort of surprise inspection, out of some misguided concern for Hazard's wellbeing.

But what Somers didn't understand was that Hazard was fine. He was perfectly, totally fine. His life, his whole existence, was like floating in bathwater: tepidly pleasant, buoying him so that he couldn't tell where he began and ended, only that sense of drifting, warmth. A boyfriend he loved. A daughter he loved. How could he not be fine?

The question came back at him at the strangest times. He'd find himself in the garage, not sure of how he'd gotten there, walking along the wall, his fingers bumping over the weedwhacker and the pruning sheers, but trailing slower over the sledgehammer, the chainsaw, the hatchet. Sometimes he would let himself look in the cabinet, up on the top shelf, where Somers had hidden the rat poison. And then he would hear the question again, with all of its knots and tangles that he tried to unravel like a man in gloves, in a blindfold, in the dark.

How could he not be fine?

CHAPTER TWO

OCTOBER 30
TUESDAY
6:47 PM

SOMERS TRIED TO CARRY all the bags from the car in one trip. It was a mistake. He was halfway through the garage, staring across the hood of his 2017 Mustang—ok, he admitted, a bit of an impulse buy, a bit of a rash decision—and wondering who had left the cabinet door open, when one of the bags split. He barely had time to register a thud, a slosh, and then a gallon of milk was spilling out of a broken jug and flooding the floor.

"Shit."

After a fumbling moment, he abandoned the milk and jumped across the growing puddle. He shouldered open the door, stepped into the kitchen, and was met with a wall of smells: hot oil, garlic, and fish. Not an unpleasant fishy smell, just . . . fish. It made his stomach rumble.

Hazard, standing over a frying pan on the stove, glanced up. He turned down the burner and moved towards Somers.

"I got it."

As usual, Hazard ignored Somers, deftly plucking some of the bags from Somers's hands and carrying them to the counter. Somers joined him, setting down the rest of the load.

"I dropped the damn milk," Somers said. "Hold on."

"Language," Hazard said in a low voice.

Before Somers could reply, he heard his daughter shrieking, "Daddy," her footsteps echoing through the house. A moment later she burst into the kitchen, her dark hair wild, her dark eyes so much like her mother's, her cheeks flushed. She hit Somers like a wrecking ball, and he grunted, laughing, and swept her up. He peppered her face with kisses until she squealed, "Down, down, down." Then he released her, and she flashed away.

"She's worked up," Somers said, staring after her.

"She's been in and out of her costume fourteen times."

Somers could feel the smile growing on his face. "Is she doing her own hair?"

"That's currently on the index of prohibited actions." Hazard was opening the bags, pulling out cucumbers, tomatoes, onions, a few summer squash that still looked good, even this late in the year.

"I'll get that," Somers said. "You've been doing—"

His mind went blank here.

"—stuff all day."

Hazard shrugged, turning toward the refrigerator. "You've been working all day."

Catching Hazard's wrist, Somers said, "Ree, please let me do it."

"Yeah," Hazard said, putting the cucumbers in the vegetable drawer. "I'll keep an eye on the fish."

"Just let me clean up the milk."

"Sure. Dinner's almost done anyway."

"It'll take two minutes, and then I'll be back and put this away."

Hazard nodded.

"Did you read that article I left?" Somers asked, studying the countertop, not quite able to bring his gaze up.

Making a noise, Hazard did something with the food.

"The one about." Somers stopped. Thought suddenly, vividly, of how good a beer would be right now. "Guys who lose their jobs. Kind of, you know, what it does to them."

Another noise.

"I left it right here on the counter."

Hazard turned away from the food, slid an arm around Somers's waist, and kissed him.

"Hi," Hazard said. "Welcome home. How was your day?"
Somers felt like flipping a coin: fight or no fight.
No fight.
"God, I'll tell you all about it."
"That bad?"
"I don't know."
Hazard kissed him again.
"Maybe not all bad," Somers said.
Hazard kissed him again.
When Somers could feel his feet again, he managed to say something that sounded like, "Kind of a good day, actually."
"Kind of?" Hazard asked with a dark heat in his voice.
"The fish is going to burn," Somers said, laughing and pushing free. "I'll be right back."
As Hazard went back to the stove, Somers stepped out into the garage. He collected the broken plastic jug and carried it outside to the recycling. Then he unspooled a length of hose, turned the water on low, and stepped back into the garage. The beauty of a cement pad and a central drain meant he could just run the hose around the perimeter of the garage, flushing the spilled milk under the Mustang and let it drain away.
He let his thumb play over the end of the hose, enjoying the water's cool pressure even at the end of October. The sensation was soothing, and Somers needed soothing. His nerves still felt like a total jangle. Work really hadn't been bad, although it hadn't been good either. It hadn't been good since Hazard had resigned. No, the shadow on Somers's day had started before work. It had started when he had come downstairs, when he had seen the omelet and the glass of juice and the glass of milk and the bacon. When he had seen Hazard standing there, shaggy-haired, bearded, silent. Waiting. Even after they had talked about the breakfasts. Even after they had talked about a fair division of household labor. Even after Somers had made a chore chart. And then, when the chore chart hadn't worked, another conversation. And then another. And then Somers had come downstairs and seen the omelet. After they had talked about all of it.

I want to do it. That was all Hazard would say about it. No matter how many times Somers tried to explain how he felt. No matter how many times he told Hazard he didn't want him doing it. Somers had tried phrasing that he'd picked up from websites. *When you do blank, I feel blank.* He'd tried rationality: if I don't want x, and it costs you energy to do x, why are you doing x? He'd tried economics: division of labor, specialization. He'd tried every language he knew Hazard spoke. And at the end, under a curtain of dark hair, those scarecrow eyes would stare out blankly and Hazard would say, *I want to do it.* The way some people said *I think I'll have a Coke.* Or *It looks like it's going to be cold today.*

I want to do it.

And Somers couldn't argue with that, not really. He could try to talk his way around it. But couldn't argue. And what was the problem, really? He loved Hazard. Hazard loved him. Hazard wanted to do something nice for him. Hazard wanted to make him breakfast. It was a kindness, really. A demonstration of what he felt for Somers. Somers knew he should feel grateful. Knew he should feel lucky to have a man who cared about him like that. And he did feel those things. Lucky, grateful, blessed, fortunate. Choose your adjective.

Happy?

Somers batted the word aside. What made the whole situation impossible was that Somers couldn't even explain what was wrong. It was just a feeling. It was the look in Hazard's eyes when he didn't know Somers was watching him. It was coming down the stairs, seeing the omelet, seeing Hazard waiting, mute and patient like a servant, and all Somers could think about was that one afternoon, that horrible fucking afternoon he had come home early from work.

Somers played the hose from side to side, pressing down on the tip, forcing the water out in a hard spray. He had come home early from work. It hadn't been like he was trying to sneak up on Hazard. It hadn't been like he was . . . spying. He had ducked out a couple of hours early, knowing that Hazard would be home, thinking they could mess around and order Thai food and maybe mess around again after dinner. It was just supposed to be fun. It was just supposed to be cute and maybe a little romantic.

Only when Somers had come home, the house had been dark. It was early afternoon. It was a bright October day, and the light came through the windows like surf off the ocean. So it was silly to say the house was dark. Only it was dark. All the lights off. Every single light. Off. And for some reason, Somers had slipped off his shoes at the door. He had been careful, removing his keys from the lock, sliding them into his pocket so they couldn't jingle. He had found himself walking on the boards he knew didn't creak. He had felt dizzy, his heartbeat in his ears. He had known, even then.

When he reached the living room, he stopped. Because it was so quiet. That was what seemed impossible: how quiet everything was. Hazard lay on the sofa perfectly still except for the rise and fall of his chest. His eyes were open, but he hadn't seen Somers. He didn't seem to see anything. And he didn't fidget. He didn't shift. The sofa's leather didn't squeak. He wasn't napping, either. That was what Somers remembered most vividly. The open eyes staring into nothing. The shallow breathing.

That had all lasted only an instant. And at the end of that instant, Hazard blinked and sat up, and he was saying something about a nap, and Somers was nodding and saying something about a nap, and it felt like some bizarre dance that neither of them really knew the steps to. But they kept doing the dance, nodding and smiling and talking about how wonderful naps were. And that had been the end of it. Neither of them had ever mentioned it again.

But an instant had been long enough. And in that instant, a dozen other puzzle pieces had fallen into place. The clearest, the most vivid, had been the realization that Hazard almost never left the house. Until that afternoon, Somers had believed—with no evidence to the contrary—that Hazard left the house to jog or to get coffee, to stop by the library, to have lunch. And now he realized that Hazard never talked about leaving the house. Never talked about going outside unless it was to pick up groceries or drop off the dry cleaning or take the car for an oil change. In that frozen instant, Somers thought about the times Hazard asked Somers to pick up a DVD on his way home from work; all the nights Hazard wanted take-out instead of dinner in a restaurant; the strange resistance, which at the time Somers had chalked up to obstinacy or a foul mood, when Somers proposed a walk through the neighborhood, or a hike in the Ozarks, or a drive to Columbia for a night out.

In the garage, with the spray of water numbing his thumb, Somers suddenly felt something holding him by the throat, clutching at him until he could barely breathe. The last of the milk swirled in the water, disappearing under the Mustang, and Somers staggered outside into the October evening, the sun swollen on the horizon. He shut off the hose and coiled it neatly around the hanger. And then he pressed his hands over his eyes and leaned against the house and breathed until he wasn't going to fall apart.

When he went back inside, Hazard was at the stove, lifting fish out of the pan on a spatula. The groceries had been put away.

Somers leaned on the quartz slab. He waited until Hazard looked at him, really looked at him, and neither of them could pretend they didn't know what this was about.

Neither of them said anything.

Hazard slid the fish onto a plate and then served roasted asparagus alongside it.

"Thank you," Somers said.

Hazard shrugged. "Pretty easy dinner tonight."

CHAPTER THREE

OCTOBER 30
TUESDAY
7:27 PM

THE HOUSE SOMERS AND HAZARD had bought was in an old Arts and Crafts neighborhood of craftsman-style homes. Located near the city center, it was within walking distance of city hall and Market Street and even the Wahredua police station. It was also within walking distance of their old apartment. Even with the location, though, and even with the valuable historical quality of the construction, the neighborhood was one of the only areas that Hazard and Somers could really afford to consider. This was entirely due to the urban blight that, Hazard believed, had been intentionally inflicted by Wahredua's former mayor and his real estate development firm.

So, although most of the houses were over a hundred years old, with wide porches and square columns, with low roofs and wide eaves, with dark beams and quality woodwork, many of the homes were falling into ruin—abandoned because empty lots had been allowed to fester, infecting the area with crime and vandalism. Hazard and Somers had bought the house cheap because of the neighborhood. And, if Hazard were honest, because the house needed a great deal of work. Work that Somers had intended to do before his sick leave ran out. Work like the leaking sink in the utility room, which had been put off again that night because of trunk or treat.

Instead of walking to city hall, though, that night they drove. Wahredua's civil servants had been putting on the trunk or treat for years. Decades, actually. The tradition had started after Hazard had been in high school, and he had been too old to take part in the actual process of collecting candy from cars parked in city lots, but he remembered the pleasure of crisp autumn nights when he could walk Jefferson Street, where city hall and the sheriff's department and public records and a dozen other city and county offices occupied grassy acres of land. He remembered watching excited children race through parking lots, collecting candy from the trunk of each car. He remembered the slightly muted thrill of seeing teenagers, kids he knew from high school, in their more adult costumes, sexy costumes that showed off thighs or abs or breasts, as they paraded for each other before disappearing into someone's basement to listen to Pearl Jam and drink Natty Lights. For him, those nights had always ended with silent walks back home. But he remembered. And the memories, especially after all these years, were strangely luminous. Something he had enjoyed more than he had realized at the time.

Now, as Hazard guided the minivan—his new car, a 2012 Honda Odyssey, gray, practically invisible—into a parking space, he felt a flicker of the same energy. He got out of the car and opened the passenger door, where Evie was already trying to rip loose the buckles on her car seat. Somers opened the other door and watched them, a crooked smile on his face.

"Somebody's excited."

Hazard slid Evie's little hands aside and unfastened the buckles. Then, lifting her out, he was treated to an ear-splitting shriek. Mostly excitement, he decoded. But a little bit of hellion too.

When he set her down, she looked up at him and extended an imperious hand. "I want my—" And then a word that Hazard couldn't understand.

"What?"

"I want my—"

He glanced over the top of her head. Somers was setting up the folding chairs at the back of the minivan, and he smirked at Hazard.

Hazard narrowed his eyes at his boyfriend.

Raising his hands innocently, Somers gestured to the back of the van. Through the glass, Hazard could see what he was pointing at.

"Oh. Your pumpkin."

"I want my pumpkin."

"Is that a nice way to ask?"

Evie did her latest performance: eyes wide and fluttering, head rolling to the side, hands clasped at her chest. "Pwease?"

"Careful," Somers said in a low, amused voice. "Your knees are melting."

Hazard shot him a glare. Then he picked up Evie, carried her around back, and passed her the bucket.

"You guys look adorable," Somers said. He got out his phone and took his place at Hazard's side. "Selfie."

"No," Hazard said.

"Smile!"

A moment later, the phone flashed, and Somers lowered it, studying the picture on the screen.

"Cute," he said, showing it to Hazard.

Hazard just grunted and lowered Evie.

"Candy," Evie shrieked, darting towards the next parked car, where an older woman was passing out candy bars that Hazard could pop down in a single bite.

Hazard caught her wrist. "Just a second, miss."

"Candy!"

"You better take her," Hazard said to Somers. "I don't know how long I can hold her."

"You take her."

"John."

"Take her."

"No, not tonight."

"I want you to, Ree. I want to see you guys out there together."

"Be real."

Somers crossed his arms. The smile died in his face. "Excuse me?"

"Um."

"What does that mean?"

"Nothing. Will you just take her? I'll sit here and pass out candy."

"It didn't mean nothing."

"Ok."

"You definitely meant something."

"Candy," Evie informed them, drawing out each syllable pathetically.

Somers's eyebrows were drawn tight. One finger was tapping a bicep. It was going to be a fight, Hazard realized. Maybe a big one. Maybe their first one since everything in July.

Then, over Somers's shoulder, Hazard saw a young couple with a swarm of children moving towards them. Young faces lit up with enthusiasm, and the swarm rushed forward.

"Noah and Rebeca," Hazard muttered.

Somers dropped his arms, putting on a smile as he turned, but the tightly-drawn eyebrows didn't relax.

The children reached Hazard and Somers first, hitting like a nuclear bomb. They ranged in age from twelve to two and a half, just a little younger than Evie. Hazard was fairly sure that there were only six children, but it felt like a pack of twenty or thirty. They were all laughing, teasing, and then two of the boys got a little rougher and they were snapping at each other, and they all wanted Hazard and Somers to see their costumes. Hazard lost count because the kids kept moving and flowing and swirling around them, but he thought all four of the boys were various forms of peace officers. He didn't have to stretch to guess that this had something to do with their recently having gotten to know John-Henry Somerset, local hero and detective with the Wahredua PD. One of the girls wore a white lab coat with ROCKET SCIENTIST on the lapel, and the youngest was dressed like Gus from Disney's *Cinderella*.

By the time Hazard realized what was happening—he had been distracted by the parade of costumes and children tugging on his hands and demanding his attention—the rocket scientist was walking away, holding Evie's hand on one side and her sister's on the other.

"I'd better—" Hazard said.

Somers snagged his shirt without looking at him.

"You don't mind if Raquel takes Evie, do you?" Rebeca's dark eyes sparkled with amusement, and Hazard guessed she had witnessed Somers catching him by the shirt. "She's obsessed with her. It would be nice if she were that interested in her own little sister, but I'll take what I can get."

Noah stretched past Rebeca to shake hands, first with Hazard, then with Somers. He had a friendly smile as he said, "I told her not to go past this line of cars, so you'll be able to keep an eye on Evie."

"It's fine," Somers said.

At the same time, Hazard managed to mutter, "Thank you."

Noah just grinned wider and slid his arm around Rebeca. "We remember what it was like to just have one. Now we could lose a few and not notice."

Hazard actually found himself smiling at that. It wasn't the words—the content was pure drivel—but at the delivery.

"Parking lot's getting full," Somers said. "Want to move your car over here?" He thumbed at an empty spot next to the Odyssey.

"We'll just bring our chairs and candy," Rebeca said. "I don't think the kids care too much about the trunk part."

They walked back down the lot, and Hazard watched them go. They made an odd pair: Rebeca short and dark, Noah tall and white. Rebeca composed and beautiful, Noah . . . kind of goofy. But they were friendly and genuine and, most importantly, smart. And they had moved into the house next door a few days after Hazard and Somers had gotten into their new home. Perhaps their best quality, in Hazard's book, was that they had no history in Wahredua; Rebeca had come for a professorship in public health at Wroxall College, and Noah wrote for a series of online blogs and websites.

Hazard dropped into one of the folding chairs, opened a bag of candy, and propped it in his lap. Somers sat next to him. The storm that had started earlier was still brewing, and Hazard waited for lightning to strike again. But after a moment, Somers let out a breath and stretched his legs in front of him. He reached over and took Hazard's hand.

"Are you glad you came now?"

"I didn't say I wouldn't come."

"So, when you tell me you're not feeling up to it, and you're tired, and you might call it a night early, I'm supposed to assume you're excited about going to trunk or treat."

"I never said I was tired."

"That was a joke."

"Kind of."

"Kind of," Somers said with a smile. "It's a nice night, right?"

It was a nice night: cool without being cold, the sky clear, stars visible even through the haze of light pollution. The smell of fallen leaves mixed with the slight prickle of Somers's cologne.

Hazard grunted.

"And you like Noah and Rebeca."

Hazard grunted again.

"Come on."

"They're fine."

"You haven't yelled at them once."

"They don't say stupid things."

"I caught you talking to Robbie about school."

"He wouldn't shut up."

"You were being very encouraging."

Hazard rolled his hand, trying to get loose from Somers.

Somers held on. "I believe your exact words were, 'You've got a lot of potential. Don't let that asshole tell you otherwise.'"

"That wasn't encouragement; I've seen his drawings. It was a statement of fact. And you and I both had Mr. Oberhausen for art. He was an asshole twenty years ago, and he's still an asshole today."

Somers was smiling broadly now. He wove his fingers between Hazard's.

"What?" Hazard said.

Somers just rolled his eyes.

Then the first wave of trick-or-treaters hit them, and they didn't have time to talk. Most of the kids were content to take a single piece of candy from the bag Hazard offered. When a few of the older kids got bold and tried to take more, Hazard stared at them. That's all it took. Just a stare. And then they'd forget about the extra three mini Twix and back away, their eyes wide.

At some point in the chaos, Rebeca and Noah arrived, setting up their chairs while kids mobbed them for candy. Rebeca took a spot next to Somers, and Noah took the spot next to her. In a few minutes, even with the rush of children, the three of them were talking about preschool. Rebeca and Noah were asking about Evie's school, already considering transferring their youngest—Rocio, Hazard heard them say, and for the hundredth time he told himself he was going to remember the names. More than once, Somers and Noah tried to draw Hazard into the conversation, but he refused to take the bait, and eventually they left him alone.

He watched the groups of children flow across the asphalt, studying their movements. He thought he could see a pattern. Not anything obvious, but a kind of rhythm to the eddies in the stream of humanity. He'd been reading about self-driving car technologies and algorithms developed from studying schools of fish; it seemed like something similar might apply here. It was the kind of thing that, a few months ago, he would have wanted to read more about. But now the thought came, lingered like an imprint, a ghost. It had no force. No vitality.

Then, like an intruder, another thought shattered his observations: Somers had been angry. Not just about the way Hazard had refused to take Evie through the trunk or treat but also about Hazard's reluctance to come out tonight. Hazard had thought he was being subtle. He had framed the possibility of staying behind in purely practical concerns. Based on how Somers had hassled him into coming, and on the way Somers had parroted back Hazard's excuses, Hazard guessed that Somers was beginning to notice. Somers was beginning to recognize the pattern. And, of course, Hazard had expected him to. Somers was a good detective. A great detective. Hazard just wished it hadn't happened so fast. He just wished Somers would be a little more clueless when it came to his boyfriend.

A boy with a wild cowlick in front sprinted down the center of the parking lot, waving something in one hand, and then a fizzing noise came over the hub of voices. Hazard had just long enough to see the bottle rocket, to recognize it, before it exploded overhead.

He was halfway out of his chair, hand dipping under his arm to the spot where he had worn a gun for most of his career, heart pounding in his chest, before he was able to stop himself. He knew it was a bottle rocket. He had seen it before it went off. But sweat stung him between the shoulder blades, and his breath sounded thin in his throat.

Somers's hand found his arm.

Shaking his head, Hazard dropped back into his seat.

"Ree," Somers said in a low voice, leaning close enough that Noah and Rebeca couldn't hear. But, of course, it didn't matter if they heard. They had seen. Rebeca, most definitely, had seen. "Are you—"

Hazard shook his head and brushed off Somers's hand. His face was heating, and he turned so that Somers and Noah and Rebeca dropped out of his field of vision. He heard Somers sigh, and then Somers's hand ran over his shoulder, down his arm, and fell away again. The murmur of voices resumed, Somers saying something easy and funny and casual that made Rebeca and Noah laugh, and then the world rolled forward.

But Hazard kept staring out at the parking lot. Somers thought he understood. Somers thought it was things like the bottle rocket, things that still sent Hazard into hyperdrive—if only for a few minutes before he could bring himself under control again.

But it wasn't just the explosion. It wasn't just his reaction. It was . . . everything. Hazard's gaze swept through the parking lot as his heart slowed and the sweat under his arms cooled. It was the fact that the kid with the bottle rocket had ignored a municipal code and committed a misdemeanor. It was the fact that, just from where he was sitting, Hazard spotted two expired vehicle registrations. It was the fact that a man two cars down had just finished a can of Miller Lite—against the city's public intoxication law. Worse, instead of stowing the empty or walking it down to a recycling bin, the man crushed it underfoot and kicked it under his car. Littering. The problem that Somers didn't understand—one of the problems—was that Hazard still saw the world as a policeman. And he wasn't police anymore.

And that was the other problem. It wasn't the simple matter of not being police. It was what he had become instead. Hazard might not have had the intense social intelligence that Somers displayed, but he wasn't an idiot either. He saw the way people looked at him. Four cars down, a group of soccer moms huddled together, wearing sporty vests and yoga pants and chafing mummy-thin arms. They were talking about him. That wasn't vanity, although Somers might have blamed Hazard's ego. It was deduction: their voices pitched too low to carry, their frequent gazes in Hazard's direction. Another time, Hazard might have thought they were lusting over Somers, but their body language was that of a threatened pack: close together, fencing out a danger. And tonight, that danger was him.

It wasn't just the soccer moms. Up the line of cars, a man sat in an old aluminum webbed folding chair. He was a big guy, and the webbing had frayed over the years; thin whiskers of polypropylene stuck out from under his ass. One more beer, and the guy was liable to split the webbing and drop right through the seat.

But the guy didn't seem worried about his ancient folding chair. He was staring at Hazard. When Hazard's gaze swept over him, he didn't blink or turn away or pretend he had been looking at something close to Hazard, something else that had drawn his attention. No, this guy locked gazes with Hazard, his eyes hard and flat. That was another old trick that went back all the way to caveman days. A threat. A challenge. After a moment, Hazard looked away.

Hazard could have played the game all night, letting himself look for the ones who were looking. But he didn't need to. In spite of his best efforts to avoid leaving the house, he still had to get groceries. Sometimes. He still had to run errands that Somers needed him to run. He saw these looks all the time.

He didn't blame the people who feared him and hated him and suspected him. What did they know? Just a simple string of facts: Emery Hazard had gone into a building with Mikey Grames, his old high school bully. Emery Hazard had left that building alive. Mikey

Grames had not. And then Emery Hazard had resigned from the police force. A kid could connect the dots.

"Better?"

Somers's voice was barely more than a whisper, and his fingers curled around Hazard's arm.

"Huh?"

Somers's gaze was tropical blue and steady. Calm.

"Yeah," Hazard finally said.

"We're almost done," Somers said. "People are packing up."

"I'm fine."

"Thank you for coming."

"John, please don't—" Hazard managed to stop himself from saying, *please don't do that*. Please, he wanted to say, don't be nice about it.

Somers cocked his head, but before Hazard could come up with a lie, a white truck swung into the parking lot. The beams from its headlights bounced across the crowd, and Hazard saw shocked faces, then fear. The truck was coming too fast. Parents screamed for kids to get out of the way. A few of the more agile adults sprinted toward their children, grabbing them by the arm, by the tail of a costume, by whatever they could reach. Hazard glanced down the line of cars, already shooting up from his seat. Ten cars down, Raquel had squirreled herself between a Jetta and a Subaru, with Evie and Rocio pressed tight against her legs. She watched the truck, one hand holding onto each girl.

The white truck was blasting music. Country. Not Emmylou Harris and Gillian Welch like Somers enjoyed. Not Dolly. Not even the country pop that had blown up on the radio lately. This was something else, and it sounded hard and angry. A furious bluegrass that had rage behind it instead of its normal wild energy.

By some miracle, the truck didn't hit anyone. It slowed, although not by much, and then, as it approached Hazard and Somers, several men riding in the bed of the truck dropped a banner across the side paneling. *STRAIGHTEN UP DORE COUNTY.*

Then the men in the truck started shouting.

"Queers."

"Snowflakes."
"Cocksuckers."
"Sheeple."
"Faggots."
"Trannies."

Hazard eyed the men. He recognized the class and species, even if he didn't know any of them by name. These were the classic Ozark Volunteer type, the local paramilitary group, a kind of neo-Nazi lite. They were all white. They ranged in age from young adult to middle age. Most of them were thin, wiry, although the older men had started to sag around the middle. All of them wore white T-shirts with the words STRAIGHTEN UP on the chest and back. All of them wore trucker hats with the same two words. All of them looked like they hadn't eaten a vegetable since last year.

As the truck drove past Hazard and Somers, Hazard squared his shoulders. He wanted to at least look these sons of bitches in the eye. But to his surprise, they didn't even glance at him. Or Somers. Their shouts were directed somewhere else. Somewhere down the line. Which didn't make any sense at all.

Hazard jogged after the truck, which had slowed as the men in the back switched from jeers to a simple chant: *Straighten up. Straighten up. Straighten up.*

"What the hell are you doing?" Somers asked, running alongside him.

"Evie."

The truck continued to roll through the crowd. Hazard and Somers stopped by Raquel and Evie and Rocio. Fear was painted on all three faces, and Hazard realized, with a start, that the trunk or treat crowd had gone completely silent. Fear was infectious; he knew that. And right then, it was racing through the men and women and children in the municipal parking lot.

At the corner, the parking lot turned into an L, with the second leg exiting onto a service drive behind city hall. It made the parking lot ideal for trunk or treat; two exits meant that people could leave quickly when the event was over, without everyone getting jammed up. Tonight, Hazard realized, it was going to provide these assholes with an escape route.

"Straighten up. Straighten up. Straighten up."

The chant was whooping, ferocious, barbaric. It raised the hairs on the back of Hazard's neck, and he realized he was hearing hate, pure and distilled.

And then a slender form darted forward at the end of the L. Maybe five feet tall, barely. Because of the distance, Hazard used the height of the panel van behind the figure to estimate. But the man didn't seem intimidated, even when the chant switched back to jeers.

"Faggot."

"Queer."

"Cocksucker snowflake."

"Tranny."

"Get out of here, assholes," the small man shouted. "This is for kids, all right? Have some goddamn respect."

One of the men rose up from the bed of the truck, his arm whipping back and forward. Hazard couldn't see what he threw, but he saw the small man stagger back, a hand going to his head. Whoops and jeers and laughter exploded out of the back of the truck.

From somewhere down the road came the chirp of a siren.

As the Ozark Volunteers broke into their chant—*Straighten up. Straighten up. Straighten up*—the white truck lurched toward the service exit, and in another minute, it was gone.

Gathering up Evie, Hazard cradled her to his chest. She wasn't freaking out, but her heart was going a mile a minute, and she buried her face in his shoulder. One pudgy hand had a death grip on the pumpkin bucket.

"You did great," Somers was telling Raquel, who had burst into tears. "You did perfectly."

Hazard rubbed Evie's back. "Did you get any candy?"

Snuffling once, she turned toward him, her head still resting on his shoulder.

"Yes."

"Good," Hazard said, still rubbing her back, slow and steady. "Because I'm going to eat it all."

"No!"

Hazard let a grin slip onto his face, and after a moment, Evie giggled.

"Let's get them back to Noah and Rebeca," Somers said, one arm around Raquel's shoulders, Rocio cradled in his other arm.

"You go on." Hazard took a step toward the small crowd that had formed at the end of the lot.

"Ree?"

"I'll be right there."

Somers hustled Raquel toward her parents, and Hazard, adjusting Evie's weight, carried his daughter toward the crowd. It was already fragmenting, splitting apart as people realized the action was over. Taillights went on, red and then white, painting the asphalt. Parents gathered up kids too quickly, and buckets spilled, spraying Jolly Ranchers and Dum-Dums and Tootsie Rolls across the ground. Lots of kids were crying now. Everybody, Hazard guessed, wanted the hell out of there. A perfect night had been ruined.

By the time Hazard had reached the small man who had shouted at the Ozark Volunteers, the crowd had dissolved. The man sat on the ground, a piece of cloth held to his head. He was obviously bleeding. Hazard saw the object: a flat, sharp-edged rock the size of his hand. Two women, one gray-haired but stylish, the other young and wearing corduroy overalls, knelt next to the injured man.

"Did one of you call for an ambulance?" Hazard asked.

Overalls looked up, blinked owlishly at Hazard, her mouth a big O.

"Ambulance," Hazard said. "He needs an ambulance."

The older woman brushed back gray hair and glanced up long enough to say, "I called."

"That's a class C felony. Second-degree assault."

The gray-haired woman was digging through her purse. Overalls was still staring up at Hazard, her mouth giving little, guppy-like flutters.

"Don't let them bullshit you into anything less," Hazard said, shifting Evie to his other arm. "If they give you boys will be boys, tell them you'll hire an attorney and sue the city for every nickel."

Gray-hair glanced up again. "Thank you."

The slender man was shaking his head. He said, "Stop, Ruth. I'm not taking aspirin."

His voice was high and clear. He looked up and met Hazard's gaze for a moment. Thin face. Hair cut into a low fade, a ginger quiff at the front. Narrow shoulders but wide hips.

Hazard did the math, and then he understood some of the Ozark Volunteers' shouts.

"Jamie," the man said, and Overalls perked up like a Labrador. "Could you find me some water?"

"I've got some," Hazard said. "Bandages, too. Disinfecting wipes. But you need a hospital."

The man just nodded. After a moment, Hazard turned. Overalls—Jamie—trotted behind him. He wondered, if he tossed a bone, if she'd play fetch.

He'd barely gone ten feet before he ran into Rebeca and Somers, who were coming towards Hazard at a steady clip.

"Evie, baby," Somers said, sliding his daughter off Hazard's shoulders and into his arms. "Are you ok?"

"Dee Dee eat all my candy."

Somers raised an eyebrow.

"It was an idle threat," Hazard said.

"Idle."

"I don't even like candy."

Somers's other eyebrow went up. "I've seen you try to fit into your jeans."

"Water," Jamie panted, the buckles on her corduroy overalls jangling as she shifted from foot to foot.

"Who's this?" Somers said.

"God only knows," Hazard muttered. "I'm getting water."

Somers peered over Hazard's shoulder. "And who's that?"

"That," Rebeca said with a smile, "is our new pastor."

"What do the Volunteers have against him?"

"With Wesley?" Rebeca frowned as though trying to pick the right thing to say.

"Aside from the obvious," Hazard said.

"I don't know," Rebeca said. "He's a good pastor. He's active in the community. He's friendly and welcoming."

"Hey, Ree, can we get out of here?" Somers said.

Jamie was still shifting from foot to foot, her buckles clattering as loud as a brass band.

"Yeah," Hazard said with a sigh. "Let me just help them first."

Acknowledgments

My deepest thanks go out to the following people:

Cheryl Oakley, for her corrections to this revised edition.

Monique Ferrell, for her consistent encouragement and support, her help with issues of procedure and investigation, and her fine sense for the subtleties of character that underlie the plots of these books. And, of course, for catching so many errors that nobody else saw!

Austin Gwin, for having, as always, an uncanny insight into what these books are actually about. As has been true for the other Hazard and Somerset books, Austin gave me the key to unlock the real ending. His insights into Hazard and Jeff's relationship, into the mayor, and into the real issues at stake in the ending helped me to write a much better version of this book. I'm infinitely grateful for his keen editorial mind.

Jo Wegstein, for helping to cover a multitude of my literary sins. These include, among other things, an exploding propane tank, what actually happened at the Yorgenson trailers, how Mikey was involved with Hollace, and which way cattle tend to stampede. There are many, many minor corrections that Jo also caught—too many to list here—but I want to thank her most of all for uncovering this related Faulkner quote, which I couldn't find a place for in the book but which deserves a spot anyway: "[T]he young man or woman writing today has forgotten the problems of the human heart in conflict with itself which alone can make good writing because only that is worth writing about, worth the agony and the sweat."

Justene Adamec, for conducting a blitzkrieg through *Guilt by Association*, *Reasonable Doubt*, and *Criminal Past*, and for hunting down countless minor errors (oh Justene, I'm still so grateful you caught and decoded 'strain destruction' that I'm mentioning it here, even though it was for another book entirely!). She also helped greatly with continuity and with general encouragement. I'll never make the mistake again (I hope) of using two different tools to pull out someone's fingernails! Lesson learned!

Jon Michaelsen, for support and encouragement with everything: engaging with a community of writers and readers; building a career; and improving my prose. Jon not only caught all sorts of specific errors but also helped point out some word crutches. His energy and commitment to our small corner of the world is inspiring, and I'm grateful for the help he has given in so many different ways.

Amy Lane, who has not yet read this book but who has been, without knowing it, a big influence. She provides unstinting encouragement and support, hilariously witty emails, and a treasure-trove of heart-warming and smile-inducing Facebook posts. She has also been a friend to talk to on the phone when I was trying to find my footing. More than that, she's shown an unbelievable degree of generosity to me and my work that I hope I can one day pay back (and, taking her example, pay forward).

And Tray Stephenson, for his support, for his kind emails, and for his careful proofing of the final text.

About the Author

Learn more about Gregory Ashe and forthcoming works at
www.gregoryashe.com.

For advanced access, exclusive content, limited-time promotions, and insider information, please sign up for my mailing list at http://bit.ly/ashemailinglist.

Printed in Great Britain
by Amazon